## ALSO BY MARITTA WOLFF

# Night
## Shift

### Maritta Wolff

*Scribner*
NEW YORK  LONDON  TORONTO  SYDNEY

SCRIBNER
1230 Avenue of the Americas
New York, NY 10020

This book is a work of fiction. Names, characters, places, and
incidents either are products of the author's imagination or are used
fictitiously. Any resemblance to actual events or locales or
persons, living or dead, is entirely coincidental.

First Scribner trade paperback edition 2006

SCRIBNER and design are trademarks of
Macmillan Library Reference USA, Inc. used under license by
Simon & Schuster, the publisher of this work.

For information regarding special discounts for bulk purchases,
please contact Simon & Schuster Special Sales at
1-800-456-6798 or business@simonandschuster.com

Manufactured in the United States of America

10  9  8  7  6  5  4  3  2  1

Library of Congress Cataloging-in-Publication Data

Wolff, Maritta, 1918–2002
Night shift / Maritta Wolff.—1st Scribner trade pbk. ed.
I. Title.

PS3545.O346N54 2006
813'.52—dc22
2006042321

ISBN-13: 978-0-7432-5487-8
ISBN-10: 0-7432-5487-2

*For Hube*

# Night Shift

# 1

THE PERSONNEL MANAGER DROPPED THE TELEPHONE back in the cradle, the radiator behind her made a little whistling sound and right after that there came a buzz from the inner mechanism of the electric clock on the corner of the desk. Wham! Whistle! Buzz! As if there was some idiotic relationship between the three noises, leading through a brief climax to a finality, Virginia Braun thought. And she almost laughed out loud.

The personnel manager shuffled the pink application blank and the little white card from the employment agency. "I'm sorry, Miss Braun," she said, "but the only opening we have here right now is for an experienced office girl. You'd have to have a professional knowledge of shorthand as well as typing. I'm sorry."

"I see," Virginia said. "Thank you."

She got up from the chair, pulling her coat around her. She had dropped one of her gloves. She noticed it then, a limp, brown cotton glove, lying alone and forlorn on the floor, the fingers curling upward pathetically, a hole in the forefinger and threads hanging where it had been mended before. Virginia picked up the glove quickly, and turned away.

The woman behind the desk smiled her professionally warm and friendly smile. "I'll keep your application on file, Miss Braun. There might be an opening for you later, maybe after the holidays. If there should be, I'll get in touch with you."

"Thank you," Virginia said again. She went on past the door into the outer office. There was a long line of girls, each with a pink-colored application blank, still waiting to be interviewed. She walked the length of the line to the elevator.

In the lobby, Virginia hesitated beside the revolving doors and turned the collar of her flimsy, tan-colored polo coat higher around her throat. Out on the street, the air was sharp and cold, the wind blowing a few fine pellets of snow with it. A patient-faced Salvation Army woman in a black bonnet stood beside a kettle and tripod, clanging her bell drearily. Virginia was swallowed up in the crowd that jammed the sidewalks, people hurrying along in both directions, shoving and bumping, their arms laden with packages.

Just then the Christmas decoration lights came on, hundreds of vari-colored bulbs amid the green festoons strung across Main Street. Above, a mist of smoke hung between the middling-tall buildings, the fine soot settling everywhere, begriming the green festoons and the patches of snow at the curb. The sky overhead was the same gray color of the smoke; and the sidewalks and fronts of buildings were colorless drab in the dull afternoon light. Restaurants and drug stores, pawn shops and all-night movie theatres punctuated the rows of garishly lighted store windows which were packed with holiday merchandise and trimmed with a glitter of tinsel and cellophane. From somewhere over the noise of the traffic came the sound of a factory whistle blowing, and then another one, the beginning of a cacophony that meant that the afternoon shifts were coming off in factories all over town. The whistles cut through the thin organ music of recorded Christmas carols broadcast through loud speakers onto the streets.

On the corner, a skinny Santa Claus with a dirty, scraggly beard appealed without enthusiasm to the passersby to contribute to some charity that guaranteed to give every child in the city a Merry Christmas.

The traffic policeman blew his whistle, gesturing with his arm, and the crowd surged across the street. There was a drug store on the corner and on the curb in front of it there was a sign that said "Bus Stop" and a schedule mounted on a metal pedestal. Virginia stopped to read the time table, her whole slight body shivering in the cold wind, one hand lifted to hold her hat. She craned her neck to see the illuminated dial of a clock in a jeweler's window across the street and then she pushed her way across the sidewalk. Inside the drug store there was a lunch counter along one wall, and Virginia climbed on the nearest stool.

"I'd like a cup of coffee, please," she said to the boy in the white coat. While she waited she opened the purse on her knees and drew out a letter, the writing blurred, the postmark smudged, the whole envelope creased and dirty from carrying. She took the one sheet of paper out of the envelope and spread it out carefully on the counter top beside her coffee. A short letter, dated "November Second" at the top and signed "love, Bill" at the bottom. In between it said that he was working hard, that he missed her, that guys with lots lower draft numbers than his still hadn't been called yet, that he wished that he could see her. She read it over many times, oblivious to the crowd around her. The corners of her mouth turned down tragically, and at last she put the letter away in her purse. She twisted around on the stool to catch a glimpse of the clock, and then she finished her coffee and picked up her check.

The cashier stamped her check and returned it to her. Virginia hesitated a moment with the little white square of paper in her hand. The lottery box was right in front of her, a pencil secured to the top of it by a chain. Virginia wrote her name and address carefully on the back of the check and then dropped it in the slot in the top of the box. There was a sheet of white cardboard on the wall above the box with a ten-dollar bill, the prize of the week, pinned to it, and beside it was printed the name of this week's lucky winner of the drawing, a Polish name, Mrs. Stanley Walezewski.

Outside the door a little knot of people had formed, waiting for the buses, shoppers with their bundles, pert, chattering office girls, and a few grimy factory workers with their dinner pails. Virginia stood close up against the plate-glass window out of the way of the crowd and the wind. A little drift of snow formed suddenly, eddied around her ankles and then was gone before the wind like a wraith. There was a hole in her silk stocking just above the top of her shoe, and the wide ladder of a runner coming up her leg. She leaned down and touched it with her finger, a helpless, hopeless gesture, with shocked concern on her face, as if it were an overwhelming catastrophe.

Just then a bus pulled up to the curb and Virginia hurried into the line of people that formed waiting to board it.

"Move to the back of the bus, please," the driver kept saying patiently over the ringing of nickels down the slot. "All right, hurry up! Step up, please!"

And over his voice and the roar of the traffic, came the sudden wail of an ambulance siren.

It happened on the chromium line just ten minutes before the day shift went off. It happened on the chromium line, where the thick, wet heat rises up from the vats and meets the dry, blue-green light pouring down—the last ten minutes of the daylight shift, at the last vat of all in the line of great vats where racks of shining automobile bumpers were doused rhythmically up and down by cables. The last vat on the line before the bumpers were dried and polished and trucked away to meet scores of other auto parts on assembly lines in Detroit and Flint.

It wasn't the vitriol vat nor the chromic-acid vat; just plain water, boiling water, nine feet of it, bubbling and boiling in a vat. The guard rail there was weak. Everybody knew it was weak—the men who worked there, the foreman, the superintendent on the chromium line. Everybody knew it was weak, but they hadn't gotten around to putting in a new one yet.

Stan Walezewski knew about it too. He never leaned against it, because he knew it wasn't safe. Stan was big, six feet tall (they hire tall men on the chromium line because it takes a tall man to reach the switches). And Stan was heavy, over two hundred pounds, two hundred pounds of big bone and flesh and smooth muscle to his strong young body. He had worked on the chromium line for three months, and he knew about the guard rail, all the boys did, but he was careful.

It was ten minutes before the day shift went off, and Stan was feeling fine. He was going home to Anna and the baby in a few minutes. He'd stop at the corner and drink a bottle of beer while he waited for the bus, and then he would go home. Anna was a fine wife, a big raw-boned Polish girl, almost as tall as Stan himself. And the baby was a fine kid. The next one would be a boy. Anna was four months gone with it. The next kid would be a boy, and he would grow up big and strong and healthy like his father. Oh, he was getting to be a reg-ular family man now, Stan exulted. And tomorrow was pay day. And tomorrow night was the wedding. Anna's kid sister was getting mar-ried to a Polish fellow from Dearborn. He was going to get drunk tomorrow afternoon, Stan gloated. He was going to get roaring drunk and dance his feet sore at the wedding and eat his belly full, and keep right on drinking and never sober up till Monday morning.

It was almost quitting time, and Stan felt fine. Another rack of bumpers came clattering along the track. Stan waved his arm and pulled his face out of shape at Joe Braun who worked beside him. Joe Braun was tall, like Stan, but skinny with a pale, sour face. Just to look at Joe always made Stan aware of what a big fine strong man he was. A real man in a fight, a real man when it came to drinking, and a real man in bed. Anna four months along with a boy. He and Anna would have lots of kids. Why not? He made good money in the factory; they could have a lot of kids.

"Hey, you, Joe! Wake up! That whistle gonna blow in a minute!" Stan yelled loud over the clatter. Joe Braun scowled at him. Stan laughed loud and long, his voice mixed in and lost with the noise here. He felt so good he'd like to yell and holler.

His eyes followed the rack of bumpers automatically, the rack slid into place on the track and automatically he moved to throw the switch. Poor old Joe, Stan was thinking, sickly sourpuss bastard! Bet he wishes he was like Stan Walezewski, bet he wishes he was fine, big man with wife and kids, bet he . . .

With the timing just right, Stan stretched up tall, reaching for the switch, stretched his tall heavy body upward, the light shining down on his thick yellow hair, turning gold-colored the hairs along his powerful bare arms, the muscles rippling under the ragged sweat-shirt, wet with the sweat of his body so that it stuck to his broad powerful back.

But the planking was wet, and, although the shoes he wore had rubber soles, his foot slipped. With his body flung upward his foot slipped and he lost his balance. He grabbed for the switch and closed his blunt fingers on the empty air. And in that second with his body out of balance falling forward, Stan Walezewski knew what was going to happen, because he knew the guard rail was weak. He thought of Anna briefly, but of himself, himself, Stan Walezewski, young and strong, and the fine good life of his body, and of pain and of death. And Stan Walezewski screamed with all the strength of his lungs.

Joe Braun saw it all. Stan's foot slipped, he missed the switch, he fell forward screaming, his face distorted, mad with terror. His heavy body crashed through that guard rail as if it had been made of paper. Water, nine feet of it, bubbling and boiling, head first, arms flailing, arc of strong smooth bare back above his trousers. As if he hung there in the air thick with heat, blue-green with light. As if he hung there in the air, oh, Jesus, as if he hung there in the air!

Joe Braun covered his face with his two hands, and his legs slowly crumpled under him and he huddled close to the wet planking. He couldn't get any air into his lungs and the hot blood pounded against the thin fragile bone of his skull. Why couldn't he quit screaming, Joe Braun was thinking frenziedly, why couldn't the goddam son of a bitch die and quit screaming, he was boiled, wasn't he? Why couldn't he quit screaming then? Christ, make him cut it out! Stop him making that noise! He was boiled, wasn't he? Shut his mouth, God! Keep him quiet! Goddam him to hell, make him stop that screaming!

Joe Braun huddled on the wet boards unnoticed, his face covered with his two hands, shaking all through his body, and the screams tearing out of his own raw, straining throat.


The dinner business at Toresca's restaurant was slow that night. It was still early, but the crowd was thinning out. Sally Otis, trim in her starched green-and-white uniform, stood beside an empty table with a stack of menus in her hand. Alertly she watched the last table of diners in her section, waiting to serve them their dessert. The room was warm and comfortably furnished and full of the modulated hum of voices. Another of the waitresses walked up the length of the counter along the wall and joined Sally by the empty table. She was a tall girl with a heavily made-up mouth and her dark hair in stiff elaborate curls. She walked with a studied sinuous motion of her hips, swinging her menus idly as she walked.

"The boss says you can go off now, if you want," she said to Sally.

Sally turned to her with her quick, warm, wide-lipped smile. "Gee, swell! Business is slow tonight, all right, but it sure wasn't this afternoon. My feet are just about dead. How about you, Lee?"

Lee shifted her weight to one foot and dabbed at the curls across the back of her head. "I just heard somebody talkin'. There was an accident out to the Kelton works this afternoon. Somebody got killed out there."

Sally's face sobered instantly and her last table of diners were momentarily forgotten. "Gosh!" she said.

"You got a brother workin' out to Kelton's, ain't you?" Lee asked, her fingers still busy with the stiff little curls.

"Yeah," Sally said worriedly. "My brother Joe works out there, and Johnny O'Connor—the O'Connors got an apartment in the same house where we live—he works out there too. You didn't hear 'em say what . . ."

"Naw," Lee said. "They just said there was an accident 'n somebody got killed."

Sally's eyes drifted back to her table again, but the worried look was still on her face. Lee shifted her weight to the other foot with an exaggerated motion of her hips and raised her little stack of menus up to her lips. "Jesus, ain't he something, though!" she murmured, with a sort of wistful awe in her voice.

"Who's that?" Sally asked automatically, her eyes still on the diners.

"Nicky Toresca. Who yuh think I'm talkin' about?" Lee went on talking softly. "Ain't he swell-looking? And smooth! Jesus, I sure could go for him, if I got the chance! They say he's terrible after women too. They say he changes women like he changes his shirts! But ain't he the smoothest-looking guy you ever saw, though?"

Sally smiled. "Why, I don't know," she said, with a little amusement in her voice. "I never seen him. I've heard about him but . . ."

"You dope!" Lee hissed behind the menus. "He's in here right now. He's been in two or three times lately!"

Sally turned to Lee with her eyes widening. "Honest? You mean the big boss? Which one is he?"

"He's alone to that table by the wall toward the back, see? Jesus, don't you think he . . ."

Sally looked down the length of the room in the direction indicated. "Oh, my gosh!" she said in a kind of amused concern. "Is that who that man is? Why, I waited on him just the other day!"

"That's who he is, all right," Lee said.

"Well, it's a good thing I didn't know," Sally said, "or I'd probably a been so nervous I'd a dropped my tray or something. Gee, he could have you fired around here as easy as he could wink his eye!"

"He sure could," Lee murmured. "But ain't he good-looking, though? He looks just like that guy in the movies, what's his name."

Sally looked at the man too. "Yeah," she said. "I know the one you mean. The one that plays gangsters and parts like that."

The man at the table by the wall sat slouched back in his chair, a cup of coffee in front of him, and a cigarette dangling from his lips. He wore a gray suit with immaculate shirt, tie and handkerchief. His hair was sleek black, his face dark and smooth and expressionless. Just then he turned his head a little, his eyes moving idly, and suddenly he looked directly at them. He kept on looking, his face not changing expression at all.

Sally looked away hastily, but Lee continued to stare. She moved her hips a little and raised one hand to her hair again, the tentative beginning of a smile on her rouged mouth.

"I wish those folks would hurry up and have their dessert," Sally said. "I got supper to get when I get home."

Lee was still looking toward Nicky Toresca's table. "Look, honey," she said, "you go ahead, if you want, I'll give 'em their dessert. I just as soon. I ain't in no hurry."

"Would you? Aw, thanks a lot, Lee. You can have the tip if you will."

"Naw, that's all right," Lee said. "I'll save the tip for yuh. I just as soon do it, I ain't in no hurry."

"Swell," Sally said gratefully. "I'll beat it then." She handed her menus to Lee and hurried toward the back of the restaurant. She pushed open the unmarked door at the back that led into the employees' washroom. It was a small, bare, cold room, with a toilet cubicle in one corner, in the other, a washbowl with a small mirror hanging above it, and hooks along one wall where coats were hung. Sally was across the room in a flash and grabbed a worn black-and-white coat and a blue felt hat from one of the hooks. She went over to the mirror, dropped the hat on top of the faucets in the washbowl and slipped the coat on hurriedly. Her fingers made quick work of the buttons and with her other hand she searched her coat pockets for her gloves.

She leaned close to the mirror to remove the pins that secured the little green-and-white cap to her hair. The light was poor, just the one dim bulb hanging from the cord above her head, and it took her a minute or two to find the pins. She stuffed the cap into her pocket and smoothed her short dark curly hair with her fingers, but in spite of the smoothing it wouldn't stay in place. It rose in unexpected peaks and curls on her head, like a child's hair.

Because she was intent and hurried, she didn't hear the door opening quietly behind her, nor did she catch a glimpse of him in the mirror when he stepped into the room. He came up behind her, walking lightly on the balls of his feet, without a sound. When he took hold of her shoulders, Sally jumped, her hat fell to the floor, and she made a little frightened strangling sound in her throat. She turned around quickly, and Nicky Toresca pulled her toward him, his face bent down to kiss her. She jerked away from him so hard that her body fell back against the edge of the washbowl. Sally's face was white and frightened. "Don't do that," she said in a small shaky voice.

Nicky Toresca's face was unperturbed and a little amused. He stood easily in front of her, his hands in his pockets. He laughed a little, easily, too, with a faint mockery in his voice.

"You're done work now. Is that right?" he said. "So put your hat on and I'll take you home." As he spoke he bent down smoothly from the waist and picked up her hat from the floor. Sally caught the odor of the oil on his sleek hair and then he offered her the hat. She took it automatically and held it with unsteady hands.

Her face looked desperate, and she licked her lips a little before she spoke. "Thanks a lot," she said, "but I can't. I—I—have to meet my sister. We go home together on the bus."

He stopped looking amused, his face went blank and expressionless again, and he just stood there close in front of her. Sally leaned further back against the washbowl and she fumbled with the hat in her hands.

"Thanks just the same, but I have to meet my sister. We always— I mean—she'd worry—I . . ." Sally's voice fluttered out helplessly.

The door opened again, but noisily this time. It was the Negro boy who cleaned up the back rooms. He came in banging his mop and pail against the door frame.

Nicky Toresca spun around toward him. "What you doin', busting in here?" he said angrily.

It was to Sally that the boy looked first, one swift glance, and then he looked up at Nicky Toresca, his eyes rolling nervously. "I'm sorry, Mist' Toresca," he said. "I sure didn't know you-all was in here. I jus' come in to clean up like I always do. I didn't know . . ."

Nicky Toresca's voice was taut with anger. "So you come busting in before the girls are outa here even. So maybe I should teach you to knock on doors. Is that right? You little sonofabitch! So maybe I should teach you to keep your nose out a what isn't none a your business. Maybe I should . . ."

"I sure am sorry, Mist' Toresca!" The boy backed out the door, rattling his mop and pail together. Sally moved then, rushing across the floor and crowding out the door with him.

"I'm late for my bus. I guess I gotta run," she mumbled to nobody in particular. She hurried through the restaurant and out the front door blindly. She was almost to the bus stop before she became aware of the sharp cold wind blowing at her hair and ears and remembered that she was still carrying her hat in her hands.

# 2

VIRGINIA HURRIED DOWN HORTON STREET, THE BIG brown paper sack of groceries in her arms. Horton Street was lined with houses, big, old-fashioned frame affairs, their architecture indeterminate in the darkness, but broken by many lighted windows. There were scant lawns in front of them and a few trees. The snow was coming down faster now, sliding along the sidewalk in front of her, sheathing street lights in whirlpools of dry fine flakes. The street was bare of traffic, dark and quiet. Only the rumble of heavy freight trucks from the main street behind her, and on the wind a muted, pulsing, thudding sound that meant they were bagging tires at the tire factory three blocks away, and, even fainter, a rhythmic, metallic hammering from the forge at Kelton's, a block beyond that.

Virginia crossed the street in the middle of the block. As she came up onto the sidewalk the quiet was split in two by a screeching, scraping sound. Two little figures bobbed up out of the darkness in front of her, a small boy first, dragging an old sled behind him, the runners grating and bouncing over the cement, and the little girl trotting after him.

"Hi, Virgie! Where you been?"

"Hey, Virgie, look! It's snowin'! We're gonna slide downhill over in Smith's driveway. His ma said we could when it snowed."

"Virgie, when we gonna have supper? I'm hungry. We ate all the orange stuff in the can in the cupboard an' the cheese n' meat in the 'frigerator. When we gonna eat, Virgie?"

"You kids come on in the house now," Virginia said. "It's awful late. Your mother'll be here in a minute and then we're going to eat. You can't go sliding downhill till there's more snow than this, and you're going to spoil that sled, dragging it around on the cement. You come on in now and get your things off. It's cold and your mother doesn't like to have you out on the street so late after dark like this."

Both children followed her obediently. The little girl slid her hand into the pocket of Virginia's coat, and the boy walked beside them, the sled rattling along behind, at the end of the loop of frayed rope.

"You suppose there'll be enough snow to go slidin' tomorrow, Virgie?" he wanted to know.

"I don't know," Virginia said. "Maybe there will."

"I bet there would be, if it kept snowing all night, huh?"

"I guess so."

"Virgie, how much snow would there be, if it kept snowing all night?" the little girl said earnestly, twisting around so that she could look up into Virginia's face. "This much, Virgie?" She held her hand up high.

The boy laughed loudly and made a funny snorting noise of derision out of his nose. "Naw, not that much! You're crazy! Girls is crazy!" He pushed against her roughly, knocking her off balance.

Virginia hoisted the sack in her arms wearily. "Buddy, don't push her like that! Marilyn, you mustn't slap him! Stop it now! Leave your sled on the porch and come on in the house, both of you."

The children clattered up the wooden porch steps behind her. Marilyn opened the door and Virginia went into the hallway first. There was a table near the foot of the stairs with a telephone on it, and several letters lying beside it. Virginia balanced her sack on one hip and shuffled through the letters hurriedly. When she was through, she sorted through them again.

The children hung over the stair railing, waiting for her.

"Virgie, you got snow all over your hair," Marilyn said. "Your hair is all wet."

Buddy hooked his knees over the railing and hung head downward, so that his red woolen cap fell off onto the hall table. "Say, Virgie," he said impishly, grinning at her upside down, "What did the big flower say to the little flower, Virgie?"

Virginia didn't answer him. She was looking at the addresses on the letters one last time. Just then the faded red curtains at the other end of the hall parted and a woman stepped through them, a big, well-built woman in a blue crepe dress, her white hair in perfect order and bright spots of rouge on her cheeks.

"Why, hello there, Virginia," she said pleasantly. "We're havin' a little snow for a change, ain't we?"

"Hello, Mrs. Gideon. There wasn't any mail for me today, was there?"

"Why, no, Virginia, just what's there on the table. Why? Was you lookin' for something special?"

"Oh, no," Virginia said quickly, the color coming up into her face. "I just thought maybe—I—I was sort of expecting a letter that was all—I . . ."

Mrs. Gideon took the toothpick out of her mouth and shook it at Virginia coyly. "Virginia, don't tell me that young man a yours is goin' back on you! You ain't had a letter from him in quite awhile! If he was a fellow a mine I believe I'd begin to wonder." She looked beyond Virginia's head at Buddy's acrobatic demonstrations on the banister. "Buddy Otis!" she said good-naturedly. "If you ain't the limit! First thing you know you're gonna break your back, all outa shape like that, or else you'll fall offa there and bust your head wide open."

"Get down, Buddy, and act like a big boy," Virginia said.

"Bud's crazy!" Marilyn said in contented admiration.

Buddy righted himself on the other side of the banister and pushed his tousled, light-colored hair out of his eyes. "Say, Mrs. Gideon, what did the big flower say to the little flower? I betcha you don't know what the big flower said to the little flower?"

Mrs. Gideon laughed and went back to picking her teeth with the toothpick. "Why, no, I guess I don't, Buddy. What did the . . ."

Marilyn hopped up and down on the stair landing. "I know. I know," she chanted. "I know what the big flower said to the . . ."

"Hey, Marilyn, you shut your mouth now. Don't you go tellin'," Buddy said warningly.

"Tell the answer and then we've got to go upstairs," Virginia said, lifting the sack again.

Buddy bobbed over the banister, his eyes shining with excitement. "You know what the big flower said to the little flower? He said, 'Hi yuh, bud!'"

Both children shrieked with laughter.

Mrs. Gideon took the toothpick out of her mouth to laugh. "Buddy, if you ain't the limit!"

"Hey, Mrs. Gideon," Buddy howled, "did yuh hear what the soap said to the . . ."

"You can ask her some other time," Virginia interrupted. "Come on now."

Just as they started up the stairs, Mrs. Gideon said, with her voice lowered a little, "Say, Virginia, did you hear that ambulance comin' out here awhile ago?"

Virginia shook her head. "Uh uh. But they were saying at the grocery store just now that there was an accident at the bumper factory."

Buddy made an ear-splitting noise in imitation of a shrieking siren, and Virginia put one hand over his mouth firmly.

"Well, I kind of thought it went to Kelton's," Mrs. Gideon said seriously. "Either there or to the tire factory. A course, Mama heard it and it kinda upset her, her bein' sick like she is, you know. I been listenin' for your brother or Johnny O'Connor to come home, so I could ask 'em about it."

"Yeah," Virginia said. "Joe should be home by now."

From someplace upstairs came a sudden raucous burst of radio music and then it was gone, as if someone had turned down the volume dial hastily.

"Say, how did you make out today, Virginia?" Mrs. Gideon asked. "You was downtown seein' about a job, wasn't you?"

Virginia shook her head. "No luck," she said briefly.

"Well, if that don't beat all," Mrs. Gideon said comfortably. "Seems like you do have the worst luck! Why, I was sayin' to Harry, Mr. Gideon, you know, I was sayin' to Harry just the other day that it certainly beat all the way you couldn't get hold a no decent job, all the job-hunting you been doin'."

Virginia dropped her eyes, flushing a little, and loosened the hair at the back of her neck with her hand, self-consciously.

"When we gonna eat, Virgie?" Buddy asked her.

"Right away."

Virginia started up the stairs again, but Mrs. Gideon drifted across the banister still talking.

"Say, did you hear about that Thomas boy up the street here? He got drafted. I was talkin' to his mother today. He has to go in about two weeks."

"Is that so?" Virginia said politely.

"I guess you don't know the Thomases, do you?" Mrs. Gideon

said. "Your sister does, though. If I forget to, you be sure an' tell Sally about the Thomas boy gettin' drafted, won't you? She'd like to know, on account she knows the Thomases . . ."

"I'll tell her."

Mrs. Gideon dug at a tooth viciously with the toothpick. "I'm goin' to the bingo game over to the Odd Fellows' tonight. Mrs. Scott is comin' over to sit with Mama. I couldn't tell you how long it's been since I been out to a bingo game now Harry, Mr. Gideon, you know, has been workin' nights like this. I sure miss playin' bingo."

"We was to the Santy Claus parade last night," Buddy said importantly. "Johnny O'Connor took me and Marilyn."

"Say, we have to go upstairs and get supper." Virginia shooed the children up the stairs ahead of her hastily, just as Mrs. Gideon opened her mouth to speak again. Their feet were noisy on the bare warped boards of the stair steps. The hall at the top was narrow and uncarpeted, with doors on either side, and dimly lighted by a small, orange-colored bulb screwed into a socket in the wall. A light shone out under the first door at the left in a bright narrow strip on the floor; there was the sound of a radio playing inside and, over that, a baby's crying. Virginia went down the hall with the children at her heels to the last door on the right-hand side. She opened the door and they went in together. The small room was dark, the shadowy outlines of furniture visible by the small light from the corner street lamp that shone in the window.

"Wait a minute," Virginia said, "I'll turn the light on."

She stumbled over the davenport, searching for the floor lamp, and put her sack down. She found the chain at last, and the bulb flared inside the battered, yellow, parchment shade. The room looked even smaller with the light on. It was cluttered with odds and ends of shabby, mismatched furniture, a heavy, old-fashioned davenport with the flowered brocade faded to a brownish monotone, a couple of overstuffed chairs of a bright blue color, a library table in one corner, stiff wooden rocking chairs, and the one window framed in limp white lace curtains.

"You kids take your things off and hang them up in the closet,"

Virginia said. She picked up her sack and walked toward the kitchen. There was a light in the kitchen but the door was closed. "Hi," she said, as she pushed it open.

The kitchen was small, cluttered with dirty dishes, the air hot and dry and full of cigarette smoke.

"Oh, hi, Fred. I thought maybe it was Sally home already."

"Naw, it's me," he said. He was a heavy squat man with broad shoulders. He was standing in front of the sink, dumping the wet soggy coffee grounds out of a dripolator top into a paper sack that was already overflowing with garbage into the tin wastebasket in which it stood. "Goddamit!" he mumbled. The last of the grounds seemed firmly stuck in the tin dripolator top. He squinted his eyes against the wisp of smoke rising from the cigarette in his mouth, and rimmed the grounds out with his finger. Most of them fell onto the floor near the garbage can. "Aw, hell!"

Virginia shoved back some of the dishes and set her sack down on the shelf by the sink. "How come you're out of bed so early, Fred? Don't you have to work tonight?"

"Sure, I haveta work," he said morosely, as he rinsed out the coffee pot under the faucet. "Is this the coffee here in this can? Hell, I ain't had no sleep today. This morning I had to go down and pay my alimony and on the way back I stopped at that hamburger joint on Clairmont. You know that dizzy dame that works there? Well, it was her afternoon off and she claimed I made a date with her last week to go to the movies next time she had a day off. Then I just about got home and sleepin' nice an' that goddam ambulance wakes me up . . ."

"They said at the grocery store that there was an accident at the bumper factory," Virginia said.

He struck a match to light the gas under the teakettle. "I figured that ambulance came out to Kelton's," he said uneasily. "You hear anything about the accident? I wonder what's keepin' Joe."

Virginia stopped with her coat half off and looked at the green-painted alarm clock on the cupboard, and the clock seemed to tick louder merely by her looking at it. "It's past time for Joe. He ought to have been home before this." Her face looked frightened, and then she said in a kind of relief, "But Johnny O'Connor isn't home, either, Mrs. Gideon said, and he works the same shift Joe does. Something must have held them up."

"Musta been an accident at Kelton's, all right," Fred said broodingly. "How long is it gonna take this goddam water to boil? Say, Virge, Gloria O'Connor come in and she says for you to come over to her place just as soon as you get home."

"Okay, I'll go over right now, and then I got to get back here and wash these dishes." Virginia hurried out of the kitchen, her coat over her arm. In the living room she nearly tripped over the children in the middle of the floor, as she went to the closet to hang up her coat and hat. Buddy was chivalrously attempting to pull off Marilyn's galoshes. Every time he pulled the wet slippery boot, the little girl slid toward him over the worn linoleum.

"Can't you hang on?" he said earnestly, his face all rosy with his exertion. "My gosh, how you 'spect me ta . . ."

"Well, I am hangin' on," Marilyn said tearfully, digging her chubby dirty hands onto the floor on either side of her as Buddy braced himself to pull again.

Virginia went into the hall. As she walked along the hallway, she heard it: a thin voice raised in song someplace in the darkness above her, a disembodied sound, floating through the upper hall. It came from the third floor, a soprano voice, high and thin and cracked, tuneless and wavering.

*"There's an' ole rugged cross*
*On a hill furrrrr away,*
*Tha em-blum of suffrin' an' shame . . ."*

The singing ceased as suddenly as it had begun, and it was followed by the sound of a voice talking unsteadily and aimlessly. Virginia shuddered a little, her face expressionless.

She stopped at the O'Connors' door and opened it a crack and stuck her head in. This living room was the counterpart of the one across the hall, the same ugly, mismatched furniture typical of all furnished apartments. All of the lights were on and the small radio on the table was grinding out a garbling of music, static and a man's voice reading a weather report. There was no one in sight, but there was a love-story magazine open over a chair arm, and a littering of candy papers strewn around an open candy box, as if Gloria had got up from the chair just a moment past.

"Gloria! Hi!" Virginia called.

The voice answered from the bedroom. "I'm in here givin' Beverly her bottle. Come on in, I got somep'n I wanta show you."

Virginia wiped sudden perspiration from her forehead, the small room was so hot. A wooden chair had been pulled up in front of the register and it was draped with the white squares of baby diapers. The diapers shifted and moved in the heat, and the acrid smell of their drying filled the room. "Look, Gloria," Virginia said. "I want to wash some dishes before Sally gets home. When you get done could you bring over what it is you want to show me?"

"Okay," Gloria answered instantly in her soft, even voice. "I'll be over in a minute, Ginny."

Virginia closed the door and hurried down the hall to her own door. Back in the living room she found a babble of confusion. Buddy had managed to remove one of Marilyn's galoshes, and now he was lying flat on his back on the davenport resting from his labors, and airily assuring his sister that it was impossible to remove the remaining boot from her foot. Marilyn sat in the middle of the floor, struggling with the overshoe herself, alternating from temper to tears back to temper again.

"Buddy Otis, you quit teasing her now," Virginia said wearily. "Get up and help her get her things off right this minute!"

In the kitchen, Fred had cleared the dirty dishes off the table and piled them in the sink. He sat now at one end of the table, his heavy body slouched back in his chair, a cup and the dripolator in front of him, and the pungent odor of coffee already permeating the air.

"Did you hear the concert just then?" he said, grinning at Virginia.

"Yeah." Virginia rolled up the sleeves of her plain yellow blouse and drew hot water from the faucet into the dishpan.

"Old lady Sipes musta been hittin' the bottle again today."

"I don't see why Mrs. Gideon lets her live here," Virginia said. "She's the horridest old woman I ever knew, always getting drunk up there and yelling and singing."

Fred poured a little coffee into the cup, and blew on it before he drank it. "Well, I guess she pays her rent and that's all old Giddy cares about. Jesus, she musta really pinned one on today by the sound of her. Virgie, hows about you runnin' out and buyin' me a dozen cans a beer, huh?"

"Uh uh. You've got to go to work tonight."

Fred laughed. "You sounded just like Sally right then."

Virginia smiled over her shoulder. When she smiled she looked much younger; her eyes warmed and crinkled smaller in her face.

"I got a letter today," Fred said, "from that gal, Betty, out in Illinois. Jesus, that gal can write the sweetest lovin'est letter you ever saw. I oughta let you read it."

"No, thanks," Virginia said, over the rattle of the dishes.

"You better read it," Fred advised. "Maybe you could use some ideas for the next letter you write to that guy Bill you're always writing to. Say, what's become a good old Bill? You ain't had a letter from him in a helluva while."

"I suppose everybody around here checks on my mail," Virginia said softly.

"Why, sure." Fred poured some more coffee out of the pot into his cup. "Christ!" he burst out suddenly. "What's keepin' that goddam Joe?"

Then it was very quiet in the kitchen, except for the rattling of the dishes and the loud monotonous ticking of the clock.

She came so quietly with the bedroom slippers on her feet that they never heard Gloria until she stood in the kitchen speaking to them.

"Look what I got! Just look what I got! Ain't it gorgeous?" She twirled around and around in front of the table, like an excited child. What she had come to show them was obviously the chubby jacket of shiny, black, long-haired fur that she was wearing over her faded housedress. But it was hard to look at anything else except Gloria herself, because Gloria O'Connor was beautiful, more beautiful than a lot of the girls in the movies and on the magazine covers. Her hair was dark yellow, with deep natural waves in it, and it hung thick to her shoulders. Her eyes were blue and her features perfect, as perfect as her full, voluptuous body. She was about Virginia's age, but she looked younger, and, by comparison with her, Virginia looked thin and small and colorless.

Fred Foster swore under his breath, looking at her. "I'd like to know what Johnny ever done to deserve this," he said plaintively. "Gloria, if you're the kinda luck the Irish have, why in hell wasn't I born under a shamrock bush?"

Gloria smiled at him graciously. "Don't you love it?" she said to Virginia, smoothing the fur of one of the wide sleeves with her fingers. "I'm just crazy about it."

"It's awfully nice, Gloria," Virginia said. "It looks wonderful on you. Black is such a good color for you."

"Yup, pretty snazzy," Fred said cheerfully. "Hey, Gloria, where's your old man? Ain't he home from work yet?"

Gloria stopped short and looked at Fred. She looked a little surprised and somehow bewildered, almost the only emotion that her perfect features ever registered. "Is it time for Johnny to come home already?" she said helplessly. "My gosh, and I ain't even cleared off the breakfast table nor bought stuff for supper or nothin'."

Fred laughed and warmed up the dregs of coffee in his cup from the pot. "Never mind," he said to Gloria consolingly. "Don't you bother your head about doin' housework. You'll keep the home fires burnin', all right."

She looked at him blankly for a second and then went back to admiring her fur jacket. "Isn't it just gorgeous?" she said happily, stroking the fur lovingly. "It's my Christmas present from Johnny. I couldn't see no sense in waitin' till Christmas. I'd rather have it right away. I been wantin' one a these for a long time."

"It's an awfully nice Christmas present," Virginia said sincerely. "And you look simply swell in it, Gloria."

"Say, I bet that set Johnny back plenty," Fred said, eyeing the jacket meditatively. "Poor old Johnny, ten to one he ain't finished payin' on that bracelet with the diamond he got you for your birthday, and now he's gotta start payin' on a coat. That's the trouble with you glamor girls, you cost a guy money."

From up above came another snatch of singing in Mrs. Sipes' cracked, drunken, old voice:

*"Come Josephine*
*In my flyin' machine*
*And away we'll go—away we'll go . . ."*

The singing broke off with a burst of laughter and the voice subsided into the disjointed aimless monologue again. Just then they heard the quick light feet coming up the stairs and along the hall. The door was thrown open with a bang, and a warm voice with a lilt to it sang out, "Well, hello, people!"

"Hi, Sally!" They all spoke together, and they all smiled together.

There was the sound of children's feet running across the living-room floor.

"Hey, Ma, when we gonna eat?"

"Ma, we're gonna slide downhill in Smith's driveway, his ma said we could when it snowed."

"When we gonna have supper, Ma?"

"Hi, giblets! Come kiss your old mother!"

There was a sound of loud smacking kisses and smothered giggles and grunts. "Look out, you kids are gettin' so big you'll knock your poor, old, broken-down mother right over. Where's your big brother? I s'pose Harold's not home from his paper route yet." The next minute Sally appeared in the kitchen door, both children still clinging to her. She and Virginia looked alike, except that Sally was older, a little heavier, her face fuller. The same dark hair, and the same dark eyes, just a little too big and a shade too serious for her pleasant, smiling face. She wore the green-and-white uniform of the restaurant, and the children were clinging to her so tightly that she could hardly walk.

"Hi, Fred," she said gayly. "If here isn't my star boarder! What are you doin' out of bed this early? Gloria O'Connor, if you didn't get a fur coat for Christmas! Honest, that husband a yours is so crazy about you that it wouldn't surprise me none if some day he come bringin' you home everything they had in the store. Ginny, you've got the dishes pretty near done! Why didn't you wait and let me help do 'em? Thanks a lot!"

She talked so fast that no one had a chance to say a word. The children were still clamoring at her. She knelt down suddenly and pulled them up against her, one in either arm.

"My goodness," she marveled. "You're gettin' so you talk pretty near as much as your mother. So you're gonna slide downhill? How's school? Did you get licked today?"

"Well, school's pretty good," Marilyn said, scowling a little.

"Hey, Ma," Buddy said, hugging her tight. "What did the big flower say to the little flower? I betcha yuh don't know what the big flower said to the little flower?"

"What did the big flower say to the little flower? Well, now, let me see . . ."

"I know," Marilyn said. "I know!"

"Don't you tell me!" her mother said warningly. "Now, you be quiet and just let me think a minute." She cocked her head over on one side while the children waited expectantly. "Now, let me see. What did the big flower say to the—now, let me think . . ."

She reached out suddenly and tweaked Buddy's small upturned nose. "Hi, bud," she said gravely. Buddy looked bewildered and perfectly astonished.

"Hey . . ." he said aggrievedly.

Marilyn burst out laughing. "She guessed it. She guessed the answer," she chanted.

Buddy was still bewildered. His mother tweaked his nose again. "Hi, bud," she said. Then Buddy burst out laughing too. They shrieked with laughter, twining their arms tight around her.

Sally stood up quickly, loosening their arms from about her. "If you'll go look in my coat pocket in the closet, there's a book of funny pictures somebody left at the restaurant today," she said briskly. "You look at it in the other room and keep out of the way till I get supper ready. Scat!"

With the children out of the kitchen, Sally pushed the hair back from her face and turned to Gloria. "Now, Gloria, let me take a look at that new coat."

Gloria turned and twisted in front of her delightedly, showing off the fur jacket. "Ain't it swell? Don't you just love it, Sally?"

"Gloria, it's just lovely! Here, turn around, let me see the back again." She rubbed her fingers along the shiny dark fur. "Why, this is just about the nicest fur coat I ever saw in my life!"

"Yup," Fred Foster said, "that's just what Johnny will think, too, when the bills on it keep rollin' in about half the rest of his life."

"Don't let him tease you, Gloria," Sally said. "He's just jealous of Johnny because he hasn't got a good-looking wife to buy coats for. When Johnny sees you in this coat, he won't care how much it costs. Imagine how I would look in a coat like this! Honest, Gloria, you're the prettiest thing I ever saw!" She hugged Gloria tight, coat and all.

Gloria was glowing with delight at Sally's appreciation. "You can wear it sometime, Sally," she said impulsively. "If you're ever goin' out someplace and I ain't usin' it right then, I'll let you wear it, honest!"

Sally laughed. "Why, thanks, Gloria. Maybe I will, sometime. Why, I'd look so dressed up nobody would know me."

"That's an idea!" Fred said. "Hey, Sally, you doll up some night and borrow Gloria's new coat and let's you and me go out and do the night spots. Is that a date?"

Sally looked sober for just a second before she laughed. "I'm afraid I couldn't keep up with you, Fred. I can't take it like I used to. I'm just an old married woman now."

"Goddam!" Fred said sadly. "It's a terrible thing the way I can't get me a date around this house. I'm scared to ask Gloria for a date for fear Johnny'd beat my head off. And Sally won't go out with me. And Virgie here, would rather set home and moon over that guy's letters than go out and drink a beer with me. What's a fellow gonna do anyway, I'd like to know."

Sally winked at Virginia before she answered him. "Oh, it's just too bad about you, Fred Foster. With all the girls you've got on the string, I guess you'll get along all right without us. Say! You go to work at ten tonight, don't you? I guess I better rustle up some supper here. You quit drinking that coffee, and I'll have something to eat here in a few minutes."

The babbling voice upstairs started in again, and there was a crashing sound, as if a chair or a table had been overturned on the floor.

Sally listened a minute, and then went on taking groceries out of the sack. "Is Mrs. Sipes at it again?" she asked.

"She's been bangin' and singin' up there all afternoon," Gloria said indifferently, leaning back against the doorjamb, her hands deep in the pockets of her jacket.

"Poor old lady," Sally said. "It makes me nervous to hear her. I'm always so afraid she'll fall down up there or something, and get hurt. Suppose she'd fall, coming down those stairs? They're so dark."

"Probably wouldn't hurt her if she did," Fred said. "I see a drunk once fall down two flights of stairs, just rolled right down 'em over and over. Hell, when he got to the bottom he just picked himself up and walked off, looking for some place to get another drink."

"Well, it's different with her. She's an old lady; her bones are all brittle." Sally paused with a pound of butter in her hand before she put it into the refrigerator. "How much did you have to pay for butter, Virgie?"

Virginia was scrubbing on a greasy frying pan. She stopped and rested her arms tracked with soapsuds on the edge of the dishpan. "Let's see. I got the groceries at Rogers'. Butter was thirty-nine cents."

Sally shook her head and put the butter into the refrigerator. "Thirty-nine cents! Wouldn't you know it! You can get it at the A. and P. for thirty-two!"

"I'm awfully sorry," Virginia said. "I was late and the A. and P. was closed. I put the change back in the cupboard."

"Fine. Oh, it's all right, but it just shows how much a body can save on groceries if they go to a chain store. But it's all right. If you were late, you couldn't help it." Sally stopped and looked at the alarm clock on top of the cupboard. "Gosh, I wonder what's keepin' Joe and

Johnny. It makes me nervous. I heard there was an accident out to Kelton's."

"Yeah," Fred said gloomily. "Ambulance went by here like a bat outa hell."

"Well, I wish those boys would hurry up and come." Sally sighed, her hands busy peeling the potatoes.

Gloria looked at the clock too, and her mind apparently reverted to a previous train of thought. "Is it time for Johnny to come home already?" she said. "My gosh, I ain't even got the table cleared off from breakfast or stuff bought for supper or nothing. I guess Johnny'n me'll have to eat out tonight."

"Well, if you got anything to eat in the icebox, bring it over here," Sally said, "and we'll all eat together. There's always room for a couple more."

"Well . . ." Gloria said. "Gee, I dunno. I kinda thought it would be fun to go out an' eat. I kinda wanted to dress up and wear my new coat and everything."

"That would be nice," Sally said. "You can leave the baby here just as well as not, if you want to go out."

"I guess maybe we will," Gloria said.

It was quiet in the kitchen then, just the snow blowing against the window hard, so that it sounded almost like hail, and the water boiling in the teakettle on the stove.

Fred Foster stood up suddenly. "Look, I'm gonna run over to the diner a minute. Some a the boys hangin' around there'll know about the accident."

"Somebody's coming in now," Virginia said. "I heard somebody in the hall."

They all were quiet to listen. Footsteps came up to the door and the door opened and somebody yelled, "Hey, anybody around here know who stole my wife?"

They listened to his noisy, affectionate greeting of the children and the next moment Johnny O'Connor appeared in the kitchen door. He had a dark-blue jacket flung around his shoulders and a dark felt hat on the side of his head, both of them powdered with the light snow. And both of his hands were wrapped in white bandaging.

"Hi, Johnny, old kid!" Fred Foster said.

Johnny sidestepped into the kitchen, weaving his bandaged hands in front of him. "Get your dukes up," he snarled.

Fred doubled his fists obediently and stepped in toward Johnny. Johnny sidled and feinted a few times and then landed a flurry of rights and lefts on a spot in the air about an inch from Fred's chin.

"Next time you oughta take my advice," Johnny said. "When I say get 'em up, sonnyboy, I mean get 'em up! Some day you're gonna come in wide open like that and somebody's gonna hang something on you, and I don't mean a bouquet, unless it's the round kind with black ribbons and a sympathy card hanging on it."

"Aw, g'wan," Fred said, grinning.

"Whatsa matter with your hands?" Gloria said in her serene, unhurried voice. "How come you got your hands all done up like that?"

Johnny turned to her instantly. "Glory be!" he said softly. There was a kind of special tenderness all over his slim mobile face when he looked at her. He put his arms around her and kissed her gently.

"Well, I'll tell you about my hands," he said. "They got next to a hot piece of steel today, and, would you believe it, they got warm!"

"Oh," she said vaguely. She squirmed out of his arms. "Look, my coat come today! How do you like it? Don't it look swell?"

"Well, I'll say it looks swell," Johnny said. "You look like a million dollars, Glory. Just look at her, isn't she . . . ?"

"You burn your hands bad, Johnny?" Fred asked him curiously.

"Naw. Just raised up a few blisters. They're all right. The doctor says I can get back on the job in a day or two."

"Well, you better be awful careful though," Sally said warningly. "You don't wanta rub those blisters off. A burn like that's no joke."

"Hell, so it was you they sent that ambulance out after," Fred said, half-joking.

"No. It wasn't me," Johnny said soberly.

"We heard there was an accident," Sally said. "Was it bad?"

"Oh, Jesus," Johnny said. "It was a bitch!" He reached for a cigarette and discovered that his clumsy bandaged hands wouldn't go into his pocket. He held both hands out in front of him and surveyed them mournfully. "My mother told me there'd be days like this, but she never said how many!"

"Here, I got one." Fred put the cigarette into Johnny's mouth and struck the match.

"Thanks," Johnny said. He took a deep drag on the cigarette. "Oh, it was a helluva thing! A Polish guy named Stan Walezewski. Maybe you heard Joe talk about him. He works on the chromium line right there next to Joe."

Sally shook her head. "I never heard Joe say. What happened? Joe wasn't . . ."

"No, Joe's all right," Johnny said quickly. The cigarette wobbled between his lips and some ash fell off onto his jacket. "Except it hit him pretty hard. He was right next to the guy when it happened. Christ, I been looking for Joe everyplace, Fry's and the Rail and all the drinking places. I finally give up. I thought he mighta come on home."

"And what's it to yuh!"

They all jumped. They had been so intent upon what Johnny was saying that none of them had heard him come until suddenly here he was. Nobody said a word. The room was still, with that strained unnatural stillness of a conversation broken off in the middle. Nobody said anything. The clock ticked loudly, the children's voices sounded, chattering together in the living room, the muffled rumble of factory noises came from beyond the window and the sound of the wind with snow borne before it.

Joe Braun stood still, just inside the door. He was not quite steady on his feet, and his dingy overcoat hung open on his gangling tall figure. His eyes were bloodshot and his face was white and sullen, with a stretched look about it, as if at any moment all of the muscles might get out of control and start to twitch and quiver. He brought a strong odor of alcohol into the small warm room with him.

Sally broke the silence first. "Well, hi, Joe!" Her voice was light and gay, with just a little effort. "You're late, mister. A few minutes more'n you woulda missed your supper."

Fred Foster got up out of his chair hurriedly. "Here, have a chair, Joey. Set down and take the load off your feet."

Joe didn't say a word to either of them. Fred remained standing awkwardly in front of the window.

"How'd you like a cup of coffee, Joe?" Sally said. "There's some all made. Supper won't be for a few minutes."

Joe still didn't say anything. From upstairs came the sound of some piece of furniture sliding heavily along the floor, and then Mrs. Sipes burst into song again, her voice wavering over the words without enthusiasm:

*"Onward Christyun sol-ol-jers*
*Marchin' asta war*
*Witha cross a Jeeee-zus*
*Goin' on before . . ."*

"Hey, Johnny," Gloria said accusingly, "you was tellin' about the guy gettin' hurt over to the factory. Why don't-cha finish tellin' about that guy gettin' hurt? Did the guy get killed?"

Joe Braun made a funny noise in his throat and walked over and sat down in the chair suddenly. "Naw, he didn't get killed," Joe said.

"Glory, wasn't that the baby crying I heard just then?" Johnny said easily. "Let's you and me go over to our house and let these folks eat their supper, huh?"

Joe Braun locked his hands tight together on the table in front of him. He was still looking at Gloria, and he had a smile across his white face. "Naw, he didn't get killed. Didn't you hear about him? Ain't Johnny told you?"

"Uh uh," Gloria said. "Johnny jus' started to tell and then . . ."

"Joe," Sally said, her voice urgent. "Joe!"

Joe kept smiling at them. "The guard rail broke," he said. "He fell in the vat. It boiled him." Joe's eyes kept roving from one face to another and the bright smile was fixed on his face. "It boiled his eyes right out of his head. Boiled the meat right off the bone a one of his arms."

"Oh, Christ!" Fred Foster said softly.

"Hell, they say he's still alive up there in the hospital. He was a big strong guy. It's gonna take a lotta killin'. He was reaching up for the switch, see, and his foot musta slipped. He fell up against the rail and it broke. Christ, you shoulda heard the way he hollered when he went into that vat."

"My, that's awful," Gloria said in her slow unmoved voice. "I betcha he dies."

Joe Braun laughed. "I wouldn't be surprised an' you're right," he said unpleasantly. His eyes could not be still in his face. He kept looking from one to the other of them. There was a defiance in his eyes and a kind of malice. "You shoulda seen him. He kept grabbin' for something all the while he was fallin', but there wasn't nothin' for him to get hold of. You oughta heard him holler when . . ."

"Cut it out, Joe," Johnny O'Connor said.

Joe stopped talking, and his eyes came to rest on Johnny's face. Johnny looked back at him steadily.

When he started to speak again, Johnny broke in. "Take it easy, Joe."

Joe's eyes were still at last, held quiet by Johnny's blue ones; but the rest of his face was breaking up and shifting. His whole body seemed to cave in. His legs stiffened out, pushing his chair back, scraping along the floor. His control was gone. "Yeah. Sure. Take it easy!" he said wildly. "My God, I tell you I saw it happen. I was working right next to him. I see it all. I heard the way he hollered when— my God! An' I know what's eatin' you, just like all the rest a them. Hell, you think I was sucker enough to go foolin' around on them slippery boards tryin' to fish him outa there, no guard rail or nothin'? Why, it's a wonder them guys that got him out didn't slip off in there, too. They got burned all over their arms, pullin' him outa there. It's a wonder they didn't go off in there, too, them slippery boards and nothin' to hang onto nor nothing. Hell, you think I was crazy? I knew he was a goner all right, soon as I seen him fall. You think I was sucker enough to try to . . ."

Joe dropped his head into his hands, and Sally spoke to him helplessly. "Aw, Joe, it's all right! We don't wanta hear nothing more about it. Don't talk about it any more or think about it. It's all right, Joe."

Johnny shook his head at her. "Look, Joe," he said gently. "How about you and me . . ."

Joe yanked his face up out of his hands. His breath was coming in half sobs. "Okay. You're damn right I was scared. I was scared to death, if you wanta know it. I was scared to death to move with that railing gone. I was scared for fear I'd go right off in there just like he done. I wasn't gonna go foolin' around trying to get him outa there. What did I care? Let him boil! I was scared. I always been scared of them goddam vats."

"Come on, Joe," Johnny said patiently. "Let's you and me go out and get a drink. I think we both could be using one. What do you say, Joe?"

"Okay, so I always been scared of them vats, and what's it to you!" Joe said wildly. "They drive me nuts. I'm all done. I'm washed up. I ain't going back. To hell with the job. I ain't goin' back there. I never wanta see them goddam vats again as long as I . . ."

"All right, Joe, okay. You don't have to go back there, nobody's trying to make you. What you need right now is a drink. How about you and me . . . ?"

Joe whirled around suddenly and pushed past Johnny to the door. They heard the sound of his stumbling over a chair, and the living-room door flung open with a bang.

"Joe, wait!" Sally called. "Where are you going, Joe? Don't go, Joe. Joe, listen to me!"

But at the kitchen door she stopped. They already heard the sound of his stumbling, running feet on the stairs.


Much later that same night, when the apartment was dark and quiet and everybody was sleeping, Sally lay sleepless in her bed. Her feet hurt and her body ached with fatigue. She lay on her back and stared into the darkness. She listened to the sound of the children's soft steady breathing as they slept, Marilyn in the bed beside her, Buddy on the cot along the wall. After awhile she heard a light rapping on the door. It startled her. She couldn't think who it could be, knocking like this late at night. Sally slid the covers back gently so as not to awaken Marilyn and got out of bed. The cold air struck her body and her teeth began to chatter instantly. Her feet groped on the cold floor boards hunting for her slippers, and she scratched her toe on a splinter before she found them. She folded Roy's old blanket-cloth bathrobe hastily over her thin pajamas and pattered out into the living room. She didn't turn on a light because Virginia slept on the davenport.

Sally sprung the night lock and opened the door softly. It was Johnny O'Connor standing on the other side of the door. She recognized him instantly, even before he spoke to her, the dim light gleaming on the white bandaging wound around his hands. "Hi, Sally," he whispered. "You musta been awake. Don't you know sleep is good for the body?"

Sally laughed a little, and stepped out into the hall beside him, pulling the door behind her. "What about you? A fine time to be just getting home."

"Look, Sally," he said, "I got to thinking about Joe, so I went around to some of the places, keeping an eye open for him."

"Yeah?"

"Well, I finally caught up with him. He's over to Nicky Toresca's night-club place and still drinking, I'm willing to bet you, right this minute."

Sally started in the dim light, and her hand rose up toward her mouth involuntarily. "Nicky Toresca's?" She repeated the name, and there was an odd sound to her voice. "I didn't know Joe ever hung around Toresca's."

"I guess he must," Johnny said, "because they seemed to know who Joe was. I didn't talk to Joe, myself. He was sitting at a table drinking with some other fellows, but I talked to Nicky a minute before I left. Nicky said to leave him where he was and not to worry about him, that he'd see to it he got sobered up and back here tomorrow morning."

"I didn't know Joe knew Nicky Toresca," Sally said again in a worried voice. "I never knew that Joe hung out at Toresca's place."

"I think he'll be all right over there. Maybe better off than he would be at home, the way he was feeling tonight."

"Well, thanks a lot, Johnny," Sally said. "It was awful nice a you to keep an eye on Joe and let me know about him. I was worried about Joe. I couldn't sleep tonight to save me. Now I feel better."

"Well, don't you worry about Joe any more. He'll be all right. He'll be home here tomorrow feeling all right, you see if he isn't."

"Thanks a lot, Johnny," Sally said again. "I don't know what we'd do around here without you."

"Yup, the indispensable man," he said, grinning as he turned away. They said good night together, and Sally slipped back inside the door. She readjusted the night lock and then hesitated a moment. Her mind was alert and full of too many things for sleeping. She pattered off toward the bathroom, her feet noiseless in her old felt-soled slippers. In the bathroom she searched the empty medicine bottles, old toothbrushes, tubes of shaving cream and toothpaste, cold-cream jars and broken combs that crammed the shelves of the little medicine cabinet over the washbowl. She was looking for a little box of sleeping pills that the doctor had prescribed for Roy once a long time ago. She couldn't find them, and she took an aspirin tablet instead. Maybe that would take the ache out of her bones, she thought. She'd just got to clean out this medicine cabinet some time. It was awful the way she let things go around the house, but with her job, it seemed like she couldn't find time to do everything.

Before she left the bathroom, she opened the other door a crack and peeked into the bedroom beyond. This was the room that Joe Braun shared with Harold. Tonight Harold slept alone in the middle of the bed; the light shone in directly on his face, his slim freckled face, with the light straggly hair. Sally smiled a little, tenderly. Harold looked so much like Roy, now, as he got older, and she was so glad. Sally closed the door and turned off the light.

From the bathroom, she went out to the kitchen. It always looked strange to her at night. It was cold and unnaturally empty of people, and of dirty dishes littering the table and piling the sink. The stove looked cold and dead, with all the burners shut off, the teakettle and coffee pot sitting primly on top of it, in readiness for breakfast. On top of the refrigerator, Sally caught sight of a crumpled cigarette package that someone had left lying there, and she took out a cigarette, lighted it, and sat down on one of the chairs pulled up to the empty table. Sally smoked rarely; she used to smoke when she and

Roy were first married, but of late years she always said that she never had time for it. It was mostly on account of the children, though, Sally admitted honestly. For some reason she was old-fashioned about it. She just didn't like to have the children see her smoking.

Sally sat alone, shivering a little with the cold, and tracing what was left of the pattern on the worn oil-cloth table cover with her finger. She puffed on the cigarette and watched the spiral of smoke drift upward. All the trouble and worry in her mind unrolled and mounted, like the streamer of smoke from the tip of her cigarette. Worry over money, and worry over Joe, worry over what had happened with Nicky Toresca at the restaurant this afternoon and the possibility that it might threaten her precious job. Worry over the visit that she would pay to Roy tomorrow afternoon. Funny, how you could look forward to a visit so much and still dread it. Oh, she missed Roy so—they needed him so! The kids—Harold was getting older now—he needed to have his father. And the little kids—they grew so fast and changed so much and forgot so many things. Why, it was almost as if their father was a stranger to them right now. And she needed Roy too—a great deep need down in herself for him all the while, day or night, whatever she did, wherever she went. The need of her physical being for his physical being, and more besides. They had always been so close—she'd never felt alone ever—they had shared everything that came to them—they had been two lucky people. And now she was so terribly alone. There was no one that she could talk to somehow—and she needed to talk to somebody so badly. But there wasn't anybody, not even Virginia, because in lots of ways Virginia seemed as young to her as Marilyn did. Now she was beginning to feel sorry for herself, Sally told herself in a sudden shift of mood, and that wouldn't do at all.

Sally got up suddenly, crushed out her cigarette in an ash tray and padded back through the darkened rooms to her bed.

Virginia heard her pass through the room, and the squeak of the bedsprings a moment later, because Virginia, too, was wide awake this night. She squirmed a little, uncomfortably, on the stiff cushions of the davenport. Outside, the wind whooped and howled, almost drowning out the factory noises. Over at the truck depot in the next block there was the roaring sound from the powerful engines of the great freight haulers as they came into the depot to load and unload cargo. Virginia knew all the night noises by heart. In about an hour the activity would start around the dairy down at the end of the street. Trucks would come in, and there would be the tinny rattling sound of milk cans as they were shoved together on the platform, from then until daylight. And any moment now Mr. Gideon would be coming home from work. There was always a set pattern of sounds connected with his homecoming.

Virginia nuzzled her face into her pillow and closed her eyes tight, determinedly. But it wasn't any use. Feet sounded along the sidewalk—the clear staccato tapping of heel plates on cement. Over at the truck depot the great engines roared and men's voices sounded as they yelled at each other over the howl of the wind.

This was a crazy town, Virginia thought, different from any town she had ever lived in before. There wasn't any real night time here. There was never a time when a part of the population wasn't up and doing, coming to and from work, going to movies, eating in hamburger places. Twenty-four hours of the day, all the day and all the night, life was going on as usual, normal, active, non-sleeping life, for a number of people. She didn't like it, and she couldn't get used to it. She hated this town.

But she shouldn't think that, Virginia reminded herself guiltily. After all, where would she be if Sally hadn't given her a home here? Sally was so sweet and wonderful. Sally had troubles that made Virginia's own worries look silly, but she never complained. She was always gay and light-hearted, doing things for other people, cheering them up, and never asking anything for herself. Virginia stared straight ahead of her into the darkness and wished that there was something she could do for Sally. If she could only find a job, then at least she could pay back the money Sally was spending, keeping her here. She was so tired of job-hunting. If she didn't find something pretty soon she was going to go to work in a factory. She didn't care what anybody said. She hated this town, and she was so lonely here. She missed Bill so, and he didn't even write to her. She could stand everything else if only Bill would write once in awhile. What would she do if he just never wrote to her again? But he wouldn't do that. Maybe Bill was sick; maybe he had lost his job and was too discouraged to tell her about it. Or maybe he had been hurt in the factory. Virginia thought about the accident in the bumper factory today, and her heart almost stopped beating. But wouldn't Bill's mother write and let her know if he was sick or hurt or anything like that? Or would she? Maybe his draft questionnaire had come. Why, maybe Bill was in the army right this minute!

A hoarse-throated factory whistle blew someplace in the wind and darkness—two long toots and a short one. Automatically Virginia's mind became busy with translation in spite of herself. That was the whistle from the tire factory. Let's see—two long blasts and one short one—why, that meant they needed electricians in the pit.

For some idiotic reason that seemed to be almost the last straw to Virginia. She rolled over on her stomach and smothered her face in her pillow and felt the warm tears ooze out of her eyes and wet the pillow slip.

Then Mr. Gideon came home. First the car in the driveway and then the slamming garage doors. His step on the back porch, and the sound of his key groping for the keyhole, the opening and closing of the kitchen door. Virginia held her breath and listened, anticipating exactly the next sound. Sure enough, a dull heavy thudding, followed in a minute by another one. That was Mr. Gideon taking off his shoes. Next came the faucet running, the water splashing in the sink. That would be Mr. Gideon getting a drink of water. He never once reversed the order. You could always count on it. You could always be sure that there would never be a time when Mr. Gideon would forget or get mixed up and get a drink of water before he took off his shoes. Then there was a silence, but Virginia knew exactly what was going to come next. She listened for it. The bang of the refrigerator door closing, the rattle of a pan on the stove.

At that point Virginia really cried, cried hard into the pillow for a long time.

# 3

SALLY AWOKE TO A COLD, STILL MORNING AT THE first raucous prompting of the alarm clock. She jumped out of bed immediately, before she had time to think about it, and went straight to the bathroom without even waiting to put on her robe. She bathed and dressed hurriedly, put her bathrobe on over her slip and went out to the kitchen to start breakfast. She only had time enough to set the table and start the cereal and coffee cooking. The real work connected with the meal fell to Virginia, along with the task of getting the children off to school.

About the time the odor of the coffee filled the kitchen, Fred Foster shambled in for his breakfast. Fred lived in the room across the hall and had contracted to board with Sally soon after she had moved into the house. They exchanged brief greetings, and he sat down heavily in the chair at the end of the table. Fred got out of work nearly an hour before, but out of deference to Sally's habitual breakfast hour he idled the time away at the diner up the street.

He sat slumped over on the table, his head between his hands, his face dull and loose with fatigue and loss of sleep. Sally looked at him sympathetically as she opened a large can of tomato juice with expert manipulation of the can opener. "Fred, you oughta try to get more sleep. You can't keep going, working nights, unless you sleep daytimes. You better talk to all them girl friends of yours and tell them they got to leave you alone, except week ends."

"Hell, don't I know it," he mumbled. "I told Giddy just now she wasn't to call me down to the telephone no matter who called up."

"That's the spirit," Sally said cheerfully. "It must be awful cold out this morning, huh?"

"Yeah," he said indifferently. "You better wear your ear flappers."

"Say, now that's an idea. Ear muffs, that's just what I need, waitin' around for the bus these cold mornings. Guess I'll have to write a letter to Santa Claus."

"Yeah! Good old Santa Claus." Fred laughed derisively.

Sally shoved some of the dishes back and set the battered old tin toaster on the table, plugged the cord into the wall, and put the bread in its waxy paper container beside it. "Well, it won't be long till Christmas now. You got your Christmas shopping done?"

"I ain't doin' any," he said. "To hell with it!"

"I know how you feel," Sally said. "Christmas around here is no joke either. But we always do a little something for the kids, and it's kind of fun. They get so excited over Christmas, you don't have to spend much money to give them a good time."

"I wasn't thinkin' about money," Fred said broodingly.

Before Sally had time to say anything more, Virginia came into the kitchen. She looked fresh and well scrubbed, but her face bore traces of sleeplessness.

"Hi," Sally said brightly. "Look, I've got to run, if I catch that quarter-after bus. Is there anybody in the bathroom? My gosh, I'm not even dressed yet! Everything is all ready for breakfast. Don't let the cereal scorch, will you? You have to watch it and keep stirring it all the time it's cooking because it scorches so easy. I put the bread for toast on the table. Use the old bread left in that loaf first before you open the new loaf and . . ."

"Okay," Virginia said. "Don't worry about us. We'll get along, all right. You go on and get dressed and get your bus."

"Honest, Ginny," Sally said, "I don't know what we'd do around here without you!"

"Yeah, Virgie's a swell girl, all right. Couldn't do without her!" Fred shut one eye the better to focus the other one on her. "My God, Virgie, what was you doin' last night? You look worse'n I do. You look like something the cat dragged in."

"You don't look so good yourself," Virginia said.

Sally was fumbling with the strings on the faded apron that she had tied on over her bathrobe. "Here, untie me will you, Ginny? I must have got a knot in it."

"Probably Virgie was mooning around about that boy friend of hers, so she couldn't sleep," Fred said. "She looks kinda lovelorn to me, don't she, Sally? You know, good old Bill!"

Fred assumed a lovelorn expression and rendered a few lines in atrocious imitation of Helen Morgan singing one of the pieces which she immortalized with her peculiar style. His voice was hardly an approximation of the night-club singer's, and the chair on which he sat was a poor substitute for the piano upon which Miss Morgan so frequently perched, but Virginia got the idea.

"When you sing you sound just about like Mrs. Sipes does," Virginia said. She flushed a little, and kept her eyes upon the hot iron spoon that she held with a holder, stirring slowly in the kettle of boiling cereal.

"Oh, say, Virgie, that makes me think." Sally stuck her head back in the kitchen doorway. "If you don't hear Mrs. Sipes stirring around up there this morning, you run up and see how she is along about noon. I'm always so nervous for fear she'll be sick up there or something and nobody would know nothing about it. She might try to call to us and nobody would hear her. She could die up there all by herself. You'll go up, won't you, Virgie?"

"Okay."

"And Virgie, I forgot to tell you. You make Marilyn put her sweater on to wear to school today, it's so cold. It's in there in the closet. It's that tan one with the buttons, you know the one. She don't like to wear it 'cause it's got a hole in the sleeve, but you make her wear it, anyway. Honest, I've been trying to get that darn sweater mended all winter. Let's see, there was something else I was going to tell you, but I can't think what it was. I had it right on the tip of my tongue. Let's see . . ."

"Say," Fred said, "I was gonna tell you. Did you hear that guy died?"

Sally stood still in the doorway. "You mean that Polish fellow that got hurt over to the factory? No, I hadn't heard he was dead yet."

"Yup," Fred said. "The boys was talking about it over to the diner this morning. He died last night. Musta lived about five or six hours after it happened."

"It was a terrible thing," Sally said, shuddering a little. "I can't bear to think about it. I hope they fixed him up so he didn't have to suffer. I feel so sorry for his wife, being left like that with a little kid and another one on the way and everything."

"That guy sure must have been tough, all right, living five or six hours like that, burnt the way he was . . ."

"I can't bear to think about it," Sally said again. She roused herself suddenly and started away almost on a run. "My gosh, what am I standing around here talking for? I gotta bus to catch. Virgie, get some frankfurters for supper, and maybe you better get some soup. Get three cans; soup always tastes good on cold days." Her voice trailed away behind her. "There's cold meat in the refrigerator for the kids lunches and . . ."

Fred Foster laughed. "My God, you can always hear Sally two minutes after you can't see her, the way she rushes around here. Some morning she is gonna miss that bus and when she does she'll just naturally run all the way downtown and get there five minutes before the bus does." He yawned and stretched his arms out wide. "Hurry up with that breakfast-food slop and cook me up some eggs, Virge. Me for a nice soft bed for the next six hours . . ."

In the bathroom, Sally wriggled her old red jersey-wool dress down over her head. "Hey, you kidlets!" she yelled, with the cloth muffling her words a little. "Time to get up! Come on, pile out now. You hadn't better be late to school! Come on now, Virgie's got breakfast all ready for you." The only answer she got was the faint sound of a bedspring squeaking from the bedroom.

She tidied her thick dark hair with a comb. No time to powder her nose, she thought. Just some lipstick to tone her up a little.

"Come on, you kids! Last stop! All out! Who wants to get into the bathroom next?"

"Hey, Ma," Buddy yelled sleepily from the bedroom, "is it still snowin', Ma?"

"No, I guess it stopped snowing, but the ground is all covered," Sally said rapidly, concentrating on her reflection in the discolored, crackled mirror, and wiping at the lipstick on her upper lip with her stiffened little finger.

"Can I take my sled to school, Ma?"

"Oh, you better not. You'll have plenty of time to play with your sled this afternoon when you get outa school."

"Mama, I wanta be next in the bathroom," Marilyn piped up. "I wanta dress in there where it's warm."

"Okay, you scoot in here then right away. Buddy, you get up and get dressed while she's in here and then you will be all ready to get washed when she's through."

"No, I ain't," Buddy said stoutly. "I'm gonna dress in there where it's warm too. I'm gonna stay in bed till she gets out. It's terrible cold in here." She was out of the bathroom in a flash but took the time to kneel down and hug Marilyn tight as the little pink-pajama'd figure came hopping out of the bedroom over the draughty floor. "Good-bye, baby. Scoot in there quick, where it's warm. Be a good girl today. Good-bye. Good-bye, everybody!"

She slammed the door behind her, and almost collided with Harold as he came slouching along from the door of the room he shared with Joe.

"Well, hi," Sally said. "Did you sleep warm enough last night? It's awful cold. I gotta run to catch my bus."

He mumbled something that sounded like "Hi," and kept his eyes on the toes of his scuffed shoes. His pale hair was rumpled, and the old green sweater bagged on his thin body.

"Bundle up good, going to school today. Wear your cap, won't you? I'm always so afraid you'll catch cold or get an earache or something, going around this cold weather without nothing on your head. Wear your cap, won't you?"

He mumbled again, a meaningless sound in his throat.

"Well, I'll be seein' you!"

But she had got no further than the top of the stairs when Sally stopped again, calling his name. "Harold!"

He stopped, the door into the living room half opened.

"Come here a minute, honey!"

He closed the door and slouched toward her. He moved so slowly that she came up to him before he took more than a couple steps. She stood close in front of him and put her hands on his shoulders, which were almost on a height with her own. Her face looked soft and tender, and her voice sounded hesitant.

"Harold!"

"Yeah," he said. He gulped a little after he spoke and looked up at her, the freckles shining all over his pale face.

Her hands tightened on his bony shoulders. "Harold, I wanted to tell you. I didn't say anything about it to the little kids, but I wanted to tell you. I'm going to see your father today."

She looked at him with her face warm and tender and a little smile on her lips. His eyes fell away and he looked down at the floor. He cleared his throat, but he didn't say anything.

"He'll ask all about you. He misses you so. He'll want to know what you're doing in school and about your paper route and how you are and everything. Of course he misses the little kids, too, but you're sort of different. You're the oldest; you're older and . . . Well, he—he'll . . . He misses you awful, honey."

A flush of color came up in Harold's face underneath the freckles. He didn't look at her or speak.

Her eyes, as she looked at him, were hurt, and somehow anxious. "Well, don't you want me to tell him 'hello' for you?"

He raised his eyes momentarily and looked at her, and then away again, down the dim hallway beyond her. "Yeah, sure," he said awkwardly.

She stood still beside him for a moment. And then she said, "Okay, I'll be sure to tell him." She reached up her hand to his fine, pale-colored hair and smoothed it, a quick caressing gesture. "G'bye." Then she was gone.

Harold turned away without looking after her. He dug his hands deep into his pockets and walked slowly along the hall toward the apartment door, with the sound of her quick steps going down the wooden stairs in his ears.

The porch steps were slippery with the light coating of snow over them, and Sally slid on the thin soles of her shoes. The air was cold. Her breath, white in the air, enveloped her face in a moment, like a veil. Once she was down on the sidewalk she ran toward the corner. The light snow covered everything, and the first sunlight touching it made a dazzle and blur before her eyes. She looked up to the corner and saw, to her relief, that a little group of people were huddled together in front of the drug store. The bus hadn't gone yet. She crossed the street with the traffic light, just as the bus came around the curve in front of the diner. The sidewalk was all but deserted, save for the huddle of people awaiting the bus: several factory workers with dinner pails, a couple of firemen from the fire-station in the next block on their way home from night duty, and a fat girl with a handkerchief tied over her head, who worked in a restaurant across from the depot half way uptown. Sally joined the bus passengers waiting at the curb, waving her hand to Mr. Smith, who owned and operated the drug store. The two firemen greeted Sally noisily; they were, all three of them, seasoned travelers on the quarter-after bus every morning.

"Hello, there. What do you think of this weather? Pretty cold morning, huh?"

"Say, you're early this mornin', ain't you? The bus ain't pulled up yet. Bet your clocks was all fast!"

Sally answered them good-naturedly. "This is no kind of weather to stand around waiting. What's the use of my getting up here till the bus comes?"

"No use getting here till the bus comes," the fireman with the mustache said slyly. "But how about all them mornings when we have to hold the bus and wait for you to powder your nose and run all the way up here from your house?"

The bus pulled in to the curb just then, and, as she clambered aboard just behind the fat girl, Sally called back over her shoulder, "Pooh! I guess you never had to wait more than a couple times for me! How about the time we had to wait for you about five minutes that day the wind was blowing and you was chasing your cap up and down the street here?"

The bus driver greeted them, grinning. "Well, don't tell me all three a you are here this morning. I knew I was a little behind schedule, but now I know I must be a hell of a way off it!"

They all laughed together and found seats as the bus jolted on down the street.

Sally kneaded her hands together to warm them. These light cotton gloves weren't any good at all in this weather, she was thinking. Next pay day she'd simply got to buy herself a pair of knitted mittens. Let's see, next pay day, and then one more till Christmas. The kids would be wanting to buy her something for Christmas. She would tell them to get her some mittens. You could buy pretty knitted mittens at the dime store for a quarter. That would please the kids too, getting something for her that they knew she wanted.

The driver sent the bus hurtling along over the uneven pavement in an effort to make up his lost time. At nearly every corner he had to make stops to pick up passengers bound for their jobs downtown. He slammed on the brakes once and caught Sally unawares, throwing her body forward against the back of the seat in front of her. She felt the jarring of it all through her body. It made her aware of herself suddenly. She straightened back in her seat again and momentarily sampled the consciousness of her own physical being. She discovered that she didn't feel so good. There was a dull heavy fatigue all through her body. There was a little gnawing pain in her right side that came from running for the bus. Her head ached, but that was probably because she was hungry; she never had time for breakfast in the morning. At the same time, she didn't feel much like eating, anyway. There was a sort of sick sensation in her stomach. That must be from the strong cheap toothpaste that she used, Sally rationalized desperately. The toothpaste, that must be it. She could taste it yet, burning and stinging on her tongue and gums. Then there was the little sore spot in her lungs, a kind of pain there when she took a deep breath. It had bothered her the last couple days. She had had a little cold and it must have sort of settled on her chest. For a moment she felt panicky. She'd have to take care of herself; she couldn't get a bad cold; she couldn't get sick. She just couldn't, that was all. She had her job; she had her family; she had to have that money to keep them going. Suppose she got sick and couldn't work and doctor bills and . . . Sally put the thought sternly away from herself. She was perfectly well, and strong and healthy; she was not working too hard. She was just being silly, sitting around and thinking about herself and how she felt like this. Sally never had time to think about herself very much, and when she did she invariably reached some point when she deliberately had to put thoughts of herself away from her in a panic.

She looked ahead of her through the windshield of the bus. The clear cold morning air sharpened the outlines of the buildings against the pallid cloudless sky. Main Street stretched away ahead of the bus, a narrow slit of a gorge between the tall buildings. The Christmas decorations hung thick across the street in the downtown area ahead, like a ceiling. The light bulbs in the decorations were still turned on, and they all ran together in a jumble of colored lights: reds, greens, yellows, blues and purples.

There, sir, Sally remembered, she had forgotten to tell Virgie to buy some electric bulbs when she did the shopping. The 60-watt bulb in the bathroom had burned out this morning.

The bus drew up to the big bus stop in front of the drug store at last, and Sally stood in line with the other passengers to pass out between the sliding doors to the sidewalk. Once she was on the street with the morning crowd pushing around her and the cold air stinging her nose, Sally felt completely her energetic self again, and moved off with her customary rapid steps.

The restaurant was in the middle of the block. It had a smart modern chromium entrance between big plate-glass windows on either side. Sally dashed in, bringing a breath of cold air with her. The breakfast trade was just beginning to trickle in, factory people, white-collar workers mostly, an early sprinkling of business and professional people. Sally called good morning to several waitresses and the boy at the counter and hurried through the restaurant to the washroom. She removed her coat and hat and rearranged her hair hurriedly in front of the mirror. She didn't wear her uniform today; this was her day to tend the cash register. Outside, Sally looked around the room with a practiced eye. A fat, oldish man was standing beside a table struggling into his overcoat, his check in his hand. Sally walked along in front of the counter to the high table where the cash register stood, and slid onto the stool behind it.

She just had time to smooth her dress over her knees when the fat man came up with his check. Sally took the green slip of paper from him, together with the dollar bill, and smiled at him brightly. "Well, good morning, Mr. Henley. It's a pretty cold morning, isn't it?"

His reply was indistinguishable over the ringing of the register and the clatter of the drawer. Sally counted out his change to him, expertly. "Fifty-five, sixty-five, seventy-five, one dollar. Thank you, Mr. Henley. Come in again soon."

"You bet I will," the fat man said jovially. He turned toward the door, drawing his coat collar over his chin. "Hate to go out in the cold," he called back to Sally. "Guess I'll call up my secretary and have her come over and do business from here today. Can I use your telephone?"

"Why, sure you can, Mr. Henley," Sally said cheerfully, impaling his check on the metal spindle in front of her.

He went out laughing, meeting an influx of customers at the door. Sally smoothed her hair, smoothed her dress, and smiled brightly at the next man who appeared in front of the cash register. "Good morning. It's pretty cold out this morning, isn't it?"

Still more customers came in. The restaurant began to fill up rapidly, even to the stools along the short-order counter. The breakfast rush was under way.

Sally worked rapidly and efficiently. She lost all track of time, all faces became a blur to her, so many hands holding out green-colored checks to her and money. Her fingers worked the cash register expertly. She smiled brightly time after time. She remembered the names of old customers automatically, and exchanged pleasant, bantering words with them. She politely invited new customers to come again. Accurately and rapidly she counted change into cupped hands that waited to receive it. She lost all sense of time and of the effort of motion and speech. She worked and smiled and spoke all in a kind of haze that was punctuated rhythmically by the noise the cash register made under her fingers, the clicking of the keys, the bell ringing, the clatter of the cash drawer as it sprang out, the bang with which it snapped back into place.

After awhile the worst of the rush was over, and the restaurant began to thin out. Sally came back to herself with a start, and she craned her neck to look at the clock over the counter. It wasn't so long until her bus time, because today was the day she went to see Roy. She'd work a little while longer, Sally decided, and then Lee or somebody could take over. The crowd would all be gone by then.

That would give her time to fix up a little and eat some breakfast before she had to go to the bus station. But she'd have to watch so she didn't miss her bus. The very idea of missing her bus terrified Sally. It would be such an awful thing. Roy would be waiting, looking at the clock, counting first the hours and then the minutes until it was time for her to come. And then, suppose she didn't come. Why, she didn't know what he would do, he'd be so disappointed. Worse than that, he'd be so worried. He'd think that she was sick, or that something had happened to her. He'd never think of such a simple thing as that she missed her bus. But then you couldn't blame him; he looked forward to her visits so. As soon as she was gone, he started counting the days until she could come again, counting first the days and then the hours and then the minutes. It was an awful thing, and he needn't worry, she'd never miss a bus. She'd never let anything like that happen.

One of the other waitresses came up suddenly. "Boss says you can quit now. I'll take over the cash," she said.

"Oh, fine," Sally said, sliding down from the stool. Sam Toresca was a swell person, all right, Sally thought, as she went toward the washroom. He never forgot that this was her day to go see Roy. He was always nice about letting her get off work in time to make her bus. Sam Toresca was an older brother of Nicky's, and he managed the restaurant. Sam always scolded about people and complained about business and the whole world, but he was one of the kindest people, Sally thought, that she had ever known. She had seen him surreptitiously feeding bums in the kitchen, and she had known him to extend credit to a customer who was down on his luck.

In the washroom Sally combed her hair and scrubbed her face with cold water, and then she applied fresh cosmetics carefully. She looked at herself anxiously in the mirror. She looked all right, and there was nothing in her face that would worry Roy. She didn't really look as if she was working too hard or had been missing sleep or was worrying or anything like that. She deliberately relaxed the muscles around her mouth and jaws and made herself smile. There, now she looked just like herself, the way that Roy liked to see her. A fresh, rounded, smooth face, with humor lines around her wide mouth, and a hint of seriousness in her dark eyes. There was a lot of warmth in her face, and a lot of youth.

She put on her coat and hat then, and just as she left the washroom Sam Toresca himself called after her. "Hey, Sally, you leavin' already?"

Sally stopped and turned around. "Yes, it's pretty near time for my bus. Did you want something, Mr. Toresca?"

"What's about your breakfast? You can't go runnin' around without no eatin', Sally."

The restaurant was empty of customers now. Some of the waitresses were sitting on the stools along the counter, chattering together over coffee and cigarettes. The Negro boy from the kitchen was sweeping the floor, cleaning up for the luncheon trade.

"You come eat, Sally," Sam Toresca scolded.

"Well, all right, I guess I better," Sally said. She sat down on the last stool at the end of the counter. Sam Toresca leaned across the counter toward her, managing to give an impression of geniality in spite of his fat, morose, sleepy face. "Well, whatcha gonna eat, huh? You might as well have the best we got, itsa goin' to waste out there in the kitchen. You see how slow business was this morning? Business shot to hell, food alla goin' to waste in the kitchen, might as well eat it. Nobodya yet ever got rich in restaurant business."

Sally smiled at him. They hadn't had a slow morning; they had had an exceptionally good breakfast trade. Sam Toresca knew it, too, and felt good about it, but the only way he had of showing it was to go around looking sad, and complaining that business was shot to hell.

"Well, let's see," Sally said. "I guess I'll just have some toast and coffee, and some orange juice—no, I'll have grapefruit juice."

"That's no kinda eatin'," Sam said. "Why don'tcha have some ham an' eggs or something? What kinda eatin' is a toast, a coffee, a juice, anyway?"

"No, honest, Mr. Toresca, I haven't got time to eat any more. Besides, I'm not hungry. I had something to eat this morning at home before I come down here."

"You tellin' lies," Sam said sadly. "Okay, so you geta thin aworkin' in a restaurant. Ain't that one helluva thing? Gettin' thin workin' in a restaurant."

He shouted her order into the kitchen and poured the fruit juice into the thin tall glass for her himself.

"Guess I have another cup of coffee myself." He drew two cups of coffee from the urn and came to sit on the stool next to Sally's, relaxing his ponderous body onto the little stool with a grunt. He was strangely silent, for Sam.

He spoke at last, keeping his voice low with an effort. "You no wanta have anything to do with tha Nicky, huh?"

Sally didn't know what to say, so she looked down at her coffee cup and shook her head.

"Thatsa good," Sam said positively. "That Nicky is a no good one witha women. Alla time women. You got sense in your head. You gotta kids, you gotta husband, no monkey business. That Nicky is a bad one. You stay away from him, Sally."

His words troubled Sally, and started her worrying again. She suddenly realized that not only had Sam Toresca noticed what had happened last night but probably everybody else who worked at the restaurant.

"Jim atella me about last night," Sam said at last, with his voice expressionless.

Sally started to spoon coffee herself. She looked up at him finally and smiled. "Oh, that last night was all right. I mean—well—gee, I hope Jim didn't make a lot of trouble for himself bustin' in like that. Because I was all right, honest. He—Mr. Nicky Toresca—just come in and said he wanted to take me home and I said no and that was all there was to it."

"That Nicky is a bad one!" Sam shook his head dolefully. "Women! Alla time women. He is no good with women."

Sally was touched by the doleful expression on Sam Toresca's face and by his obvious concern over her. She put her hand on his arm impulsively. "Aw, don't you worry, Mr. Toresca. It's all right. Your brother just thought—I mean—well, now he knows I don't wanta have anything to do with him, why, he'll never pay any more attention to me."

But Sam shook his head sadly and doubtfully. "Well, I don'ta know. That Nicky is a bad one witha women." And then, in a sudden burst of confidence that amazed Sally, "That Nicky he is justa plaina bad one. Not just women—everything. He thinksa everybody gotta do just what he say. He thinks he smart, he thinks he know it all, he thinks he tough. Now me, I been justa like the poppa to Nicky. I take carea Nicky when he justa little boy. I been like the poppa to him. He won'ta never do nothing like I tell him to. He tellsa me what to do, and I gotta do it. Alla time he keepa tellin' me what to do and I gotta do it. I tell him somethin' and he say shut up my trap and doa like he tells me. Me, that's been just like the poppa to Nicky. I'm gettin' damn sick of it. Sally, some day I'm gonna justa pack up and go away and never come back here no more. I'm gettin' damn sick of it."

He stopped talking and drank down his whole cup of coffee at a draught.

Sally said, self-consciously, "Gosh, I better get goin' if I want to get that bus."

"Okay," Sam Toresca said mournfully. "G'bye Sally."

"Good-bye."

As she hurried up the street toward the bus station, turning up her coat collar against the cold, Sally kept thinking about what Sam had said to her. It troubled her in spite of herself. Nicky Toresca could have her fired so easily. But last night wasn't really important, Sally reassured herself. It wasn't as if she was some glamor girl that Nicky Toresca might start chasing. Then Sally put the whole thing out of her mind, because today was the day she went to visit Roy, and she had more important things to think about.

At the bus station she stood in line at the ticket window, sorting several bills out of her purse. She wished it didn't cost so much. Not that she wasn't willing to pay the money in order to see him, but there were so many other things that she ought to do with that money, and seeing Roy always seemed like such a natural thing to her that she hadn't ought to have to pay money for it. She exchanged the bills for a long strip of tickets and put the envelope away in her purse.

Just then her bus came in, so she went out immediately and climbed aboard. She took a seat near the window toward the back, being careful to see that it wasn't the seat over the wheel which rode rougher than any other. She found the lever on the seat by which the back was lowered and adjusted it to a comfortable recline. At this stage of her journey she always closed up her mind tight. She didn't think about anything, not where she was going or why or even who she was. At this stage of the journey she might be just anybody going anywhere. She settled herself comfortably in her seat, stretched her feet on the footrest, removed her hat, so that she could lean her head back on the square clean piece of toweling pinned to the back of the blue velvet upholstery. Passengers were coming aboard and the bus was slowly filling up. A blonde girl in a bright blue coat with a big fluffy fur collar took the seat next to Sally's. As soon as she sat down she went about the ritual of retouching her lipstick, readjusting her hat with the bright feather in it, poking and smoothing her curls. Then she lighted a cigarette, flapped open a magazine and began to read a story. Sally was glad that she didn't want to talk. At this stage of the journey she never felt like talking much.

In a minute, the bus driver came through the bus collecting the tickets. Sally offered him the envelope from her purse. He took out the long string of tickets and tore off one section and returned the envelope to Sally. She put it back in her purse. Now with that over she could sleep. After many trips like this, she had trained herself to sleep. Then the bus driver took his seat, pulled the lever that closed the door. The great powerful motor of the bus roared, and he wheeled the big unwieldy body across the runway back of the bus station and onto the street. He pointed the nose of the machine west, and the bus picked up speed. Sally always kept her eyes open for just a moment, watching the old familiar buildings whizz by beyond the window. These were the streets that she walked every day of her life: the post-office building, the city-hall building, the familiar store fronts bright with the Christmas decorations, and Toresca's restaurant. Half a block down was the big bus-stop place in front of the drug store. After that Sally closed her eyes, and relaxed her body completely. After so many trips like this, she had established a routine for herself. At this stage of the journey she deliberately cleared out her mind and kept it quiet. If she didn't do that she had too much time to think and she got jittery. So she carefully and deliberately kept her mind still. She didn't look at the other passengers; she didn't look at the scenery out of the windows. She just sat still and relaxed in the seat and submerged her whole consciousness in the roaring sound of the motor and the lurching, rocking motion of the bus. In just a few moments, Sally was asleep. That was as it should be. That was a definite part of her schedule for these trips.

The bus went whizzing along, full of the noise of idle small talk, the rattling of magazine pages, smoke drifting up as passengers in the rear seats took advantage of the fact that smoking was permitted in the back of the bus. The bus driver drove skillfully, making stops in villages along the way, checking passengers on and off, swinging luggage up and down from the luggage compartments over the seats, telling old ladies how many miles to such and such a place and approximately how long before the bus would arrive there, making complete stops before crossing railroad tracks, weaving in and out of traffic, sounding the powerful horn as he passed the slow-moving, heavy freight trucks, obeying traffic signals, stopping for red lights, waving a hand in salutation to the drivers of buses that he met. And Sally slept. She slept deeply and peacefully, her body relaxed, her breathing slow and even, her body swaying with the motion of the bus.

When she awoke suddenly the powerful motor was still and the bus was full of the confusion of passengers getting out of their seats, careful not to bump their heads on the luggage compartment as they stood up, putting hats on, lifting baggage down into the aisles. The bus driver was saying over and over, "All out, please. This is the last stop. All passengers change buses here. All out, please."

Sally slid over the vacated seat next to hers and stood up in the aisle. She was still groggy with sleep, half bewildered, and thankful that this longest part of the trip was over, even though the hardest part of it was yet to come. She climbed out of the bus and went into the small, crowded depot. She had seven minutes before her next bus left. She knew that without having to ask. Seven minutes. Now came the time when she started thinking. Now was the time when she couldn't fool herself any longer, this was the day, this was the hour, and she was really on her way to see Roy. She went to the cigar counter. The young man with the glasses greeted her genially. "Hello, there. Haven't seen you since the last trip. Pretty cold today, isn't it?"

Without Sally's having to tell him, he reached around in back of the counter for the carton of cigarettes of the brand that Roy smoked.

"Anything else for you today?" he said, setting the long carton down on the glass-topped counter.

"Well, let's see," Sally said. She selected three candy bars from the boxes on the counter, and then two packages of chewing gum, and after a little hesitation a small cellophane sack of salted peanuts.

"That'll be all," she said. More money out of her purse. She watched it go regretfully as the man manipulated the cash register. Not that she begrudged the money spent on these few little things for Roy. She only wished that she could spend more. It was just that she always thought of money as she spent it in terms of all the things that she needed to spend it for and couldn't.

She picked up the cigarettes and the sack with the candy and gum in it and moved on to the magazine racks. There she hesitated longer. It was always a problem to her, because Roy didn't care much about reading. Even at home he had never cared about reading. At last she chose several magazines that contained mostly pictures, and a smaller more expensive magazine dealing with popular science and mechanics. Roy ought to like that, because he had always been tinkering around machinery as long as she had known him. More money out of her purse to the smiling girl who sold the magazines and papers.

Just as she turned away she remembered post cards and stamps. She usually brought those from home. She looked into her purse to make sure that she had them.

There weren't any empty seats in the waiting room, so she went to stand near the door out of the way of the crowd. While she waited, she looked around at the crowd, spotting a familiar face here and there. She did not acknowledge any of them, and none of them paid any attention to her. Men and women who made the trip the same day that she did every two weeks. It was a curious thing. Sally always wondered about it. At this stage of the trip they were always loath to come together and to talk. Maybe it was because, like herself, for just as long as possible they liked to be just anybody going anywhere, and, even after they couldn't fool themselves with that any more, they had their own thoughts to think and they didn't feel like talking. Not yet, they didn't.

Just then the bus was called, and a number of people detached themselves from the confusion of the waiting room and a line formed waiting to get on the bus, Sally and all the familiar faces and others as well. Even aboard the bus they still avoided each other, all these familiar faces, and scattered around sharing seats with other passengers. Sally took a seat beside a heavy lady with dyed red hair and pearl-button earrings. The lady was reading a magazine. She didn't look like the kind of person who would prove to be talkative. This bus was altogether different from the other one, and so were the passengers. This bus was bound for a destination in another state. These passengers were bored, long-distance travelers, with the faint scorn of the sophisticated for these incidental, short-run passengers who climbed aboard at one jerkwater stop and got off again at the next. The bus driver was an unpleasant-looking fellow. He collected the tickets rapidly and efficiently. He always scowled over Sally's, as if he too felt scorn and distaste for these short-distance travelers.

The bus left the depot strictly on scheduled time. This bus rode smoother; these seats were more comfortable. But Sally made no attempt to sleep. She sat tensed in her seat instead, staring out of the window, her packages in her lap. Now the time had come when evasions were impossible, and the jitters began to set in. It was the funniest thing, Sally kept thinking, she always felt the same way. And these fellow travelers of hers, the people with the familiar faces, apparently they all felt just the way that she did too.

Sally kept staring out of the window. The bus left the town behind and took a broad, smoothly paved highway through the open country. On either side of the road the bleak, partially snow-covered fields stretched away, unfertile-looking land, with a look about it today as if it were pinched with cold. There was a scattering of frame farmhouses and red-painted barns behind them, and occasionally a sparse, partially cleared woodlot. But mostly just the flat fields stretching away, neatly boxed with wire fences, the light snow lying over them. Once the bus came up over a slight incline fast, a bridge it was, and Sally caught a glimpse of ice with snow over it, a dark moist track in the middle where ice was just forming and the water still ran free. Then that was all for several miles, just the flat, barren-looking land on either side.

It wouldn't be long now, Sally kept thinking, if she kept looking off to the horizon over there to the right; it wouldn't be long now before she would see it. Sally kept her eyes fixed on the horizon line away off to the right of the highway, and her mouth took on a pinched look. The familiar faces scattered all over the bus turned to the right too, sets of eyes fixed on that spot on the horizon, as if some magnetic pole there had them all within its field.

And then suddenly she saw it—away off there on the horizon to the right of the highway. Tan-colored brick walls rising up stark from the land. Neat, tan-brick buildings set together in precise relation-ship of rows. No trees here, not even fences, just wide open fields, and in the midst of them the tan-brick buildings lined up each to each in order and precision in the pattern of a square. Far away like this, they looked very sharp-cornered and small, like children's blocks, Sally thought, stacked together by a logician in the middle of an empty floor. From the midst of them a tall chimney rose, so slim as to be all but indiscernible against the pale, colorless sky. A heavy drift of vaporous smoke had come out of it and hung motion-less in the air over the buildings, as if entirely unrelated to them or the chimney or the land or the sky or anything.

The road curved and the view was cut off. Sally gathered her parcels and her magazines together in her arms and slid forward to the edge of her seat.

The bus came down a hill and around another curve, and came to an abrupt stop with a raucous sound of brakes. Still only the unbroken fields on either side, but close to the main highway there was a winding narrow dirt road cutting away at right angles to it. At the corner there was an unpainted, run-down-looking gas station, and beside it a roadhouse. Beer and dancing, the sign read.

The bus driver operated the door lever and got to his feet as soon as the bus stopped. "All out here for State Hospital," he said tonelessly. Sally climbed out of her seat into the aisle and moved to the front of the bus together with the people with the familiar faces. The bus driver slammed the door shut behind the last of them impatiently and the bus roared off down the smooth white cement highway, the sound of its motor receding in the thin cold air.

Sally and the people with the familiar faces were left huddled on the highway, in the midst of the bleak landscape, with not another living soul in sight.

"I don't see anything of the cars coming," one of the women said at last. They all looked away down the winding dirt road, but there was no sign of any automobiles, just the double track running away across the snow.

"Seems like they'd get them out here to meet the bus," another woman said.

"Oh, hell," the fat, oldish man said. "We might as well go in where it's warm and call up."

Together they trooped across the snowy expanse in front of the gas pumps to the door of the roadhouse. The fat, oldish man opened the door with a flourish and the men drew back, the women walking out around them to enter the door first. Sally walked with her feet dragging. She felt numb with depression and a kind of vague misery.

The inside of the roadhouse was one vast room, with tables and chairs pushed over to the walls and a big open space in the middle of the floor for dancing. There was a bar at one end of it, attended by a man in shirtsleeves. Several men with stubby beards, obviously farmers in their overalls and blue denim jackets, were clustered around one of the tables, drinking beer. They turned their heads in concerted rotation to look curiously at the newcomers. The air in here was warm, but there was something about the place as bleak and cheerless as the landscape outside.

"Want to use your telephone," the fat man yelled, and his voice boomed and re-echoed in the big bare room.

The man behind the bar jerked his head indifferently to a phone booth in the corner.

"I'll call 'em up and tell 'em to get those cars down here," the fat man said unnecessarily to the group by the door.

He walked away over the bare floor toward the phone booth and his shoes squeaked loudly with every step he took.

The group at the door shifted uneasily on their feet, waiting, and conversation came in little spurts, mostly in concern over the fact that the automobiles had not been sent down to meet the bus as they should have been. A slim young man in a greenish overcoat and felt hat detached himself from the group and drifted over to the big, multi-colored juke-box that stood to the left of the door against the wall. He shifted the parcels he was carrying all under one arm and leaned down with his overcoat flapping open to read the record titles listed on the front of it. Sally noticed him particularly. She had never seen him before, the one strange face among all the familiar ones. She was willing to bet this was his first visit. He was acting so nervously, and his face looked so unhappy. Sally felt sorry for him. She wished she could talk to him and tell him that it wasn't going to be as bad as he probably expected it to be.

The young man pressed one of the numbered knobs on the front of the juke-box and then changed his mind and pushed the big chromium knob that canceled his selection. He bent over, studying the list of titles in frowning concentration, groping his cigarette package out of his pocket with his one free hand. At last he pushed another number button and inserted the nickel in the slot. The machine remained quite still and no music came out of it. The young man waited a moment and then looked helplessly toward the man behind the bar, but the bartender was rearranging bottles on the shelves and paid no attention to him. The young man turned back to the silent juke-box and struck it a hard thump on the side next to the slot with the flat of his hand. There was an audible rattle as the nickel was dislodged and dropped into place, and the sound of machinery in motion sounded.

Just then the fat man came out of the phone booth and yelled at them the length of the room. "Cars'll be right here." He started back toward them, his shoes squeaking loudly again.

Inside the juke-box, the record dropped into place on the turntable and music blared forth suddenly. It was gay, hot, swing music, slightly raucous and very loud.

The conversation thinned out and ceased. Even the fat man seemed to be silenced. Everybody looked at the juke-box in a kind of helpless disapproval. The music was so fearfully loud and so fearfully bright and gay in that bare cheerless place in the midst of those bleak fields.

The young man in the green overcoat drifted back to the edge of the group uncertainly, as if he felt himself outcast from them by the enormity of his misdemeanor in creating such music here.

The music ground on and on. Matches flared and smoke drifted up as an epidemic of cigarette lighting swept the group. Even Sally began rummaging through her purse on the off chance that she might find some cigarettes there. The blatant music began to eat at her nerves. Such music had no place here. Would the record never come to an end, Sally wondered desperately. Just then the drums set up a deafening, fiendish tattooing, and then the brass took it on the beat with a squawk. The young man who had inserted the nickel turned around and looked at the juke-box with an expression of guilty horror on his face. He looked desperate, Sally thought, as if he was contemplating smashing the box to bits, or throwing it bodily out of the door. Sally had a quick visual image of the box bouncing over the empty fields end over end, emitting the awful squawks and thumpings at every bounce.

Out of her own desperation and pity for him, Sally walked over to the young man in the green overcoat and said, "Have you got an extra cigarette?"

He turned around to her with a look of gratitude on his face. He cleared his throat as he began to rummage hurriedly in his pocket. "Yes, certainly, just a minute."

Sally smiled at him, her warm friendly smile, and waggled the cigarette carton in her hand. "Imagine me bumming cigarettes with a whole carton of 'em right here."

The young man laughed a little. "It's perfectly all right," he said. He offered her the package and then struck a match for her.

"Thanks." Because she didn't know what else to say to him, she said, "The cars oughta be here any time now. I don't know what's the matter with 'em lately. They don't have the cars down here when the bus gets in."

The young man murmured something unintelligible in his throat.

And in the meantime the music went on and on, as if it had no intention of ever ceasing. And then all at once it did. Just stopped without warning, one last squawk and a couple of thumps and it stopped. The silence closed in then like a tangible thing, ominously. The silence after the music was over was really much worse than the music had been. The young man cleared his throat again. Someplace in the direction of the bar a board squeaked audibly.

Oh, God, Sally was thinking, oh, God.

Then they all heard the sound of motors outside and one of the women said, with the words all rushed together, "There they are!"

They trooped out together, and climbed into the two battered, old, seven-passenger automobiles that waited to receive them. Sally found herself wedged in a corner of the seat with the young man in the green overcoat beside her, and a faded, oldish woman on one of the folding seats in front of her.

The driver slammed the door shut, and devoted himself to the task of getting the wheezy old motor started. He had trouble with it, and the other car was out of sight by the time that he got it going. He turned the car around, cutting a great swath in the snow in front of the gas station, and then started up the narrow dirt road away from the highway. The car shook and rattled over the bumps. Why, the old wreck wasn't even airtight, Sally thought to herself, shivering a little at the draught of cold air on her feet. The narrow track of road wound back and forth over the snow for no apparent reason. It seemed to take all the skill and concentration of which the driver was capable to keep the car headed in the right direction, bumping and bouncing as it did over the frozen ruts.

After awhile the road took another wind, and there were the brick buildings again, only much nearer this time. The car left the road at this point and turned into a graveled driveway, a wide, well-graveled drive that came out in a perfectly straight line from the rows of buildings. Here, at least, the going was smoother, but to the rattling noise the old car made was added the spat-spat of gravel stones on the fenders, until the noise was deafening. Sally always wondered if the driveway seemed straighter than it really was, because of the interminable winding of the road behind. How could it be humanly possible to build a driveway in such a straight line? Along the edges of the drive on either side little trees had been planted equidistant to one another. They stuck up out of the snow like bare twigs. Looking at them, with the car rushing along, was like looking at a picket fence, Sally thought.

The tan-colored brick boxes loomed closer and closer, and then suddenly they were there. The car drove straight ahead into the very midst of the square the buildings formed. The driver stopped the car with a jerk in front of the cement sidewalk leading up to the entrance of one of the buildings, and got out and came around on the other side of the car and opened the doors. There was no one in sight, no stir of human activity around the buildings.

Sally was the last one to get out of the car, and, when she stood up, the sack slipped out of her hands, and the gum and candy bars spilled out on the floor of the car. The young man in the green coat had just stepped down from the running board, and he turned around and helped her pick them up.

"Well, I guess they aren't hurt much," Sally said, as she crammed them back into the sack. "It's lucky I didn't drop them out there in the snow, though."

The young man answered her with his polite, wordless murmur in his throat.

He helped her out of the car then, and they stood together on the sidewalk. The wind blew hard and Sally and the young man grabbed for their hats at the same instant. The wind always blew harder here. It must suck down between the buildings, Sally thought. The other passengers had already disappeared from view, and the car behind them drove away immediately, leaving them quite alone in the midst of those bare, tenantless-looking buildings. The young man hesitated, looking from one to another of the buildings despairingly. So she had been right about him, after all, Sally thought. This was his first visit here.

Just as she was about to speak to him again, a motley crew of people came around the corner of the building in front of them. They were women, all of them, led by a tall, elderly nurse, trim in white uniform with a blue cloak wrapped around her. The women followed her, in two-by-two rows, with a few stragglers. They were all ages of women and all manner of women. Some of them wore fur coats and boots; others were scantily protected against the cold by short cloth jackets over cotton print dresses; one of them was wrapped in a gray blanket, her face hidden from them by a corner of the blanket flapped down. The nurse set a brisk pace for them, and they followed her, most of them with dropped heads, some of them talking together as they walked.

They passed by, close to Sally and the man in the green over-coat, along the sidewalk that ran parallel between them and the building. Sally and the young man stepped back a little to let them pass. Sally saw the taut look on his face as he stared at them.

Neither the nurse nor any of the women paid any attention to them as they brushed by. Not one of them paid any attention until the last one, a gaunt, dark-haired girl in a fur coat who straggled along behind the others. When she came abreast of Sally and the young man she stopped dead still and looked at them. She looked at them, but her face was a blank mask and her eyes seemed to look through them rather than at them. Sally looked at the young man, and the young man looked back at Sally helplessly. The dark girl stood perfectly motionless in front of them. Then suddenly the mask of her face was broken. She gave them a look of venomous, contemptuous loathing. And then she spat at them. She stood there in front of them with a kind of horrible, complete lack of motion and that look of despising them on her face. She spat at them again. Then her face suddenly went masklike again, and she began to cry in a toneless, emotionless monotone.

The young man kept looking at Sally, and she put her hand on his arm as if to reassure him. She called out in her clear voice, "Nurse! Nurse!"

The entire group of women came to a dead halt instantly. The nurse stepped out to the side, so that she could look back. She said immediately in a calm, firm voice, "Mary! Come along, now!"

The dark girl turned away obediently and rejoined the group. The nurse designated another of the women to walk with her, and then returned to her position at the front of the column. They began to move again, disappearing around the corner of the building, walking briskly.

The young man stood still beside Sally, staring after them, and then just staring at the spot where they had disappeared, working the parcels nervously in his hands.

"It's your first visit, isn't it?" Sally said to him kindly.

He nodded his head and cleared his throat. "Yes, it is. My—my wife—she . . ."

"You go in over here," Sally said, indicating the entrance of the building in front of them. "That's 'A Building,' the administration building, you know. All visitors always go in there first. I'll show you where to go when we get in there."

"Thank you," he said. He hesitated for just one more minute and looked up at that building, looked up at those neat rows of precise, barred windows. He stood like that for just a minute, with his head lifted, and then he took a deep breath and fell into step with Sally as she started up the cement walk to the steps. He pulled open the heavy door for her and they stepped into a severe, wide corridor, with glass-topped doors on either side.

"These are the doctors' offices, and stuff," Sally explained to him. "The waiting room is straight back."

They walked along the corridor together, their feet echoing. Here, inside the building, there was an atmosphere of teeming life and activity in sudden contrast to the deserted, lifeless appearance of the exterior. There were faint sounds of voices and footsteps, and the air was filled with the high, muted ringing of the bells that summoned doctors to various parts of the hospital.

Sally conducted the young man the length of the corridor, into a vast waiting room with chairs lining three walls and a long information desk with a switchboard on the other side.

"You go over there to that desk," Sally explained. "You tell the woman your name and who you want to see. I guess probably you'll have to fill out a card, if this is the first time you come here to visit, but she'll tell you."

"Thanks very much," he said. "It was good of you to . . ."

"Oh, that's all right," Sally said, smiling. "I can still remember the first visit I made here."

The young man's face looked strained as he turned away. "Yes," he said, "I imagine you always would remember your first visit out here."

He started toward the desk and Sally dodged into the ladies' room that opened off to the right.

Inside, she put her parcels down on a shelf and retouched her make-up in front of the mirror. She combed her hair again and put on more lipstick without really seeing her reflection in the mirror at all. She was nervous; worse than that, she admitted, she was scared to death. Her legs felt weak and her heart was beating too fast. She picked up her parcels again, and practiced taking a couple of long slow deep breaths. Then she didn't dare to delay it a moment more, so she walked out the door, and through the crowd directly to the information desk. She waited her turn behind an elderly couple and, when they finished, she stepped up to the desk and said, "I'd like to see Roy Otis, please. I'm his wife."

The heavy, dark-haired woman behind the desk smiled at her. "Why, hello there, Mrs. Otis. How are you? Did you bring anything for your husband today?"

"Just cigarettes and some magazines and this candy," Sally held out the paper sack to her as she spoke.

The woman glanced at it and went on filling out the little slip of paper. "Uh huh. That's all right. I thought maybe you were bringing him some Christmas presents today. It's kept us busy the last couple days, so many people visiting that won't be here again before Christmas, so they are bringing their gifts in early."

Sally murmured something politely in answer.

The woman finished filling out the paper form, and tore it off the pad and handed it to Sally. "Just a moment, please," she said.

Sally watched her thick white hands as she swiveled around the circular name index. She found the right card, and slid her finger swiftly down the list of names there. "Otis—Otis, Roy," she murmured. "Ah, yes. Here we are."

Now came the thing that Sally always dreaded. This was the moment that she always had to brace herself for. It was silly of her, she realized, but she couldn't help herself. As many times as she had visited Roy here, and as simple and inconsequential as this thing was, still she always dreaded it.

The woman pulled the telephone toward her, removed it from the cradle and dialed one number. While she waited, she beat a gentle tattoo on the desk with her long, sharp-pointed yellow pencil. And then she said into the phone, "Is Roy Otis comfortable enough to see his wife today?" That was what she always said, in her cool competent voice with an even inflection. "Is Roy Otis comfortable enough to see his wife today?" with just the shade of emphasis on the one word "comfortable" that always made the chills creep all through Sally's body.

The woman put the phone down briskly and smiled at Sally. "If you'll just sit down, please, the nurse will come for you in a moment."

Sally said, "Thank you," and turned away from the desk. The waiting room was crowded today, but at last she saw an empty chair near the door and she went to it and sat down, arranging her parcels on her lap. She never got tired of looking at the people in the waiting room, all kinds and manner of people mixed together here, waiting to make their visits, all classes and nationalities. Sally had never known anything like it before, so many different kinds of people all brought together in one place.

Sally shifted the piece of paper in her hand, waiting for the nurse to come for her, and watched the people around her curiously. Some of them she had talked to, and she knew the exact set of circumstances that brought them here. But she felt sorry for all of them. That was why these visits always depressed her so much. Not because of herself and Roy entirely, although that was bad enough, but because of all these other people who came and went in the waiting room on a similar errand.

She lifted her feet out of the way absently, as Freddie pushed the wide cleaning brush under her chair. "Hello, Freddie," she said. "How are you today?"

"Oh, I'm fine, thank you," Freddie said in his startling clear soprano. He had a pretty, white, round, fat face. Glandular. He would probably be an inmate here most of his life. He loved to sweep the floor, so they let him do it. All during visitors' hours, he kept sweeping up the broad marble floor of the waiting room incessantly, pushing away at the brush, ambling around as if it were an effort to move his fat, clumsy body, his trousers tight over his fat, rounded buttocks. He always looked sad. Sally used to feel sorry for him, but now she knew why Freddie always looked so sad. He had told her all about it once. Freddie couldn't stand it if the marble floor wasn't perfectly clean and shining. And when visitors came they smoked all the while and spilled ashes on the floor and dropped cigarette butts all around their chairs, and, try as hard as he could, poor Freddie couldn't keep that floor clean. It made him feel awfully bad. Why, keeping that floor clean was all the life that Freddie had or was ever likely to have. That floor was his whole life in this world, the only life that he had, and it had to be clean and shining all the time. Visiting days nearly drove Freddie crazy. Sally saw the nurse from Roy's ward coming toward her. She gathered her parcels and got up from her chair. The nurse was young and rather pretty. She came up to Sally, the keys jangling in her hand as she walked. "Hello, Mrs. Otis," she said pleasantly. "I'm sorry I had to keep you waiting, but something came up, so I was delayed."

"Oh, that's all right," Sally said as she fell into step with her. They walked across the waiting room to a corridor toward the back. Roy had been on the third floor in this building ever since they had found out about his back injury. For a long time he had been in a cast, and they kept such patients in this building. Sally could never quite understand about it. The doctors had decided that this back injury of Roy's had been the cause of his psychosis. But now his back was all right again. They had taken off the cast a long time ago, and still they were always vague and indefinite when she talked to them about when Roy could be released. Oh, they were very definite about saying that he would soon be able to be released, a complete recovery, it was just that they were never definite about just when.

The nurse unlocked a door from the corridor that led to a flight of stairs. On the other side of it, Sally stood and waited for her while she relocked it, and then they started up the stairs together.

"How has he been?" Sally said, over the sound of their feet echoing in the small marbled enclosure of the stairs.

"Pretty good," the nurse said briskly. "Oh, he had several blue days, but on the whole he has been feeling pretty good."

"I'm so glad," Sally said.

At the head of the stairs there was another door to be unlocked and relocked. Only three or four paces down the second-floor corridor was the door to the stairway that led to the third floor. Again the nurse selected a key from the heavy ring she carried in her hand. Two sounds, Sally often thought, would remind her of this place as long as she lived: the rattle of keys, and the muted clangor of the call bells that went on incessantly, so high and soft that you got used to the sound and only noticed it occasionally.

As they climbed the stairs to third floor, the nurse said, "Of course, he has been more contented lately because he is counting on coming home for Christmas. He doesn't talk about anything else."

"I know."

"Tell me," the nurse said casually, "has the doctor given his consent yet? I mean has he really signed the order?"

"Well, no. Not exactly. He just said that he thought . . ."

At the head of the stairs the nurse hesitated a moment over selecting her key. "I don't know," she said. "I hope the order comes through all right. Your husband is going to be an awfully bitter and disappointed man if he doesn't get this Christmas parole."

The nurse unlocked the last door, and then they were in the ward where Roy had been kept the last few months. At the desk the nurse dropped Sally's visiting slip into the open file box.

Sally said, explaining her parcels, "I've just got candy and cigarettes and a couple magazines."

"You better leave the carton of cigarettes here. Just take him a couple packages out of it. I'll mark the carton for him."

Sally handed over the carton and the nurse wrote Roy's name on the box with ink.

"Now, then!" the nurse said, slamming and locking the drawer on the cigarettes. They started off along the corridor, open doors on either side furnishing glimpses of patients in bed, patients in chairs, patients in the recreation room with radios, playing cards and reading magazines, and a scattering of male nurses and orderlies among them.

"Just one thing," the nurse said, lowering her voice a little. "I wouldn't talk to him too much about the holiday. Don't let him get excited talking about it to you. Don't make too many plans for it with him, or anything like that. It's better for him not to get excited, and then, besides, if something should happen so that he didn't get leave, after all . . ."

"I understand," Sally said.

They came around a corner in the hallway, and there, standing in the doorway to a single room, was Roy. Tall and thin, brown trousers, and a faded blue shirt open at the neck. His hair was pale-colored as Harold's was. Harold looked so much like Roy, and his face was thin and pale and lifeless. Oh, he had aged so much here, Sally thought despairingly, he had aged so much!

"Hello, darling!" Sally called out with her voice tender and a little thick with feeling.

He said her name, "Sally," and came to meet her, walking slowly, his hands outstretched and his face working a little.

"Darling, how are you?" Sally said incoherently.

He took her in his arms gently, packages and all, and held her close against him. Her hat slipped back on her head, held on only by the elastic in the back, and he buried his face in her tously dark hair. She clung to him, talking incoherently all the while. "You're looking better, Roy, honest! Darling, how have you been? It's been so long since I was here. Roy, you . . . Oh, Roy!"

The nurse stood by, watching them vigilantly, clinking her keys in her hand.

He didn't say anything. He just stood there holding her gently, his face buried in her hair, as if he would never let her go again.

"I thought you'd rather visit in here," the nurse said. "Your husband is sleeping in a five-bed ward now, but I thought it would be more pleasant for you to visit here."

Sally heard the pleasant, impersonal voice, and it recalled her to herself, and what was expected of her. She stepped back from Roy, out of his arms, and smiled gayly, and made her voice gay to match it.

"Oh, that'll be fine! Thanks a lot. It'll be a lot quieter than in the ward. Did you write to me that you had been moved into a ward, Roy? I don't believe you did. A fine thing, letting me get behind on all the news."

They walked into the single room, all three of them. The nurse pulled the two straight wooden chairs around facing each other in front of the metal tall-legged table. "There you are," she said cheerfully.

"Thanks a lot," Sally said again.

Sally waited a minute for Roy to sit down, and then sat down herself.

"Have a good visit," the nurse said. She went out, adjusting the door carelessly so that it stood wide open.

Sally and Roy sat together silently then and looked at each other. The room was almost oppressively small and plain, the bare white walls, the hospital bed, the one window with the thick screen of metal and beyond that the bars, the plain empty metal table.

Roy never moved his eyes from her face, as if he couldn't get enough of looking at her, seeing her, knowing that she was really here with him. His face was so thin and worn that it almost broke Sally's heart. He had a slump to his shoulders that he never used to have. Oh, God, Sally was thinking, if I could just put my arms around him and hold him tight and tell him that he was looking better and that he'd be out of here soon, tell him that we all miss him, that we all want him back, tell him that I love him and I always will and that I can't live unless he gets better and comes home!

But that wouldn't do at all. It wouldn't do at all, and Sally knew it. And if they didn't start talking, in just about two minutes an orderly would be sticking his head in at the door.

Sally made a great effort and smiled her warm generous smile at

Roy. She held out the parcels, showing them to him. "See, I brought some candy and some magazines. I brought a whole carton of cigarettes. The nurse is keeping them out there at the desk. All you have to do is ask her for them when you run out. Did you have enough cigarettes to last you this week? I think you smoke too much, anyway, but I guess it's all right. I got your letter day before yesterday . . ." Sally lied desperately now, "I read parts of it out loud to the kids. Gee, they get the biggest kick out of your letters, hearing how you are and all that, you know . . ."

"How are you, Sally?" he said. "You ain't workin' too hard, are you? You look tired; you look like you're worrying. Ain't nothin' the matter is it, Sally?"

Sally laughed at him. "You silly! Of course there isn't anything the matter! I'm not working too hard. I feel fine. Virginia does just about all the housework. She's been just wonderful with the kids, and taking hold with the work and everything."

"She hasn't got a job yet?"

"Oh, not yet," Sally babbled, her hands busy tearing the cellophane on one of the packages of cigarettes. "But she'll be getting something before long. Honest, I never knew anybody that tried harder than she has. She just haunts that employment office. She answers just about every ad in the paper. She'll get a job, all right. But, you know, I wouldn't really care if she didn't, she's been such a lot of help to me. But of course I shouldn't say that. I can't afford to pay her anything, and she wants a job and to be earnin' money . . ."

"I don't see how you get along," Roy said tonelessly. "You don't make much money, and the kids and Virginia and everything."

"Oh, you'd be surprised," Sally scoffed. "We get along fine! Joe's working every day, and I get his board money, and Fred Foster's board money. Don't you worry about us, Roy. We get along fine."

"Just the same, you look worried," he said. "Somethin's bothering you, I can tell, just looking at you."

"Pooey! What could be bothering me? You're getting better, I've got my job, the kids are fine. Everything is all right, honest, it is. You gotta believe me when I tell you, Roy. Everything is all right. Don't you start worrying, because everything is all right."

He looked at her hard without answering.

"Here, have a cigarette." She held out the package to him and he took one. She took one too, and then began a scramble through her purse for matches.

"How is Harold?" Roy asked her.

"Oh, Harold is just fine," Sally said brightly, her eyes lowered to the inside of her purse. "He's getting so big, why, he's gonna be grown up before we know it. He's still got his paper route and he works at it faithful every day, rain or shine. He's a lot of help to me. He's older now, you know, and I can talk things over with him. Why, he's just—he's the man of the family, while you're away. He talks about you a lot to me. This morning we was talking and he told me to be sure to tell you hello and that he sent you his love. He's always so interested to know how you are when I've been down here and everything."

"I'm glad he's a help to you like he is," Roy said. "Course, he's getting older and all that, but you know how some kids are. When they git to be Harold's age a lot of them start actin' smart. They get funny about their folks, won't talk to 'em or tell 'em nothin'. And then, if you don't watch out, they get to chasin' around and get into trouble the first thing you know. It kinda worries me. It's hard for the mother to look after a kid Harold's age, if he acts like that . . ."

"Oh, Harold isn't a bit like that," Sally bragged recklessly. "He talks to me about everything, just like he always did. He's more help to me."

She was still rummaging in her purse. She didn't look at Roy when she said it. He looked at her hard. For just a moment his face looked suspicious and worried, and then blank again.

"You better get some matches from the nurse," he said.

"I guess I'll have to. I thought I had some, but I can't find 'em. Gosh, if I did have any I probably couldn't find 'em anyway, the mess of junk I carry around in this purse. Oh—here's some stamps and postal cards I brought you. I'm glad I come across them. I bet I'd have forgot 'em as sure as anything."

"Thanks." He took them from her and stuck them in the pocket of his shirt.

"You got enough envelopes and paper and stuff?"

"Yeah."

Sally got up. "I'll go ask the nurse for some matches." Outside the door, she met an orderly in the hall and stopped him, instead of walking all the way back to the desk.

He gave her the little paper folder. "You keep 'em," he said. "It'll be all right, and then if he wants more cigarettes you can light 'em for him while you're here. But don't forget!"

He grinned at her when he said it, and Sally laughed. "That's right," she said. "I take 'em when I leave."

She went back to Roy with the matches.

"I got 'em. A whole package of them."

She struck a match and lighted his cigarette and then her own.

"Have you seen the doctor yet?" Roy asked, after she was seated again.

"Not today," Sally said. "But I want to see him before I leave. I guess I'll have to kind of cut our visit short this time, if I get to see the doctor before the bus goes."

Roy nodded. "Well, I want you to be sure and see the doctor. By now he oughta know for sure about my Christmas parole."

"Oh, I was planning to see him."

"Have you told the kids yet?" Roy asked her.

"Huh?" Sally said, "Oh, you mean about . . ."

"About my coming home for Christmas," he said.

"Oh, no, I haven't told 'em," Sally said hurriedly. "I thought, well, you know, something might turn up that you couldn't come or something and then they'd be so disappointed that it would just spoil their whole Christmas, and then . . . I—I—well, you know, I wanted to kind of make it a surprise for them, you know . . ." Sally's voice trailed off helplessly.

Roy nodded. "Yeah. Sure." He puffed on his cigarette hard. "God," he said, "they sure will be tickled about it!"

Sally was busy improvising an ash tray out of a card from her purse.

"They will be tickled about it, won't they?" he said sharply.

Sally looked up at him quickly with her face tragic for just a moment. "Aw, Roy, you know they will! They'll be tickled to death. What did you think!"

He looked at his cigarette carefully, he was trying to keep his face steady, but his chin was quivering a little. "And you'll be glad, you will be glad, won't you, Sally? You want me to come home for Christmas, you want me to come home, don't you, Sally?"

"Oh, Roy," she said. It was such an effort for her to keep the tears back that her whole face stretched tight. "Roy!"

Oh, God, she was thinking, how can I sit still in this chair like this? How can I just sit here and smile and act gay and flip and keep my hands off him? It's too much for them to ask of me. It's too much. I'm only human. I can't stand it when he feels like this.

The tears came into her eyes in spite of herself, but she did not shed them. She looked at him, and he was only a blur that swam before her eyes. I'm only making it harder for him when I act like this, she kept saying over and over. It only makes it harder for him.

She forced the smile onto her lips, and tipped her chin up high. Her voice was even gay and somehow light; she could hear it. "Darling, you shouldn't say things like that. You know I want you. You know the kids want you too. Why, darling, we're all of us just—just—living along, counting on the time when you can come home to stay. You mustn't say such things. You mustn't even think 'em. What makes you say things like that to me?"

He got himself under control again with an effort. When he answered her, his voice was low, with a quality of humility in it, and shame. "Oh, God, Sally, I don't know. Sometimes I just get to thinkin'. I don't know. Lately I been thinking a lot and I can begin to remember some of the things I done and the way I acted to home before you brought me down here, when I was outa my head. I think about it, and it makes me sick, what you an' the kids musta thoughta me. I musta been awful. I musta done a lota crazy things I can't even remember. I don't see how you can feel the same about me, or the kids or nobody."

"Roy, honey, don't even think about it! You was sick. I understand; I made the kids understand. You don't have to feel bad about it. You was just sick. Some people get pneumonia or appendicitis and stuff like that, and you hurt your back and it just made you, well, sick in your head. Roy, you make me feel bad when you talk like this. Do you suppose somethin' like this could make me feel any different about you? You know better'n that, Roy. None of it was your fault, you couldn't help it, you was sick!"

She leaned close to him, across the table, the tears shining in her eyes. He reached out and cupped her face with his hand. "I'm sorry, honey. I didn't wanta make you feel bad. It's just that sometimes I get to thinkin' about things and I can't stop and I get all mixed up and . . . I know, Sally. I know how swell you are. The way you acted when I got sick, the way you write to me and come to see me every chance you get. I guess you're the best wife any guy ever had . . ."

Sally smiled and dropped her face and kissed his hand, and then she sat up straight in her chair again. "You're not such a bad husband, either, Mr. Otis."

They laughed together, and the room suddenly became warm and cheerful and pleasant. They could both feel it.

"We'll have the best Christmas we ever had," Roy said to her firmly.

She nodded to him, and then turned the conversation away as skillfully as she could.

"Well, how have you really been since I was here last time? Have you been feelin' good? Whatcha been doin'?"

"Oh, hell!" he said. "The same old thing. It's always the same here. I been feelin' about the same. I'm still kinda weak yet after them fixin' up my back and them treatments they give me. Oh, I don't know. I play cards with some of the other fellows sometimes, and then I listen to the radio lots. I dunno, I don't do much a anything."

"You're gonna be feelin' good enough to go over to O.T. again pretty soon, aren't you?" she said brightly.

He grinned at her weakly. "Oh, God! Make baskets, I suppose!"

She laughed with him. "Well, anyway, it would help pass the time away. Look, you want another cigarette. Here, I'll light it for you."

"Tell me about you," he said, after he had puffed on the cigarette to get it burning. "What you been doin'? How's your job?"

"Oh, my job is fine. Mr. Toresca is the nicest man to work for. When you come home I wantcha to meet him. You'd like him a lot. He's kind of funny, Greek or Italian or something, but he's been awful nice to me. I get along with my job fine. That's all I do, work, and then go home at night and get supper and spend some time with the kids. They're all busy with their school stuff, and excited about Christmas now. That's all there is to tell. Everything is just about always the same for me every day too."

I dunno," he said. "You look kinda thin, you know, peaked, or somethin'. Like you ain't eatin' right, or you're worrying about somethin' . . ."

"Pooey," she said. "You're just imaginin' it! I been cuttin' down a little on eatin' lately because I was getting too fat. I look better if I keep my weight down. I get enough to eat, don't you worry about that. Imagine working in a restaurant and then not getting enough to eat! How's the food been around here lately?"

"Oh, God," he said, "I told you what the food was like around here."

Sally laughed. "Darling, the first day you're home we'll go out and blow ourselves to the best chicken dinner we can buy. You wait and see!"

"You seen Mr. Hunter lately?" he asked her.

"Well, not just lately. The last time I saw him, he come into the restaurant to eat, and he asked after you and said to tell you hello for him. And he said to tell you not to worry about a thing, that when you came home your old job would be right there waitin' for you."

"Hunter's a swell egg!" Roy said.

"He sure is!"

"If you ever get in a jam or somethin'," Roy said to her, "you know, if somethin' should ever come up and you needed money or anything, you go to Hunter. Hunter'd fix it up for you. I been workin' for him for years and I don't know of a better guy."

"They been havin' any good movies down here lately?" Sally asked him.

"Yeah, they had one just the other night, but, hell, I was feelin' kind of tired, so I didn't even bother to go."

"Aw, you oughta go, Roy. You always liked to go to the movies."

"Yeah, sure," he said. "But I never cared nothin' about going to the movies alone. I always liked to go with you."

They sat quietly together for a moment, with the memories of all the happy Saturday night dates, movies and dancing and beer, sliding by, like bright beads on a string stretching between them.

Sally stirred in her chair. "You know, if I'm gonna get downstairs and talk to that doctor before bus time, I've gotta leave in a minute."

"Aw, you just got here!"

"I know it. If there was only another bus I could take. But the next one is so late that it makes me awful late gettin' home. And then I have to wait over an hour to make connections."

"Yeah," he said. "You better take this next bus back all right. Hell, I should kick. I'd be glad to see you if it wasn't more'n for two minutes. You comin' down here to see me is all that keeps me goin', that, and knowin' that you're there waitin' for me to get better and get back home again."

"That's right," Sally said. "It's just like I always tell you. We both gotta job to do. Your job is to do everything you can to help yourself get better, and my job is to keep things goin' till you can come home again. Your job is the hardest; but when this is all over, why, things will be just like they used to be, and it'll mean more to us even than it did before."

"Sally," he said simply, "I wouldn't wanta get better, or I wouldn't even wanta live, if it wasn't for you."

She stood up from her chair hastily. "Roy, honey, I'll just have to go, honest. I'll probably have to wait awhile to see the doctor and that darn old bus goes so soon."

He stood up too, and came close to her and took hold of her hands. "Okay, sweetheart."

She looked up to him with her face shining with tenderness. "You be good and do what they tell you to, and don't worry about anything. And write, won't you? And I'll be seein' you . . ."

"Christmas," he prompted.

"Yeah, I'll be seein' you Christmas—and—and—just—hurry up and get well, won't you, darling?"

He held her hands tight, looking down into her face. "Everything is all right, isn't it, Sally?"

Her eyes never blinked or faltered and her voice was clear and sure. "Everything is all right, Roy."

Then he drew her into his arms. She stretched up on her toes, her arms around his neck to kiss him. They kissed and then he buried his face in her neck. "Little Sally!" he whispered with a catch in his voice.

She held him tight to her, her hands moving on his back and shoulders, her warm body pressed to the long length of his.

The nurse's pleasant, impersonal voice spoke from behind them, "Leaving already, Mrs. Otis?"

They stepped apart almost guiltily, and Sally fussed with readjusting her hat. "Yes, I have to go. I want to see the doctor, and my darn bus goes so soon. Seems like I just get here and then I have to start back."

The nurse laughed pleasantly. "Well, Mr. Otis, I think it does you a lot of good to see your wife. You look better already."

Roy smiled back at her. "Yeah," he said. "You bet it does me a lot of good. I couldn't get along at all, if she didn't come down."

"Well, I really gotta go," Sally said.

She took hold of his hand in her warm firm one. "Write, won't you, Roy? And if you run out of cigarettes or there's anything else you want, you let me know, won't you? And I'll be seein' you . . ."

"Christmas," he said.

"That's right." Sally squeezed his hand tight. "Take good care of him," she said to the nurse, smiling.

"He's a good patient," the nurse said. "He takes good care of himself now."

"Good-bye, darling," Sally stood up on her toes quickly and kissed him lightly on the mouth. Then she picked up her purse from the table and turned away.

"Good-bye," he called after her. "Good-bye, Sally—till Christmas . . ."

And, as Sally walked along with the nurse, she wondered how it was that you could be so sorry to leave someone, and at the same time feel such a release and relief with a visit over.

"Well, I hope your husband gets his Christmas parole, all right," the nurse said, as she unlocked the door for Sally to leave.

"I hope so too."

One of the orderlies guided Sally back to the waiting room, unlocking and locking the endless doors they had to pass through. Once in the waiting room again, Sally hurried down the corridor to the door marked with the name of the doctor who had special charge of Roy's case: "Dr. Tace," neat black lettering on the glass.

She always hated to go and see him. He was a pleasant, youngish man. He had been kind to her, and kind to Roy. She trusted him. It was simply that he had such a vast realm of knowledge that was beyond her understanding where Roy and his illness were concerned; it was simply that he had come to hold such a strange power over Roy and her both and their future happiness. Because he alone could set the date for Roy's final discharge.

And now there was this business of the Christmas parole, but she would be glad to get that settled one way or the other. She couldn't be sure how she felt about the Christmas parole business. Oh, of course she wanted Roy to come, and he was planning on it so. It would nearly kill him if they wouldn't let him come. But there were so many problems connected with it, problems of just herself and Roy, and problems where the children were concerned. She didn't know how she could explain it to the children or how they would act. The trouble was that Roy was going to expect them to act just as if he'd been away for days instead of months, as if he had just stepped out of the house to go over to the drug store to buy a package of cigarettes, and had come back again. She was so afraid that the children would hurt his feelings. But she'd have to get along with it some way. Things would work out. Things would have to work out.

She hesitated a minute before the door, and then took hold of the knob firmly and turned it.

Inside the office, a perky, well-dressed office girl greeted her from behind the desk. "How do you do? The doctor isn't in just now. Would you care to wait?"

Sally stood still, with her heart sinking to her shoes. "How long before he'll be in, do you know?"

"I really couldn't say. Something came up in another part of the hospital and he was called."

"You see, my bus leaves pretty soon," Sally said helplessly. "I wanted to talk to the doctor before I leave. It's very important."

"Oh, I see," the girl said. "Well, I don't believe I could get in touch with him, and I really can't tell you when he'll get back here to his office. Wait a minute, you're not Mrs. Otis, are you?"

"Yes. Yes, I am."

"Oh, yes. The doctor was expecting you to come in today. He spoke about it to me. He left a memorandum for you."

"Yes?" Sally was frightened for a minute, and her heart beat against her ribs loudly.

The office girl rummaged through some papers on the desk until she found it, a little piece of white paper torn off a desk pad. She read it over, frowning a little.

"You had applied for a Christmas parole for your husband, Roy Otis—is that right?" she said at last.

Sally murmured something in assent.

"I'm awfully sorry, Mrs. Otis," the girl said with real sincerity in her voice, "but after reviewing the case the doctor left word for you that he cannot grant it. He doesn't believe that it would be wise, especially just at this particular stage of your husband's recovery, for him to leave the hospital."

The words sounded strange in Sally's ears and all but meaningless. She heard herself saying rather stupidly, "Oh, there must be some mistake. He talked to my husband about it. My husband is planning on it. Why, he's so sure about it, I don't know how he'll ever . . ."

"I'm awfully sorry," the girl said. "Dr. Tace reviewed the entire case history thoroughly before he decided. He talked about it to several other doctors who are familiar with your husband's case. They all agreed with Dr. Tace that it wouldn't be best for your husband to leave the hospital right now."

"Yes, of course." Sally murmured. "I understand. I just . . ."

"I know it's a big disappointment for you," the girl said. "But I'm sure that above all you want to do what's best for your husband's recovery."

"Yes, of course," Sally said again. Oh, it isn't myself, she was thinking, but Roy, what about Roy? He has been planning on this so. What will he do?

The girl kept looking at her, and Sally spoke to her with an effort. "I was thinking about my next visiting day. I wonder if I could come earlier in the week. I'll be awfully busy just before Christmas and . . ."

The girl shook her head. "I was just going to tell you about that. The doctor made a special note of it. He thinks it would be better if you didn't come again until the week after Christmas."

"The week after Christmas," Sally said. "Oh, but, but—my husband will be expecting me. He'll expect to see me again before then."

"The doctor thought it would be better if you didn't come," the girl said sympathetically. "Your husband has been counting on going home for Christmas so much. It would only upset him terribly if he saw you again before then. Dr. Tace thinks it will be much better for him if you wait until the week following to come again."

The enormity of the whole thing in terms of Roy's disappointment was beginning to overwhelm Sally. And to think that she had been selfish and petty enough to worry about how things would be if Roy came home for Christmas. When he wanted to come so much, and had been planning on it so. And now he couldn't come.

Sally made a desperate decision. "I was just thinking. Could I come down here Christmas day? Could I spend Christmas afternoon with him?"

"I'm sorry," the girl said. "But you know the rules. No visitors whatsoever are allowed on holidays like that. It's really much better for all the patients."

Sally turned away from the desk with a kind of numbness all through her body.

The girl called after her, "Dr. Tace wanted to know if he had your permission to continue the form of treatment he is using."

"Yes," Sally said as she groped for the doorknob. "It's all right."

Sally stumbled out of the door and went straight to the ladies' room. She stayed in there until just time for the cars to leave for the bus. She combed her hair time after time, and took minutes to put fresh lipstick on her mouth. She didn't cry; she didn't even think about it very much. She just didn't feel like talking to anybody. She still felt numb.

When it was time to leave, she went out and climbed into the car together with a number of the people with familiar faces. The people were talkative and friendly now. It was always this way, the release of tension that they all felt when the cars rolled away down the driveway with the hospital behind them. They talked about themselves, but mostly about the cases of their relatives back there in the hospital. They always talked a lot, going back, they felt banded together, and kindly and friendly now, interested in each other, and sympathetic. And they felt good, to be driving away, with the hospital behind them, a return to the normal life, in spite of themselves. But this trip Sally didn't feel that way, or any particular way. She talked a little, and asked questions politely and then didn't hear the answers that were made to her.

The cars arrived at the main highway just as the bus was coming. She found the envelope with her tickets in it, and handed it to the bus driver. On the bus she chose a seat by herself, and sat up stiff and straight in it, looking out of the windows with unseeing eyes.

Back at the depot where she changed buses, she bid good-bye to a number of the people with familiar faces who were leaving the depot on different buses. She wished them a Merry Christmas in a cheerful voice, and smiled her wide friendly smile many times. She bought a chocolate bar at the candy counter and ate it without enthusiasm, more from habit than because she noticed that she was hungry. And then she bought herself a package of cigarettes, which was unusual for her, and smoked two of them, one after another while she waited for her bus.

It came at last and she climbed aboard. She took a seat next to the window with an empty seat beside it, and adjusted the back to a comfortable angle. She gave the bus driver the last piece of the long orange strip of tickets with which she had begun her journey.

With tickets all collected, the driver returned to the front of the bus, closed the door and switched off the interior lights. In a moment the noisy motor was roaring, and the driver wheeled the bus out into the street, and Sally was headed for home. She didn't look out of the window, nor did she pay any attention to the other passengers. She didn't sleep either.

She rode with her eyes wide open, staring at the back of the seat in front of her. She lighted cigarettes several times.

And when suddenly she realized that, aside from his disappointment and everything else, just how much she herself had been planning on having Roy with her at home for Christmas, Sally cried a little. She turned her face toward the window and pressed it against the back of the seat and cried very quietly, so that nobody would hear her. She didn't cry long, just for a few minutes. After that she wiped her eyes and blew her nose, and lighted another cigarette. It was getting dark now, lights were coming on, and she looked steadily out of the window, sitting motionless, the cigarette glowing in her fingers.

The bus roared along, doggedly on schedule, up hill and down, along the dark snow-covered countryside, and through the bright-lighted hustle-bustle of small villages.

There, sir! Sally thought, she had forgotten to tell Virginia to buy some tapioca today. She had intended to make a tapioca pudding for supper and they were all out of tapioca. What in the world was she going to fix for dessert tonight, if she didn't have tapioca pudding?

# 4

THE NEXT DAY WAS SATURDAY AND IT GAVE PROMISE of being the coldest day of the winter. The temperature had fallen during the night. The apartment windows were coated with a thick crystalline tracery of ice. Outside, the sky was white as frost; there was a slight wind blowing; the air seemed visible to the eye, sparkling and electric as if the very atmosphere itself had frozen into a granular form that moved and shifted with the wind.

There was heat enough in the apartment, thanks to the combined efforts of Mr. and Mrs. Gideon, who had got the furnace going full blast long before daylight; but the heat seemed to have a deceptive superficial quality over an underlying chilliness all over the house that no amount of heat from the furnace could disperse.

Virginia and Sally arose at their customary early hour and shivered over hurried preparations for breakfast. This morning, the entire family congregated in the kitchen long before breakfast was ready, as if the cold had penetrated to their very beds and driven them out before their usual hour of arising. The one morning that the children were free to stay in bed as long as they pleased was invariably the one day of the week when sleeping late appeared uninviting to them. They cluttered up the kitchen, always underfoot, no matter which way Sally or Virginia turned. Buddy, for some diabolical reason, convinced Marilyn that her grade at school was going to hold classes on Saturdays the same as other days of the week in order to make up some of the time they would miss during the Christmas vacation. In spite of Sally's repeated assurances that Buddy was only teasing her, a germ of doubt was implanted in the little girl's mind. Buddy harried her relentlessly in a kind of fiendish delight. He painted horrible pictures for her of the dire fate that would overtake her if she was absent from school this Saturday morning. Just as he got her firmly determined to start off for school, he switched his tactics and gave her a gruesome account, complete with lurid details, of how extremely slight her chances were of getting to school before she froze to death (an ear dropping off at this street corner, an arm at the next). Marilyn, in the face of this dilemma, broke down and began to cry at the top of her lungs. Buddy howled with delight and poked her in the ribs and pulled her hair. Sally slapped his face and assured him that if it wasn't that she was late for her bus that very minute, she would give him a good spanking. Buddy hooted with glee and hopped up and down all over the kitchen floor. Harold attempted to enforce discipline on the young rebel, and a scuffle ensued. Buddy began to cry too. Immediately, Marilyn leagued with him and the two younger children presented a solid, rebellious front to their older brother. Sally lost her patience and assured all three of her children that they would drive her crazy just as sure as anything in the world and then she hoped that they would be satisfied. Virginia, in a desperate attempt to be helpful, suggested that they had better be good or Santa Claus would cross them off his list.

Sally was gone at last like a whirlwind, bundled up with sweaters and scarves and a pair of wool mittens that belonged to Buddy pulled over her own cotton gloves.

Joe, after innumerable cups of hot black coffee gulped down as rapidly as possible, sullenly prepared to depart for the factory. In direct defiance of the elements, he wore his customary workday garb, a thin, sleazy, old overcoat and a greasy gray felt hat and no gloves at all. He accepted the brown paper sack containing the lunch that Virginia had packed for him and ambled off with it reluctantly. But a moment later, before Virginia had managed to quite make her head stop whirling from the morning's confusion, she heard a flurry of feet in the hall. Joe burst back into the apartment on a run. It appeared that a block away from the house he had suddenly discovered that he had forgotten the badge that was necessary to gain admittance at the factory gates. He had unpinned it in the midst of his alcoholic rebellion of the day before when he had been determined never to do another day of factory work as long as he lived. He had unpinned it and thrown it down someplace, and now, with the clock hands moving on inexorably, just minutes from the hour his shift went on, he could not find the badge. Virginia and the children joined in the frantic search. Joe's reddened face and clumsy, numbed hands gave testimony to the coldness of the weather. The vast quantity of hot coffee he had drunk just before leaving was producing ill effects of gas and indigestion. Joe collapsed into a chair in a condition bordering on hysteria. It was no use, he babbled. He couldn't stand any more of this. To hell with the job, to hell with everything. He was all done, he was finished, he was washed up. To hell with it, to hell with everything.

Nobody paid any attention to him. The search for his missing badge went on furiously. It was Marilyn who at last discovered the missing button, lying all but smothered in the thick rolls of gray dust under Joe's bed.

It was no use, Joe said, waving it away from him with a languid hand. It was no good to him now. It was too late, he could never get there on time. Virginia could just throw that goddam badge out the window or stick it, whichever she preferred. It didn't matter to him. He was all done with it forever.

Then Virginia lost all control of her nerves and temper and turned on him in a savage fury that surprised even herself. She all but dragged him bodily out of the chair, jabbed the pin of the badge through his coat and crammed the sack of lunch into his hands. She pushed him out of the door, saying over and over again, "Go on now, you've got time if you hurry. Go on, get out of here, you've all the time . . . Oh, you make me so mad. If I was Sally I'd . . . Go on now, hurry up, get out of here! If you don't get out of here I'll—I'll—I'll hit you!"

Joe went, protesting that he couldn't understand why it was that everyone always picked on him so, and that he hoped that he froze to death standing around the gate trying to argue the guard to let him in late. But he ran all the way down the stairs, and out of the door, slamming it violently behind him.

Virginia was exhausted after her effort to get Joe on his way to work. She told the children sharply to stay out of the kitchen while she cleaned up, and slammed the door shut on their chattering and confusion.

Before she had regained her composure a telephone call came that lifted Virginia's spirits sky high and sent her scrambling into her coat and hat and sweaters. The employment agency telephoned to say that a certain office downtown was hiring girls that morning, to go to work immediately. Virginia raided the cracked cup in the kitchen cupboard, repository for household funds, for bus fare and lunch money. She left the children in Harold's care with instructions for preparing their lunch, and then she fled down the hall, her heels beating out a gay, confident syncopation over the bare floor boards.

She got to the corner just in time to catch a bus downtown. The bus was cold, too. Passengers huddled in the front seats, talking about the weather, speculating about the exact temperature, comparing rumors of fantastic numbers of degrees below zero reported from various sections of the city.

Downtown, Virginia hurried to the employment agency to pick up the address and her reference card. The address, she was glad to note, was that of one of the larger office buildings in the immediate downtown area. Virginia went directly there, and, by the time that she walked through the revolving door into the lobby, she felt almost frozen. Her feet and hands were clumsy and her whole body felt numbed. She would simply have to stop at the ladies' lounge and get thawed out a little, Virginia decided.

As soon as her hands were able to handle a comb without trembling too much she went about tidying her hair. Her skin looked chapped and blotchy with cold. She tried to retouch her lipstick and her hand was so unsteady that she was clumsy with it and made a streak of red out from one corner of her mouth. No amount of scrubbing with her handkerchief could wipe it away. Oh, gosh, what was the use, she thought despairingly, nobody would ever hire her, the way she looked. Virginia was getting panicky and she decided that she had better go up there to that office quick, before she got any more nervous about it. She tugged at the stretchy, sagging neck of her old green sweater in disgust. Please God, let this be the time, please, God, let me get this job! Then she stuck her chin out, held her head high and walked to the elevator briskly. She got out of the elevator at the ninth floor and took the slip of paper out of her purse to make sure of the address: 918, that was it, 918, and the man's name was Mr. Sultky. She tried to make herself walk slowly and to keep her body erect and poised, as if she already belonged in this building, as if she had worked here for years, as if she were the brisk and efficient Miss Braun, you know, Miss Braun, private secretary to Mr. Sultky in 918, one of the most efficient young business women in the city . . .

She came to the door at last, and, from long experience, she did not allow herself to hesitate. She took hold of the knob directly and walked in, smiling a cool friendly smile.

The office into which she stepped was not in the least imposing. Merely one big desk in the middle of a gray rug that covered the floor, with windows behind the desk to the left, and, to the right, another door marked "Mr. Sultky, Private." There was a young woman sitting behind the desk, a rather young and friendly-looking person, not at all like the efficient middle-aged personnel women whom Virginia had come to know so well and to hate.

She looked up from some papers and greeted Virginia with a smile. "Hello, there, are you another one of the girls from the employment service? You girls don't seem to mind the weather when it comes to a job, do you? Won't you sit down?"

For some reason or other Virginia turned wary of this rather unorthodox person. She took the chair that was indicated, murmuring her thanks.

The girl at the desk took her card and glanced at it casually. "Okay, Miss Braun. Now, maybe, I'd better tell you something about the job. Mr. Sultky, as you might possibly know, is the editor and publisher of a little bimonthly journal that is the official organ for one of the two major political parties here in the city. Mr. Sultky has decided to start a drive to increase the circulation of the paper. He is planning to get out a special extra-large Christmas edition to be sold on the newsstands as well as mailed to the regular subscribers. In order to do that he needs ads, lots of ads. The job that is open here for you, if you want it, is ad soliciting. You know, you go around to different places of business and try to sell them ads. I don't suppose you've ever done any ad soliciting before?"

"Well, no, no, I haven't, but I . . ."

"Oh, sure you could," the girl behind the desk said easily, with her friendly smile. "You'll get along fine with it. Now, let's see, I've made up some lists here of places to go. Two or three other girls have already started out soliciting this morning. I'll have to see what places are left."

"Now, let's see," she said rapidly. "How would you like this one— mostly beauty shops? They aren't hard to find. You know the streets around here, don't you? You won't have to do so much walking. Here is a copy of the paper and an advertising rate card.

"Another thing, I almost forgot." The girl leaned down and opened a desk drawer and took out an order pad. "If anybody should want to subscribe to the paper, here are some subscription blanks. It's a dollar and a half a year."

Virginia crammed the subscription blanks into her purse along with the other materials that the girl had given to her.

"Well," the girl said with her friendly smile, "I hope you have good luck and sell just lots and lots of ads."

Virginia recognized a dismissal and got up from her chair. The cold had made one of her ears ache a little; she was conscious of the sharp stabbing pain in her ear.

"Oh, I almost forgot to tell you," the girl said, "you get a commission on the ads and subscriptions you sell; you know, you get paid on the commission basis. That's all right with you, isn't it?"

The words stuck in Virginia's throat a little. "Yes, of course."

"Good-bye then. I'll be seeing you. Good luck!"

Virginia crossed the office to the door, feeling confused, feeling somehow as if there were all kinds of questions that she should ask the girl, and yet she couldn't think of any specific ones. It just seemed all wrong to her. She wasn't exactly disappointed, but the enthusiasm she had expected to feel at getting a job was strangely lacking.

Virginia closed the door behind her and walked down the corridor to the elevators. While she waited, she consulted the list of addresses and made tentative groupings of those that were in the same vicinities. While the elevator dropped to the main floor, she glanced over the list of prices for various sized ads, her face serious with concentration. She had never tried to do any work like this before. She was interested and curious and a little excited about it already. Though it was not quite as she had expected it to be, she felt some measure of elation. After all, a job was a job, and she had a job now.

She arrived at her first destination, another office building in which were located several of the beauty shops that appeared on her list. The first place was an imposing chromium-and-leather affair on the ground floor of the building. Virginia hesitated only one second. Let's see, first she would ask to see the advertising manager, or the proprietor of the shop. Virginia had given up hesitating outside of doors long ago. She took a deep breath, opened the door and walked in with as much assurance as she could muster.

And so her hegira began.

She visited nineteen beauty shops in rapid succession, one after another. The results fell into a pattern amazingly soon. Either they never did any advertising—a satisfied customer is our best advertisement—or, if they did, they were not disposed to do any through the paper that Virginia suddenly found herself representing. Their quota for Christmas advertising was filled. None of them had ever heard of the paper; none of them cared if they never did hear of it and not one of them saw any advantage in wasting any money on an advertisement in such a publication. She stopped at a drug-store lunch counter for a cup of coffee and a sandwich. She gulped down her food in a hurry, eager to be on her way again. She hadn't quite lost hope. She didn't think about much of anything as she gulped down the steaming hot coffee that did not seem to warm her body at all. It was as if her thoughts and her feelings were congealed by the cold. She was conscious of one thing only: a great desire to go to every single address on the list.

The afternoon was infinitely worse than the morning had been. Virginia lost all track of time and the number of shops she visited. The small shop located on the second floor of a dingy building on a side street was unexpectedly expensive in its furnishings for all of its somewhat unfavorable location. One of the girls in the front of the shop had sent Virginia out back. There the proprietress herself was seated at one of the tiny chromium-and-glass tables, giving a manicure to a special customer. The woman had been kind enough, and even rather friendly. She simply never spent any money on advertising, she told Virginia, as she spread the red polish on the nails with swift deft strokes of the brush. She was not impressed by the sample of the paper. She had never heard of it, and she suggested to Virginia that she was afraid that most people hadn't ever heard of it either. She said it was a cold day, and she commented that Virginia looked simply frozen to death.

Virginia thanked her for her time and trouble and turned away. And, as she walked toward the front of the shop, she heard the clear, well-bred voice of the aristocratic-looking, gray-haired customer who was having the manicure, and who had been an interested listener to the entire conversation. "What a pathetic-looking little creature," the woman said. "She must be desperate for a job to do something like that. How miserable of the people that run the paper to send her out on a day like this! Nobody would ever run an ad in an unknown paper like that. I'll bet they've got her working on a commission, too."

The proprietress of the shop made some answer to the customer, but Virginia did not hear what it was. A wave of feeling suddenly broke in upon the numbness of her brain. There was a big, full-length mirror just inside the door, and Virginia suddenly saw herself in it while the woman's words were still dinning in her ears. "What a pathetic-looking little creature! What a pathetic-looking little creature!" Virginia took one look at her image in that mirror and fled. She was pinched with the cold. Her hair was disarrayed and straggling down from under her plain brown felt hat that had slid on her head to a peculiarly unbecoming angle. The make-up was gone from her face and there was a smudge of soot across her nose and another across her cheek. The old tan polo coat was wrapped around her, so pitifully inadequate a protection against the extremity of the weather. The scuffed brown shoes and the cotton gloves with the split finger seams somehow made the whole picture complete. Then the dogged, blind, hurt look on her face. "What a pathetic-looking little creature!"

The first thing she did when she reached the street was to tear the list of beauty shops to bits and scatter the pieces to the wind. She was angry, angry at that pretty, flip girl in that office who had started her out on this fool's chase, angry at herself for being taken in by it. Then there was her disappointment. To think that she had thought that this was a job, to think that she had thought that this was her lucky day, to think of all the plans she had made, her happiness at the thought of working again, having money of her own, and how she had planned to surprise Sally with the news.

Virginia wanted to cry. She opened her purse to get her handkerchief and the first thing her fingers touched was the sample copy of the little journal that the girl in the office had given her. Virginia tore that into bits too, and took a savage pleasure in doing it. She threw away the price list, too, and she all but threw away the pad of subscription blanks, but she checked herself. After all, that was worth money. She would have to return them. Subscriptions! Oh, that was a joke! Who would even want a subscription to such a paper? It wasn't fair, Virginia thought desperately, it just wasn't fair. Other people had jobs, why couldn't she get one? She had looked so hard, she had been disappointed like this so many times. It seemed as if she couldn't take any more of it.

There was a drug store just up the street a little, and Virginia turned in there. The booths were filled with exhausted women shoppers who compared notes on purchases and gossiped over hot-fudge sundaes and whipped-cream-trimmed dessert concoctions. Virginia sat at the counter and gave her order for coffee to a waitress who put a glass of water down in front of her and wiped up the counter with a rag, all in one gesture. One of four or five giggling high-school girls, who filled a booth in the corner, came up and put a nickel in the juke-box. A male vocalist, with a voice overflowing with a kind of synthetic joy, started to sing "Jingle Bells."

"It's terrible cold out today, isn't it?" the waitress said, as she took the nickel that Virginia handed her above the coffee cup.

"Yes, it is," Virginia said. She listened to the noise of the cash register as the girl deposited her nickel, and it made Virginia feel guilty. She had no business to spend Sally's money foolishly like this for a cup of coffee.

Then a wave of despair overwhelmed Virginia. She couldn't go on like this much longer, she thought. She wasn't being dramatic about it, or silly or emotional. It was just the plain fact. She couldn't go on like this much longer, living from day to day, not being able to find a job, haunted by that feeling that there was no place for her anywhere in the world, that she was of no use to anything or anybody. Virginia remembered something she had heard a girl say long ago, and the words took on a new significance for her now as she recalled them. "God forgot us when he made the world!" That was what the girl had said. And it's true Virginia thought, God forgot us when he made the world. People like me there just isn't any place for. No job, no place, nobody, nothing! And not only that, Virginia thought despairingly, she was a detriment to Sally, a kind of additional millstone tied around Sally's neck. Sally had enough, too much already, without her. If she had any courage, what she ought to do was run away, go someplace alone to some other city where Sally didn't even know where she was, and there either find a job or starve, live or die, all to herself. But Virginia knew that she wouldn't do that because she didn't have the courage. She was weak, and she wanted to live.

The coffee cooled in front of her, and Virginia closed her lips tight together and blinked back tears. Oh, Bill, she was thinking, I don't see how I can go on living, if I don't get a letter from you pretty soon! If I don't get a letter from you pretty soon, I won't want to go on living.

Then she thought about Bill for a long time, recalled good times they had had together, speculated as to why he didn't write to her. And she tried to decide what to buy him for Christmas. There was the Two Dollars. The Two Dollars was the very last money of her own that Virginia had in the world. When her money started dwindling so fast, she had hidden the Two Dollars away in her old suitcase, for this very purpose, a Christmas present for Bill. The package to him should be in the mail already. Virginia thought of all the things she saw in store windows. Buying this gift for Bill was going to be all the Christmas that she had this year, but she didn't care. That was Christmas enough for her.

She sat there for a long time, and then a sudden glimpse at the clock sent her scurrying out of the drug store to return the subscription pad before bus time. It was almost dark outdoors, and the streets were crowded. The Christmas carols played over the streets loudly and monotonously. Virginia thought that the air felt a little warmer, but she couldn't be sure; maybe it was because she herself had thawed out a little from the warmth of the drug store and the hot coffee. Stores were ablaze with light and glittering with all the color and tinsel of Christmas. The aisles were choked with shoppers, clerks hurried here and there with tired set faces. Saturday was a long hard day for the clerks. And to think that she couldn't even get a job working in a store over the holiday rush, Virginia thought bitterly.

She took the elevator up to the ninth floor and turned down the corridor toward Mr. Sultky's office. She saw the light shining through the crinkled glass in the door before she got to it. She came up to the door, rapped on it lightly and turned the knob at the same time. When she went in, the office was flooded with soft light from the tall standard lamp on the desk. The girl was sitting at the desk with the typewriter in front of her, typing. She did not even look up as Virginia came in.

Finally she leaned back in the chair and stretched, her arms wide above her head. "Well, hello, there!" she said brightly. "We were wondering what had become of you. The other girls came back ages ago."

Virginia cleared her throat. "I brought back the subscription blanks," Virginia said determinedly.

"How did you make out?" the girl asked.

Virginia shook her head. "I didn't get any. Nobody would—they all said . . ."

The girl swung her chair around and wiped her ink-stained hands on a clean sheet of typing paper. "Oh, that's all right," she said to Virginia brightly. "You'll have better luck with it tomorrow, Monday, I mean."

It seemed inconceivable to Virginia that these people should think that she was willing to continue such a hopeless job as this one had turned out to be. The fact that they did made her even angrier. She stammered a little when she spoke.

"I—I—won't be back Monday!"

"You won't!" the girl said blankly, her hand groping over the desk for her cigarette package. "What do you mean you won't be back Monday?"

The anger and bitterness were knotting up tight inside of Virginia. "I mean I won't be back Monday. I—I—don't want to do it any more."

The girl turned to Virginia again, and the pleasant look was gone from her face. "You girls make me sick," she said conversationally. "You really do. You hang around employment agencies all the while and complain because you can't get a job, and then when you do get one you don't want it!"

The bright anger exploded in Virginia. "A job," she said bitterly. "You call this a job! Just—just go out and try it yourself! Nobody's ever heard of this paper, nobody's ever seen it before. They all do advertising in the daily papers. A swell job this is!" Virginia pulled her coat around her, picked up her purse and gloves and started for the door.

As she did so the office girl took some money out of a coin purse in the pocket of her jacket. "Here," she said.

Virginia stopped at the door. "I don't want your charity," she said. "I took the job on a commission basis. I didn't sell any ads, so there isn't any money coming to me."

"Don't be silly," the girl said impatiently. "Mr. Sultky wanted to give something to each of you girls for your trouble."

She held the money out, a dollar bill, under the light, and Virginia saw it. Virginia stopped still and her face went white. A dollar bill! Virginia saw it in terms of what she owed to Sally, and the Two Dollars home in the suitcase, and a pair of new silk hose, a tube of toothpaste maybe, and maybe some warm mittens.

Her face was white and still as a mask. She walked across the floor slowly and took the bill out of the girl's hand. "Thank you," she said. She walked back across the floor with all the anger gone out of her, and the despair choking her again.

As she closed the door, the girl at the desk said almost penitently, "Good-bye. I'm sorry the job didn't turn out better. Merry Christmas!"

# 5

VIRGINIA CLIMBED THE STAIRS AT HOME WEARILY. There was no letter waiting for her on the hall table, and she was so tired that she didn't particularly care. The door to the apartment was unlocked, and she stepped into a living room that bore testimony to the children's activities of the day: papers and books lit-tered everywhere, furniture out of place and the pillows from the davenport scattered over the floor. There was light and the sound of voices from the kitchen. Virginia dropped her purse and gloves on the library table in the corner, and walked toward the kitchen, loos-ening her coat as she went.

Fred Foster and Joe were seated at opposite ends of the kitchen table, the dirty breakfast dishes, just as Virginia had left them that morning, pushed back out of the way to make room for the beer cans between them. Buddy and Marilyn were eating sandwiches so liber-ally spread with jam that the thin purple stuff oozed out with every bite they took. Harold was nowhere in sight.

"Hi, Ginny!" Fred Foster said. His face was already a little flushed from the beer, and he was wearing his good suit of clothes, a sure indication that this was a Saturday night, with no more work until Monday.

"Hello." Virginia glanced at the empty beer cans disapprovingly. Apparently the two of them had been drinking beer steadily ever since Joe had come home from work. It happened every Saturday, but still Virginia did not approve.

"Hey, Virgie, when we gonna eat?" the children chorused at her.

"Did you have any lunch?" Virginia asked them.

"Jus' some bread and stuff."

"Didn't Harold fix the soup the way I told him to?"

"Uh uh," Buddy said, licking jam off as much of his face as he could reach. "He went away someplace. He hada go sell papers."

"Well, after you finish those sandwiches you better wait and not eat anything more till supper." Virginia walked back into the other room to take off her coat.

"Vir—jinny," Fred Foster said, as she walked away. He took another drink out of his beer glass and called after her, "I hear you got a job, huh?"

"No," Virginia said. She stripped the baggy green sweater over her head and hung it on a nail in the closet.

"The kids said you went downtown early this morning to see about a job."

Virginia walked over to the sink, pushing up her dress sleeves, without answering him. Fred watched her curiously.

"Hey, hey, what goes on here?" he said teasingly. "If you wasn't workin', where was you all day? This looks bad."

Virginia stacked dishes in the dishpan noisily and said nothing.

Fred winked at Joe elaborately. "Say, Joe, you better keep an eye on your kid sister. Looks to me like she's up to something. I bet she's gotta boy friend we don't know nothin' about."

Joe brooded over his beer glass. He laughed unpleasantly at Fred's words.

"Hey, Virgie," Buddy said. He was trying to lick jam from the tip of his nose. He screwed up his face and twisted his head back and forth in the effort. "Hey, Virgie," he said again.

Virginia paid no attention to him. He opened his mouth wide and roared her name, "Virgie!"

"For Christ's sakes cut out that yellin'," Joe said.

"What do you want, Buddy?"

Virginia carried a stack of dirty dishes from the table and piled them up on the sink shelf in the space she had cleared there.

"A letter come for you today in the mail, Virgie," Buddy said.

Virginia dropped a cup. It broke in three pieces and the handle scuttled across the floor under the table. She turned on him in a flash, her eyes enormous in her face. "Why didn't you tell me? Where is it? It wasn't down on the table. What did you do with it?"

Fred reached into his inside coat pocket and drew out the slightly bent medium-sized white envelope. "I'm sorry, Virge," he said, as he handed it to her. "I just wanted to kid you a little. I didn't know it was gonna make you feel bad."

"It's all right," Virginia said, as she took the letter from his hand. "I was just feeling kind of cross tonight, that was all."

She looked at the envelope with a kind of curiosity. She just looked at it for a moment, and then she walked toward the door into the living room with it in her hand.

The children started to trail after her, but Fred called them back sharply. "Hey, you kids, lay off! You stay out here and let Virgie read her letter."

Virginia walked into the living room, feeling somehow stiff and self-conscious. The floor lamp near the davenport was turned on, and, without thinking, she pulled the chain, making the room suddenly dark. Then she pulled the chain again quickly. She stood still with the letter in her hand. She picked up a couple of the pillows from the floor at her feet and put them back on the davenport. She sat down on the edge of the davenport, turning the letter in her hands, seeing Bill's writing and the right postmark. Then she just stared at it. A funny thing, she was thinking, she had looked for this letter twice a day for a month and a half at least, maybe more. She had looked for this letter, she had prayed for this letter, she had cried over this letter and worried over it. Now here it was at last. It was funny. She couldn't understand it. Why didn't she tear it open, Virginia wondered. Why didn't she rip the envelope quickly? She ought to be all trembling with excitement and happiness. She ought to have had the letter open and read over twice by now. But she wasn't excited. If anything, she was abnormally cold and still inside. She turned the letter over again and stared at it. She swallowed hard and closed her eyes a minute, because she was looking at it so hard that the handwriting all ran together in front of her eyes. You're acting silly; you must be crazy, she told herself. Why don't you open it? Why don't you read it? It's a letter from Bill, you dope, from Bill. You've waited for this letter so long!

Suddenly she realized that she was afraid to open that letter, more afraid than she had ever been before in her life, afraid of what he might have written there, or more of what he might not have written.

Out of that realization she slid her finger under the flap of the envelope and slowly tore it open.

It was a very short letter, a few lines scrawled across a single sheet of paper. It took her but a moment to read it. She read it with her face set and still. When she was through she put it into the envelope without re-reading it. She got up from the davenport and opened the closet door. Her old gray suitcase was on the floor, pushed to the back of the closet. She pulled it out, the dust coming off on her hands. She opened the cover of the suitcase and put the envelope with a small pack like it in one of the pockets in the side of the suitcase. She closed the lid and shoved it back against the wall.

For a moment she remained where she was, squatting on her heels on the floor. The light shone on her dusty hands. She looked at her hands, noticed the dust, and rubbed them together.

As easily and as quickly as that it happened. Virginia just gave up. Bill was suddenly gone from her, lost, finished, done with. Not what the letter had said, unless maybe that one phrase about "no Christmas present, please," but what the letter hadn't said. A wooden, formal letter, polite, but no more than that, not even a friendly letter, so little about himself, nothing at all about her. Just the kind of letter that a person writes with an effort in answer to the letter of another person that one does not wish to correspond with but whose feelings in the matter one hesitates to hurt. Just a few impersonal lines scrawled on a sheet of paper and signed simply with his name—"Bill"; not "love" or "as ever" or anything. Just Bill. It was the first letter she had ever had from him that he hadn't signed "love." This was the end. She had seen it coming; she had dreaded it, and now it was here. She had struggled so long to keep it going, but now she had given up. The odds were too great against her. Oh, the odds had been too great for both of them, she thought with a flash of rebellion. And then she sank back into that curious vacuous state of mind and feeling. A vacuum before readjustment, such a readjustment as she could not now even conceive. For so long now, Bill had been the focus of her life; he had given her aim and direction. She wondered briefly and without emotion how in the world she was ever to go on living without him.

The voices from the kitchen ran into a blur in her ears. For a time she remained where she was, squatted there on her heels at the open closet door. She didn't think about much of anything and she rubbed at the dust on her hands aimlessly. In a minute or two she came back to consciousness of herself. The muscle in her ankle had cramped; she felt the pain from it stabbing up through her leg. Virginia stood up then, stumbling a little because her legs were cramped and stiff. She closed the closet door and turned around and walked into the kitchen.

She went to the sink and began to draw hot water from the tap into the dishpan. Fred Foster watched her curiously over the top of his beer glass.

"Well, what did good old Bill have to say for himself, Virge?" he said banteringly. "Now you got that letter, maybe somebody will catch you with a smile on your face for a change. God knows, you been going around here like a sourpuss lately."

Virginia's face was set and still. She poured soap powder out of the big box into the side of the dishpan liberally, stirring the water with her hand to make suds.

Marilyn slid down over the edge of a chair seat on her back, her fat, round, little stomach arching up in the air. "Virgie's got a boy friend!"

"I'll say she has," Fred said heartily. "Did he say he still loved you, Virgie?"

The dishes rattled together noisily in the pan as she washed them, but Virginia gave him no answer.

"Well, well! So she won't talk!" Fred winked across the table at Joe elaborately. "I bet they had a fight about something and this was a mad letter. Is that right, Virgie?"

Joe said, "You got any more cigarettes, Fred?"

"Yeah, sure."

Fred slid the crumpled package of cigarettes across the table, with an expansive, sweeping gesture of his arm.

"Hey, Virgie," Fred said in mock alarm, "don't tell me he's ditched you for another girl! My God, don't tell me old Bill wrote you a letter to tell you he's got himself another girl friend!"

Virginia went on washing dishes, her face deliberately turned away from him.

"No, sir, you can't get a word out of her," Fred explained to Joe. Joe, alone with his beer, wrapped in a thick cloud of cigarette smoke, paid no attention to him.

Fred emptied another beer can into his glass and shoved the empty among the other cans clustered along the back of the table. He turned the glass around and around in his hand and watched Virginia steadily.

"Hey, Virgie!" he said suddenly.

Virginia kept her head bent over the dishpan, industriously scratching a blob of dried egg yolk from a wet slippery plate with her fingernails.

"Virgie, look around here a minute!"

She did not turn around. Fred stuck his cigarette in his mouth and pulled himself up out of his chair. He walked over behind her, dropped his hand on her shoulder and bent down to peer at her face. "Whatsa matter, Virgie, you mad or feeling bad or what?"

She shook his hand from her shoulder and turned her set, strained face away from him.

Fred retreated a little and leaned against the corner of the refrigerator. "Aw, come on, Virgie, tell us about it. Something must be the matter with you and that guy. He waits around a couple a months without writing to you, and then, when you finally do get a letter from him, you go around here with your face a mile long. Whatsa matter, Virgie?"

She made a little sound in her throat as if she was clearing it, and her hands moved faster with the dishes.

Fred cocked his head on one side to look at her. "I tell you what," he said jovially. "How about you going out and drinking some beer with me tonight? I bet that would be good for what ails you. Hell, I ain't got no date so special I couldn't break it. You need to get out someplace and drink a little beer. How about it, Virgie?"

He waited a minute and then he said, "Huh? How about it?"

She shook her head a little without turning around.

"Virge," Fred said judiciously, "somethin' musta hit you hard. You look sick, no kiddin'. What did that lug say to you in that letter, anyway? I'd like to punch his nose in, playin' around with a nice little kid like you."

Virginia knelt down and scraped garbage out of a dish into the can under the sink.

"Aw, come on, Virgie, spill it! You'll feel better if you do. Did that bastard write you a letter and tell you he was through with you?"

Virginia's lips started to tremble, but she tightened them rigidly again. "Fred, please!" she said.

They heard the door open and shut, and Johnny O'Connor appeared in the doorway, his coat draped around his shoulders.

"Hi!" he said. "Been h'isting a few off the table, I see. Saturday night in the old home town! Hello, Ginny."

"Howza boy, Johnny?" Fred said expansively. "Sit down and drink a beer."

Johnny held one of his bandaged hands up, a mock shade for his eyes, and looked at Fred. Then he shook his head dolefully. "Freddie, my lad," he said, "either I am seein' things or you are slippin', or else you got a damn early start on yourself this afternoon. If you don't watch it you're gonna be lookin' up countin' the wads of chewing gum stuck to the underside of a table someplace before the night is over."

"Aw, don't you worry about me, Johnny."

Johnny looked past him to Virginia at the sink. "Well, honey, how did that job business come out? I hear you was down to see about a job? Did you get it?"

"No," Virginia said.

Johnny's face was instantly touched with concern. "Oh, that's tough! I thought maybe this was gonna be the day when things broke for you. Never you mind, Ginny, you'll be getting a job some of these days yet, you wait and see."

"You better not pick on her, Johnny," Fred said ponderously. "She ain't feeling so good. She got a letter today from that stinkin' bastard boy friend of hers she's been writing to ever since she came out here. He ditched her!"

Virginia let dishes clatter out of her hands and whirled around suddenly. Her whole face was shifting and trembling. "Oh, stop it!" she said. "Why can't you leave me alone? Why can't you quit talking about it!"

The whole kitchen went quiet. The children crept up from the other room and peered in around Johnny, their eyes wide. Joe leaned over across the table and pulled another beer can to him. "Oh, Jesus!" Joe said softly in disgust. He poured beer out of the can into his glass carelessly, a splashing larrup of sound, the collar of foam rising high. He took a drink and wiped the bubbles of foam off his mouth with the back of his hand.

Virginia stood still, twisting at her apron with her wet, red, puckery hands. She was trying hard to make her face still and controlled again, trying very hard to keep from crying out loud.

Johnny O'Connor spoke to her gently. "Hell, don't feel so bad, honey. He ain't worth it; no guy is worth it. If that was all he cared about you, why, it's better you found it out now instead of later sometime. Just let him go to hell and forget about him. There are a lot of other guys around that are worth a lot more than he is. Why, some day you'll look back to this and laugh about it, Ginny . . ."

"No, I won't," Virginia said. "I'll never laugh about this, not ever. I'll never laugh about it as long as I live!"

Fred Foster laughed at her tolerantly. "Oh, yes, you will. Why, Virge, if I had a buck for ever' time I felt just the way you do, I'd buy me a second-hand automobile! First thing you know you'll meet somebody else and you'll forget this guy Bill was ever on earth. Besides, what kind of a guy was this Bill, anyway, keepin' you all upset and writing to him all the while instead of comin' right out and sayin' . . ."

Virginia's voice rose hysterically. "No. You haven't got any business to talk about Bill like that! Bill is the swellest and the best . . . This isn't his fault. He isn't to blame. He wanted to marry me. But how could we get married? How could we even plan on it? What's the use of our ever planning on anything?"

"Hey, hey, Virge! Take it easy!"

But Virginia had gone too far to stop now. "What chance did Bill and I ever have, I'd like to know! He can't get a good job till he finishes his engineering course, and it's gonna take a lot of money to do that. He has to help support his mother. He doesn't make much, working in a factory. He's got debts to pay. And now the draft, he'll probably get called in the spring. How could we ever plan on anything? It isn't his fault. You haven't got any business to say nasty things about Bill. He couldn't help this. Nor I couldn't. Nobody could. It isn't fair, we never even had a chance!"

Virginia was struggling so hard with her tears that her whole body was trembling. She pushed past Johnny out of the kitchen, and they heard the slam of the bedroom door behind her.

# 6

FRED FOSTER LEFT TO KEEP A DATE, AND JOE LINGERED awhile longer in the kitchen, alone over the beer cans. He had a date himself, but not till later on. He was just beginning to feel the beer; he knew he ought to eat something, but he didn't feel like eating. Anyway, he would have to lay off the beer if he was going to be in any kind of shape later in the evening. Joe went to the bathroom and then he unbolted both doors and went on into his bedroom. He didn't have to change his clothes just yet, so it might not be a bad idea if he took a nap, Joe decided. He didn't bother to turn on the light. He groped across the room in the semi-darkness to the bed. Joe lowered his long body onto the untidy, tumbled coverlets without bothering to remove his shoes. He stretched out his legs luxuriously, and pillowed his head on his doubled arms. The beer had made him sleepy and he fell immediately into a light slumber.

He slept for awhile but the room was cold and it half-wakened him. He began to dream then, caught between sleeping and waking, with part awareness that it was a dream. He was in a room someplace, and there was a girl with him, a blonde girl who looked a little like Gloria O'Connor, except her hair was lighter and longer and shinier. The girl was dressed like a girl he had seen in a picture the other day, a black sheer negligee splitting open in the front, long black mesh hose on her legs. The girl kept smiling at him and saying nice things to him, and he was excited because he knew that he was going to have her in a minute. But when he came close to her to take hold of her, she backed away from him and her face looked very sad. He kept following her, and the room got bigger and bigger. He followed her, stumbling over furniture, his hands outstretched and fumbling, but he couldn't get hold of her. "No, Joe, we mustn't," she kept saying. "Why not?" he asked her. And she said, "Because you were afraid to ride your bicycle over the railroad bridge, remember?" They started laughing then, a lot of voices raised in loud derisive laughter. It wasn't the room any more, it was a bar someplace, filled with drinkers. The girl was still there, and Stan Walezewski, and Joe hated Stan Walezewski so much he wanted to kill him. Stan was wet, a puddle of water on the floor around him, and his face was swollen and distorted, as if he had the mumps. The girl had her arms around Stan's neck and she was laughing at Joe, and so was Stan and everybody. He ran out of the room to get away from them, but the door only opened into another and larger room and everybody in there was laughing at him too. They pointed at him as he came into the room, and they laughed at him. He began to run. He ran as hard as he could, the laughter following him, sometimes loud and sometimes faint. Then suddenly he was safe, completely safe and hidden away from them in some small dark place. He rested there and he knew that he was safe now, that they never would find him. But they did find him, and they began to batter the door down. He was suddenly aware that his hideaway was high in the air and the height made him dizzy. He was trapped and frightened, and they were trying to smash the door down. He yelled at them, threatened them; they would be sorry if they opened this door! But the door splintered open at last, and the light poured in. Joe perceived the reason for his terror: he was half-clothed; he wore no trousers. His hideaway was a sort of shallow ledge high up in a wall. He jumped down into the crowd and ran away, half-naked as he was, and they chased him, laughing.

Joe stirred uneasily on the bed and made a moaning sound in his throat. Outside the bedroom a board squeaked and snapped suddenly, and the cheap tinny doorknob began to turn gently and noiselessly. The door inched open without a sound. For a second Harold Otis was silhouetted against the dim light of the hallway, looking back over his shoulder furtively. Then he slipped through the door and closed it quickly behind him. The doorcatch sprang back in place with an audible snap. Harold leaned his back against the door for a moment, and his breathing was suddenly flurried and noisy.

In a moment he groped his way in the darkness along the footrail of the iron bed to the dresser against the opposite wall. He felt the edge of the dresser with his hand and then stretched up on his toes and fumbled above his head for the chain on the light bulb. He couldn't find it for a minute. His hand at arm's reach made short choppy motions in the air. He gave it up and felt along the dresser edge again to get the exact location. He took a step sideways to the right until he stood in front of the exact center of the dresser, where the beveled edge came together in a slight indentation that he could feel with his fingers. He reached for the light chain again and this time he found it on the first attempt. He pulled it and the room was full of light.

Harold was looking up when he pulled the chain and the sudden glaring illumination dazzled his eyes. He closed them, and let his body sag forward against the edge of the cheap, cluttered dresser top. When he opened them he looked at his reflection in the mirror anxiously. His light hair was rumpled and streaked with dirt, and there was a smear of blood over his right ear. His face was dirty and very white. There was a large bloody scab forming on his forehead where the skin had been scraped away. One of his eyes was red and swollen nearly shut, the swelling extending down into his cheek to give the whole side of his face a distorted contour. His jacket and trousers were streaked with dirt, and there was a big gaping hole torn in the fabric of his trousers over one knee.

His face was absolutely expressionless as he contemplated his reflection. He rubbed at some of the dirt on his face with an equally dirty and blood-smeared hand. He felt the swelling around his eye gingerly with his fingers, moving the swollen, discolored eyelid just perceptibly. He lowered his hand and examined his scraped knuckles. They were still bleeding a little and smarting. He stood still and sucked at them, looking at himself in the mirror, and he snuffed a couple of times, miserably. When he took his hand away from his mouth, his lips were quivering a little, although his face was still controlled and expressionless. He pulled a brown knitted woolen cap out of the pocket of his jacket, dislodging it with difficulty, and dropped it on top of the brushes, dirty handkerchiefs, and empty matchfolders that littered the dresser top.

In spite of the effort he made to hold them still, his lips quivered more and more. He turned away from the mirror with a little half-sound in his throat, like a smothered sob. He walked across the floor stiffly toward the bed. Then he saw Joe Braun.

Joe moved and stretched his arms. "Huh?" he said, drowsily, his eyes still closed.

Harold stopped crying instantly. He unzipped the fastener on his jacket, took it off and flung it over the footrail of the bed. He walked back to the dresser and drew himself up tall in front of the mirror, swaggering a little, his thin shoulders very straight under the baggy old sweater. He examined his swollen eye, tenderly and admiringly. Then he began to whistle softly, a shrill sound from between his teeth. He felt the big puckery scab on his forehead with one gentle finger, and explored cautiously for a similar one on his head under the hair just over his right ear. He gave that up and contemplated his skinned knuckles, and his whistling grew increasingly loud and shrill. He coughed, cleared his throat noisily, and went on whistling.

Joe rolled over on the bed suddenly, and blinked his eyes open.

"Hi yuh," he said to Harold without looking at him. He was looking at the clock on the dresser instead. "Jesus, why didn't somebody call me?" He stretched hard once more and then he bounded off the bed and went to the door of the clothes closet. Harold looked at Joe quickly, and then turned back to the mirror and went through extravagantly exaggerated motions of examining his eye again, which was swelling by the moment and rapidly discoloring.

But Joe didn't notice him. Joe was searching out shirts hung among the other clothing in the closet. As he found each one, he removed the hanger from the rod and held the shirt around to the light to compare it for cleanliness with the one he was wearing.

"Oh, God!" he said at last, giving up the search. He stepped back from the closet door a little and buttoned his shirt collar, then started rolling down the sleeves so he could fasten the cuffs.

Harold watched him attentively in silence, standing with his back to the mirror now, and carrying his head twisted to one side slightly, so that the light from the bulb above him shone down directly on his swollen, discolored eye.

Joe finished with his cuffs and smoothed out some of the wrinkles in his shirt, but still he didn't notice Harold. He went back to the closet and picked up a pair of shoes from the floor. They were black, with pointed toes, and in each one was stuck a crumpled, bright-colored silk sock. Joe took them over to the bed, dusting the pointed toes of the shoes lovingly with the palm of his hand. He sat down on the edge of the bed heavily, dropping the pair of shoes to the floor with a thud, and began to pick at the laces of the ones he was wearing.

Harold began to whistle again, loud and shrill. He leaned down and brushed some of the dirt off his trousers with a wide sweeping gesture of his arm, designed to catch Joe's eye. Then immediately he turned around to the mirror again, swaggering out his thin chest, and repeating the exaggerated motions of feeling his swollen face.

This time his luck was better. Joe glanced up at him, and, catching sight of Harold's reflection in the mirror, sat still, staring.

"Goddam! Look at you!" Joe said.

"Yup!" Harold said happily. He made a clucking sound out of the corner of his mouth, expressing both admiration and concern for his injury, and went through the elaborate pattern of examining it once again, whistling shrilly all the while.

Joe stuck his feet into his shoes and got up from the bed without waiting to tie the laces. He came over to the dresser and stood beside Harold.

"Here, lemme see it." He reached down and cupped the boy's chin in his hand and tipped his face up to the light.

Harold raised his face willingly, grinning, and swelled out his chest. Joe looked at his eye critically and then took note of the other marks of conflict upon Harold's person and clothing. Then Joe looked at the eye again, tipping his head to one side, and squinting his own eyes at it judiciously.

"Shoulda had some raw meat on it," he said at last. "Jesus, ain't that gonna be a sight tomorrow, though!" He whistled shortly. "Kid, somebody sure hung one on yuh!"

"Jeez, yuh oughta see the other guy!" Harold bragged. "An he's a whole lot bigger'n me. Boy, you oughta see him! Jeez, I sure fixed him up!"

Joe let go of his face and turned back to the bed, laughing his dry, unpleasant laughter. While he tied his shoes, his head tipped down between his knees, his hair glistening with oil, he said to

Harold, "You better keep away from your mother, kid. Jesus, wait'll she sees you!"

"Aw, hell," Harold said. "What's it to her? I guess it ain't none a her business what I do!"

Joe Braun laughed again. "Gettin' pretty tough, ain'tcha," Joe said. "Gettin' too big for your britches!"

Harold's grin broadened across his face in delight. "And I ain't through with this guy yet, see!" he bragged. "Boy, I'm really gonna fix him for this, you just wait!"

Joe Braun studied his own reflection in the mirror admiringly, and swaggered a little himself. "Attaboy!" he said to Harold, slapping him across the back condescendingly. "You get him! Don't let nobody pull nothin' on you."

"Don't you worry!" Harold said.

Joe finished dressing and took his overcoat off the wire hanger. When he turned around, he was just in time to see Harold slide a couple of cigarettes out of the half-filled package he had dropped on the dresser top, cupping them quickly in his hand.

"And that's another thing," Joe said. "You better not smoke them around here, 'cause if your mother ever catches you at it she's gonna beat hell outa you!"

"I guess she ain't never caught me doin' it yet," Harold said proudly.

Joe came back to the mirror and looked at himself again. Then he opened one of the small drawers at the top of the dresser and took out a cheap white rayon neck scarf with fringe on it and folded it carefully around his neck, smoothing his overcoat collar over it.

"I smoke cigarettes alla time," Harold said. "All us guys do. I guess smokin' ain't gonna hurt nobody."

The door closed behind Joe, and Harold looked after him admiringly for a moment. He picked up a folder of matches and stuck it in his pocket and the two cigarettes after it, carefully, so as not to bend them. Then he turned out the light and went through the door into the bathroom. He pulled the chain on the electric bulb and bolted the door behind him and also the door on the other side of the bathroom that opened out into the living room of his mother's apartment.

Yessir, with the cigarette in his mouth and that black eye he sure looked tough, all right, just the way Joe said he was. But just the same he was a little scared about what his mother was going to say when she saw him. She was going to feel bad. She was going to make a fuss. She was going to ask him questions about being in a fight. And when he didn't tell her anything about it, she was going to feel worse. Maybe she would even cry. Harold felt a twinge all through him, in spite of himself, at the thought of his mother crying about it. He weakened suddenly and a lump formed in his throat. Maybe he would tell her. Maybe he would go and tell her all about it, and let her fuss around him and feel sorry for him. Then he knew suddenly that he couldn't tell his mother about this, even if he wanted to, because it was something that would make her feel worse than anything. The lump got bigger in his throat. He puffed on his cigarette ferociously and scowled into the mirror, trying to look plenty tough, but it wasn't so good because he had to go easy with the scowl on account of his swollen face.

His eyes were smarting from the cigarette smoke, or something. He lit the other cigarette from the butt of the first one, and threw the butt into the toilet.

Just then, someone tried the knob of the door from the living room. Harold swung around on his heels, alert and wary, and instantly threw the freshly lighted cigarette into the toilet, all in the same motion.

"Hey, who's in there?" he heard Buddy saying. "I wanta go to the bathroom."

Harold was overcome with disgust for himself for throwing the cigarette away in his panic.

"Get to hell away from that door and lemme alone," he said.

"You been in there a long time," Buddy said accusingly. "I wanta come in. I gotta go to the bathroom."

"You heard what I said. Git away from that door and shut your mouth, will yuh? I ain't coming outa here till I'm good'n ready, see?"

Buddy retreated. "I'm gonna tell Ma on you."

Harold looked regretfully at the cigarette floating in the water, the paper soaked away and the tobacco floating out in a little puddle.

He slicked down his hair once more and flushed the toilet. He let the window stay the way it was, unbolted the door from the living room and turned off the light.

Then he unlocked the door and went back into his and Joe's room, because he wanted to look at his black eye some more.

7

SUNDAY WAS USUALLY THE DAY THAT SALLY DID THE washing for her family. There were a washing machine and tubs available to her in Mrs. Gideon's basement, and ample line space there to hang the clothes during the cold weather. Saturday and Sunday nights Sally worked late at the restaurant, and so on Sunday she did not have to go to work until the middle of the afternoon. It had become her custom to utilize her free time Sunday morning to do the weekly washing, but this Sunday she had decided to treat herself to a Sunday morning in bed, and keep the washing over until Monday night after work.

She awakened Sunday forenoon when Buddy and Marilyn got out of bed because, in spite of their elaborate precautions not to awaken her, the bedroom door was closed behind them with a deafening slam. Sally awoke with a start with the fearful feeling that she had overslept. But just as she started to fling back the covers to jump out of bed she remembered that this was Sunday. She lay down again, pulled the covers up to her chin and snuggled her head on the pillow contentedly. A morning in bed was a rare treat for Sally. Why, she wouldn't trade this chance to stay in bed for ten dollars, she thought. Oh, of course, for ten dollars she'd get out of this bed quick enough, she corrected herself, but anyway it seemed awfully good to stay in bed for once and there wasn't going to be anybody around offering her ten dollars to get up, so it looked as if she was safe. She wasn't sleepy now and probably couldn't get back to sleep again, she decided, but just the same she would lie right here all morning, and enjoy it. Just as she settled herself down for several hours of the enjoyment of luxurious living, she fell asleep again, and slept deeply and quietly for hours.

When she awakened the second time, Buddy and Marilyn were perched on the edge of her bed, gently poking and patting her. As soon as she was awake they informed her accusingly that it was almost time to go to the movies. The matinee at the neighborhood movie house six or seven blocks away was the traditional Sunday treat for the children. Sally hugged and kissed each one of them and asked them what movie they were going to see today. Neither one of them knew, but the main attraction for them was the eleventh installment of the Green Hornet serial. They gave Sally a complete résumé of the adventures of the Green Hornet in the previous ten installments, both of them talking at once excitedly.

Sally got out of bed and into her bathrobe with energy and went to find her purse for the show money. The children trailed at her heels, assuring her that they had eaten, that they had had their baths, that they were ready to go immediately. The only other member of her family who was in evidence was Virginia, who was sitting at the kitchen table manicuring her fingernails. At the sight of Virginia's sober white face and the discouraged slump of her shoulders, Sally insisted that she accompany the children to the movies. Virginia protested without much enthusiasm, and Sally overrode all of her objections. The children waited impatiently for Virginia's fingernails to dry so that she could change her dress. In the meantime, Virginia recounted the news of the morning to Sally. Lunch was over and the dishes had all been washed. There was enough cold meat left in the refrigerator for supper. Harold had gone out someplace, his eye looked simply awful this morning. Nobody had seen anything of Joe all day. He wasn't in his room. She had forgotten to ask Harold if he came home last night at all. Fred Foster had been in at lunch time, but he had such an awful hang-over that he couldn't eat a thing. He had drunk about three bottles of Coca-Cola and he had gone to bed again. Buddy had knocked a stack of water glasses off the corner of the table and broken three of them. Buddy defended himself at this point by adding that Marilyn had pushed him into the table. Marilyn defended her own honor by slapping Buddy's face. A slight skirmish ensued, which Sally quelled with the threat that if they didn't behave they couldn't go to the movies. At the prospect of not being on hand for the Hornet's anticipated miraculous escape from a burning building, the children were sufficiently sobered to go into the living room and sit quietly on chairs until Virginia was ready to go.

Sally followed them to the door and, once the door closed behind them, found herself in possession of another rare luxury: the apartment all to herself for once. She put the water on for coffee and took a leisurely warm bath. The apartment seemed strangely quiet and deserted to her. She kept wishing that Harold would come home because this would be such a good chance for her to talk to him. She hadn't had a chance to say much of anything to him last night with everybody around and with the evasive attitude that he had assumed. But she couldn't help but worry about him and she thought that she ought to talk to him. Of course, she supposed, there really wasn't anything wrong with boys his age getting into fights once in awhile, but this seemed somehow more serious than other fights he had been in, and he had acted so funny about it, as if he thought that it was smart to be all beat up with a terrible black eye and cuts and scratches and bruises. Sally sighed a little as she got back into her bathrobe. She just didn't know what to do about Harold. She wished he didn't hang around Joe so much of the time. She wished that Roy was here to look after him.

Then Sally's thoughts scattered in several directions all at once. Roy—the letter she would have to write to him tonight—the terrible disappointment he would feel when he found that he couldn't come home for Christmas. How to give the children a nice Christmas when she had so little money—how to make the day pleasant for Roy when she couldn't be with him, and he had to sit alone locked up in that place of keys and call-bells.

Such thoughts depressed her, and the unnatural quiet of the empty apartment weighed upon her. She stirred her coffee disconsolately. She had lost all taste for her own company and the leisurely quiet breakfast alone with the Sunday papers. Sally moved to remedy matters with characteristic energy. She put the coffee pot back on the stove and went out into the hall. Sally put her foot on the bottom step of the flight of stairs leading upward, and called, "Mrs. Sipes! Are you there, Mrs. Sipes?"

There was a complete silence from the floor above. Sally waited, looking up the flight of bare, warped, uneven stair steps. They had been painted at some time or another with a queer shade of yellow-ish paint, but the paint had worn off and chipped away under the tread of many feet, and the very boards sagged in the middle of each step. Those stairs weren't safe, Sally thought, and for an old lady like that, too, particularly when so many times she used them she was unsteady with alcohol.

"Mrs. Sipes!" Sally called her name again.

This time she was answered with a sound from above, as if some piece of furniture had been pushed along the floor. Sally smiled to herself; according to the sounds from up there you would think that Mrs. Sipes spent most of her time moving the furniture over the bare floor from one part of the room to another.

There was the sound of slow heavy footsteps from above and then another period of silence. After that Mrs. Sipes answered in her wavering broken voice. "Is that you, Sally?"

"Yes. How are you today, Mrs. Sipes? I'm just eating a lunch before I have to go to work, and I thought maybe you'd like to come down and have some coffee with me, or something. Everybody's out. Virginia took the kids to the movies, and I guess I got kind of lone-some down here all by myself."

"Why, I'd be pleased to," Mrs. Sipes said, in an artificial, minc-ingly polite voice. "I'd be simply pleased to, Sally."

The next moment Mrs. Sipes herself appeared at the top of the stairs. It was all that Sally could do to stifle an audible gasp at the sight of her. Where in the world did that poor old woman find such ridiculous and unbecoming clothes, Sally thought, as Mrs. Sipes descended the stairs a trifle unsteadily but with a slow and ponder-ous dignity. Today she was wearing some sort of a negligee of an astounding bright purple color. It was of a satin material trimmed with ruffles of chiffon in the same color, ruffles at the neck and sleeves and all down the front and layers of them around the bottom. The whole garment was disgustingly wrinkled, stained and dirty, but Mrs. Sipes held it in place wrapped tight around her gaunt lumpy old body as if it were the most elegant gown in the world. That negligee combined with Mrs. Sipes' appalling hennared hair, her black, horn-rimmed glasses and the rouge spots on her cheeks made her just about the weirdest sight Sally had ever seen in her life.

Mrs. Sipes made the last step, and Sally stood aside for her to precede her down the hallway. Mrs. Sipes stood still a moment, either to get her breath again or her sense of direction. From someplace out of the mass of crumpled purple ruffles over her breast she pulled a dirty handkerchief, and she rocked on her feet a little, pressing the handkerchief over her mouth.

Sally waited, smiling. "My, there certainly has been another change in the weather again, hasn't there?" she said, conversationally. "Those awful cold days, and now it's almost warm outdoors again. I wish it had stayed cold. Seems like there is always so much more colds and flu and sickness around when we have a mild winter."

Mrs. Sipes removed the handkerchief from her mouth and smiled at Sally. "Lots of my friends invite me to go out on Sundays, but I don't never do it," she said brightly. "I just like to loll around at home on Sundays."

Sally took hold of her arm and they walked down the hall together. "I think that's a swell idea. Of course, working the way I do, Sunday morning is just about the only chance I get to lay around. Why, today I never got out of bed until just a little while ago."

Mrs. Sipes nodded her head solemnly as if Sally had made some profound observation. She kept on nodding her head all the way down the hall, her lips folded tight together and her head bobbing up and down slowly.

"Here we are." Sally led her through the living room to the kitchen. "Isn't it awful, the mess a couple of kids can make with two or three Sunday papers? This place always looks like a cyclone hit it all day Sunday."

"Awfully cold out today," Mrs. Sipes said politely. "Awfully cold!"

Sally pulled a chair up to the kitchen table for her, and Mrs. Sipes sat down.

"Now, what can I fix you to eat with your coffee?" Sally said brightly. "I'm just having toast and coffee myself. Would you like some toast? Or I'll tell you, there's some coffee cake left. Did you ever try those big round coffee cakes they sell at the A. and P.? My family is just crazy for 'em. And they're so big, one of them is enough to go around." Sally set down the plate with several slices of coffee cake on it. "Or maybe you'd like some eggs and bacon. Are you hungry? I could scramble some eggs for you in just a second. Would you like some eggs and bacon?"

Mrs. Sipes was busy with settling and straightening all her ruffles. Her hands were loaded with ten-cent-store rings, and with every motion of her veined hands two or three big colored glass sets shone in the light. She appeared to give Sally's suggestions due consideration, her fingers picking at the ruffles under her chin.

At last she shook her finger coyly at Sally. "Now, Sally, don't you bother. Just some coffee. Don't you go to no bother over me!" But as soon as she said it, her eyes darted away over the table, as if she was taking count of every bit of food in sight.

Sally put the frying pan on the stove and got a couple of eggs out of the refrigerator. "Oh, you better have some eggs," she said. "It's no bother to fix 'em. It'll only take a second." Poor old lady, Sally thought, as she poured the coffee for her, no telling when she had eaten last, no telling whether she had the money to eat or not, and drinking like she did all the time. Even if she did have the money, she probably didn't eat regularly.

By the time Sally had the coffee poured for her, Mrs. Sipes had eaten all the coffee cake and was just starting in on Sally's toast. She patted the purple ruffles at her breast, crumbs of toast falling out of her mouth and she chewed it noisily. "I was out with my gentleman friend last night," she said. She tipped her head to one side, coquettishly. "Didn't we have a time! Didn't we have a time!"

"Why, that's fine, Mrs. Sipes," Sally said. She cut the rest of the coffee cake and got it to the table just as the last of the toast vanished.

Mrs. Sipes smiled at her, her glasses glinting in the light. "Didn't we have a time!" she said again. "I was out with my gentleman friend last night, you know!"

"Yes, that's what you were telling me. I'll bet you had a lot of fun, didn't you?" Sally gave up the idea of any more food for herself. It wouldn't be any use, she thought in amusement. Because if she put it down on the table and looked away for a minute, Mrs. Sipes would have eaten it up.

Mrs. Sipes had started nodding her head again, but it did not interfere with her eating.

Sally filled her coffee cup again, and Mrs. Sipes drank out of it immediately, slopping some of it on her ruffles.

"Here you are." Sally put the plate with eggs and bacon in front of her. "I'll get you a fork out of the cupboard." For a moment she thought Mrs. Sipes was going to dive right into those scrambled eggs with her fingers. She got the fork for her, and Mrs. Sipes acknowledged it with an extra low nod of her head, eating bacon all the while which she held in one hand with the little finger curled out daintily and elegantly.

"I guess I better fill up my cup before I set down," Sally said. As she rinsed the dregs out of the bottom of her cup under the faucet, Sally wondered if Mrs. Sipes could eat like this indefinitely. She had never known her to stop eating so long as there was a bit of food within reach. Poor old lady, maybe she did go hungry most of the time. Anyway, Sally thought, this morning she was getting enough to keep her going the rest of the day.

"Well, it won't be long till Christmas, now, will it?" Sally said conversationally, as she sat down across the table from Mrs. Sipes with her coffee cup. "And the days always go so much faster when it gets close like this."

Mrs. Sipes stopped nodding her head and appeared to be thinking over what Sally had said. She finished the last of the eggs and she said with a kind of well-bred elegant concern in her broken old voice, "Christmas! Must get at my shopping, dear!"

Sally laughed her warm, pleasant laughter. "Well, it isn't going to take me long to do my Christmas shopping this year! Just a few things for the children is all I can manage. I guess just one evening at the dime store and I'll have all my Christmas shopping done."

Mrs. Sipes sorted through the purple ruffles and found a chunk of scrambled egg. She looked at it almost tenderly and then popped it into her mouth. "So much shopping. So many friends," she said sadly. "So many, many friends!"

"Yes, I suppose it is a job if you have a lot of people to remember," Sally said. "Christmas for me is just for the kids, you know. They get so excited about it, and, honestly, we have the best time. We never spend a great deal of money because we never have it to spend, but we have an awful lot of fun. The kids are real good about it. They don't get their hearts set on a lot of expensive things and then get all mad and disappointed when they don't get 'em, like some kids do. Oh, of course, there's things they want every year that we don't have the money to get for 'em, but they don't seem to mind so awful much. Whatever little things you give 'em they always seem to be crazy about. Then Christmas Eve we always have a big party, trimming the tree and putting our presents for each other underneath it. Christmas is an awful lot of fun when you have a family of kids."

After she said that, Sally looked at Mrs. Sipes a little apprehensively. Mrs. Sipes was still hunting through the ruffles for more mislaid scraps of food, but her search was becoming half-hearted.

Poor old creature, Sally thought. Christmas must be a pretty dismal day for her, that is, if it made any difference to her, if it was any different to her than any other day. But of course it must be. After all, she must have memories about it, she must have had happy Christmases in the past.

"Mrs. Sipes, are you going someplace for Christmas this year?" Sally asked impulsively.

Mrs. Sipes looked at her blankly for a moment, the light glinting on the black-rimmed glasses, prominent on the dead whiteness of her powdered face, with the terribly red cheeks and the terribly red straggling hair.

"Christmas?" she said vaguely.

"I said, are you going someplace for Christmas this year, or are you planning on staying home?"

For a moment more, Mrs. Sipes' face was perfectly blank and vague. Then she drew herself up straight in her chair in her most elegant and dignified manner. "Why, I tell you, Sally," she said. She put her elbows on the edge of the table, and folded her hands together under her chin. "Why, I tell you. I got so many friends who want me, so many friends. But I always say . . ." she paused for emphasis and appeared to lose the thought momentarily. While she struggled to recapture it, Sally felt a sudden lump in her throat. She reached out her hand to Mrs. Sipes' arm and squeezed it hard. "Why, I tell you what, Mrs. Sipes, why don't . . ."

But Mrs. Sipes had recollected herself and she broke in on Sally with superb assurance in her wavering old voice. "I always say—" she paused for emphasis again, but this time she went on after the proper interval—"that Christmas—is in the home! That's what I always say—that Christmas is in the home! Yes!" She began to nod her head slowly and solemnly.

"Why, I think you are right," Sally said kindly. "Of course you're right. But I tell you, if you are going to be home this year, why don't you come to our party Christmas Eve and help trim the Christmas tree? We always make a kind of party of it, you know, popcorn and candy, and then the kids always recite the pieces and stuff they learn at school and sing the Christmas songs they learn every year. We have an awful lot of fun. We'd love to have you come, if you're not doing something else that night."

"Why, I'd be pleased to," Mrs. Sipes said, after just the right amount of polite hesitation of consideration. "I'd be simply pleased to, Sally."

Sally patted her arm. "That's fine, Mrs. Sipes. I'm glad you can come."

Sally drank the last of her coffee and twisted around to look at the clock on top of the cupboard apprehensively. "Say, I've got to get dressed, or I'm going to be late to work. I have to go to work this afternoon, you know. Why don't you come in the other room and sit in a comfortable chair while I change my clothes, huh?"

Mrs. Sipes scrambled to her feet in a kind of guilty haste with all her ruffles flying. She got hold of her handkerchief again and held it hard over her mouth.

"Oh, you don't have to go yet," Sally said. "You come on in the other room and then we can talk while I'm getting ready if you want to. I'm sorry to have to hurry you, but I gotta catch the bus, you know."

"No, I have to go upstairs now. I have to . . ." Mrs. Sipes' voice trailed off as the thought got away from her.

"Well, all right, if you have to go." Sally put her arm around her shoulders and walked into the living room with her. Mrs. Sipes walked in small mincing steps, holding up her ruffles daintily.

At the door Sally said, "You'll come down again sometime, won't you?"

Mrs. Sipes looked at her blankly, but her hands worried her handkerchief until several of the sets in her rings rattled. Suddenly her face changed, caved in, an awful kind of settling together around the mouth, that made her look like an old, old woman, and as if she was going to cry. She worked her lips a little and licked them with her tongue and then her face was smooth again. "Have to go upstairs now," she said to Sally with a coy smile and a coy wriggle of her shoulders. "Have to go upstairs and get dressed. I'm kind of looking for company. I have to get dressed. My gentleman friend might come, you know."

"All right," Sally said. "You come again sometime when you can stay longer, won't you? Good-bye."

She closed the door quickly and felt a kind of relief at the sound of Mrs. Sipes' stumbling footsteps down the hall. The tears were just behind Sally's eyelids. What a terrible, terrible thing! A terrible thing to happen to anybody and to a woman, especially. She must have had a husband once and a home, maybe even children. Now here she was living out the last of her life all alone in a miserable, cold room with no one to look after her and nobody to care if she was alive or dead.

Sally's heels beat out a quick staccato flurry across the living-room linoleum. As usual, she had only minutes to spare before her bus. It was only after she had left the house and was hurrying up the street that she suddenly remembered that this was Sunday and she had read something in the paper about the bus schedule changing for Sundays. She hurried up the street to the corner, hoping for the reassuring sight of several more bus passengers who might be gathered on the corner in front of the drug store. But there wasn't a soul in sight. Though it was only the middle of the afternoon, it was almost dark already.

A cold damp wind blew hard around the corner. Sally pulled her hat more securely down on her head, and then turned up her collar and tried to pull her coat together where it gaped apart in the front. Then she pulled at her hat again. It happened right then, while she had her arm lifted, pulling at her hat, and just as she stepped down from the curb to cross the street to go over to the filling station to find out about the buses.

A big shiny automobile that came so fast, and pulled up to a stop so close to her that Sally stepped back on the curb in alarm. The door on her side of the car opened. Sally had to step back a little, as the heavy door swung open toward her over the curb. There was a man alone in the car, but the light was so dim that Sally couldn't see who it was at first. He had on a dark overcoat and a dark felt hat. He sat behind the wheel easily, with one arm resting over it. He said, "Hello, Sally," casually, as if he were someone she had known all her life.

But still Sally couldn't tell who it was. She only felt puzzled, and she stepped back from the car a little. Goodness, nobody she knew ever went driving around in such a swell automobile, but it must be somebody who knew her because he had called her by name. Oh, it must be a customer at the restaurant. That was it! Lots of old customers who had been coming regularly ever since she had gone to work there knew her by name. She thought of that all in a split second, but before the second was over, with the restaurant in her mind, she suddenly knew who this man was, this man who said "Hello, Sally" to her as easily and casually as if he had known her all her life.

Her heart almost stopped beating—because she knew then that it was Nicky Toresca. Sally took another step backward away from the open car door.

Nicky spoke again then. "Get in, Sally. I'll take you downtown." His voice was low and even and unhurried. He didn't sound impatient or commanding or anything, except a little amused, maybe.

Sally didn't know what to do. She couldn't just say, "No, thank you," as she might have to any other man, and then turn away and walk off up the street. With Nicky it was different; with him it was her job, and jobs were scarce. There was her family, and there were long agonizing weeks in employment agencies with no money coming in.

Sally took a deep breath. Her thoughts were all going around and around in her head. It seemed to her that it must have been five long minutes ago at least since Nicky Toresca had asked her to get into his car, and she had to make some answer to him.

She tried to make her voice sound natural. Light, friendly, but not too friendly, and, most of all, casual.

"Oh, I don't want to bother you, Mr. Toresca. The bus'll be along any minute. Thanks just the same."

"No trouble," Nicky Toresca said calmly. "I'm going right by the restaurant, anyway. You don't want to wait around for no bus. They changed the bus times all around. You might have to stand here ten, twenty minutes."

Well, I guess that takes care of that, Sally said to herself. There was some part of her that was detached enough to find a kind of ironic humor in her predicament and her stupidity in handling it.

She heard herself say meekly, "Thank you, Mr. Toresca," and she saw herself climb meekly into the car beside him. She slammed the door shut, but her fingers, she discovered, were trembling and there was no strength in her wrist. The door was big and heavy. It swung to, but it didn't shut tight. She still had the nickel for bus fare in her right hand, the hand with which she tried to shut the door, and she dropped the nickel onto the floor of the car. She fumbled with the door handle to push the door open, so she could slam it again.

"Wait. I'll get it."

She murmured something about she could get it all right, but her hand fell away from the handle into her lap. Why, she was shaking all over like a leaf, Sally discovered. Why, she was acting like a fool.

She had got to get hold of herself. After all, she wasn't some thirteen-year-old girl whose parents had just warned her not to get into automobiles with strange men.

Nicky Toresca leaned over in the seat toward her and reached his arm out in front of her to the door handle. He was wearing thin leather gloves, some kind of thin, light-colored leather, that fitted his hand smoothly, without weight or bulk.

He pulled at the door again, and when he bent his arm toward her to slam the door, Sally flattened her body hard against the back of the seat, so that his arm didn't touch her.

The door slammed shut. But still Nicky Toresca didn't drive away.

"You drop something?" He looked down toward the floor of the car.

Sally was in such a panic of nerves that she nearly screamed out loud and got out of the car and ran away. She spoke too fast, with the words tumbling out of her mouth and her voice panicky and unnatural. "Oh, that's—that's—that's all right, Mr. Toresca. Oh, never mind! Don't bother with it. It—it was just a nickel, anyway. I had my bus fare in my hand and when I was shutting the door I . . . Oh, let it go. Never mind, it was just a nickel, it . . ."

Her voice ran out.

Nicky Toresca bent over around the wheel, his dark smooth face turned toward the floor, feeling with his gloved hand around Sally's feet.

"You should throw nickels away on your salary?" He made a little clucking noise with his tongue in his mouth. Just then his hand touched the side of Sally's foot, and she jerked her feet away instantly, so hard that they thudded into the side of the car.

"Oh, don't bother to look for it, please." She heard herself babbling again, but there didn't seem to be much she could do to stop herself. "Please, it was just a nickel. It's dark; maybe it rolled out of the car when the door was open. Please let it go, Mr. Toresca."

Nicky Toresca went on about his search calmly, but he did not touch her feet again. At last he sat up leisurely and smoothed his overcoat.

"I tell you," he said easily, with that slight hint of amusement in his voice, "I'll probably find it tomorrow when it's daylight, and then I'll bring it over to you. How will that be? Will you trust me?" He sat with both hands resting on the steering wheel, and he turned his face toward Sally when he spoke. His face was dark and smooth, with just the suggestion of a smile at the corners of his mouth.

Sally looked at him and then away again immediately. All the traffic on the busy street ran together in a blur before her eyes. The drug store, that familiar building in front of which she waited for a bus every day of her life, looked entirely out of place to her. She was surprised to see it here, like finding an old familiar face in the midst of a strange and terrible nightmare. Her nerves were stretching and twanging.

"Oh, you shouldn't bother with it. Let's forget all about it. It was just a nickel. Please, it isn't worth all this fuss. I—I'd rather just . . ." Her voice thinned out again, because suddenly she felt ridiculous. Why, she had been taking what he said seriously. Of course he had only meant that as a joke, saying he would bring the nickel to her tomorrow. He was just joking, and she had acted as if she took him seriously. She had made a fool of herself. Sally all but cried with humiliation.

At last the car slid away from the curb.

My God, Sally thought, they must have been sitting here for an hour. She must be hours late to work. It must be a month ago that she left the house and ran up to the corner to take a bus.

Nicky Toresca handled the car easily, driving fast but not too fast, and snapping the tuning buttons of the car radio. He found some dance music and left that on, turned down low.

"It's a nasty day, huh?" he said to her. "How about a drink? Let's stop someplace on the way downtown and have a drink, huh?"

Panic grabbed at Sally again. This was what she had been afraid of.

"I know just the place," Nicky Toresca said. "We'll stop in there and have a drink. All right?"

"Oh, I'm sorry, Mr. Toresca, but I'm afraid I can't," Sally said desperately, fighting to keep her voice natural and even and casual. "I'm pretty near late to work now. I haven't got time to stop any place, honest. Thanks, just the same."

The corners of Nicky Toresca's mouth twitched and he looked at her. When he spoke, there was mockery in his voice. "So you're late to work, so what? Who's gonna bawl you out? Who's gonna fire you? Sammy, maybe? We ought to be friendly, Sally," he said lightly. "Friends should have a drink together, huh?"

Sally heard herself using another variation of the only excuse that she had. "No, to tell the truth, Mr. Toresca, I don't drink. I felt funny, I guess, about coming right out and saying it at first, but I never drink a thing. Thanks, just the same."

"Why, Sally!" Nicky Toresca said in a kind of mock surprise. "You don't drink coffee? I thought we'd stop at this place I know and have a cup of coffee!"

Why, you fiend, Sally thought suddenly. You're not even human! You set these traps for me to fall into on purpose. You like to see me do it. You like to humiliate me. You do all this on purpose, all that business about that nickel, and now this stuff about having a drink. You know exactly how I feel and what I am thinking, and you set little traps for me to fall into, just for the fun of it. For the first time Sally's anger rose, and got the better of her fear.

Sally looked hard at Nicky Toresca for a moment—Nicky Toresca with his smooth, blank, dark face, the cigarette dangling from his thin lips. The anger put ready words into her mouth, and a touch of malice into her voice.

"Why, Mr. Toresca! I didn't think you really meant it! I didn't think a good-looking young fellow like you, all dressed up swell and everything, would really want to be seen even in a coffee place with somebody that looks the way I do." Sally laughed quite naturally. "I look awful dowdy and dumpy in this restaurant uniform and today, especially, when I didn't have time to comb my hair or fix my face or nothin', before I left home."

There, that ought to hold him, Sally exulted. His vanity. That was the only thing she knew about him to go on, but any fellow that was as vain about his clothes and the way he looked and all that, must be awfully vain about the women he was seen with. She bet she had him stopped cold this time.

Nicky Toresca laughed too, the first time Sally had heard him laugh, a dry laughter without any particular humor in it. When he spoke, it was exactly as if he could read her mind, as if he knew exactly what she had been thinking.

"You women!" Nicky Toresca said lightly. "Always worryin' about how you look and who'll see you! You're all alike, I guess. Okay, Sally, so it's a date for some other time when you have a chance to change your dress and get all prettied up special for me."

All the anger and the fight went out of Sally then. It was no use, she just wasn't any match for him. She wasn't clever enough. He was too smart. No matter what she could ever say to him, he could always find a way to twist it around so that it made everything worse for her and humiliated her and frightened her still more.

Nicky Toresca swung his automobile expertly around a couple of cars that had double parked and down a side street. They were in the downtown area now, not far from the restaurant. Sally looked straight ahead of her dully. She felt that strange exhaustion and helplessness in herself again. Temporarily, she just couldn't try to cope with this situation any more. They had turned off from Main Street, where the restaurant was located. She didn't know where Nicky Toresca was taking her or why, but she was too tired momentarily to care about it, or try to think of ways to be evasive with him. She was all done, Sally thought. She had tried to be clever with him and she had failed. She had given up.

Nicky Toresca sent his car shuttling back and forth through side streets. He didn't say a word for a long time. The dance music kept coming out of the radio, bright and cheerful. If he thought she was going to start babbling about where was he taking her and having to get to the restaurant and all that, Sally kept thinking, he was mistaken. She wasn't going to say a word to him. But just let him stop this car or touch her and she would scream and scream until half the policemen in town heard her.

Nicky Toresca swung his car into an alley, and out of it again, making a sharp turn, and bringing the car to a dead stop with a grinding of brakes. Miraculously they were back on Main Street and stopped directly in front of the door to the restaurant. For a moment Sally was dazed, blinking her eyes in the lights. She sat quite still for just a moment.

"There you are," Nicky Toresca said.

Sally gave a guilty start and reached for the door handle. But his hand got there first. He turned the handle and the big heavy door swung open for her.

Sally slid over on the seat, hoping there was strength enough left in her knees to carry her, so that she didn't fall flat on her face on the sidewalk.

Without turning around, while she was getting out, Sally said, "Thanks for the ride downtown," with as much dignity as she could.

"I'll be seein' you," Nicky Toresca said as he slammed the door shut again behind her.

Sally discovered that although her legs felt wobbly they seemed to work all right as she walked across the narrow strip of sidewalk and into the restaurant. She wondered if anybody had seen her getting out of Nicky Toresca's car. She hoped not, more than anything. Several of the girls nodded to her as she walked back through the restaurant. She couldn't tell whether they had noticed or not. Oh, well, she'd find out soon enough if they had seen her, Sally thought grimly.

Just as she went into the washroom, she heard Sam Toresca's voice from the kitchen. Thank goodness he hadn't seen her, anyway. For some reason, she would have preferred anybody, and, if necessary, everybody else who worked here to have seen her rather than Sam Toresca, after all those things he had said to her about his brother. Why, he might even think that she wanted to ride around with Nicky, Sally thought in horror, and she'd be so hurt and ashamed if he should ever come to think that about her.

Sally hurried out of the washroom, picked up a stack of menus from the counter and walked to the center of the restaurant to take up her position. She met Lee, and, as she brushed past her, she said unpleasantly, with her mouth close to Sally's ear, "You're late! My, you was traveling around in pretty fast company tonight, wasn't you? You must tell me about it, sometime. I bet he's pretty hot stuff, huh?"

# 8

THE NEXT NIGHT AS SALLY PLODDED UP THE STAIRS at home after work, the outside door down below was flung open with a bang and Johnny O'Connor came up behind her in a couple of bounds.

"Mist all Chrighty!" he said. "It's a real blizzard outdoors, you know that! I'm soakin' wet! I had to go over to the shop to get my hands dressed. I stood out so long, waitin' for a taxi, that if I'da had an extra tin can on me, I coulda made one of those Fords! This weather is really winter, and it isn't kiddin'!"

"Well, hi, Johnny," Sally said. "What did the doctor say about your hands?"

"Oh, they're fine," Johnny said carelessly. "Just a couple of blisters and a little bit tender. I'll be workin' in a day or two."

"You better be careful and do as the doctor tells you," Sally said. "You don't want to rub those blisters off." They reached the top of the stairs and she continued, "Here, let me open the door for you."

"Thanks. Come on in and set a spell, why don't yuh, Sally? We haven't seen you in a coon's age."

"Well . . ." she hesitated momentarily.

"Sure, come on!" Johnny urged. He ushered her in ahead of him with a flourish.

The O'Connor apartment was a blaze of light, a jumble of loud radio music and the close air tinctured with the smell of the diapers drying over the register. Gloria O'Connor sat curled up in the big, overstuffed chair, a pulp romance magazine open on her lap, and one of her perfectly shaped bare legs swinging idly over the arm of the chair, a blue satin slipper with feathers on it hanging from the tip of her toes.

She looked up as they came in. Her eyes were very blue and very calm. The heat in the room had made her perspire a little, and her thick golden hair hung in curls. "Hello," she said.

Johnny went to her immediately. He leaned down to her, one hand on either arm of the chair. She raised her face to him slowly, and he rubbed his nose against hers. "Glory be!" he said, with that peculiar quality of gentle wonderment in his voice.

"My gosh, you're wet!" She leaned away from him, shivering. "Must be snowin' hard outdoors."

"Honey baby, you ain't just saying it!"

He bent over to kiss her, and she leaned further back in her chair. "Don't, Johnny, you're cold!"

Sally walked across the room to the davenport. There, in one corner, behind a doubled pillow, was the baby, a dirty pink blanket tucked over her. Her bottle was propped up on the pillow and she was sucking on it rhythmically, one tiny spidery hand resting delicately on the neck of the bottle. The blanket had come untucked over her feet, and, with her free feet, she traced intricate patterns in the air incessantly.

Sally caught one of the small bare feet and closed her hand over it, holding it still. "Well, hi there, Beverly! Aren't you getting to be a great big girl, takin' your bottle all by yourself! How are you, huh? Are you hungry, huh? You eatin' your supper, Beverly?"

The baby looked up at her out of her dark-blue eyes that were exactly the same shade as her father's. She looked a lot like Johnny, the same dark-blue eyes, the same fine features, and what hair she had was dark like his, too. She looked up at Sally seriously for a moment, and then she smiled. Sally laughed back at her and squeezed her foot tight.

"I swear, Johnny O'Connor, this baby looks more like you every day," Sally said. She touched her hand against the glass feeding bottle as she spoke. "Gloria, this milk is stone cold. You ought to heat it a little!"

"Is it cold?" Gloria said. "I don't see why it oughta be cold. I warmed it. Anyway, I think I warmed it. Maybe it just cooled off while she was drinkin' it."

Johnny came over and stood beside Sally in front of the davenport. "Hi yuh, wee one! Can you say good evening to your old father and your Aunt Sally, huh?"

The baby caught his eye and smiled immediately and then she hiccoughed.

"Aw, that nasty old cold milk!" Sally said. "It makes her have gas on her stomach!"

The baby hiccoughed again.

"Whoops!" Johnny said, mocking her.

"Gloria, honey," Sally said, "why don't you warm up that milk in her bottle again? I'll hold her till you get it fixed."

Gloria gave up the task of trying to select a piece of candy out of the box on the corner of the table. "Okay, Sally. I'll go fix it right now." She got up from her chair leisurely and took the bottle from the davenport, disappearing into the kitchen with it.

"Say, Johnny," Sally said slowly, patting the baby's back gently again as she spoke. "I meant to ask you. I been thinkin' about it. Why do you suppose Joe went over to Toresca's place the other night? I supposed it cost a lot of money to go there, and everything. I never knew Joe was any hand to hang around night-club places like that."

"Now you're talking a mystery to me too, sister!" Johnny said. He drew hard on his cigarette and blew out a little puff of smoke, and then he sucked it up his nose, dividing it into two thin streamers that wafted in the air momentarily and vanished. "No, Sally, your guess is just as good as mine about that. I give up."

"It just seems kind of funny, that's all," Sally said. She stroked the baby's soft hair thoughtfully.

"How is Joe?"

"Oh, he's fine," she said abstractedly.

"I went to the funeral yesterday," Johnny said. "A lot of the guys turned out."

"My, that was an awful thing," Sally said. "I feel so sorry for his wife with another baby on the way, and everything. Will the factory pay her money, Johnny?"

"Oh, hell, I dunno," he said seriously. "Those bastards! Some day we're gonna get a union in over there and then things are gonna be a lot different."

Sally spoke to the baby suddenly. "Hey, Bevvy! Don't you go to sleep now! Your mother is gonna have your bottle ready in a minute. You got some more eatin' to do yet before you can go to sleep."

"Hey, Glory, hurry up with that bottle, can't you?" Johnny yelled over the noise of the radio.

"Just a minute, it's heatin'," Gloria answered in her serene voice.

In a few minutes she came in from the kitchen, handed the bottle over to Sally and went back to her chair. She doubled her arms against the chair back and rested her shining blonde head on them. "Johnny," she drawled. "What we gonna have for supper, huh?"

"Back to the davenport for you," Sally said to the baby. "I gotta go home and get my supper, did you know that?" She put the baby down and tucked the blanket around her, adjusting the pillow beside her and propping up the bottle at exactly the right angle.

While Sally was bent over the davenport, her hands busy with the baby, and her back to Johnny, she spoke to him, raising her voice over the radio music. "Johnny," she said. "Johnny, what kind of a fellow is Nicky Toresca?"

Johnny walked over to the radio and snapped it off with a clumsy motion of his bandaged hand. He looked at Sally keenly before he answered, but her back was still to him. She was still fussing over the baby, arranging and rearranging the pillow and the blanket and the bottle.

"Oh, I don't know," Johnny said in the dead silence after the radio was off. "Why?"

"Oh, I just wondered," Sally said hastily in a voice that was a shade too casual. "I've always heard a lot about him and I just wondered what kind of a fellow he was. I knew that you knew him and so . . ."

"Did you ever see Nicky Toresca?"

"Yes. Yes, I have," Sally said almost reluctantly. "I just wondered what kind of a . . ."

Johnny kept on looking at her, but she didn't turn around. "Don't tell me tricky Nicky's took to hangin' around the restaurant lately!" Johnny said.

"Oh, no." Sally said. "He—he just comes in once in awhile, and I've seen him and you hear so much about him, I just wondered about him, that's all."

"You mean on account of Joe?"

"No, not on account of Joe, honest. I—or—or yes, you know, it was sort of funny Joe going over to Toresca's to drink that night, and Nicky acting just like he knew Joe and all that. I just got to wondering . . ."

Johnny didn't say anything for a minute, and Sally gave one last tuck to the blanket and turned around to him. She looked a little flushed and flustered, and her smile came just a little too quick. "I just asked," she said. "I knew you knew him and I just thought . . ."

Johnny was looking at her hard and he opened his mouth to speak, but Gloria spoke first. "You talking about Nicky Toresca?" she said, sliding her hands along her satiny-smooth white legs as she dangled them over the chair arm. "I think Nicky Toresca's good-looking. Johnny, when are we goin' to Toresca's to drink? I like to go there. That's a swell place. We never been there since I had my fur coat. Let's go there some night, Johnny."

Johnny rumpled up Gloria's hair lightly and sat down on the other arm of her chair. But he was still looking at Sally.

"Oh, I don't know what you'd say about the Nicky," Johnny said. "I don't see much of him any more. I knew him years ago when we was both kids. We both went to the same school up to about the seventh or eighth grade or something like that. Nicky was a kind of quiet, funny, little kid and Sam was always riding him to do this or do that. There was a whole bunch of us kids that lived over there in that part of town that all run around together for awhile. That's when I knew Nicky. He had a kind of mean streak in him when he was a kid. I remember once he and a couple other kids ganged up on . . . Oh, I don't know, I don't know much about him now he's got to be a big shot. Sometimes I go in his place and have a drink and sometimes he comes over and talks to me a minute, but that's about all. I know Sam better than I do the Nicky. Sam Toresca is a good guy and a hundred per cent all right."

"Oh, I like Sam Toresca a lot," Sally said. "He's awful nice to work for. Gee, I really have gotta get home. Virgie'll think I got lost tonight or something." She picked up her purse and gloves and started for the door.

"If it's my private opinion that you want," Johnny said, "I think that the Nicky is a stinker."

"Good-bye, Beverly," Sally called out from the door. "Aw, look, she's just about asleep. You'll have to pinch her or something to keep her awake to finish her bottle."

"And furthermore," Johnny said, "if I was a female of the species and tricky Nicky come anywhere within ten feet of me I'd wrap a chair around his head and holler 'murder,' wouldn't you, Glory?"

Gloria looked up at Johnny with her strange expression of bewilderment. "Oh. You're talkin' about Nicky Toresca. I think he's good-looking."

"Well, so long, kids," Sally said as she slid out the door. "I'll be seein' you. Gloria, honey, any time you wanta go out, bring the baby over, it'll be all right."

"Okay," Johnny said. "So long, Sally."

Gloria yawned and stretched and snuggled closer to Johnny as the door shut behind Sally. "Johnny, what we gonna have for supper?"

Johnny laughed gently and put both arms around her, pulling her over against him. He dropped his face down onto her shining hair. "Ah, Glory, you're the nicest wife I ever had!" She turned her head a little and started to say something, and he stopped her, covering her mouth with his hand. She relaxed against him obediently and was silent. They sat together so for several minutes. The baby sucked a couple of times loud on the rubber nipple and then dropped off into sound sleep. The nipple slid out of her mouth as her mouth relaxed, and the bottle, out of balance, slipped down from the pillow and bounced off the davenport onto the floor.

"Um—ummm—" Johnny sighed contentedly. He tilted Gloria's face up and kissed her hard on the mouth, and then pushed her away from him. "My God," he said lazily. "I'm about to starve to death! Come on, honey baby, let's you and me go out to the kitchen and see if we can find the can opener."

Gloria twisted around in the chair to face him. "Johnny, you gonna work tomorrow?"

He frowned without answering her for a moment. "Well, just between you and me, honey, I guess not. I can't figure out what's eatin' that screw of a doctor over there. My hands are all healed over. I coulda worked today, just as well as not." Johnny scowled over the problem and then he looked at Gloria again. "Why? Look, Glory, don't you be worrying your pretty little head about . . ."

"Oh, I wasn't worryin'," she said. "I'm glad you ain't workin' tomorrow, then you can stay with the baby."

Johnny's face relaxed and he smiled at her. "Why, sure I can stay with the baby. Are you steppin' out tomorrow and you never told Papa?"

"Why, I thought I told you," Gloria said. She pondered and then snapped her fingers suddenly. "No, it was Mrs. Gideon I was tellin' it to, right after I got the phone call."

"Well, give out to your husband, baby!"

Gloria sat up straight in the chair, and dropped her hands to her knees as she explained. "Well. Marjorie called up on the telephone today, and we're goin' downtown tomorrow all day. We're gonna go Christmas shopping, and then, late in the afternoon, we're goin' to that movie at the Majestic and maybe we're gonna eat downtown someplace and I'm gonna wear my fur jacket and my black dress and we're gonna do all our Christmas shopping. And then we can send the packages home in a taxi, so we won't have to lug 'em along to the movie and . . ."

Johnny stopped smiling as she talked and his face looked sober and set. He studied the bandaging on his hands fixedly while Gloria chattered on.

"Marjorie knows about a new restaurant that just opened up that has music and everything and we're gonna eat there maybe and"— Gloria bounced up and down a little on the chair cushion—"and everything. Gee, we're gonna have a lota fun!"

Johnny didn't look at her. "Sure, that's nice, you girls'll have a lota fun. But look, Glory, how's about puttin' it off a few days, huh?"

Gloria stopped talking abruptly. She looked at him with her beautiful face blank and expressionless. "No!" she said.

"Just to please me, huh, Glory?"

"No." She explained it to him patiently. "We're gonna go tomorrow. Marjorie and me talked about it on the phone today. We got it all fixed. We're goin' tomorrow."

Johnny got up stiffly and lit a cigarette, his hands clumsy with the big wooden match. He spoke with his back still to her. "Glory, baby, let's talk about it. I'm not just trying to be mean, see? I want you to go downtown and have fun. You know that. But I haven't been working the last few days, and I can't go back to work tomorrow, and God knows when that crazy screw of a doctor will . . ."

"I know you ain't goin' to work tomorrow 'cause that's what you said. And so you can stay with the baby then because I was just wondering who I was gonna get to stay with her tomorrow because we want to get downtown before noon and we don't know what time it will be before we get home again. But if you ain't gonna work tomorrow you can stay with the baby and that will be swell."

Johnny turned around to her then. Even his face was stiff, as if he were undergoing some physical pain that was almost more than he could bear. He walked over and took her hand in both of his gently. When he spoke his voice was soft and hoarse, hardly more than a whisper. "Glory, honey, it's money, don't you see?"

"Money?" Her face was expressionless and a little bewildered. "Oh, Johnny, I forgot to tell yuh! I'm gonna need a lot a money because we're gonna do Christmas shopping and . . ."

"That's just it, darling," he said gently. "Right now we haven't got a lot of money. But later . . ."

"I don't wanta go later, I wanta go tomorrow. We got it all fixed to go tomorrow!"

Johnny was silent. He kept stroking her hand without looking at her.

Gloria never took her eyes from his face. "We're gonna go tomorrow," she repeated at last.

Still Johnny did not answer or look at her. Gloria kept watching him. Suddenly in one of her quick changes of mood that always came without warning, she began to cry.

She sobbed without restraint, like a child, and she flung her arms around him and buried her face in his neck. "We had it all fixed to go tomorrow! I talked to Marjorie on the telephone! We was gonna have a lot of fun! Oh, I wanta go! Please, Johnny, please let me go!"

Johnny pulled her up against him with a convulsive motion of his arms and then held her tight. "Oh, Glory, Glory!" he said. For just a moment he dropped his face down into her thick crumpled hair and let her cry. When he lifted it, his face was grim and his eyes were very bright. He pushed her away from him a little and began to stroke her hair back from her face with his bandaged hand.

"There, darling, there! Don't cry like that, baby! It's all right. Why, sure it is! You can go tomorrow if you want to. If you wanta go as bad as all that, why, you can go tomorrow. Baby, listen to me, you can go, I said. Honey, don't cry like this! Don't I always let you do what you want to? You know that. Now, don't cry about it any more. You can go tomorrow, of course you can go!"

Gloria sat up straight suddenly and looked at him, the tears still running down her face, and her breath still coming in sobs. "Johnny! You mean it? You mean it's all right and I can go tomorrow?"

He held her hands and looked into her eyes steadily. "Sure. That's what I said. You can go with Marjorie tomorrow. It's all right."

Her smile came slowly until her whole face shone with delight. "Aw, Johnny!"

She flung herself on him and hugged him with all her strength.

His hands, moving over her shoulders and back, were unsteady, like his breathing.

"Oh, baby, baby!" he whispered.

# 9

THE NEXT MORNING, VIRGINIA AWAKENED TO FIND that her head ached, her throat was sore and that every bone in her body ached. She crawled out of bed and got into her clothes with an effort. She didn't say anything to Sally, but as soon as Sally was out of the house and the children off to school, she launched a frenzied campaign to combat the cold. She gargled her throat with strong hot salt water. She dosed herself with soda and as many aspirin tablets as she dared to take at one time.

As the forenoon advanced she felt worse instead of better, and her panic increased. Suppose this wasn't any ordinary cold, suppose this was the flu. There was a regular epidemic of flu around this winter, suppose that was what she had. She sat down in the cluttered kitchen amid the dirty dishes that she felt too ill to wash, and struggled to keep the tears back. She felt so miserable, she hated to be sick, and then suppose she would have to have a doctor and bills would accumulate that Sally would have to pay. Oh please, please, don't let me get sick, Virginia prayed over and over to nobody in particular. Just don't let me get sick now and I'll never complain about anything again. I've been so silly to make such a fuss about my troubles and worries. Just don't let me get sick now and I'll never complain again, honest I won't.

Out of Fred Foster's little radio that he had left connected in the kitchen came a man's gay voice singing:

*"You better be good, you better not cry*
*Santa Claus is coming to town!"*

Virginia choked down a sob in her throat and got up and shut off the radio with a snap.

By afternoon, she was on the davenport, with chills and dizziness and a steadily mounting temperature. She felt warm and relaxed and drowsy now. She slept intermittently, and she lay on her back wide-eyed, watching the furniture chase itself around and around the room.

When Sally came home from work she found her lying there, and Sally took immediate action. She heated hot water for a gargle; she fed Virginia fever-reducing medicine left over from a cold that Marilyn had had in the fall; she rubbed medicated salve into her throat and chest. She helped her to undress and then tucked her into Buddy's bed in the bedroom.

With Virginia in bed and already half asleep, Sally hurried out to the kitchen and began to stack up the day's accumulation of dirty dishes. Virginia had been too ill to buy the groceries; by now the stores were all closed and Sally wondered what in the world she was going to feed her family.

The children were under her feet whichever way she turned, both of them talking at once, regaling her with long, incoherent stories of the events of the day at school. "Look," Sally said at last, her mind still busy with the problem of the evening meal, "why don't you kids go in the other room and look at pictures or something? Then you can tell me all about this after supper, when I'm not so busy. But you be quiet in there, won't you, cause Ginny is trying to go to sleep."

As they left the kitchen she called after them, "Where's Harold? Did he come home after school with you? He oughta be in from his paper route by now. You seen him?"

"Naw," Buddy said. "We ain't seen him since we was home for dinner this noon."

"So Harold got lunch for you, huh?" Sally kicked the pieces of a broken dish together as she spoke, and sighed a little.

The children left the kitchen, and Sally poured soap flakes and hot water into the dishpan and began to wash the dishes swiftly and deftly. Ah, she knew what she could have for supper. There was almost a whole bag of pancake flour. It was a long hot job when there were so many of them, but that was the only thing she could do. Pancakes, and, besides that, there were a lot of odds and ends of meat in the refrigerator that she could fry to go with them.

While she was still washing dishes, she heard Johnny O'Connor's voice in the living room, talking to the children, and in a minute he appeared in the doorway. He was in working clothes, his felt hat pulled to a jaunty angle and he seemed to be in an inordinate good humor, even for Johnny.

"Well, hi," Sally said. "What are you grinnin' about from ear to ear? What became of that wife of yours? I heard the baby downstairs when I came home. I bet you went back to work today, that's what I bet you, that's what you're grinning about. What did the doctor say about your hands? Are they all healed up now?"

"Why, Sally, honey, didn't you hear?" Johnny said sweetly. "My business went bankrupt, my yatch sunk, I got drafted, and my wife run off with the ice man. Say, how is Virginia feeling tonight?"

"Gee, not so good, Johnny," Sally said soberly. "I got her to bed in there, but if she isn't feeling better in the morning I'm gonna call a doctor. She's got quite a high fever, I think. I gave her some fever medicine I had around here, maybe that will help. I guess that's about all a doctor could do for her. I'm afraid it's the flu all right, there's so much of it around."

"Yeah," Johnny said. "Well, you watch it, baby, and take plenty of soda. We don't want you catching the flu, too."

"I know it," Sally said. "It kind of worries me. Knock on wood." Sally laughed, and tapped with her wet knuckles on the edge of the wooden shelf above her head. "Say, where did Gloria go today?"

"Oh, God, I'm a ruined man," Johnny said, grinning. "She and that friend of hers, that Anderson girl, are havin' themselves a day on the town. Christmas shopping, the movies, some new restaurant dump for dinner, and God alone knows what all. Can I borrow ten dollars till Monday?"

Sally joined in his laughter. "Oh, it's nice for Gloria, though. She's stayed pretty close to home ever since the baby come. It does her good to get out once in awhile, and she has such a good time. She's just as tickled as a kid at something like that."

"Well, you'll never hear me kicking," Johnny said. "Glory comes cheap at the price!"

"Oh, I guess Gloria didn't do so bad either," Sally said affectionately. "So they let you go back to work today. Your hands are all better, huh?"

"My hands are fine," Johnny said shortly. He bent his fingers into a fist, stiffly, and rubbed at some of the dirt and grease on the bandaging.

Sally looked up curiously. "How come you still have to wear bandages if they're healed up enough for you to go to work? Those bandages look awful dirty. You oughta be careful. How come the doctor didn't change the bandages when you got done work tonight?"

"Oh, Christ," Johnny said, his eyes still lowered to his hands. "I guess I can change them bandages myself. I don't figure I really need 'em on any more, anyway."

Sally kept looking at him, and suddenly she put down the dish and drying towel on the shelf and put her hands on her hips. "Johnny O'Connor! Now what are you up to? You didn't go back to work over at the shop today with them hands all done up like that. The doctor wouldn't let you, and, if he had of, he'd have seen to it you come in after work and got fresh dressings on 'em."

Johnny began to grin again. He shoved his hat back on his head and lighted a cigarette. "Sure, Sally, and when did I ever tell you I went back to work over at the shop today?"

"Johnny O'Connor," Sally was wide-eyed in consternation. "You can't fool me, so don't you try to. You've been working someplace today. Look at the dirt and grease on those bandages. My gosh, don't you know you'll get into trouble? What would they ever do over to the shop if they found out you was drawing compensation and then working someplace else on the side?"

Johnny stopped smiling, and his easy mobile face froze. "Look, Sally . . ."

"There aren't any ifs or buts about it," Sally scolded, "and you know that just as well as I do. Oh, Johnny, you'll get into trouble as sure as anything. Where are you working?"

"Now, listen a minute, and let me tell you, will you?" Johnny said. "In the first place, the compensation you get over to the shop is a laugh, you know that. You couldn't keep a canary bird alive on what they give a guy with a family for compensation in that damn place. That's number one thing. The other thing is that my hands are fine, and there isn't any reason I shouldn't be workin', except that that goddam crazy screw of a doctor says I can't. The other thing is that what they don't know over to that shop isn't gonna hurt 'em a damn bit. I know a guy that runs a little shop the other side a town, and there isn't ever a time when he can't use an extra guy at the forge. He's a friend of mine and he'll keep his mouth shut, see?"

"Aw, Johnny," Sally said. "You're acting foolish, honest, you are. Even if you don't get in trouble at the shop, suppose you get your hands infected or something. How can them blisters ever heal up if you've gone and got yourself another job at the forge in that awful heat? Johnny, it isn't right and you know it."

"My hands are perfectly all right," Johnny repeated. "They're all healed up."

"Then let me see them," Sally said. "I'll have to see them to believe that. If they're all healed up, take those dirty nasty bandages off and show me."

Johnny took a hard drag on his cigarette. He blew a little cloud of smoke out of his mouth and then inhaled it into his nose, the smoke dividing into two little streamers into either nostril. He didn't say a word.

Sally picked up the dish and the towel again and slowly dried it and put it away in the cupboard. Her face was very serious.

"And another thing," she said at last. "Johnny, they'll find out as sure as the world. You have to go back over to the shop for that company doctor to dress your hands, and don't you think that he'll be able to tell by the looks of them that you're working around a forge again?"

Still Johnny didn't answer her.

Sally kept on talking with her voice very gentle. "If you was that hard up for some money, you coulda borrowed some, or you could have got a drag on the money you'll make when you get back to work over at the shop."

Johnny smiled at her crookedly. "Just try to get a drag when you're off with an injury. Believe me, I did. I went the rounds over there the past couple days."

"Well," Sally said, "I don't know. All I know is that you can get along some way. Anyway, you wouldn't starve, you know that. I couldn't lend you any money, but we always have enough to eat around here and there's always enough for you folks. Mrs. Gideon would carry you on the rent too, and you know it. I guess you could get along all right, if you didn't work for awhile. Of course, I know you. I know just what happened. You went to see that doctor today, and he told you you couldn't go back to work, and you got all mad and excited, and quick without thinking you just rushed over there and got that job. Well, now you go right downstairs to the telephone and call that man up and tell him you're not going to work for him any more."

Johnny shook his head. "Uh uh. No can do. Tim Roscoe is a good friend a mine. He gave me a job today and he gave me the money I said I needed, and all without asking a question or saying a word. He's hard up for men on the forge over there, and he's got a lot of orders to fill. He's working the men night and day, and it's a hard thing to find a good man with the tongs. Hell, I can't call him up and tell him I've changed my mind. Instead a that, I'm going back over there tonight and work the night shift and damn glad of the overtime and don't you think I'm not."

"All right, Johnny, you go right ahead," there was an edge of exasperation in Sally's voice that she was fighting to keep under control. "Go right ahead. Just work night and day with those blistered hands of yours till you drop. You know better than that. Why, my gosh, as far as money goes, if you had saved the money today that you must have handed out to . . ." Sally stopped short and bit her lip.

"Yes?" Johnny's eyes were very bright and his voice was very soft.

The silence in the kitchen grew uncomfortable. Sally dumped the dish water and dried the pan without answering, but still Johnny waited.

Sally spoke at last. "Well, let's not talk about it," she said. "I guess you know what I was going to say all right, without my having to say it, and I'm sorry. It isn't any of my business. It just seems awful foolish to me, that's all. Suppose you get sick from this or lose your job? Then who's gonna hand her out a pocketbook full of money to spend?"

Johnny's face was tense and angry, and Sally looked at him out of the corners of her eyes apprehensively.

"Johnny, don't get me wrong. I'm not saying a thing against Gloria. My gosh, it isn't her I blame. It isn't her fault. You're the one, you dope. Gloria is a sweet baby, and nobody could ever blame her for nothing. You're the one. Gosh, you oughta have your head examined. Honest, Johnny, and I used to think that you were quite bright, too. Honest, of all the dumb things I ever heard of in my life, if you aren't . . ."

As she talked Sally's voice became good-humored and affectionate again, teasing and cajoling, and a better apology than any words
she might have spoken to him.

In a moment, Johnny was relaxed and smiling again. And in
another minute, his hat was pulled down at the old jaunty angle. "Aw,
who's a dope?" he scoffed back at Sally. "Lady, mind what you're saying there! Who's a dope, I'd like to know. Sally, my girl, you just keep
your eye on Mrs. O'Connor's little boy Johnny. He'll do all right, and
don't you worry about that for a minute."

Sally measured pancake flour out of the small paper sack with an
old chipped cup without a handle, and dumped it into a big green
mixing bowl.

"We're gonna have pancakes for supper," she said conversationally. "You better stick around, Johnny. I wonder what's become of
Fred. Honest, as slow as I am, if I don't hurry up around here, Fred
isn't gonna have time to eat before he goes on the job at ten o'clock.
I don't know what's the matter with me. I guess I must be getting old."

The living-room door opened and closed noisily, and Johnny
cocked his head to one side to listen.

"I guess that must be Fred," Sally said. "Poor Fred, I'll bet he's
wondering if we're ever going to eat around here. Unless maybe it's
Harold. He oughta be home. He usually gets home here from the
paper route about . . ."

But it was neither Fred nor Harold who walked into the kitchen.
It was Joe Braun, in his dress-up clothes and overcoat, white scarf
with the fringe on it, and an air of slightly alcoholic good humor
about him, to match the odor of whisky that he brought into the
room.

"Well, hello there, Johnny. How's the boy?" he said with unusual
joviality. "Hi, Sis, how you doin'?"

"Well, stranger, if it isn't just about time you were showing up
around here for a meal," Sally said good-naturedly. "Honestly,
Johnny, what am I gonna do with this fellow? He pays me good
money for board every single week and then . . ."

"Oh, oh"—Johnny shaded his eyes the better to look at the large
pasteboard box that Joe was carrying under his arm—"oh, oh! Some-

body's got a new suit! Well, what do you know about that? The best-dressed guy on Horton Street already, and then he goes and buys himself another new suit!"

Joe looked down at the box as if for the first time he was aware of it. "New suit, hell," he said. "I wish it was! Naw, that's a little present for my sister. Here you are, Sis!"

He held it out to her, and Sally stared at him, her eyes round in her face, too surprised to take the box he offered her. "Well, what in the world . . ." she said.

"Aw, wait a minute here," Johnny said. "It ain't Christmas yet. She's got to save it till Christmas. Jesus, if this isn't just like you, Joe. A hell of a guy you are! Why don't you save it till Christmas? Why do you want to come lugging it home now for and handing it out to her when . . ."

Joe laughed loud and long, and set the box down on the edge of the table. "Oh, I figure this is one present she won't be wanting to save till Christmas," he said. He laughed again, as if he were the possessor of some joke that was unknown to the rest of them. "Go ahead an' open it," he said to Sally. "Go ahead."

Sally was so bewildered that she could only stare from Joe to the box and back to Joe again.

"Well, if that is how he feels about it, you may as well open it," Johnny said. "Well, sure, why not? But get this, Joey, if she opens it now it don't count for a Christmas present, and you gotta buy her another to go under the tree."

Sally got a little kitchen knife with a sharp blade and a bright-red handle and came back to the box on the table. "Oh, gosh, Joe, you shouldn't have done this," she said softly. She tackled the string with the knife slowly and deliberately, as if she wanted to prolong the moment before opening the package as long as possible, to get the full pleasure of anticipation out of it. "Joe, you shouldn't have," she murmured. "You went and spent a lot of money that you shouldn't have, and I know it. A poor old broken-down thing like me . . . I'm not worth it. I guess you can't fool me on this label."

She tipped the box up for Johnny to see, indicating the label of the smart dress shop with her finger.

Johnny whistled softly. "Well, whatcha know, Joe! Joey, I didn't think you had it in you, son. When you do something, you do it right, don't you?"

Sally cut the string and fumbled at the box cover with unsteady fingers. "Oh, I can't wait to see what's in here. Joe, if this isn't the nicest thing I ever heard of! It's so sweet of you, but honest, you shouldn't have spent all this money on me."

She lifted the cover from the box and started to fold back the tissue paper. Johnny came closer to the table, so that he, too, could see what the box contained.

Sally smoothed back the thin rattling paper. "Oh, Joe! Oh, it's beautiful!" She picked up the dress by the shoulders and held it up out of the box. "Why, Joe, this is the most beautiful dress I ever saw in my life!"

It was a beautiful dress, a dull warm shade of red in a rich soft material. It was almost severely plain, but with a smartness and elegance about it that were unmistakable.

"That's all right!" Johnny said. "That's all right! Sally, you'll look like a picture right out of a magazine. Hold it up to you. Let's see how you look."

Sally's eyes were full of quick warm tears. "Oh, Joe, it's the prettiest dress I ever had in all my life! Oh, I love it!" She lifted it out of the box carefully, holding the shoulders of it up to her own shoulders. And, as she lifted it, the little white card fell out of a fold of the material and landed on the floor right at Johnny O'Connor's feet.

"Card and everything," Johnny said, as he bent to pick it up. "Joe, I have to hand it to you. When you do something, you do it right, with all the trimmings."

"That color looks all right on you," Joe said to Sally without any particular enthusiasm.

"Why, sure it does," Sally held the dress to her with her chin and one hand, and stretched out a sleeve of it with the other. "Red is my favorite color, and this is the prettiest red I ever saw. Joe, honest, I don't know what to say to you!"

Johnny had trouble scooping the little white card up from the floor, but he got hold of it at last and held it out to Sally.

"Yeah, the color is just right with your dark hair," he said.

Sally took the card that he offered her, but she kept on examining the dress as if she couldn't take her eyes off it. "Oh, gosh," she murmured. "I'm crazy about this! Why, I haven't had a new dress in so long that—and never such a nice one as this, Joe!"

Sally held the dress under her chin with one hand and examined the card that Johnny had handed to her. It was just a plain little white card and she turned it over in her hand to see if there was writing on the other side of it. There was. Just a few words written in black ink, in a sprawling hand across the card. It didn't take Sally more than a second to read what was written there, and then the smile was gone from her face, and she turned red from her neck to the roots of her hair.

Just a few words on a card, written sprawling in very black ink: "For that date we have, remember?" and then the initial underneath, the one letter "N," half printed, half written, a tall arrogant capital "N" that was somehow just as mocking and supercilious as Nicky Toresca's face.

Sally threw the card back into the box as if it had burned her fingers. She began to fold up the dress, and now her hands were shaking noticeably.

Joe Braun laughed again. "I told you you'd be surprised," he said.

Sally bit her lips, but she didn't even look at him. She was folding the dress again as quickly as she could with her clumsy, shaking hands.

Johnny O'Connor looked from one to the other of them alertly, with a puzzled look on his face. "Hey, hey, what gives?" he said.

The kitchen was very quiet. Nobody answered him. Sally was having trouble getting the dress folded smoothly into the box, and the tissue paper kept rattling. She kept her lips pressed tight together, but tears shone suddenly on her cheeks, in spite of herself. Joe shifted his feet awkwardly and cleared his throat loud.

Johnny moved uneasily himself. He kept looking from one to the other, as if he couldn't make up his mind whether to say something more or whether to walk out of the kitchen and leave them alone together. He looked at Sally again, and the hurt look on her face seemed to make the decision for him. He whirled around on his heel and came closer to Joe. "Okay, Joe," he said softly. "What's all this about?"

But it was Sally who answered him immediately in her clear voice. "No, it's all right, Johnny. It was just a mistake, that's all. It—it—the dress doesn't belong to me, that's all. I—I . . ." Sally's voice faded out, and she was trying to jam the cover back on the box and trying to keep from crying.

"Joe, you bastard," Johnny said softly. He moved suddenly, and before Sally knew what he was doing he had the cover off the box again and was fumbling for the card in the bottom of the box.

"No, Johnny, please!" Sally said.

"Maybe this isn't any of my business," Johnny said, "and on the other hand, maybe it is."

He got hold of the card at last, and Sally took hold of his wrist and held it hard. "Johnny, please!"

Johnny looked at her steadily for just a minute. "Looky, Sally, nobody is ever gonna catch me flat-footed when they hand you out a kick in the teeth."

He freed his hand from her fingers with a sudden sharp twist of his wrist and lifted the card to read it. He read it once, and then he read it again, and then he just stood there and looked at it for a minute.

"Oh," he said at last softly, "so that's it!"

"No, it isn't Johnny," Sally said. "No. It isn't the way you think it is."

"Oh, yes, it is," he said. "It all adds up now and makes sense. That lousy bastard!"

Johnny threw the card back on top of the red dress. He patted Sally on the shoulder gently with his bandaged hand. "Don't you worry, honey. This is something that is right down Johnny's alley! It looks like I got a little call to make tonight when I get outa work."

"Oh, no, you don't," Sally said determinedly. "I'm not gonna have you getting mixed up in this, and maybe making trouble for yourself. I can take care of this myself and it's my place to."

"You just relax and don't worry."

"Johnny, promise me you won't go over there," Sally said desperately. "I don't want you to, please. Anyway, promise me you won't go over there tonight. Promise me you won't do nothing till we talk it over, please."

Johnny hesitated a minute and then he said. "Well, okay, if that's the way you want it. But, lady, you and me are due for a talk, and don't you forget it!"

He turned around and walked out of the kitchen, and, when he passed Joe, he looked at him just once and Joe seemed to wilt down into his overcoat collar. He went out and they heard the slam of the door behind him.

Then Joe started for the kitchen door himself. "I guess I better get goin'," he mumbled. "I gotta go and see . . ."

"Oh, no, Joe," Sally said. The tears were gone now and her voice was tight with anger. "You're gonna stay right here. I wanta talk to you!"

Joe came back into the kitchen and sat in the chair near the table.

"Now, look," he said plaintively. "So you're mad about this. Okay, so what the hell, it ain't my fault, is it? How was I supposed to know? Nicky gives me the goddam box and he says . . ."

"Well, I shoulda thought you mighta known," Sally said. "I don't know what you must think I am, Joe."

"Oh, hell," Joe said again. "I don't get it. Whatcha mean, you don't know what I think you are? A guy buys a girl a dress, so what?"

"That's right," Sally said. "So what?"

"Oh, Jesus!" Joe laughed shortly. "Well, there are some people in this family that ain't so particular as all that!"

"I suppose you're talking about Petey now," Sally said steadily. "Well, Petey is my sister and I don't never say a word about her. What she does is her business. But I live a whole lot different kinda life than Petey does, and you know it, Joe."

"Well, I still don't see whatcha haveta get sore at me about," Joe said.

"I guess you're right," Sally said surprisingly, as she stirred the batter in the big green bowl. "If you can't see why I should be sore at you, Joe, why, that's all right. That wasn't what I wanted to talk to you about, anyway."

Joe was puzzled and he stared at Sally uneasily. "Okay, if you got somethin' you wanta say to me go ahead and say it. I ain't got all night."

Sally kept stirring the batter, as if she was trying to think of the right words to say.

"Well, I ain't no mind reader," Joe sneered. "If you got something on your mind, spill it."

"I got so much on my mind, I don't know where to start," Sally said softly, "nor I don't know how to say it."

Joe laughed unpleasantly.

"I'm worried about you, Joe."

"Well, thanks!"

"No, I mean it, Joe. Joe, how come you're hanging around with Nicky Toresca all the time lately?"

Joe began to scowl and his voice, when he answered her, was uneven and angry. "Nicky's a friend a mine, and what's it to you?"

"A friend of yours!" Sally repeated. "That's just what worries me, Joe. You call Nicky Toresca a friend of yours. It just isn't right. Nicky Toresca is—well—he's bad. He isn't the right kind of a fellow for you to be friends with, Joe, and you know it. He's something—something altogether different from what you are, Joe. Can't you see that? He runs that night club, and he makes a lot of money and they say he's crooked. I don't know about that. And, besides that, he's just a bad person. I know he is. You're not like he is, Joe. You work in a factory and you don't have a lot of money to throw around the way he does. You're younger than he is, and you work hard for a living. You've always been a nice, quiet, hard-working boy. I don't know what has got into you lately. You act so smart and tough and nasty. I don't think it's doing you a bit of good to hang around with Nicky Toresca."

"I guess it ain't none of your goddam business what I do," Joe said angrily.

"Maybe it isn't," Sally said. "But I can't help it. You're my brother, Joe, and I don't want to see you make any mistakes or get into any trouble if I can help it. That's just natural."

"Well, don't worry about me," Joe said. "Nicky Toresca is the best friend I ever had, and he's one hell of a swell guy if I ever met one. If you don't happen to like him, that's your business. And if I happen to like him, that's my business. It ain't hurtin' you none, so what's it to yuh?"

"That's just it, Joe," Sally said softly. "It is hurting me, though. Since you been hanging around with him, you been acting different. You're changing; I can tell. And that ain't all . . ."

"What do you mean, that ain't all?"

Sally hesitated a little. "Well, on account of Harold."

"Whatcha mean, on account of Harold?"

"Well, I don't know how to say it to you, Joe. But you know that Harold is crazy about you. He follows you around all the time. It's different with him than with some other kids, his father being gone now, and everything. It's just natural for a boy that age to look up to somebody, and with Harold it's you. Don't you see what I'm drivin' at, Joe? Now you're changing, Harold's changing too, because he copies after you, and there isn't anything I can do about it. I been wantin' to talk to you about it, but . . ."

"Oh, Jesus!" Joe said. "So the kid gets a black eye in a fight and I'm to blame for it. That proves he's changing because I'm changing and a whole lot more crap. You don't even talk sense. I suppose if I quit seein' Nicky Toresca then everything would be fine around here and . . ."

Sally leaned across the table toward him and spoke to him earnestly. "Joe, try to understand what I said the way I meant it, and please don't get sore. Maybe I didn't say it right. It's hard for me to say things I think out in words sometimes, but try to understand what I mean. You know yourself, if you'd just admit it, that Nicky Toresca isn't our kind of folks, that he isn't any good."

"Well, I don't know any such a goddam thing!" Joe said, looking back at her defiantly. "I guess I know a damn fine guy when I come across one, and Nicky Toresca is it. He's done a lot for me and that ain't all . . ."

"Yes, he's certainly done a lot for you!" Sally said.

Joe's temper flared up instantly. "Okay, okay, go right ahead and pick on me. That's all anybody ever does around here, is pick on me.

Pick, pick, pick, I get so goddam sick of it, it seems like I can't hardly stand it. Nothing I ever do is right, everything that happens around this goddam place I'm always to blame for. Well, I'm getting good and sick of it. Jesus, I work my head off in that rat trap of a factory day after day and kick my money in here to help you keep goin', and what thanks do I ever git for it . . . ?"

"Joe!" Sally said. "Joe, listen! Have I ever asked you to give me any money? You offered to room here and share the room with Harold; you offered yourself to board with me and pay for it. Have I ever asked you for a cent of money, ever? I've never asked a thing of you. If that's the way you feel about it, why you can quit your job over at the shop tomorrow and . . ."

"Yes, you bet I can!" Joe shouted. "You bet I can, and that's just what I'm gonna do, too, by Jesus! That's just what I'm agonna do."

"Okay, Joe," Sally said wearily. "I'm sorry I said a word to you. It doesn't do any good to try to talk to you, because you won't listen or try to understand. You just get sore and start yellin' and talking crazy and . . ."

"Who's yellin' and who's talkin' crazy?" Joe said furiously. "So you think I'm just talkin', huh? Well, wait and see! I said I was quittin' over there to the shop once before and then like a sucker I went back. Well, this time I ain't agonna do it. I'm all done over there, you wait and see."

"Joe, you get all worked up and talk like a ten-year-old kid! It's all right for you to talk big and say you'll quit your job. Maybe you don't like that kind of work—lots of people don't like it—but what are you going to do? You have to work, don't you? My gosh, I don't like my job, either. Do you think that I work over there at that restaurant just for fun? Of course I don't. I work to make the money to keep this place going. And you have to work to get the money to keep yourself going. Joe, I wish I could say to you, all right, if you don't like factory work, you just quit and I'll keep you going until you find some other kind of a job. But I can't do that, and you know it. Suppose you do quit your job over there tomorrow. What will you do then? Factory jobs are just about the only kind of work there is around this town. What would you do if you quit your job, Joe? What would become of you? Just think about that for a minute."

Joe laughed in her face. "Oh, so you think a factory job is all I'm good for? So you think hanging around some goddam machine day in and day out waiting for it to bite my hand off is all I'm good for? Well, I'll show you. I'll step into another job tomorrow morning, you wait and see. Nicky Toresca will give me a job. He offered me a job any time I wanted one."

"Doing what, Joe? Do you think Nicky Toresca is gonna pay you to set around at a table in his place and drink up his liquor?"

"Hell, he hires a lot a guys," Joe said. "He's got enough work for a lot a guys, drive cars, run errands for him, and stuff like that, and he'll pay me good money, don't you think he won't, and if that ain't a hell of a lot better than workin' my head off in some stinkin' rat trap of a shop day in and day out, you're crazy."

Sally rubbed a piece of bacon rind across the sizzling-hot pancake griddle. "Joe, you don't really mean it, do you?" she said slowly. "You don't really mean that you're goin' to quit your job over at the factory and go to work for Nicky Toresca!"

Joe laughed again as he got up from his chair. "Hell, what have I just been tellin' yuh? I worked my last day in that goddam rat race today. I handed in my badge. I'm all through. You think I was just talkin' to hear myself talk?"

Sally was silenced, and Joe swaggered toward the kitchen door. "You got anything more you wanta say?" he sneered.

Sally shook her head slowly. "I don't see what there is for me to say, now, Joe. You know how I feel about it; but if this is the way it is, why I guess there isn't anything else I can say, is there?"

Joe stopped before he got to the door. He felt around in his pocket and pulled out a roll of bills. He peeled a five-dollar bill off the outside of the roll carelessly and threw it down on the table. "There's your board money for this week."

"No, I don't want it, Joe," she said. "You don't eat here any more enough to pay, anyway."

"Aw, think nothing of it," Joe said patronizingly. "I eat here every once in awhile. You take it."

"No, I don't want it." Sally smiled a little, mirthlessly. "Maybe I'm a sucker, Joe, but I guess I don't want any of your money that you get from Nicky Toresca."

"That's a laugh!" Joe said. "Where the hell you think the money you earn over there to the restaurant comes from—Santa Claus?"

Sally turned her back on him without answering. Just as he started to push open the kitchen door she spoke his name. "Joe."

He stopped with his hand on the door and she said, still without looking at him, "Seein' you're working for Nicky Toresca now, Joe, there's one little job you can do for him right away."

"Whatcha mean?"

"This." Sally kicked at the edge of the dress box on the floor with her foot. "You better take this back to him."

Joe hesitated, and she said. "Go on, get it out of here."

"Okay, have it your way," Joe said. He went over and picked up the box. As he went out he said to her, mockingly, "Any message?"

"No, there isn't any message, thanks."

As soon as Joe was gone, Sally called to Buddy in the front room. "Buddy, you want to go over to Fred's room and tell him we're ready to eat now? And then you kids get washed up because we're eatin' right now."

"Okay," Buddy called back.

Sally ladled batter out of the green bowl into little puddles on the pancake griddle. As she leaned over the griddle, watching the batter spread out and fry, she rested her forehead on her hand wearily.

She was afraid, and she didn't mind admitting it to herself. It seemed as if the ground was whirling around under her feet and slipping away faster and faster. Roy's release was something that still remained in a far and indefinite future. Her job hung by so slender a thread, why, she might not even have her job by tomorrow morning. Virginia was sick, and there would be doctor bills. Some of the children might catch it, too. If they didn't catch it from Virginia, they could pick up flu at school as easy as not, there was so much of it around now. Then Joe quitting his work at the shop and taking on some indefinite job doing God knew what for Nicky Toresca. Harold going around copying the way Joe walked and the way Joe talked and how much more than that she couldn't even guess. Why, it was as if Harold was to be touched by the influence of Nicky himself almost, and nothing she could do about it, unless she kicked Joe out of the house, and he was her brother, and she couldn't do that. She felt that things were getting beyond her power to cope with, the job was becoming too big for her. She had tried to keep things going, but she had failed. "Oh, Roy," she whispered. "Oh, Roy, I can't do it, darling. I'll have to give up. It's too much for me, and I'm so tired. Darling, I'll just have to give up!"

Just then Marilyn bounced out into the kitchen. She had apparently adopted hopping as a means of locomotion. She arrived at her mother's side with a couple of last jumps that set the dishes in the cupboard rattling together.

"Whatcha doin'?" she asked.

Sally cleared her throat a little to answer her. "Makin' pancakes, dolly. How many pancakes can you eat for supper? I bet you're awful hungry, aren't you?"

"Yup," Marilyn said. "I can eat 'bout 'leven."

Sally laughed and squeezed her tight as she expertly flipped over the cakes on the griddle.

"Say, Ma," Marilyn said artlessly, as she hugged her mother tight, "say, Ma, do you think Santa Claus is gonna bring me a great big doll that goes to sleep and talks and has clothes to change and . . ."

"Well, I can't really tell," Sally said. "Of course, he has an awful lot of little girls on his list this year. I wouldn't be surprised if he brought you some kind of a doll, though."

"It would be nice to have a doll bed'n a buggy'n a table with chairs and dishes'n stuff, wouldn't it?" Marilyn said tentatively.

"Now, wait a minute," her mother said. "I don't believe Santa Claus could bring all that to just one little girl, do you?"

"I suppose not," Marilyn said regretfully. She burrowed her head into her mother's stomach, still hugging her tight. "Ma," she said contentedly, "what did the big toe say to the little toe, huh, Ma?"

"Gosh, I couldn't even try to guess that one," Sally said. "You got me stuck, honey. What did the big toe say to the little toe?"

"The big toe said to the little toe, 'Who was that dirty heel I seen following you?'"

Marilyn laughed uproariously, and Sally knelt down suddenly and scooped the little girl up in her arms. "Oh, baby, do you love your mother?" she whispered, burying her face in the soft dark hair at the back of Marilyn's neck. "If you do, give her a great big hug and kiss. Aw, harder than that, you can hug me tighter'n that. Aw, that's better, that's more like it! Uuuumph!"

# 10

THE NEXT MORNING VIRGINIA WAS NO BETTER, AND Sally announced over her protests that she was going to call a doctor. She left Virginia crying dismally into her pillow. Downstairs she telephoned the doctor before she left the house, and then she hurried up to the drug store on the corner, with minutes to spare before her bus. In the drug store she selected a bright-colored Christmas card and addressed it to Roy. She had been sending him one every morning, a part of her campaign to cheer him up. As she dropped the envelope in the mailbox, she reflected that his box of Christmas gifts ought to be in the mail by tomorrow at the very latest, and she hadn't yet bought a single gift for him. Christmas had caught Sally unawares one more year. All the way downtown on the bus she thought about Christmas. It did not seem possible to her that it was so near. She wondered where in the world she was going to find the time and energy to do all the things that she must do before the holiday. Already her mind was busy with tentative plans for the children, and tentative budgeting of her money. Oh, she would make out all right, Sally decided. She owed it to those kids of hers, and there wasn't anything in the world that was going to stop her. Or hardly anything. Sally got out of the bus and looked quizzically up the street toward the shining smooth façade of the restaurant. It just occurred to her that she might not even have a job any more. Nicky Toresca, Sally said to herself grimly, don't you dare to have me fired.

Don't you dare! You just try it and I'll—I'll—kick your teeth in, so help me God, I'll kick your teeth in!

But whatever Nicky Toresca's intentions were in regard to Sally's job, it was still open to her apparently, at least for the time being.

When the lunch rush had begun to clear out, Sally asked Sam Toresca's permission to do her shopping for Roy's package, explaining to him the urgency of the situation. Sam didn't approve of Christmas, he said, nor the excessive spending that went with it. He was disappointed in Sally that she would allow herself to be taken in by it. However, she was to run along and do her shopping on the condition that she would eat a good lunch when she returned to the restaurant.

Sally did her shopping as quickly as she could in the crowded stores and returned to the restaurant, to the stipulated lunch, an hour or so later. While she ate, a sullen, distant Lee drifted over to her. She might be interested to know, Lee said, that Nicky Toresca had been in looking for her while she was gone.

Sally had that to worry about the rest of the afternoon, while the other girls watched her with sullen animosity, whispering about her behind their lifted menus. Sally couldn't help but be aware of their jealous disapproval. If the whole thing wasn't so serious, it would be very funny, Sally decided.

Sally got home that night later than usual, due to the rush of business at the restaurant. She was tired and wet, chilled by the rain that was falling. She came home to a cluttered house, dirty dishes and scraps of food littering the kitchen. The groceries that she had had the foresight to order from the store by telephone were in a box in the middle of the kitchen floor. Buddy and Marilyn were wild with delight at the sight of the armful of packages she carried. They danced around her, demanding to see what she had. No, sir, she told them. It was pretty near Christmas, and Christmas meant surprises. She was going to put all the packages away in the bedroom and they were to leave them alone. Santa Claus couldn't tolerate kids who snooped around into packages just at Christmas time. This warning elicited more squeals of excitement from the children. Had there been any mail, Sally wanted to know as she carried the packages away, and they answered her that there had been none. Sally sighed a little as she limped into the bedroom on her tired, aching feet. Another day, and not a word from Roy. He must be taking this Christmas business just terribly hard and she couldn't get to him or find out how he was, or anything.

The bedroom was dark, damp and cheerless. Sally dumped the packages on the floor behind the door and turned on the light. Virginia was still in Buddy's bed, the covers pulled up over her head. Sally flung her coat and hat on the bed, unlaced her shoes and took them off her swollen, aching feet. Virginia, in the meantime, pulled the covers back from her face and gave Sally the briefest of smiles in greeting. Sally sat down beside her on the edge of the bed, curling her toes luxuriously in an old tattered pair of felt slippers that belonged to Roy. Virginia was feeling a little better. She could talk a little in a strained, hoarse voice. The doctor had come and had left her medicine which she had been taking as he had prescribed. He had pronounced her case flu, and he had painted her throat with silver nitrate. Mrs. Gideon had brought her up some lunch. The children had been just as naughty and noisy as they could be. Harold had failed to come home at lunch time, and they had had to forage food for themselves. No, she wasn't in the least bit hungry; there wasn't a thing Sally could fix her to eat. Mrs. Gideon had brought up a bowl of broth just awhile ago and she had eaten part of it, but she wasn't really hungry. Besides, everything she ate tasted like silver nitrate, and it made her sick. Mrs. Gideon said that Mrs. Sipes fell coming up the porch steps tonight and had a terrible big bruise on the side of her head; she must be drinking again. No, it wasn't time for her medicine, she had just taken it before Sally came. No, there wasn't a thing Sally could do to make her more comfortable. Sally was to just go ahead and get supper. She was perfectly all right, and if she wanted anything she would call, and she wished that Sally wouldn't kiss her because then she would catch the flu, too. Yes, the doctor was coming again tomorrow, but she wished that Sally wouldn't let him because she was perfectly all right.

As soon as Sally was out of the room, Virginia covered her head again, and wept quiet warm weak tears into the pillow. She was so miserable that she wished that she was dead. She thought her chances of dying at the moment were pretty good—the way her throat felt, and her temperature so high, and the way she ached all over, and if she was going to die she wished she would hurry up and get it over with, because she was so miserable that she didn't see how she could stand another hour of it, let alone another day of it.

In the kitchen, Sally flew into the work of cleaning up the dishes so she could get the belated supper on the table. The children crowded underfoot, so excited and full of talk about Christmas that their mother didn't have the heart to send them into the other room out of her way. She promised them that they could stay and talk to her if they would sit quietly in their chairs and keep out of her way. They must be very good, she said, and keep from underfoot so she could hurry with supper because after supper before they went to bed they had to help her do up the Christmas packages for Daddy. She was answered with squeals of delight again. But that was mostly over the prospect of packages to be done up. Sally was too weary to try to combat this mysterious vagueness both children seemed to feel where Daddy was concerned. How they could forget Roy so soon when he had been such a good father to them, and when they had loved him so, was beyond her.

Pushing that thought from her mind, Sally adroitly changed the subject. Had the children seen Johnny O'Connor today? They argued about it for five minutes and finally came to unanimous agreement that they hadn't seen Johnny O'Connor since he had been in the apartment last night. Sally wondered about that. She wondered if he had kept his promise to her, or whether he had gone to talk to Nicky Toresca. If he did, it would just make matters worse, as far as Sally could see. It would make Nicky terribly mad; it would lead to trouble for Johnny. Suppose Johnny had talked to Nicky, suppose Nicky had gotten very angry, suppose that was why he was down at the restaurant looking for her today.

As soon as she finished the dishes and had the frankfurters in the kettle to boil, Sally slipped down the hall to the O'Connor apartment. No need to knock with the radio blaring like that; no one could possibly hear. Sally opened the door a little and stuck her head in. She found Gloria alone, curled up in the corner of the davenport with a magazine. Johnny, she found out, was in bed. He was just terrible tired. Gloria couldn't understand it. He never got home from work last night until this morning sometime, Gloria couldn't remember just when, and he had slept a little then, and then gotten up and gone back and worked a few hours more, until late in the afternoon. Now he was in bed once more and he had the clock fixed and he was going back to work again at one o'clock tonight. Gloria couldn't understand it; he never worked such crazy hours before. She didn't like it. She had wanted to go downtown to the movies tonight and wear her new fur jacket, drink some beer afterwards at some swell place like maybe Nicky Toresca's, but Johnny wouldn't do it because he said he had to work. She didn't like to have Johnny work such crazy hours. Why, he was working all the time. She just didn't like it, and she had told him so.

Sally told her she didn't like it either. She didn't think it was right for Johnny to work all the time. Sally went back down the hall, thinking about Johnny. He would work until he dropped; he'd get sick; he'd get infection in his hands, she just knew it, and Gloria just sitting around there, making a fuss because he couldn't take her out to the movies and to some night club where everybody would look at her because she was so beautiful. But that wasn't being quite fair to Gloria, Sally reminded herself. Gloria was just as sweet a little kid as ever drew breath; it was just that Johnny had spoiled her so, and that she wasn't over-quick about catching on to things.

Anyway, one thing about it, Sally thought, with Johnny either working or sleeping twenty-four hours a day, he wasn't going to have any time to go and talk to Nicky Toresca. That was a load off her mind.

Sally got the supper on at last and sent Buddy to wake up Fred Foster. There was no sign of Joe tonight, and Sally hadn't even bothered to set a place for him at the table. She didn't know whether he even had come home last night or not. Harold wasn't home yet, either. What did you do when a boy got to be Harold's age and lived a life of his own and wouldn't even talk to you about it? What did other parents do? Sally left food on the back of the stove with the burners turned down low, so that there would be warm food for Harold or Joe whenever they did come home.

Fred Foster ambled into the kitchen, yawning, Buddy at his heels. They sat down at the table immediately. It seemed to Sally that her family had shrunk considerably, only the four of them gathered around the table. But the children more than made up for the missing members in noise, in spite of all that Sally could do to quiet them. They were beside themselves with excitement over the prospect of wrapping packages after supper. They explained the project to Fred, both of them talking at once at the top of their lungs. Fred was not particularly interested, nor in particularly good spirits. Sally quieted the children and tried to tease him back into good humor. What about all these girl friends of his, she wanted to know, for how many of them was he going to buy Christmas gifts? None of 'em, Fred said sullenly, not a goddam one of 'em. That was why he wasn't dating this week. He didn't dare to, because if he dated a single one of them this close to Christmas they would be sure to glam on to him for a present, and he wasn't going to buy them any presents. None of them was worth it, and he couldn't afford it, anyway. Sally laughed merrily. Well, she said, it would serve him right if they all dropped him after Christmas. It would serve him right if he couldn't even get a date for New Year's Eve. Oh, hell, Fred observed cynically, she needn't worry about that, a pack of gold-digging chiselers like that would take anything they could get off a guy. If they missed on Christmas, hell, they would try to make up for it on New Year's.

The children were impatient to get at the package wrapping. Sally cleared the table and stacked the dirty dishes in the sink. Fred Foster drifted toward the kitchen door aimlessly, so Sally asked him why he didn't hang around and help do up packages. Fred sat down immediately and said that he was no good at wrapping but that he would just as soon watch.

Sally instructed the children to sit down and be quiet, and then she went to the bedroom for her purchases. She discovered that Virginia was asleep and she tiptoed out with the presents for Roy. She spread them out over the kitchen table, unwrapping a little Christmas tree last of all, and setting it in the middle of the table with the other gifts all around it. The children were delighted, and sudden warm tears came to Sally's eyes. It was all a sort of miniature of Christmas at home, the little tree, with all the presents around it. She envisioned Roy opening the box and piling the gifts around the little tree like this, there on a white metal table beside a white metal bed in a plain, white-painted ward in that place of keys and bars and muted call-bells. Oh, she was so glad now that she had got the tree, Sally thought. To the other gifts she added oranges and bananas, the carton of cigarettes, a little package of mixed nuts, another package in cellophane of the traditional Christmas rock candy. She had forgotten to buy magazines, but it would be all right this time. She was never really sure that he cared about reading them, anyway.

Fred volunteered to go downstairs to Mrs. Gideon's basement and find a box large enough to hold all the gifts. The children hovered around the table, examining each article that Sally had purchased. They were each to pick out the article that they wanted to send to Daddy, Sally instructed them, then they were to help wrap it, and write his name and their own on the card attached. Buddy immediately chose a blue glass ash tray with a silver-colored airplane, but Marilyn was more painstaking. She handled a little case with pencils in it for a long time, and then surprisingly demanded that she be allowed to send the necktie to Daddy. Sally hesitated a moment. It was the most pretentious gift of the lot, the necktie, and the one that she had mentally set aside as the gift to Roy that was to bear her name. But she would not spoil Marilyn's pleasure. Of course you can send Daddy the necktie, dolly. Isn't that a pretty one? Gee, he's gonna be crazy about that necktie, and he'll think so much of it, because you gave it to him.

Fred came back just then with a box in either hand. After both of them were duly examined for sturdiness and measured for size, one of them was selected and put aside. Marilyn's present was wrapped first because she was the sleepiest: white tissue paper wrapped smoothly over the flat cheap Christmas box that contained the necktie, the flaps of paper secured at either end with red poinsettia stickers, red cord wrapped around and tied in a neat flat bow. When the card was selected, Fred offered his fountain pen. Marilyn painstakingly wrote the message on the little smooth white card. "To Daddy, with love from Marilyn." But the card was too small and the message too long and a huge blot of ink in the middle of it broke Marilyn's heart.

Buddy's ash tray offered a greater problem. He was determined to wrap it in green tissue, since Marilyn's gift had been wrapped in white. But the green paper didn't look so well with the blue ash tray, Sally suggested gently. Buddy thought that it looked very well, so Sally conceded her point without protest. The tissue was thin and the ash tray had a number of sharp edges that kept tearing through, no matter how careful Sally was with it. In the midst of this difficulty Harold arrived, and Sally had to stop the wrapping and serve him his supper. She explained to him gaily what they were doing, and invited him to make a selection of a gift next. But Harold was not enthusiastic. He took his plate of food and withdrew to a corner of the kitchen, well out of the way of the activities. Sally struggled on with Buddy's package, while he watched her anxiously, the card to go with it already written and in his hand. At last, with innumerable layers of tissue and a maze of string wound around it in all directions, Sally announced that that was the best she could do with it. Buddy attached the card himself, punching a hole in one corner of it and hanging it to the bow with a loop of cord. Then he stuck stickers of all sizes and shapes all over the package until his mother called a halt. In the meantime, in a burst of Christmas spirit, Fred Foster had done up a Santa Claus figure with a pack of peppermint drops in another sheet of green tissue, and trimmed the package with a great rosette of the red wrapping cord. Sally insisted then that he put his name on a card and attach it to this gift. Roy had heard her mention Fred, she said, and it would please him.

When the three packages had been duly admired, Sally sent the children off to bed. Harold started to follow them, but Sally called him back. He hadn't selected the present for his father yet, she reminded him. He must select a gift, wrap it and write the card for it. Harold hesitated, and then returned to the table, with a scowl on his face. Without more than one glance at the remaining articles, he indicated the box of stationery as his choice. He declined to wrap it himself, and hastily wrote the card for it, and then went off to bed.

Fred Foster sat hunched over the edge of the table, his chin in his hand, a cigarette hanging from his lips and watched Sally silently while she did up the stationery, and then the three boxes of candy that she was including for Roy to use for gifts in case they had a Christmas party at the hospital. She did up the pencil case and put Virginia's name on the card, and then, after a little hesitation, she did up the package of candied fruit and affixed Joe's name to it.

Fred Foster burst out laughing as Sally piled the bright packages together on the table.

"What's the matter?" she said, looking at him in surprise.

"I'm laughing at you," Fred said. "You're the limit, Sally. You got a package there for everybody, but you ain't got one with your name on it. You sure are the limit. You go buy all this stuff and make sure it's fixed up to look like a present from everybody, and then you ain't got no present there from you. What's he gonna think, gettin' a present from everybody but his wife?"

"My gosh, you're right!" Sally sat down in the chair across the table and stared at the presents in wide-eyed concern. "Gee, I sure am a nitwit!" She joined in Fred's laughter and accepted the cigarette he offered her.

"Well, I tell you what you could do," Fred said. "Why can't you put your name on one of them boxes a candy? Hell, what's the difference, he probably is gonna know you bought all this stuff, anyway. Why can't you do that?"

"Well—I suppose I could do that," Sally said a little doubtfully.

"Or why don't you change the card on the necktie?" Fred offered. "Hell, the kid ain't gonna know the difference. Put her card on the box a candy and you send him the necktie."

"No . . ." Sally deliberated. "That wouldn't be right. Marilyn picked that out to send to him and she helped wrap it up and put her card on it and everything. I couldn't do that.

"I know what!" said Sally suddenly, "I'll put my name on this!" She drew the little Christmas tree toward her over the table top.

"Jesus, that ain't no kind of a present," Fred said. "I still think you oughta put your name on the necktie."

Sally fingered the little Christmas tree lovingly. "No, I tell you, Fred. I'd rather put my name on this. Honest, I'd rather put my name on this than on the necktie or any of the other stuff."

"Why?" Fred asked curiously.

Sally kept turning the little tree in her hands, watching the light catch the cellophane-wrapped balls of candy that decorated it. "Oh, I don't know. You'll prob'ly laugh if I tell you . . ."

"No, I won't. Why?"

"Well—" Sally hesitated, "I'm not so good at saying things in words, but you know how it is; it isn't the money you spend that counts, it's just givin' the present. We never been able to spend a lot of money on swell presents in this family, so it ain't that part of it that counts. I guess there's nothin' in the world I'd rather send to Roy for Christmas this year than a little Christmas tree. You see, a Christmas tree means something terrible special to Roy and me."

Sally kept her eyes lowered to the tree self-consciously as she talked, and a little flush colored her face. "You know, Roy and I got married in November, and we couldn't hardly wait, that first year, for Christmas. We didn't have much money, but we had a little tree and we bought a few trimmings to go on it and set it up in the corner of the little bedroom we was living in, in the roomin' house, and gosh, it meant more to us than an eleven-foot tree and a house to go with it woulda meant to some folks. You see, it was kinda funny with Roy and me. Neither one of us ever had a real home. My mother died when I was just a little kid and our whole family split up all over. Why, I was out workin', doin' housework for folks when I was fourteen. It was the same way with Roy. His folks died when he was a baby and he lived around with relatives all his life. We got married awful young, you know. People made fun of us. They said we was too young to get married, and all that stuff. But Roy and me knew what we wanted. We'd never had a home, either one of us, and we met and got crazy about each other, and we wanted to get married and make a home together. And we did, too, right from the very beginning. I guess that's why a home and a family and all that means so much more to Roy and me than anything else in the world, more'n it does to a lot of folks. The Christmas tree sort of stands for all that to us. We couldn't hardly wait to get that tree that first year, and we never missed a year havin' one since. Then, after awhile, we had the kids and they begin to get old enough to know what Christmas was about, and then it begun to mean even more to us. We always make a party of trimming the tree Christmas Eve, because that was what Roy and I did the first time. This is gonna be the first Christmas Roy and I ever been separated. I guess that was why I couldn't give up the idea of sending him some kind of a Christmas tree, even if it was only a little toy one like this. I'd rather send Roy this little Christmas tree than anything else in the world. It don't look like much of a present, just looking at it, but there ain't nothin' I'd rather send him, nor nothin' I bet, that Roy would rather have me send."

Sally looked up to Fred suddenly, and her eyes were bright with tears. Fred's face was very sober. "Jesus, Sally," he said, "that's all right! It sure is! You know, you and Roy are damn lucky, at that."

Sally thought about it a minute. "Yes, I guess we are. I've often thought about that. I think we're awfully lucky. Of course, right now, it might sound funny, me saying that. But we are lucky. Right now things are kinda hard for us, but they'll straighten out again. Roy is getting better, and he'll be able to come home after awhile and get back to work again, and then we'll go on just like we always was. Nothin' like this or anything else is ever gonna spoil the way Roy and me feel about our home and our kids and bein' together."

"You bet you're lucky, damn lucky," Fred brooded. "Jesus, look at what happened to me. There never was a guy that wanted a home and family more than I did, and look how it turned out. Christ, I get so homesick sometimes and so lonesome for them kids of mine that I can't hardly stand it. I get so goddam sick of livin' in a roomin' house and knocking around nights, I can't hardly stand it. But look at the spot I'm in. I can't git the kids away from her. I can't git married again and live decent, the way I want to, with that alimony rolling around every week when I get my pay check."

"Did you ever think of goin' back to Betty?" Sally asked.

"Oh, hell, yes. She's all the time scheming and using the kids to try to get me to come back there."

"Maybe if you went back things would be different this time, Fred. Maybe she'd do things different."

Fred shook his head slowly. "Naw, there ain't no use me kiddin' myself about that. Jesus, Sally, you don't know what kind a woman she is. She's dirty and sloppy, and drinkin' all the time and naggin' me. Why, she's the jealousest woman that ever drew breath. She gets outa her head, jealous of me over nothing. And she ain't no kind of mother to them kids. She don't care nothin' about kids. She only had them two we got because she was scared I was fixin' to divorce her even then, and she figured I wouldn't if we had kids, me bein' crazy to have a family, and all. And Jesus, the thing that scares me sometimes is that I'll get so lonesome and homesick that I will go back over there, just on account of them kids of mine."

"Well, of course it isn't any of my business," Sally said carefully, "and you'll probably fly mad if I tell you this, but it seems like to me your best bet is to find some nice girl and settle down with her and then go to the judge and I bet he'd give you the kids as quick as a wink."

"Hell, yes," Fred said. "You ain't tellin' me nothin' I don't know. But that ain't so easy as it sounds. I can't just pick up a nice girl off a street corner someplace tomorrow night and . . ."

"No," Sally said. "You bet you don't pick up a nice girl that would make a good wife and mother off from no street corner someplace. That's just the trouble with you, Fred. How you ever expect to meet a nice girl and settle down, the way you do, drinking all the time and hanging out with a bunch of tough women in tough beer gardens night after night?"

"Hell, don't I know it? But what's a guy gonna do? I get lonesome. I can't just set around by myself all the time. A guy has to go out and have a little fun once in awhile, don't he?"

"Well, I don't know . . ." Sally said. Fred's face had turned sulky, and he jerked a cigarette out of the package on the table.

Sally got to her feet instantly. "Say, what am I setting around here gabbing for, like I didn't have a thing in the world to do! I gotta get this package done up, and wash the dishes and get to bed sometime tonight."

Fred was apparently just as willing to drop the conversation as she was. "Here, why don't I help you?" he said pleasantly. "I still got time before I go to work. I can do up some packages for you, if you figure I can do it good enough."

"Well, thanks," Sally said. "But I just gotta do up the Christmas tree, and that's all." She tried a piece of white paper against the tree, tentatively, and then a piece of the green, her forehead wrinkling. "Oh, wait a minute, I know what! I almost forgot."

She was out of the kitchen like a flash, and Fred heard her rummaging in the closet off the living room. In a moment she returned with a double sheet of heavy, silver-colored paper, like lead-foil, with great red poinsettias splashed across it.

Fred whistled. "Boy, ain't that something? That sure musta cost you somethin', paper like that. Hell, I bet that paper cost more'n the present you had done up in it!"

Sally laughed. "Oh, I didn't buy that, don't worry. That come around a present that was sent to us. Ain't it pretty, though, the way it shines in the light? I think it'll be big enough, don't you? Oh, sure, plenty big enough. And it's as good as new, too, just this one edge that's torn a little, and I can trim that off and still have more'n enough left to do it up in."

"Jesus, that sure is pretty," Fred said. "I never seen any paper as swell as that before. Who sent you a present all done up swell like that?"

"Oh, I guess that musta been done around a package Petey sent," Sally said. "And look, here was the ribbon that come on it. Ain't that pretty?" She held up a long length of filmy red ribbon about four inches wide, with a double stripe of silver through it. "I'll press that out with the iron and use it again. That'll sure make a pretty package."

"Who's Petey?" Fred asked curiously. "He sure must have a lot of money, whoever he is."

Sally stopped still with the ribbon in her hand and threw her head back and filled the kitchen with her warm pleasant laughter.

"Whatsa matter?" Fred asked suspiciously. "What's so funny? I just said the guy musta had a lotta money to buy fancy wrapping stuff like that and . . . Of course, it ain't none of my business who he is and . . ."

"No, it's perfectly all right, Fred. What you said was all right; that wasn't why I was laughing. I was just laughin' because people always think Petey's a man on account of her name. Petey's my sister."

"She is!" Fred said incredulously. "Where'd she ever git a name like that? That ain't a girl's name. What's her name, anyway? Sounds like Pete, Peter. I never heard no girl being named that before."

Sally plugged the iron into the wall socket and smoothed the ribbon in her fingers while she waited for it to heat.

"Petey is just a nickname," she explained. "Her real name is Mildred, but that name never seemed to fit her, somehow. When she was just a little kid she was a terrible tomboy and my dad always used to call her Pete. I don't know, we all got to callin' her that, Pete and Petey. Nobody ever calls her Mildred. Petey just seems to fit her, I guess."

"Jesus, that's funny," Fred said. "I never heard you mention her before. I never knew you even had another sister. She older than you?"

"No, she's younger. She's the one next to me," Sally said. "You see, I was the oldest in our family, and Petey next, then we had a brother and a sister in between that both died when they was kids. Joe was next, and Virginia was the baby. After Ma died and Pop got sick our family all split up. There was some neighbors named Clark, kind of oldish people, they took Virginia when she was just a baby and moved away with her, and I never even saw her again until she was a big girl after old Mrs. Clark died. Joe went to live with Pop's brother's family."

"What become a you and Petey?"

Sally tested the iron with a quick motion of her hand. "Well, Petey and I went to stay with a cousin of my mother's. She was the only relative Ma had living. We didn't get along so good. I guess it was because we were older, and they already had a lot of kids in the family and not much money. Oh, they was always nice enough to us. After all, they took Petey and me in and give us a home when we didn't have no other place to go, but it just didn't work out so good. We was only there a couple years. As soon as we got old enough to get out and work and take care of ourselves, we left. Gosh, I remember how Petey and I used to lay awake at night and plan about how we was going to get away and get jobs and go to some big city and live in an apartment together and make a lot of money and have swell clothes. We always said we weren't never gonna get married, that we was gonna stay together. Funny, how you make plans like that when you're a kid, and then your life comes out all different."

"Jesus, it's too bad, a family getting split up like that," Fred said reflectively. "How old was you and Petey when you went to work?"

Sally spread the ribbon out on a sheet of tissue paper and tested the iron again to see if it was hot enough for pressing. "Well, let me see . . . I was fourteen, a little over, and Petey was only thirteen, but she was awful big for her age and looked older. I remember how we packed up what few clothes and stuff we had in a suitcase and sneaked out of there one night. We had been saving up a little money and we took a train to the nearest big town, about fifty miles away. It was the first time either one a us had ever rode a train. Boy, we was scared to death. We was so afraid they could tell just by looking at us that we was running away and that they would try to send us back. Why, I remember, I was so scared and riding on the train and all it made me sick to my stomach. I remember how I went in the toilet and cried, and Petey come in and shook me till my teeth rattled to make me stop crying. A long time afterwards, Petey told me that she was scared to death too, but she never let on she was then."

"God, she sure musta had a lot of guts, a little kid like that only thirteen years old," Fred said.

Sally began to press the wrinkles out of the red ribbon, slowly and carefully. "Yes, she sure did. She had a lot more spunk and sense than I did. If it hadn't been for her, I'd a got scared and gone back home, I'll bet you anything. Why, I can remember that night yet, as plain as day. I guess I always will. There we was in that little toilet with the door locked and the train a rushing along, black as pitch outside. We hadn't ever been to the city either one a us, and we didn't know no more than nothing what we was gonna do or what was goin' to become of us once we got there. I remember how Petey shook me and slapped me and everything else to make me quit crying. Then she opened up her pocketbook and pulled out some lipstick and powder that she had swiped somewhere and fixed us all up. You know, combed our hair different and stuff, so that we would look older, she said." Sally shook her head reminiscently. "Gosh, that sure was a night, though!"

"Jesus, it sure musta been. Tell me what happened. What did you do when you got off the train?" Fred asked curiously.

The room was full of the warm musty smell the iron made against the wide gauze ribbon. Sally held it up in her hand, and the tinsel stripes in it caught the light and sparkled. Sally pulled the cord out of the wall socket. "Well, it was the funniest thing," she said. "You wouldn't hardly believe it. We got off the train in that big waiting room, and we didn't have any more idea where to go than nothing. We went up and asked somebody at one of the ticket windows where we could get a cheap place to stay all night, because we didn't hardly have any money left at all after we bought them train tickets. The fellow told us we better go to the Y.W.C.A. He kept looking at us kind of funny, and Petey got scared. She figured he was gonna call a cop or something and have us sent home. Believe me, I was so scared that if he had of, they wouldn't have heard a word out of me. I'd just of trotted right along home and darn glad to get there. But not Petey. She thanked the guy as cool as you please and picked up our suitcase and we walked out of there. When we got out on the street I tried to get her to go over to the Y.W. to stay all night, but no, sir, she wouldn't hear of it. She said if we went over there the first thing they would do was start askin' us questions and stuff, and the first thing we would know they would be shipping us right back where we come from."

Fred listened to the story with his chin propped on his hand, a cigarette burning down unnoticed between his fingers. He shook his head admiringly. "Say, that Petey wasn't so dumb, was she? She musta been just about as smart as they come. How'd she ever have sense enough to figure all that out, just a little kid like that?"

"Well, sir, I don't know," Sally said. "I guess Petey musta just been born with a kind of knack for lookin' out for herself. She was just as smart as a whip when it come to gettin' along on her own like that and lookin' out for herself. Gosh, I was the oldest, but I was nothin' but a baby compared to Petey!"

"Well, what happened then?" Fred asked impatiently. "What did you do after you walked out of the depot?"

Sally sat down in the chair across the table again, and fingered the smooth wide ribbon lovingly as she talked. "Well, there we was out on the street. It was late at night, dark as pitch and the rain kind of drizzling down. I wanted to go to the Y.W. and stay all night and Petey wouldn't hear of it. I'd never been out alone that late after dark before in my life, and a strange place, but Petey told me if I started crying again she'd knock my head off. She picked up that suitcase and started walking along with her head up in the air as big as you please. I kept asking her where we was gonna go, and she kept saying never mind, we'd just keep walking, that if we started standing around on street corners we'd get into trouble just as sure as anything. So we just kept walking for awhile, Petey turning up this street and that street just as if she'd lived there all her life and knew just where she was going. Finally, she said the thing for us to do was stop someplace and get something to eat. I kept trying to tell her that maybe we didn't have money enough, that maybe we oughta stop under a street light and count our money first, but nope, Petey wouldn't do it. There was still some restaurants open along the streets, with electric signs turned on and people in them. Petey kept looking along at all of them as we went past. Finally, we come to one that looked not so swell as some of the others, like the food would be cheaper. There wasn't hardly nobody in it at all, except a coupla waiters and some folks at one table. I wanted to stop there. Petey didn't want to do it. We had a regular fight right then and there. I said I wasn't gonna go a step further. Petey was awful mad at me, but finally she said okay, if I wanted to, we'd stop there. Gosh, if that wasn't the funniest thing," Sally paused a moment, smiling.

"Well, go on," Fred said. "This beats any true-story magazine I ever read. So where did you go after you ate to the restaurant?"

"Well, wait a minute, just let me tell you," Sally said. "Petey didn't want to go in there at all, and she was plenty sore at me, but we finally went in. We ordered coffee and the cheapest sandwiches there was on the menu. I was about starved to death, and I started in eating without paying no attention to nothing. But I remember how Petey just set there, spooning her coffee, her eyes going this and that way, not missing a thing around there. Finally, she says to me, there was something funny going on around here! Well, that just about scared the living daylights out of me, and I asked her what she meant, and she said it was nothing to get scared of, there was just something funny about this place. Then she told me to watch, and, sure enough, just like she said, there were quite a few people coming in the place, and they would go back and say something to one of the waiters and then go through a door that was marked kitchen. Well, I didn't think that was so funny. I kept telling Petey maybe these folks all worked there. Anyway, they was all going out into the kitchen for something. Petey didn't say another word about it to me, but she just set there watching what was going on for all she was worth. All of a sudden the waiter fellow went out back by another door and Petey jumped up from that table quick as a flash. She told me to set still right where I was at that table, and then before I could say a word, I'll be darned if she didn't head for that kitchen door like a streak and out there she went. Don't think I wasn't scared—her goin' out back and me there all alone at that table!"

Fred raised his hand and shook one finger at Sally. "Don't tell me," he crowed, "don't tell me, lemme guess. You kids walked right into a speakie! I got around some during prohibition, myself, and I sure know a speakie when I hear about one. What did they do, toss Petey out on her ear for crashing in there?"

"Toss her out on her ear nothing!" Sally laughed. "You don't know Petey! Yes, sir, that was just what that place was, a speakeasy where they was selling liquor! Afterwards, Petey always kidded me about it. She said I certainly could pick a joint. The funny thing was, lots of them other restaurants we come past, we found out later, were perfectly all right, just regular restaurants, you know, but this place where I talked Petey into stopping was one of the biggest speakeasies in that part of the town. Petey sure used to kid me about that!"

"Well, go on," Fred said. "Jesus, hurry up and tell what happened, I gotta go to work in a minute."

"Well," Sally went on, "Petey went out back and left me setting there at that table. She didn't come back and she didn't come back. Of course I didn't know what was out back there no more than nothing, and I was just scared to death. I thought something terrible must have happened to her when she didn't come back, and I set there just froze to my chair, not knowing what to do. I didn't have enough nerve to get up and walk out back like she done, besides, the waiter was standing right there in front of the door. I couldn't get up and leave, because Petey was still in there. I figured something terrible had happened to her and I ought to call the police, but I didn't know how to do that, either. Finally, why, I remember just as plain as day, I made up my mind that if she didn't come back in a minute I was just gonna start screaming my head off."

"Well, cut the details, what was she doin' out there?" broke in Fred.

Sally helped herself to one of his cigarettes, and he hurried to strike a match for her. Sally puffed on it a few times comfortably before she went on. "Well, just about the time I was ready to start screaming or crying or just plain drop dead, I don't know which, the door opened and out come Petey, sailing along with her head up in the air, grinning like a million dollars. I tell you, I was never so glad to see anybody in my whole life. Petey come sailing up to the table and told me to leave my sandwich go, that there was a nice man out back who was gonna buy us a drink, to come on with her. Well, before I had a chance to get my mouth open to say, no, sir, that it wasn't right, that we wasn't gonna do any such a thing, Petey hissed at me to keep my mouth shut and do just as she told me or she'd skin me alive. Believe me I got up and tagged along behind her just as meek as a little lamb. It never does you no good to argue with Petey when she gets set on something like that. You just go right along and do like she tells you. Well, you should have seen that waiter fellow open that door for us, smiling at Petey for all he was worth. When we got out back it was a regular speakeasy, all right, a bar and tables and a lot of people and a little orchestra playin'. I'd heard the music when we come in, but I figured it was just a radio playin'. Well, sir, I'd never been in such a place before in my life, and neither had Petey, but she walked over to that bar as if she'd been doin' it for years, and me taggin' right along behind her. Well, the fellow that was gonna buy us the drink, he was kind of the manager of the place, was waiting for us there by the bar, and Petey crawled up on the stool next to him and the next thing I knew she was introducing me to him as her kid sister. She made him order a beer for me, but she took a shot of whisky or some kind of liquor, gosh, and neither one of us had ever had a drink before in our lives. I'll never forget how Petey looked, setting up there on that stool as big as you please. She was flirtin' with that guy for all she was worth. She pulled out that lipstick out of her pocketbook and a little mirror and started putting more on her mouth, a-smiling and a-looking at him out of the corner of her eyes. When he offered her a cigarette she took it and let him light it for her and started puffing away on it. Afterwards, I asked her how she ever dared do it. Most people are afraid to smoke and drink like that the first time for fear it will make them sick, you know. So I asked Petey about that once, and she said, well, she was kind of scared, but she figured everybody else was doin' it and it didn't seem to hurt them none, so why should it hurt her!"

Sally stopped to laugh, and Fred laughed, too.

"Jesus, that Petey musta been some kid, all right," he said. "She sure didn't waste any time once she got started there, did she? She musta been pretty cute. What did she look like?"

"Oh, Petey's the best-looking one in our family," Sally said easily. "She's dark, like the rest of us, but she's a big, tall girl. She's got a real deep voice. Oh, I guess it isn't that she's so pretty really, I mean she isn't swell-looking like Gloria O'Connor is, for instance, but there is just something about her. She's got a terrible lot of pep—she's—she's—well, she's sort of like electricity crinklin' in the air."

"Say! She sounds all right!" Fred said admiringly. "So you had the drink with this guy, then what?"

"Well, just wait'll I tell you," Sally said. "This guy was hanging around her, and you just oughta heard the story Petey spieled off to him. She told him she was eighteen years old and that she had had a good job in Chicago, but she had to give it up and come out here to look after me, on account of I was her little sister and the aunt I had been livin' with had just died. He wanted to know why she didn't take me back to Chicago with her, and Petey answered him right off straight that that was what she was aimin' to do, but the only trouble was that she had had to spend most of her money for burying this aunt I was supposed to have been living with, and now she had to pick up a job here to get a little money ahead to get back to Chicago on. Well, I just set there with my mouth wide open, listening to her, and every once in awhile Petey'd look around at me and say 'Isn't that right, Sally?' She'd be smilin', but she'd give me a terrible look, and I'd just about fall off my stool saying yes, that was right, yes, that was just like she said. I'll never forget if I live to be a hundred how once like that, Petey leaned over and put one arm around me and kissed me and turned around to that man and said, wasn't I cute, I was so young and bashful. That little snip, and there I was a whole year older'n she was, and neither one of us had seen fifteen yet!"

"Jesus, what a gal!" Fred said. "She oughta been on the stage!"

"She sure oughta," Sally agreed. "Well, pretty soon this man wanted to buy her another drink, but Petey said, no, thanks, we had to go. The man got kind of interested in where we was going and stuff, but Petey said, oh, no, we'd be perfectly all right, she had a friend in town, she'd sent him a wire when to expect us. Then she pulled her face down and looked real sad. I couldn't get head nor tail to what she was talking about, of course, but the man sure seemed to know what it was all about. He got real excited and swelled out his chest, and said no, sir, he wasn't going to let her do that. Petey just looked at him real sad, as if she was going to bust out crying. Honest, if that Petey isn't the limit! She looked at him real sad and then she said in that deep voice of hers kind of quavery, as if she was trying hard not to cry, for him not to worry, she'd be all right. Of course, she said, kind of forlorn like, this man wasn't a very nice fellow, she'd rather not get mixed up with him, but what was she gonna do, she had her little sister to take care of now, and all that stuff. Well, this guy she was talking to, just seemed to eat that stuff up. He started patting her on the shoulder, and the first thing I knew he pulled a big roll of bills outa his pocket. Gosh, I remember how my eyes glued onto that roll of bills. I'd never seen so much money before in my life, and we didn't have more'n two dollars to our names. We didn't even have that much, after we'd bought them sandwiches. Well, he peeled off a couple of them bills and started to give 'em to Petey, and I started to draw the first easy breath I had all night. And then I pretty near did fall off the stool because, no, sir, Petey wouldn't take 'em."

Sally stopped to laugh again. "You can sure see how dumb I was!"

"Damned if they couldn't put this in the moving pictures," Fred said incredulously. "My God, that Petey kid musta been born knowin' all the answers."

"Well, I guess she musta been, all right. The man kind of argued with her. He said he knew just the place for us to go and stay at and he'd take care of us, and Petey needn't worry her little head another minute about this other guy, and all that stuff. But Petey just kept saying no. She kept thanking him and telling him how swell he'd been to us and all that, but that she just couldn't take his money. There was just one thing, she said to him, kind of wistful like. I'll never forget, she must have been pretty scared right then, because she reached over and took hold of my hand in my lap and hung onto it so hard that her fingernails cut right in, and it was all I could do to keep from yellin'. The guy says, what was that? What was on her mind? Well, Petey said, she kind of thought maybe he'd give her a job, that she'd worked in a lot of places like this before in Chicago, and she'd kind of thought maybe he'd help her out by giving her a job for awhile, so she'd have a chance to save up a little money. Well, the minute Petey said job, the guy was all off in a minute. No, he didn't have any jobs, and he sounded kind of sore all in a minute. Well, Petey said, that was certainly too bad, she'd kind of thought maybe he could help her. Then she started sliding off the stool. She said we'd have to go right away because her friend was expecting her and we was late already. When she got off the stool she kind of caught her heel, and when he went to steady her, she give him one long last look out of those great big eyes a hers. Honest, I can laugh about it now but . . ."

"And she had the guy sold a hundred percent," Fred broke in. "She musta had him hook, line and sinker."

"Well, she certainly did," Sally finished. "He said he'd try her out right that night, carrying drinks to tables, and she could keep the tips she made. I'll be darned if she didn't tie a white apron on and park me and the suitcase out back in the ladies' room, and work till that place closed up early in the morning, sometime. She made enough money to buy us both a good breakfast and rent us a room in a cheap rooming-house place, just off the tips she picked up around there that night. She only worked at that place about a couple weeks after that, though. The manager guy kept getting fresher and fresher with her, and I'll be darned if she didn't pick herself up a job peddling cigarettes around on a tray in a real classy speakeasy place on the other side of town. The fellow that run it seen her in there waiting on tables one night and offered her the job."

Sally got up and picked up the piece of paper in which she was going to wrap the Christmas tree. "Gosh, I been talking my head off," she said, "but that sure was a night, though."

But Fred was still curious. "Well, what happened to her after that?" he wanted to know. "How long did she work at that place selling cigarettes?"

"Oh," Sally said, her hands busy with the paper. "Four or five months, I guess. She made pretty good money there. It looked like a fortune to us. I got a housework job, from an ad in the paper, and we moved out to a better room and bought us some decent clothes and stuff."

"What become of her after that? You said she worked there four or five months. I bet she got married, huh?"

Sally laughed a little. "Uh uh, not Petey. No, there wasn't any stopping her, once she got started. She quit that job she had as cigarette girl and went to work in some little place that was just getting started. She got a job as kind of hostess. She set at the tables with fellows and had drinks with 'em and danced with 'em, if they wanted to. She didn't care much about doin' that kind of work, but the thing was she got a chance to sing in there, and that was what she was aimin' at."

"Was she a good singer?" Fred asked.

"Gosh, yes, she did all right, singin'," Sally said. "I never knew she could sing, that is, sing good enough for something like that out in front of people up till then. I guess she got the idea while she was workin' to this other place. They hired a girl to sing in there and Petey always used to say she could do better'n that girl did, if she ever got a chance. I guess she knew what she was talkin' about, too, because the next job she had was singin' in some speakeasy place in Chicago. The guy that owned the place heard her singin' one night and signed her up. Petey was always lucky picking up jobs like that."

Sally smoothed the paper carefully around the little Christmas tree and then wound the ribbon around it painstakingly, so as not to wrinkle it.

"It's funny," Fred said, "I never heard you talk about your sister before. I never knew you had another sister besides Virge. What did Petey do then, get married?"

"Uh uh," Sally said. She tied the knot tight, and began to loop the ribbon carefully for the bow.

Fred looked at her curiously, but she didn't say anything more. Outside, a wash of sleet pelted against the windows. "Jesus, what a night!" Fred said. "Sleetin' and wet, and I gotta walk over to that goddam factory and go to work right now."

"I got your lunch all put up," Sally said. "It's there on the shelf in the paper sack."

Sally pulled the loops of ribbon through and separated them into a great fluffy bow on the broad side of the package.

Fred walked over and picked up his sack of lunch, but still he lingered. "Where is your sister now?" he asked Sally.

"Huh? Oh, Petey?" Sally's eyes were on the package as she fussed with the bow of ribbon. "Well," she said at last, "I don't really know where she is right now. I haven't seen her in a couple years. The last I heard from her was early last summer, I mean this last summer. She was in New York someplace then. We wrote a couple letters back and forth. But I guess she left there."

"New York, huh," Fred said. "Jesus, she really gets around, don't she? She musta done pretty good for herself. What was she doing, working down there, singin' or something?"

Still Sally kept her eyes lowered to the ribbon bow, pulling at it gently with her fingers. "Well, no, no, she wasn't," Sally said slowly. "She was sort of on a vacation, I guess."

"Oh," Fred said. He watched Sally a moment curiously. "Well, I didn't mean to be nosy or nothin', asking all them questions about her," he said. "If she ever gets out in this part of the country I sure would like to meet up with that gal!"

"Okay, Fred, it's a promise, if she ever comes out here I'll see to it you get a chance to meet her," Sally said, laughing. She held up the package for his inspection. "There. How does that look? Gee, I think that is one swell-looking package, if I did wrap it up myself. Don't that ribbon look pretty with that paper?"

"Yup, it sure does." Fred turned around to look as he went out. "That's all right, Sally. I'll see you in the morning. Good night."

"Good night, Fred," Sally called after him. "Watch those front steps, going down in the dark. They're just terrible slippery."

"Okay, don't worry, I'll watch 'em. See yuh in the morning!"

After he was gone Sally carefully lined the big cardboard box with tissue and put all of the packages for Roy into it carefully, the bright package that was the Christmas tree in the middle, and all the others around it, filling in the cracks and corners with oranges, apples and bananas. When she was all done, she looked at it admiringly. It was certainly a pretty box. Then she remembered the little note she was going to include about the three extra boxes of candy. She supposed it was illegal to include writing in a parcel, but just a little note like that wouldn't hurt. She wrote several lines on a scrap of paper with Fred's leaky fountain pen and slipped it under the cord on one of the candy boxes. She took one last look at the array of parcels and then folded the tissue over them and folded the flaps of the top of the box together. She tied it shut with quantities of white cord, and then searched for a clean piece of heavy brown wrapping paper, large enough to cover it. When it was all done, and the address plainly written on both sides of the parcel, Sally sat down again with a sigh of relief. At least, she had this much done toward Christmas, and it was really the most important thing of all. She would put it in the mail the first thing tomorrow morning, and Roy would be sure to get it before Christmas. She picked up the large package and shook it a little. No, it didn't rattle, and the cord was tight. It ought to go through the mail without any damage. For just a moment, Sally sat by the table, holding the package in her hands. She could visualize Roy in the hospital receiving this package (it would be opened, of course, before he received it, and the paper wrapped loosely around it again, the strings dangling). She could imagine how he might sit holding it just like this for a moment, before he opened the box. Oh, surely, he couldn't help but feel all the love and care that had gone into this package, Sally thought. The presents didn't amount to much; she wished she could have done more. Surely, he would understand how much they all loved him, and how much they missed him, how sorry they were that he couldn't be home for Christmas, how much they wanted to include him in their festivities, whether he was actually with them or not. Sally had a lump in her throat, and she kept looking at the box and thinking about Roy, as if this feeling she had was something that could be transmitted to this plain brown-paper-wrapped parcel, like some kind of perfume, perhaps, so that when the parcel was given into Roy's hands at the other end of its journey, he might be immediately aware of it.

Sally put it down on the table suddenly, got up and went to the sink. She was tired and sleepy, and her feet hurt, but there were dishes to be done before she could go to bed tonight.

# 11

THE DAYS UNTIL CHRISTMAS PASSED RAPIDLY, AS crammed with the activity of preparation as Sally had anticipated. She budgeted her every waking hour away from the restaurant in terms of things yet to be done. There was one night when she stood over the hot stove for hours baking cookies and making candy. It was four o'clock when she limped off to bed leaving sheets of brown paper spread all over the kitchen, covered with the little thin sugar cookies in the shapes of stars, Christmas trees, Santa Clauses, men, women and animals, frosted in pink and white, gay with a sprinkling of colored sugar and little round red cinnamon candies for eyes. Sally had a reward for her hard work in the growing excitement of Buddy and Marilyn, who shared preparations with her as the holiday drew near.

It was Fred Foster who finally took the children downtown on Thursday afternoon so that their gifts for the school party Friday might be purchased and wrapped in plenty of time. Sally gave each one of them a dollar with the admonition that it must be stretched to include their entire shopping for this Christmas. But when she arrived home Thursday night and the children showed her their cache of packages hidden behind the davenport, Sally decided that they must have received substantial financial aid from Fred. When she tried to scold Fred about it, he denied it. While Sally got supper, all three of them talked to her at once, and she couldn't tell who had had the most fun on the shopping expedition, Fred or the children. At any rate, Fred had revised his plans for Christmas. He had boasted that he intended to get drunk that day by way of celebration. Now he mentioned casually that he believed he would accept his ex-wife's invitation for Christmas dinner and spend the day with his own children.

Virginia worried Sally. She remained in bed, cross and listless, with the doctor coming every morning to swab out her throat with the hated silver nitrate. She told Sally about the two dollars, but when Sally offered to do some shopping for her, Virginia declined. No, she didn't have any money, so she would have to skip Christmas this year. She wished that everybody would remember that and not embarrass her by giving her any gifts. But what about the two dollars? Sally argued. That was Virginia's money; she had been saving it. The two dollars, Virginia said firmly, was to be applied to her doctor bill, and, if Sally wouldn't do that, then she was to take it and buy something that she needed for herself. Sally suspected the purpose for which Virginia had hoarded the two dollars so carefully, so she gently suggested to her that if Virginia would tell her what to get she would be glad to buy a present for Bill and mail it to him. No, Virginia said stiffly, she wasn't sending him a present. Then how about cards, Sally suggested. Surely Virginia had friends she would like to remember. Virginia shook her head forlornly. She wished that Sally wouldn't keep talking about Christmas to her; she wasn't having any this year. Sally laughed at her. She was afraid she would have to have Christmas, whether she wanted to or not, Sally teased. This whole family was a bunch of crazy nuts about Christmas. She couldn't see how Virginia was going to get away from it. But Virginia refused to be cheered or comforted, and Sally worried about her. She tried to tempt Virginia's appetite with little cardboard cups of ice-cream from the drug store. She gave her cheerful accounts of holiday preparations, and asked her advice about presents for the children.

Friday night, two days before Christmas, the stores were remaining open until eleven o'clock. Sally and Fred Foster decided to do their shopping together on that night.

Sam Toresca granted Sally's request for her pay check for the week's work Friday night instead of the customary Saturday. In spite of the fact that Friday was an interminably long and harried day at the restaurant, Sally was in high spirits over her shopping tour.

As soon as the dinner crowd began to thin out a little, Sally flew to the washroom for her coat and hat. She found Fred at the agreed meeting place, the corner drug store, sitting on a stool hunched over a cup of coffee. Sally crawled up on the stool beside him and recklessly ordered a cup of coffee for herself. While her coffee cooled, she pulled out her shopping list and went over each item on it, making frequent additions and an occasional deletion, chattering all the while to Fred. The drug store had a festive atmosphere about it. The lunch counter was crowded with shoppers. The juke-box was alternating between two recordings, it seemed, one of Bing Crosby singing "Adeste Fidelis" in Latin, and one of Kate Smith singing "Silent Night" in German. The holiday spirit was reflected in every glittering tinsel wreath, every winking electric bulb, the rustle of paper sacks and packages, the mixture of gay voices. Over all the other din, the girl at the cash register gave the traditional holiday greeting in a high, synthetic, sweet voice, "Thank you, come in again, and Merry Christmas!"

Sally chattered on about her list and surreptitiously counted her money in her purse. The tips had been good. The pay check was not as fat as it might be, with one day missing. Sally decided recklessly to pay only part of her rent this week, and make it up later, after the holidays. Mrs. Gideon wouldn't care, she was sure of that, and by skimping a little later she would be able to make it up all night. Fred recounted the sad story of the two hours he had spent at the big community bingo party down the street that afternoon, with no luck whatsoever in his attempt to win a turkey or a goose for Christmas dinner. Pooh, who wanted turkey or goose anyway? Sally consoled him. She had already ordered two chickens for their Christmas dinner, Sally confided. She knew it was extravagant, but she just made up her mind to do it anyway, because the children liked it so, and they hadn't had chicken in she couldn't remember how long.

Fred caught the gay spirit after looking at Sally's smeared, crumbled, shopping list, and pulled out his leaky fountain pen with a flourish and started writing a list of his own. His notepaper happened to be the back of a receipt for an alimony payment, which, he decided bitterly, was a very fitting thing for him to use as a shopping list. His decision in regard to his family was amazingly simple: shirts for his father and brothers and brothers-in-law, silk stockings for all the women. He and Sally had a consultation about sizes in women's hosiery. What size stocking did she wear? What size did Virginia wear? he inquired artlessly. Why, bless his old heart, Sally thought, as if she couldn't guess what he was up to. Sally immediately made a mental addition to her own list, a pair of socks, or maybe a necktie for Fred Foster. When they had finished their coffee they started pushing their way toward the cash register, making frequent stops to examine articles displayed on the counters. At the cosmetic display a brightly wrapped box, including face powder, rouge, lipstick and perfume, all for sixty-nine cents, caught Sally's eye. Why, that was just the thing for Virginia, she said to Fred. Poor kid, she wasn't going to have a very happy Christmas, sick like she was, and worried about money and not having a job, and all that. Sally decided she'd buy one of those boxes for Virginia. It was expensive, but, Sally defended herself, it was something Virginia could use, and every girl liked nice cosmetics, instead of that dime-store stuff. Fred applauded the idea and the box was bought. The next stop was a bin of Christmas candy. Fred purchased one of the enormous three-pound sacks of it, after Sally assured him that it wouldn't hurt the kids to eat it, in spite of its gay coloration. Kids sure got a kick out of that candy. You remember how crazy you used to be for it when you was a kid, Fred reminisced. Sure thing, Sally said. When she was a kid, that was just about all the Christmas they got, too, hardtack candy and an orange apiece, and maybe a few nuts. Sally bought a pound of it for her own children. They moved on toward the door. Almost at the cash register they came across a bin full of fluffy white toy rabbits with enormous pink ears and enormous glass eyes. A tired young salesman explained the peculiar virtues of these toys. These were no ordinary toy rabbits. When you squeezed the rabbit's stomach it squeaked, like this, see? And when you pinched this little rubber bulb suspended from the collar around the rabbit's neck, the rabbit's eyes lighted up with real light, like this. He explained the mechanism of tiny flashlight bulbs concealed behind the glass eyes, and the battery located some place in the depths of the animal's anatomy. Then he pinched the bulb a couple of times and the rabbit's eyes shone with a wild green glare. Well, what did you know about that? Sally marveled. What in the world would they think of for kids next? Did you ever see anything cuter than that in your life?

Fred was completely won by the bright-eyed rabbits. How much were they? he asked weakly. Only sixty cents, the salesman confided. What did he think of that? Of course, they had been marked down from a dollar, because the store wanted to close them out before Christmas.

Fred ordered one wrapped up immediately. It would be just the thing for his baby, he told Sally.

Sally stroked one of the soft downy bunnies wistfully, while they waited, and squeezed the bulb a couple of times. Gosh, if they weren't the cutest things, she lamented, as the rabbit gave her a lurid green wink. Why, she knew what! She just believed that she would buy one of these for little Beverly O'Connor. Johnny was always doing so much for her kids, and everything.

"I'll take one of them, too," Sally told the clerk happily, when he came back with Fred's package. Aw, he could see through her, Fred teased her. She just wanted one of these batty-eyed bunnies to play with herself. Ten to one the battery would be worn out before Beverly ever got it. Well, maybe he was right, Sally agreed, joining in his laughter. But, anyway, she thought they were just about the cutest toys she had ever seen. She wished in a way that her kids hadn't got too old for stuff like this. Now, look at Buddy, for instance. Did Fred know what Buddy wanted for Christmas this year? Sally confided somberly. One of those big sets of toy soldiers from the dime store, one of those terrible ones that had soldiers running with bayonets, and soldiers with machine guns, and tanks and ambulances, and even wounded soldiers and stretchers and Red Cross nurses, and all that stuff. Wasn't that just awful?

Fred couldn't see what was awful about it. What did she expect? Kids heard people talk about the war. They heard about it at school and on the radio and at the movies.

Well, just the same, Sally protested. War was a terrible, terrible thing. She hated to buy toys like that for a kid. Just think about all those poor little kids over in Europe where all the terrible bombing was!

The clerk brought her package just then, and they moved over to the cashier's counter to pay their coffee checks. Just as they went out, Sally looked back over her shoulder, and she looked straight into Nicky Toresca's eyes. He was leaning on one elbow at the tobacco counter, leisurely stripping cellophane off a new package of cigarettes while he waited for his change. Sally looked away from him hastily, and shivered a little involuntarily.

"What's the matter, you cold?" Fred inquired solicitously. "This weather sure is a bitch. This damp goes right through yuh, worse'n cold. I wish it would freeze up again."

"Yeah," Sally said. "This sure is awful Christmas weather. I wish it would snow, don't you?"

They came to the entrances of the big five-and-dime store, and pushed their way through the crowd. The store was a nightmare of crowd and confusion.

"My gosh, will you look at this!" Sally gasped despairingly, as they elbowed their way through the entrance.

"Yeah," Fred said morosely. "I guess everybody and their uncle will be down here shoppin' tonight."

Sally grabbed for her hat, dislodged by the shoulder of a tall man in a suede jacket who almost knocked her over as he crowded past her, his arms full of packages.

"Oh, well," Sally said philosophically, as she jammed her hat down securely on her head again, "just think what it will be like tomorrow night, with everybody coming down here to get the things they forgot to buy, and lots of the shops don't give out pay checks till tomorrow, either. Tomorrow night will be even worse than this."

"Hell, it couldn't be," Fred said. "Lead on, I'm right behind you."

"Well, okay," Sally called back over her shoulder. "And I tell you what, Fred, if we get separated in all this crowd, let's wait for each other at the Coca-Cola counter, huh?"

After almost an hour and a half, Sally and Fred held consultation at the Coca-Cola counter and decided to move on to a department store where some of the larger items on their lists could be purchased. They fought their way out of the store and moved on up the street. Inside the less crowded shop, they combined purchases into fewer sacks and plunged into their shopping again. Most of the larger articles to be bought here were on Fred's list. Sally went with him and held the packages while he selected shirts in the men's department. They moved on to the hosiery counter and Fred bought four or five pairs of hosiery in various sizes. Then he consulted his list once more and looked at Sally slyly. Wouldn't she like to go to the ladies' room? he suggested innocently. He would wait for her right here. Why, that would be swell, Sally assured him with equal innocence. Sally turned away and pushed through the crowd toward the elevators. Gosh, wasn't it sweet of Fred to buy something for her, like this? She just bet anything there would be some nice stockings for her and Virginia from him. Sally took a detour back to the men's department and bought a blue workshirt in Fred's size. That was a little more money than she had really counted on spending, but just the same, Christmas only came once a year, Sally decided recklessly, and Fred had been so nice to her and the kids, like bringing the kids downtown shopping the other day, and giving them extra money to spend, she just knew it.

A rack of bright neckties caught her eye. She wondered about Johnny O'Connor. She hadn't planned on giving him anything. She thought just a little something for the baby would be enough. After all, Johnny knew how scarce money was with her, and he would understand. But if she was going to give something to Fred she would certainly have to give something with all their names on it to Johnny. The ties were a dollar, real good ones. Sally fingered one of them appreciatively. She hated to pick out ties. Roy always used to tell her that she didn't have any kind of head on her when it came to picking out men's neckties. Every time she used to buy a tie for Roy he always went and changed it. She always picked out the ones that she thought were pretty, but it must be that men had different opinions about it. This time she decided to be smart and leave the actual selection up to the male clerk. She gave him the colors in suits that Johnny wore most frequently, and he had dark hair and blue eyes, she contributed helpfully. The clerk selected a tie that he was sure was just the thing. Sally personally thought it very dull. She was more in favor of the bright blue satin one, but she had better take the one the man picked out. Remember what Roy always said, she warned herself. While the clerk was doing it up for her in bright Christmas paper, Sally deliberated over whether she should buy another one of these ties for Joe. Goodness, she guessed Joe was mad at her, the way he acted, and there wasn't any telling whether he would show up for Christmas or not. He hadn't been home to eat in days. But just the same, he was part of the family, she ought to get something. He was her brother, and she loved him. She remembered how she used to take care of him when he could just toddle around, how he used to hang onto her; he wouldn't let anybody else put him to bed, nights.

Sally went into consultation with the clerk again about an appropriate necktie for Joe. But the last minute she impulsively disregarded his advice and bought the tie that she herself thought was the prettiest one on the rack, almost the prettiest tie she had ever seen in her life. You couldn't tell her that Joe wouldn't like that beautiful tie with stripes better than that dirty-looking, old, bluish-colored one with the little specks of figures in it that the clerk recommended. Sally hurried back through the store to rejoin Fred Foster at the hosiery counter.

He had decided to buy a snow suit for Tommy, and Sally went with him to help pick it out and offer her suggestion on size. They finally agreed on a dark brown one, complete with helmet, mittens, long trousers and jacket. That sure was all right, Fred kept saying in delight. That was gonna be just the thing for Tommy. It would keep him warm, all right, nice, thick, woolly cloth like that. It would be big enough so Tommy could wear it next year, too, unless he grew a lot. Sally watched the clerk fold it in the box a little wistfully. She wished she could afford something like that for Buddy. Poor kid, he always had to wear the old clothes that Harold had outgrown. The best she had been able to do for Buddy this year was a new pair of corduroy knickers, and a new cap and mittens from the dime store.

Fred and Sally moved on to the sweater department. Sally had decided on a new sweater for Harold and one of the button-up kind for Marilyn. The garment for Harold offered no problem, but Sally wavered over a twin sweater set for Marilyn for a dollar more, instead of just a single sweater. It was so cute: a little tiny red sweater with short sleeves and then the navy-blue one that buttoned over the top and had long sleeves. It would be so warm and nice for her to wear to school, and, besides, it would tickle Marilyn so, a real grown-up sweater set. Sally weakened eventually, as she knew she would, when she first laid eyes on the set. She paid for it a little apprehensively. My gosh, it certainly didn't take you long to run through money, once you started out buying things like this.

Eventually, after another examination of their shopping lists, they decided that the balance of their purchases could be made back at the dime store. Maybe by this time the crowd had begun to thin out a little. Just as they left the department store, Sally stopped again before a counter of costume jewelry. A big flower pin with many colored stones caught her eye. It was for a suit lapel, the clerk explained. Also lots of women were wearing them on their fur coats this season. Sally turned the glittering pin in her hands lovingly. It was just about the prettiest she had ever seen in her life. Marked down to fifty cents, too, the clerk assured her. See, here was the original price tag still on it, eighty-nine cents, see. You know what, Sally said to Fred, I have a notion to buy that for Gloria O'Connor. I bet she'd be crazy about this, and it would be just the thing for her, too. She could wear it on her new fur coat. Fred was of the opinion that Gloria had enough fixings and doodads without Sally spending her good money to buy her some more. No, I think I'll take that, please, Sally said to the clerk, hitching the bundles in her arms in order to get her purse open.

They returned to the dime store, which, if anything, was more crowded than it had been before. With most of the major items off their lists, they were able to go on a little spree of petty buying. Sally remembered to buy spare Christmas-tree bulbs. Fred bought five or six large cellophane wreaths and bells at the same counter. They would trim up Sally's apartment awful nice, he said, and, if he was coming to the tree-trimmin' party tomorrow night, he ought to contribute something. He also bought an entire box of tree ornaments, and Sally recklessly bought half a dozen red candles. She loved to see real candles burning at Christmas time, she told Fred. They made another stop at the candy novelty counter. Sally bought a ten-cent set of little carved gold-colored button earrings for Virginia. She also bought a little football for Buddy for a quarter. In some subconscious way she felt that that might counteract the effect of the set of toy soldiers.

Eventually their shopping lists were completed and thrown away, and, after a few more reckless random purchases, they made their way out to the street once more. At some time during the evening they had invested in several heavy paper shopping bags, and they were no sooner on the street than the handles tore out of one of them that Fred was carrying. They both grabbed for the bag and somehow managed to catch it between them so that the catastrophe of spilled packages and sacks was averted. With a great deal of laughter, they managed to lift it so that Fred could carry it securely in one arm. With the loss of faith in the durability of handles on shopping bags, they hoisted up the other one that Fred was carrying, so that he was loaded down with a shopping bag in each arm, and the large box that contained Tommy's snow suit wedged precariously between one of the bags and his chest. Sally was so loaded with packages that Fred said he was just able to see the tip of her nose over them when she stood on tiptoe and flung her head back. Just as they got all the packages reloaded and started off down the street in the direction of the bus stop, Sally stopped still in her tracks. Fred Foster, you know what I forgot? I forgot to buy a single blessed thing for old Mrs. Sipes. Isn't that terrible? How did I ever happen to forget that? Isn't it the luckiest thing that I remembered it before we got home? We'll have to go right back and get something for her now.

For Christ's sakes, Fred protested, did she mean they had to go back there into that madhouse just to buy something for old lady Sipes? To hell with it! Give her a bottle of beer with a red ribbon tied on it, if you was so crazy to give her something for Christmas.

That was no way to talk, Sally scolded him. Poor old lady, she didn't have anybody to remember her at Christmas time. She was coming to the party tomorrow night, and wouldn't it be a fine thing not to have a present under the tree for her! Maybe Mrs. Sipes was old and kind of foolish-acting, and maybe she drank too much and all that, but Sally guessed that she had feelings, just the same as other people. You ought to be careful what you said about people like Mrs. Sipes, because your own life wasn't over yet, and you never could tell how you'd end up yourself. Why, Fred Foster, for all you know, maybe you'll be an old man some day living all alone in an attic room without any friends or relatives to take care of you, and then I guess you'd know how much it means to have somebody remember you at Christmas.

Fred was silenced, but not quite convinced. Okay, he said, so they would go back and buy something for old lady Sipes. Hell, he supposed Sally even expected him to buy a present for the old girl. Well, she didn't see why not, Sally said. She guessed it wouldn't hurt him to buy her a little something, for goodness' sakes.

They turned around and, by the time they were back in the store, good humor was restored again. Fred good-naturedly stood by, while Sally selected two or three bright-colored handkerchiefs and a ten-cent gold pin with bright-red stones in it. Fred himself bought one of the quarter boxes of chocolate-covered cherries at Sally's recommendation. That ought to be just the thing for the old girl, he observed, she would gobble them all down just as soon as she got the box, but then for the next six weeks she would be picking cherries out of her hair and her coat collar, so she wouldn't starve to death. Sally had to laugh in spite of herself.

Once they were back on the street, Fred announced importantly that they weren't gonna bother with no bus tonight, they were going to go home in a cab. Sally tried to dissuade him, but Fred was adamant. No, sir, they were going home in a taxi, in style. They walked on down the street to the taxi stand at the corner. A sleety rain was beginning to fall, freezing on the streets in a hard thin coating of ice that made walking difficult and traffic hazardous.

While the cab skidded over the streets at breakneck speed Sally luxuriously relaxed her body on the seat.

The cab drew up in front of 218 Horton Street, and Sally and Fred loaded up their packages once more. The cab driver called a cheery Merry Christmas after them, and Sally turned around and called back to him for mercy sakes to be careful driving that cab tonight or his family wouldn't have a very Merry Christmas either. The cab driver wheeled around into the street and then solicitously kept his headlights turned onto the porch while Fred and Sally, loaded with their packages, wobbled up the icy steps.

The front door was locked, and, with a great deal of laughter and rattling of packages, both Sally and Fred tried to find their keys. In the midst of the struggle, the door was opened for them by Mrs. Gideon herself.

"Well, for mercy sakes!" she said, peering out at them. "Would you look at you folks? Well, I tell you, I'm glad I got all my Christmas shopping done, because I guess you musta bought out the stores tonight. Here, Sally, let me take some of them packages before you drop them."

"No, thank you," Sally said gayly. "I got hold of 'em just right, and if you take a single package outa this armload the whole mess of them is gonna fall right on the floor."

"My, ain't this a terrible night?" Mrs. Gideon said, as she closed the door behind them. "It's still raining, ain't it?"

"Yup, and freezing on," Fred said. "Jesus, them streets are just like glass."

Sally and Fred were edging away from her up the stairs as she talked.

When they passed the door to the O'Connors' apartment, a slit of light shone out from under it across the dark hallway, and they heard the familiar blare of radio music.

"Wanta stop in and say hello?" Fred suggested. "Let's show 'em all the packages we got, huh?"

"Well, okay," Sally said reluctantly. "But let's not stay. I'm awful tired, and them kids of mine will be sitting up over there waitin' for me to get home, you know."

"Hell, I ain't gonna stay," Fred said. "I gotta go to work in a few minutes."

"Say, that's right. Look, Fred, why don't you stop and I'll go on home and pack your lunch. You'll have to go in a minute, and I better get your lunch put up."

"No, sir," Fred said. "You come on in here now and set down a minute. You're ready to drop, and you ain't gonna go in there and pack no lunch for me tonight. I can buy my lunch in the cafeteria over there for once, I guess. You ain't gonna bother to pack no lunch for me tonight."

"Well, all right," Sally said. "Gosh, I'm not gonna argue with you, if you do wanta buy your lunch tonight. I ain't got strength enough left to do it."

Fred juggled his sacks around and freed one hand. He rapped on the door and then rattled the doorknob. "Anybody to home in there?" he yelled. "Christ, you wouldn't hear the house if it fell down, that radio goin'!"

Johnny opened the door instantly. "Well, I'll be damned," he said, grinning at them. "If here isn't Mr. and Mrs. Santa Claus in person. I'll bet a lot of stores downtown went out of business tonight when you came home. Come on in, for God's sakes, Sally, and set down before you fall down."

"Oh, Fred, look!" Sally cried as they walked into the room. "Gee, doesn't that look pretty! Just look!"

The table in the corner of the living room had been pulled away from the wall a little and a small-sized Christmas tree mounted on it, resplendent in shining silver icicles, glass balls and colored bulbs.

"That's all right," Fred agreed. "God, it looks like Christmas around here!"

"Well, you don't look like the Fourth of July yourself, toting all them packages," Johnny said.

Gloria dropped her magazine and stretched, her arms doubled above her shining head. "We put it up tonight after Johnny got home," she explained.

"Jesus, Sally, will you set down before you fall on your face?" Johnny scolded, pulling a chair around for her. "Sit down, Freddy."

Sally sank down in the chair, her eyes still on the gay little Christmas tree. "Gee, it's awful pretty, Gloria. Don't you love 'em? I never can wait to put 'em up, and then I always hate to take them down. Gosh, I bet Beverly is crazy about it. Has she seen it yet?"

"Yeah, she likes it," Gloria said. "We didn't have no tree last year, but this year Johnny said we had to have one on account of the baby. I claimed she was too young for a tree, but Johnny said she wasn't."

"The hell she's too young," Johnny said. "You oughta seen her when we plugged the lights in after we got it all trimmed. She kept looking and looking at it, squealin' and yelling. I held her up close, so she could look at it, and damned if she didn't grab one of them icicles quicker than a flash and start shoving it in her mouth. She's crazy about the tree. She cried her head off when we took her in the bedroom and put her to bed with her bottle."

"Of course, she isn't too young for a tree," Sally agreed. "She don't know what it is yet or anything like that, but she notices it. I think it was awful nice to have it for her."

"I'm gettin' a tree for my kids," Fred announced importantly. "I wanta be over there first thing in the morning, so I can see 'em when they get up and find their presents."

Johnny walked the length of the room to the cigarette stand and turned his back to them while he lighted a cigarette. "Hell, Freddy, you'll have to get up in the morning if you get over there to see them find their presents. Tommy'll be outa bed before six o'clock, I'll lay you a dollar to a nickel on it."

"Johnny says we have to hang up a stocking for Bev," Gloria said. "I think it's silly when she's so little, but Johnny says we have to."

"Why, sure you do," Sally said. "That's just part of Christmas when you got a baby." There was a pause in the conversation, broken at last by Sally.

"Say, what do you think? Mrs. Gideon went to the bingo tonight and she won a turkey and two chickens and a big basket of groceries, all in about an hour, she said. Doesn't she beat anything you ever heard of? Honest, that woman is the luckiest person I ever knew in my life . . ."

"Oh, God," Fred complained, "ain't she the limit, though! Some of these days, Giddy is gonna part with enough money all at once to buy a Sweepstakes ticket and then you know what's gonna happen, don't you?"

"Well, I wouldn't be surprised a bit, with luck like she has," Sally said. "I tell you what, let's take up a collection and buy her a Sweepstakes ticket and then, after she wins, maybe she'll deed the house over to us, huh?"

"Ha, ha," Fred said. "Fat chance, not the way Giddy pinches her pennies. Hey, O'Connor, got a light?"

Johnny was moving around the room restlessly, a cigarette hanging from his lips, his hands jammed in his pockets. He apparently did not hear Fred. He paid no attention.

Fred waved the unlighted cigarette at him. "Hey, hey, I said, you gotta match?"

"Get a match for Fred," Gloria said, "and then for goodness' sakes set down someplace, Johnny. You make me nervous, walkin' up and down like that."

Johnny came back to himself with a noticeable start. "I'm sorry. Here you are, Freddy."

He walked over to Fred, searching for matches in his pocket, and Sally looked at him curiously.

"What's a matter, Johnny, aren't you feeling good?" she asked him. "You look awful tired, and your face is kind of flushed. And you're kind of quiet tonight. I guess that's always a sign there's something wrong with you, or me either. What's a matter, isn't he feeling good, Gloria?"

"You should talk about lookin' tired, Sally, my girl," Johnny scoffed, "and you so tired you can hardly sit up on that chair and your face as white as a sheet."

"Well, I am tired," Sally admitted readily. "Boy, we sure had a day of it down there to that restaurant, don't think we didn't. And then shopping in that crowd tonight. My feet hurt and my head aches and, boy, wouldn't a bed feel good to me right now? But instead a that I got to wrap packages tonight. I'm not gonna have no chance to do it before the party tomorrow night, and we always put the presents under the tree after we get the tree trimmed. Say, don't you folks forget you got a date to come over to my place tomorrow night for the tree trimming. We couldn't have the party without you, you know and—Johnny O'Connor!"

Johnny stopped still at Sally's startled voice, the match poised in front of Fred's cigarette.

Sally jumped out of her chair, dropping packages in all directions. "Johnny O'Connor, look at your hand! Oh, Johnny, my gosh!"

As she came close to him, Johnny waved the match out and drew away from her. "Now take it easy, Sally," he said plaintively. "It's just swelled up a little tonight, that's all . . ."

"Swelled up a little!" Sally echoed. "Well, I guess it is! Johnny, let me see it, please."

He held his right hand out to her silently. It was huge and misshapen with swelling, the fingers covered with a clean bandaging, wrapped loosely and awkwardly around it.

Sally took hold of it gently, her face anxious and concerned. When she turned it over, she cried out again. "Oh, Johnny, my God, look at your wrist, and way up your arm!" With quick trembling fingers she loosened his shirt cuff, and pushed the sleeve back. The wrist was swollen too, and hot to the touch, and long livid streaks of red extended up his forearm. "Oh, gosh," Sally said, tracing the streaks of red with a gentle, trembling finger. "No wonder you couldn't sit still tonight. Why, this hand and arm must be paining you something terrible, just throbbing with fever, I bet. Oh, Johnny, I'll bet you anything you've got infection in them burns. I was so afraid of that. I never seen anything before that looked as ugly as your wrist and arm does. Here, let's take that bandage off and look. I never saw infection before, but I'm so afraid that, that . . ."

Johnny pulled his hand away from her and smiled at her ruefully. "You don't want to look at that hand, Sally, it don't look so good. It's been paining like this all afternoon."

"Well, Jesus," Fred Foster said, "what you waiting for? Go see a doctor!"

"Johnny, you better," Sally said. "You mustn't fool with it any longer. You'll just have to go to a doctor right away."

"Oh, hell," Johnny said with his three-cornered grin. "It's late tonight, and I don't figure I'll die before morning so . . ."

"No, Johnny," Sally said sharply, "honest, you know yourself that you shouldn't fool with anything like this. You mustn't let it go another hour. Infection is risky business, you know that. I'm just afraid right now, it's got a terrible start. Look at those streaks right up your arms. And look, your left hand is swelled, too. Johnny, you got to have a doctor!"

"Oh, hell," Johnny said, fumbling for another cigarette. "Now, look . . ."

Sally turned around to Gloria. "Gloria," she said, "Gloria, you make him do it. You make him have a doctor over here right tonight. Honey, he's awful sick, don't you understand? He's got infection in that hand, and it's goin' right up his arm. You've got to get a doctor for him, honey."

"Is it where he got burned?" Gloria said helplessly. "Unguentine stuff is awful good for burns. I got some Unguentine in the bathroom, should I . . ."

"Oh, Unguentine hell," Fred Foster said angrily. "Jesus Christ!"

Sally whirled around to Johnny again. "Johnny, I'm going downstairs and call a doctor. I guess I know what's on your mind. You're smart enough to know that you need a doctor, all right. You're just worrying about getting into trouble over at the shop about this. Well, maybe you will, I don't know anything about that. All I know is you have to have a doctor right away. Johnny, maybe I'll get you into a mess of trouble, but I have to call a doctor for you."

"Now wait," Johnny said with authority in his voice. "Will you let me talk for just a minute, Sally? Sure, I'm no fool, I know I got a bad hand here. It's been getting worse, the last day or two. I been using salt water and stuff on it. I thought I could beat the infection. Well, it's been getting worse right along, so I didn't dare go back to the doctor over at the shop. Today, while I'm working, I get a telephone call here at the house, see? The doctor from the shop calls up and says if I don't come in today for him to look at my hands, the compensation stops and I lose my job. So I gotta go in and see him, but I can't go in before tomorrow morning because . . ."

"Tomorrow morning nothing," Sally broke in determinedly. "You're going over there right this minute!"

"Now, wait," Johnny said. "Wait just a minute. I've got to have more time. I've been soakin' my hands, but I got to have more time. My God, the way they are now, the doctor is gonna take one look at my hands and he is going to know damn well I been working on a forge someplace again. Do you know what that heat at the forge did to them blisters on my hands? Dried them right down into little shells! Do you see what's gonna happen to me when the doctor hands in his report that I've been drawing compensation over there and working on the side? If I have a little more time to soak 'em, those dried-up blister things will soften up a little so I can cut 'em off with a razor blade and then . . ."

"Johnny!" Sally took hold of his arm tight in both her hands. "Listen to me, you mustn't dare to touch those blisters with any old razor blade. You've fooled with that hand long enough, soaking it and cutting at it. You know better than that! Do you want to end up by losing two or three fingers or your whole hand maybe?"

Fred Foster got up from his chair and came to stand in front of Johnny. "Look, she's right. You can't fool around. You better get your hat and coat on and go over and see that doctor right now. Hell, I know you're in a spot. After that doctor's report goes in, your number is gonna be up, and what I mean is up in every shop in this town. You're gonna be way out there on the limb if you have doctor bills, because you'll never get another cent compensation now, from no place. But that ain't the thing now. Sally's right. You could maybe lose your hand, if you keep fooling around like this. Hell, no amount of soakin' and cuttin' is gonna fix up that hand a yours, but what that doctor over there can tell in a minute you been up to something."

"Okay, okay, so I go see the doctor tonight," Johnny mumbled.

Suddenly, without warning, Gloria began to cry, a soft miserable sniveling sound. Johnny went to her instantly and touched her soft hair with his hand.

"Sshshsh—Glory, baby! Don't cry. Everything is all right. There isn't nothin' for you to be worrying about. Everything is gonna be all right."

"Jesus, Johnny," Fred said, "I wish I could go over with you to see the doctor. I would just as soon as not, but I gotta go to work in a few minutes."

"You better take a cab over there," Sally said. "You want me to call it for you right away? You're all ready to go, aren't you?"

Johnny's face looked blank and bewildered, and he rubbed it hard in the crook of his arm. "That goddam fever musta spread up to my head, I can't even think straight," he said. "Look, there must be an angle to this someplace I'm missin'. Now, suppose I went to some other doctor tonight besides the company doctor. Maybe he could do something to fix me up, and then, if I went in to see the company doctor the first thing in the morning, why, maybe . . ."

Johnny's voice trailed out, and he closed his eyes and shook his head hard a couple times. "Jesus, I can't even think straight," he murmured.

"Hell, Johnny," Fred broke in, "there ain't nothing that no doctor can do that is gonna fix up that hand a yours between now and tomorrow morning. What's the use of putting out good money to some other doctor? You're better off to go over there and let the company doctor take a look at it for nothing, ain't you?"

"There must be an angle to this somewhere that I'm missin',"

Johnny said again, helplessly. "Jesus, if I go over there I'm gonna be in a hell of a spot!"

Sally and Fred stared at each other silently.

"Oh, gosh, Johnny," Sally said at last. "I don't know what to say. Maybe we're telling you to do the wrong thing, I don't know. But the thing is you've just got to get to a doctor."

Johnny shrugged his shoulders suddenly. "Okay," he said. "So I go see the doctor. Give me a cigarette, will you, Fred?"

"I'll go call a cab for you," Sally said, hurrying toward the door. "What's the number, two four two four, isn't it? I'll tell them to hurry a cab right over."

Sally ran all the way down the stairs in the dim light, quickly and lightly, her sore feet forgotten. When she got back upstairs again, Johnny had his hat and jacket on and was pacing the floor again restlessly, rolling his cigarette between his lips, nervously.

"They said they'd send a cab right over," Sally said, as she closed the door behind her.

"Thanks a lot, Sally," Johnny said. He walked over toward Gloria on the davenport, and, as he approached her, she began to cry again.

"Oh, Glory, don't cry," he said, putting his arms around her. "It's all right. I can't stand to see you cry. Come on and smile for me just once, huh?"

Gloria wound both arms around his neck and hung on hard and cried louder than ever. "Don't go, Johnny," she sobbed. "Don't go over there tonight, I don't want you to. You stay here. Don't you go over there, please, Johnny!"

"Glory, listen, honey . . ."

"No, Johnny, don't you go over there! You stay here. I don't want you to go over there!"

"Jesus Christ," Fred said to her, angrily. "Johnny's sick! You want him to go to a doctor, don't you? What you talking about!"

Just then they heard the muffled sound of a horn blowing from the street outside.

"There's your cab, Johnny," Sally said.

Johnny loosened Gloria's arms gently. "So long, baby, I'll see you in a minute," he said. He leaned down and kissed her lightly on the lips and then turned around and hurried for the door. He was slightly unsteady on his feet, he staggered a little and knocked against a corner of the table, setting all the icicles on the little Christmas tree dancing.

"Oh, gosh," Sally whispered under her breath, as the door closed behind him. "Oh, gosh!"

There was another period of silence, broken only by Gloria's crying. And then they heard the roar of the motor down below, and the splashing of water as the cab drove away down the street.

Fred Foster cleared his throat awkwardly. "Well, I better go get my clothes changed. I gotta go to work in a minute." He stooped down and began to gather up his packages that he had placed on a chair.

Sally went over and sat down beside Gloria on the davenport, and put her arm around the girl's shoulders. "There now, Gloria, don't cry so," she said softly. "Johnny's gonna be all right. He had to go see the doctor, that's all. The doctor'll fix him up. He's gonna be all right, honey!"

Gloria jerked away from her and covered her face in her hands. "No," she said. "I didn't want him to go over there. I wanted Johnny to stay home. You talked him into goin', and I wanted him to stay home."

"Wait a minute, Fred," Sally called. "Don't shut the door, I'm going home right now, soon as I pick up these packages."

She patted Gloria on the shoulder and got up and began to pick up the sacks and parcels, while Fred waited for her silently in the doorway. "Look, Gloria," she said, when she was ready to go. "I have to go home and get my kids to bed, but if you want me you holler, and if you don't want to stay alone you come over, won't you?"

Gloria did not answer, or pay any attention to their leavetaking.

Sally put the children to bed, and hurriedly looked through the little stack of Christmas cards that had come in the mail that day. But not a word from Roy and nothing from Petey. She straightened up the kitchen a little, and put water on to boil for tea. Then she carried all her packages out and piled them on the kitchen table. There were all these presents to be wrapped before she could go to bed tonight. And the grocery list, too, she mustn't forget to order all the stuff for Christmas dinner, and the popcorn for the party tomorrow night. Sally sat down with a scrap of paper and a pencil and began to write her list, wrinkling her forehead in thought. Her head ached so that it was hard for her to think, and she couldn't get Johnny O'Connor out of her mind. There was a cigarette package on top of the cupboard, and just as Sally was lighting a cigarette she heard a gentle insistent knocking on her door.

There, that must be Johnny now, she thought, though it didn't seem hardly like he'd had time to get back already, or maybe it was Gloria. But when Sally opened the door it was Mrs. Gideon who stood outside, holding a kimono wrapped around her.

"Say, Sally," Mrs. Gideon said urgently, "there's somebody wants to talk to you on the telephone. They're holdin' the line, so you better hurry."

"Thanks a lot," Sally said automatically. Telephone calls late at night always frightened her. She was always afraid that Roy was sick or something had happened to him. For the second time that evening, Sally ran down the flight of stairs.

"Hello," she said softly. "This is Sally Otis. Hello."

"Hello, Sally." It was a man's voice, and it sounded somehow a little blurred and indistinct, and Sally couldn't place it for a minute.

"This is Sally," she repeated. "Who is it, please?"

"It's me," he said. "Johnny. Look, Sally . . ."

"Oh, Johnny," she said. "Gosh, I didn't recognize your voice at first. Johnny, what did the doctor say? Where are you? How do you feel? What did the doctor say . . . ?"

"Listen, Sally, I only got a minute . . ." He stopped then as if he were reluctant to go on.

Sally waited and then she said, "Yes, Johnny, I'm right here, I'm listening. What is it?"

"Sally, I want you to tell Gloria. But don't let her get upset and worry, because I'm all right. The doctor looked at my hand, see, and he said it didn't look so good. So the thing is this: he wants me to go on over to the hospital and stay there tonight. They can treat me over there, and watch it to see if it gets any worse. See what I mean? You tell Gloria, but don't let her get upset. Tell her I'll be home the first thing tomorrow morning, will you?"

Sally felt a little wave of fear for him, but she kept her voice controlled and steady. "Sure, I'll tell her, Johnny. And don't you worry about her, because I'll look after her. I'll stay with her tonight or anything she wants me to do. So don't you worry."

"Oh, good. I knew I could depend on you, Sally," he said.

"Sure," she answered. "Don't you worry about a thing. I think it's a swell idea for you to go to the hospital where they got everything to do with to fix up your hand and then keep an eye on it tonight."

"Look, I gotta go," Johnny said.

"Which hospital is he taking you to, Johnny?"

"Huh? Oh, Receivin', I guess. I'll see you in the morning."

"Okay, and don't you worry, everything will be all right. I'll see you tomorrow. Good night, Johnny." Sally's voice was very cheerful and steady. She marveled at the sound of it.

"Good night," he said.

She waited until she heard the click of the receiver in her ear, and then slowly she put the telephone back in its cradle.

She paused a moment outside Gloria's door before she knocked. She was just like some little kid. You never could depend on her to act like a grown-up woman about nothing. And, of course, under the circumstances, you couldn't blame her if she was upset. Sally felt so weary. Why was it, she wondered, that when you got just terribly tired like this, that one hard thing came up right after another, with no letup and no rest?

She knocked softly, and in a moment opened the door. Gloria was still sitting on the davenport, and she looked at Sally silently with a resentful, tear-streaked face.

Sally closed the door and went over to her, mentally rehearsing words she might say to her, choosing phrases and discarding them. She sat down beside her and took hold of her hand, and still she couldn't quite decide on any words to say to her.

"Honey, listen," she heard herself begin weakly. "Now, you mustn't get all upset about this or scared. Johnny just called on the telephone. I was talking to him, and he wanted me to tell you . . ."

"Johnny was talking to you on the telephone," Gloria said, with a shade of resentment in her voice.

"He wanted me to tell you," Sally went on, "the doctor looked at his hand, and then he wanted Johnny to go over to Receiving Hospital to have it treated where they got everything to do with. Seein' it was so late an' everything, he thought maybe it would be better if Johnny stayed over there all night, so they could treat his hand and watch it, so it couldn't get no worse. Johnny said to tell you, and that he would be home here the very first thing in the morning."

Gloria listened to her with her face expressionless. Sally expected tears or some outcry from her, but nothing happened.

"See," Gloria said at last accusingly. "See, I told you. I didn't want Johnny to go over there tonight, but you talked him into it. Now, see!"

"I'm sorry you feel that way about it, honey," Sally said. "I wasn't trying to butt in to somebody else's business or nothing. Johnny was sick, and I thought he ought to go and see a doctor. You don't want Johnny to get bad sick, do you?"

"See," Gloria said again, accusingly. "I didn't want Johnny to go over there, but you talked him into it, and now they've put him in the hospital!"

Sally was so tired, and she controlled a wild impulse to burst out laughing right in Gloria's face. As if the whole thing was her fault, as if by the simple fact that she had persuaded Johnny that he ought to see a doctor, he automatically became so ill that hospitalization was necessary. But she didn't have any right to lose her temper with poor little Gloria, Sally thought penitently. Gloria was just like a little kid, and of course she was upset about Johnny now, so you wouldn't expect her to hardly know what she was saying.

"I tell you what, Gloria," she said, trying to make her voice light and affectionate. "I thought a nice cup of hot tea would taste good to me. Wouldn't you like a cup of tea? Why don't you come on over to my place and we'll drink some tea and have a little lunch outa the icebox before we go to bed."

"No," Gloria said positively. "I don't want any tea."

"Well, come on over, anyway. I got to wrap up a lot of Christmas packages tonight. You don't want to go to bed already, do you? Why don't you come on over and keep me company while I wrap packages?"

"No, I don't want to." Gloria's voice was as flat and expressionless as her face.

Sally got up and moved slowly toward the door. "Okay," she said. "Honey, would you—would you—want me to stay over here with you tonight?"

"No."

"Gloria, if there's anything you want, if there's anything in the world I can do for you, you'll come on over, won't you?"

"I'm all right. I don't want nothing."

"But if you should want something, you'll come over, won't you? Good night, honey, and don't worry too much about Johnny, he'll be all right."

"Good night," Gloria said flatly.

Well, she just gave up, Sally thought, as she went back to her apartment. She couldn't figure Gloria out. She had expected her to cry and take on and go all to pieces, and instead she had taken it all as cool as a cucumber.

Sally went back to the kitchen, her body heavy and numb with fatigue. She stared at the pile of packages on the table. Oh, there was nothing like Christmas, she thought idiotically. The teakettle on the stove had almost boiled dry. She guessed she didn't want any tea, after all. Her head was still aching; she had heard people say that they had thumping headaches; this must be what they meant. It really did thump, didn't it, Sally thought objectively. Thump, thump, thump, a kind of rhythm to it, like some tune. It was familiar, why, it was thumping out some tune, some tune that she knew. Sally sat still and listened hard to her head thumping. Why, it was a tune! Why, she knew what it was! It was "Piccolo Pete." Her head was actually thumping out the tune to that silly old song, "Piccolo Pete." Sally giggled to herself. Oh, my gosh! Silly old head going thump thump thump on its piccolo, no . . .

My gosh, take it easy now, Sally said to herself sternly. She picked up her pencil again and determinedly studied her grocery list. There, she knew she had forgotten something, cranberries. Cranberries were a traditional part of holiday dinners in her family, cranberries for Thanksgiving, cranberries for Christmas. Why, the kids wouldn't have thought it was really Christmas if she had forgotten the cranberries.

Sally wet the pencil lead between her lips and wrote in firm black script at the bottom of the list, "Cranberries."

# 12

SALLY HAD HER WISH ABOUT SNOW FOR CHRISTMAS. The snow began to fall the next day about noon, great wet chunks of it that melted on the icy streets as soon it fell. But now it really looked like Christmas, Sally exulted, when she found a moment to look out of the great plate-glass window at the front of the restaurant.

At lunch time, she telephoned her grocery order. She called Mrs. Gideon, too, and learned that Johnny O'Connor was still in the hospital, and that Gloria had gone to see him. But Sally had little time to worry about Johnny with the rush of business at the restaurant.

There was a holiday atmosphere around the place that Saturday. The waitresses chattered together over plans for the holidays, gifts received and gifts given. The restaurant was closing early tonight, and there was a rumor afloat that each employee was to receive a holiday bonus.

The dinner trade started earlier than usual. At seven-thirty sharp, Sam Toresca closed the door with a flourish behind a last party of customers, put on the night lock and announced that business was done for the day and that everybody was to set right down and have themselves a turkey dinner. He was answered by a shrill wave of cheering from the waitresses. All the girls began to kiss each other and wish each other a Merry Christmas. A campaign to kiss Mr. Toresca formed immediately and Sam fled to the kitchen. The trays with the surprise turkey dinner were already set up. Sam insisted that the entire kitchen staff, even to the dishwashers, come out to the front of the restaurant and join in the festivities. Sally found herself at a table with Sam Toresca himself, Jim, the Negro boy who cleaned the floors, and the chef, an aged Italian who spoke scarcely a dozen words of English.

The party was a hilarious one. The room rang with voices and laughter. When the dessert came in, it proved to be the de-luxe special of the week, a little mold of red-colored ice-cream in the shape of a bell. Sam Toresca turned off the overhead lights, and they ate by the light of the little wall lamps and the blue bulbs that trimmed the two huge Christmas trees in the front of the restaurant.

Oh, this was just lovely, Sally kept telling Sam Toresca. This was the nicest party! It was so nice of him to do this for them. Sam kept scowling. He guessed it was alla right if you liked thisa goddam fool Christmas stuff! But Sally caught the twinkle in his eyes and called his bluff. He couldn't fool her, she teased him, he was having just as much fun as anybody else.

After the dessert was finished, a spontaneous movement formed to carry the dirty dishes to the kitchen to save time for the dishwashers, who would still have work to do after the rest of the staff were free for the evening.

Then Sam Toresca called them together for the distribution of the pay envelopes. The first girl to receive one ripped it open immediately, and her squeal of delight when she looked inside assured the rest of them that the talk of a bonus had been something besides a mere rumor.

After the envelopes were distributed, the group disintegrated rapidly. There was such a stampede for the washroom that Sally lagged behind a little, making a special trip to the kitchen to wish Sam, Jim, Chef and the dishwashers all a Merry Christmas.

By the time she got to the washroom, no one remained there but Lee, who was making up her face in front of the mirror. They chattered together over their respective plans for the holiday and then left the restaurant together.

The wet thick snow was still falling, softening the brightly colored lights of the street decorations overhead, the riot of Neon signs up and down the street, and the garish store fronts. Crowds of last-minute shoppers packed the streets, and the Christmas carols blared out of the loud speakers in the shopping section for the last time this year.

Sally and Lee stood together for a moment in front of the restaurant, turning up their coat collars against the thick wet snow.

"You go the other way, don't you?" Sally said. "I get my bus at the drug store. Well, gee, Lee, have a nice Christmas, won't you, and I'll see you Monday, and I hope your date turns out good and . . ."

Lee was looking over Sally's shoulder behind her, but suddenly she looked back at Sally again. When she spoke it was with unaccustomed warmth and friendliness. "Gee, thanks, honey, and the same to you!" She bent down and kissed Sally on the cheek, squeezing her tight with one arm about her shoulders.

Then she stepped back a little and looked up over Sally's shoulder again. "Why, hello, Mr. Toresca," Lee said, with a note of artificial surprise in her voice. "Merry Christmas!" She looked back at Sally again, the sweet smile on her face, and patted her arm lightly. "Well, good-bye now, I gotta run for my bus. I'll be seein' yuh. Merry Christmas."

"Good-bye, Merry Christmas," Sally answered her automatically.

Lee hurried off down the street, and for a second Sally stood quite still, aware suddenly of the damp and cold of the wet snow, and of a curious lifeless feeling in herself.

"Hello, Sally." It was Nicky Toresca's voice, all right, and his fluid ease of speech when he said those two words that Sally had come to know and hate. He stepped around from behind her then and stood still in front of her.

"Hello, Mr. Toresca." She had forgotten he was so tall, Sally was thinking objectively out of this curious lifelessness she felt. He had his coat collar up and his hat pulled down against the snow. Sally watched the way the chunks of snow melted on the shoulders of his dark overcoat and on his hatbrim.

Nicky Toresca pulled one hand out of his pocket and took hold of Sally's arm. "This is no weather to stand around in," he said. "The car is around the corner. Come on, I'll take you home."

Sally heard her voice answering him without any particular volition on her part. "Well, thanks a lot, Mr. Toresca, but I'm not going home right now. I have some shopping to do first."

"Okay," he said. "We'll go do that first, and then I'll take you home. Where you want to go, Horner's?" He nodded his head toward the large department store up the street.

Sally heard herself answer him again with a total lack of emotion. "No. I have to get a Christmas tree. I'll get off the bus at the grocery right near my place. They got a lot of them there."

Sally found herself walking down the street beside him, under the pressure of his hand on her arm. "You don't want to go running around in this snow lugging no Christmas tree," he said. "We'll get your tree, and I'll give you a ride home with it. That's a lot better than lugging a tree in this snow storm, is that right?"

"I guess so," Sally said. "Thank you very much."

They walked around the corner, and there was Nicky Toresca's big automobile parked at the curb. He opened the door and helped Sally in solicitously. During that short moment while she was alone in the warm, dark interior of the automobile while Nicky Toresca was walking around to get in on the other side, Sally thought dispassionately: why not just say to him, Mr. Toresca, I hate you. I'll quit my job right now. I'm going to the drug store and catch my bus, good night and Merry Christmas.

Nicky Toresca slid under the wheel, and bent down, fumbling with his keys.

He raced the motor a little, and slid the car away from the curb smoothly.

"There's a vacant lot over on Mills Street where they got a lot of trees for sale. We'll get one over there."

Sally didn't answer. Strangely enough, at that moment she wasn't even thinking about Nicky Toresca. She was sitting very still with her hands folded over the purse in her lap, looking straight ahead of her at the blur of lights and the swirling snow. She was thinking about Roy, and that he hadn't even written to her, not a Christmas card, not anything. This was the first Christmas Eve that they hadn't spent together since they had first known each other. She felt an aching in her even through the numbed lifelessness. How terrible Roy must be feeling tonight, sitting alone down there in that place of keys and bells, with the snow beating at the windows. How terribly lonely he must feel, how miserable, how hopeless. How terribly easy it was for people to take happiness for granted, when in just a few short months two people's happy life could turn into such misery for both of them. What was the use? Where was the end to it? Oh, what was the use!

Nicky Toresca parked the car at the curb. "Jesus, they got enough trees left!" he said. "You ought to be able to find one just like you want here, all right."

He got out first and opened the door for her, and Sally stepped out into the snow again. There was a little wooden shanty set up close to the sidewalk, lights shining out of a window, into the snow, and a regular forest of Christmas trees of all sizes behind it.

As they crossed the sidewalk, the shanty door opened and a man stuck out his head. "Lots a trees left, folks," he said. "Go on out and pick out what you want. We're sellin' 'em off cheap tonight."

"Okay," Nicky Toresca said. "We'll go take a look and bring the one we want back here. You stay in outa the snow, huh, it might be bad for your health."

"Well, Jesus," the man said plaintively. "The prices are all marked on 'em, what's the sense a me comin' out and standing around while you spend half an hour maybe lookin' at trees . . ."

"So I said okay, didn't I?" Nicky said.

The man slammed the shanty door shut, and Nicky took hold of Sally's arm again and led her around the shanty into the little forest of trees that covered the vacant lot. There was a dim lighting here from strings of electric bulbs strung up between wooden posts driven into the ground.

"How big a tree you want?" he asked her.

"Just a small one," Sally said. "Not so big as these."

"I guess they got the smaller ones back here."

They walked in among the trees farther back in the lot. Why, it was like a regular forest, Sally thought. All the trees, and the snow falling. Even with the roar of the traffic still discernible, here among the trees, with the sound of the wind and the snow, it was like being far away from the city, out in the country someplace in a woods.

"I hear you're havin' a party tonight," Nicky Toresca said to her. "Joe was tellin' me. I give him the night off so he could come home. Joe's okay, a pretty smart kid, is that right?"

"I guess these trees here are just about right," Sally said steadily.

They stood still then, and Nicky said, "You don't want none of them trees here, they look scrubby. How about that one over there?"

They walked over to it. A small tree, thick with branches and perfect in shape, and covered with little tight clusters of cones.

"It's awful nice, but it's too big," Sally said.

Nicky studied it critically as he sheltered a match for his cigarette. "It ain't so big. If it's the price that's too big, forget it. This one is on me."

This was all a little like a nightmare, Sally thought. If anybody had ever told her that she would be picking out her Christmas tree this year with Nicky Toresca, she would have thought they were crazy. But here she was.

"All right," she said tonelessly. "It's an awful nice tree." She started to turn away, but Nicky Toresca reached out suddenly and stopped her with a hand on her shoulder.

"Wait a minute," he said easily. "I want to talk to you, Sally."

She stopped obediently and waited for him to speak. Her face was perfectly expressionless, except for the way that her mouth turned down at the corners that was sadder than tears. Roy, oh, Roy, she was thinking, it's Christmas Eve tonight, and you're locked up in that place, and Nicky Toresca is buying our Christmas tree!

"You sent back the dress," Nicky Toresca said flatly. "What's the matter, you didn't like it, maybe?"

Sally felt only a little stirring inside of her. "Mr. Toresca," she heard herself saying, "I been wanting to talk to you, too. I guess you got things a little mixed up about me. I sent the dress back because I don't want presents like that from you. Nor I don't like you taking me home or taking me to work in your automobile and talking about having dates with me. I'm married. My husband happens to be sick and in the hospital right now, but I don't have dates. I never did, and I don't now."

Nicky Toresca sent his cigarette flipping off the tips of his fingers into a wide rosy arc in the snow. "That sounds very nice, Sally," he said. "But don't forget I saw you downtown with your boy friend the other night."

"I don't have boy friends," Sally said steadily. "You saw me downtown with Fred Foster. He rooms where I do and he asked me to go along shopping with him and help him pick out presents for his family, that's all."

"I guess if you can go out with one man you can with another. Is that right?" Nicky Toresca said. "Maybe you just got it in your head you don't like me. Well, that's too bad. Because I could do a lot for you, Sally. If you got such a thing in your head, that's too bad."

"No, I don't like you," Sally said. "And you've got a lot of ideas about me that are all wrong. Just because I happen to work for you . . ."

Nicky Toresca's fingers closed hard on Sally's shoulders. "Yes, it just happens you do work for me," he said softly. "And, as far as that goes, so does your brother, is that right? You got some kids to take care of, and, if you are smart like I think you are, you don't want to lose a nice job that pays pretty good money right in the middle of the winter. Do you, Sally?"

"Yes, you're right," Sally said. "Workin' in the restaurant is a good job that pays me good money that I need bad, and it isn't easy to get jobs in this town that pay good money. But I guess this is one job I can't keep. I think maybe I better quit, don't you?"

"No, I don't think you better quit," he said. "You need that job, and hell, I guess I can take a hint."

Sally looked up at him questioningly.

Without warning he pulled her up against him and kissed her, his mouth bruising hard against her lips. Sally's body went perfectly rigid and unresisting. With unblinking eyes she watched snow filtering down among innumerable pine trees and feathering the branches with white.

Nick Toresca put her away from him suddenly, his hands still tight on her shoulders. "Sally," he said, with that peculiar liquid inflection of her name, "Sally, I have been nice and friendly with you, is that right? But sometimes I ain't so friendly to people. It's a funny thing. You can ask anybody in this town, and they will tell you the same. It's a hell of a lot better for anybody to have me nice and friendly, a hell of a lot better."

He released her shoulders and turned around and picked up the little Christmas tree in his gloved hand, reaching in among the thick branches to get hold of the slender trunk. "Maybe you better think about that," he said.

Sally turned around and they started picking their way among the trees back toward the shanty.

"As far as your job goes," Nicky said from behind her, "you can quit or not, just as you please. It's nothing to me. I don't give a damn whether you work at the restaurant or where you work."

Sally felt the snow brushing wet against her face. Idiotically, as they walked out through the trees, a line of a poem that Harold had had to learn once in school came back into her mind. He used to recite it to her, and she had learned it along with him. Something about America and how good it was to be in America and in a friendly Western woodland where nature has her way, in a friendly Western woodland where nature has her way or maybe sway, in a friendly Western woodland where nature has her—in a friendly winter wonderland, bells are ringing, dum de dum dum, people singing, dum de dum dum . . .

Sally stood by silently while Nicky Toresca paid the man in the shanty for the Christmas tree. She stood by silently while the man and Nicky maneuvered the tree into the back of the car.

She got in then, and Nicky slammed the door behind her. He swung the car around with skillful ease and headed directly into the driving snow, toward Horton Street. He didn't speak again, and neither did Sally. The thick snow swirled around the car and packed onto the windshield, so that the wiper moved slowly and made a squeaking noise as it cleared a wide swath on the glass in front of the steering wheel. With the traffic and the storm, the car moved slowly, too. Traffic lights at corners flashed the Christmas colors intermittently. Christmas Eve. This isn't me, and this isn't really Christmas Eve, Sally kept thinking without emotion. This is some bad dream I am having. This is a nightmare where all kinds of wild, impossible things happen, all mixed up with an approximation of reality. There are Christmas presents wrapped up in bright paper, and the children will hang up their stockings, and I will fill them, and there will be the Christmas Eve party tonight, but I mustn't let that fool me, because it isn't real. It couldn't be. We're not living in our own home on Toomis Road, we're in a strange apartment on Horton Street. Roy isn't even there, so it couldn't be home. And Nicky Toresca just bought our Christmas tree and kissed me in a vacant lot among the Christmas trees and said strange threatening things to me that I can't understand. So it can't be true. This is a bad dream I am having. I must keep remembering that. It's a bad dream and that's why I feel so funny, so lifeless, as if I wasn't here or there or anywhere, as if I didn't really exist at all.

Nicky Toresca stopped the car at the curb, and, for a moment, Sally couldn't tell where she was, with the snow falling so thick and this strange dream in which she was caught. Then she recognized the familiar steps and the familiar warped, sloping boards of the narrow porch across the front of the house at Mrs. Gideon's.

"This is the right place, huh?" Nicky Toresca said to her.

"Yes," Sally said. She reached out her hand to the shiny metal door handle. There was no strength in her fingers. Nicky opened the door for her, his gloved hand over hers, pinching her fingers between his hand and the door handle. The heavy door swung open noiselessly and Sally stepped out into the cold and darkness.

"I'll get the tree out for you," he said.

He came around on her side of the car, and Sally stood quietly with the snow wet against her face and catching at her eyelashes, while Nicky Toresca folded the front seat forward and carefully removed the tree from the back seat, turning it this way and that, so that none of the branches would be broken.

He paused with the tree in his hand, looking over the top of it at Sally. "You want me to bring it in for you?"

"No," Sally said, reaching out her hand to take it. "I can make it, all right. Thank you."

They stood together momentarily with the little tree between them catching the snow in a thousand spiny fingers. "Merry Christmas, Sally," Nicky Toresca said. His voice was as soft and expressionless as ever, but the odd liquid inflection that he gave her name was more pronounced.

Out of the detachment from which you watch yourself performing in a dream when you realize that it is only a dream, Sally saw herself grasp the Christmas tree firmly in her hand, and heard herself say in a polite, even voice, "Merry Christmas."

She turned away then and walked up to the porch, carrying the tree at arm's length. Some of the tree branches caught on one of the thin columns on the porch, and she had to stop on the steps and disentangle it. The front door opened just as she got to it, and Mrs. Gideon stood framed in the light of the doorway.

"Hello, there," Mrs. Gideon said warmly. "Why, Sally, if that ain't the prettiest little tree I ever seen! You was later tonight than you planned on, wasn't you? Them kids a yours like to wore out the stairs running down here every time they heard the door open, to see if it wasn't you coming home. My, look at that snow coming down! It's real, old-fashioned Christmas weather tonight, ain't it?"

Sally listened to herself answering Mrs. Gideon a little anxiously, but it was all right. Apparently her role in this strange dream was to be that of her natural cheery talkative self. "Isn't the snow nice, though! I love to have it snow for Christmas. I think this is the nicest Christmas weather we've had in years. Gosh, I thought I never would get home. I had to stop and get the tree, and I was tied up later at the restaurant than I figured, and then with the storm and traffic and all I thought I never would get home."

"I see you got a ride home," Mrs. Gideon said pleasantly. "That was nice. It woulda been awful hard walking in this storm, lugging that tree."

"Yes," Sally said brightly. "I was awful lucky. I got a ride home with someone from the restaurant."

But just then there was a clatter of noise from above, and Buddy and Marilyn came running down the stairs. "Hey, Ma, is that you down there? Ma, did you get the Christmas tree? Ma, we been looking for you! Can we have the party now, Ma? Ma, we got our stockings hung up."

"Hi, darlings, be careful on those stairs! Was I awful late? Did you think your old mother wasn't coming?" Sally set down the Christmas tree and held out her arms to them.

They smothered her with hugs and kisses, but their attention immediately shifted to the Christmas tree. They swarmed around it, examining it from every angle. Buddy whistled loud and shrill through his teeth. "Oh, boy, that's a swell tree!"

Sally never took her eyes from their flushed, excited faces. "Do you like it, darlings? Is it all right? I wish you could have been along to help mother pick it out. Do you think it's big enough?"

"Oh, boy, it's keen," Buddy said. "Where we gonna put it, Ma? Can we have the party now?"

Mrs. Gideon watched them too, with a smile on her broad face. "Kids sure get a kick out of a tree," she said to Sally, fussing with the neck of her new print dress.

"Oh, I meant to ask you," Sally said to her, "was there any mail for me today?"

Mrs. Gideon smoothed her hair surreptitiously, as she thought. "Why, yes, Sally. I think there was. Just five or six Christmas cards. The kids took 'em upstairs. They wasn't no letters though—just . . ."

Buddy was tugging at Sally's coat sleeve. "Can I, Ma? Can I carry the tree upstairs now? Can I?"

"Oh, you better let me. It's kind of a job getting it up the narrow stairs with all those branches sticking out. I better carry it and you can open the door for me."

"Well, come on then," Buddy said impatiently. "Everybody's waiting for the party. Come on!"

"My gosh," Sally said, smiling. "Has the party started already? Who's up there, Buddy?"

"Oh, Fred," he said, "an' Joe an' Miss Sipes an' everybody." He took hold of Mrs. Gideon's hand and said to her artlessly, "An' you're all ready for the party, ain't you?"

"I sure am, Buddy," she said.

"Well, I tell you," Sally said, "you two kids go on ahead and tell them the party is starting, and then you hold the door open and me and Mrs. Gideon will bring the tree. How's that?"

"Okay," he said. He took the lower stair steps in a couple of jumps, but Marilyn lingered behind, close to her mother. Her face was very sober, and she had been less talkative than usual.

"What's the matter, dolly?" her mother said. "You go on up with Buddy, and Mother'll be up in just a minute. I bet you was afraid we wasn't gonna have the party when I was so late. Of course we're gonna have it."

"I want to whisper," Marilyn said gravely.

"All right," Sally said with equal gravity. She leaned down, and the little girl put her arms around her neck and whispered with her lips close to Sally's ear. "Mama, Harold didn't hang up no stocking. He said it was a lot of crap, and he wasn't gonna do it."

"Well, he shouldn't have said that because that's a bad word," Sally whispered back. "But don't you worry, honey. Harold is just getting too old to hang up his stocking. Santa Claus is for little kids like you and Buddy. Santa Claus don't never forget little kids that still believe in him and hang up their stockings."

Marilyn thought over what her mother had said. "Well, I betcha I never get too big to hang up my stocking," she said at last, practically.

Sally squeezed her tight. "Well, don't you dare, baby. Not for a long, long time. Why, what would be the fun a Christmas if Santa Claus couldn't stop here for somebody? Now, you run along upstairs and we'll come with the tree." Buddy's voice filled the hallway as he jumped up and down in the door. "Here they come! Here they come! Here comes the Christmas tree!"

"Well, hi, everybody," Sally said. "Did you think I was never gonna get home here? A fine thing, I invite people to a party, and then I'm not even home when you git here!" The small room was full of people and noise and confusion. Sally carried the Christmas tree in to the middle of the floor, and Mrs. Gideon stopped just inside the door.

"Mrs. Sipes, I'm so glad you could come," Sally chattered. "My, you look nice tonight. That's such a pretty dress. You look so nice."

The dress in question was a dismal red crepe, ripped at the seams, faded in streaks and incredibly dirty. In honor of the festive occasion, Mrs. Sipes was wielding a wobbly, moth-eaten fan of black feathers. Her henna-colored hair was piled high on her head, struggling loose at the neck and forehead. She kept bobbing her head back and forth at Sally, the horn-rimmed glasses shining on her chalky white and red face, and saying, "I was pleased to come," over and over again.

"About time you showed up, Mrs. Otis," Fred Foster howled over the confusion of voices. "About two minutes more'n we'da brought Mrs. Gideon's hat rack up here and trimmed that and had the party without you. Neat lookin' tree you got there."

Fred was standing on a chair, hammer in hand, tacking one of the cellophane wreaths he had bought at the dime store the night before at the top of the window. "Well, hi, Fred," Sally said. "Gee, aren't those wreaths pretty? Look how they shine in the light. Gosh, it certainly does look like Christmas around this place. Those wreaths sure trim the place up." Fred had scattered them around the walls, and they winked red and green on every side.

"Ma, where we gonna set the tree? Where does the tree go, Ma?"

To the children's clamoring, Sally answered, "Sshssh, not so loud. Over there by the window, I guess. Wait till Fred gets down, and we'll try it and see how it looks there."

Sally pulled her hat off and scrambled out of her coat. "Joey," she said, lifting her voice again, "oh, I'm so glad you could come! It wouldn't have been Christmas without my baby brother."

"Hi yuh, Sis, Merry Christmas," Joe said awkwardly from his seat in the corner where Harold lurked behind his chair like a little shadow. On her way to the closet to hang up her coat and hat, Sally dropped a kiss on Joe's forehead. The part of Sally that watched the dream in which she was lost, said, see, this couldn't be real, that couldn't really be Joe, not that fellow in the brand-new suit with his hair slicked back so smooth, lolling there in that chair with a cigarette hanging out of his mouth, like a cheap carbon copy of Nicky Toresca.

Sally slammed the closet door, and stopped to kiss Virginia, who was curled up on the end of the davenport with a blanket over her feet and legs. "How you feel, honey? You look fine."

Virginia was in bathrobe and slippers, and her dark hair was combed back neatly from her pinched white face. "Oh, I feel all right," she said in her hoarse voice. "I'll stay up for awhile, I guess."

"That's fine," Sally said. "And if you start feeling bad or gettin' too tired, you just go on back to bed, won't you?"

Fred Foster clambered down from his chair laboriously and surveyed his handiwork, the shiny red-cellophane wreath swinging at the top of the window. "That's all right," he said appreciatively. "Where you want the tree, Sally, over here by the window?"

"Yes, don't you think, Fred? Here, wait a minute, I'll pin the curtains back out of the way." Sally scurried over to the library table in the corner and searched for pins in the drawer. On a corner of the table top she saw the little stack of envelopes, the mail from that day's delivery. She slipped them into the pocket of her uniform and then went to the window and folded up the curtains, securing them with pins.

Fred carried the little tree over and placed it in front of the window. "How should it go?" he said, twisting it this way and that. "Which is the best-lookin' side of it? You oughta have the best-lookin' side of it facing out in the room."

"Why, Fred, I don't think it matters which side you have facin' out," Mrs. Gideon said critically from the davenport. "That tree is just about shaped perfect. I don't think it makes much difference."

"Very nice tree, very nice," Mrs. Sipes murmured, fluttering her fan in front of her face. Little pieces of the feathers came loose every time she shook the fan and floated in the air around her, like a black snow storm.

"That'll be fine, Fred," Sally said. "Just the way you got it now. Does it stand level on the standard the way it is now?"

"Seems to," Fred said, squatting on the floor to study the little standard of rough boards that held the tree upright on the floor. Buddy and Marilyn squatted on the floor too, one on either side of him.

"Let's cover up the standard with some tissue paper," Sally suggested. "You kids know where it is. You go find Mother some sheets of tissue paper, will you?"

The children ran off to the kitchen, stumbling against each other in their haste.

"I can do that, Sally," Fred said. "What you want, just some paper wrapped around them boards?"

"Yeah, it makes it look a little nicer. If you'd just as soon, Fred. I wanta skip in and change my dress."

"You go ahead," he said. "We'll handle it, won't we, kidlets?"

Once she was in the bedroom with the door shut behind her, Sally looked over the stack of Christmas cards that had come in the mail that day. She shuffled through them rapidly without opening them, looking only at handwriting and postmarks. Nothing from Roy. Nothing from Petey. Sally changed her dress and tidied her hair.

Back in the living room, she said, "Gee, that looks fine, Fred. Now, before we start trimmin' the tree, I wanta run over to O'Connor's a minute and see if I can't get Gloria to come over."

The voices thinned out a little, and Fred said soberly, "How is Johnny, anyway?"

"Well, not so good, I guess," Sally answered. "He had to stay in the hospital, you know."

For a moment the room was quiet and then Sally went on. "Look," she said, "after Gloria gets over here, let's not talk about Johnny, huh? She knows we all like Johnny and how worried we are about him and all that, so if we just keep talking about him it'll only remind her and make her feel bad. Let's just not say anything about him after she gets here."

Sally slipped out and hurried down the dark cold hall. The radio sounded loud from the other side of the door, so she opened it without knocking. Gloria sat alone on the end of the davenport, with her hands folded in her lap, and the little Christmas tree that Johnny had trimmed the night before was shining bravely in the small hot room.

Gloria raised her eyes slowly as Sally came in. "Hello," she said, distantly.

Sally's heart was touched, Gloria looked so lonely and forlorn and so very lovely. Her hair was combed out loose, shining thick and golden to her shoulders. She had on a pink dress of some soft material, with a myriad of tiny ruffles at the neck and wrists.

Sally went to her and took hold of her hand. "We're getting ready to trim the tree now," she said, "and we want you to come. Come on, honey, we'll leave the doors open and then if Bevvy cries we can hear her. You come on, you'll feel a lot better than just sitting around here alone. Worrying isn't gonna help Johnny any. He wants you to come and have a good time, honey."

"I don't want to come," Gloria said.

"Oh, sure you do!" Sally urged, tugging at her hand. "You'll have a good time, Gloria. We can't have any fun, thinking about you sitting over here all alone. We're all just as worried about Johnny as you are almost, but Johnny don't want us to sit around and worry. He wants us to go ahead and have a good time, the same as if he was here."

Gloria's voice sounded close to tears. "I don't want to come," she said. "Everything's spoiled. Johnny is staying in the hospital and my whole Christmas is spoiled."

"Well, he can't help that, honey," Sally said patiently. "It's all spoiled for him, too. Just think how bad he feels about it. You come on over now and help us trim the tree."

Gloria was weakening a little. "Well . . ." she said doubtfully.

Sally tugged at her hand again, pulling her up from the davenport. "Sure, you want to come, honey. You'll have a good time, you wait and see."

As they started to leave, Sally went back and snapped off the radio. "So we will be sure to hear Bevvy if she wakes up," she explained. They left the door ajar and went down the hall toward Sally's apartment where the sound of the conglomeration of voices floated out into the hallway.

When they went in, Fred Foster whistled loud and long. "Oh, boy, here comes the angel for the Christmas tree," he said appreciatively. "Hi yuh, Gloria."

"Hi," Gloria said. Her manner was still a little distant, and she stood awkwardly just inside the door.

"Wait, I'll get you a chair from the bedroom," Sally said to her, slipping around her toward the bedroom door.

"Ma, now can we trim the tree? Are we all ready now?" The children called after her.

"Yup, now we're gonna trim the tree," Sally told them. She brought the chair for Gloria and then got the boxes of trimmings out of the closet.

"This is how we do it," Buddy explained to everybody importantly. "First Ma puts the lights on the tree, and then me and Marilyn hand her the other stuff and she hangs it on the tree for us."

"That's right," Sally said, laughing. "And it's up to you folks to help me and tell me if I'm doing it right and where to put stuff."

Fred Foster came up and whispered into Sally's ear elaborately, just as she lifted the first string of lights out of the box. "Look, how's about me going out in the kitchen and popping the popcorn for you? I'm a good hand at popping corn, and then it will be all ready to eat when you get the trimmings on the tree, huh?"

"Well, that would be swell, if you want to, Fred. That would be a big help."

"Okay," he said, "so it's settled." As he started for the kitchen door he beckoned to Joe. "Come on, Joey," he said. "Let's you and me go pop corn. I bet you shake a mean corn popper, Joey."

As Joe got up from his chair, Fred winked at him. "I got the refrigerator all stocked up this afternoon when I heard you was comin', pal."

Sally raised her voice above the laughter. "Well, that's fine, boys. But the popcorn's right there in that sack on the shelf by the cupboard, and if we don't hear it poppin' inside of five minutes we'll be coming out in the kitchen to see what you're doing."

Just as she started to hang the string of lights over the branches, Sally saw Harold out of the corner of her eye, sliding toward the kitchen door after Joe and Fred. She said instantly, "Harold, you want to come and help me with these lights? You hold this part of it, while I get these up by the top of the tree."

Harold came to her slowly and reluctantly and held the lights as she directed. Sally only had two strings of lights, and it took a great deal of stretching and maneuvering to make them do for a tree of this size. When she had them all arranged, she said, "Now everybody close your eyes while I plug in the lights to see if they are working. Nobody but me is supposed to see the tree lighted till it's all fixed."

With joking and laughter everyone promised to close their eyes, even Mrs. Sipes. Sally plugged the double socket into the floor plug and watched the little bulbs wink on all over the tree. Two red bulbs together there near the top. Sally unscrewed the little hot bulb, gingerly, and exchanged it for a blue one in one of the lower branches. She pulled out the socket from the wall. "Everything is fine, you can open your eyes now," she said.

The rest of the tree trimming moved more slowly. The children took infinite time, poring over the boxes, before they selected just the ornament that they thought ought to go onto the tree next. Sally waited for them patiently and hung the colored balls, and squat Santa Clauses, and tinsel bells over the tree, pausing frequently to ask advice from her audience. Finally all the ornaments were hung except the battered old tinsel star which, according to family tradition, went at the very top of the tree, and by the same tradition was always put on the tree last. The sound of corn popping came from the kitchen intermittently, and once Sally called out and asked Fred and Joe to put the coffee water on to boil. Next came the strands of tinsel rope which were woven in and out among the branches. Now the tree was taking on sparkle and color. It was no longer a squat sturdy little spruce from the north woods, it was a Christmas tree.

The tinfoil icicles came last of all, and everybody was invited to participate in hanging them from the branches. The children, Harold, and Mrs. Gideon immediately volunteered, and Sally stood back a little with a handful of them, filling the spots on the tree that the rest of them neglected from time to time.

At last the very last icicle was hung. The two younger children were almost trembling with excitement. "Now, is it time for the star? Now, is it time for the star?" they chanted.

"Yes," Sally said gravely. "Now it's time for the star." They squabbled together momentarily as to which of them was to have the honor of bringing the star to their mother. Sally settled the argument by suggesting that they both bring the box to her. They carried the box together, and Sally lifted the battered old star out of the tissue paper tenderly. Their Christmas tree star, the star that had been on the very first Christmas tree that she and Roy had had together. The children knew all about the star. Other tree ornaments were broken and thrown away from year to year. But this star was special, this star always crowned their Christmas tree, year after year. Sally stood on tiptoe to affix it to the tip of the topmost branch of the little tree. Funny how a dream could be so real, she thought. Here she was hanging up their Christmas star on another tree, as she had done so many years before, but this was only a dream, she knew it was.

Once the star shone above the tree, the children were so excited they couldn't stand still. "Now, is it time?" they wanted to know of their mother, breathlessly.

"In just a minute," Sally said. "Tell Fred and Joe to come in now, and then when everybody's here, it'll be time."

The children ran shrieking to the kitchen, and when Fred and Joe appeared in the doorway, the children dragging them by the hands, Sally explained the next step in the ritual. Now that the tree was all trimmed, the next thing was the presents. She would give a signal, and then everybody ran to where their presents for each other were hidden and brought them out and put them under the tree. Then when the presents were all under the tree, the lights were lighted. "I'll say one, two, three, go," Sally explained, while the children waited with held breath, like runners before a hundred-yard dash.

"Oh, boy, is this gonna be a scramble," Fred Foster said, rubbing his hands together. "Okay, Sally, we're all ready, give us the signal!"

"All right," she said, "here I go!" She counted slowly and dramatically, spacing the words in rising climax. "One—two—three—go!"

All the tension in the room broke up into a riot of confusion. Buddy and Marilyn flopped down on their stomachs instantly, and began pawing their presents out from under the davenport, where their joint cache had been hidden. Fred disappeared at a gallop in the direction of his room, Joe and Harold in the direction of the room they shared. Only Mrs. Sipes and Virginia remained still. Sally saw Gloria O'Connor slide out the door. Good, she was glad now she had presents for all the O'Connors. She just wished now that it had been more, with Johnny sick and everything. And there went Mrs. Gideon too, running awkwardly, puffing for breath. There, Sally thought, she might of known that Mrs. Gideon would have some little remembrance for them, and she had never thought to get a thing for the Gideons. Oh, well, she had an extra box of the quarter candy all wrapped for just such an emergency as this. She would put that under the tree with Mrs. Gideon's name on it tonight, and tomorrow she'd take down a little remembrance for Mr. Gideon and the old lady. Cigarettes for him, maybe, and a handkerchief or something like that for Mrs. Gideon's mother.

Sally hurried off to the bedroom closet where she had hidden her own gifts. In the bedroom she hurriedly scribbled Mrs. Gideon's name on the plain white tissue in which the candy box was wrapped. Then she gathered up all the packages until both arms were full of them, and went back to the living room. The little Christmas tree was all but hidden from view with people crowding around trying to get near enough to arrange their armload of presents at the bottom of it. Laughter and confusion filled the little room. Fred Foster openly confessed that it was going to take him another trip, that he still had more presents to come. Where in the world did all these packages come from, Sally marveled, when she got near enough to the tree to deposit her own load. Why, there were piles of packages! All those bunchy ones, clumsily wrapped and conspicuously sprinkled with stickers, must be Buddy and Marilyn's gifts. That stack of shining, elegantly wrapped ones, so apparently the product of a department-store wrapping service, must be Joe's. Fred Foster came hurrying back with another armload of big packages of strange irregular shapes. Toys for the kids, Sally diagnosed them. She had told him not to buy them a lot of stuff. Fred didn't have much money, but he had the biggest heart in the world, and once he got excited about Christmas there just wasn't any stopping him.

At last all the presents were deposited, a shining multi-colored heap all out of proportion to the little tree it surrounded. Then everybody returned to their chairs and Sally plugged in the light switch. The twenty or thirty little bulbs came alive with color, shining over the tree and the pile of presents. The children shrieked in a kind of contented excitement.

"Now what happens? Do we open the presents?" Fred wanted to know.

"No, sir," Sally said positively. "No presents get opened around here until Christmas morning. Now comes coffee and popcorn and candy."

Sally hurried to the kitchen. Fred followed her out and volunteered his services; but when she assured him there was nothing he could do to help her, he poured a beer apiece for Joe and himself and went back to the living room. Sally worked quickly. The coffee first and after that plates of the little frosted cookies of many shapes that the children loved, plates of her homemade candy, a couple of bowls of hard candy, a big dish of nuts, one of fruit.

Joe and Fred came to assist her in carrying in the cups of hot coffee and the dishes of food. Sally found time to get three or four of her red Christmas candles from the cupboard. They were complete with little green tin holders. She put one on the library table, one on the little table at the end of the davenport, and one on the window sill, well out of the way of the Christmas tree. That one was for Santa Claus, she explained. Then, after the food was distributed, plates loaded with cookies and candy and fruit, she lighted the candles and turned off the electric lights. The room shone with the soft light from the Christmas tree bulbs and from the flickering candles. Fred's cellophane wreaths danced brighter in the soft light and the room smelled of warm pine needles.

Why, this was just wonderful, Mrs. Gideon said in a warm, almost tearful voice. Everything was so beautiful, the candles and the tree and all. She really believed that this was the nicest Christmas party she had ever been to in all her life. She just wished that Mama could be here to see it all and enjoy it. Yes, it was certainly very nice, Mrs. Sipes said, fluttering her fan vaguely. She was certainly very pleased to be here.

The children sat with their plates on the floor at Sally's feet. How would Buddy like to recite the piece he learned for the Christmas program at school? Sally suggested. Buddy needed little urging. With his mouth full of candy he began to rattle off the rhymed words so rapidly that no one could understand what he was talking about. Sally stopped him and suggested that he start all over again, and slower this time. So Buddy started again, without so much assurance, and, with several promptings from his mother, was able to recite the entire rhyme. Marilyn became a little tearful. She didn't have a piece to recite, she protested. She had been in a play, and her lines didn't make sense without the others to go with them, even if she could remember them. Sally suggested that she should recite the last four lines, the little ditty that came last of all in the play. Marilyn became a little shy about it, and everybody had to coax her before she was persuaded to recite the four short lines in such a soft voice that the words were all but indistinguishable. At that point Fred Foster wanted to know in an aggrieved voice if they didn't want him to recite his piece. Upon everyone's assurance that they most certainly did, he started forth on the traditional "'Twas the night before Christmas and all through the house . . ." Before he was half through with it his memory failed him and he went down in ignominious defeat. But, surprisingly enough, it was Mrs. Sipes who saved the situation for him. She knew the rest of it and proceeded to recite it in her shaking, quavering, old voice, to a round of applause at the end.

In the flickering candle light, Sally looked at Harold and asked him cautiously if he would like to tell the Christmas story. Other years it had been customary for him to tell the Christmas story for the benefit of his younger brother and sister. But Harold became agonizingly embarrassed and declined hastily. Sally did not press the point. Well, that was all right, she said. She guessed everybody knew the Christmas story, anyway.

Now, was it time for the singing? the younger children wanted to know, looking up to their mother expectantly. Yes, she guessed it was, if they wanted to sing. They led off with "Jingle Bells," which everyone in the room knew and joined in enthusiastically. After that Sally started "It Came upon the Midnight Clear." She did not get such full and enthusiastic support on that. No one seemed to remember all of the words except Sally herself and the children, who had occasion to sing it each year in school. After it was over, without hardly pausing for breath, Buddy and Marilyn started again in their shrill, sweet, off-key voices, and Sally joined with them on the old familiar words:

> *"Silent night, holy night*
> *All is calm, all is bright . . ."*

Once that song was finished the room was all but still. Buddy and Marilyn started again, a duet sustained by their mother's humming of the melody, the old Luther cradle hymn, made appealing by their childish voices:

> *"Away in a manger*
> *No crib for his bed,*
> *The little Lord Jesus*
> *Lay down his sweet head . . ."*

Sally watched their small upturned faces, as they sang together, stumbling over the words a little, a little uncertain of the key, but enrapt and lost in the old familiar words and melody. Beyond the dream world where Sally watched it all, she felt warm tears come to her eyes. When the song was finished she leaned down and drew Marilyn up against her knees and kissed her. She heard herself saying softly into the little girl's ear, in a warm, broken voice, "Aw, baby, I miss Daddy, don't you?" But Marilyn's face was quite blank and uncomprehending. "Don't you wish Daddy could be with us tonight?" Sally said again softly. Marilyn wrinkled her forehead a little in thought. "Well, I guess so," she said, and then she added in her practical, matter-of-fact voice, looking up into her mother's face, "but Daddy's dead, ain't he, Mama?"

The tears rolled down Sally's cheeks then. "Oh, no, no, lover, no," she said. "Daddy isn't dead. He's away in the hospital, sick. He loves you so much, dolly. And he wanted to be home with you for Christmas. I've told you, can't you remember?"

Buddy was tugging at her skirt insistently. "Come on, Ma," he said impatiently. "Now it's time for your song. Now you gotta sing your song. It's time. Come on, Ma."

"Oh, Buddy," Sally said. "Nobody wants to hear me sing all alone. I don't sing very good all by myself. Let's not have that song tonight."

"You gotta," Buddy insisted earnestly. "It's part of the party. You gotta sing your song."

"Sure," Marilyn chimed. "You gotta!"

"Come on, Sally," Fred Foster said. "We don't want to miss none of the party. Let's hear your song."

"Well, I'm not very good at singing," Sally said, "it's just something the kids like to hear."

She waited a minute, trying to force the tears back out of her voice. Not this song, not now. It wasn't anything about the song, except that to her it always seemed the sweetest of all the Christmas songs, and for some unaccountable reason very sad. They knew she liked it, Roy and the children, and they always made her sing it. But tonight was a dream. How could she sing it when Roy wasn't here to squeeze her hand when it was over, and joke her a little about the tears that it always brought to her eyes?

The children waited expectantly, and Sally began the song bravely in her high clear voice:

*"Oh, little town of Bethlehem*
*How still I see thee lie*
*Above thy deep and dreamless sleep*
*The silent stars go by*
*But in thy dark streets, shineth*
*The everlasting light*
*The hopes and fears of all the years*
*Are met in thee tonight."*

Sally started on the second verse, but the tears were welling up faster, and it was all she could do to keep them back. Oh, she couldn't go on, she couldn't finish it. This dream must end, somehow. She couldn't go on dreaming it, it was too painful, there were too many memories. Sally clenched her hands tight and struggled on, struggled to keep the tears back and her voice even, but her voice began to waver, in spite of herself. She couldn't go on, she couldn't!

Then the interruption came, and Sally stopped singing. Nobody noticed, because they were all listening to the cyclone of sounds below—doors banging, a rich booming laughter, and then a clatter of feet coming up the stairs. A rich, deep, loud voice from the hallway. "Jesus, brother, watch that top step, it's darker'n Tut's Tomb in this joint!" Then the voice grew louder and the rush of steps came down the hall. "Hey, hey! Does Sally Otis live someplace in this house? Sally! Where are you, honey! Sally!"

Sally jumped to her feet, her face suddenly white and tense. The door stood ajar, and the first thing that came in view was a long, silk-stockinged leg with a black suede pump as the door was kicked open—and there she was. A tall girl, who seemed to fill the whole doorway and then the whole room. A tall girl with a mane of black curly hair to her shoulders, dressed in black, with the tails of a couple of silver foxes bumping at her knees, and a silly little hat stuck on the back of her head, with a couple of yards of veil trailing behind her. Her arms were filled to overflowing with the sparkle and color of paper- and ribbon-wrapped packages.

"Sally, baby!" she said in her amazing deep voice.

"Oh, Petey, Petey!" Sally said. Suddenly the dream was over for Sally, and it became reality. She crumpled up into the chair and began to cry as if her heart would break, as if she would never stop crying again.

Petey unceremoniously dumped her armload of packages into Fred Foster's lap. "Here, hold these a minute," she said, "and, for Christ's sakes, don't drop 'em. Some of 'em break."

In two strides she was across the little room and her arms were around Sally. "Aw, Sally! Things have been tough for you, kid, haven't they? Why didn't you let me know? Why didn't you let me help?"

"Oh, Petey! Petey!" Sally sobbed again. She was shaking convulsively with her crying, and she hung on to Petey tight.

"Relax, honey. Don't hang on so tight," Petey said with an incredible gentleness in her deep voice. "You know I'll never go away and leave you in this mess, don't you? Everything is gonna be all right, kid. Petey's come home for Christmas!"

She pulled the little hat off her thick dark hair suddenly, shook it hard and dropped it on the floor. "Ugh, wet," she said to everybody in the room in particular. "It's snowin' outdoors like the other side a Siberia!"

She turned back to Sally and pushed her away from her gently, holding her by the shoulders. "Don't cry so, Sally. I've been bad, haven't I? I should have come here as soon as you wrote me last spring about the mess you were in. But, kid, I never figured things were going so bad, for you, honest."

"Say, lady," a man's voice said plaintively from the doorway. Everybody in the room jumped, because everybody in the room was looking at Petey.

Petey's laughter filled the room. "Pal, for a minute here you musta thought you were the forgotten man."

It was the taxi driver, who had trailed Petey up the stairs with another armload of Christmas gifts, standing patiently inside the door, with packages piled in his arms up to his nose.

"Here, I'll take part of those," Petey said. "By the looks of things around here, I guess you unload over here by the tree."

Together, she and the driver deposited the packages with the rest of them by the tree, and then Petey snapped open the big suede purse she carried under her arm. "Well, Merry Christmas, Joe," she said, handing him a couple of bills rolled up small in her hand.

The taxi driver glanced at the bills surreptitiously as he pocketed them and smiled broadly. "Thank you," he said. "Merry Christmas."

As Petey swung around from the door, her eye caught Joe, sitting on the chair in the corner. She paused, transfixed, and then moved toward him slowly, her hands outstretched. "Joey! Little brother Joey!" she marveled. "Honey, I haven't seen you more'n three times since you been out of diapers. Come here and give me a big kiss. I bet you don't even remember me. My God, maybe you don't even know who I am!"

Joe got up to meet her a little awkwardly. "Well, I remember a little and I heard a lot," he said, "and seeing there couldn't be anybody else like you in the world, that makes you my sister Petey."

"It certainly does," Fred Foster murmured ecstatically, still holding her packages carefully just as she had dropped them upon him.

Petey kissed Joe and hugged him hard, and then she turned back to the others. "Now wait a minute," she said. "Maybe I've got some more relatives mixed up in this party." Here eyes traveled from one face to another. "I don't mean you, dear," she added, snapping her fingers at the goggle-eyed Fred Foster. "Joe's the only man in this family."

Her eyes came to rest momentarily on Gloria O'Connor, and she tilted her head, looking up and down appreciatively. "And it wouldn't be you, sweet," she murmured. "We don't grow blondes in our family."

Then she saw Virginia huddled in her corner of the davenport. Petey was across the room instantly, with her amazing long stride. Virginia raised her small white face to her mutely, and Petey was silent for a moment. "You're Virginia," she said at last. "You see, I've got all the advantage. I can remember you when you were a baby. But I bet I know what you feel like when a great big grown-up woman that you've never seen before in your life comes busting in here and tells you she's your sister." Petey stooped suddenly and kissed Virginia on the forehead. "Never mind, darling," she said, "some of these days we'll take a day off and get acquainted, you wait and see."

As she straightened up, Petey shook a finger at Harold. "And I don't need to look but once to tell who you are. I know your father, so I couldn't miss on you. Hi yuh, Harold." And then all in one sudden motion she scooped up the children from the floor, one in either arm. "You're Buddy," she said, kissing his astonished little face hard. "And you're Marilyn." She kissed her too, and then she kissed them both again. "And who am I?" she said. "Quick, now, one, two, three, four, five, six . . ."

"Aunt Petey!" both children screamed together, winding their arms around her neck and covering her face with kisses. Petey shook her thick hair back, and her great laugh boomed in the little room. "There," she said, as she put the children down, "that's better. That's the kind of welcome home I like to get." She knelt down suddenly in front of the children and said to them gravely, "Say, I want to tell you before I forget. I went to see Santa Claus last week, and while I was there I took a peek at his list, you know, all the kids where he had to stop tonight. And darned if right up there near the top of the list I didn't see your names, honest. There they were, Marilyn Otis, Buddy Otis, just like that, right up there at the top among the best kids in the country. You got your stockings hung up?"

"Sure," Buddy said importantly. "That's mine right over there, see?" He pointed to the limp stocking hanging from the top of the chair in which Joe Braun was sitting.

"And that one's mine," Marilyn said pointing to another.

"That's good, that's fine," Petey said. "Now, the thing is for you to get to bed pretty soon so Santa Claus can come. You don't wanta hold him up, you know. He's got an awful lotta places to stop tonight."

Sally got up from her chair then and came to Petey's side. In that short space of time, Sally had gotten control of herself again. Her eyes were swollen, her face flushed with tears, and her voice still a little uneven, but her crying had stopped. "I'm terribly sorry, Petey," she said. "I'm terribly sorry, everybody. I guess I must have been tired out or something, to go to pieces like that." She took hold of Petey's hand firmly in her own. "I want you all to meet my sister, Petey. Petey, this is Mrs. Gideon, she's our landlady from downstairs. And this is Gloria O'Connor, the O'Connors live down the hall. This is Mrs. Sipes from upstairs, and this is Fred Foster . . ."

"From across the hall," Fred broke in. "It's a neighborhood party. Hi!"

"Hi, Fred," Petey said. "Looky, you don't have to set around here all night holding those packages of mine. I'm sorry, let me take part of them, and let's put 'em under the tree."

As they knelt in front of the tree to unload the packages, Petey kept on talking. "I know all about Sally's Christmas parties. What gives next? I see I'm too late for the tree trimmin', and, from the sound when I come in down below, I'm late for the singing. What I really hope I'm not too late for is some coffee and some of them good cookies Sally makes. How about it, Sally?"

"Oh, gosh, Petey, I shoulda thought!" Sally said penitently. "Look, I'll get you a cup a hot coffee right away. Gee, a fine thing, you come home here, and what do I do, I cry my eyes out and forget to introduce you to folks, and don't feed you and . . ."

"Sure, isn't she awful!" Petey said.

Sally hurried out to the kitchen, and Mrs. Gideon got to her feet. "Well, I have to be getting along downstairs," she said. "My mother is with me and she's sick in bed," she confided to Petey, "and I better get back and see how she is." Mrs. Gideon raised her voice a little. "Sally, I had an awful nice time to your party. And, Sally, I was thinking, now your sister's come, I know you ain't got a mite of extra room up here, why don't you have her sleep in that extra bedroom of mine downstairs? It's awful little, an' it ain't fancy, but she's just as welcome to have it as she can be . . ."

"Aw, thanks, Mrs. Gideon," Petey said, taking her hand and squeezing it hard. "That's awfully sweet of you. But I've visited Sally before, and I know how it is when you've got a small place and kids and everything. So I took a room at the hotel and left my bags and everything there before I came over here. Thanks, just the same, anyway."

"Well, you're welcome any time," Mrs. Gideon said warmly. "I'll see you again while you're here. I think it's just awful nice for Sally that you could come."

Everyone took their cue from Mrs. Gideon and the party melted away, Gloria, and Mrs. Sipes, Fred Foster last of all, lingering in the doorway regretfully. Harold and Virginia went off to bed, and the small children began the old argument about whose turn it was first in the bathroom. Joe too got to his feet, and went to the closet for his coat and hat, where he had hung them as he came in. Petey shoved her coat and furs to the other end of the davenport and sat down, kicking off her shoes and stretching her long arms and legs luxuriously.

"You goin' someplace, Joey?"

"Yeah, I got some things to tend to yet tonight. I gotta job, you know. I'm workin' for Nicky Toresca," he added impressively.

"Well, I wouldn't know," Petey said sweetly. "I never heard of the gent."

"Well, you will, if you stay around this town long enough," Joe bragged.

"Well, fine," Petey said. She studied Joe quizzically from under her long black lashes as he got into his coat and hat.

"I'll have your coffee in a minute, Petey," Sally called from the kitchen. "I made some fresh."

"Oh, you shouldn't have bothered," Petey said. "So long, Joey, we'll see you tomorrow. Don't forget to hang up your stocking and eat the bananas before they get black."

She watched Joe leave, a look of speculation on her face, her head resting on her doubled arms. The moment the door shut behind him, she was off the davenport in a bound and out to the kitchen.

"Hey, hey, what gives?" she said to Sally. "What kind of job has our little brother Joey got that takes him out this late at night and makes him strut around here like he was God's right-hand angel?"

Sally poured coffee into two cups without answering. "Wait till I get your lunch ready and then we'll talk," she answered.

Petey studied Sally's face, her own face puzzled. "Just coffee for me and lots of it, and let's have it here in the kitchen, huh, just like old times. I'll help you clear off this table."

The sisters removed the clutter of dirty cups, paper sacks and empty beer bottles from the table, and Sally wiped the oil cloth carefully with the dishcloth.

"Go ahead and set down," Petey said. "I'll go get my cigarettes." She was back in an instant with her long quick stride and took the chair across the table from Sally.

"Oh, boy, this is good," she said to Sally affectionately, as she ripped open the cigarette package. "It was worth the trip, honey."

After their cigarettes were lighted, the sisters studied each other across the table unashamedly.

"It must be three years," Sally said wonderingly.

"Oh, Jesus," Petey said.

And still they looked at each other.

"Sally, how do you do it?" Petey burst out at last. "You have trouble, hard work, worry, but you never get a day older. Just look at you! A little tired around the edges maybe, but not a day older! My God, you'll stay about fourteen as long as you live."

Sally smiled her warm, wide-lipped smile. She tried to smooth down her short tousled hair, and she fussed with the frayed neck of her old red jersey dress. "I look a mess," she said half-apologetically. "I always do. I never have time to fix myself up, and what would be the use if I did?"

"Fancy clothes, beauty shops," Petey dismissed them all with a gesture of her long slim hand, with nails painted so red they were almost black. "You don't need 'em, honey. You got something there."

Sally laughed a little. "Well, I oughta have white hair and wrinkles by now. If I look the same, I guess it's because I stay young with the kids. You should talk about staying young! You look younger every time I see you."

"Me! Ha ha!" Petey's laughter boomed. "Honey, you need glasses. I'm an old hag! Look at me! I pull out a handful of white hairs every month. I'm wrinkled, I've got suitcases under the eyes . . ."

"You're beautiful, and you know it," Sally said firmly.

And, in a way, Petey was beautiful. Her big, well-formed body, slender in the tight-fitting black dress. Her smooth dark skin, tanned evenly by the sun. The great mass of blue-black curly hair to her shoulders. Her eyes were large and brown, with long dark lashes, and great smudges of shadow underneath them. Her restless red mouth with the laughter wrinkles at the corners. Above all was the vitality about her that you felt even when she was sitting still like this, as if she were really on her feet and pacing the little room with her long nervous stride.

"You're so tanned," Sally marveled. "Where have you been since New York? Where did you come from?"

"Since New York? Oh, God! Florida, Cuba, Bermuda, Nassau . . ." Petey ticked them off on her fingers. "Way to hell and gone! I came up here from Florida. Nice country down below. I have a notion to bleach my hair and try South America."

"Gee!" Sally laid her cigarette down on the ash tray and stared at her sister, chin propped on her hand. "Gosh, it must be wonderful to go to places way off like that! Me, I've never been five hundred miles away from home in my life. That's just wonderful, Petey." Then she added, with just a strain of carefulness in her voice, "How did you happen to be way off there in all them places? Was you working down there?"

Petey's left eyebrow had a trick of twitching a little and then doubling up into a little v-shape pointing up her forehead when she was amused, turning her momentarily into a handsome Mephistopheles. "Working?" she said cheerfully. "Not this child!"

Sally was silent, and a little disapproval showed on her face in spite of herself.

"It was all right," Petey said. "Lots of fun, lots of sunshine, lots of boatrides, lots of music, lots of dancing. When I bailed out, we shook hands on it. I got a trunkful a new clothes, enough money to come up here on, and move on again in a few days." Petey hunched her shoulders and turned her hands palms outward.

Sally knocked the ashes from the tip of her cigarette carefully without speaking.

Petey reached out and closed one of Sally's hands tight in hers. "Yeah, I know, honey. Come on, now it's your turn to give me the little pep talk. It wouldn't seem like I'd come home, if you don't."

"Well, gosh," Sally burst out at last. "It doesn't do the slightest bit of good for me to say anything. You know what I'm going to say before I say it, and you don't pay no attention to it. I hate to go sticking my nose in and tellin' you what to do. It isn't any of my business, but I just can't help it. I don't like the way you live, and I can't help it. I don't think it's right; it isn't right, either. Maybe it's all right for some people, if that's the way they want to live and they don't know any better. But not for you, Petey. You're not that kind of a woman. It isn't the right kind of a life for you. Maybe it's kind of fun at the time, bein' on the loose, fancy clothes, new places and new—people, but what is it going to get you? Petey, honey, why don't you . . ."

Petey drowned her out with her laughter. "I know, why don't I get married and settle down and have some kids," she mimicked in a singsong voice. Then her face turned more serious again, and she patted Sally's hand affectionately. "No, darling, you got me wrong. I been a bachelor too long. There'll never be no one man for me, nor no one house nor no one place. Uh uh. It just wasn't meant that way, and I haven't got any kick coming. You have your life, and I have mine. It's just the way we are."

"Well, don't be so sure about it," Sally said warningly. "Some day you may meet a man somewhere . . ."

"Honey, I have!" Petey was laughing again. "I've met a whole slew of men. I've met practically every kind of man there is. Of course, I love 'em. I love 'em all."

"You know what I mean," Sally said.

"Sure, I do. But I'm not worrying." Petey jumped up and got the coffee pot from the stove and filled their cups again. "Looky, let's talk about you. I got a feeling you got plenty to tell me. I knew that the minute I walked in here tonight and saw your face."

"Oh, gosh." Sally sighed deeply as she stirred the sugar into her coffee.

"Maybe you're too tired to talk tonight," Petey said sympathetically. "You look tired, Sally. Maybe we better postpone this little session till tomorrow night or sometime, huh?"

Sally shook her head. "I am tired, but I'd rather talk, honest. Gee, Petey, if you knew how long it's been since I've had a chance to talk to anybody. It seems like I'd bust if I didn't talk. But maybe you're too tired, maybe you don't want to hear all about my little old troubles. I guess it won't be very interesting for you, just having to sit here while I spill my head off and . . ."

"Hey, hey!" Petey stopped her. "Now wait a minute! Where'd you get that in your head? Has there ever been a time in our lives that we didn't tell each other just what was on our minds or that one of us didn't want to do everything we could to help the other if the other of us was in a jam? That's what families are for, and we're the only family each other's got. You give with the trouble, and I'll take it, don't you worry about that."

"You'll never know how glad I was to see you walk in tonight," Sally said. "Honest, Petey, you'll never know how glad I was. Once in awhile things get all balled up for me till it seems like I can't go on for another day. I don't know what in the world I'd of ever done if you hadn't come tonight."

"There, that's more like it," Petey said.

She leaned back in her chair, and lit another cigarette, waving the match slowly in the air to extinguish it, her eyes on Sally's face.

Sally turned her coffee cup in her saucer slowly. At last she looked up to Petey with a little laugh that was almost a sob. "Honest, I've got so much to tell, I don't know where to begin."

"Well, let's start with Roy," Petey said. "Is he better or worse? When is he gonna get out of that place?"

And then Sally started talking, the words rushing out, and she talked for a long time. All her troubles and worries. Roy and Harold and Virginia and Joe. Financial troubles, her job, and finally, Nicky Toresca and her fear of him. Petey asked quick questions about Nicky Toresca and Sally described him as best she could. They talked of many things and the cigarette butts piled up in the saucers and the coffee grew cold and forgotten. Finally they happened to notice the clock. My God, Petey said, they better get to bed and give poor old Santa Claus a break around here.

Sally refused Petey's offer to help her fill the children's stockings. She thought Petey ought to get back to the hotel and get some sleep. She must be tired and she would want to be over early tomorrow to see the kids undo their presents.

Petey agreed with unexpected alacrity and got into her black velvet coat again, and the silly little hat. She stopped to powder her nose, and outline her mouth in vivid red lipstick. Sally stood beside her and picked up her heavy furs, stroked them lovingly, enjoying their softness and beauty and the faint sweetness of Petey's perfume that clung to them.

Petey swept a handful of veil back from her face and dropped a light sticky kiss on Sally's forehead. She would see her the first thing in the morning. She was to sleep and not worry any more about anything, and a very merry Christmas. Petey took the furs and was gone before Sally had a chance to walk to the door with her.

Petey was down the stairs in a second, being careful to walk on her toes so that her tall heels would not clatter on the bare steps and awaken the sleepers in the house. In the hall below she stopped at the telephone and consulted the directory for the number of the local taxi service. She ordered her cab, and told them to hurry because she was catching a train, an old and automatic lie with her because she always wanted taxi-cabs in a hurry.

She waited in the hall impatiently, looking out of the door from time to time. It was still snowing, the streets were dark and treacherous with slush. Petey hitched her heavy furs to a more comfortable angle across her shoulders, and pulled up her stockings, checking to see that each black seam was perfectly straight up her leg. She swept back the veil from her face again with an impatient hand and lighted a cigarette. She paced the little hallway, light and noiseless on her feet, puffing smoke out behind her.

At last she saw the auto headlights come up the street, cutting through the darkness and the wet mushy snow ahead of them. Petey never waited. After all, at this time of night and on this quiet deserted street, that was bound to be her cab. She closed the door silently behind her and was down the porch steps and on the sidewalk before the cab pulled up to the curb.

"Hi, Joe," she said to the taxi driver cheerfully as he opened the door for her. "Jesus H. Christ, I stepped in a puddle back there the size of Lake Michigan!" She turned the overhead light on, once she was in the cab, and studied her wet pump and the spots of water splashed on her sheer black nylon hose, dabbling at them with a finger of her black suede glove.

The driver swung the cab around and started toward town. "Sure is an awful night out," he said. "Them folks always hollering about having snow for Christmas is sure welcome to it. Where you want to go, lady?"

Petey snapped off the light and settled herself on the seat, crossing her legs becomingly. "Looky, Joe," she said, "you know where this Nicky Toresca joint is?"

"I sure do," the cabby said.

"Well, step on it," Petey said, "what you waiting for? It's already Christmas, brother, so open her up."

The cab driver stepped on the gas obligingly. There was very little traffic on the streets at this hour. The cab went skidding down the street, the snow whirling around it, and water splashing out from the wheels behind them.

Petey looked out of the windows, singing softly to herself in her deep rich voice, blue and hot:

> *"I have never been aboard a steamer*
> *I have been content to be a dreamer*
> *Even if I could afford a steamer*
> *I'd still take a ferryboat everytime . . ."*

"Hey, that's all right," the cab driver said approvingly. "You sing, lady?"

"Not so's you'd notice it," Petey said, a little abstractedly.

"Sure sounds all right to me," the cab driver said. "You oughta get a job singin' on the radio, no kiddin'."

Petey's laughter boomed out in the small glass-enclosed space of the taxi-cab.

She sat forward in her seat suddenly, leaning her elbows on the back of the seat ahead of her. "How much further, Joe?"

"Just a couple more blocks," he reassured her. He swung the cab around a corner fast, the wheels slid in the slush, and he spun the wheel, straightening the cab out again.

"Guess you must be a stranger in town," he said to her conversationally. "Just about everybody around here knows where Toresca's is."

"Is that so?" Petey said politely.

The driver swung around another corner and came to a stop with a squeaking of brakes and a splashing of water. The front looked closed and dark, but the big Neon sign across the front proclaimed that this was Toresca's.

The driver hesitated, his hand on the door handle. "Look's like it's closed," he said.

Petey struggled to wiggle her wrist watch out from under her dress sleeve and the top of her glove. "Christ, what kind of a town is this?" she said crossly. "They close the joints up with the chickens?"

The driver scratched his head. "Gee, lady, I dunno. It oughta be still open. What time is it?"

Petey turned the little diamond watch toward the light, and lowered her face close to it. "It's about three o'clock."

The driver scratched his head again. "Gee, I dunno. It oughta be open."

Petey hesitated, frowning, with her own hand on the door handle.

"Oh, gosh! Sure, it's closed!" the driver said triumphantly. "Now I remember. They closed 'em all early tonight on account of it was Christmas Eve. They been having so many traffic accidents around town, so many folks gettin' drunk and smashin' cars up, that the city closed 'em all up early tonight. I guess they closed 'em up at twelve o'clock sharp."

Petey shrugged her shoulders and settled back in the seat again. "Well, Merry Christmas and a Happy New Year," she said. "Take me over to Grant Hotel, Joe."

"Sure am sorry," he said, as he pulled away from the curb. "It just slipped my mind about 'em closin' 'em tonight. Could just as well a saved you the trip over here." He reached over and turned off the meter as he spoke.

"Oh, never mind," Petey said. "I'll make it some other night."

And as the cab splashed on down the street, Petey looked back, watching the winking red sign that proclaimed that that was Toresca's until they turned a corner and it was out of sight.

# 13

CHRISTMAS DAY AT SALLY'S WAS A PLEASANT, LAZY day, given to over-eating and the unwrapping of the presents under the tree. Buddy and Marilyn were out of bed early to explore the contents of their stockings, and once that was done they launched a determined campaign to unwrap the presents under the tree immediately. No, their mother said, they would have to wait until Joe and Aunt Petey came.

Fred Foster, too, was out of bed at an unwontedly early hour for a holiday, and stopped in for a cup of coffee before he went over to his wife's apartment to spend the day with his children. At the last moment Fred's holiday mood deserted him. He lingered in the kitchen, smoking innumerable cigarettes and complaining to Sally. For two cents he wouldn't go near that place over there. He knew what that dame was up to. All the time she was scheming how to get him to come back to her, and the children were her best bet and she knew it. Would she let him take Tommy and go home to his folks for Christmas? No, she would not. Instead of that, she set Tommy up to coaxing him to come over there, and now she was cooking up a fancy dinner and she would put on a heavy mama-and-papa act in front of Tommy, he knew. What he ought to do was just stay away from there entirely. What he ought to do was go downtown and get drunk. When did Sally expect Petey to come over, anyway?

Sally soothed him as best she could, while she cleaned the two chickens for the Christmas dinner. She knew just how he felt, and it was a shame. But right now he should think about Tommy and the baby. Think how disappointed Tommy would be if his father didn't come. He wanted Tommy to keep loving him and grow up close to him, didn't he? Well, then, if he had promised Tommy to come he would just have to go. He needn't think for a moment that Tommy was too little to feel bad and be disappointed if he didn't keep his word to him.

Fred swore vilely, consigning his ex-wife to the most unendurable section of hell for all eternity, and went for his overcoat.

Sally found time to slip down the hall to the O'Connors' apartment to invite Gloria over for Christmas dinner. She found Gloria still in bed, the baby awake and whining in its crib. No, Gloria said, it was very nice of Sally to ask her, but she had already promised her girl friend to come over to her house today. However, she would be very grateful if Sally would keep the baby. Sally said that she would be only too glad to do anything she could to help Gloria.

She leaned over the crib and teased the baby into smiling. Didn't Beverly know that this was Christmas? Didn't she want to see what Santa Claus had left in her stocking?

There wasn't any stocking, Gloria said, yawning in the bed. She had been too tired last night to bother with it. Besides, Bevvy was too young to know what it was all about, that had just been a foolish notion of Johnny's.

Gloria was going over to the hospital to see Johnny sometime today, of course, Sally said. Oh, sure, Gloria thought she would go over late in the afternoon.

Would he be able to have visitors? Sally wanted to know. She would like to go over and see him herself, sometime this afternoon. It would be just about the only chance she would have. She would be back at work again tomorrow.

Well, Gloria said, a little coldly, she didn't believe it was any use for Sally to go over there. She didn't think they would let her in. Johnny was pretty sick, his high temperature and all, and they didn't want him to have visitors.

In that case, Sally decided it would probably be better if she didn't go. But would Gloria be sure to tell him that they all sent him their love and hoped that he was feeling better and that he would be able to come home soon?

When Sally got back to the apartment she found Buddy and Marilyn scrambling among the presents under the tree, trying to find packages that bore their names. When she scolded them, they protested indignantly that they weren't opening the old presents. Couldn't they just look at them? Oh, sure, Sally said, but how about that package right there with Buddy's name on it, and a hole in the paper at one corner. She supposed the mice had torn that hole in the paper. Well, they must have, Buddy said, he certainly didn't know how that hole got in the paper.

They had both just better come out in the kitchen with her, Sally said, she didn't trust them around that tree. What would Santa Claus say, if he could see the way they were behaving?

Buddy laughed triumphantly and unrepentingly. The joke was on his mother and Santa Claus both, he bragged; Santa Claus had already been there. Well, there was another year coming, Sally reminded him.

The children tagged her out to the kitchen reluctantly. When, oh, when, they wanted to know, could they open the presents? Not till Joe and Aunt Petey came. She had already told them that about a million times. This was Christmas. Couldn't they be good children and not tease and bother her just this once?

The moment her back was turned they both slipped away. They sneaked into the bedroom where Joe Braun was fast asleep and awakened him by the rudest methods. Get up quick, they told him, they were all ready to start opening the presents.

Well, then, for Christ's sakes, go ahead and open them, Joe howled. Go ahead and open the goddam presents, but get to hell out of here and leave him alone.

And in the midst of that disturbance, Virginia discovered Harold just in from his paper deliveries, doing a little exploring among the presents himself.

Well, for gosh sakes, Sally scolded, she would have expected that of the little kids, but she thought Harold was a grown-up boy and old enough to know better, not to go snooping around like some little kid. Harold's pride was hurt, and he said, okay, he didn't give a damn about any old presents anyway, he didn't want their old presents. Now, wasn't he ashamed, Sally said desperately. If he didn't cut out that swearing she was going to scrub out his mouth with soap and water, and she didn't care if it was Christmas.

For once the younger children combined with Harold to present a solid front of mutiny to their mother. All right, then, when, they wanted to know, could they open the presents?

Sally said if they didn't keep quiet about it for the next five minutes they wouldn't open them till New Year's. How would they like that?

Virginia languidly raided the icebox for a combination breakfast and lunch, and Sally sat down with a cup of coffee. A fine kind of mother, she was, she reproached herself, making a ruckus and scolding the kids like this on Christmas. Why, Christmas was their big day. It was only natural for them to get impatient with all those mysterious presents spread out in front of their eyes. A fine mother she was!

A moment later Petey arrived, as fresh and sparkling as the Christmas tree itself. My God, hadn't they got around to opening up all those presents yet? she wanted to know. A fine thing, afternoon on Christmas day, and presents still unopened. The children were overjoyed to find such an energetic and influential supporter of their cause. Petey never stopped even to take off her coat. She went to Joe's bedroom and hauled down the bed covers and pummeled him out of bed. There were plenty of days to lay abed, for God's sakes, she told him cheerfully, but this was Christmas. Joe went off to the bathroom with hardly a grumble. He was still a little too much in awe of this energetic, newfound sister to make the protests that he normally would have made at such treatment from any other member of his family.

Fifteen minutes later he appeared on the scene, sketchily clothed, and Petey organized the distribution of gifts. Everyone was to sit down, and the children, with Harold's assistance, were to distribute them. So the packages were distributed and opened and the mound of paper wrappings and ribbons grew in the middle of the floor. Buddy and Marilyn, in spite of the fact that they received more gifts than other members of the family, got theirs undone first, and then immediately wanted to see how the other and slower members of the family had fared. Sally finished last of all, undoing each ribbon and sticker carefully, exclaiming over the beauty of the package, first, and then the beauty and appropriateness of the gift it contained. Petey suggested that each one of them exhibit the gifts he had received to the entire group.

Petey, the unexpected guest, was surprised and delighted to find a number of gifts with her name on them, such makeshift gifts of candy and cigarettes and cheap cotton handkerchiefs as Sally had been able to achieve. Only Joe had been able to procure a real gift for her, a large and ornate atomizer of cologne, that Petey proclaimed to be her favorite scent and sprayed over everybody liberally on the spot.

Several hours slipped by and suddenly Sally jumped to her feet.

For heaven's sakes, she had all but forgotten about dinner, she cried guiltily. All these perfectly beautiful presents she had received, so much more than she had ever anticipated or deserved, must have gone to her head. She would fly into it and get dinner on the table immediately. Everybody must be starving to death. Why hadn't somebody reminded her that she had something else to do today besides sit around and gloat over her presents?

Petey followed her to the kitchen, demanding an apron, so that she might help her. But even with Petey's assistance it was nearly five o'clock and quite dark outside before dinner was on the table. The children, who had fared well on candy all day long, had to be forcibly dragged away from their toys to the table. Once there, they gulped down their food hurriedly and were back in the living room in ten minutes. But the elder members of the family lingered over the table. Sally kicked off her shoes luxuriously over coffee and chocolate mints (Petey's contribution) and cigarettes. This had been the nicest Christmas, didn't everybody think so? She, at least, had gotten the loveliest presents she had ever dreamed of. Everybody had been too generous with her. Particularly Petey and Joe. She just wished they wouldn't spend so much money on her when she could do so little in return.

Virginia was particularly silent at that point. She felt that it was she who had been dealt with most generously, considering the fact that she had been unable to make any gifts at all this year, but she was too shy to say so.

Petey overrode all of Sally's objections. As if she hadn't done so much for them all their lives, as if she still didn't. As if they ever could repay her with just a few little old presents at Christmas time! Sally was more touched than ever by these declarations and grew a little tearful. No, sir, just the same, she protested.

Petey switched the topic to the weather. Jesus H. Christ, if it wasn't snowing again! What kind of a town was this? Just look out-doors; if this wasn't the darkest, dampest, dismalest town she had ever seen in all her life! A look at the darkness outside recalled the time to Joe, and once Petey had consulted her wrist watch for him, he got to his feet immediately. He had got to be getting along. After all, he was a working man. Neither Sally nor Petey had any comment to make to that statement, but they exchanged glances.

The dinner had been all right, Joe said. Thanks for the necktie, and thanks for the shaving kit. With his social duties disposed of, Joe bade them good night and swaggered off to his bedroom for his coat and hat. Sally's lips narrowed into a disapproving line as she watched him go, and Petey's vagrant eyebrow mounted her forehead in satanic amusement.

Petey got to her feet immediately and tied on her apron. Sally and Virginia were to rest; she was going to wash the dishes and clean up the kitchen. Virginia, particularly, was looking so tired and peaked that her suggestion was that she take a nice warm bath and hop into bed. They didn't want to take any chances on her having a relapse of this mean old flu.

Virginia admitted that she was a little tired and that perhaps bed was the place for her. At the kitchen door, she paused and, in an awkward, shy voice, that broke in spite of her, she said that she wanted to thank them both for being so terribly nice and giving her all these lovely presents when she had been unable to do anything for anybody this year. She was particularly grateful to Petey, who had brought beautiful gifts to a young, unknown sister whom she hadn't seen since she was a baby. Petey put an end to Virginia's little speech with a hug and kiss. She was the lucky one, she protested, to have a sweet little sister like this to do things for. Virginia was just to forget all about it.

While Petey cleared the table and stacked the dishes, Sally prepared the bottle of milk for young Beverly O'Connor, who slept quietly on her bed in the bedroom. But Petey wasn't to start washing dishes until she was back, Sally warned. There was no sense in Petey ruining her beautiful manicure over a few old dishes that Sally could wash in a minute.

When Sally returned to the kitchen, Petey had half the dishes washed, but Sally shooed her away from the dishpan, and they finished them together. My, it had been a nice Christmas, hadn't it? Sally kept saying. It would have been just perfect if only Roy could have been here. Just think, it was the first Christmas that they had all been together like this since they were kids. Wouldn't it have been wonderful if Pa could have only lived to see them all grown up and together here today? Wouldn't he have loved to have seen Sally's kids, though, his grandchildren? Wouldn't he have been proud of his big, grown-up family, though?

While they cleared the kitchen they reminisced together, funny things that had happened when they were kids, funny things Pa had said, funny things Pa had done.

Once the dishes were done, Petey glanced at her watch and said casually that she believed she would go on back over to the hotel. Why, it was early yet, Sally protested, the evening was just beginning. Petey agreed, but she protested that she was a little tired, she hadn't slept too well last night. She had some phone calls to make and then she believed she would pile into bed and see if she couldn't get some sleep. She suggested that Sally do the same. Well, gee, of course, if she were tired, Sally said penitently. After all, Petey hadn't had much chance to sleep last night, the way Sally had kept her up, talking to her half the night. After all, they would have other times to be together while Petey was here. Petey wouldn't be rushing off someplace right away, now that she had finally come home, would she? Sally added wistfully.

No, Petey assured her, she had no intention of rushing off any place. Sally needn't worry about that. In a twinkling, Petey had her coat and furs on again. She had had the best Christmas of her life, she told Sally, and she would be over tomorrow night, after Sally was through work. Sally was to go to bed early; rest was what she needed.

Sally followed her down the stairs and waited with her for the taxi-cab while Petey went through the familiar ritual. Hitching her furs to the comfortable position, straightening her stocking seams, puffing the cigarette impatiently. When the cab came, Sally watched Petey run out through the snow to the open cab door.

"Hi yuh, Joe," Petey greeted her driver. "Hotel Grant, and step on it!" At the hotel she paid her driver and saluted him with a generous tip, her own cheerful wide grin and a Merry Christmas. Petey walked in through the wide doors into the lobby, her heels clicking smartly, her body erect. She walked on through the lobby to the bar at the far side of the hotel. It was a small bar and rather ornately decorated. Tonight it was quite deserted, except for a bored and lonesome bartender.

Petey loosened the furs at her shoulders, shaking drops of water in all directions, and slid up on the red leather seat of the first stool at the end of the bar.

"Hello, Joe," Petey said to the bartender cheerfully. "You're certainly doing a rush business around here tonight, aren't you?"

"Well, you know how it is," he answered her in a strange nasal voice. "A day like Christmas most everybody spends at home. There may be more business later, though; it's still early yet."

He dropped a little square paper napkin in front of Petey on the shining bar top. "What'll yours be?"

"Scotch and plain water." Petey cupped her chin on her hand as he turned away to select a bottle from the shining array spread out on the shelf below the mirror. "It's tough having to work Christmas. I bet you can think of a lot of places you'd rather be tonight than stuck here behind this bar."

"Oh, it ain't so bad," the bartender said. "I had the whole day off to stay home with my wife and kids. I don't mind so much, except you get pretty tired just standing around here when there ain't much business like tonight."

"That's right," Petey said sympathetically. "I knew a pretty good bartender once that went stir crazy standing around on a slow night like this is. He decided to break it up a little by taking a drink out of every bottle, beginning at the left end of the bar."

"Yeah?" the bartender said, as he filled the little shot glass in front of her and corked the bottle again.

"Yup," Petey said, mixing her own drink energetically. "He got just two bottles beyond the cash register. He was a big guy and the waiters had a hell of a time carrying him out from behind that bar."

The bartender grinned a little in spite of himself and struck a match for Petey's cigarette. "You stayin' here at the hotel?"

Petey nodded her head as she puffed on the cigarette to light it.

"I guess it ain't much of a Christmas for you, havin' to spend it in a hotel room."

"Oh, I got a sister here in town with a family of kids. I spent the day with them."

"Oh. That's all right." The bartender leaned on one elbow conversationally, as Petey sipped her drink.

"Yup, one of those nice quiet home parties!" Petey slanted her eyes at him, grinning. "I bailed out early to do a little holiday celebratin' on my own. You know what I mean, a few drinks, some bright lights, a little music . . ." Petey let her voice trail off and rolled her hand over palm upward to him.

"Well, there's probably a lot of better towns to do your celebratin' in than this one," the bartender said. He looked Petey over speculatively as he spoke. "Where you from, Chicago?"

"Oh, I been around," Petey said carelessly. "Chicago, New York—I just came up here from Key West."

"Is that so!" There was an interested note in his voice, and he kept looking at Petey. "Then I guess you ain't gonna find much in this town like you're used to."

"Oh, I don't know," Petey said. "It looks like a pretty alive town to me. I tell you what, Joe, just between you and me, and that bottle of Scotch over there, if you been around a lot, pretty soon you get wise to it. Joints are pretty much the same, and it doesn't matter where you find 'em."

"Well, I guess you got something there, at that," the bartender said meditatively. "Course I never been to New York or big-time places like that, but I used to work in Chicago once, and I guess I get what you mean, all right."

Petey grinned at him. "Yeah, and from your side of the bar, Joe, they're even more alike. Am I right?"

"Lady, you sure are! Oh, you know, the only difference is the guy you're working for. Sometimes he's a good guy and sometimes he's a bad guy. But the business? The business is all alike, you sure said it! Say, lady, you talk like you been in this business yourself!"

Petey nodded her head, her face sober momentarily. "Yeah, Joe. I been in and around this business more years'n I like to remember."

The bartender looked curious, but just as he opened his mouth to speak again, Petey drained her drink and set the glass down hard on top of the little damp square of paper. She slid back on the stool and hitched her furs up onto her shoulders again.

The bartender reached for her glass. "Here, have another one on the house for a Christmas present. We gotta get your celebration started right!"

Petey shook her head. "Nope, thanks just the same, Joe. I'll be in again, and then I'll collect that free drink I got coming." As she sorted change from her purse, she added, "I tell you, Joe, if you wanta get my celebration off to a good start you could tip me off to some good spots in this town. I'm quite a stranger here."

"Well, there ain't too much to pick from," he said over the ringing of the cash register. "Of course, there's two or three real nice bars in town, like this one, for instance, but I figure you ain't interested in just setting around a plain ordinary bar tonight."

"That's right," Petey said.

"I tell you, there's one real swell night-club place in town, I mean real class, like you'd find in a big city, and that's Toresca's."

"Toresca's?" Petey repeated the name after him. "That's a funny name."

"Yeah," he said. "Must be Greek or Italian or somethin'. It's named after Nicky Toresca, the guy that owns the place. He's quite a big shot around here."

"Oh?" Petey said. "Well, I believe I'll go over and take a look at your Toresca place. Thanks, Joe. I'll see you again."

"Yeah, come in again," the bartender called after her. "I hope you enjoy yourself over there, all right. Just tell the cab driver, they all know where Toresca's is."

"Okay. Merry Christmas!"

Once again Petey crossed the lobby, and gave her floor number to the elevator boy. She stepped out of the elevator and walked half the length of the corridor, her feet noiseless in the thick carpet, swinging her room key in her hand. Once the door was closed behind her and the lights were on in the small, well-furnished room, Petey tossed her furs and hat onto the bed carelessly. She went over to the little desk by the windows and sat down in the chair. She took the small money purse out of her big suede bag and spilled its contents, bills and change onto the clean desk blotter in front of her. She counted the money rapidly, and then rummaged in her purse again. She removed a small packet of letters, and from several of the envelopes she removed additional bills that she added to the money on the desk top. Once again she counted, and then she slowly returned all of the money to her purse. She sat quite still for a moment, tapping one long red fingernail against her lower lip reflectively. She lighted a cigarette and stood beside her chair smoking, her face thoughtful. With a sudden quick energy she dabbed out the cigarette in the ash tray and crossed the room to the clothespress. She flung it open and stripped the dress over her head. She undressed rapidly, folded a heavy, red satin robe about her and made off for the bathroom with her quick long stride. She snapped the light on and started the shower running into the tub.

A few moments later Petey faced her reflection in the full-length mirror on the bathroom door. She wore a slim black dinner dress of a heavy silk material that looked as if it had been painted over her smooth rounded body. It was cut with a startling square neckline, low on her full breasts, and the neckline further accented heavily with blue-black sequins. The sleeves were long and straight and ended with dramatic points on the backs of Petey's long slim hands, and more sequins. The tight skirt had a slash up the front to the knees that was filled in with a slashing of solid sequin trimming. Petey brushed away an infinitesimal smudge of white powder from the fabric over one hip, and her vagrant eyebrow climbed up onto her forehead. "Nicky Toresca!" she said sardonically.

The elevator boy goggled after her in open-mouthed admiration and she created a furor in the lobby among the two or three bellhops on duty, all of them scrambling to call her cab. Even the cab driver whistled a little as he opened the door and Petey crossed the sidewalk and stooped to enter the cab.

"Hi yuh, Joe," Petey said cheerfully, as she settled herself on the cab seat and crossed her legs comfortably. "Nicky Toresca's, and I'm in a hurry!"

The cab driver apparently took her at her word. He slammed the door shut and sent the cab hurtling away from the curb. The heavy wet snow was still falling in the dark streets between the buildings, melting into treacherous ice on cement, hanging in the heavy damp air to blur the multi-colored Neon signs the length of Main Street. It was warm inside the cab, and Petey tapped out a dance rhythm noiselessly in the air with the shiny toe of her sandal, and sniffed her own perfume appreciatively. Her destination was only several blocks away from the hotel, and in a couple minutes the cab pulled up at the curb in front of the smart, modern façade that bore the one word in big Neon letters, "Toresca's." From the entrance a cold, disgruntled-looking doorman in trim uniform stared at the cab dubiously and then reluctantly stepped out into the wet snow to open the door.

Petey paused in the snow only long enough to hand a bill to the doorman. "You boys split the difference," she said carelessly, and then she strode across the wet sidewalk to the entrance, her glittering skirt swishing around her heels. She pulled open the heavy door without waiting for the doorman and stepped into the warm interior. Inside, she stopped a moment. In front of her was a sort of narrow ramp, thickly carpeted, leading to the bar on a higher floor level directly ahead. To the right were several phone booths, and to the left a small checkroom. Petey stood still and cocked her ear to the faint strains of the orchestra that drifted out over the confusion of voices from the crowded bar.

A thin, blonde girl, in a short black dress with a conglomeration of too vivid make-up spread over her face, was leaning over the counter, talking to the hat-check girl, a tray of cigarettes beside her. They both stopped talking at the sight of Petey, and stared at her curiously, their two faces, turned to her, expressionless blobs of white flesh under thick coatings of cosmetics. Just as Petey glanced at them as she started to walk up the ramp, the blonde girl, without taking her eyes off Petey once, whispered something to the other behind a raised hand. Petey smiled at them sweetly as she went past and, without pausing, patted the blonde girl on the shoulder. "Anyway, honey, my slip doesn't show," she murmured, with just the proper inflection, so that the blonde girl's eyes immediately dropped to her own short hemline in spite of herself. Petey walked the rest of the way up the ramp and into the bar. It was a long bar, rather tastefully decorated in light shades of blue and green, in contrast to the thick dark-green rug underfoot. Tonight the bar was crowded with drinkers nearly two deep, and two bartenders were on duty. A waiter came up to Petey instantly. "You want a table? A small one, or do you have a party coming in later?"

Before she answered, Petey walked to the top of one of the two short flights of steps that led down to the small dance floor and the tables. Petey looked the room over at her leisure, oblivious of the heads turned in her direction.

"I'd like that one in the corner at the back," she said at last, and she started down the steps, the waiter at her heels.

"Don't you want a table up front? Got a lot of nice tables left right on the floor."

Petey ignored him and walked to the table of her choice, pausing for him to pull out the chair for her before she sat down. She gave the order for her drink and then leaned back in her chair and loosened her cape at the throat. The table Petey had chosen was a small one for two, set in a shadowy intimate corner in the back of the room. She was sitting in the chair against the wall, so that the whole room was in front of her. It was a small room, rather elegantly furnished, with a scattering of tables on three sides of a smaller dance floor. The orchestra played from a stand at the back of the room, and for a time they held Petey's attention as she slowly lighted a cigarette. There were three or four couples dancing, and about two-thirds of the tables were filled. Petey studied the crowd next, reflectively. They were a well-dressed crowd, several tables of them in evening clothes, and there was a liberal scattering of alert-looking waiters at strategic points around the room. The room was neither noisy nor subdued, the lighting was pleasurably soft through the inevitable drift of cigarette smoke, and an atmosphere of holiday gaiety prevailed. By craning her neck a little, Petey could see back to the bar, where the voices were a little louder and where the crowd was a little more variegated. Her eyes at last drifted back to the orchestra again, and she continued to watch them idly until the waiter set her drink down before her.

The waiter mixed the drink for her and, as he turned away, she beckoned him back, the huge stone in her ring glittering in the dim light. He turned back and bent over the table, and Petey raised her face and spoke confidentially. "Looky, Joe. Is Mr. Toresca around?"

The waiter's voice and his pale face were both noncommittal when he answered her. "I dunno." He looked at Petey speculatively, and then he added, "You got a date with Mr. Toresca?"

Petey ignored that question completely. She opened her bag and slid a bill out onto the table top underneath her fingers, folded, so that the denomination showed.

"You think maybe you could find out if Mr. Toresca was around?" She slid the bill back and forth a little under her fingers as she spoke.

The waiter looked at the bill appreciatively, but his voice was still noncommittal. "I dunno. Maybe he's out back in his office. He's got an office out back there. Maybe I could find out, I dunno."

"Aw, I bet you could, Joe. You look like a bright boy," Petey said sardonically.

The waiter suddenly pocketed the bill. "Okay," he said. "What you want me to tell him, in case he's around?"

Petey leaned back in her chair once more and took a sip of her drink. "That's better," she said. "Now, looky, Joe, get this straight. You tell Mr. Toresca that Joe Braun's sister is out in front and wants to see him, and that it's important. You get that?"

"Sure, sure," he said impatiently. "Joe Braun's sister is out in front and wants to talk to him and it's important."

"That's fine," Petey said. "No, now wait a minute. If he says to bring her back to his office, you tell him no soap. Tell him she wouldn't come back to the office. She wants to talk to him out here. You got that? No, now wait! And if he asks you any more questions, you don't know nothing from nothing, you got the message from one of the other waiters and you don't know nothing about it nor her nor nothing. Can you remember that?"

"Aw, hey! Wait a minute," the waiter said suspiciously.

"Now, Joey!" Petey stopped him with a wagging finger and her wide, good-humored grin. "Look, you do just like I told you. It's all right. You're not gonna get in any jam. It's perfectly all right. It's a little surprise for Mr. Toresca, that's all."

"Now look, lady," he said plaintively. "I don't want to get into any trouble."

"You're not gonna get into any trouble. How many times do I have to tell you?" Petey repeated the words in a singsong voice. "It's a surprise for Mr. Toresca! Now g'wan, g'wan, g'wan!"

The waiter turned away, muttering something that sounded like he didn't know nothing about it, he didn't have nothing to do with it and how should he know.

Several minutes slid by, and Petey did not move. Suddenly the door back of the orchestra opened and Nicky Toresca emerged. He wore evening clothes, his hands thrust easily into his pockets. He stood still momentarily, his eyes roving over the room. Heads turned in his direction immediately, and several people from different tables called greetings to him. He answered them with a slight gesture of his hand, something between a wave and a fascist salute. His eyes roved over the room, and when they came to Petey, they stopped momentarily, and Petey half smiled at him. He looked away, his face still blank and contained. He started walking slowly toward the flight of steps up to the bar. He did not look at Petey again.

Just as he passed her table, Petey spoke in her low deep voice with just the faintest shade of amusement in it. "Good evening, Mr. Toresca."

He stopped then and looked at her. Then his eyes darted away to the bar and beyond the bar toward the checkroom.

Petey waited just the space of a second or two and then she said, still with the faint amusement in her voice, "Joe Braun has three sisters, did you know that, Mr. Toresca?"

He looked at her again then, and this time he did not look away. He looked at her hard, his eyes unblinking, at her face, her hair, her gown, down to the glittering slit in the bottom of the skirt that revealed a provocative glimpse of a shining slim leg crossed over the other one, up again to her face, his eyes lingering a little at the low-cut neckline of her dress. He walked over to the edge of the table then and spoke with the cigarette bobbing in his mouth. "So?" he said flatly.

Petey looked away, the faint smile still lingering at her mouth.

She studied the cigarette in her fingers. Then she looked up at him suddenly, and dropped her eyes again. She flicked a piece of ash from the glowing tip of her cigarette.

Nicky Toresca pulled out the other chair at her table and sat down. A waiter, threading in and out among the tables, came toward him instantly. Nicky Toresca nodded his head briefly, and the waiter hurried up the steps to the bar.

Petey raised her eyes then and looked at Nicky Toresca across the table, looked at him with her eyes as steady as his own. Neither one of them spoke. The waiter brought the drink and moved away again.

At last Nicky Toresca broke the silence. "You must be a stranger in town."

"That's right," Petey said. She took a sip from her drink and said, "It's a nice town. The more I see of it, the better I like it."

"Is that right!" Nicky Toresca said politely.

"That's right."

He raised his own glass from the table then. After that he puffed on his cigarette a couple of times. "Maybe you oughta stick around."

"I was just thinking about that," Petey said readily. "You think maybe I should?"

"I think maybe it would be very nice," Nicky said smoothly.

Petey laughed softly, her low-pitched husky laughter. "So?" she mimicked.

Nicky Toresca smiled then for the first time, and slid down in his chair a little, his hands deep in his pockets, his eyes fixed on Petey steadily. "I think maybe this town could do a lot for you," he said at last.

Petey sat up suddenly and twirled her glass in her fingers. The sudden motion made all the sequins on her dress reflect the light in tiny glittering points. "I think maybe I could do quite a lot for this town," she said.

"Is that right!"

"Uh huh," Petey said. "I'm awful handy to have around."

Nicky Toresca looked at her appreciatively. "I think you might be, at that," he said with amusement in his voice.

"Yup, I am," Petey said. "I'm nice—and I know an awful lot of things—and—I sing. People like it." She jerked her head at the crowded tables.

"Is that right!" The interest and the amusement were plain on Nicky Toresca's face now.

"Yup! Maybe you'd like a sample of that?"

"Go ahead," he said. "I'm listening."

Petey stood up suddenly and tossed her hair back and pulled her cape securely across her shoulders. "You wanta come up and introduce me, Mr. Toresca?" she said teasingly.

"Uh uh. I hear better back here." Nicky Toresca tipped his head back and studied Petey again even more appreciatively, now that she was on her feet.

Petey's eyebrow bent double in amusement, and she turned away and walked off toward the orchestra stand. Heads turned her way again and eyes followed her as she walked the length of the room in her long quick stride with the faint strut to it.

She mounted the steps to the orchestra stand confidently, and said, "Hi yuh, boys," to the six or seven astonished musicians. The young orchestra leader looked away to Nicky Toresca in the back of the room questioningly. Nicky had turned his chair around sideways to the table. He nodded his head in answer, smiling all across his dark face. The orchestra leader brought the selection they were playing to an end in a couple more bars and then turned to Petey.

Petey slipped her hand through his arm, and spoke to him and to the others in a confidential voice. "Look, boys, I want a job singing here, and I need it bad. We'll have to mug through without any rehearsin', but I think we can make it fine. Are you with me?"

Several of the musicians answered her instantly. "Sure, sure thing—atta girl . . ."

She looked back to the leader and he patted her hand patronizingly. "We're willing, and I guess we can keep with you. What number you want?"

"How about 'There'll be Some Changes Made'?"

The leader shook his head. "Uh uh. That's a new one. We never played that one yet."

"Well, looky, some of you know it, don't you?" Petey said urgently.

The piano player rolled the cigarette in his mouth and squinted his eyes away from the smoke. "I heard it on the radio the other day. It's a new one out here. Ain't even on the juke-boxes yet."

"My, my," Petey said. "I don't suppose you ever take a chance on nothing until it's been on the juke-boxes for two months! Look, it's a swell number, you can play it, can't you?"

"Sure, I can play it," the piano player said, indignantly. "Didn't I just tell you I heard it on a radio the other day, for Chris' sakes!"

"Well, fine," Petey said. "Then we'll make out swell, and if any of you other boys want to come along for the ride on the second chorus, come ahead, don't mind me."

"How you want it?" the piano player said morosely.

Petey leaned over his shoulder and struck a chord softly with her fingers.

"Way down there?" the piano player said doubtfully.

"That's right. That's where my voice is, way down there."

Petey dropped her fur cape over the back of his chair and walked out to the edge of the orchestra stand. She adjusted the small microphone up to her height with the competent ease of familiarity. When it was ready, she spoke into it with her low warm husky voice, easily and pleasantly.

"Good evening, Ladies and Gentlemen." Her voice did not suffer over the microphone at all, and almost immediately voices began to thin out as even more eyes were turned in her direction.

She spoke with a sort of confidential intimacy that in some mysterious way seemed to set up an instantaneous and personal contact between herself and each person in her audience.

"I heard a new song the other day, and it's been running around in my head ever since. I was just talking to the band boys about it, and Joe here, at the piano, says he heard it too. We're going to pass it along to you, and I hope you like it. Ladies and Gentlemen, this is gonna be strictly on the house!"

Petey's own infectious laughter drew a ready response, and amid that laughter and a scattering of applause she nodded her head to the morose and doubtful piano player. She moved over nearer to the piano as he played a few opening bars for her, and nodded her head approvingly and then walked back to the microphone.

*"There'll be a change in the weather*
*And a change in the sea*
*From now on there'll be a change in me.*
*My walk will be different my talk an' my name*
*Nothin' about me's gonna be the same . . ."*

Her voice was very low and husky and oddly musical, but, more than her voice, it was Petey herself, and her terrific vitality and this mysterious contact she could establish with an audience that put her song across. She had a roar of applause after the first chorus and she took it again with the band coming in behind her.

*"I'll change my way of livin'*
*And if that ain't enough*
*Why then I'll change the way I strut my stuff*
*Cause nobody wants you when you're old and gray . . ."*

Petey finished the song to even more applause, which she acknowledged with a graceful half-curtsy, her head dropped low, and then she turned away and picked up her cape from the chair back.

"Thanks a lot, boys. Maybe I'll see you around again."

But the applause had not stopped, and, as she slung the cape over one shoulder and walked down from the stand, it grew even louder. She turned, laughing, and waved her hand, but the applause continued. The blond young band leader made what capital he could of the situation, joining in the applause heartily and finally leading Petey back to the center of the band stand again.

"What you want this time?" he asked with a faint wariness and suspicion in his voice.

Petey hesitated for only a second, and then she laughed. "Boys, this is probably gonna kill you. But it's an oldie, and I bet you still remember it . . ."

"What is it?"

"You remember 'Little Man, You've Had a Busy Day'?"

"Yeah, sure," the band leader said. There was no comment from any of the musicians, but the expression on their faces seemed to say that they were glad that this was her funeral and none of theirs.

The band leader raised his baton and they gave her a few opening bars that quieted the applause. Petey walked back to the microphone once more.

"Thank you, Ladies and Gentlemen," she said. She paused until the room was quiet and attention was centered upon her again. She spoke quietly and simply. "Well, today was a big day for the kids, wasn't it? Santa Claus came last night and they were all out of bed early to see what was in their stockings. They had packages to open and candy to eat and new toys to play with. Oh, it was a big day for the kids, all right! Right now, all over the country, they're goin' off to bed. Oh, they don't wanta go to bed yet, but they're tired and cross and sleepy. Here's an old song you all remember. Let's dedicate it now to all the kids all over the country, in the hope that every one of them had a very Merry Christmas—'Little Man, You've Had a Busy Day.'"

She sang the song with tenderness in her voice, and with a wistful nostalgia that made a blues song of it. Whatever response she had anticipated from this song, she must have been more than satisfied. In the midst of the applause that followed, she glanced at the table in the corner at the back of the room. Nicky Toresca was still sitting there, slid down in his chair, not applauding, but watching her intently.

As the room quieted a little, she spoke into the microphone again. "Thank you, Ladies and Gentlemen. That's all for now. Stick around, and I'll be back—maybe."

She waved her hand, nodded to the musicians once more and left the orchestra stand, while the orchestra leader picked up his program where she had interrupted it. She walked in and out among the tables, this time smiling at the faces that were turned toward her. She made her way to the table in the back of the room and sat down in the chair across from Nicky Toresca. He had ordered a fresh drink for her, and she took a sip of it gratefully. He struck the match for her cigarette and she thanked him with a nod of her head. After awhile she said, "So?"

"What's your name?" he asked her.

She shrugged her shoulders a little. "Most folks call me Petey."

Nicky Toresca leaned forward in his chair and closed his hand tight over hers on the table top. "I don't guess this town could get along without you, Petey," he said softly.

Petey slid her hand out from under his, but she looked at him and dropped her eyelashes provocatively.

# 14

THE NEXT DAY WAS A BUSY ONE FOR PETEY. SHE WAS awakened about noon by a phone call from Nicky Toresca, suggesting that she meet him for lunch. She accepted the invitation with alacrity. Once the phone was back on the hook, she snuggled down regretfully in the soft warmth of her bed, but in a moment she flung the covers back suddenly and ran for her shower. She met Nicky at the appointed place and time, and over a leisurely breakfast-lunch she haggled with him charmingly over a salary and contract for her services at his night club. Nicky, too, was charming about it, as if she were a child to be humored in the matter, but back of that was a wariness. When it came to talk of actual terms, she found him bent on driving a hard bargain with her. He exhibited a penuriousness in money matters that she had anticipated. It took all of her wit and charm to arrive at a suitable understanding. As soon as lunch was finished she suggested they run right off to his lawyer and put the whole thing in writing while they were still in agreement. Nicky tried to put her off, but Petey resorted to a charming childlike stubbornness and imperiousness, and he finally capitulated. Once her copy of the brief contract form was in her purse, with Nicky Toresca's signature at the bottom of it, Petey, in high spirits, hailed a cab to keep a beauty-shop appointment.

Next, the afternoon rehearsal which went as well as she had anticipated. She made a special effort to win the good will of the musicians, as well as of every other employee at the club with whom she came in contact. She found them friendly enough, but already they had set her apart, as Nicky Toresca's current favorite and consequently as someone to be treated with more care and reserve than the average employee. That was something that Petey had anticipated too and she knew how to deal with it. She was not impressed with her fellow entertainers, but there was a comic whom Petey liked from the first glimpse at his face, which was battered like that of an ex-prize fighter's. He bore the unbelievable name of Tommy Terwilliger and his repertoire included burlesques on singing, tap dancing and magic. He was also, she learned, a competent bartender who sometimes was pressed into service at the bar on busy nights, or on the regular bartender's night off.

Rehearsals were lengthy, slipshod and ill-organized, and Petey became bored. How any sort of well-organized floor show was ever presented here was a mystery to her. In the meantime, Petey was on the alert for any other signs of activity that might be going on around Nicky Toresca's. There were rooms upstairs, which would mean girls or gambling or both. From the short time she had spent here the preceding evening, it was apparent that whatever went on upstairs, Nicky Toresca never allowed it to spread to the downstairs part of his enterprise. The bar did not open for the cocktail business until five-thirty. It was deserted now, except for a solitary bartender who was apparently taking an inventory of liquor supplies, ice, cash and mixers, before the opening.

Three bleach-blonde chorus girls were working over a new dance variation suggested to them by the bleary-eyed master of ceremonies who seemed to double for dance director. Petey watched them critically for a moment and then turned to Terwilliger, the battered-face stubby comedian who lounged at a near-by table, twisting a burned-out cigar stub in his fingers nervously.

"Hi," she said cheerfully. "Let's you and me skip the agony and go up to the bar and have a beer, how's about it?"

"Sure, if you want to," he said, looking at her a little dubiously. He got up and shuffled after Petey's clicking heels toward the steps up to the bar. He was a funny little guy, Petey was thinking. Before he had answered her, he had looked behind him and in all directions, as if to make quite sure that it was actually to him that she was speaking. Something in that involuntary mannerism touched Petey. The poor lonesome little guy! She wondered what was the matter with him, rum-dum or punchy—he certainly looked like an ex-pug—or maybe a combination of the two.

Petey led the way to the bar and climbed up on a stool, hooking her heels in the rung comfortably. "Hi, how'd yuh like to set us up a couple beers on the house," she said to the bartender. "We sure need 'em."

The little man named Terwilliger edged up on the stool next to hers timidly. While the bartender poured the beer, Petey hummed the tune the orchestra was playing and watched the efforts of the chorus girls as they rehearsed their routine.

"How long you been workin' here?" she asked him kindly.

Again he looked over his shoulder quickly, as if he expected to find someone standing right behind him to whom Petey was speaking. "Me? Oh—oh, I dunno. A long time. Two years, I guess. Ever since Mr. Toresca started up this place."

Petey smiled at him encouragingly and propped her chin on her hand. "Gosh, you must be good," she said admiringly. She wondered how long she would have to talk to him before he would quit looking startled everytime she addressed a remark to him.

"Aw, naw!" he said quickly, as if he wanted to set her right on the error of such a belief as soon as possible. "Naw! I ain't always been in the show, neither. Sometimes I jus' tend bar, sometimes I jus' help clean up the place. Mr. Toresca's been awful nice to me."

He looked at Petey again timidly, and started, as if he were surprised to find her still listening and smiling at him sympathetically. Then he said self-consciously, "People been awful nice to me. You know how it is, lots a the old-timers remember back when I was fighting. They been awful nice."

Petey tasted her beer meditatively. Yes, she could imagine that it would give Nicky Toresca quite a kick to make an ostentatious show of keeping someone like Terwilliger employed around his place.

"Yeah, I thought you was a fighter when I first saw you," Petey said. Tommy grinned and ran his hand over his battered features. "Yeah, I guess you couldn't miss. I wasn't so good at it, but I done a lot of fightin' in my day."

Petey grinned and patted his hand. "Aw, I bet you were, too, good. You're just bein' modest. How did you happen to get in show business?"

Tommy was beginning to warm up to her, he grinned back at her shyly. "Oh, I was in show business, so to speak, before I ever took up fightin'. My dad was a piano player; he showed me how ta play the piano. I had a job playin' piano when I was twelve er thirteen years old."

"Well, look at you!" Petey said admiringly. "I guess you could just about run this joint single-handed."

"Oh, I don't play piano much no more," Tommy said. "My hands . . ." He held out his stubby hands as he spoke, both of them knobby with broken fingers. "I never was much good at it, anyways. I never learned how to play by music nor nothin' fancy, jus' picked up a little that my dad showed me . . ."

"How did you get to doin' funny stuff?"

The little man seemed delighted to talk, now that he was relaxing a little and coming to trust the sincerity of Petey's interest. "Oh, that was sorta by accident. I never could sing or dance or anythin' like that worth nothin'. Everytime I usta try, it'ud make folks laugh. I got to cuttin' up like that when I was a kid playin' piano, cause it made everybody laugh."

"That's all right!" Petey patted his hand again. "And sometime I want you to play the piano for me. I bet you're a swell piano player, too. Gosh, I wish I could play. I never could put two notes together worth nothing."

With his pleasure, Tommy grinned so widely that his scarred features drew up into a grimace. "Aw, I bet you could play if yuh tried," he said delightedly. "Anyways, what you wanta play for? You sing awful nice, Miss—Miss . . ."

"My name's Petey."

She held out her hand and he shook it carefully.

"I'm pleased to know you, Miss Petey," he said.

Petey squeezed his hand tight, and for some reason she felt warm tears stinging behind her eyelids. Well, look at me, she thought, getting all weepy over an old stumblebum hanging around a night club. But, just the same, she thought defensively, I bet I'll never have a better friend in this joint, or in this town, or in the whole world.

"You got any family, Tommy?" she asked him. "You don't come from this part of the country, do you?"

"Nope. I was born down South, but I been up North here for a number a years. I guess all the family I got left now is my son," he finished proudly.

"Oh! You gotta son? Is he here in town with you?"

"Yup," Tommy said happily. "He's goin' to the Junior College now."

"Gosh, good for him!" Petey said admiringly. "Does he take after his father?"

Tommy's face shadowed momentarily, and he twisted his beer glass several times in his knobby fingers. "Well, I tell you, Miss Petey. He's kinda handy with his fists, Jimmy is, and he's kinda got it in his head lately to be crazy over fightin'. But I keep a tellin' him fightin' ain't nothin' but a bum's racket. Lord a'mighty, if he don't believe it, all he's gotta do is look at me." Tommy smiled crookedly as he said it.

Petey was silent, her face warm with sympathy. The orchestra leader finally called to Petey that he was ready to rehearse her number.

"Jesus H. Christ, it's about time." She paused to swallow the last of her beer and drop her cigarette in the ash tray on the bar. "See you later, Tommy." She patted his arm and was gone down the steps, the skirt of her trim navy-blue suit swirling around her knees, and a length of navy-blue veiling from her hat trailing in the air behind her.

Tommy Terwilliger watched her go regretfully, with admiration and dumb affection on his face.

That night, on her way to Toresca's, Petey paid Sally a brief call. She ran up the stairs, holding up her long skirt in either hand, and pounded on the door, wanting to know cheerfully if there wasn't anybody home at Sally's house. She burst through the door into the living room, just as Sally got up from her chair.

No, Petey couldn't sit down, she assured Sally. Her cab was waiting out in front and she was late now. Where in the world was she going all dressed up so fancy, Sally wanted to know. Hadn't Joe told her? Petey asked in surprise. How in the world could Joe have told her anything, Sally complained, it was getting so that she didn't see Joe more than twice a week, the hours he kept. What was Petey up to now, anyway?

Why, Petey was a working woman now, she said triumphantly, and triumphantly she pulled her contract with Nicky Toresca out of her evening bag and waved it under Sally's eyes. Sally stared at it, half-incredulous and half-disapproving. Well, what did you know about that! Petey had been in town about three days, why, less than that, and here she had a wonderful job singing at Nicky Toresca's night club.

"Gosh, Petey," Sally said. "It'll be so nice to have you here in town for awhile." But she could not keep the disapproval from showing on her face.

Petey took hold of Sally's shoulders and shook her gently. "Aw, honey, don't you go all sourpuss on me like this. It's all right! Hey, hey, don't tell me you're afraid I'll vamp your boy friend away from you!"

Sally smiled in spite of herself, but then her face was serious again. "No, Petey, you can joke about it all you want to, but I just don't like you gettin' mixed up with Nicky Toresca. Things are bad enough right now, with Joe and everything. I wish to goodness I'd known enough to keep my fool mouth shut about him!"

"My God, what kind of talk is that?" Petey said. "Aw, now, looky, honey, don't we always tell each other our troubles? Aren't we family?" She was silent a moment, and then she took hold of the starched lapel of Sally's green-and-white uniform and spoke slowly, "Looky, dear, I—I—don't think you'll have to worry about Nicky Toresca hanging around you for awhile anyway. I guess—fickle is the word for Nicky, you see what I mean?"

"Of course I do," Sally burst out. "That's just the trouble; that's just what I don't like."

"You know how it is," Petey went on carefully, "I come along, I'm something new, I wear fancy clothes, I sing a couple songs, I . . ."

"Petey Braun!" Sally's face was incredulous. "Why, Petey Braun! You talk as if—why anybody'd think you was afraid that I'd feel—feel—jealous or something, because—because you come along and Nicky Toresca starts running after you and forgets all about me! Why, why shouldn't he, for goodness' sakes! You're beautiful an'—why look at us right this minute, you're all beautiful and shiny an'—like something right out of a magazine, and me—all sloppy and dumpy, my hair hanging, like a regular old hag and . . ."

"Aw, no, Sally, don't say that," Petey's deep voice was uneven with feeling. "No, it's not like that at all. Why, you're the one! You're fresh and young and beautiful. Why, if we needed anything to prove that Nicky Toresca wasn't nothin' but a goddam fool this would be it, that he'd pass up somebody like you for—for—something like me, nothing but a mess of glitter an' a pair of rolling eyes—and—and a pair of wigglin' hips and . . ."

"Aw, Petey!" Sally put both arms around her and hugged her tight. "You haven't changed a bit, have you? You're just the same big sweet kid, so 'fraid a hurtin' somebody's feelin's that you'd . . ." Sally hugged her tight and then she burst out laughing. "Why, Petey, you're acting just like I cared something about Nicky Toresca, as if I wanted him hanging around me, as if I cared if he died or run off with two dozen other women or what. You know it isn't like that. You know all that's worrying me is that I hate Nicky Toresca so, and I don't want you getting mixed up with him and him—him—makin' love to you and stuff like that! That's all I care about!"

Petey's laughter boomed. "Well, sure! Listen to us playin' a heavy dramatic scene over that beetle-brained clothes-horse bastard!"

"Why, sure!" Sally echoed; and the face she turned toward Petey was warm with affection.

"Looky," Petey said. "Don't you go worrying your head about me and the Nicky! This is strictly business. I needed the job and I wanted the heat off you. Well, that's fine, and I can keep him running around in circles for quite awhile. Christ, I really gotta run," she finished. "I can hear that taxi meter tickin' way up here, can't you?" She opened her purse hurriedly and slipped a couple bills into Sally's hand, closing her fingers tight over them.

"Oh, no," Sally said. "No, Petey, really. Look, I—I won't take it. It's your money. I don't need it, honest, I don't. Now, Petey, please!"

"Aw, skip it! I got paid a week in advance today, and I got so much money I don't know what to do with it. No, looky, you got doctor bills for Virginia and stuff and she's my sister too, and it's just as much up to me as it is up to you. You take that money and shut up or I'll knock your pretty little teeth right down your pretty little throat, you hear me?"

She turned away down the hall and Sally wailed after her, "Petey, it's too much! I won't take all this money. Why, this is enough to pay for all the doctor and the medicine, and a lot more besides! I won't take all this money!"

"My God, anybody'd think I handed you the San Francisco mint!" Petey marveled. "Quit yellin' at the top a your voice about all that money or all the stick-up boys over in the prison will hear you and break jail! Jesus Peter Piper! I bet that taxi Joe thinks I died up here. I'll be seein' yuh!"

# 15

PETEY WORKED HARD AT HER JOB AT TORESCA'S AND was rewarded by a growing following among the customers. Between work, rehearsals and beauty-shop appointments she located a comfortable furnished apartment and moved over from the hotel. She also found time to order some new clothing and play a little poker in the well-equipped gambling rooms on the second floor at Toresca's. The third floor, she learned, was given over to rooms for private parties, girls furnished at a price. One day, when she walked into the Nicky's office to meet him for a lunch date, she interrupted him in the process of haggling over financial matters with a stout, over-dressed madame. That was her first taste of the famous Toresca temper, and the Nicky's positive belief in the advisability of making his visitors knock on all doors at all times.

She didn't get out to Sally's again for three or four days, until one damp dark afternoon when it suddenly occurred to her that Virginia must be feeling very lonely and dismal, confined to the house as she was, with such cheerless weather crowding at the windows. As she climbed the porch steps she heard the factory noises; the dampness of the atmosphere muted the metallic quality of the sound until it merely seemed that the moisture-hung air itself was pulsing continually with great dull thudding vibrations. Petey paused momentarily to listen. She liked factory noises and she liked factory towns. They were alive. They had a vitality all their own that other towns seemed to lack. This town was booming, she had heard, with work on war contracts. Petey made a mental note to find out more about that, what the produce of these factories was, what percentage of the town's population they employed. Another thing, Petey decided, some Saturday night between her spots on the program at Toresca's she wanted to go around to some of the joints where the factory boys went with their girl friends to drink beer. Those places had a vitality, too, that made Toresca's seem anemic. Petey thought she would like to sing in such places. Probably she would have her wish about that, too, some day, Petey grinned wickedly to herself as she climbed the stairs to Sally's apartment. She could just see herself a few years from now, crawling around from one cheesy beer joint to another, probably with a guitar and a tin cup, singing old, out-of-date songs in a whisky voice. Oh, well, with a hi ho and the wind and the rain and the rain it raineth every day!

Petey beat a tattoo on the door with her fist. "Anybody home to Sally's house?"

She heard a voice answer, the words indistinguishable, so she opened the door and walked in. The living room was deserted, lighted only by the bulb lights on the Christmas tree in front of the window. Just then the bathroom door opened, the bright light streaming out, and Virginia appeared, a towel partially wrapped around her dripping hair.

"Oh, hello," Virginia said a little shyly. "I was just coming to let you in."

"Hi," Petey said. "What you doing, washing your hair? Looky, young lady, don't you know you'll catch cold, running around with your head all wet like that? It's awful easy to catch cold after the flu, and a relapse is no joke. You rinse your hair off a little and get out here over this register but quick."

"You think I'll catch cold?" Virginia said in a troubled voice. "I thought it would be all right to wash it, seeing I was going to stay right here in the house."

"Oh, I guess it'll be all right if you hurry up and get out here over this register." Petey tested the air over the register with her hand. "There's a lot of heat coming up here."

"I'll be right there," Virginia said hastily. She disappeared from the doorway, and there came the sound of water splashing in the bowl.

Petey slid out of her damp coat and furs, and kicked off her shoes, holding first one damp foot and then the other over the register. "Jesus, it's wet outdoors! Does the sun ever shine around this town? Where are the kids? If they're playin' outdoors someplace they're gonna be soaked."

The sound of splashing water ceased, and Virginia came out of the bathroom.

Petey pulled up a chair to the edge of the floor register. "Here, sit down," she said, "rub your head good with that towel and then lean over the register."

Virginia sat down obediently, and began to rub and squeeze her fine dark hair with the bath towel. "Where's the kids?" Petey asked again.

"Oh, they went home with some boy to see his Christmas stuff. They were going to play over at his house awhile. Gee, I suppose they'll get soakin' wet, coming home. I guess Harold is out delivering his papers. He has a paper route, you know."

"Oh, does he? Good for him," Petey said absently. "How you feelin', Ginny?"

"Oh, I'm fine," Virginia said. "I—I feel a lot better. I'm all right now."

"Shaky in the knees, I betcha!"

Virginia smiled a little, across her white serious face. "Uh huh."

Petey looked at Virginia hard for a moment, and then she said suddenly with the curious gentleness that sometimes crept into her deep voice, "Looky, honey, would you like to have me do the front of your hair up in pin curls for you?"

"Oh, there isn't any sense in bothering with it," Virginia said listlessly. "Thanks, anyway."

"Oh, it won't take but a minute," Petey coaxed. "It'll take it a little longer to dry, but it'll be so much easier to comb. Did you ever wear it back from your forehead in a big curl with a little bow or something? I think it would look awfully cute that way. Let's try it, huh?"

Virginia started to protest again, but Petey interrupted her. "Is there a comb and hairpins in the bathroom? No, sit still, I'll get 'em. You stay here where it's warm."

Petey went off to the bathroom, and returned in a minute with a little paper package of hairpins and a comb in her hands. She dropped them in Virginia's lap. "Here we are! Guess we better have some more light here." She switched on the floor lamp and then came back to stand near Virginia's chair. "You better put that towel around your shoulders. I'll have to comb your hair out, and it might be a little wet for you. I'll yell when I'm ready and you can hand me hairpins. If I pull your hair too hard, you holler, won't you?"

Petey wound little flat curls on Virginia's head expertly, chattering to her all the while. The door from the hall opened suddenly and Petey looked around over her shoulder. "Well, hi," she said cheerfully. "If it isn't little brother Joey! You're just in time, you can be next. What'll you have, wave, pin curls, page boy . . ."

"Hi," Joe said. He closed the door behind him, and stood still a moment, watching Petey's fingers with the long, red-painted nails as she fastened another curl with a couple of hairpins. "Gone into the hair-dressin' business, huh? Jesus, it's wet and cold out!"

"It's warm in here. Take your coat off and stand over here by this register and dry out, why don't you?"

Joe went to the icebox instead, returning with a can of beer to sit in morose silence while he drank it. "Christ, you're a sociable sour-puss today," Petey said to Joe, with a teasing note in her voice. "Old mood indigo! What's eatin' yuh, Joey?"

"Goddam sloppy weather gets on your nerves," Joe mumbled.

Petey pinned down a curl industriously. "Joey, didn't you used to work at the factory where what's his name O'Connor does?"

"Yeah," Joe said flatly.

"What happened? Did you get promoted outa there on your can?"

"Naw, I quit."

"How come?" Petey asked with frank curiosity in her voice. "I thought the way these shops was booming with war work everybody was making fancy big money. Gosh, practically everybody I know is looking for a factory job!"

"Hell with a factory job," Joe said.

"Why? Whatcha mean?"

"To hell with shop work, that's all," Joe said sulkily.

"There we are," Petey said to Virginia as she slipped the last pin in place. "You know how I mean to comb it out when it's dry, don't you? Get it all together in your hand and comb it right back from your forehead smooth, and then make a big curl over your hand. Fasten it down right in front of the curl with pins, and then fix a little tiny ribbon bow in front of the curl. It'll look cute."

Virginia patted the curls with her hand carefully. "Thanks an awful lot," she said shyly. "It was awful nice of you to take the trouble."

"No trouble," Petey said. She put her arm around Virginia's

shoulders and squeezed her tight up against her. She walked over to the table and rummaged in her oversized purse for cigarettes.

"You mean you just don't like shop work, huh, Joey?"

"That's right!" Joe said. Petey was silent. She tipped her face up to her cigarette, and the light from the floor lamp behind the davenport poured down on her. Without much make-up, in such a strong light, her face looked a shade older than it ordinarily did, and her eyes a little tired.

Virginia sat quietly, her shoulders hunched, her head bent over the register, but she listened to them attentively.

Petey broke the silence at last. "How do you stand with the local draft board, Joey?"

Joe's body went tense in his chair, and he didn't answer for a moment. Then he took a deep breath, and let his body relax gradually. "I gotta high number."

"You look pretty healthy to me," Petey said. "You think they'll get you, all right?"

This time Joe made no answer at all. The room was very still, except for a faint crackling from the Christmas tree, the sound of the wind outside, and the factory noises just perceptible. Petey glanced at him casually, but his face was hidden in the shadow.

"They'll probably get you, all right, huh?" she said.

"Now is it my turn to ask questions or should we talk about the weather?" Joe said with a nasty edge to his voice.

"I'm sorry," Petey said. "I was just interested, that's all. You know how it is, I haven't seen neither one a you kids in so long I sorta have to ask questions to catch up with what gives with you." She waited a minute, but Joe didn't say anything, so she went on abruptly. "Joey, why don't you fool 'em and enlist in the army?"

Joe started in his chair. "Enlist?" he echoed incredulously. He laughed shortly, and his voice was suddenly raw and jumping with nerves. "Like hell I'll enlist! By God, if they want me, they're gonna have ta come and get me!"

Petey stared at Joe. His body had tensed again, and for a moment there had been naked fear in his voice.

She spoke to him soothingly, a sort of puzzlement on her face. "I don't guess the army is as bad as you think it is, Joey. Besides, this isn't some plot the government cooked up just to get you, Joe Braun, into a uniform. It's happening to everybody. Lots of guys aren't so crazy about going, they got good jobs, they're married, something like that." She shrugged her shoulders. "But—what can they do about it? The draft is in, it's a law. They gotta go, whether they want to or not. You're no different than anybody else. Suppose it does turn out to be two years instead a one? What can you do about it? Maybe it won't be so much fun, but there's lots of worse things than being in the army. You don't have to worry about a job for awhile, you see some country . . ."

Joe interrupted her. "Don't gimme that bull!" he said in a strained voice. "I can see what's comin' just as straight as the next guy. It's okay to set around and talk about what a nice healthy life the army is, but hell, you can't fool me! This country is gettin' into the war. Everybody knows it! Jesus, the war! I seen them newsreels! Sure, the army is a fine place to be in! I seen them newsreels!"

Petey almost jumped herself, because Joe Braun's voice was suddenly thin and uneven with a fear that was almost terror, because his terror-stricken voice suddenly brought into that quiet room the whine of falling shells, the explosion of bombs, the roar of great guns, rumbling tanks, shrieking dive bombers. Petey shut her eyes to the memory of a couple of newsreels that she, too, would never forget. Virginia sat up straight in her chair and looked from one to the other, her eyes wide in her face.

Petey spoke with the gentleness in her voice. "Yeah, Joe, I've seen those newsreels, too. We sit here and look at the pictures, but over there in Europe that stuff is happening to an awful lotta people."

Joe was making a visible effort to get control of himself again.

Petey spoke quietly. "Okay, Joe. So maybe this country might get into the war. So just thinking about the war scares the pants right off you. Suppose everybody felt the same way about it you do. I've seen movie pictures about Hitler's concentration camps, and they weren't so cute either. Take your pick, Joey!"

Joe jumped up out of his chair suddenly, his face driven, his nerves beyond control. "I don't wanta talk about it," he shouted. "I ain't gonna talk about it no more!"

Petey spoke rapidly as Joe began to fumble for his overcoat. "Joey, get wise to yourself, kid, for God's sakes! If just thinkin' about the draft has got you wore down to a bundle a nerves and all scared inside, get wise to yourself and do something about it! Get outa this town and go get yourself a nice job in an airplane factory or something like that, so you can get deferred to do defense work!"

Joe was struggling into his overcoat, his long arms waving in the air, as he tried to find the armholes. "Sure! Go getta factory job! Getta factory job! Jesus, I get so goddam sick a people yellin' that, I could puke! Maybe I just as soon be in the army as hang around a shop day in day out waitin' for one a them big bastard machines to gnaw an arm off or a leg off. Sure! It's all right for you to talk, you never . . ."

Petey was on her feet suddenly and across the room in front of Joe. "Joey," she said. "Joey! Now I get it why you hang around Nicky Toresca! Now I know! But Joey, you're all wrong. Now I know why you copy after Nicky Toresca, but you're wrong, Joey! Christ, you couldn't be more wrong! You think Nicky Toresca is pretty tough, don't you? You think he's hard and tough. You think he ain't afraid of nothing! You think he hasn't got a nerve in his body! Joey, you poor little sucker! Joey, Nicky Toresca isn't a bit different than you are right now! Nicky Toresca is a scared jittery little yellow sneak! He makes a big noise, like he's tough, but he isn't. You're never gonna learn about guts from Nicky Toresca, Joey! Joey!"

He slammed the door in her face, and a moment later there came the sound of his feet clattering down the bare uncarpeted steps. Petey turned around slowly, and looked into Virginia's pale frightened face. She patted her on the shoulder automatically. "It's all right, honey, so we did a lot of yelling. That's all it amounts to. Gosh, I'm a dope! There I go and hop all over Joey, instead of takin' it slow and easy, the way I would have done if I'd a had a brain in my head! I mean about him and the Nicky. Once things start clickin' in my head, what do I do but jump up and start hoppin' all over Joey. You think I'd know better at my age. I guess I'll never learn to keep my damn fool mouth shut! I guess I'll never learn to keep my goddam nose outa other people's business. I'm always buttin' in—telling folks what do do. You have to keep an eye on me, Ginny."

"Well," she added, after a moment's silence, "I gotta get back to my place and start thinkin' about gettin' some dinner. Just a poor working gal, that's me!"

"I know Sally would want you to stay to supper," Virginia said timidly. "We—we don't eat till sort of late but . . ."

"Aw, don't bother about me," Petey said cheerfully. You've got enough to feed around here. Gosh, I wish you knew where the kids were, and I'd stop by with the cab and bring 'em home, they're gonna get sopping."

"They ought to be home by now," Virginia said. "I told them they weren't to stay long."

Petey got into her trim black coat, singing idly in her deep voice. She looked up suddenly and found Virginia staring at her, and she burst out laughing.

"The old pipes sound a little foggy, huh?"

"Oh, no," Virginia said. "I—I—just never heard you sing before, that was all. I—it's swell."

"Aw, you're sweet!" Petey said. "You'll have to come over to Toresca's some night and see how I do it. I know what. Why don't you come to the New Year's Eve party over there? You'll be out doing a little celebrating anyway, won't you?"

Virginia shook her head slowly. "Uh uh. No, I don't know anybody or anything and . . ."

"Now there is something we'll have to fix up," Petey said positively. She made a mental note to ask Tommy Terwilliger if his boy Jimmy had a girl friend.

Petey jammed her hat on her head and gathered up her heavy furs. Just then there was a clatter of feet in the hall, and the door opened. Buddy and Marilyn burst into the room.

"Hello kids," Petey boomed. "Look at you! Soakin, soppin', drippin', drizzlin'! Come on, get your things off quick! C'mon, c'mon, get 'em off! Quick, quick!" She knelt down and unbuttoned first one coat, then the other, pulled their caps and mittens off, unbuckled overshoes, while the children shrieked with laughter, dancing about her, pressing wet sticky kisses on her face.

# 16

SALLY HAD NEVER DREADED A VISIT TO ROY AS MUCH as she dreaded that visit the week after Christmas. Roy had been so hurt, so disappointed. To look forward to a release was one thing, a vague indefinite date sometime in the future, one never knew just when, but to look forward to a Christmas parole was another. That meant to count days on a calendar, to go to sleep at night, saying this day is past and tomorrow there will be only this many days left before I go home for Christmas; a Christmas parole meant saying on visiting days, this many more visits you will make and then comes the one when I will go home with you. That was what a Christmas parole meant, and Roy had counted on it for weeks. Oh, Sally thought, there was nothing in the world that she wouldn't give, if that could have happened to her instead of to Roy. Roy had been so brave and so patient; he asked for so little, and he had counted on this one thing so much, a small thing, when you thought of it, but a couple days away from keys and bars and call-bells, a couple days at home, the chance to spend Christmas with his family, just the simple thing that most people took for granted. But it hadn't happened that way for Roy. Oh, there wasn't any use, Sally told herself, in wasting time now in regretting, and crying over it, and vainly wishing that this could have happened to her instead of to him. That was very easy to do; the harder thing, and the thing that she had to do now, was somehow to make it up to him, somehow to cheer him up, somehow to take the hurt and disappointment out of him, make him understand that what was past was past and not worth hurt and bitterness. But how was she to do that? Oh, I can't, it's too big a job for me, Sally cried desperately over and over. I'm not a very smart person, I can't think of things to do and say like some other people can, somebody'll have to help me, somebody'll have to tell me what to do. I just love him more than anything in the world, but sometimes just loving isn't enough. Sometimes you have to be smart too, and think with the head as unerringly as you feel with the heart. And I'm not a smart person at all, and I love him so!

But the hours passed and the days, and the day of the visit drew near. It was like the game Sally had played as a child, you scurried desperately when the call came: "A bushel of wheat, a bushel of rye, who isn't ready holler aye!" Because right after that came the inexorable call: "Here I come, ready or not!" Oh, yes, Sally told herself grimly, the day would come, ready or not, and there would be a bus trip and at the other end of it a meeting with Roy. All living was like that, "Here I come, ready or not!"

So the hours dwindled, and Sally's fears mounted increasingly. It was something she couldn't talk about, not even to Petey. This was so peculiarly her problem, hers and Roy's. The night before, Sally lay sleepless in her bed and said little, broken, inarticulate prayers to nobody in particular—not help for me because of me, but for Roy's sake. Because Roy is the finest person in the whole world, and he must have the best, the very best . . . Oh, I love him so, but the loving isn't enough. Oh, no, it isn't, because just the loving alone can harm sometimes, just as sometimes it is the only help. You have to be smart with the head, too, and know the things to do and the words to say. Oh, please, please, not for me, but for Roy's sake, please, because I love him so . . .

She awoke to a jangling alarm clock in a gray dawn with a feeling of fatigue through her body, like a physical presence there, heavy and dull as lead. She went through the business of breakfast and dressing in a sort of haze, all faces a blur and all voices a jangling confusion, and all the while the clock ticking away the minutes slowly and distinctly. She caught her bus downtown and went through her work at the restaurant like an automaton. Before it was time for her to leave for the bus station, Sam Toresca came to her and insisted that she eat something. She sat down at the counter obediently, but when the food came, she was aware suddenly of a nervous pain and nausea in her stomach that made food seem impossible to her. That frightened Sally, and roused her to an awareness of herself. Now look, you've got to snap out of it, she told herself firmly, you can't get sick, you can't go to pieces like this. You've got to be strong, you've got to be alert and controlled for Roy's sake. You can have all the nerves and fears and jitters you want after this visit is over, but now you can't have any at all because of Roy. Sally ate all the food set before her and drank two cups of strong hot coffee before she went to the washroom for her coat and hat. She combed her hair, put the lipstick on her mouth and forced the muscles of her face to relax into the smile that she must have when Roy caught sight of her this afternoon.

She slept on the first and longest part of her bus trip, not so much from habit as from sheer nervous fatigue. Through her sleep and through her waking moments during the rest of the trip, it ran like a refrain, "Here I come, ready or not! Ready or not!" At the hospital she didn't see the nurse until she touched her on the shoulder. "Hello, Mrs. Otis, how are you?" the girl said, smiling. "I'm sorry to keep you waiting, but I was delayed." Sally gathered up her packages and rose to follow.

"Well, did you have a nice Christmas?" the nurse asked cheerfully as they walked along the corridor.

Sally's voice stuck in her throat. There were so many, many things that she must ask in the short space of time before she saw Roy. Sally cleared her throat, and listened to her own voice, warm and natural, saying, "Yes, we had an awful nice Christmas, thank you."

They paused then, while the young woman went through the ritual of unlocking and locking doors, and then they mounted the stairs together.

"My husband," Sally said, "how—how has he been?"

"Fairly well, Mrs. Otis. I think there has been a decided improvement in his case." She answered Sally briskly, without hesitation.

"He must have been terribly disappointed and blue, hasn't he?" Sally insisted desperately. "About not getting the parole, I mean. He planned on it so, and the doctor wouldn't let me come to see him again before Christmas, and he hasn't written a word to me, and I've been so worried."

They paused again, while the nurse relocked another door behind them. Her keys rattling together sounded very loud in the narrow corridor. "Well, of course, Mrs. Otis, he was very disappointed. I think I warned you about that, your last visit." The nurse's voice was friendly. "He planned on it so much. Naturally, he has been very depressed. These last few days he's been a little—difficult."

"Difficult?" Sally echoed the word in a voice that almost trembled.

"Oh, nothing serious, really," the nurse hastened to reassure her. "He simply refused to talk, or associate with the other patients, and we had a little trouble in getting him to eat and take his medicine. I'm sure he will show an improvement after your visit. Your visits always mean a great deal to him."

Sally was silent with the fear pressing at her lungs.

"You must be very cheerful today," the nurse said, kindly. "Don't make too big a fuss over him. He mustn't be encouraged to feel sorry for himself."

Not to make too big a fuss over him, the words repeated themselves in Sally's ears. Not to make too big a fuss over him. Oh, how could they ask that? She was a human being, she wasn't made of steel, she was flesh and blood and bone, and she loved him, and she wanted to comfort him and fuss over him in the only way that she knew how. They couldn't ask that, they couldn't expect her to be light and flip and gay, not this visit. It wasn't any use, she couldn't do it, oh, she couldn't! "Here I come, ready or not!"

The nurse relocked the last door behind them and said, "You better leave the cigarettes here at the desk. I'll mark them with his name."

Sally stripped the paper wrapping off the long carton with steady fingers, and removed one package of cigarettes before she handed it over to the nurse. The nurse scribbled Roy's name across the cardboard flap, as Sally watched her. Then she searched for the key to unlock the drawer where cigarettes were kept.

"Oh, Mrs. Otis, I want to thank you," the nurse said. "Mr. Otis gave me the box of candy Christmas day. It was very thoughtful of you. I only wish that the relatives of more patients would remember that we keep Christmas the same as they do, or we try to."

Sally made a little sound in her throat in answer. The drawer clicked shut and they started off down the corridor. "I thought you'd like to have your visit in a private room again," the nurse said. "It's a little more pleasant, I think, than trying to visit in the ward."

"Thank you," Sally murmured.

The nurse lowered her voice a little as they approached the turn in the corridor. "Another thing. Mr. Otis may act a little resentful toward you at first. If he does, I would try to ignore it, if I were you."

Resentful toward her? Why, that had never occurred to her once in all her worrying about this visit, Sally thought. Hurt, disappointment, depression, all of those things she had anticipated, but never resentment toward her. Why, that was where half the fear of these visits came from, Sally realized suddenly. The normal emotional reactions were hard enough to cope with, and then there was always the unspoken fear of the non-normal reactions that it was impossible to anticipate or to cope with at all.

They came to the turn in the corridor, and Sally put the smile on her face, and felt her heart beat, quick, dull thudding in her body. They turned the corner, and there was Roy standing motionless in the doorway down the corridor on the left. Sally felt first the shock she always felt, noticing each time she came how thin he was and how stooped his shoulders. The next second she forgot everything, except her joy to be seeing Roy once again, after separation.

She called out to him, her voice uneven with tenderness, "Oh, Roy! Hi, darling!"

He didn't answer her or come to meet her. He just kept looking at her with his face set and serious.

"Look who's come to see you," the nurse said cheerfully. "We've missed her, haven't we, Mr. Otis?"

They came up to him then, but he still didn't smile, or speak or touch her. Sally closed her fingers tight on his arm and stretched up on tiptoe to kiss him. He stood quite still and rigid. Even on tiptoe, Sally couldn't reach his mouth. She kissed him on the chin. "Oh, darling," she said softly, "how've you been? How are you? Why in the world didn't you write to me? Aw, it's been so long!"

Roy cleared his throat. "Yeah, it has, hasn't it?"

A little chill went through Sally, and the tears came to her eyes.

It was there all right, the sullen resentment, on his face and in his voice.

The nurse ushered them into the room then, and pulled the two plain, straight-backed chairs around to face each other. The same little bare room, the one forbidding window, the high narrow bed against the white wall, the metal table, the two chairs.

"There you are," she said cheerfully. "Have a nice visit now!" She patted Roy's arm as she stepped past him toward the door. She left the door wide open with care and disappeared down the corridor, her stiff, starched, uniform skirt rustling after her.

She left them standing there awkwardly, and even after she was gone, Roy didn't speak or move. Sally put her candy and magazines down on the table miserably. "Roy, what's the matter, dear?" She knew she shouldn't have said it, but somehow she couldn't help it.

He sat down on one of the chairs then, stiffly, but still he did not answer her.

Sally sat down too, and fumbled the package of cigarettes in her hands, tearing loose the cellophane wrapping. She'd got to snap out of it, Sally told herself. The nurse had been right, she had to be cheerful, and, if Roy didn't act right, she had got to ignore it. It wasn't that he wanted to act like this, it was just that he'd been hurt and blue and lonely.

"You—you want a cigarette now?" Sally said, trying out her new cheerful voice.

He shook his head. Sally withdrew the package she had offered him and took out one for herself. She started the old search for matches in her bulging, battered, old purse. "Darn it," she murmured, her voice desperately gay and natural, "never can find anything in this pocketbook. More junk in here . . ." She found the little book of matches finally and struck one for her cigarette.

Just then, after she struck the match, Roy made a little sound and, when she looked at him, his face was twisted and contorted as he cried silently, with great sobs shaking his thin body. It startled Sally so that she almost burst out crying herself. The tears ran down her cheeks helplessly, but in a flash she was kneeling on the floor beside him, one hand tight on his knee, the other tugging at his thin wrist as he covered his face with his hand. "Roy, my darling, don't," she said brokenly. "Don't cry like this, please don't! It's all right, darling, I understand. I understand, but don't cry like this, please. Please, don't! Roy, they'll make me go away if you don't stop crying, honey. They won't let me come again. Roy, if you don't stop you're gonna make me cry too, darling!"

She looked up into his face anxiously, her own lips quivering, and she kept smoothing his hand with her own warm one.

He moved suddenly and pushed her hand away roughly. He talked as best he could, his voice shaking and hoarse with his crying. "I always knew it'ud happen," he said. "I always knew after awhile you'd get sick of comin' down here, that you wouldn't wanta bother with me no more. I mighta known from the way you talked that you didn't really want me ta come home for Christmas. I always knew it'ud happen!"

"Oh, Roy, don't!" Sally said urgently, her face suddenly white and drawn. "Don't say that, don't even think it! Roy, listen to me! Of course I wanted you to come home for Christmas, we all did. We were all as disappointed as you were. When the doctor said you couldn't come, it just about made me sick. But the doctor said you couldn't. I couldn't help it; there wasn't nothin' I could do. Darling, I come to see you just as soon as I could! The doctor wouldn't let me come again before Christmas. I come today just as soon as I could. You can ask the doctor, or the nurse or anybody, darling. Roy, darling, don't say things like that to me! You know yourself when you say them that they aren't true!"

"I guess I know," Roy said. "The doctor told me all along I could go home for Christmas. But that last time you come you went down there and told him you didn't want me! Nor you didn't come near me the next visitin' day, did you! You can fix up all the stories with the doctor you wanta, but I guess I know!"

"Oh, Roy!" Sally whispered his name. She closed her eyes, and bit her lips tight to stop her crying.

Sally heard the rustling of the nurse's uniform outside the door, and then her pleasant voice in the room itself. "Well! What's going on in here?"

Sally rose to her feet as the nurse approached Roy's chair. "I'm awfully sorry, Nurse," she said. "I didn't do nothing to upset him, honest. He just started crying. He—he's got it in his head that I fixed it up with the doctor so he couldn't come home. He thinks I didn't want to come to see him. I . . ."

Sally couldn't talk any more, and she turned away.

The nurse went over to Roy and shook his shoulder gently. Her voice was still even and pleasant. "Why, Mr. Otis! Aren't you ashamed of yourself? Your wife comes all the way down here to see you and then you act like this! The doctor explained to you himself why he thought it wasn't best for you to go home, or for your wife to visit you again before Christmas. It was just because you've made such an improvement that he didn't want to risk any setbacks from the excitement of going home. You're going to be discharged some of these days, and that's a lot better than any two-day parole, isn't it? If you don't stop crying now, your wife will have to leave, and you don't want her to have to leave, do you? There, that's better. You're almost well now. You don't do things like this any more. Think about your wife. Aren't you ashamed to make her feel badly and say things to hurt her after she comes all the way down here to see you so faithfully?"

Roy began to stop his crying. He hunted a handkerchief out of his pocket and blew his nose noisily. Sally stood quietly by the table while the nurse talked to him, her face stark and tragic. I mustn't let him hurt me so, she kept telling herself. It isn't as if he really meant it when he says things like that. It's just that he's sick and nervous and not quite himself. I have to understand that. She lighted another cigarette to busy her hands, and when the nurse stepped away she held out the package to Roy once more. "Don't you want a cigarette, now, dear?" she said, her voice steady and controlled and tender.

"Thanks," he mumbled. He took one, and she struck the match for him, before she sat down again.

"There, that's better," the nurse said. "Now, let's forget all about this and have a nice visit together. Your wife doesn't have very much time to spend with you, you know."

Roy's crying had almost stopped. He kept his eyes lowered to the cigarette burning in his fingers. The nurse lingered a moment longer, her alert eyes on his face, and then she smiled at Sally and disappeared once more.

Sally began to talk cheerfully. "Gosh, I don't have much time left. I don't know where the time goes to, do you? I'll have to hurry and tell you all the news. Not that there ever is much news. We're all fine; the kids are well. They're havin' vacation from school this week, of course. They all sent you their love. I keep workin' every day, same as always. The restaurant is really a swell place to work. Mr. Toresca is so nice to all of us, why . . ." Sally stopped momentarily. She had started to tell about the Christmas party Sam Toresca had had for his employees, but maybe it would be better to make no mention of the holidays at all. "Why, you couldn't ask for a better boss than Mr. Toresca. I want you to meet him when you get home, you'll like him a lot. Oh! You remember me tellin' you about the O'Connors, the folks with the little baby that live down the hall? Well, Johnny O'Connor has been in the hospital. He works at the forge in the bumper factory and he burnt his hands on hot steel, and then he got infection in the burns and had to go to the hospital. He was real sick, but Gloria, that's his wife, said he was comin' home in a day or two. Of course, he won't be able to work for a long time. I guess things will be pretty tough for them. It's too bad, they're both such nice kids."

Roy blew his nose again, and then puffed on his cigarette. Sally couldn't really tell if he was listening to her or not, but she went on talking gaily.

"Virginia had the flu. She's just getting around from it now. You know, there's been a regular epidemic a flu around this winter, I guess on account of so much wet weather. Pa always used to say that a warm winter meant a lotta new graves in the cemetery by spring. Oh, Virginia didn't have it bad; she feels pretty good now. I guess we was lucky, none of the rest of us caught it from her. Joe's got a new job. I guess I didn't tell you, when I wrote last, did I? You know he never liked factory work much. It's a pretty good job, he's—he's working for some man that—that owns a couple restaurants and stuff. Oh! And this is something I didn't write you about! Just guess who's in town, guess!"

She waited a minute, smiling at him, and Roy cleared his throat. "Who?" he said.

"Oh, you'd never guess! Petey! Isn't it swell? And she's gonna stay awhile. She's got herself a little apartment. I haven't been over to see it yet, but she says it's awful cute. She'll come along with me to see you some of these days. She's looking awful well, younger than ever and pretty as a picture. She's just the same big sweet kid. Gosh, it seems so good to have her around again!"

Roy dropped his cigarette butt to the floor and stepped on it. "You better keep away from her," he said morosely. "She's no good!"

"Oh, Roy," Sally said gently. She twisted her hands together in her lap. She was silent just a moment. "Petey's got a job. She's—she's workin' awful hard. She paid all a Virginia's doctor bills and . . ."

"What's she doin'?" Roy asked shortly.

"She's singing—in a night club. She . . ."

"That's a good place for her," Roy said. "She'll have lotsa chance to pick up her kind of money on the side in a place like that. You better keep away from her."

Sally's eyes dropped to her nervous hands again, and she made him answer this time. When she looked up at him again, she was smiling tenderly. "I guess that's all the news," she said. "Now tell me how you been. You didn't write, you know, and I been so worried about you. How have you been feeling and what you been doing?"

"Oh, I been all right," he said. "I just been settin' around here, same as always."

She wanted to ask him if he had received her Christmas package, and about the Christmas-day festivities at the hospital, but once again she decided to avoid any mention of the holiday.

"Well, I brought you some cigarettes," she said. "They're out there at the desk. And here's some magazines and candy and stuff. And some stamps and post cards." She took them out of her purse as she spoke and laid them on top of the magazines on the table. "This time you use 'em, dear. We missed your letters so! You know I can't help but worry when you don't write. You write, won't you?"

He nodded his head, and reached for the pack of cigarettes on the table. She hurried to strike the match for him, and then returned the matches to her purse. She fidgeted with her purse and gloves and finally she said, "Darling, I guess I have to go now. Seems like the time goes so fast. I don't no more than get here and I have to think about leavin' again."

She stood up slowly, pulling her coat tighter around her, and he got up too. "Well, take care a yourself, dear," she said a little uncertainly, "and write often, won't you? Hurry up and get better and . . ."

He moved over to her suddenly and took hold of her shoulders tight in his fingers. "Sally," he said, "don't stay away. Don't you never leave me, Sally. And don't let Petey get you mixed up in no . . ."

"Oh, Roy, darling!" Sally lifted her face up to him, with all of her love for him shining on it.

He took her in his arms suddenly, pressing her tight, and he kissed her almost savagely, his mouth hard against hers so long that she was breathless. "Darling, everything's all right, isn't it?" Sally whispered.

He was holding her so tight that he was hurting her. "Oh, Sally, sweetheart!"

"Leaving already, Mrs. Otis?" The nurse's voice was cool and pleasant as she appeared in the doorway.

Roy held her tight for just a moment longer and then he released her. Sally straightened the felt hat on her head and smiled at the nurse, as she backed away from him. "Seems like the time goes so fast, I no more than get here, and then . . ." her voice trailed off. She fussed with her coat and purse and stood on tiptoe to kiss Roy lightly once again. "Good-bye, darling. Take good care of yourself, and write often, won't you? I'll be back next visiting day. You will write, won't you? Good-bye, darling, good-bye!"

"Good-bye, Sally," he said steadily.

Sally turned away abruptly. Her knees were suddenly unsteady, and she discovered that she was walking too rapidly.

The nurse looked at her a little curiously after they passed the turn in the corridor. "How did the rest of your visit go? Was everything all right?"

"Oh, yes, yes," Sally said hastily. "Everything was fine. I'm sorry, though, about him getting upset like that when I first came. I . . ."

"Oh, I'm sure it wasn't your fault, Mrs. Otis," the nurse said. "Maybe it was a good thing for him, even. He apparently had been brooding over that idea for quite awhile; it was probably good for him to get it out of his system like that."

When they came to the desk, the nurse said, "One of the order-lies is going down. He'll take you down with him, Mrs. Otis."

Sally followed the young man through the maze of doors and corridors and stairways, blindly. Once she was in the main waiting room, she took refuge in the women's powder room. She took off her hat and combed her hair in front of the mirror, staring at the reflection of her white face. Her knees were weak, and she was trembling all over. She couldn't understand herself, she felt so very queer, and somehow frightened. It was, of course, because it had been such a hard visit, she explained to herself. She had dreaded it so to begin with, and it had been so different than she had expected. Roy had not been himself, and for a long time now he had been so natural; oh, maybe blue or depressed, but himself, so they could laugh and talk together. But today was different. His crying like that had hurt her so, and saying those things to her, even if she knew that he didn't mean them. After the nurse had left, he had been so strange and silent, saying those things to her about Petey, and all. Sally knew then that she was really avoiding what had upset her most of all. Yes, it had been the very last, when he had kissed her like that, her mouth was still stiff and sore from it. Oh, that was it, Sally admitted to herself desperately. It was then that Roy had been least like himself. Then he had been a stranger to her. It had been all wrong. That was why, Sally knew now, that she had been frightened, that was why she had almost run away from him. It was an enormous thing to Sally, and her mind turned this way and that, helplessly and desperately, for some explanation or some excuse, but she could find none.

Most of the bus trip home that fear clung to her, to plague her and bewilder her. After awhile, she put it aside a little, and she thought again of Roy's face and how he had cried, and she turned her face toward the window in the dark warm bus, and cried to herself softly. But the fear was still there. Sally lighted a cigarette and stared straight ahead into the darkness, her eyes wide and unblinking till they ached, but she never noticed. The bus motor droned and throbbed, water splashed under the huge tires, and the wind pulled and knocked at the window beside her.

As New Year's Eve drew near, the city was marked with preparation, just as definitely as it had been before Christmas, but preparation of a different sort. Every bar, beer garden and night club in town as well as the theatres, clubs and churches advertised special programs in celebration of that night, in an attempt to attract prospective merry-makers. The traffic division of the local police department launched a crusade in the papers and over the local radio station to combat drunken-driving accidents and fatalities. Celebrants were urged on every hand to use taxis and to leave their automobiles at home.

Nicky Toresca had planned a New Year's Eve party which he firmly expected to outdo anything else of its kind in town and in the surrounding areas as well, so his advertisements stated. He had hired an entire floor show from out of town, in which only Petey and his regular orchestra would participate. The out-of-town enter-tainers arrived several days before the big night, and afternoon rehearsals suddenly became much more strict and far better organ-ized. Petey received special billing in the advertisements and the best spot on the program. She worked carefully over her selection of songs, the patter to go with them, and a selection of songs for group singing. In the meanwhile the big cardboard boxes containing the noisemakers, favors and confetti that were to be distributed among the merrymakers piled up in Nicky Toresca's office. Decorators and electricians crawled over the place, planning the festive redecora-tion of the interior. But even in the midst of work, rehearsals, dress- and beauty-shop appointments Petey found time to worry about Sally and Virginia. New Year's Eve, Petey firmly believed, was the one night in all the year that no female, regardless of age or status, could sit at home without feeling the smallest bit sorry for herself. With a man it was different. He could go out to a bar and get drunk, but all a female could do was sit at home alone, listen to the radio and give the evening over to self-pity. Petey was determined that both her sisters were to participate in the festivities. In fact, she wanted both of them to be present for the celebration at Toresca's. Nicky Toresca had already promised her a table reservation, but that was the least of her difficulties. Sally was the chief one. She knew that there was no use in trying to arrange a date for Sally. She would have no part of it, so Petey decided that it would be up to Joe, whether he liked it or not, to act as Sally's escort for the evening. She revealed her schemes to Sally first, and Sally cheerfully and affectionately turned them down. No, Sally said, she was past the stage of her life where she got a kick out of night-clubbing. She would love to come, just to see Petey and hear her sing, but she would rather come some other night when there wouldn't be such a crowd. Petey was puzzled and disbelieving, but Sally refused to argue about it. She appreciated Petey's thoughtfulness, and all that, but she would just rather not come. But, Sally said, with Virginia it was different. She thought it would be just wonderful for Ginny if Petey could fix up a date for her to go to Toresca's that night, seeing that Petey would be around to sort of keep an eye on her. Petey shifted her plans rapidly. All right, she said, so Sally didn't want to come to Toresca's. Okay then, she had a better idea. She would get the tickets and Sally could take the kids and go to the midnight movie at one of the theatres. Again Sally disagreed with her. No, the kids would get so tired and cross, staying up that late, and there would be such a crowd at the theatre, so much drinking and rough carryings on, that she would rather not. Petey was not to give it another thought. Sally intended just to stay home with the children. Maybe they would have a little party all their own. The kids got sort of excited hearing about New Year's Eve, and they would borrow Fred Foster's radio and just have a little party at home and all go to bed early. Truly, Sally said earnestly, she would lots rather do that, thanks just the same. So Petey at last was forced to give up that part of her scheme. But she was still dissatisfied, thinking regretfully of the new dress she had intended to buy for Sally, and the corsage of flowers and the other fixings to go with it. The first opportunity she had, Petey cornered old Tommy Terwilliger. Did his boy Jimmy have a girl friend, she wanted to know, artlessly. Well, no, Tommy said, in some surprise, Jimmy didn't. Jimmy was quite a hand for the girls, but no one girl for very long. Well, that was fine, Petey said cheerfully, she was glad to hear it. And now, did Tommy know what Jimmy's plans were for New Year's Eve? Well, Tommy wasn't sure about that. Jimmy had wanted some extra money. He had made plans involving some girl, but at the last moment the girl had changed her plans and left town for a week end of merrymaking with some friends, and Jimmy had been very hurt and indignant about the whole thing. If he had made new plans Tommy hadn't heard about them. Petey put her cards on the table then. There was Virginia, and there was the table reserved at Toresca's. Tommy was delighted and volunteered Jimmy's services on the spot, but Petey said no, the decision was really Jimmy's. If Jimmy was interested, have him drop in the next afternoon during rehearsals and they could talk it over. Jimmy Terwilliger appeared the next afternoon, a big, dark, curly-headed boy, who met with Petey's approval. By his martyred expression, Petey deduced that he was still sulking over the disruption of his former plans, but had resigned himself to the fact that a blind date is better than no date at all, especially when a table reservation at Toresca's went with it. Well, that would be up to Virginia, Petey decided, to make him forget that the other girl even existed. In very short order Jimmy Terwilliger fell under the spell of Petey's charms, and agreed to all of her proposals for the evening. He even agreed to an immediate introduction to a shy and self-conscious Virginia, via telephone. At least things were breaking her way where Virginia was concerned, Petey congratulated herself.

The next day Petey invited Virginia to meet her downtown for lunch. After lunch she suggested that Virginia come along with her to a dress shop where she was due for a fitting. Before they were out of there, Petey had a complete outfit chosen for Virginia, a soft blue velvet dress with a short swinging skirt and innumerable tiny buttons from the high neck to the very hem, shoes, hose, gloves, purse, and a gay little hat that was more veil than hat and at the same time very young and becoming to Virginia. The problem of a coat Petey disposed of easily. Virginia was to wear Petey's own black fur cape. It might be a little large and long on Virginia, but Petey thought it would do quite nicely. After the shopping Petey shooed Virginia off to a beauty shop where an appointment was already made for her. Virginia was incoherent in her pleasure and gratitude. Why, she was the lucky one, Petey said, kissing Virginia affectionately. Imagine the fun it was suddenly to have a little sister to do things like this for.

The last day of December rolled around, the gloomiest, wettest day, Petey thought, of all the wet gloomy days since she had been in town. Water stood over the sidewalks. There was a damp cold wind that cut to the bone, and yet the mist hung in the air as thick as fog. Petey gargled her throat carefully, a fine thing, if she should get a cold or lose her voice today of all days.

She had to get up earlier than usual to finish up shopping and keep a lengthy appointment at the beauty shop. Rehearsals that afternoon were long and wearing, with everyone's temper worn a little thin, and the added nervous strain of trying to rehearse over the shouting and pounding of the decorators and electricians who were hurriedly at work on the last-minute decorating. To add to the strain, Nicky himself materialized from someplace and sat at the bar with an impassive face, viewing the proceedings. It was with a conscious effort that Petey kept herself good-humored and relaxed.

When rehearsals were over at last, and the lights and decorations were completed, Nicky Toresca and Petey had dinner together in a quiet hotel dining room. Nicky Toresca was too out of sorts to talk, and Petey was too tired. Once he broke the silence to ask Petey if her dress had been finished all right, and Petey nodded. Her dress for tonight had been a little splurge by courtesy of the management. That was fine, Nicky said. Her flowers would be over right away. Petey thanked him with a brief smile. In the cab going over to her apartment, Nicky informed her that he had reserved a small table for themselves. He didn't see any reason why they weren't entitled to some celebrating of their own. When Petey got out of the cab, she relented a little and patted Nicky on the hand. Relax, she told him. By twelve o'clock nobody would be sober enough to see the decorations or care about the floor show; the party was going to be fine. Nicky leaned out after her and kissed her, his fingers tight in her thick hair.

In her apartment Petey undressed and lay down for an hour or so. She didn't sleep; she kept the radio turned low and lighted a cigarette from time to time. She could remember so many New Year's Eve celebrations, in so many places. She stretched back in memory through the years. She heard the faint thin echo of her voice singing a lot of songs. She saw blizzards of confetti and tangled mazes of tape, the confusion of so many faces, so much laughter, so many glasses raised from table tops. Sometimes she had been working, sometimes she hadn't. The pattern of New Year's Eve celebrations was all the same. Petey spun the glittering little merry-go-round of memory idly; it made her neither sad nor happy. It didn't make much sense, when you looked back like this, in terms of one night when a year ended and another year began. But then, nothing in her whole life so far made much sense either, Petey thought dispassionately.

Petey drew a luxurious bubble bath for herself, and then dressed carefully and rapidly. The dress was pure white, heavily accented with a glitter of silver-blue, like ice, a misleadingly simple dress, fitted perfectly, cut very low. It was very effective with Petey's tanned skin and dark hair, and she knew it. Oh, well, there weren't too many years left that she could wear a white dress like this. In accord with the simplicity of her dress, she combed her hair out loose and simple, heavy to her shoulders, and put in a few of the gardenias Nicky had sent. She clustered more of them and fastened them securely to her glittering belt. The rest she fastened to her evening purse. Her only other adornments were heavy bracelets on either arm. They weren't diamonds, Petey thought, as she fastened them on carefully, but they were darned expensive imitations. For a wrap she wore a full scarlet cape to the floor, cut military style, accented in gold.

She called a cab and went out to Horton Street for a brief call on Sally before going on to her job at Toresca's. The mist was thick like fog, veiling the buildings, distorting the lights. She instructed the taxi driver to wait for her, and stepped out daintily, holding up her skirts carefully as she crossed the wet sidewalk.

As she burst in the door Petey called a general "Hello." She took in the scene quickly and, before Sally could make any introductions, she went on, "I guess you don't have to introduce me." She smiled at Johnny O'Connor as she spoke. "I know who you are. I've heard all about you. You're the missin' mainspring around this house! Hi, Johnny!"

"That's me," Johnny said. "O'Connor, the indispensable man! And you must be Petey, and, may I say right this minute, though I've heard a lot about you, they never said it would be like this!" He indicated Petey's glittering dress, the scarlet cape flung back from her shoulders, with his clumsy bandaged paw, and smiled at her in undisguised admiration.

Petey's deep hearty laughter filled the room. Without thinking, she started to extend a hand to him.

"Sorry, lady," Johnny said gaily, "we'll have to shake on that one later."

"Petey Braun," Sally said solemnly. "You never looked beautifuller in your whole life. I just wish I had a picture to keep of you the way you look right this minute!"

Petey smiled at her affectionately and kissed her lightly on the forehead. "Happy New Year, Sally," she said gently, with the rich warm feeling in her husky voice.

"Johnny, I wanta go home," Gloria O'Connor said.

"Okay, sugar puss," Johnny said.

"Aw, no, you just got here," Sally protested. "Johnny O'Connor, you just get home from the hospital tonight, and you dodge in here two minutes and then run away again. Why, I've hardly had time to look at you even!"

"Tough luck," Petey said with a significant motion of her own hands. "How you feeling, Johnny?"

"Oh, fit as a fiddle," Johnny said cheerfully. "A bit weak in the knees, a bit light in the head, but I'm fine. You can't kill an Irishman."

Gloria was edging toward the door, and Petey glanced at her curiously. Her beautiful face was a little sulky, and Petey thought there were tear stains on it.

Johnny followed her obediently. "See you later," he said to Sally, and he winked at her significantly over the children's heads.

"All right, Johnny," Sally said pleasantly.

He paused beside Petey for a moment. "The Nicky must be

pitchin' quite a party over there tonight, if I can take this for an indication."

"Yup," Petey said. "Complete with confetti, balloons and all the fixin's."

"Well, he wasted the money on the confetti and the balloons," Johnny said. He slipped his arm around Gloria as he spoke, and dropped his cheek against hers. "Take a good look at that dress, baby," he said, "because some day I'm gonna buy you one just like it."

As they went out the door, Petey said, "Good night, see you again. Happy New Year!"

"And the same to you and many more of them," Johnny called back. "Stop in and see us sometime. I guess you'll be findin' the O'Connors home for quite awhile now."

The door closed behind them and Petey said, "Looky, Sally, honey, I gotta run! I just stopped to say Happy New Year. My taxi Joe is waitin'. Jesus, whata night out! You're lucky you're staying in."

"Isn't it an awful night, though?" Sally said. "Be careful, won't you? Don't let your taxi driver go too fast. Virginia left quite awhile ago. Gosh, she looked as pretty as could be, and I know she was real excited about it, though she wasn't letting on much. This Jimmy come after her and he looked like an awful nice fellow. And what do you think? He sent her a corsage of pink roses. I know Virginia was tickled to death with 'em. It was awful nice a you to do all this for her, Petey."

"Oh, hell," Petey said lightly. "It's no more than what should be coming to Ginny. Every gal that age should have a few pretty clothes and some parties."

"Every gal should, but they don't all get them," Sally said. She smiled at Petey as she spoke, and for a moment they were silent together, both of them thinking back through all the years to a time when they were Virginia's age, and much younger even, and there was nobody in the world to give them anything.

Petey bent down and hugged the children and then said once more, "Looky, I gotta run!"

Sally followed her out into the hall. "I'm so glad you stopped in," she said honestly. "It sort of makes a whole party for me just seeing you all dressed up so beautiful like this."

Petey loosened one of the gardenias from the cluster on her purse and stuck the stem carefully through a buttonhole on the front of Sally's uniform. "I wish you was going out someplace tonight and doing a little celebrating, Sally."

"Oh, I am," Sally said. "After the kids are to bed I'm going over to the O'Connors' to see the New Year in. They can't go out tonight on account of Johnny just gettin' out of the hospital and all, so we're gonna have a little party for ourselves over there."

"That's fine," Petey said, and then she added curiously, "What's the matter with the beautiful blonde? She didn't look like the happy wife whose husband just got outa the hospital to me."

Sally lowered her voice a little. "Oh, I guess Gloria was just feeling kind a bad about having to stay in tonight. She's a regular little kid, you know, and she loves to go out places and have a good time. I guess she kind of wanted to go over to Toresca's tonight, but Johnny didn't feel like it, of course, and I don't suppose they have the money either, with him outa work and all."

Petey shrugged her shoulders. "Keep your eye on little Beautiful! There's gonna be trouble there!"

"Oh, I hope not," Sally said. "Johnny is an awful nice fellow and you see how he is, he's just crazy about her. Gloria's a funny little kid, but I don't think . . ."

Petey gathered her cape about her and started down the hallway. "I'll see you tomorrow, honey. Have a good time tonight. Don't drink too much gin and don't do nothin' I wouldn't do. Happy New Year!"

"Happy New Year! See Virginia gets home all right, won't you? Thanks for my pretty posy! Have a good time tonight, yourself! Honest, you're the most beautiful thing in this town. I'll bet the men will probably all be fightin' over you at Toresca's tonight . . ."

"That's all right with me," Petey called back, "just so long as the best man wins."

They laughed together as Petey started down the stairs. Just then, even amid their laughter, they heard the sound of muffled crying from the O'Connor apartment. Well, Petey thought reflectively as she ran down the stairs, that made a nice homecoming for Johnny O'Connor. A wife who cried because she couldn't go out and get drunk New Year's Eve instead of being thankful that he hadn't died in the hospital. Well, that was what a guy got for marrying a glamor girl, or to be more exact about it, that was what happened to a gal who had bright lights in her eyes and got herself tied down to some guy and an apartment and a baby.

The moment Petey stepped in the door at Toresca's she knew that the New Year's Eve party was going to be a financial success for the Nicky. She flung her cape back carelessly, and she knew very well that she was attracting a great deal of attention as she walked down the short flight of steps slowly, her dress glittering in the lights, her head lifted as she looked out over the crowd.

Nicky's head waiter met her at the foot of the stairs and stared at her appreciatively. "Good evening, Miss Braun. You're in kind of early. Mr. Toresca's table is down there. You want to sit down now?"

Petey shook her head. "Hello, Joe. No, I'm looking for some friends of mine. Looky, do you know Tommy Terwilliger's kid, Jimmy?"

"He's with a girl right over there," the waiter said instantly. Petey followed his eyes and saw them. Virginia's back was toward her, but Jimmy Terwilliger saw her approaching and he was on his feet instantly. "Hello, there, Miss Braun!"

Petey dropped her hand on Virginia's shoulder. "Boo! Oh, gosh, you look lovely, honey. How are you, Jimmy?"

Virginia was a very different-looking girl, Petey reflected, than that sad, bedraggled-looking little creature she had first seen Christmas Eve, just a week ago this very night, curled up on the end of Sally's davenport in a faded bathrobe, with a pale drawn face and stringy hair. Was it the clothes and the excitement that did all this, or could it be that Jimmy Terwilliger had something to do with it, Petey wondered.

The waiter set a chair for her. "Well, what gives with you?" she asked them. "Having fun?"

They both said yes together, and Petey wondered if it wasn't a little too dutiful. Oh, well, probably they hadn't had much of a chance to get acquainted yet.

Jimmy Terwilliger was a tall, well-built boy with curly dark hair and dark eyes. He looked a little like his father, despite his father's battered features, and despite the fact that he was a couple of heads taller. Something in the set of his broad shoulders, Petey noted, was very like his father's, even today, and she remembered Tommy's words that Jimmy had it in his head to be crazy about fighting.

"You look wonderful, Miss Braun," Jimmy said awkwardly. "I guess you're gonna steal the whole show around here tonight."

"Oh, you look lovely," Virginia said softly, and Petey squeezed her hand.

"I can't stay but a minute," Petey said. "I'm just a workin' gal. The rest of you can celebrate all you want to, but I have work to do tonight."

"What time is the show on?" Jimmy asked.

"Oh, about eleven-thirty. I don't go on for quite awhile."

Just then a waiter appeared behind Petey's chair. "Say, Miss Braun," he said urgently. "Al Riley just come in. He wants to see you right away. He says it's important."

A little interest flickered on Petey's face momentarily and vanished. She picked up her drink again. "Never heard of him," she said cheerfully.

"He works here," the waiter said. "He said to tell you he had to see you, that it was important, on the level. He said to tell you it was about your brother."

Petey's vagrant amused eyebrow straightened out suddenly and she stopped with the drink at her lips. Her eyes narrowed a little, but her face was imperturbed. Then she set her unfinished drink down on the table. "Okay, Joe," she said. "Where is he, out back?"

"No, he's up at the bar."

"I'll see you kids later," she said. "Have fun, honey." She patted Virginia's shoulder as she got up, and she moved leisurely away in and out among the tables in the direction of the steps. The bar was packed and even noisier than the tables were. Petey mounted the steps slowly. At the top she stood still and went about lighting a cigarette, her eyes drifting down the line in front of the bar. She saw him step back from the far end of the bar, up against the wall, a short guy whose face she recognized.

Petey went to meet him impatiently. "You could be Riley," she said. "Well, what gives?"

"I'm sorry to bother you, Miss Braun," Riley said nervously. "Look, this is important. Can't we go someplace where it's quiet and . . ."

"C'mon, c'mon," Petey said impatiently. "I ain't got all night, brother."

Riley licked his lips. "Look, Miss Braun," he said again, "this is confidential. Couldn't we go someplace where . . . This is important, Miss Braun. Joe's in a jam!"

For the second time his eyes strayed away from her, and this time Petey knew what they were watching. It was the little wooden door at the end of the orchestra stand that opened out to Nicky Toresca's office, among other things.

Petey glanced around the bar. If there was any quiet place left in the world tonight, she'd like to know where it was, and, even if there was a quiet spot around here, it would not be one where they could talk without Nicky Toresca's knowledge, if that was what was bothering Riley.

"Looky, pal," Petey said again. "I told you I haven't got all night. This is as good a place to talk as there is. Spill it!"

Riley was panicky. He spoke again and Petey had to lean close to hear what he said amid the uproar.

"Miss Braun this is serious. Joe's in jail. The boss is gonna raise hell!"

"I wouldn't be surprised 'n he did! Why didn't you say so in the first place?" Petey snapped. "What's Joey been up to?"

Riley made one last effort, his face almost agonized. "Miss Braun, there's a bar right around the corner . . ."

"Okay, so you won't talk here," Petey said, "come on!"

She led the way down the ramp to the entrance, pulling her cape tighter around her and picking up her skirts before they stepped out into the wet. Out on the sidewalk, Petey said to the doorman, "Think you can whistle up a cab?"

"Sure thing," he said jovially. Petey stared at his red, smiling face suspiciously as he waved for the cab with elaborate gestures of his arm that almost upset his balance.

"Give you ten to one that that Joe is flat on his face before 1941!" Petey said sourly to Al Riley. She stepped into the cab with Riley at her heels, and said to the driver, "Take a run around the block, Joe, and no hurry, we like the scenery around here."

Out of the penetrating, damp, night air again, Petey shivered a little and, as the cab started up, she said to Riley, "Okay, now spill it! What's Joey been up too?"

"Well, he got in a fight and . . ."

"Oh, Christ!" Petey said. "So you drag me out on a wet night to tell me Joey got drunk, took a smack at somebody, and was bundled off in the nanny wagon!"

"Naw, wait, lemme tell you," Riley said plaintively. "He didn't just get in no fight. The boss is gonna raise hell about this!"

"Okay! Go on and talk, why don't you?"

Riley lowered his voice. "We was over on Mill Street, a joint over there, me and Joe, see? He gets in this fight with the guy that runs the place. He picks the fight over nothing, see? Jesus, the boss is gonna be sorer . . ."

"I don't get it," Petey said flatly.

"We was over there on business, see?" Riley said. "The boss got a whole back room fulla slot machines over there. Me and Joe was over there on business, and he picks a fight with the guy that runs the place over nothin'. Joe gets to acting smart and talking big and the guy gets sore and Joe takes a swing at the guy!"

"So," Petey said.

Riley went on. "So the guy takes a swing at Joe, and you know Joe, he goes all to pieces he gets so scared, but the guy is sore at him. The guy is gonna beat hell outa Joe. Then a big mug that is settin' there in a booth lets the guy have it over the head with a beer bottle. The guy goes out like a light. The guy's wife already gets the police. They pick up Joe and the mug with the beer bottle. The boss is gonna raise hell about this. We ain't supposed to get in no trouble when we're out on business. We ain't supposed to get in no fights with the customers. The boss is gonna . . ."

"Yeah, so you said," Petey said impatiently. "How come you're on the loose?"

"The guy's wife didn't even know I was with Joe," Riley said. "I couldn't do nothin'. I beat it right over here."

Petey lighted another cigarette and threw the butt out and rolled up the window again against the sudden draught of chill, mist-laden air. "So what am I supposed to do?" she said.

"Well . . ." Riley said. "Joe yells at me just as the police come in, he's scared half to death, see, he says for me to come tell you. I don't wanta get in no trouble, Miss Braun. I gotta report this to the boss, ain't I?"

It looked to Petey as if this breach between Joe and Toresca might be exactly what she had been hoping for. But, on the other hand, Joe had trusted her. She had never consciously let anybody down who had trusted her in her whole life, and Joe was her brother.

"I don't get it," Petey said again. "Joey's in the soup. There ain't nothin' I can do now."

"Well," Riley said, "maybe Joe figured you being a good friend of the boss, if you was to talk to him, see?"

"So maybe Joe figured!" Petey mimicked.

Riley tried again. "Well, so maybe Joe figured you'd come over and pay his fine, an' I'd keep my mouth shut to the boss. But I don't wanta get in no trouble, see? The boss is gonna hear about it, anyway, Miss Braun. That guy that runs the joint was plenty sore. Hell, I try to help Joe if I can, but I don't wanta get in no trouble."

"Sure, sure," Petey said, her forehead wrinkled in thought.

"Maybe Joe figured you'd pay his fine an' he'd sorta lay low a day or two till the boss cooled off about it?"

Another thought suddenly occurred to Petey, and she turned to Riley. "Looky, pal, the boss will pay the fine all right, won't he? He'll get Joey outa the clink tonight?"

Riley hesitated a little. "Well, sure, he'll pay the fine. He don't want no trouble, see. Maybe if he's plenty sore he'll leave Joe in the clink a day or two, but . . ."

The decision was made for Petey. "Look, pal," she said rapidly, "you got any money on yuh? I wanta borrow it. My credit's good."

"Well, sure," Riley said, a little reluctantly.

"Come on, hand it over, I ain't got all night."

Riley handed her the little roll of bills, and Petey glanced at them by the light through the steamed-over cab window. "That's fine," she said. "With what I got, that oughta cover it. Now, look, I'll drop you off here, and you go in and tell your little story to the Nicky, see, and I'll beat it over and spring Joey. Thanks for tipping me off about it. Hey, fella, pull over will you?"

The cab driver pulled over to the curb obediently and Riley opened the door.

Petey reached out her hand and they shook. "Is it all right?" she said.

"Sure, Miss Braun," Riley said. "I hate to tell the boss about Joe, but I don't wanta get in no trouble, see?"

"That's all right," Petey said.

Riley got out of the cab, turning up his coat collar, and slammed the door shut behind him.

"The jail," Petey told her cab driver. "And I bet I'm the first person you ever come across that was in a hurry to get there."

The cab driver pulled up suddenly before the impressive entrance of a large new building.

"Here you are, lady," he said, pulling down the little flagged lever to stop the meter.

Petey gave him his money before she got out of the cab.

"You go right in that door," the driver said. "You go down the hall aways and then there's a door to your left to where the desk is."

"Thanks," Petey said. "Happy New Year."

She slammed the cab door behind her and pulled her cape closer. Just as the cab pulled away, before she even got to the steps, Petey stopped. Through the glass door, she saw Joe Braun coming down the corridor. He turned up his overcoat collar before he opened the door. He paused at the top of the broad cement steps and lighted a cigarette, cupping the match carefully, the little flare of light illuminating his face under his hat brim. He either didn't see Petey, or he didn't recognize her in the thick mist.

"Well, well," Petey said mockingly. "Who you won't run into, when you ain't carrying a gun! What is this, a gag?"

Joe jumped and burned his hands on the match flame. "Jesus, I didn't see you standing there! I thought I was hearin' things. Hi!" He came down the steps to meet her, swaggering a little, a bravado to cover his nervousness.

Petey's face was angry as she shivered there on the wet sidewalk. "Next time you're in jail, don't forget to write!" she said.

"You seen Riley, huh?" Joe said.

"Why, no," Petey said sarcastically. "I'm just out for a walk because it's such a beautiful night out! Fancy meeting you here!"

"I didn't know whether Riley'd tell you or not," Joe said. "Thanks for comin' over, anyway."

"Look," Petey said, "maybe you like this neighborhood, but I don't. I gotta show to give yet tonight. Where am I gonna get a taxicab but quick?"

"Well, I dunno. They don't cruise this street much."

Petey's voice was sharp with exasperation. "To hell with it. Where's a telephone?"

"I think there's a drug store around the corner about a block."

Petey started walking rapidly, and Joe fell into step with her.

"It was nice of you to come over like this," Joe said. Petey was silent. She walked rapidly with her skirts held high, kicking her way around puddles of water.

Joe was plainly nervous. He tried the shaky swaggering front again. "As it worked out, I didn't need no help. Jesus, I sure talked myself outa that neat!" He laughed loudly, but Petey did not look impressed. "They picked up this big dummy along with me, see? So I tell the cop at the desk that the big dummy jumped Barney, and I get mixed up in it, trying to stop the fight. The big dummy just stands there without saying nothing. So they tell me to beat it and the big dummy gets the book!" Joe laughed again.

"That wasn't the way I heard it," Petey said. "What did they do, slap a fine on the guy?"

"Yeah," Joe said. "Except he didn't have no money, I guess. I guess they had to lock him up."

Petey stopped dead still and Joe looked at her in surprise. "Christ, Joey, you're startin' the New Year like a good little rat, aren't yuh? According to your pal Riley, I hear the big guy got picked up just because he took a ride on a beer bottle to keep you from gettin' the bejesus beat outa you!"

Joe's front cracked a little. "Hell," Joe said plaintively. "The big dummy just stood there without sayin' nothin'! He musta been nuts or drunk or something. I told you, he was a dumb sucker!"

Petey was scowling but she started walking again. They rounded the corner and the Neon sign over the drug store shone just ahead. Joe walked silently beside her. When they got there, Joe pulled open the door for her and they stepped into the little cluttered cut-rate drug store. Petey looked first to the clock on the wall that showed a few minutes yet before twelve. Her face was expressionless, but her eyes were narrowed and there was not the faintest trace of her habitual good humor. Joe glanced at her out of the corner of his eyes apprehensively.

"There's a phone booth down back," Joe said. "You want I should . . ."

"Wait a minute . . ."

There was a silence, and suddenly Joe's brave front collapsed entirely. "Look, I'm in a jam!" he said desperately. "The boss is gonna be sore as hell at me. Maybe if you was to talk to him about it, huh?"

"Oh, shut up!" Petey said. She threw her cigarette down, an abrupt movement of her bare arm that set the heavy bracelets sparkling. "I'm goin' back and spring that guy outa the clink," she said briefly. "I'm just a dumb sucker myself, from way back. What name they book him?"

Joe was so preoccupied now with his own plight that he scarcely noticed what she was saying. "He didn't give no name. I told you he wouldn't say nothing. Look, for God's sakes, you could try talkin' to him, couldn't you? I ain't goin' in till tomorrow and if you was to talk to him tonight, why . . ."

"I see a cab. See you later, Joey!" And with a whisk of her skirts Petey was gone, leaving her smoldering, lipstick-smeared cigarette on the floor and the faint odor of perfume, and Joe standing alone with his mouth foolishly still half open.

At the jail, while her cab waited, Petey climbed the steps and pulled open the heavy glass door. She walked down the corridor rapidly. The door to the left was open, the light pouring out, and Petey stepped to the doorway. A plain room, a big man in uniform at a desk trimmed with a couple of telephones, a ledger and several sheaves of papers. He was reading a newspaper, and several other uniformed men were lounging in the room, talking idly with cigarette smoke drifting upward. They all looked up at the sound of Petey's footsteps. She paused momentarily in the door and then she walked across the room to the desk with her long stride with a strut to it. They looked at her curiously. She was so out of place here, with her long dress, her flowers and her heavy, glittering bracelets.

"Hello, boys," Petey said briefly, and then she addressed herself to the man behind the desk as he slowly lowered his newspaper. "A friend of mine was just picked up in a joint over on Mill Street. I'll pay his fine."

The big man shifted in his chair ponderously and looked at the ledger in front of him and then he looked at Petey curiously. "What's his name?"

"Search me," Petey said. She pulled the little wad of bills out of her purse, holding them folded close in her hand.

One of the uniformed men, who was looking at Petey admiringly, spoke up then. "She must mean the big, light-haired guy they just brought in. You remember, the guy that . . ."

The man behind the desk cut him short with a grunt. Then he cleared his throat and looked at Petey. "His fine'll be twenty-five dollars, miss. He's booked on a couple charges. He . . ."

Petey laid the bills on the desk in front of him. "I don't care about the charges," she said. "Here's your money."

He picked up the bills slowly and nodded his head to one of the uniformed men who disappeared through a door at the back of the room. The room was very quiet then, except for the scratch of a pen as the man behind the desk scrawled something in the ledger.

With her business at the desk concluded, Petey walked back to the door into the corridor. She stepped over the threshold and lighted a cigarette. As she waited she leaned one shoulder against the doorjamb, her cloak falling back in thick folds. She held her cigarette with one bare arm lifted, the elbow supported in her palm. A moment or two slipped by, but she did not move.

The door opened again and the man in uniform and the prisoner entered. The latter glanced at the desk first, and then his eyes moved away slowly across the room to Petey and stopped. He stood quite still a moment, looking at her, but with no curiosity on his face, nor any expression at all. He was big, all right. He seemed to fill the entire doorway. He wore no overcoat or hat, just a worn, wrinkled, tweedy-looking suit of nondescript grayish color. His hair was light, bleached-looking, almost the color of his skin, and his eyebrows the same. He looked as if at some time or other he had been out in the sun for a long, long time. His features were rough-hewn, with angles and planes of bones at the chin, cheekbones and forehead. His face was like a crude drawing and had a strange quality, that, like a drawing of a face, it was unlikely ever to alter or ever to give expression.

When he walked across the room he moved slowly and easily, the arms swinging a little. His body was like that of an athlete, but one who has long been out of condition and is just beginning to go to fat.

As he approached, Petey drew in her breath a little and stepped back from the doorway. He came to the door and stopped beside her. When he looked at her his eyes were pale, no darker really than his hair, and like his face so devoid of expression that they were almost like the eyes of the blind.

"Look," Petey said. "I know this must seem funny to you. I mean, my bailing you outa here like this. I mean you don't know me or anything . . ." For the first time in her life, Petey heard herself stumbling over words. Her voice trailed off, and she looked into his face. He gave no impression of hearing her and but little of seeing her. She fumbled with the gardenia-trimmed bag in her hands.

"So?" When he spoke, his voice was expressionless too, yet unrelated to him as any voice would be unrelated to him, as the very act of speaking at all seemed unrelated to him.

Petey drew in her breath again. "That kid over there in the joint on Mill Street was my brother. He was scared to death, and that's why he . . . That's why I waited to talk to you. I wanted you to know.

He—he—didn't want to leave you in the clink like that. That's why I came to get you out."

He looked at her for just a moment longer, and then he turned and started walking down the corridor. Petey walked with him. Even with her long stride she had to take a quick extra step now and then to keep pace with him. They came to the door and Petey pushed it open. Just as they stepped onto the steps, she heard the bells tolling. There was an uncanny second or two of silence and after that a cacophony of sound broke loose. Automobile horns, shouting voices, factory whistles, bells, pounding, and, though it was loud, all of it curiously far away from this quiet dark side street where the mist hung thick.

They both stood still together. The big man didn't seem to be looking at anything; he didn't seem to be hearing, not with his ears anyway; it was as if he soaked in all sensation through his pores. Why, Petey thought, it was as if all the life there had ever been in this man had retreated someplace far into his great body and burned there with a tiny flickering flame.

The faraway racket of noise increased and became a din. Petey felt the mist cool against her face. She looked at him, and he turned his head slowly and looked down into her face. "Nineteen hundred and forty-one," Petey said softly. For a moment they stood like that, looking at each other, and then the moment was gone. He moved down the steps.

Petey was oddly breathless and she stumbled over the words. "My cab is waiting. I could drop you off someplace, if you want . . . I'm in a hurry, but I'd like to drop you someplace . . ."

"No," he said. He didn't pause, or look back. He walked away up the street slowly, his feet careless of puddles. He walked as if it were a function only, not walking to any place or away from any place.

Petey stood there on the sidewalk and looked after him. The mist swallowed him up, and then suddenly his great body was silhouetted momentarily in the bright light at the street corner. He turned the corner then and disappeared. Petey walked over to her cab and opened the door.

\* \* \*

Once Petey was back at Toresca's, she walked up the ramp hurriedly, shaking drops of moisture out of the folds of her heavy cloak.

"Gosh, Miss Braun, you're late," the hat-check girl said to her cheerfully. "Show's on already."

"I know it," Petey said. She pushed her heavy mop of hair back on her shoulders. "Jesus, me for the ladies' room and a quick repair job! It's drippin' wet outdoors."

"Oh, you look gorgeous, Miss Braun." The hat-check girl dropped her elbows on the shelf. "Gee, Mr. Toresca has been tearing this place apart tryin' to find you!"

"My, it's nice to know that you're missed," Petey said over her shoulder.

A few minutes later, Petey adjusted the microphone, her glittering vivacious self. "Ladies and Gentlemen, a Happy New Year!"

Her act was a success. She stopped the show. Petey smiled her smile, gave her patter and sang her songs, and a hilarious, rather alcoholic, crowd applauded her enthusiastically. She skillfully selected songs that they all knew and led them in the singing herself. She sang her own concluding number then, and for encores she volunteered to sing requests. From the numbers shouted to her she chose good solid songs that she had sung many a New Year's Eve before, which would still be good for many more such nights to come.

In the midst of acknowledging her last applause, she remembered to wink at Virginia, who still sat at the table near the wall with Jimmy Terwilliger amid a sea of confetti and tape. She was also conscious of Nicky Toresca waiting for her at a table down in front. His face was bland, half-smiling, but he was angry; she could have told it just by looking at him, if she hadn't known it anyway. She made a last graceful half-curtsy, her head bowed low, the thick hair falling around her face. She waved her hand, smiling once more, and stepped away from the microphone. She stepped aside skillfully so that a drunk with a paper hat and horn who lurched up out of a chair at her fell against another table in bewilderment. Her rich laughter boomed, and the crowd laughed with her. She helped the drunk to right himself, dusted him off elaborately, and stuck one of her gardenias in his buttonhole.

The floor cleared for dancing, and Nicky Toresca kicked out the other chair at his table for Petey. Her drink was waiting on the table for her, and Petey picked it up with a little sound of contented pleasure. Still half-smiling, Nicky Toresca handed her the cigarette he had just lighted, and she thanked him with a little bow, her eyebrow bending up against her forehead. "Happy New Year," she said, raising her glass to him before she drank.

"Where the hell were yuh?" Nicky said, and the anger crept into his voice.

"Oh, around and about," Petey said sweetly, smiling at him. "I had business."

"You went over to the jail to bail out Joe, is that right?" Nicky said smoothly.

"Uh huh," Petey said.

"I am going to bat Joey's ears off over this," Nicky said, with the faint anger in his voice.

"So go ahead," Petey said. "So bat his ears off. Joey's got it coming." She glanced away out to the small floor space filled with dancers.

"But it so happened you didn't have to bail Joe out. He already talked himself outa jail before you got there, is that right?"

"You know all the answers tonight, don't you?" Petey said.

Nicky Toresca smiled at her. He was in immaculate evening clothes, and they became him very well, Petey admitted, as she glanced at his dark handsome face, his slim body, and his studied suavity of manner.

"So then?" he asked softly.

"So then what?"

"So then where did you go that was nicer than seein' the New Year in with me?"

"So I got in a crap game with the boys over to the jail," Petey snapped. She discovered suddenly that her head ached, and her throat was raw from singing, that she was tired, nerves on edge. This room was too small, too hot, too smoky, too many silly people, making altogether too much goddam senseless noise. She felt again cool mist on her face, momentarily, and a dim misty street that was easy on the eyes, with all the noise and confusion there, but somehow far away. And there was a big man beside her when she heard her voice again saying softly, "Nineteen hundred and forty-one," a big man who saw you without looking at you, heard you without listening to you, and walked away up a street.

You better snap outa that, Petey told herself sharply. She looked at Nicky again, and his face was closed and smooth with all his anger bunched at the mouth.

Petey grinned at him suddenly, fluttered her eyelashes up and down, and spoke softly in an exaggerated Southern accent.

"Wah, Mista Tahresca, honey, wah, sugah, ah do balee-av youah jealous a pooah li'l ole me! Whyah, honey, cain't a gal have no little secrets a-tall?"

"I guess we'll dance this one," Nicky said. The music had stopped temporarily, but Petey got up obediently. Nicky Toresca followed her out onto the floor and made a little sign to the orchestra leader who nodded in answer and lifted his baton. "This is my kind of music," Nicky said, and he swung Petey around to face him with his fingers very tight on her wrist. It was a rumba, and Petey smiled in Nicky Toresca's face, as the rhythm of it caught in her body.

It was a long dance and, when it was over, they went back to the table again, and Nicky Toresca signaled the waiter for more drinks. They were silent for a long time.

Nicky Toresca spoke at last. "Petey, I hate to play games. People get in trouble who try to play games with me."

"Is that right?" Petey said. Out of the corner of her eye, she saw Jimmy Terwilliger assisting Virginia with her cape, and she turned around in her chair a little to wave good-bye to them. She hoped Jimmy took Virginia straight home. Sally would worry if Virginia stayed out much later.

Nicky Toresca's fingers closed tight on Petey's wrist on the table top, like thin steel clamps, and his voice was tight with anger. "When I'm talking to you I want you to listen to me!"

Petey didn't move her hand in his fingers. She turned around to face him again very slowly, and her eyebrow doubling. "Why, Mr. Toresca," she said, "I don't remember a thing in my contract that says I'm drawin' my money here for listening to you talk!"

Nicky Toresca withdrew his hand from hers in a moment, casually, and stuck it in his pocket. "You're awful independent, aren't you?" he said easily. "It's too bad Joe don't take after you. Joe always listens when I talk." He finished with a half smile on his face, his eyes goading her.

That odd feeling stole over Petey again, a sort of fatigue all the way through her to the bone. She was tired of this place, she discovered, and tired of making double talk with Nicky Toresca, and tired of singing. She didn't want to walk up to that microphone, but she didn't want to sit here at this table any longer, either. She wanted to get out of this joint, but she didn't know where she wanted to go. She didn't want to go home, and she didn't want to go to Sally's. She didn't want to go any place or do anything that she could think of, and she didn't want to stay here and keep on doing this. Just then, clear with the mind's eye she saw him again, the big, light-haired man, walking toward her across that bare room in the jail, walking slowly and easily, with his arms swinging a little, his wrinkled tweed suit bagged at the knees, his strange unseeing eyes fixed on her. She tried to shut the vision out of her mind. What was he to her—a big rum-dummy she had sprung out of the clink, and he walked off and left her without even as much as saying thank you? A big overgrown rum-dummy she sprung out of the clink one night and would never see again as long as she lived. Just thinking about him, she felt again that sudden loss of all her self-assurance, that strange uncertainty, that he had made her feel those few moments they had been together. What's the matter with me? Petey asked herself. I never felt like this before. This town must be getting me. I better get to hell out a here. I better get moving. Something is wrong. I don't feel so good. Everything is wrong.

Petey got up to sing again, and she didn't care whether she sang or not. She asked the orchestra leader for a song they hadn't ever rehearsed, just because she felt like singing it, she couldn't tell why. And when she sang it, there was a loneliness and a nostalgia in her voice:

*"It's only a shanty, in old shanty-town.*
*The roof is so slanty it touches the ground,*

*A tumble-down shack, by an old railroad track*
*Like a millionaire's mansion, it's calling me back . . ."*

When Petey returned to the table, Nicky Toresca's mood had changed completely, either his anger was gone, or he was concealing it well, or he had decided on a complete change of tactics. Petey didn't feel like trying to figure out which.

When she sat down he spoke to her with the nearest thing to good humor that he could approximate. "You know, the trouble is," he said, "everybody is out celebratin' but us. We need some drinkin' and dancin', is that right? We need a change of scenery. This place can keep running without us around."

"I think you've got something there," Petey said.

So they did a great deal of drinking and dancing. They went from place to place, all over town, and to several roadhouses beyond the outskirts. When the sky lightened into a dismal dawn, they found a restaurant open for business and ordered breakfast. While they waited for their order they discovered that the juke-box had a Cugat recording. They danced to it in the little aisle between the counter and the booths, to the disgust of the sleepy young waiter, who was quite apparently nursing a hangover.

After breakfast they caught a cab on the corner in the thin morning daylight. Petey gave a cluster of her fading gardenias to the cab driver because he said they were pretty. Put 'em in the icebox, she told him sleepily, and they would be as good as new.

When they arrived at her apartment house, she told Nicky not to bother to get out with her. No bother, he said, laughing, he was coming up anyway. But Petey was definite about it, uh uh, not tonight.

"Still playin' games, is that right?" the Nicky said, half angrily.

"Uh huh," Petey said sleepily. "That's right."

In the middle of her yawn he took her in his arms, his face tightening, and kissed her, a long kiss, his mouth hard against hers. When he finally let her go he said, "Happy New Year, Petey."

Petey got out of the cab and crossed the sidewalk amid the curious stares of early-morning passersby. Just as the cab pulled away from the curb, Nicky Toresca stuck his head out of the window, amusement and mockery on his face.

"Pattycake, pattycake, baker's old man!" he shouted after her.

Petey paused in front of her doorway in the bleak chill morning air, and flung her head back, laughing.

# 17

IT WAS EARLY AFTERNOON ON NEW YEAR'S DAY BEFORE Joe Braun had his hangover and his nerves under sufficient control to pay the dreaded call to Nicky Toresca's office. Joe was so frightened that he could hardly make his legs carry him without trembling, and he could hear his thudding heartbeats.

Nicky Toresca was sitting behind his big, flat-topped desk. The desk light was on, the rest of the room was dim. There were some papers strewn on the desk and the Nicky had a pencil in his hand. He looked up as Joe came in. Joe let the door shut behind him and stood still just inside the door, with his knees shaking and a light dew of perspiration across his forehead and his upper lip, even though this was a cold day.

Nicky looked him over leisurely and then he said, "Set down," and looked back to a paper covered with figures in front of him. Joe walked over to the nearest chair and sat in it. Oh, this was going to be a session, all right, Joe thought, his fears sweeping over him. Joe sat very still and tried to quiet his breathing that seemed inordinately loud to him in this quiet room. He didn't want Nicky Toresca to hear his nervous, uneven breaths. His fingers were stiff and clumsy with his cigarette. The ash fell off onto the rug, and Joe covered it up guiltily with his foot, rubbing it into the rug silently and gently. From time to time he stole a glance at Nicky Toresca. The Nicky was impeccably dressed in a well-cut business suit, his sleek hair was in order and shone in the light as he bent over the desk. There was a cigarette in his mouth, and he squinted his eyes from the stream of smoke. Nicky was apparently checking over the figures on the sheet of paper. Joe watched him in dread as the pencil point traveled slowly and inexorably to the bottom of the column.

Suddenly Nicky got up from his chair, and Joe sucked in his breath noisily and held it. But the Nicky went to the window behind the desk. He pulled the cord a couple of times, rattling the Venetian blind. He raised the blind a little, pushed up the window a bit from the sill to clear out the smoke that hung heavy in the small room. He lowered the Venetian blind, all this with Joe's eyes on him in an agony of fascinated terror that held him numbed.

The Nicky walked around in front of his desk slowly and stood facing Joe. He spoke abruptly at last, with his voice soft and deadly. "So I tell you how I want things done, and it goes in one ear and out the other. Number one thing I tell you, no drinking, no fighting when you're on the job, is that right? Maybe you think I'm just talking! What do you do? You shoot off your mouth to Barney Krazowski, make trouble, start a fight, the cops have to come in. I don't do business that way. You don't do business that way when you're workin' for me."

Nicky Toresca paused, his eyes never leaving Joe's frightened face. "You hear what I'm saying to you?"

Joe nodded. He cleared his throat and stuttered out the words. "Yeah. Sure, I do! But if you'd just lemme tell yuh, it wasn't my fault. Barney Krazowski, he . . ."

Nicky Toresca came a step nearer to him. "When I'm talkin' to you, you don't talk back, is that right?"

"Sure! I just . . . I . . ." The words died out, a stutter of sound in Joe's throat.

Nicky walked up close to him, a couple of quick steps, so quick Joe didn't see him coming. He slapped Joe's face hard, two or three times, on each side, with the flat of his hand. "You don't talk back," Nicky said patiently. "You don't make alibis. What happened happened already. You listen when I talk, and you don't talk back!"

The first time Nicky struck him, Joe ducked a little involuntarily, and his arm raised a little, as if to shield his face. Then he sat perfectly still while Nicky slapped him a few more times. His eyes were fixed on Nicky's face, dumb and agonized and pleading.

Nicky stuck his hand back in his pocket. "You snivelin' little yellow bastard!" Nicky said gently. "I ought to kick your teeth in and tell you to get to hell outa here and stay out! Some day maybe I will!"

He turned his back on Joe then and returned to the window and closed it. He stood still a moment, looking through the slats in the blind at the dismal criss-cross of alleys, and ash cans and empty packing boxes. When he turned around to Joe again he had the mocking half smile on his dark face. "I got a job for you," he said. "It'll take you all week. I was goin' to hire a special man to do it, but I think you can handle it. I think maybe it is right down your alley, Joe."

Joe listened attentively, the livid finger marks across his cheeks. He listened attentively with a sort of trapped wariness and bewilderment on his face.

"You're gonna do a little work in the advertisin' department, Joe," Nicky said silkily.

There was a large cardboard box on the floor behind Nicky's desk. As he spoke he lifted it onto the desk top and removed the cover. He looked at Joe then, the half smile on his face. He lifted first from the box a wad of coarse brown material. He shook it out in front of Joe's bewildered eyes. It was a large baggy sort of coverall suit, with baggy legs and long full sleeves. Nicky spread it out over the corner of the desk in front of Joe. He reached into the box again and came up with a large mask, designed to cover an entire head down to the shoulders. The mask was an animal head, long floppy ears, short stumps of horns, an elongated nose with a hilariously comic lopsided toothy grin. Nicky looked at Joe again, smiling, and then carefully placed the mask on top of the suit on the desk. Joe's face was still bewildered and uncomprehending. Nicky reached into the box once more, and this time he drew out before Joe's suddenly horrified and unbelieving eyes a large sandwich sign of heavy painted canvas, that announced in screaming red-and-blue letters that Toresca's was the gayest spot in town.

Nicky Toresca put the sign down on the desk, too, and tossed the empty box back onto the floor next to the wastebasket. Joe looked from Nicky to the paraphernalia on the desk, and back to Nicky again. There was a look of shocked horror on his face, and still a kind of disbelief.

"You can start right now," Nicky said softly. "You work every afternoon this week, from about one o'clock maybe on till about six. You can cover just Main Street, through the business section. If you keep movin', you won't get so cold. You better wear a jacket or sweater or something under the suit."

Joe's eyes dropped once more to the grinning comic mask, the gaudy sign, the baggy suit, and his fingers closed tight on the arms of his chair till the knuckles went white.

"Go on," Nicky said wearily. "Take that stuff and get out of here." He looked at his wrist watch as he spoke. "You're gettin' a late start today. You shoulda been on the street two hours ago. Snap into it and get movin'."

Joe got up from his chair slowly. He looked at Nicky and then he looked back to the stuff on the desk. Suddenly, Joe realized that Nicky Toresca was in earnest about this; that he was to put on this silly costume and carry that sign up and down Main Street, like any street-corner bum that Nicky could have hired to do it for a quarter an hour. This would be a joke the boys would never get over. This would be something they would never let Joe forget.

Joe looked at Nicky with a last desperate dumb appeal on his face but Nicky showed no sign of relenting. He stood easily with his hands in his pockets watching Joe with a mocking smile. And then he stopped smiling as Joe stood there.

"I said get goin'!"

Joe had done a lot of boasting about what a good job he had with Nicky Toresca. He had bragged a lot about how valuable he already was to the Toresca enterprises. There was going to be a lot of people doing a lot of laughing when this story got out. There would even be quite a few people who would consider it worth a special trip up to Main Street any day to see Joe walking a beat in this garb and carrying a sandwich sign for Nicky Toresca.

Joe reached out his hands toward the silly grinning mask, but at the last moment he couldn't quite do it.

"Oh, no!" he said desperately. "Aw, Christ!"

This time Nicky hit him with his fist, and hard. The blow sent Joe sprawling against the desk, his hand to his jaw. The heavy ring Nicky wore tore the skin. The blood ran out from under Joe's hand, trickled down his wrist and stained his shirt cuff. The grinning mask toppled off the desk and rolled at Joe's feet, the ears flopping.

"Now go on and get into that outfit and get walkin'!" Nicky said.

Joe stooped down and picked the mask up from the floor. He took the other stuff from the desk and left the room without another word.

# 18

AFTER NEW YEAR'S IT TURNED COLD. IT HAD SNOWED most of the night, and the day was clear and bright, with a covering of snow over the ground that was already begrimed by smoke and soot. Petey felt as if she were going to have a cold, and went to work energetically with every remedy she could think of. She telephoned Toresca's that she wouldn't be in that night until late, and not at all if her cold developed. But by dinner time all traces of the cold had disappeared; nevertheless, Petey decided to abide by her original plan. She wouldn't go to work until late tonight; she had a perfect alibi. She would spend an evening with Sally instead. She took a cab out to Horton Street. At the top of the stairs she met Gloria O'Connor pattering down the hall in a pair of sloppy bedroom slippers and an old faded housedress.

"Hi," Petey said cheerfully. "How's Johnny comin'?"

Gloria's face did not look friendly. "All right," she said.

"Fine! We're havin' some winter weather for a change. I like to froze my fanny just comin' from the cab to the house."

Gloria made no answer, and she stared after Petey as she went down the hall toward Sally's door. Gloria stood quite still for a moment looking after Petey, watching the way she walked, memorizing the clothes she was wearing.

Petey found Sally and Fred Foster in the kitchen, Sally busy with the dishes, and Fred playing solitaire on the kitchen table to kill the time before he went to work. They greeted Petey heartily and pulled a chair up to the table where she settled herself comfortably over the last cup of coffee left in the pot. Petey had a project in mind for Virginia and as she explained it she paused from time to time to kibitz Fred's solitaire game, pointing out plays that he had missed. Petey said she had been thinking about Virginia. She knew how crazy Virginia was to get a job, but she thought it would be a lot smarter if Virginia held off a little longer before she took a factory job. There was bound to be a lot of clerking and office jobs opening up these days, with the defense-program boom, and the draft taking so many boys from their jobs, and making girls preferable in the eyes of lots of employers. If Virginia just stuck to it, Petey was of the opinion that she would pick up some sort of office job, and that would be experience for her against a better job in the future. In the meantime, Petey was willing to pay Virginia something, if Ginny would care to come over to her place in the afternoon and straighten the place up a little. It wouldn't be hard work, and it wouldn't take Virginia long to do it, but it would at least bring her a little something, and make her feel that she was doing something while her job-hunting went on. Sally was delighted with the idea. She knew Virginia would be only too pleased to start in the very next afternoon.

Fred broke into the conversation. He was getting damn sick of solitaire. It seemed funny to him that no one would play cards with him. Petey agreed to play on the spot, but Sally protested that the only game she knew was rummy. Petey and Fred assured her that if there was anything they liked to play it was a nice lively game of rummy. Sally consented at last, hung up her dishcloth and pulled up a chair at the opposite end of the table. Fred dealt the first hand while Sally, the appointed score-keeper, went to find paper and pencil. They squabbled together good-naturedly over the turn of the cards, keeping a broken conversation going over the slight demands the game made on them.

A hand ended and Sally picked up her pencil. "Fred, how did you come out?"

Fred counted the cards in front of him rapidly and audibly and then he said, "Gimme sixty. Not so bad, huh?"

Sally wrote it down industriously. "That's sixty for you. And I got fifty-five and I had fifteen left. I made forty—how about you, Petey?"

Petey was gathering up the cards to shuffle them. "Put me twenty in the hole this trip."

"Look at Wrong Way Corrigan!" Fred chortled.

Sally studied her figures as Petey dealt the cards around. "That puts you ahead, Fred, and Petey is next, and I'm right behind her. I guess this is still anybody's game."

"Oh, I'll go out this hand," Fred boasted. "I gotta go to work in a minute. I'll just have time to win the game this hand before I leave."

"Say, Petey," Sally said earnestly, "is something the matter with Joe? Has he had trouble on his job or something?"

"Why?" Petey asked.

Sally scowled over her cards, rearranging them in her hand before she answered. "My first play? Well, I dunno, he acts sort of funny. He—he's been hanging around home a lot, and he acts—well, he acts more like he used to, don't you think so, Fred?"

Fred spread a four run of hearts out in front of him with a flourish. "Yeah. Joe musta banged his head against somep'n. He sure pulled his horns in the last couple days."

Petey didn't even hesitate. "I dunno," she said. "His job is coming along fine, I hear."

"What's that noise?" Sally broke in, cocking her head to listen.

Petey turned her own head attentively. "What kinda noise?"

"I don't know," Sally said. "A kind of moaning noise. Spooky!" She shivered a little, smiling.

Petey laughed at her. "Honey, you got the heeby-jeebies! Come on, play cards! We gotta tie Freddie up about a hundred in the hole this time."

"Yeah? Fat chance you got! Not this boy! Look what I got on the board already."

"Yeah, and look at that fist full of cards you're setting there with," Petey teased him. "I'm gonna go out in a minute and then . . ."

Sally dropped her cards on the table. "There! I did too hear a noise. There it is again, listen!"

This time they all heard it. A sort of low wail, an animal noise, but strangely close, muffled and eerie.

Sally stared from one to the other of them nervously. "Hear it?"

"Must be a dog," Fred said.

After several repetitions of the hideous sound Petey said, "This is gettin' to be not so funny as it was. There's something out there. We gotta find out what it is."

She walked to the door, but before she got it open another sound came that agitated them all still more. There was an animal-like scratching on the other side, then a rattling of the doorknob, that grew until the whole door seemed to be shaking on its hinges.

"Jesus!" said Fred Foster and even Petey stepped back a little, indecision on her face.

Then the shaking stopped suddenly. There was a rapid scuffling sound in the hall, and the scratching and shaking resumed immediately, but this time on a door further down the hall. Over the sound came Gloria O'Connor's shrill, terror-stricken scream. The mad, weird cry came again, and suddenly the cry took words, but in a voice like no human voice. "Sally, lemme in! Lemme in, Sally! I ain't agonna hurt nobody. Sally, Lemme in! Sally!"

Petey got the door open, just as Johnny O'Connor appeared down the hall. There was a scuffle of sound, the mad howling cries began again, quick footsteps on the stairs, and the outside door was flung open down below. Petey went out into the hall, and through the open door they could hear the scuffle of steps on the porch, a thudding sound, and then quiet.

"It's the old lady upstairs," Petey called back to them. "She must have the DT's or she's gone off her nut."

They all poured out into the hall then, Sally and the children, Fred, Johnny and a white-faced, weeping Gloria. From down below they heard Mrs. Gideon weeping noisily.

"May I never live to hear a noise like that again," Johnny O'Connor said soberly.

"Oh, the poor old lady," Sally said. "The poor old soul!"

"She musta gone bats," Petey said. "From the sound of it, I guess she took a dive off the porch. We better go down and see. She coulda broke her neck."

"I'll go with you," Johnny said. But before they even started, the howling cries began again. From the front of the house, from the side, and from the front again.

"Jesus, she must be running around in circles out there, crazier than a bedbug!" Fred's hands were trembling as he lighted a cigarette.

"Poor old lady," Sally murmured. "Oh, if she only wouldn't holler like that. I'll never forget her hollering like this as long as I live."

Johnny came to the door, his jacket over his shoulders, and Petey said, "You gotta flashlight?"

"Yeah." Johnny turned back, and Gloria trailed after him. "Johnny, don't go outdoors. I don't want you to! Johnny, I'm scared."

"You better not go out there," Fred said to Petey nervously. "She's gone nuts. She could tear yuh to pieces. Look at the way she was shaking that door, like to tore it off the hinges. It ain't safe to go out there where she is, she could jump on yuh in the dark and . . ."

"We gotta catch her and get a doctor," Petey said impatiently. "Christ, she's runnin' around out there with no coat on or nothing. Maybe she hurt herself when she took the pitch off the porch, you can't tell. What you wanta do, just let her run around out there and yell her head off till she busts a blood vessel?"

Johnny appeared in the door, lugging the flashlight clumsily. "Here, you better take it," he said to Petey. "Come on, let's go. She was yellin' from back of the house while I was huntin' the flashlight. I think if we was to go around the house on the other side, why, maybe . . ."

Petey took the flashlight and jammed her arms into her coatsleeves hurriedly.

As they started down the stairs they met Mrs. Gideon on her way up. She was white-faced and round-eyed. She had stopped crying, but she was out of breath and trembling.

"For mercy sakes, wasn't that awful?" she gasped. "Why, she like to scared Mama and me to death! We was all alone. Harry, Mr. Gideon, you know, has gone to work. You folks all right up there? What ever got into that poor old woman to carry on like this? You suppose she's sick or drunk or what? For mercy sakes, what'll we do? She's arunnin' around outdoors there without a coat on, and yellin' and wavin' her arms. I just don't know what we oughta do . . ."

Petey opened the door below, and she and Johnny stepped out into the crisp cold darkness. The cries had stopped, and they hesitated on the porch steps. From other houses up and down the block, they saw faces pressed to the panes of lighted windows.

They went down the steps together, across the sidewalk to the side of the house. It was very dark, and the dry snow crunched noisily under their feet. Petey kept the flashlight beam swinging ahead of them.

Petey took hold of Johnny's arm suddenly as she spoke. "Hey, hey," she said softly.

"Where?" Johnny whispered, and they stood still together.

"Over by the front of the garage, just standin' there, right about opposite that big tree."

Petey kept the flashlight beam pointed at the snow just ahead of them. Johnny looked in the direction she had indicated, blinking his eyes to accustom them to the darkness.

"I see her," he whispered.

"I'll put the light on her," Petey said. "We'll see what happens then. Stand by for some action maybe!"

Petey flicked the beam directly on her then, suddenly, without warning. It was Mrs. Sipes all right, in a wrinkled dark dress, torn and dirty. Her face was wild and distorted, hair hanging in disorder and blood was running from a big scraped gash on her forehead. She stood quite still, looking into the light.

"The light has blinded her for a minute," Petey whispered. "She musta hit her head when she dove off the porch."

Petey spoke to the old woman in a gentle, friendly voice. "Come on now, Mrs. Sipes. You better come back in the house and get your coat on. You're gonna catch cold out here. This is Sally, Mrs. Sipes, you remember Sally. She's your friend. Come on back in the house now. Come on, Mrs. Sipes. It's all right, Sally wants you to come back in the house now, Mrs. Sipes, before you catch cold . . ."

Mrs. Sipes moved suddenly toward them, and Johnny said, "Watch it!" sharply. But the old lady went by them like a streak, running to the front of the house again.

They turned around to follow. "No soap," Petey said. "Looks like the only way we're gonna get her back in the house is to carry her in, if we can catch her. She's a spry old girl. She went by us like a bat outa hell. I'll douse the beam. We oughta be able to see her around here by the street lights and maybe we can sneak up on her."

They rounded the corner of the house, walking as softly as they could in the squeaking snow.

Petey caught Johnny's arm once again and nodded her head vigorously. Mrs. Sipes was standing on the edge of the sidewalk with her back to them, looking up and down the street wildly.

They separated and advanced cautiously on the old woman, sneaking up quietly like children playing Indian. Johnny came up directly behind her, and Petey cut a circle off to the right, bringing herself between Mrs. Sipes and the house, but keeping the timing just right, so that Mrs. Sipes would not catch a glimpse of her before Johnny reached her.

But apparently Mrs. Sipes had eyes in the back of her head tonight. Just as Johnny came up behind her she was off again like lightning. Johnny lunged, but she was gone. Petey ran like a streak, but she got past her up the sidewalk. Mrs. Sipes didn't go far; she just retreated out of reach, and then stood still, looking back at them, her face literally covered with the blood from her head now, a horrible sticky red mask.

Johnny and Petey joined forces again, and stood still together, looking up the sidewalk at Mrs. Sipes, who stared right back at them. They were both out of breath.

"Well, it was a good try," Johnny said, grimly. "But I don't think we'll be sneakin' up on the old girl, not tonight. We better put in a neighborhood alarm. It's gonna take some help and a little doin' to corner her."

"An' me without my butterfly net!" Petey said bitterly. She stood on one foot, holding Johnny's arm, and removed one of her high-heeled pumps and whacked the snow out of it vigorously. "My favorite winter sport—chasing loonies on dark nights!"

Automobile lights cut the snow behind them. "Oh, Jesus," Petey said. "Here comes a car. If the old girl should take it into her head to dodge out across the street, it's gonna be just too bad."

The car came slowly, slid next to the curb, and drew up beside them.

"It's a police car. Here come the recruits! Somebody on the street must have phoned in an alarm," Johnny said.

One of the uniformed men in the car opened the door and leaned out. "What's the disturbance around here?"

Petey was emptying her other shoe and she pointed up the street with it, holding the pump by the slim heel. "There she is, boys," she said cheerfully. "And you're sure welcome!"

The officers looked up the street toward Mrs. Sipes dubiously. "A drunk?" the other one asked.

"It's an old lady who lives here in this house," Johnny explained. "She started yelling around and making a disturbance tonight, and finally she ran outdoors here. We've been trying to get her back in the house, but we couldn't catch her."

The officer flashed his own flashlight up the street into the old woman's face. "There's blood on her head. How'd that happen?" he asked. Mrs. Sipes stood quite still, blinking into the beam of light.

"She fell off the porch when she run outdoors," Johnny said. "She must have hit her head then."

The two officers got out of the car. They advanced toward Mrs. Sipes slowly and one of them yelled, "What's goin' on here?" Mrs. Sipes retreated a little further up the sidewalk as they advanced.

"You won't be catchin' her that way," Johnny advised.

The officers stopped momentarily in indecision.

"Looky," Petey said. "Why don't you get back here by the car and turn the lights out. Then we'll go across the street and come up sort of behind her. Then maybe she'll run back this way and then you can nab her. If she runs the other way you can catch up with her in the car easy."

The officers looked at each other, frowning a little, and then one of them said, "No harm tryin'. Go ahead."

Johnny and Petey crossed the street. Mrs. Sipes watched them dubiously, but she stood still. When they were just about opposite her, they started to cross the street again in her direction. She hesitated, but as they drew near, she ran again, back toward the house. The two officers stepped out of the shadows beside their automobile and caught hold of her easily. She struggled only for a moment, and then she said in her wavering, high-pitched, old voice, "Lemme alone. I ain't a hurtin' nobody. What you wanta grab hold of me for? I ain't a hurtin' nobody!"

Johnny and Petey approached them slowly. One of the officers was holding the old woman by the arm. "She's drunk, all right," he said to them. "She got any family here? What does she do, live alone?"

"I'm Mrs. John Sipes an' I live right here in that house," Mrs. Sipes said unevenly. "Lemme go. I ain't a hurtin' nobody!"

"Yeah, she lives alone," Johnny said. There was a faint scowl on his face as he spoke.

The other officer jotted down the house number on his pad and climbed into the car.

"Well, we'll take her along," the officer said, maneuvering her toward the car.

Petey stepped toward him suddenly. "Wait a minute. Whatcha gonna do with her?"

"Lock her up, lady, get her off the streets!" The officer said a little impatiently.

Petey's eyes narrowed, but her voice was laconic. "I think the hospital is the place for her!"

"They'll stick a bandage on her head over to the jail," he said. "Come on, in you go!" He shoved Mrs. Sipes into the car. She didn't resist much, her voice had sunk to a mumble now.

"I don't just mean that gash in her head," Petey said. "She may have been drinkin', all right, but I don't think that's all that's wrong with her. I think she's sick."

The officer got into the car after Mrs. Sipes and slammed the door. "Look, lady," he said, "if you handled as many cases a this kind a thing every week as we do . . . !"

The motor raced, and the car pulled away from the curb. Even over the noise of the motor, with the windows closed as they were, came Mrs. Sipes' quavering wail. "Lemme go, I ain't a hurtin' nobody! Sally! Sally!"

The car went on up the street, slowed down for the traffic and then turned the corner. Johnny and Petey stood motionless until it was out of sight. "Not so good," Johnny said. "Poor old gal!"

"Well," Petey said. "So, maybe she was drunk, I don't know. It's a wonder her breath didn't tip that officer's cap, but just the same, I wish we'd a got hold of her before the busy boys got here, and got a doctor for her."

They walked back to the house together. "Maybe they got somebody around the jail that can look her over," Johnny said with no conviction.

Petey laughed shortly. "Yeah! They'll toss her in a cell and forget about her."

They met Fred coming down the stairs on his way to work. "The police picked the old lady up, huh?" he said with some of his old cheerfulness. "God, she sure scared the bejesus outa me, yellin' around like that. She must be crazier'n a bedbug! What they gonna do with her?"

"Toss her in the clink, I guess," Petey said.

"Well, they better double lock the door," Fred said cheerfully. "Hell, she ain't drunk, she's gone bats!"

Johnny and Petey went on up the stairs. "If she's really sick they'll know so by tomorrow," Johnny said consolingly. "They'll send her to the hospital then."

"Oh, sure, they'll send her to the hospital tomorrow," Petey said briefly, "after the liquor is off her breath. The only trouble is I knew a case like that once when tomorrow come about five hours too late that morning."

Sally's door was ajar and they went in together. Sally and Gloria were sitting on the davenport, the children were back in bed. Mrs. Gideon sat in the rocking chair. They heard the sound of her voice as they came in.

Petey went to her purse for a cigarette and Johnny lounged in the doorway.

"She got any relatives or friends here in town?" Petey asked Mrs. Gideon.

"Well, I was just sayin'," Mrs. Gideon said. "No, sir, she hasn't. She hasn't got a soul left in this world that cares what becomes of her. That's what makes it seem so sort of sad. Not a soul ever come here to see her all the while she lived here, and she never got one single speck a mail, not even at Christmas time."

Mrs. Gideon hesitated a moment, and then she spoke with genuine feeling in her voice. "I suppose you all wondered why I let her live here. Harry, Mr. Gideon, you know, never liked to have her around, and I know she was kind of a nuisance, with her drinkin' and all. You see, I've known that poor woman all my life, not really known her, exactly, but I've known of her. She used to live right near us when we had the house over on the other side of town. I knew her when her husband was alive. John Sipes, his name was."

They all listened attentively, and Mrs. Gideon went on. "John Sipes worked in one a the shops, he was a real, steady, hardworkin' man. But he was terrible close; he never spent a penny on nothin'. They never had but the one kid I guess, and it died when it was real little. The poor woman just stayed to home and worked without hardly a decent rag to her back all the while her husband was alive. He was an awful close man. I remember the neighbors out there used to tell a story about 'em. Seems once after the talking pictures come in, she teased him into taking her and going to the movies one night. I guess they'd never been to the movies before. Anyway, they went to the show and on the way home stopped for coffee and hamburgers or something, the way you will. Somebody they knew was there where they was eatin' and they told it afterwards. Mrs. Sipes was real smilin' and tickled about it, and she said to John, 'Now, didn't we have a nice time tonight, though!' And her husband said, 'Yes, we did, but we can't never do it again. It costs too much money.' Well, I guess it was like that as long as he lived."

"So I guess I know the next chapter to this story," Petey said.

Mrs. Gideon smiled a little, and the rockers of her chair kept squeaking. "Well, I guess it's a common enough story. The minute that man was buried, an awful change came over her, and I don't know as you could blame her. Her husband left quite a lot of money, insurance and in the bank and all. Lord knows he should of, he never spent a penny or let her while he lived. Well, the first thing she did— it was in the winter that he died—was buy herself some clothes and go off to Florida. When she come back in the spring there was a man hanging after her, quite a lot younger'n she was. He lived right there at the house with her. I remember some woman that lived near by tried to talk to her. But Mrs. Sipes just said, no, sir, what if he was after her money, she didn't care, she was goin' to spend that money and have a good time. She said she had it comin' to her. Well, she spent the money, all right. She finally sold the house, too. I hadn't heard what had become of her the last couple years till she come here looking for a room. I hardly recognized her, her hair dyed like that, and all. All the money she has in the world is her old-age pension. It wasn't much. I don't know how she ever gets along on it, with her drinkin' like that and all . . ."

"Oh, gosh," Sally said. "The poor old lady, and then to think of her bein' locked up in jail like this tonight. I tell you some awful things can happen to people, and none of us know what's ahead of us or how we're gonna end up, either."

"You're right about that, Sally," Mrs. Gideon said.

Petey narrowed her eyes from the cigarette smoke, and her breath caught in her throat suddenly.

# 19

IT WAS SO LATE BY THE TIME PETEY GOT BACK TO HER apartment that she had half a notion to stay away from Toresca's altogether. But on the other hand it was too early for her to go to bed, accustomed to late hours as she was, and she felt a sort of restlessness. The walls of the small apartment seemed to close in on her, and the quiet was loud in her ears. Regular old firehorse, Petey thought somberly, as she started the shower running. She was always mourning because she never had the chance to spend an evening at home, and then if she did get the chance, what always happened? Why, along about this time of night she would find herself scrambling into a long dress and heading out for the bright lights someplace.

She hunted out an old dress that she hadn't worn in a long time, a plain black dinner dress with long sleeves and completely unadorned. She added a wide gold suede girdle studded with brilliants, heavy long gold earrings and a heavy ring with a huge brilliant stone, and let it go at that.

When she arrived at Toresca's, she found, as she had suspected, only the remnants of a crowd remaining. She stopped at the bar for a drink.

"Hello, Joe," she said without enthusiasm, as she swung up onto a stool. "Whatcha hear from the mob?"

"We been having a slow evenin' all night," the bartender said, as he mixed her drink. "You shoulda been around, Miss Braun, maybe you coulda pepped the place up a little."

"Yeah," Petey said. "Just call me dynamite!"

The bartender drew himself a short beer and drank it.

Petey sipped her drink, her chin on her hand, and watched the musicians beating out music for the two or three couples dancing without enthusiasm.

"Some day that outfit is gonna go so sound asleep they'll wake up here in the mornin' still playing 'Rosetta,'" Petey said.

She watched them idly, and suddenly she saw Nicky Toresca enter from the back, in hat and overcoat.

Nicky paused beside Petey and lighted a cigarette without speaking. "It got so late I thought you wasn't comin' in tonight," he said, extinguishing the match with a short sharp motion and doubling it in his fingers.

"Oh, you know me," Petey said. "Do or die for my alma mama."

"I thought you was sick. I pretty near sent flowers."

"Jesus! Too bad I lived!"

Nicky Toresca's face was morose as he looked at her. "You don't look like you been sick," he said. "I thought you had a cold."

"Mama, shall I cough for the man?" Petey mocked.

"Maybe you just didn't feel like workin'," Nicky said. "Maybe you had a date tonight, is that right?"

Petey's eyebrow bent slowly as she took a drink. "Here we go again!"

"Don't bother to haul your contract outa the front of your brassiere," Nicky said softly. "It's just a little hunk a paper!"

"Why, Mr. Toresca," Petey said. "I'm awful glad to hear you say that! I was just thinkin' tonight I might need a change. My, if I started singin' some other spot in this town I bet you'd be surprised how many a your customers would come along!"

Nicky's face turned angry.

"Wanta take a bet on it?" Petey asked, smiling sweetly.

He turned on his heel without another word, and strode down the ramp and out the front entrance.

Petey watched him go, and after him another party of customers. She slid down from her stool slowly. "Well, I guess I better go up and do my bit before you carry out the last customer and lock the door," Petey said to the bartender. She pushed her drink away, still unfinished. "Joe, it's a cruel cold world, did anybody ever tell you?"

She walked down to the front of the room in front of the orchestra stand, her cape slung over one shoulder and her heels clicking.

She greeted the musicians, dropped her cape on a chair, and adjusted the microphone. There weren't more than six customers left, besides a few at the bar. Petey looked them over, smiled a greeting at a couple that she recognized, and called the number she wanted over her shoulder to the orchestra. While the piano player picked the melody up in her key, with an idle ripple of notes for introduction, Petey reflected that there probably wasn't a soul in the joint that gave a damn whether she sang or not. She didn't bother to give the song any build up, she just sang it. She let all the stoppers out and sang it very blue.

*"Tonight I mustn't think of him,*
*Music, maestro, please!*
*Tonight, tonight I must forget*
*Those precious hours,*
*but no hearts and flowers . . ."*

A part of her listened to herself singing and was amused. Nothing but a little old ordinary pop tune and listen to me tearing the heart out of it, as if it was important, or even good music. Jesus, I yawp like a bitch in labor!

She finished that song and sang a couple more of them, and all of them turned out to be blues songs tonight, for some reason. One song always reminded her of another, when she was singing like this without anything definitely rehearsed.

Some new customers came in—three men. They passed the bar and came down the steps. Petey looked at them curiously. Just three men, except that one of them was the big blond guy that she got out of the jail New Year's Eve. At the sight of him, Petey felt as if her heart stopped beating. Then it started again, but it beat too rapidly. Just looking at him she got that strange feeling, a sort of loss of confidence, a vague fear. He didn't even look at Petey. He came down the steps behind the two other men and they took a table toward the back of the room. The big guy sat down easily. He didn't have a hat on and his hair shone bleached, almost white, in the light. He wore the same wrinkled, tweedy suit, but tonight he was wearing a light gabardine raincoat over it, unbuttoned, and the fabric stretched tight across his tremendous shoulders.

The pianist finished his introduction, but for once Petey missed her cue, and he had to take it over again for her. She didn't want to sing. She wanted to walk away from this microphone and get to hell out of this joint.

When she started singing, the big guy turned around to look. She watched the slow turning of his head and a shock went through her like needles, in anticipation of the moment when he would look directly at her with his strange pale eyes. He looked at her, all right. Petey met his eyes momentarily, and then she looked away up to the bar. Jesus, what did he wanta turn up here for? she thought angrily. She never expected to see that big gorilla again in her life, and then he comes rambling in here tonight, like a—like a goddam old ghost!

When the song was over, Petey glanced again at that table toward the back. She couldn't help it; she had to do it in spite of herself. The two men were applauding, but the big man wasn't. He sat quietly in his chair. He was still looking at her, but there was no glimmer of recognition on his face.

For no reason that she could understand, Petey was getting angrier by the minute. Who did that big lug think he was anyway? She had gone out of her way on a wet, cold night—not to mention the twenty-five smackers—to spring him out of the clink. What did he do? Why, he never as much as said thank you. And now he comes in tonight and sets there and gives her the fish-eye. Who did he think he was anyway?

In spite of the applause when the song ended, Petey took her bows, picked up her cape from the chair and walked away from the microphone to the bar.

The bartender had her drink ready for her. "Say, Miss Braun," he said, admiringly. "You was sure doin' all right tonight!"

"Thanks, Joe," Petey said.

The bartender moved off to draw a couple of beers, and Petey glanced out of the corner of her eyes down below to the table where the big man was sitting. The two men with him were talking earnestly, leaning across the table toward each other. She had never seen either one of them before. They were well dressed, one middle-aged, one younger. They could be business men, they could be anything, they could be anybody. The big man wasn't talking. He just sat there, though once in a while one of the men would turn and look at him, as if to include him in the conversation. The big guy had finished his drink already, although the other men were so busy talking that their drinks sat almost untouched. He had finished his drink, and the waiter was bringing him another one just as Petey looked. She watched him toss off the whisky straight, and take a sip out of the chaser. Rum-dum, she said to herself viciously.

It was on the tip of her tongue to ask the bartender who the three men were, and that made Petey even angrier. The hell she'd ask! She didn't give a damn who they were. She deliberately tried to put all thought of them out of her mind. She deliberately tried to forget that the big man was here now in this very room with her.

Closing time approached, and most of the customers drifted out. The musicians packed up their instruments. It's getting late. I ought to go on home, Petey thought, but she made no move to go. The big man and the two men with him were the last customers at the tables. The bar was deserted, except for Petey herself, and a pudgy little drunk at the far end who was waving a bill in the bartender's face and noisily demanding just one more beer. The bartender explained good-naturedly that it was after curfew, polishing the bar with the barcloth as he talked.

The three men got up in a minute, pushed back their chairs noisily and started up the short flight of stairs. Petey looked straight down at her drink, but she knew that the last moment she would look around, and she did. She looked over her shoulder, and she looked right into the big man's face, because he was looking at her too. They looked at each other for just a moment. There was no recognition on his face; he did not even pause. They went down the ramp, all three of them, and stopped momentarily while the other two men got their hats and coats from the check booth. Then they went out together. Petey suddenly felt very tired.

She stared down at her drink for a moment without even tasting it. It didn't seem worth the effort somehow to get up from this stool, climb into a cab and go home.

She watched the waiter pushing the wide broom across the floor. From someplace she heard a factory whistle blowing.

The door to the back opened and Tommy Terwilliger drifted in, stopping to talk to the waiter. Petey felt better suddenly just at the sight of the stubby little man with his battered, scarred face. She smiled all of a sudden, and she said to the bartender, "Hey, Joe, mix up one for Tommy, whatever he drinks, huh?"

"Sure thing," he said. He grinned as he uncorked the bottle. "This is where the profits go!"

Petey took the drink, picked up her own drink in her other hand and went down the steps.

"Hi, Tommy," she called. "How's about havin' a drink with me? I never was cut out to be a solitary drinker."

Tommy Terwilliger turned to her with his shy, pleased smile. "Why, hello, there, Miss Petey. You're hangin' around kinda late tonight. Sure, I'd be glad to have a drink with you."

They lifted two chairs down from the top of a table out of range of the broom the waiter was wielding, and sat down.

"Here you are," Petey said, smiling as she pushed his drink toward him across the table.

"Say, this is kind of nice," Tommy said.

"Yup, the joint is all ours. What gives with you, Tommy?"

"Oh, not much a nothin'," Tommy said. "I heard you was sick, Miss Petey?"

"Just a cold hangin' around," Petey said. "I'm fine now."

"Just the same, you look kinda peaked tonight," Tommy said with a shade of concern in his voice. "You better look after yourself good. A cold ain't nothin' to take chances with."

"Aw, I'm all right." Petey pulled another cigarette out of her package. Tommy groped in his pocket for a match, but Petey lighted it herself.

"Tommy?"

"Yeah, Miss Petey?"

Petey waited a minute, twirling her glass slowly in her fingers. "Tommy, was you ever in a town somewhere, and all of a sudden everything just played out for you? All of a sudden you was fed up with it till you couldn't stand it, and you wanted to get to hell outa there quick, it didn't make no difference where you went just as long as you got movin' outa there?"

"Sure," Tommy said. "Many a time."

"There ain't but the one remedy for it, is there?" she said.

"If there is another, then I never heard about it."

"No," Petey said. "There isn't. You just pack up the old suitcases again, and catch another train."

Tommy's face looked sympathetic and worried all at once. He was silent a moment, and then he began to talk with a determined cheerfulness. "Say, Miss Petey, did I ever tell you about MacGorham? He was a heavyweight that usta fight outa here ten, fifteen years ago . . ."

Petey reached out and squeezed Tommy's hand tight. "You're a swell egg, Tommy!" she said.

Tommy looked pleased and bewildered, and shy suddenly. He took a sudden gulp of his drink.

"Tommy," Petey said again, "Tommy, was you around tonight when those three guys come in and set down at that table in the back? They was here till after closing time."

"Naw," Tommy said. "I was out back. I never come out here till just now. Why, what about 'em?"

"Oh, I was just wonderin' who they were," Petey said. "I never saw them in here before. One of them was a big guy, real big. He had real light hair and . . ."

"Oh, that musta been San," Tommy said.

"San?" Petey repeated the name.

"Yeah, a real big guy, never wears no hat an' his hair looks kinda bleached out and he . . ."

"That's him all right," Petey said. "Who is he, anyway?"

"Well, I don't rightly know," Tommy said. "I never heard nobody tell much about him. He's been around town now about a year I guess, but I don't know where he come from before that. He comes upstairs here to play cards quite a lot. He ain't a very talkative guy, and he ain't got no special friends that I know of. He's quite a heavy drinker, but he ain't no hand to talk. He sure is a big guy. I always wondered about him. I betcha . . ."

"San." Petey repeated the name again. "That's a funny name. Must be a nickname. What's his real name?"

"You got me," Tommy said. "Everybody calls him San, and I guess that's his name all right, or I guess his name is really 'Sans.'"

"Sans!"

"Well," Tommy explained, "I guess nobody ever heard him say his name. He ain't a very friendly guy. But he was in here one night right soon after he first come into town, I guess. And he signed a check for some liquor, and that's the name he wrote on the check—Sans."

Petey grinned suddenly all the way across her face. "I guess that's a French name," she said.

"Yeah?"

"Uh huh," Petey said. "I learned the French words to some songs once, and I remember that name."

Tommy looked a little dubious. "Well, maybe he's French," he said. "But he don't look like no Frenchman to me. I'd a said he was a Swede or a German, maybe. He sure is a big guy. I've always wondered about him. I betcha . . ."

Petey broke in. "Tommy, you remember you promised to play the piano for me sometime? You'll never have a better chance. Come on and play for me, huh?"

"Aw, you don't wanta hear me play the piano," Tommy said. "I ain't no fancy player. I never learned to play off music or nothin' like that."

"The hell with that talk," Petey said. "Come on and play, Tommy."

"Well, okay, if you want me too," Tommy said reluctantly. He got up, his drink in his hand, and walked over to the orchestra stand.

He rubbed his knobby hands together as he sat down, his eyes fixed on the stained row of keys in front of him. He spread his hands out on the keys lightly then, hesitating a moment before he struck them. In that moment before he began to play he hitched his shoulders in a peculiar gesture and ducked his head down.

He struck the keys hard with his square short-fingered hands, and the noise was loud in the empty room. It was power piano playing, with the bass rolling out under his left hand like the roll of a drum.

Petey's face was delighted, and she got up from the table, drink in hand and moved closer to the piano. "Hey," she said. "That's all right!"

"Aw, it's kinda old-fashioned piano playin'," Tommy said apologetically. "Folks don't like it much now days."

"The hell they don't!" Petey said, as she came to lean over a corner of the piano.

She watched his hands in fascination. He didn't go in for a lot of melodic intricacies. He played it lean and clean, like the old-timers, Yancey and the rest, that she had heard on recordings.

When Tommy stopped playing, Petey was breathless. "Aw, don't stop! Jesus, I love it," she said in sincere tribute. "I guess this is just my kind a music, that's all."

Tommy finished his drink and put the glass down again. "It's funny to hear you say that, Miss Petey," he said shyly. "Because music like this sort a reminds me a you. Sometimes, when I see you walk up here to the microphone like you do, or when you're laughin' and singin' up here, I kind of hear this kinda music playin' in my head. I guess this is your kinda music, all right."

Petey's great laughter echoed. Then she said quickly, "No, it's all right, Tommy. I guess when you stop to think of it, that's just about one of the nicest things anybody ever said to me. Give me more of it!"

They didn't talk any more, and Tommy played for a long time. Petey couldn't get enough of it. It was almost morning when he grew tired and got up from the piano at last.

Petey climbed into a cab for home, and rolled the windows down a little so the cold air could blow in. She felt good now, strong and rested, the way good music always made her feel. After all, she thought, there wasn't anything in the world like great music, real jazz, to take the crimps out of you when you got to feeling rotten. Suppose I had lammed outa here on a train tonight, she said to herself, where would the percentage a been? I'd still have been feeling lousy, and I'd a been running away from something instead of staying to look it in the face. The trouble with you is, she told herself objectively, you've taken a dive for that big blond lug they call San. He's gone deep with you already, too deep. Nothing like this has ever happened to you before, has it? So maybe your number is up, and you aren't any different or any luckier than anybody else. This is the kind of thing that happens to lots of people. Now let's see how well you can stand up and take it. All the while she was thinking that, she was aware that by tomorrow she couldn't feel strong and objective about it any more. By tomorrow she'd feel lousy again, and she'd run away from it again, even in her own thinking. But that was tomorrow. Tonight she felt good.

When she got out of the cab, it was beginning to snow. The cold and the snow on her face were good to Petey. She felt alive and good. Why, for two cents she wouldn't go to bed at all. Instead, she'd go out someplace and have a big breakfast, and maybe take a walk. She didn't get a chance to walk much lately, and then she would . . .

Hey, wait a minute now, Petey grinned at herself. Listen to superwoman! You better go flop for awhile. This is too good to last, and you've got things to do today, and rehearsals and a show to give tonight.

But the good feeling lasted. Petey took in her bottle of milk and put it in the refrigerator. Nothing could hurt her really, and if the breaks didn't come her way, she could take it.

Petey turned on the radio for the early-morning war news, and undressed for bed, closing blinds against the morning light that was not far away.

# 20

SATURDAY NIGHT THAT WEEK SALLY WORKED LATE at the restaurant as usual. Once work was over, she scrambled into her wraps and ran all the way to the drug store to get the next bus. She was tired; Saturday was always a long hard day for her. Her body ached as it jolted with the motion of the lumbering motor. Sally sighed, and, as she rode along, she hunted paper and a stub of pencil out of her purse to write her grocery list. She didn't ride the bus all the way to Horton Street, this night. She got out at the big A. and P. store several blocks before her stop. The big market was still open, and it was Sally's custom to do her shopping for Saturday-night supper and for Sunday herself.

The store was crowded. Sally stood in line for one of the little pushcarts, with double-deck wire trays. She maneuvered it in and out among the shelves, selecting a few items painstakingly, smiling as she made way for women like herself, pushing the little carts laden with groceries. All the time she was formulating hypothetical menus for dinner tonight, and mid-day Sunday dinner. Oh, if she just had ten dollars to spend here tonight, couldn't she plan menus easily, Sally thought. No matter what they said, prices were beginning to edge upward. Sally bet they would keep going up, too, higher and higher. She remembered a little, and she had heard a lot of stories about how high prices went in the last war, the food rationing and all the rest of it. Feeding a family the size of hers with what little money she had was no joke when conditions were normal, and goodness knew how she would make out if prices kept really mounting till they were sky-high. She was vaguely aware that there were such things as vitamins and balanced diets that kids had to have if they were to keep well and healthy, particularly in the winter time. That reminded her of the vitamin tablets the doctor had said Virginia should have once she got over the flu. In fact, the doctor had recommended them for the entire family, because there was so much sickness around that winter. Sally felt a little sinking sensation in her stomach; they cost so much money. Funny, when she was a kid nobody ever thought of such a thing as taking vitamin tablets, and now that was all you heard about, as if it wasn't possible to live without them. Well, if it wasn't, why did they cost so much, and what were you going to do when you just didn't have the money to buy them?

Sally completed her shopping at last, stood by while the competent young man in a white coat added up the items of her purchase on an adding machine. She parted with the bills regretfully, and pocketed the change, while he packed her groceries into two huge brown paper sacks, milk bottles in the bottom, eggs on top. Her groceries had cost her a little more than the mental estimate Sally had kept as she selected them and, for no reason, that frightened her. It wasn't any joke feeding a family like hers. What would she do if it wasn't for Fred Foster's board money? What would she do when Petey left town, as she surely would eventually, and Sally had nothing left but her own pay check in a world of mounting prices and new taxes?

Sally stuck her purse in the top of one of the two paper bags and lifted them, carrying one in each arm. Someone opened the door for her. Sally smiled her wide cheerful grin and said "Thanks."

Out on the street, she trudged off toward home. It was cold, and snowing a little, now and then a lazy flake floating down. Sally's spirits drooped as she plodded along, and she made a conscious effort to combat the feeling of depression. After all, there were many people a lot worse off than they were; she was making out all right. This was Saturday night. Her hardest work day of all the week was over, and she was on her way home to get supper for the kids. Tomorrow was Sunday and she didn't have to get up early and she didn't have to go to work till late afternoon.

She climbed up the porch steps at Gideon's at last. Her arms ached from carrying the heavy bags, and her face and hands and feet were stiff with cold. She bunched the parcels together tight against her and managed to turn the doorknob and kick the door open. The hallway was warm and cozy with light. There were a couple of letters on the table by the telephone, and Sally paused to see if they belonged to her. The one on top was hers, all right: Roy's familiar handwriting and the familiar postmark. Sally lowered one of her sacks to the chair near the table to pick it up. The letter underneath was hers too, addressed in neat typewriting to Mrs. Roy Otis, but not an ad, a personal letter and postmarked this city. Sally examined it curiously.

Just then Mrs. Gideon stuck her head out between the curtains. Her eyes were red with weeping, and she said, "Oh, Sally, what do you suppose? Mrs. Sipes is gone!"

Sally felt a little chill through her body. "For goodness' sakes! You mean she . . ."

Yes, Mrs. Gideon said, she died this afternoon. Mrs. Gideon had got to wondering about her this morning, so she called up the jail and they had told her that Mrs. Sipes had been taken to the hospital. It seemed that the morning after they picked her up the matron was unable to arouse her. She was unconscious. They sent her to the hospital then, and she had died there this afternoon, without ever recovering consciousness. In a coma, the hospital people called it. They said that what was wrong with her was something to do with hardening of the arteries, something had happened in her brain, a clot or something, Mrs. Gideon didn't just understand. Anyway, Mrs. Sipes was dead.

The quick tears came to Sally's eyes. She was so sorry, she said. She supposed that it was wrong to wish the poor old lady back, she probably was better off, but wasn't it awful that she should have had to go the way she did? It seemed so awful to think that the last thing the poor old woman was conscious of in this world had to be arrest by the police and being locked up in jail.

Yes, Mrs. Gideon agreed tremulously, that was the way she felt about it too.

Would there be a funeral or what? Sally asked. She'd want to get off work whenever it was, because there would be so few people to go.

Mrs. Gideon cried openly. No, there wouldn't be a funeral, she said. She thought it was just terrible. There wasn't anybody to claim the body or pay for the burying, so they were going to send it to the State University Medical School. Didn't that seem just awful?

"Oh, gosh!" Sally said softly. They talked together awhile longer, and then Sally picked up her sacks again and climbed the stairs. The news about Mrs. Sipes brought back her depression and with it a kind of melancholy of hopelessness that was even harder to combat. Her door was unlocked; she managed to turn the knob, and as the door swung open she cried, "Well, hi, everybody," in her warm cheerful voice.

Buddy and Marilyn swarmed to meet her enthusiastically, holding up their faces to be kissed. Harold was stretched out on the davenport with a section of the paper. Sally was so glad to see him home that she dropped a quick kiss on his forehead, although she knew it made him angry and self-conscious these days to have her fuss over him.

"Booo, it's cold," she said. "I'm glad you're here to home tonight, where it's all warm and nice, mister."

She hurried to the kitchen with her groceries. The kitchen was cleaned up, spotless and shining. Virginia and Fred Foster were sharing a lunch of coffee and icebox leftovers on the table. Fred was dressed in his good suit, his hat shoved to the back of his head, and Virginia was in a bathrobe, her hair wound on curlers in the front.

What was going on here? Sally wanted to know. Didn't they know they were going to spoil their supper?

Neither one of them, they explained, had time to wait for supper. Virginia had a date for the movies with Jimmy Terwilliger, and Fred announced that he had a heavy date with the most beautiful girl that he bet Sally had ever set eyes on. While Sally unloaded her sacks, Fred went on talking about his date. She was a Kentucky girl and was up here visiting some relatives. He had met her the other night when he stopped into the Myles Café to have a beer before he went to work. She had been there with a bunch of people he knew. He guessed she went for him, all right. He asked her what she was doing Saturday night and she said why, not a thing, and looked at him real loving out of her great big brown eyes. Oh, baby, Fred said happily, gulping down a slice of cold boiled potato, decorated with a splash of catsup.

My gosh, Sally scolded good-naturedly, her family was getting to be nothing but a bunch of gadders, she never saw anything like it. Joe always out someplace, and now Fred and Virginia were getting to be pretty near as bad. She set out cheese, and a couple of packages of cupcakes to amend their lunch. Didn't they have time for some soup? she urged them. They could split a can, it wouldn't take but a second for it to heat. They both protested that they were leaving this very second. Sally contented herself with filling up their coffee cups a second time. They were going to need it going out in the cold tonight, she said, and then she went into the other room to hang up her coat and hat.

Once Fred and Virginia were out of the kitchen, she cleaned up the remains of their lunch and started to prepare supper. Buddy and Marilyn kept underfoot, regaling her with stories about school and sliding downhill in Smith's driveway. Sally listened to them, smiling, and asked a question from time to time. This, she thought, was the nicest part of her day. Suppose they did get underfoot and slowed down her supper preparations, what did that matter? Poor kids, she was home with them so little. Home, Sally echoed grimly, with unaccustomed bitterness. Did she call this a home? Why, really it was nothing but a railroad station. What kind of a home was this for the kids, with her gone so much of the time, their father absent entirely and other members of the family always either coming or going.

The patties of hamburger fried noisily in the big skillet, and Sally opened a can of tomatoes which she dumped in on top of the meat, as a special Saturday-night treat for the children. She found time to open Roy's letter and read it hastily. It was a short letter, and a depressing one. There was nothing to write, he said. He just sat around day in and day out, like he always did. He hoped they were all well. Love, Roy. Sally put it back in her pocket, sighing a little. She would have to write to him tonight; she would make it a long and cheerful letter, somehow. That was the least she could do to help him.

Then Sally ripped open her other letter, and glanced at its contents while the children chattered around her. Her face looked very serious as she read it. She went through it twice before she returned it to her pocket.

Once dinner was over and the children had left the table, Sally called to Harold. Why didn't he stay out here with her and keep her company while she drank her coffee? The younger children lingered, too, as Harold slouched back to his chair awkwardly. But Sally told them to run along, they had talked to her before supper, now it was Harold's turn. The children drifted into the other room reluctantly.

Sally spooned her coffee, stealing a quick look at Harold. He sat slouched down in his chair. His pale hair was rumpled over his thin small face that was so like Roy's. He didn't look at her. He stared straight ahead of him and he cleared his throat once, nervously. His face was closed and secret. Why, she couldn't even guess what he was thinking about, Sally thought despairingly. Was this what always happened as children grew older, did they turn away from their family to a life of their own, did they close up and stop telling you about what they did and what they thought?

"Gosh, it certainly is cold," Sally said at last. "Feel that draught from that window every once in awhile. I bet that wind is gonna blow up some more snow."

Harold squirmed in his chair a little, but he made her no answer.

Sally felt his awkwardness in herself now, and she thought rebelliously, no, this is all wrong, I can't let it go on like this. Why should there ever be awkwardness and self-consciousness between a mother and a son? I must have been neglecting Harold. I should talk to him more. I should never have let a barrier like this grow up between us.

While she was thinking that, Sally smiled at him affectionately and said, "How's the paper route coming, hon?"

"It's all right," Harold said briefly.

"Mrs. Gideon said you got the job of shovelin' off her sidewalk this morning?"

"Yeah," Harold said, and he cleared his throat. "I shoveled off a lot a walks today."

"Well, good for you," Sally said. "Gosh, you must be makin' a lot of money. What you gonna do with all this money?"

"I dunno," Harold said vaguely. "Maybe I'll git me a jacket. I could have enough money for that next week, maybe."

"Well, that would be nice too," Sally said. "I wish you'd get one of those with a hood on like the boys wear now. I'm always so 'fraid you'll catch cold runnin' around without a cap like you do half the time. This is bad weather for earaches and stuff if you're gonna run around without a cap."

Harold made no answer. He moved on his chair restlessly.

"How's school?"

"It's all right."

Sally took a sip of the hot coffee and tried to think of the words she had to say to him.

"It don't seem to me that you talk to me about school this year like you always used to. Is everything all right at school? You always liked to go to school. Do you like it this year? What studies do you like best?"

"Oh, I dunno," Harold said. "School's all right."

"Do you like the kids in your class? Do you like your teacher, what's her name, Miss Marsh?"

"Yeah, Miss Marsh."

"Do you like her?" Sally said with gentle insistence.

"Oh, she's all right."

This was all wrong, Sally thought again, despairingly. How could he be so closed and evasive? Maybe she had been too easy with him, maybe there should be more discipline. Maybe she had overdone this business of letting him have more freedom now as he grew older. She had been so afraid of antagonizing him and driving him even further away from her. But, after all, he wasn't so very old, eleven going on twelve isn't very old. At any rate, things had somehow got to be different.

"You're sure you like school this year? You're sure everything is all right?" Sally said with a shade more seriousness in her voice.

Harold's fair skin turned pink in his embarrassment. "Sure. It's . . ."

She hesitated a little and then she said, "Hon, I don't think you're telling me just the truth about that. I don't think everything is all right. It isn't really, is it?"

Harold wriggled on his chair without answering. He wouldn't look at her, and his face was nervous. She knew that more than anything else he wanted to get up from that chair and run away from her and from what she was saying to him. Oh, gosh, Sally thought, it wasn't right, it wasn't fair to pin a kid down and bully him like this. But what else could she do?

"Harold, you didn't answer what I asked you," Sally said, and she let some of the sternness creep into her voice.

"You see, hon, I got a letter from your teacher, Miss Marsh, today."

Sally pulled the letter out of her pocket slowly as she spoke.

Harold glanced at her quickly, at the letter, and then he looked away, his face miserable and frightened and trapped.

"Accordin' to what Miss Marsh says, I know things aren't goin' so good at school for you," Sally said, her heart aching at the sight of his face. "She says you been skippin' school a lot without no excuse. She says you don't co-operate with her, nor in your classes. An' she says you're in trouble with the other kids all the time, gettin' into fights and stuff like that."

The hot red color mounted into Harold's light hair, and crept down into the collar of his shirt.

"Aw, Harold," Sally pleaded. "You never got into any trouble at school before. You always liked school and you always done so well in your studies. Can't you tell me what the matter is, and we'll talk it over, and maybe we can fix things up? Tell me?"

Harold cleared his throat again, and licked his lips with his tongue but he made her no answer.

It wasn't any use, Sally thought despairingly. She'd just got to be strict and hard with him.

"Harold, I asked you what the matter was, and I want you to tell me the truth about it!"

She waited a little, but he didn't answer her.

Sally spoke determinedly. "All right, Harold. I guess you won't talk to me about it. You're gettin' to be a big boy now, and I can't make you talk to me unless you want to. But if you won't tell me what the matter is and let me help you fix it up, you've just got to fix it up all by yourself. Because you've got to do different than you been doin' at school. I mean it, Harold! I'm gonna have Miss Marsh write to me again in a couple weeks, and I want to hear that you're doin' better. No more skippin' school, and no more fightin' with the kids. You've always done good in school, and I know something is the matter now, or you wouldn't be gettin' in trouble like this. I'd like to have you tell me about it and let me help you, but you won't do it. You'll just have to work it out by yourself then, because, I mean it, this kind of foolin' around has got to stop."

Harold's face was agonized. "Aw, Miss Marsh, she . . ." he mumbled.

"I don't know anything about Miss Marsh," Sally said, "except she wrote me an awful nice letter. Are you tryin' to say that she just made up all that stuff about you?"

Harold gathered up all his courage visibly, although he would not look his mother in the eye. "Aw, school ain't so much," he said in a thin voice. "I been thinkin' about quittin' and—and—gettin' a job!"

Sally felt panic, but she kept her voice controlled and steady. "That's a kind of silly thing for you to say, hon. There's laws in this state that says you have to go to school for years yet, so you might just as well get it in your head that you've got to settle down in school and get along good. Aw, Harold, you used to like school so much, and you done so good in your studies. Me and your father was always so proud of you. You see we never had much chance to go to school, neither one of us. We didn't have no parents nor home nor nothing, we had to get out and work, instead a goin' to school. We want it to be different with you. We want you to go to school, we're gonna give you the chance. We want you to go to school and high school and graduate and everything. Aw, hon, think how bad it would make your father feel if he knew you was gettin' in trouble to school, and talkin' like this."

Sally's lips trembled a little in spite of herself, and she had to stop talking. Harold's face stretched taut, and his eyes were agonized as he looked at her.

Sally got up from the table hurriedly and began to stack the dishes together. "We won't talk about it no more," she said. "I know you're gonna do better, hon, and we won't have to talk about it no more."

Harold sensed a dismissal and he slid off his chair and vanished into the other room.

Oh, she'd handled it so badly, she'd said everything all wrong, Sally thought despairingly. Oh, she wished that Roy . . . Sally put the thought out of her mind determinedly. She carried dirty dishes to the sink and turned on the water, which ran noisily out of the faucets.

# 21

AFTER HER FIRST GROUP OF SONGS THAT NIGHT BEFORE a fairly good-sized Saturday-night crowd, Petey held up her hand for silence. "Ladies and Gentlemen," she said. "I have a very special surprise for you tonight. A couple of nights ago I was hangin' around in here after closing time, finishing up a drink. Tommy Terwilliger was around here, too. The orchestra boys had all left, and after awhile Tommy drifted up there to the piano and began to play." Petey paused dramatically and then she laughed. "Well, to tell you the truth, I kept Tommy here playin' till daylight. That's how his piano playin' hit me. Then I got to thinking that it wasn't fair for me to keep Tommy to myself, because I know you'll get just as big a kick out of what he can do to a piano as I do. That's why you're going to have a chance to hear him here tonight." She paused again, while the waiters pushed the piano into place on the dance floor behind her. "I could say a lot of things about boogie-woogie," Petey said. "If I really knew music, I could give a whole lecture on it. I'd rather just let Tommy speak for himself. When you've heard Tommy play you'll know how lucky we are to have him here to play for us. Ladies and Gentlemen, let's give Tommy Terwilliger a big hand."

She got a round of enthusiastic applause, and Tommy Terwilliger stumbled up from the direction of the bar in his ill-fitting, shiny tuxedo. Petey took his hand, and, when the applause died out, she said, "I know you've all laughed at Tommy's funny stuff here in our show. You've even seen Tommy out there doing double duty at the bar some nights. Now you're going to have a chance to see Tommy where he really belongs, at the piano."

Amid more applause she led him to the piano. As he sat down she leaned over the corner of the piano top. "Let 'em have it, Tommy," she said softly, as she clasped her hands together and shook them gravely. Tommy was set to go, first the odd little weave of his shoulders, then his head ducked down, and he began to play.

Petey noted that voices faded out and the crowd was giving

Tommy and his music full attention. Then she forgot about the crowd altogether because Tommy was playing very well. She was lost in her delight in the terrific vitality of this music, the infinite variety of the style. This music was alive, it had the quality of life as Petey knew it. She could feel it deep inside of her.

When Tommy finished, Petey broke into spontaneous applause herself, and watched the reaction of the crowd anxiously. There was even more applause than Petey had dared hope for, not quite as much as she would have liked to have heard, but more than enough. Tommy grinned shyly in his pleasure and relief.

"Give 'em a little more," Petey said to him softly. "Not too much, though. You're the star of the show around here, and we can't have you sitting around playin' encores all night."

Tommy played again and, when he finished, Petey led him away from the piano in spite of the applause. She was triumphant and delighted with his success and took him up to the bar for a drink. Her enthusiasm was contagious. She welded the entire bar full of people into one appreciative unit, with Tommy Terwilliger the center of all attention, to his self-conscious bewilderment. Petey's contagious, noisy, vibrant good-humor made the bar immediately the gayest spot in the place. Newcomers chose to remain there in preference to a table, until the bar was packed several deep. Later on Nicky Toresca came down from the gambling rooms on the second floor, and Petey danced with him for awhile. They both drifted back to the bar eventually. Nicky stayed for the space of a drink and disappeared upstairs again.

When it came time for Petey to sing again, the place was filled. Once again Petey gave Tommy Terwilliger an introduction for the benefit of the newcomers. When Tommy was seated at the piano, Petey walked away toward the back of the room in the direction of the bar. She looked back over her shoulder, watching Tommy's odd ritual of getting set to play, the spotlight shining on his sparse hair and battered features, his broad shoulders, and his thick square hands, the stubby fingers stretched over the keys.

It was just as Tommy began to play, just as she reached the steps up to the bar that she saw him, the big man with the light hair, the big man they called San, sitting alone at a small table at the back of the room. Petey never hesitated, she never stopped to think about it, it seemed to her at that moment such a natural thing to do. She walked over to his table and she said, "Hello, do you mind?" He kicked the chair out for her with his foot. She signaled the waiter for a drink as she sat down, and then she slid around in her chair, her back half turned to the big man, the better to listen. Tommy finished playing, and played again, and yet again.

Petey turned around suddenly and picked up her drink. She looked very lovely, her dress shining red and gold in the dim light, her face vibrant with excitement. She made an impatient motion as she shook back her heavy hair. The big man was looking at her and she spoke to him easily, without thinking, because it seemed so natural to her that she should be sitting here across a table from him. "Jesus, I'm so glad the crowd likes it," she said softly. "But how could they help it? I love that playin'. It's like nothin' else in this world. It's—it's alive . . . It's . . ."

"It's like you," he said.

She felt the little shock of associating voice or even the act of speaking with his huge quiet body, his chiseled, expressionless face and the pale blank eyes.

"It's funny you should say that," Petey said. "That's what Tommy said to me just the other night, too."

She caught the cue for her next song from the orchestra just then and got up hurriedly, leaving her drink unfinished on the table. She felt an elation in her, a complete alertness, the brink of things to come. The song was one on which she had done a lot of rehearsing, a trick song with a chorus punctuated with crescendos of mad, sad, wild laughter. There had never been a time in her life, Petey thought, that she felt more like singing. She took the verse part easily with all her accustomed humor and vitality. Then she flung her arms wide with the first burst of the startling, wild, sadder-than-tears laughter of the chorus:

> "He had the laughin' boy blues
> They kept him laughin' all the day
> He had the laughin' boy blues . . ."

When she was through singing she came back to the table, where her drink was standing as she had left it. She sat down and took a sip of it, and never missed the fresh cold drink that Nicky Toresca would have had waiting for her. The big man did not speak to her, and she felt no need to say anything to him. She offered him a cigarette from her package and struck the match for both of them. With this curious elation and excitement she lost track of time; she could not have told whether it was minutes she had been sitting here opposite him, or hours.

"I'm glad you come," she said to him at last, simply. "I was afraid you wouldn't."

He made a little sound in his throat, and Petey's slim white fingers moved in intricate rhythms on the table beside her drink, which somehow she had forgotten.

Quite a while later she said, "Let's scram out of this place, huh? I could use some food."

"Right," he said.

Petey went for her wrap then, and she joined him again in front of the checkroom. He was hatless and had merely the light gabardine raincoat for protection against the winter weather. When they came out onto the sidewalk snow was falling.

The big man paused, and he said, "I know a place, but it's quite a ways."

Petey laughed a little. "Aw, that's all right," she said. "I don't mind the snow. The walk would be good for me."

She didn't mind the walk. She felt very much alive, with all sensations sharpened. Once she slipped a little on a stretch of ice hidden by the fresh snow. He took hold of her arm, and then his hand slid down to her hand. His hand was so big that hers was lost in it, and his fingers were very warm. As they walked close together Petey looked up to his face from time to time. It was a long walk, but Petey never noticed it. The air was not too cold, nor the snow too wet. The flakes clung to her hair and her furs a long time before they melted. Just as it fell now, the snow was fresh and clean. It glistened over the sidewalk, piled up at the curbs and swirled around automobiles on the street, the colored Neon signs and street lights.

They came to the place at last, a big hamburger joint almost at the outskirts of town. It was a place where truck drivers stopped. There was a large space in front of it parked full of trucks, and more of the huge trailered vehicles lined the street in either direction. Inside was a big room with a long counter and booths, very warm and brilliantly lighted.

Petey and the big man took a booth toward the back. They ordered hamburgers and coffee. Petey got a handful of nickels and fed them into the juke-box. The steam over the plate-glass windows shut out the storm, save for the shadows of the falling flakes against the glass. The whole room shook with the rumbling vibrations of the trucks as the truck drivers in caps and leather jackets came and went continually.

Petey gulped her hot coffee and wriggled in her furs contentedly. "Aw, this is good!" she said, and the big man nodded. Still they did not talk. They listened to the idle conversation of the men at the counter, the music from the juke-box, and the sizzling of the hamburgers frying.

Petey felt very good and a million miles away from everything and everybody she had ever known.

"This is a funny town," she said suddenly.

"Why?" he asked her.

"Oh, I dunno," she said. "I was just thinkin' about it, setting here. On one side a town there's the prison, and on the other side the whorehouses. In the middle there's the beer joints and the movies and all around is the factory bums."

"So?" he said.

"So here's the factory bums workin' their guts out makin' little gadgets that they ship away and put together into automobiles, but the closest thing to a finished automobile the guys see here is the ones that come rolling through here at night, four to a truck, and then the guys point and say see there's one with one of the bumpers that we make. They work their guts out and they never make enough money to get along. They get drunk on Saturday nights, and they gamble on everything all the while, slot machines, bingo games, poker games, craps, and dice shootin' for cigarettes at the drug store.

The women go to the fortune-tellers, spiritualists, palm readers, tea leaves and cards. Jesus!"

"Yeah," he said. "It's a funny town."

They were silent after that. They ordered more of the hot coffee, and then they just sat for a long time in this warm place shut away from the whole world by the storm and the rumbling trucks.

At last by mutual unspoken consent they got into their coats and got up to leave. The big man paid the waiter at the counter and they stepped out into the darkness and the snow. Outside they stopped quite still. The wind and snow howled about them and the world went suddenly cold and bleak and dark for Petey.

"Where are you going?" she had to shout the words over the noise the trucks made here.

He answered her with a motion of his shoulders.

They stood together quietly for a long moment. Then Petey stretched her arms up, a hand on each of his broad shoulders. She leaned close to him and tipped her face up, her lips at a level with his chin to make herself heard over the confusion of noise.

"No, San," she said. "It's late, and it's cold and there isn't any place to go. Come home, San."

He looked down into her face hard, and then suddenly he took her in his arms and kissed her. He released her slowly, and she took a step back out of his arms slowly. They looked at each other, and then Petey took hold of his hand and held it tight, and they turned and started back downtown in the snow together.

# 22

SUNDAY WAS A DULL DARK DAY, WITH SNOW HEAVY underfoot and deep on window ledges. Sally held up dinner as long as she could, but Petey did not come, nor did she telephone. Sally was disappointed, and she strained her ears for the familiar quick tread on the stairs even after they were seated at the table. Once dinner was through, Sally accepted Virginia's offer to do the dishes and clean up the kitchen, and hurried into the living room where an oversized stack of mending awaited her. As the needle wormed in and out, leaving a trail of firm even stitches behind it, Sally thought about Harold, and about the letter she had received the night before. Sally was apprehensive. She had always told Roy with such an easy conviction that during this hard time they each had a job to do. His job was not to worry and to help himself get well as soon as he could; her job was to keep the family until he was able to return to them, and normal life could be resumed. It sounded easy enough, but just how well had she been doing her job, Sally questioned herself. There was more to her job than providing the children a place to stay, and food to eat and clothes to keep them warm. There was much more to this bargain she had made with Roy than that. Harold was their firstborn, with a face like his father's, and a thin, straight body like Roy's own. There was something special and different in Roy's feeling toward Harold, a quiet pride, a special inarticulate tenderness. But now things were not going quite right with Harold, and the fault was hers, Sally thought. She had failed him and in failing him she had failed Roy. Sally had a feeling that this year might be perhaps the most important year in Harold's life. If this was so, whatever she did now or didn't do was going to have a direct bearing on the future. This was no time for her to be panic-stricken or undecided, no time for her to sit around and wish that Roy might be here to share the responsibility with her. This was a time for clear, straight thinking and for decisive action.

It was not until she was on the bus bound for her work downtown through the snowy twilight streets that the idea came to Sally. As soon as it occurred to her she knew that it was the thing that was best for her to do. She would go and talk to this teacher of Harold's. Miss Marsh had written her a nice letter, and she apparently was interested in Harold. Perhaps she could give advice. Sally immediately felt relieved and made her plans hastily. Monday was always a slow day at the restaurant. There would be a lull in the afternoon before the first of the dinner trade came in. That dull spot in the afternoon coincided with the hour when school was dismissed. If she went to the school she could perhaps talk to Miss Marsh before the teacher left the building. Sally was certain that Sam Toresca would give her an hour off to make her call.

The next afternoon she boarded the bus up East Williams. She got off at the corner, two blocks from the school. It was a cold, bright afternoon. Sally had calculated her time just right; school should be out any moment now. Sally pulled the collar of her coat tighter at the neck and hurried up the street, past a row of dingy store fronts, several groceries, a dry cleaner's office, in the direction of the school building. It was a large, rather old brick building in the middle of a bare expanse of playground, partially covered with dingy snow that was packed down and tracked by hundreds of children's feet. Even as Sally looked, the first of the children began to pour out of the building. They came straggling out in groups, shouting and whistling to one another, cumbersome in heavy jackets, mittens and snow suits. They poured out of every door until the playground was covered with them, the shrill chattering of their voices rising in crescendo. There was a long depression in the ground at the edge of the play-ground, where, Sally surmised, swings stood in the summertime. Water had collected there and frozen into a long strip of ice, worn hard and shiny smooth by a myriad of sliding feet. The children slid across it now, dozens of them. They came on a run and slid the length of it, feet wide apart, arms flailing. Sally smiled at the sight, at their shouts and laughter, their frequent sprawling tumbles. Sally walked more slowly now, her eyes alert for a glimpse of her own children amid this melee. She hadn't thought about them, and she hesitated a little. She would prefer that the younger children, and Harold, too, for that matter, did not see her coming to the school. Just then, Sally caught a glimpse of Harold coming out. Quickly, without thinking, Sally stepped into the entrance of a cigar and candy store. It would be much better, she reflected, if he didn't see her coming to the school like this. She was out of direct line of vision, and, besides, he wouldn't be expecting to see her here in this neighborhood at this time of day. Sally stood close to the plate-glass window filled with cigarette ads on large cardboard signs, shivering a little in the cold, and watched

Harold walk across the school yard, her face warm and tender. Harold came alone, slouching along, his hands deep in his pockets, threading his way among the groups of children. He walked quickly, his head bent down. Sally felt a little rush of tenderness all through her, watching him. He was so little, after all, only eleven, and his body was so slight and thin under the worn jacket, and the old trousers that bagged at the knees as he walked.

Harold cut across the playground diagonally, without pausing once, not paying any attention to the children around him. He came up toward the sidewalk just at the end of the strip of ice where the children were sliding. There was a group of children milling around there just at the end of the ice, little boys they were, no bigger than Buddy. As Sally watched, the little group turned around and stared at Harold, the sliding forgotten. Harold walked more rapidly, and the little group of children stood quite still, staring at him with blank faces. Then a burst of laughter spread among them, and a nudging and activity with it. One impish voice started the cry and the others joined in a mocking chant. "Harold's old man's a loony! Harold's old man's a loony!"

Harold moved faster, almost running now. Sally heard his thin voice, "Aw, shut your goddam dirty mouths!"

The little boys shrieked with delight, and closed in on him from every side, seven or eight of them, packing around him, poking and jostling and shouting their taunting cry: "Harold's old man's a loony! Harold's old man's a loony!"

They hemmed him in and shoved at him until he staggered to keep on his feet, his fair head bobbing over the tops of theirs. "You go on and lemme alone or I'll sock you!" He shouted at them. Sally saw him lunge at them, and the little boys ducked away, laughing derisively, closing in from a different angle. Harold moved slowly toward the sidewalk, swinging his fists at the ducking rosy faces of the children, saying words that Sally couldn't hear over the laughter and the taunting chant.

He broke away from them at last and reached the sidewalk. The children stood together and yelled after him. "Harold's old man's a loony!" Harold turned around then. Sally saw his face quite plainly, with the anger and hurt and defiance on it. "Aw, shut up and lemme alone," he shouted back at them. "That's a goddam lie! My old man's dead! Shut up your goddam mouths!"

The children howled derisively.

Harold had one parting word for them. "Bastards!" he shouted. He turned away up the street then. He stuck his hands in his pockets. He tried to walk slowly with a swagger, but he couldn't quite make it. He walked faster and faster until he was almost running.

Even with the great wave of sickness that she felt, Sally's one thought was, oh, he mustn't see me here, he mustn't see me here now after this! She opened the door to the cigar store with her trembling hands and stepped inside. Inside the dim interior a thin pasty-faced man with a mustache asked her what he could do for her.

"I'll—I'll have a bottle of Coca-Cola," Sally said. She fumbled the nickel out of her purse automatically and took the uncapped bottle that he offered her. She moved away a little in front of the magazine rack to drink it. She stood there with the ice-cold bottle in her hand and stared for a long time at a magazine that had on the cover a picture of a girl clad in scanty underwear, and, underneath, the caption "The Truth about White Slavery in America." She took several sips out of the bottle. She wasn't thinking about much of anything, and there was a sickness in her, an actual nausea.

Sally drank about half the Coca-Cola out of the bottle, then she set it down on the counter and left the store. She walked back up to the corner again and waited for the bus. She didn't have to wait long. It wasn't until she was on the bus and headed back downtown again that the crying began inside of her and the agonized sobbing voice that said over and over, "Oh, Roy, oh, darling, darling, oh, Roy!"

As Sally plodded up the stairs that night, she met Johnny O'Connor just coming down, and they stopped to talk a minute. Johnny looked at Sally critically. Her face was pale, the smudges of shadows darker around her eyes, and he thought that her wide friendly smile was just a second slow in coming.

"You look tired," he said. "You must have had a hard day."

"Oh, not specially," Sally answered. "I am sorta tired, though. How are you? What does the doctor say about your hands?"

"Aw, they're fine," Johnny said. "It'll be just a matter a time now and they'll be as good as new."

"Well, I'm glad. Gosh, you sure were lucky to get out of it as easy as this. You coulda lost two or three fingers just as easy as not."

"And that's no joke! I still count 'em every once in awhile, just to make sure." Johnny fumbled for a cigarette, and the paper of matches fell to the step at his feet.

Sally bent to pick it up. "Wait, I'll light it for you. Could you spare an extra cigarette?"

"I'm sorry," Johnny said, hastening to flip a cigarette out of the package for her. "You never seem to be smokin' more'n six times a year. I forget to ask you."

Sally struck the match for them, and then she leaned back against the balustrade and took a deep drag from her cigarette. Her shoulders were sagging a little, and her face in the dim light of the stairway was very sober.

"Hey, Sally!" Johnny said. "You don't look so good. Something wouldn't be the matter, could it?"

Sally smiled a little and sighed. "No. Nothin's the matter more than usual. I guess this is just my blue day, or something."

"You and Gloria both," Johnny said. "She's been goin' around all day today like any minute if yuh blinked your eye you'd find her cryin'."

"Aw, women are like that, Johnny," Sally said.

"You tellin' me!" Johnny grinned, and then his face sobered. "Things have been kinda tough for her lately, you know. We haven't had the money to go places and do things like we always do. It's tough for Glory to have to just set around home day in and day out, poor little kid!"

There was just a shade of exasperation in Sally's voice. "I guess it ain't any tougher for her than it is for you having to set around and wait for your hands to heal up, not bein' able to work or nothin'."

"Yeah," he said, "but with Glory it's different. Look, maybe you could be droppin' in for a minute to make a little female talk with her, huh? I been tryin' to cheer her up all day, without any luck you could notice. She wouldn't even talk to me much or tell me what the matter was. Maybe she'd talk to you and then she'd feel better."

"Okay," Sally said. "I'll stop in a minute now before I go on home. It would seem good to set down a minute before I start gettin' supper."

Johnny patted Sally's arm. "Well, fine," he said. "Now you girls let down your hair and have a good cry together and then you'll both be feelin' better. No kiddin' though, thanks a lot, Sally."

Sally laughed over her shoulder, and Johnny went on down the stairs and out the front door. Sally came to the top of the stairs and paused momentarily outside the door to the O'Connors' apartment. The familiar blast of loud radio music blared out from the other side of the door, and made knocking useless.

Sally turned the knob and called out "Hi!" as the door swung open.

Gloria, in a print housecoat that fit snugly to the curves of her soft body, was curled up on the end of the davenport, her head buried in her arms, her long fair hair falling over her knees. The face she lifted to Sally was marked with tears, her eyes reddened.

"Hello," she said.

Sally closed the door behind her, and sat down on the nearest chair, stretching her feet up from the floor gratefully. "I thought I'd stop in a minute before I go home and pitch into gettin' supper. I haven't seen you in a month of Sundays, Gloria. How are you? How's the baby?"

"I'm all right. Bevvy's fine," Gloria said. When she stopped talking, her eyes wandered away, and her mouth drooped down at the corners, tragically.

"I just met Johnny goin' out," Sally said. "He says his hands are healin' up fine. I'm glad to hear it."

"Yeah. Johnny just went out to get something for supper."

"You don't mean to tell me you haven't eaten yet!" Sally made an attempt at lightness and cheerfulness in her voice. "My gosh, I thought we was always the last ones to eat around this house."

Gloria made no answer. Her eyes dropped to the bedroom slipper that she dangled from the toe of her white foot, an old mule with a run-over high heel, and pink fluffy feathers on it, that were now scraggly and soiled.

In the silence Sally sighed a little, the sound lost in the blaring radio music. "Gosh, I hate to go in there and get supper," she said. "I got the blues right tonight. For two cents I could just bust out cryin' or run away someplace. Johnny said you'd been having the blues today, too. I wonder what's the matter with us."

Suddenly, without warning, the tears ran down Gloria's face again, and the muscles in her smooth white throat bunched and contracted as she swallowed a sob. "I feel just awful," she said, in a shaking voice. "I'm gettin' so tired of this, I just can't hardly stand it!"

Sally got up from the chair and walked over to the radio and tuned it down. Her face looked very serious. "You're gettin' so tired of what, Gloria, that you can't hardly stand it?"

"This place!" Gloria gestured around the little crowded living room as she spoke. "Just settin' around here all the time. I can't go downtown shoppin'. I can't go to the movies. We can't dress up and go eat in restaurants nor go places nor nothin'. Johnny says we can't. I just have to set around here all the time. I'm gettin' so sick of it, I can't hardly stand it!"

For the first time since Sally had known her, she lost her patience completely with Gloria. For two cents, Sally thought, she would walk right over there and shake her until her teeth rattled. Why, you half-baked little simpleton, Sally thought with unaccustomed viciousness, you don't even know what trouble is. You sit around here whining and sniveling and—why, I could just . . .

But when Sally spoke her voice was controlled and almost gentle. "Gloria," she said, "you're talking just like some little kid instead of a grown-up woman with a husband and a baby. You're actin' just like you thought Johnny was making you stay home here just to be mean or something, and you know better than that. Nobody ever had a better husband in the world than Johnny is to you. You know how crazy he is about you. You know there isn't nothin' in the world he wouldn't do for you, or let you do if he could. You know Johnny's had a run of bad luck. He's been sick and he can't work yet, and he's lost his job. He just hasn't got the money to take you places or buy you things. You've been darn lucky that he's been able to give you a place to stay and enough to eat. I don't see how he's done it."

"But when's Johnny gonna have the money?" Gloria wailed. "Johnny always used to have the money. He said when he had the money I could buy a whole lot a new clothes and we'd go someplace every night, and we'd go to Toresca's and everything! When's Johnny gonna have the money?"

Sally's face tightened a little. "All right then," she said brusquely. "If that's the way you feel about it, why don't you go out and get a job? I should think you would, anyway, to help Johnny tide things over until he can get back to work again. If you get a job you'll be earnin' money and then you can go places again and buy things, and, besides, it'll help Johnny out till he gets back on his feet. Why, it might be weeks before he can work again; it might even be months. I don't see how Johnny is ever gonna swing it unless you pitch in and get yourself a job and help him."

Gloria's crying stopped as suddenly as it had begun. She stared at Sally with a blank, bewildered face. "Get a job?" she said. "You mean, get a job—like Johnny used to have a job?"

"Why not?" Sally said impatiently. "You're young and strong, you could work. And while Johnny can't work, he could look after the baby. Then, when his hands get healed up and he can work again, you wouldn't have to any more. It would help Johnny out a lot till he gets back on his feet again. It would be a change for you, and it might give you a little spendin' money so you could go out nights like you like to."

Gloria's face was incredulous, but something like a glimmer of interest showed on it as well. "Where could I get a job?" she said. "I don't know how to do nothin'. What kinda job?"

Sally unbuttoned her coat and slid it back on her shoulders in the warmth of the room. "Well," she said readily, "I bet you could get a job as a waitress someplace easy. They don't need any extra help at the restaurant where I work right now, but I'll bet there is some restaurant here in town that would hire you in a minute. You're young and you're awful pretty; you wouldn't have no trouble gettin' a waitress job, and it isn't such awful hard work, either."

Gloria was still staring at Sally, her blue eyes wide, and she spaced her words carefully, like a child repeating a lesson it has learned. "You mean, I could get a job—an' earn money, an' then we could do things like we usta?"

The sight of Gloria's bewildered face as she struggled with this new idea touched Sally. Sally went over to her and hugged her hard. As she straightened up she caught a glimpse of the clock on top of the radio. "Oh, my gosh," she said. "Look how late it's gettin'! I gotta get home right this minute and get supper started."

As Sally hurried down the hall her own troubles were all but forgotten temporarily. Why hadn't she thought to talk to Gloria about getting a job sooner? Why, that was just the thing for Gloria. She wouldn't have any trouble at all picking up a job, anybody as young and pretty as she was, and it would be so good for her. It might help her to grow up a little, to have the responsibilities of a job like other people. Johnny probably wouldn't like the idea just at first, but it wouldn't be as if Gloria would have to work forever.

At home, once her greetings to the children were over, her coat hung in the closet, Sally hurried to the kitchen. Virginia was finishing the last of the dishes.

"Well, good for you," Sally said. "You got the potatoes peeled and the dishes done and everything!" She kissed Virginia affectionately. "Now, let's see . . ."

With preparations well under way, Sally sank down in a chair to catch her breath. "This today's paper?" Sally lifted it out of Virginia's way as she spoke.

Virginia nodded.

Sally stared at the front page for a moment, the glaring black headlines that announced the latest war news. Sally shivered a little. To Sally, Europe was a remote place, where vast armies marched back and forth continually, and little children died horribly as bombers flew thick in the dark night skies. "That darn Hitler!" she murmured, and then she opened up the paper to the local news that was so much less alarming.

"You didn't see anything of Petey today, did you?" Sally asked, without looking up from her paper.

"No, I didn't," Virginia said. "I was over there and cleaned up her place late this afternoon, but she wasn't around. I guess she must have been at rehearsals."

"I been kind of worrying about her," Sally said. "I was afraid maybe she was sick or something."

"I guess she can't be sick," replied Virginia, "according to all the stuff she had on that grocery list for me to get for supper tonight. She was ordering enough stuff for about four people."

Sally turned over a page, the paper crumpling together. "Oh, well, she probably had a date or something and didn't get a chance to call. I wouldn't be surprised 'n she came over tonight on her way to work or called or something."

Virginia turned down the burner under the potatoes a little, then got the canned peaches out of the icebox and began to dish them up into the small fruit dishes with a tablespoon. The kitchen was warm and steamy, fragrant with cooking odors, and silent, save for the boiling of the kettles and the rattle of Sally's newspaper. Sally turned another page and asked, "Has Harold been home yet?"

"Uh uh. I don't think so. He hasn't been here since I got home, anyway."

"Gosh, I wish he wouldn't stay out so late after dark. He musta finished his paper route a long time ago." There was almost a tremble in Sally's voice, and Virginia turned around and looked at her in surprise. With the last dish of peaches filled, Virginia licked the syrup out of the spoon appreciatively. "Well, why don't you . . . I mean it's none of my business," Virginia said carefully, "but I don't think it's right for Harold to run around so late nights, especially when you don't know where he is or what he's doing. Why don't you make him get home here before dark? Couldn't you tell him that if he doesn't get home on time you'll make him give up his paper route, or—or—something like that?"

"I suppose I'll have to," Sally said. She was silent a moment, her eyes still on the paper, and then she sighed. "Aw, poor little kid," she said, and this time there was no mistaking the tremble in her voice. Virginia looked at her curiously as she carried the dishes of fruit to the table. Sally turned over the sheets of the newspaper again, to the very back, and out of long habit glanced down the Help Wanted column.

Suddenly Sally sat up straight in her chair, and her face looked both pleased and excited. "Say!" she said, her eyes still on the employment column. She got up from her chair suddenly, the paper still in her hand. "I'm goin' over to O'Connors' a second," she said to Virginia rapidly. "Here's something I wanta show to Gloria."

Sally was out of the living room in a flash and hurrying down the hall, the paper rustling in her hand. At the O'Connor door, Sally rapped a little and then turned the knob and pushed it open. The living room was deserted. The light was on in the bedroom, and a series of grunts and squeals gave testimony that the baby was awake. The light was on in the kitchen too, and Sally caught a glimpse of Gloria's housecoat through the door.

"Is that you, Johnny?" Gloria called.

Sally hurried out to the kitchen where Gloria was leisurely preparing the baby's bottle.

"Gloria, honey, you're a thirty-six, aren't you?" Sally asked excitedly.

"Huh?" Gloria said, setting the milk bottle down hard on the shelf.

"I mean you're a size thirty-six, aren't you?" Sally repeated impatiently. "You buy size eighteen—I guess it is—dresses, don't you?"

"Sure," Gloria said. "I buy size eighteen. Course, sometimes the sizes run different, sometimes I've bought . . ."

"Oh, I was just sure you were a thirty-six," Sally said happily. "Look here!" She held the paper out to Gloria, indicating one of the items in the employment column with her finger.

Gloria looked at it obediently, and after a moment she said, "What is it?" curiously, as if the printed word held no meaning for her.

"It's an ad from the corset factory here in town," Sally explained rapidly. "They want a perfect thirty-six for a model. Oh, I bet you could get that job without half trying, anybody with a perfect figure like you got, and that's your size. See, it says they pay good, too!"

Gloria looked at Sally and then at the paper and at Sally again, her face bewildered. "You mean it's a job? You mean they want some-body just to try on corsets, they'll pay money for it?"

"That's what it says," Sally said triumphantly. "They are trying to find a perfect thirty-six for a model, and they'll pay good money. Aw, it doesn't matter how many women try out for it, I bet all you've got to do is go over there and the job is yours! Look, it says they're inter-viewin' people Wednesday morning. Why don't you get up early Wednesday morning and go up there? You know where the corset factory is, don't you? You take the bus uptown, and then go down that street where the Majestic Theatre is. You know where the Majestic Theatre is? Well, the corset factory is on that same street, on the same side of the street where the theatre is, about two blocks down . . ."

"I know where it is," Gloria said slowly. "I seen the sign once when . . . Well, maybe I will."

"Good!" said Sally. "I thought of you the minute I saw this ad. I don't care if there's fifty other women there, I bet you'll get the job. Now, don't forget."

Sally walked back into the living room and stuck her head in the bedroom doorway. "Well, hi there, Bevvy! How are you anyway, huh? How are you—aw—you're a nice girl, that's what you are!"

The blankets of the crib were turned back, and the baby was kick-ing her bare legs energetically. Although she was clad only in a diaper, her dark hair was wet with perspiration in the warm little room. She looked up at Sally with her dark-blue eyes, so absurdly like Johnny O'Connor's, and smiled her incredibly wise and knowing smile.

Sally leaned over the crib, catching one of the baby's tiny hands tight. She kissed her, and nuzzled her face in the baby's soft neck. "Yessir, Bevvy, you're a nice girl, that's what you are. I bet you're a perfect size half-a-scrap-a-nothin', aren't you? You remember your Aunt Sally, don't you? Of course you do! Aw, you're a sweetheart, that's what you are!"

Sally kissed the baby once more and backed away from the crib. "No, sir, I can't stay and play with you. I gotta go home and get my supper on. Your mother is fixing your supper right now, did you know that?"

Sally waved her hand at the baby, and raised her voice a little as she lingered in the doorway. "Gloria, this baby has grown, just since I've seen her! Honestly, she get's to look more like Johnny every day, doesn't she? Aw, you're a cutie, that's what you are, flirtin' with your Aunt Sally like that! Good-bye Bevvy, I'll see you again, sure—see you again!"

Sally retreated into the living room. "Don't forget, Wednesday morning," she called to Gloria. At the door she hesitated a little. "Gloria?"

"Yeah?"

"Look, Gloria, if I was you I wouldn't say anything at all about going over to the corset factory, or gettin' a job, or anything just yet, to Johnny. Why don't you wait till Wednesday and see if you get the job and then surprise him, huh? Will you do that?"

"Well, sure . . ." Gloria said slowly, "I could wait till Wednesday and surprise Johnny."

"Sure, you could just tell him you was goin' out for a walk or something Wednesday morning. Aw, I'm sure you'll get the job, though. I thought about you the minute I saw that ad. Good night."

# 23

IT WAS ALMOST NINE O'CLOCK BEFORE GLORIA GOT home Wednesday night. She ran all the way up the stairs at Gideon's because she was feeling happy and excited after her visit to the corset factory. She had spent the day with her girl friend. After dinner some strange people had dropped in at Marjorie's apartment, and Gloria had found herself the center of attention, both for her personable self, and because of the news of her job which they had considered novel.

She flung open the door of their little apartment and called, "Hello, Johnny!"

"Hi, sugar puss!" Johnny was seated in his favorite comfortable chair by the radio. The baby was nestled in his arm, and he was supporting her bottle for her with his bandaged hand, the radio humming soft music beside him. "Well, if here don't come draggin' in my youngest wife, the one they call Gloria. Woman, this here tearin' around nights has gotta stop, do you hear me? Come here and kiss your old man, baby!"

Gloria crossed the room and kissed him obediently.

"Glory be!" Johnny said softly. "Jesus, we missed you! Did you have a good time today?"

"Umm, I hada swell time," Gloria said contentedly. She stripped off her coat and threw it over a chair and sat down on the davenport, bouncing on the edge of it a little.

Johnny watched her with pleasure and affection on his slim, mobile face. "So you had a good time, huh? Tell me all about it, honey!"

"Well . . ." Gloria began, and then she paused as if she were trying to think where to begin first in her recital. She stretched her arms and legs out wide and straight, and then relaxed them suddenly and curled up on the end of the davenport, with a sensuous, catlike motion. Her face was shining with happiness and excitement. "Ooooh, I had a swell time!" she said again.

"Bevvy," Johnny said in a mock-plaintive voice, "your mother is altogether too wonderful and beautiful for the likes of plain folks like us, did you know that? Sometimes I wonder why she ever bothers to pay any attention to us at all!"

"First I got to tell you about the surprise," Gloria said. "Sally said I should wait and that you'd be surprised. I went this morning and there was a whole lotta girls there and they measured us and stuff and they picked me. The man said my figure was just perfect and that I was better than anybody they'd ever had. He's a nice man. I bet it's gonna be fun, and I get twenty-seven fifty, that's what the man said. Twenty-seven fifty a week!"

Johnny's face suddenly went blank and rigid, only his eyes were alert and moving. "Glory, baby, now wait a minute," he said. "What's this surprise you're tryin' to tell me? What's all this you're talking about?"

"It's about the job I got," Gloria said impatiently. "Sally said you was gonna be surprised. I gotta job at the corset factory. Sally seen the ad in the paper and I went and the man picked me and said I was the perfect thirty-six. He said I had the perfectest figure he ever saw. They're gonna show me how to be a model, and I bet it's gonna be fun. I git twenty-seven fifty a week! Sally said you was gonna be surprised. Ain't you surprised, Johnny?"

"Yeah, I'm surprised," Johnny said. He got up from his chair suddenly. The baby was asleep, the bottle all but empty. He set the bottle down on top of the radio and carried the baby carefully into the bedroom to her crib.

Gloria went on talking, lifting her voice a little. "The man over there is awful nice. He said I was gonna be in his department. I don't know how to be a model, but they said they'd teach me how, that there wasn't nothin' to it. I betcha it's gonna be fun. They said I was to start workin' tomorrow. And I git twenty-seven fifty. I went over and told Sally and she said that was awful good. Sally said first thing I knew I was gonna be rich!"

Johnny came out of the bedroom again and picked up his cigarette package, fumbling with the matches. He lighted the cigarette and took a deep drag. "Glory, baby," he said. "I don't want you taking that job. You call up the corset factory tomorrow and tell 'em they'll have to find somebody else to stand around with their goddam corsets on. I know Sally only meant to help, but don't you see, I don't want you to get no job. You don't need no job, baby. You got me to take care of you and get you the things you want, you always will have. I know things are kinda tough right now, but I'll be back to work before you know it, and then you'll have more money in your pocketbook than you can think up ways to spend it. You don't have to have any job, honey."

Gloria stared at him incredulously, her mood of happy excitement completely vanished. "No! I'm gonna be the model, and it's gonna be a lot of fun and I get twenty-seven fifty. Sally said you was gonna be surprised. She said it was gonna help you and that you'd be proud a me."

Johnny's voice was tender with feeling. "Sure, and I am proud of you, darlin'. You don't know how good it makes me feel to think you wanted to go out and get a job to help me. Of course I'm proud of you!"

He went over to her and gathered her into his arms and held her tight against him for a moment. He released her then, brushed the hair back from her face and kissed her. "But you don't have to get a job, see, honey? We'll make out fine till I get back to work again. Sally was wrong about it, that's all." His face broke into a little humorous grimace. "You suppose I want my wife standin' around in her underwear over to that corset factory with a lot a strange guys lookin' at her? No, baby! You don't have to get no job, not while you got me to take care of you. I don't want you havin' any job. I want you here, keepin' house for me and taking care of the baby and goin' out and having a good time like you like to do. That's the way it's always gonna be. I'm the one that works in this family."

"No!" Gloria pushed him away a little and there was a sort of sullen stubbornness on her perfect face. "I'm gonna work to the corset factory, like they said I could!"

"Glory—" Johnny began.

She broke in on him, her voice rising higher. "No, I don't care what you say! I'm tired a setting around here. I'm not gonna do it any more. Sally said maybe it would be weeks or months before you could work again, and while you ain't working I just gotta set around here and I'm not gonna do it any more. I'm gonna work to the corset factory and get twenty-seven fifty, and then I can buy things and go places and have a good time like we used to. No, I don't care what you say, I'm gonna work over there like they said I could."

Johnny's face was twisted and he had to moisten his lips with his tongue before he could speak. He touched his bandaged hands together gently, his eyes upon them, and his voice was very soft. "Glory, honey, what can I say to you, when you put it like that? All I know is what a heel I am for lettin' you down like this. All I know is you're entitled to nice things and fun if anybody ever was in this whole world, and I can't give 'em to you now. Jesus, you don't know what a heel it makes me feel like. You dunno how ashamed I am to look you in the face . . ."

Gloria was crying a little, but he made no move to touch her. He got up from the davenport slowly, as if his body was so heavy that he could barely lift it. He walked back in front of the radio and fumbled with the cigarettes and matches again.

After a little he spoke again, and there was a timid humility in his voice. "Glory, honey, if you could trust me and wait just a little longer. The doctor says my hands are comin' fine, and I'll be working again in no time. Then we'll have fun like we used to. It's even gonna be better than it used to. That's a promise. Did I ever break a promise to you, baby? If you could just wait a little longer."

Gloria was crying, but even through her tears the sullen stubbornness was in her face and in her voice. "No, I'm gonna go to work over there tomorrow. Please, Johnny! I'm tired a just settin' around here. They gonna pay me twenty-seven fifty and Sally said first thing I knew I was gonna be rich! Please, Johnny!"

Johnny's face twisted as if he were in pain, and his voice was lifeless. "Darling, there's nothin' more I can say. If you wanta go to work over there it's all right. What can I say? If I can't give you the things you want, how can I say no when you wanta go out and get 'em for yourself? It's all right!"

"Aw, Johnny!" She held her arms out to him like a child, but Johnny didn't go to her. He walked into the bedroom instead and when he came out he had his hat and jacket on.

"Johnny, where you goin'?" she said.

"I'm goin' out and get a little fresh air and buy a paper," he said. "I'll be back in a little while. It's all right, honey."

"Is it all right?" Gloria said. "You mean I can go to work over there tomorrow, like they said I could?"

"Yeah, sure," Johnny said steadily. "You can go to work over there tomorrow like they said you could. I'll be back in a little while, honey."

He closed the door behind him gently. He stood still for just a moment, one hand lifted to his face. He turned suddenly and almost ran toward the stairs. He was going so fast, his head ducked down, that he almost collided with Petey, who was running up the stairs two steps at a time, clutching the skirt of her sequin-trimmed black dress, her furs loose at her shoulders revealing the startling, low-cut neckline.

"Well, hi, there, Johnny O'Connor," she said cheerfully. "You been chasin' any more loonies these dark nights? How are you? How are your hands coming?"

"Well, hi, there, Petey Braun," Johnny said. "All dressed up like the million-dollar baby! Woman, you sparkle tonight! You mind if I'm shadin' my eyes to look at you?"

Petey's warm, husky laughter echoed up and down the stairs. "How the hands coming, Johnny?"

"Aw, fine, thank you," he said. "I don't have to be askin' you how you are. Even from where I'm standin' I can see you're doing all right."

"Well, that's more than I can say for you!" Petey cocked her head and squinted her eyes at him elaborately. "Man, if I ever saw anybody that looked like they needed a good stiff drink right now, you're it."

Johnny smiled a lopsided grin. "Lady, where did you think I was heading for, coming down these stairs like a bat outa hell?"

"Well, don't let me keep you," Petey said. "I can see this is urgent. Better tell the barkeep a double shot, and turn down an empty glass for me, will yuh? I may not look it, but I need one myself!"

Petey continued up the stairs and down the hall. The door to Sally's apartment was open and Sally herself was standing in it.

"Hi, there," Sally called. "I thought I heard you down there. It's about time you was showing up around here. How are you anyway?"

"Aw, fine, I couldn't be better!" Petey stooped and kissed Sally lightly. "How you doin', honey?"

Sally looked at her critically. "Say, what's the matter with you? You look as if you could hardly keep from bustin' all over the place tonight."

"Ha, ha," Petey mocked. "Aw, 'tis many the aching heart that's hid behind a smile!"

"Humph," Sally said suspiciously. "We're just eating. Why don't you come on and have a bite?"

"Some coffee would be fine," Petey said. "No, don't bother to lug a chair out, I can't stay but a minute."

"What you mean is you can't set still," Sally said, laughing as she led the way to the kitchen.

"Hi, everybody," Petey said. "What's cookin' by all a you? Hey, you kidlets, I got something for you, but you can't have it till you eat your supper." She pulled a big white sack of candy out from under her fur cape and dropped it on top of the cupboard.

"Say, where you been keepin' yourself, tall, dark and beautiful?" Fred Foster said. "We ain't seen nothin' of you around here in a hell of awhile! You can't treat your family like this!"

"Hi, Freddy, did you miss me?" Petey said.

"Did I miss you? Listen to her! She says did I miss her! Well, look at me, here I am a shaking, shattered wreck of . . ."

"Ha, cigarette nerves," Petey scoffed. "Thanks, honey." She took the cup of coffee Sally brought her and leaned one elbow on top of the cupboard comfortably.

"She can't stay but just a minute," Sally complained, as she sat down at the table again. "And we haven't seen nothin' of you in days. My gosh, I was worried about you! I thought you must be sick or something."

"I know it," Petey said penitently. "I been bad. I didn't show up, I didn't telephone or anything. I been bad. C'mon and beat me! Beat me, Daddy, eight to the bar—a plink, a plink, a plink plank plink plank plunk plink!"

"No, really, I was sort of worried," Sally said seriously.

"I'm sorry, honest," Petey said. "I got tied up and busy, but that's no excuse. I'm sorry, honey."

"Oh, it's all right," Sally said.

Petey sipped her coffee. "Looky, what's the matter with your neighbor down the hall? I met him coming down the stairs right now looking like grim death, and pub-galloping if I've ever seen it."

"Oh, gosh, I bet I know," Sally said. "Gloria got a job today, and I suppose he is feelin' sorta bad to think that she has to . . ."

"Jesus H. Christ!" Petey's eyebrow bent in her amusement. "What kind of a job would anybody give Beautiful? What's she gonna do, model bathing suits in a store window?"

Sally laughed a little. "Well, that's a pretty good guess. She got a job over to the corset factory. They had an ad in the paper for a perfect size thirty-six. She went over there and got the job this morning. She's gonna model corsets. The pay is real good, she . . ."

"Oh, man, oh, man!" Fred Foster chortled. "Out of the way, everybody! I'm on my way to the corset factory to get a job right now! Jesus, are the boys over there gonna get a treat!"

"Poor Johnny," Petey said. "No wonder he was headin' out for a stiff drink. He's looking right at trouble now, little Beautiful running around over there in her scanties!"

"Oh, gosh!" Sally's face was incredulous and apprehensive. "Why, I never thought of that! Maybe I never should have showed her that ad. Of course Johnny would feel just awful thinkin' about her . . . Oh, darn it, I'm so dumb! Why, I thought, you know—that—that it would be just women, that . . ."

"Women, hell!" Fred said cheerfully. "All the designers and stuff like that over there are men. The lucky stiffs! Boy, they sure got something to look forward to, startin' tomorrow!"

"Oh, darn it!" Sally said dolefully.

"You should worry," Petey said. "The strip-tease gal over at Toresca's went in business this year to support a sick husband and a baby, and, Jesus, any guy that looked cross-eyed at that little gal once her act is over, she'd bat his ears off!"

"Well, just the same," Sally said, "I bet Johnny feels rotten about this. Darn it anyway, you'd think I'd learn to keep my nose outa other people's business, or, if I'm gonna stick it in, that I wouldn't be so dumb."

"Ginny, you're doin' a fine job, cleaning up my joint," Petey broke in. "But don't work too hard at it. Oh, while I think of it, I saw your boy friend this afternoon."

Virginia blushed a little. "I'm glad you think I'm cleaning up your place all right."

"Jimmy's a nice kid," Petey persisted. "He came in just as rehearsals broke up and I had a beer with him. I guess he thinks you're pretty all right, Ginny."

Fred Foster dropped his head on his hand and looked at Virginia in mock wonderment. "My, ain't love wonderful," he marveled.

"Jesus, you wouldn't even know Virgie was the same kid around here lately. She sure spruced up and . . ."

"Well, of course," Sally said reprovingly, "any girl feels a lot better when she's interested in some fellow and . . ."

"Oh, my gosh," Virginia said awkwardly. "The way you people talk you'd think I was in love with Jimmy Terwilliger! Does a girl have to be in love with a man just because she lets him take her out places to have a good time?"

"There you are!" Fred pointed at her triumphantly. "Women!" he said bitterly. "Women! My God, they're all alike. Nothing but a bunch of goddam gold diggers. They glam on to some poor guy just to get everything out of him they can. They don't care nothing about a guy, unless he can take them places and buy them things. They're all alike, every goddam one of 'em. Women!"

Petey laughed her deep laughter. "This is where I came in," she mocked. "I know you, Freddy, you can't do with 'em and you can't do without 'em." She set her coffee cup on the cupboard shelf. "Well, take it easy everybody, baby's gotta go and earn an honest dollar."

"Have you got to go?" Sally got up from her chair and followed Petey into the living room, a chorus of good nights called after them. "Seems like you just got here." Sally opened the door and followed Petey out into the hall.

"Aw, I'll come again when I can stay longer," Petey said. "Maybe next Sunday, huh? No, now wait a minute, don't tell me you've heard that one before. So maybe this time I'll fool you. Take it easy, honey."

Sally looked at Petey suspiciously, as she stood there smiling, her dress shining in the dimly lighted hallway. "Petey, what's the matter? You act like something's hit you that's just about knocked you to pieces. You talk too fast and keep fidgetin' around like you couldn't stay still. What's the matter, Petey?"

"Aw, I'm all right," Petey said. "You're just imaginin' things, honey."

Sally looked at her hard, and then suddenly she put both arms around her in an oddly protective gesture.

"Hey, hey, what gives?" Petey said. "Don't you start worrying about me, honey. I'm the gal who's been all around the town, remember? I can take it."

Sally's voice was troubled. "You're so swell, Petey, and you're so good to everybody. It's just that I can't stand to think of anybody or anything ever hurtin' you."

"You're sweet!" Petey said. "Jesus, I gotta beat it. The Nicky is sour enough these days without me bein' late for the first show."

Sally's face was worried and puzzled. She closed the door slowly on Petey's quick footsteps and her laughter.

# 24

ON A DARK COLD AFTERNOON, SEVERAL WEEKS LATER, Virginia was on her way downtown to meet Jimmy Terwilliger. Ginny was feeling good these days, better than she ever had before since she had been in this town. Jimmy Terwilliger was giving her back her self-confidence and she hardly ever thought of Bill any more. She was confident about the job she was going to get soon, too. It was Petey, Ginny believed, who had done this for her. She loved Petey. She wanted to be just like her. When there was nobody around, Ginny often tried to imitate Petey's deep, rich, loud laughter, her expressions too, and the way she walked. It was a kind of game she played. People didn't know it yet, Ginny thought, but pretty soon now she was going to be just like Petey.

She got off the bus and hurried up the street past the five-and-ten and the cheap department stores. She was late. Her old tan polo coat was wrapped tight around her and her brown felt hat was pulled low on her forehead against the cold. It was Virginia's custom to do the cleaning at Petey's apartment late in the afternoon at an hour that she knew Petey would be out at rehearsals. Several days a week that hour nearly coincided with the time that Jimmy Terwilliger got out of his last afternoon class at the Junior College. Sometimes they met for a cup of coffee, perhaps to dance a little to juke-box music at some soda-fountain place. Today they were to meet in the restaurant at the back of a cut-rate drug store near the street on which Petey's apartment was located. There were a counter and a few booths on a shining, clean, black-and-white tiled floor, a big juke-box with a gaudy illuminated front, a number of small chromium-and-leather tables and chairs. Jimmy Terwilliger was already there waiting for her in one of the booths toward the back. He waved at Virginia as she came in, and she smiled and waved back at him. She felt a tiny complacency in her. This drug store was a hangout for other young people like themselves, students of high schools and colleges all over the town. It was often crowded at this hour in the afternoon. Lots of the kids who came here were friends of Jimmy's. Some of his friends were girls, but it was for her that he was waiting. Virginia took pride in that. She liked to come in late like this if the place was crowded, so that all of them could see that Jimmy was waiting for her. She liked to feel the eyes of the other girls upon her. Jimmy was very popular; he was so big and handsome, to say nothing of his local renown as an athlete. Virginia walked across the tiled floor toward the booth where he was sitting. She carried her head high, and she tried to walk a little like Petey did.

"Hi, Jimmy, I'm terribly sorry I'm late," she said.

"That's okay. Better late than never, huh, kid?"

Jimmy stood up, towering above her, to help her off with her coat. He hung it up for her on the hook at the end of the booth.

"Boo, cold!" Virginia said, shivering a little as she slid into the seat.

"Some hot coffee'll fix you up," Jimmy said. "You want coffee or would you rather have something else, a soda or something?"

"Coffee is fine," Virginia said.

While Jimmy waved at a waitress, Virginia wriggled comfortably in the warmth and pulled at the sleeves of her sweater.

Virginia fitted into the picture here, and she knew it. She wore the same kind of clothes that the other girls did—what amounted to a uniform with them. Out of the money that Petey had paid her she had bought a few things for herself—the soft pink wool cardigan that she was wearing, the brief tan-and-brown plaid skirt, pink ankle socks bright above her old saddle shoes, which she had left over from her own school days. Virginia knew that she looked well in these clothes, with her hair combed out soft and fluffy and bright-red lipstick on her mouth.

They'd have to make this short, Jimmy was explaining to her, he was due over to the gymnasium right now. While he talked, Virginia sipped her hot coffee gingerly.

Virginia cut into Jimmy's conversation idly. "I don't see why you're so crazy to get in this Golden Gloves stuff," she said. "I bet you'll miss out on a lot of school work you'll only have to make up later. Besides, it must be dangerous. Aren't you afraid you'll get hurt?"

Jimmy smiled at her in magnificent, amused tolerance. "Not this boy," he said cheerfully. "I can take care of myself with any guy in any ring around this town! I'm a cinch to go right through to the finals at Grand Rapids! After that, maybe Chicago, how can you tell?"

None of this particularly interested Virginia, and it was almost Jimmy's sole topic of conversation these days.

"Suppose you did get to go to Chicago, so what?" Virginia said. "I just don't get it. Would that help you graduate from college this year? Would it help you get a job? Besides, you're liable to get hurt bad, you can't tell me."

"Aw, you talk just like my dad," Jimmy said, grinning. "In the first place, I won't get hurt, see? I got what it takes; I'm good," he said modestly. "Nicky Toresca has seen me work out. If I wasn't good do you suppose Nicky Toresca would back me the way he is? He got me the best trainer there is around here, and one of the sweetest handlers from the corner you'll ever want to see. As far as graduating and getting a job next year, you know where I'll be next year—toting a gun around for Uncle Sam. It's gonna be a big help to me in the army if I clean up some Gloves Titles this year. It gives me a sendoff and a lot of experience to do some fighting after I'm in the army. You can't never tell how it might work out. Look at Gene Tunney!"

Virginia was scarcely listening; she had heard all of this before. "Well, just the same," she said.

"Aw, you just don't get how it is," Jimmy went on. "Fighting's in my blood. I keep trying to tell that to Dad. It's all right for Dad to tell me that fighting's a bum's racket. Would that a stopped him years ago when he was fighting? Hell, no! I'm crazy about fighting and I can't help it. I'm just the same as Dad was when he was my age. That's what I keep telling him."

Jimmy went on talking, and Virginia only half listened. She listened to the music from the juke-box, and she looked at the other people in the room covertly. She thought about herself, Virginia Braun, alive and glad to be alive, with her hair combed out fluffy, sitting across a table from a good-looking young man who liked her very much.

When she finished her coffee she told Jimmy that she had to go. It was getting late and she had the work to do at Petey's. Jimmy got up instantly and helped her with her coat. He had to go too, he said. On the way out they discussed a tentative movie date for the next night. Jimmy promised to telephone her late the next afternoon to confirm it. They lingered a trifle longer in front of the drug store, moving about to keep a semblance of warmth in the cold.

Virginia snuggled her chin into her coat collar, pulled her hat down and walked rapidly into the wind. She kept her head lowered as she hurried along, but she kept her eyes on the store windows. She saw things she wanted all up the line, some of which perhaps she could have, if she handled her money wisely. She noted a fancy ornate necklace and bracelet to match, a slim youthful woolen sports dress, a fluffy angora sweater, a pair of tall white rubber boots. She turned the corner at last, out of the wind, and hurried down the street toward Petey's place. She reached the warmth of the apartment building at last, and slipped her hand into Petey's mailbox for the key.

Petey's apartment was on the third floor, and Virginia was breathless by the time she reached the door. Her hands were cold and she fumbled with the key, but at last she pushed open the door. She caught the faint sound of the radio, and for a moment she wondered guiltily if Petey could be home already. Then she remembered the key in her hand. At that moment she saw the big man with the light hair and the pale eyes sitting there in the living room, a newspaper in his lap. She had seen him here several times before.

"Hello," Virginia said distantly as she came in. The man nodded his head at her without bothering to look at her, and Virginia tossed her coat and hat on a chair near the door in silence. She surmised that he must be a friend of Petey's, and a rather good one, if Petey was willing to let him have the run of her apartment when she was out. Virginia didn't particularly like him. She thought he was a very strange and unfriendly sort of person. He had never said as many as two words to her. The first time she had found him here he had made her nervous; he was so quiet, his big body so motionless, and there was something strange about his eyes. It had made her clumsy and awkward with her work that first time, knowing that he was sitting there, but now she didn't mind him any more. She had intended to ask Petey about him, but she had never gotten around to it, somehow. As a matter of fact, he was sort of good-looking in a strange way, Virginia decided, as she stole a look at him on her way to the kitchen. Virginia switched on the light in the kitchen. There were only a handful of dishes in the sink; apparently Petey had not eaten at home the night before. Virginia washed the dishes and cleaned up the kitchen, working swiftly and competently. She sang softly as she worked, and listened to her voice appreciatively. It wasn't such a bad voice, and perhaps she could learn to use it to better advantage. Perhaps she could sing sometimes like Petey did; she thought that she would like that.

With the kitchen in good order, Virginia turned off the light and went back into the living room on her way to the bedroom. The big man had dropped his paper to the floor carelessly, and sat with a cigarette burning in his fingers. He watched Virginia as she crossed the room. She felt his eyes on her. He really was good-looking, Virginia decided. She was pleasurably aware of his eyes following her, such strange pale eyes, and his big body so motionless in the chair. She just wished Jimmy Terwilliger could see this man. Jimmy was pretty proud of his physique, but he would look like a weakling beside this man. Virginia felt his eyes on her, and she felt a little glow of pleasure inside of her. She wondered what he was thinking of her when he watched her like that. Virginia walked into the bedroom with her own special imitation of Petey's strut. As she cleaned up the bedroom, she sang again softly, and she was aware every minute of the big man sitting out there in his chair. But though she was aware of it, it didn't make her clumsy and awkward this time. It made her surer and more deft in her work, and pleasantly aware of the motions and gestures of her own body. Virginia couldn't quite understand why that should be when she was out of the range of his eyes, but, just the same, it was true. She sang a little louder, and she was aware of the graceful arc of her body as she leaned across the bed to remove an infinitesimal wrinkle in the spread. There wasn't much work to be done in the bedroom, either. Petey, Virginia had discovered, was a very neat person. She didn't leave clothing scattered around, and she didn't leave drifts of powder over everything on top of her dressing table. Virginia finished tidying the bedroom in no time. Now there was the living room to be dusted and straightened up. Then there were several pairs of Petey's sheer hose to be washed out in the bathroom basin, the bathroom cleaned, and the work would be done.

When Virginia came out into the living room she stole a glance at the big man. She couldn't tell if he was looking at her or not. Just the same she sang softly to herself, and walked slowly across the floor to the kitchen, with her head high, and her legs moving from the hips, the way Petey walked. She got the dustcloth from the cupboard in the kitchen and came back into the living room. Now she had to work directly under his eyes, and she was more aware of him than ever. The singing died in her throat as she bent to dust a chair, and she was aware of the flex of her muscles, the way her hair fell against her cheeks. She postured her arms gracefully, the sweater sleeves pushed up a little, her arms half bare. She moved on to the bookcase where Petey kept piles of magazines. Virginia lingered there, unconsciously posing a little in front of the shelves, still full of the awareness of herself and how she must look to this man. She bet he was thinking that she was attractive, Virginia thought; well, why shouldn't he, she was attractive. She bet that right this minute he was thinking, gosh, what a cute little sister Petey has; when she gets older she'll look quite a lot like Petey does. Virginia spread her hands gracefully, stacking magazines into a neat pile, and enjoyed the sinuous motions of her arms.

The next item of furniture was the table beside his chair. Because Virginia was feeling very confident and very assured of herself, she walked directly up to him. "Excuse me," she said softly. She leaned over in front of him slowly, picked up the ash tray from the table and carefully dusted the table top. Again she was almost breathtakingly aware of the poise and balance of her body bent like this, and the easy motion of her arms. She dusted the top of the table over again, and, on the sweeping motion, her arm touched his sleeve lightly. Virginia was very much aware of it. She straightened up, twisting her body a little at the waist, the ash tray in her hand. She turned around quickly, feeling the skirt swirling against her legs, and walked to the kitchen to empty it, walking slowly in the studied way, singing again softly. She emptied the big glass ash tray, rinsed it under the faucet and dried it neatly on a towel. Usually she brought all the ash trays out at once, but today she had forgotten—she didn't care. She didn't have to think about the big man as she wiped the ash tray; she simply felt him and was aware of him. She caught a glimpse of her tiny distorted reflection in the glass, all pink and soft fair skin and dark hair falling, and that gave her pleasure, too. She hung up the towel and carried the ash tray back into the living room with her slow studied walk. She anticipated the moment when she would lean over close in front of him to return the ash tray to the table top. The moment came. Virginia leaned over very slowly and put the big ash tray down carefully, and slowly slid it along to the exact middle of the table. If she slid it just a little farther, Virginia was thinking, her arm would brush his sleeve again, and without thinking much about it she started pushing the ash tray across the smooth, polished table top. While she was still moving the ash tray, he dropped his cigarette butt in it suddenly. Her eyes clung fascinated somehow to that little paper-wrapped wad of smoldering tobacco, lying there in the middle of the big glass dish. Then she felt his hands tight on her shoulders, pulling her toward him as he rose from his seat. At the touch of his hands a quick warm glow went through her like quicksilver, and the glow became half pleasure, half pain, like a billion needles pricking ever so lightly. None of it made sense to Virginia, because she had never felt quite like this before. He kissed her then, and Virginia thought suddenly with triumph, so he did find me attractive, after all. She didn't struggle in his hands, because the kiss was good to her and this warm prickling glow of her body was good to her, too. Then he took her in his arms and kissed her again, the whole length of her slight body held tight against his. He kissed her until she was breathless, and still Virginia felt the triumph. In a minute, when he released her, she knew already what she would do. She would step away, shaking her hair back from her face, and she would smile—maybe she could bend an eyebrow upward the way Petey did—and she would say, half-mocking, "Well, really!" or something like that. Then she would go back to her work with the good tight triumphant awareness of herself, and of him, and of him watching her. Except that he didn't release her. Suddenly Virginia became afraid. She didn't say anything, but she struggled a little. His arms were so strong and he held her so tightly that she could scarcely move at all. The pleasure was gone suddenly for Virginia, and the triumph, and only the fear was left. He kissed her again, though she tried to turn away, and his lips were hard against her face, and his arms were hurting her. She heard him say something, a murmur in his throat that she couldn't understand. He moved then, carrying Virginia with him. She didn't understand, and she was more frightened than she had ever been in her life, and she kept struggling to break away from him with all the strength she had, with a single and absolute concentration of her mind and her energy. The big studio couch was just behind them, but Virginia didn't think about it. She didn't think about it at all until she stumbled against it, lost her footing, felt her feet leave the floor suddenly, falling but not falling really, since his arms were about her, and then felt the softness of the cushions under her back and the weight of his body above her. He was so heavy that the breath was half-crushed from her lungs. She felt his lips on her face again, and on her neck, and his hands on her body. The fear turned into terror for Virginia. She didn't scream; she had no breath for that. She only said, her voice a hoarse insistent whisper, "No! Stop, please! Let me go, please!" She was struggling, but he was so heavy that somehow she felt the power of motion seep out of her muscles before it ever came to be actual motion. He pulled her body down a little, his body unbearably heavy upon hers. She felt his hands tugging at her clothing, and then the cool air against her bare thighs. "No," she said again, in the dry soft whisper of her terror. "Don't do that! Please, stop! Let me go, please, let me go!" Why doesn't Petey come, she thought then, oh, why doesn't Petey come home?

She was still struggling, but the absolute concentration on that one thing was gone, she realized it, and the terror was choking her breath. She heard the dry whisper again. "No, don't, please . . ."

Then the whole thing became a nightmare. The struggling stopped, and the whisper too. Only the nightmare, the nightmare of unreality and pain, something happening that she couldn't understand. In the nightmare, time stood still. She couldn't tell how long or how short the time was, but after awhile he released her a little, the full pressure of his body was removed. Virginia discovered that she could still move. She slid off the end of the studio couch suddenly and onto her feet. She didn't see him at all, only as a sort of blur before her eyes in the dim light. Her legs almost buckled under her, and she had to catch hold of the end of the studio couch for support. She couldn't be sure if he put out his hand to steady her or to take hold of her again, but she pushed his hand away. The terror had hold of her, and she listened to a fluid, hysterical voice that said, "Don't touch me! Get out of here and leave me alone! Oh, go on, get out of here!"

She didn't wait. Somehow her legs carried her toward the bathroom and she closed the door behind her—good solid wood—and slid the bolt, good solid metal. In a moment she heard the apartment door open and slam shut again. Virginia didn't cry. She turned on the light and she stared at her reflection in the mirror.

Petey was running up the steps, two at a time, when she met the big man coming down the stairs, his coat over his arm.

"Hi," Petey called gaily. "Jesus God, what an afternoon I've had! I'm worn to a frazzle!" The hall was deserted and Petey stood on tiptoe, her hands on his arms, and kissed him lightly. "Where you goin', Sam?"

"Out," he said tonelessly.

"Well, if you don't get back," she said, "I'll meet you for dinner same place, same time."

"Will you?" he said in his odd, disassociated voice.

"Uh huh," Petey said. "Isn't it funny!" She looked at him affectionately, pulled her hat off, and rumpled her hair loose and free at her neck. "Jesus, I'm tired! What a day!" she said again simply.

Then she started up the stairs again. "Me for a hot bath. I'll see you."

He started down the stairs, and suddenly she called his name: "San!"

He stopped and turned around slowly, one hand on the balustrade.

Petey stood still, and suddenly she laughed. "It's all right. I was so tired, I just wanted to see your face again." She laughed again, and made a mock binocular with her fist. "My very dearest person," she said, "if that is lipstick I see on your chin from here, it's the wrong color!"

He stood quite still, looking at her, with his pale eyes with their odd, sightless quality.

"You know—your face rests me," Petey said, a queer irrelevance in her voice, as if she spoke a thought aloud to herself alone.

"See you at dinner, San."

The living room was fairly tidy, Petey noted, and it looked wonderfully inviting, dim and quiet and peaceful to her. "Hi, Ginny!" she called. She threw her hat and her coat and furs over a chair and sank down on the studio couch gratefully. Virginia wasn't in sight, but Petey saw the light beyond the bathroom door and heard running water. Toresca's had been a madhouse that afternoon, Petey reflected. Rehearsals couldn't have been worse. The Nicky was in a temper. Somebody told her something had gone wrong upstairs. Her nerves were stretched tight even now. Must be she was getting old; must be she couldn't take it any more the way she used to. Petey shifted her body comfortably on the studio couch, the cushion soft under her, and fumbled for a cigarette. She didn't want the lights on just yet. It was more soothing in the half darkness like this. Oh, she was tired; her nerves were stretched and worn raw.

The cigarette didn't taste good to her. No wonder, Petey thought, she had been chain-smoking all afternoon. She wished she had a drink. Probably half the trouble was she hadn't had a drink all afternoon. She wondered idly if she could teach Virginia to mix a decent whisky sour just by yelling the instructions to her from here. Petey wadded the pillows behind her back comfortably and stretched out her long slim legs, the ankles crossed neatly. Her hair was loose around her face, and, although she looked tired, she looked young, somehow, in the plain black dress she was wearing.

"Hey, Ginny, come here a minute," she yelled. There was still no answer from the bathroom, though the sound of running water had stopped. "What's a matter? You haven't fallen in, have you?" Petey called good-naturedly. "Open the door, I want to talk to you a minute." Why, I'm so tired I'm practically silly tired, Petey thought idiotically.

In a moment the bathroom door swung open, the light shining out. Virginia didn't come out, though. "Hi," she said. Petey caught a glimpse of her. Virginia was in front of the mirror, straightening her hair with unsteady fingers.

There was something wrong about this; there was something wrong in the way Virginia was acting, the little warning bells rang in Petey's head. I'm tired, I'm imagining things, she answered herself. But she looked at Virginia curiously, and she knew that she wasn't imagining things. Virginia didn't speak; she didn't come out of the bathroom; she didn't even look at Petey. She just kept fussing with her hair in front of the mirror, and her hair needed fussing with, it was all mussed up, sticking every which way in the back.

The cigarette burned in Petey's fingers, and she kept looking at Virginia and trying to figure out what it was that was wrong about the way Virginia was acting. Then suddenly she knew; it was guilt, for some strange reason Virginia was acting guilty. She couldn't seem to look Petey in the face, much less come out of the bathroom and talk to her. That's silly, Petey reasoned, why should Virginia be acting guilty before me like this? But it was guilt, all right, guilt in every sagging line of her body, and in her small white face with the lipstick smudged away from the lips. Then Petey heard her own voice in her ears with startling clarity. "My very dearest person, if that is lipstick I see on your chin from here, it's the wrong color!"

The anger caught Petey, a blind vicious anger, and because she was so tired she felt hot tears behind her eyelids. Petey was off the studio couch in one bound. The words came all in a rush, and she made no attempt to stem them. "You little tramp!" Petey said. "So now I know why you're hiding around in the bathroom without the guts to look me in the face. So that's it! I thought you were different, but no, you're just like all the other little mantraps your age. Any man you're around five minutes, you start mugging. It just happens that guy means something to me, see? But what do you care? You're like all the rest of them. I thought you were different. I've been nice to you, and what's the thanks I get for it? Behind my back the first chance you get, you wiggle your fanny around here and start mugging around. Oh, you make me sick, go on, get your things on and get out of here. And you don't need to bother to come back right away, either. I'll clean up this place for myself. Go on, get out, before I say a lot more things we'll both be sorry for."

Virginia got out all right, like a frightened mouse running to cover, her face stricken and miserable. Once the door was shut behind her, Petey was so hurt, and so disgusted with herself for her tirade, that she could have cried. She lit another cigarette and went out to the kitchen to mix her own whisky sour, blinking tears back at every step. Just because I'm tired and on edge tonight I have to fly off the handle, she thought, and say a lot of nasty things like that to the poor kid. Yeah, but just the same . . . So what? She mugged around with San a little; he kissed her a few times. What should I get excited about? Why should I care, what difference does it make? Except that she is attractive in her own fresh young way, and I feel old as the hills tonight and full of wrinkles and gray hairs. Oh, God, damn it to hell anyway! Petey poured a strong double shot of the whisky and dumped it in the glass. You're acting like a stupid jealous fool, Petey told herself objectively. You better not let San know that you even guessed anything about this, and tomorrow you better call up Virginia and apologize for those things you said to her. Just the same, the stubborn voice of the hurt inside her insisted, just the same!

Oh, God damn it to hell anyway! Petey walked back into the other room and, as she walked, some of the liquor slopped out of her glass; she felt it splattering cold and wet against her legs. "Oh, God damn it to hell anyway!" Petey said, loudly and distinctly.

# 25

VIRGINIA WALKED BACK PAST THE ROW OF GLITTER-ing store fronts, but this time she didn't notice them. She didn't notice the cold, either. She just walked without thinking much of anything, not even where she was going. It never occurred to her to go home. It was somehow as if everything in her life up till this afternoon was now unrelated to her, like being a strange person in a strange city. It was getting dark rapidly now, street lights were on, and the traffic rushed by noisily in the streets, but she didn't notice that, either.

After quite awhile, she stopped on a curb for a traffic light, her feet stumbling a little. Then she discovered that she was cold. She was shivering and her feet felt shriveled up and clumsy in her shoes. With that sensation she became aware of others. Her body felt sore and aching, her face was flushed and feverish. She felt nauseated and her head ached. She couldn't walk any more; she would have to sit down someplace, she thought. She looked about her, reconnoitering. She would find a lunch-counter place and go in for a cup of coffee, she decided. Some instinct in her kept her walking, searching for an unfamiliar place, where she would not be likely to see anyone that she knew. She cut back and forth, through several side streets, all the while thinking that she could not walk a step farther, that she would have to sit down, even if it was right here on a curbstone. At last she saw a Neon restaurant sign ahead, and she turned in at the door. It was a small place that she had never seen before, untidy and not too clean-looking, but she went in. Inside the air was very hot and laden with the pungent smell of onions and other unidentifiable foodstuffs. The place was almost empty, except for two or three men in working clothes, unshaven and dirty, sitting at a table with their beer. Too late, Virginia saw that this was more beer-garden than restaurant. But it was too late to turn back now. She walked the length of the room to a booth in the very back, wedged in between the wall and the juke-box. The counterman followed her. Just as she sat down he said, "What'll it be for you?"

"I'll have a cup of coffee, please," she said. She noticed that speaking was an effort for her, that she had had to strain her throat to get the words out.

As the man turned away he stuck a nickel in the juke-box, shoved the metal coin-carrier into the slot carelessly and then went back toward the counter. Virginia huddled in the far corner and, as the juke-box blared forth suddenly, she felt the vibrations from it all through her body. A plaintive nasal male voice sang over the music:

*"You are my sunshine, my only sunshine . . ."*

Suddenly, without warning, Virginia felt tears in her eyes, and she was herself again, sick and aching and bewildered, but herself. Now she started thinking; thoughts came quickly one after another, as if they had been dammed up too long, and with them a feeling of such misery as she had never known before in her life. First came the incredulity that this thing could have happened to her. Things like this sometimes happened to other people, she supposed, but, oh, it couldn't have happened to her. But her memory, as if eager to help her, offered her the testimony of clear, vivid recollection, and Virginia turned away from it with a little spasm of revulsion. Oh, it had happened, all right. She had a quick visual image suddenly of the big man's face as he had looked sitting there so quietly in that chair, his pale eyes following her. Oh, he was a horrible creature, Virginia thought. She never wanted to see him again as long as she lived. He ought to be in prison; he ought to be killed. She felt unclean, as if she ought to take a bath, but she knew at the same time that no amount of soap and water was going to take that feeling from her. Why, even Petey, her own sister, had called her a tramp and ordered her out of her apartment and told her to stay away. It was a funny thing, Virginia thought seriously and undramatically, how you and your whole life could be ruined in just the space of a few minutes, less than an hour.

The nasal male voice sang out of the juke-box again in lugubrious complaint over a blighted love.

Virginia dropped her head in her hands.


She wasn't clean, she wasn't decent any more, Virginia kept thinking. Nice people would never want to have anything to do with her again. Even worse, somehow, she felt that same way toward herself. How could she ever bear to live with herself after this? Oh, this wasn't fair, Virginia thought with a little flare of rebellion, this shouldn't have happened to her. What happened back there at the apartment wasn't her fault. Or was it? She had liked it at first when the man kissed her. Why, yes, she supposed she had even wanted him to kiss her. Shame and revulsion swept over Virginia, and she leaned her forehead on her hand, the steam rising up from her coffee cup against her white, tragic face.

The counterman appeared suddenly at the opening of the booth. He looked profoundly bored. "Gents up front wanta know if you wanta have a beer with 'em," he said to Virginia without enthusiasm.

She started a little. "Huh? Oh! Oh, no, thank you."

He disappeared without a word.

For no tangible reason, that made Virginia's sense of her own degradation complete. She supposed they could tell what she was, just by looking at her, Virginia thought lifelessly. She supposed she would get used to this kind of thing.

All of a sudden out of another corner of her thinking came a totally different thought without warning, and a fear with it that momentarily paralyzed Virginia. Oh, my God, she thought in her despair, why didn't I think of that before, why have I been so dumb? It isn't as if what happened back there at Petey's apartment was the worst of it, the worst of it is yet to come. What would ever happen to her if she became pregnant? The humiliation and shame were lost in this new fear that turned into a desperation of self-preservation. She had no money; she had no place to go. She could never tell Sally, nor Petey either, now, after the way Petey had talked to her. What would she ever do?

The juke-box blared forth again, a fanfare of bugles and then a chorus of male voices:

*"We're in the army now, we ain't behind the plow!"*

Virginia was numbed. Pregnancy! She regarded it now as an inescapable certainty. It was a reality too big for her to cope with; there was no solution for her. She was trapped, and there was no way out. She couldn't put the thought away; she couldn't think of anything else.

Virginia got up after awhile and left the restaurant. She turned back to Main Street automatically, and went down the street to the drug-store bus stop. She waited a few moments until the East Williams bus came in and climbed aboard.

When she came home, Sally's voice called to her cheerfully from the kitchen, over the eating sounds, "Hi, there, is that you, Ginny? About time you was showin' up around here, young lady. Where you been? I was about ready to send the police lookin' for you!"

"Yeah, give an account a yourself. Where you been?" Fred Foster yelled.

"I met Jimmy downtown," Virginia heard her own voice answer.

"Well, I thought as much," Sally called back.

Virginia got out of her coat and hat, and put them away in the closet.

"You better hurry up and get out here while there's still something left to eat," Sally called again.

"I don't want anything, thank you," Virginia said. "I ate downtown."

She went into the bathroom and closed the door behind her.

When she came out she hesitated a second and then she called out to Sally, "I'm not feeling very good. I guess I'll go to bed now. Is it all right if I go in your bed, till you're ready?"

"Why, sure!" There was puzzlement in Sally's voice. "I'm sorry you aren't feelin' good, honey. Look, you can sleep in my bed all night if you want to, I just as soon . . ."

"No," Virginia said. "When you're ready I'll come out on the davenport. I'd rather, honest. Good night."

She closed the bedroom door behind her, and she didn't bother to turn on the light. She undressed by what little light there was from the window and slid into the middle of Sally's big bed. She stretched out her aching body, and lay very still, staring wide-eyed into the darkness. No escape, nothing she could do, no way out.

Out in the kitchen over her second cup of coffee, Sally was saying, "Oh, dear! I just bet you anything that Ginny and that Terwilliger fellow have had a fight!"

"Ah, that's love for yuh!" Fred Foster said. "The craziest goddamdest thing they ever invented!"

# 26

SALLY MOUNTED THE BUS FOR THE STATE HOSPITAL the next day with unusual exuberance. It was not that she was totally without misgivings concerning this visit to Roy, nor was her mood something caught from the bright sunshine that poured down from a clear blue sky, melting snow and ice into slushy puddles. Sally's exuberance was due almost entirely to a new hat. Such things were not frequent in her life. For two winters now there had only been one hat, a battered shabby felt that she thought of seldom and vaguely as being merely "my hat." But today Sally had a new one. It was the first time she had worn it, and that fact gave her a pleasant sense of being dressed up. Added to that was the knowledge that it was most becoming. That hat had been a gift from Petey together with a huge black fabric purse that she guaranteed would hold at least twice as much as Sally's bulging old pocketbook, and a sheer, bright woolen scarf. Sally was initiating all three gifts, and the novelty of a new outfit somehow made the day and the familiar bus ride something festive.

During her wait between buses, Sally went about the business of selecting magazines and candy for Roy with a fresh enthusiasm. Whatever frame of mind she would find Roy in today, she was quite sure she could handle it. She felt pretty and young and strong; she loved Roy and he loved her, so what was there in the world for her to be afraid of?

That feeling lasted right through to the end of her journey, and to the time when she was pulling open the heavy glass door into the corridor of Administration Building. Inside, as she walked toward the information desk, Sally listened with approval to the sound of her feet against the marble floor. Sometimes her tread had been dull and heavy and slow, sometimes her feet had dragged and caught forlornly; today her footsteps were light, rapid and rhythmic.

When her visitor's slip was okayed she sat down in a chair in the corner of the waiting room in front of the window. The sun shone in brightly through the window, and Sally felt its warmth against her knees. Beyond the window, water splashed down in streams from melting icicles, and, as Sally glanced out, a great chunk of ice dislodged from the edge of the roof fell to the ground with a heavy plopping noise. This day was a sort of preview of the spring to come and it matched the lightness and exuberance of Sally's mood. Spring is a renewal of faith after a hard cold winter, and faith was something that Sally felt strong within herself as she sat waiting.

"Hello, there, Mrs. Otis. Sorry to keep you waiting," the nurse said pleasantly when she finally appeared. "Goodness, you look pretty today! You're going to be a regular breath of spring weather upstairs there, which is something I think all of us could use."

A shaft of sunlight dissecting the room shone directly into the nurse's face as she spoke, and Sally noticed that in the strong light the nurse's sweet rather attractive face looked strained and tired with great shadows of weariness about her eyes. With a little shock, Sally thought of this person, whom she always took as much for granted as the heavy key-ring or the muted call-bells, as an individual, a young woman who had a hard and responsible job to do, and performed it cheerfully and well. Why, she didn't even know this girl's name, Sally thought guiltily.

"How are you today?" Sally said, and, as she fell into step with the nurse, she added impulsively, "You know, I was just thinking. As often as I come down here and as nice as you've always been to me and to my husband too, I don't even know your name!"

The nurse laughed a little over the loud rustling of her starched white skirt. "That isn't so strange, Mrs. Otis. Few people that come here to visit as you do ever think much about those of us who work here. You all have too much else on your mind, I think. My name is Smith."

"There! Now I feel better," Sally said with her warm smile. "It is sort of late for us to be getting introduced like this, but better late than never, they always say."

As they paused for the nurse to unlock the door to the stairway, Sally spoke the question that had really been first in her mind since the very first glimpse she had had of this familiar, white-garbed figure. "How has my husband been, Miss Smith?"

The nurse hesitated a little, closing the door behind them and relocking it, with a noisy rattle of keys. "Well, as you know, Mrs. Otis, your husband has been very depressed ever since the holidays."

"Yes, I know," Sally said. "He was so terribly disappointed about not coming home. But I thought that would kind of wear off after awhile. I thought maybe he'd be feelin' better this week."

"Well, I don't think it is anything to be too alarmed about," Miss Smith said as they mounted the stairs, "but his fit of depression hasn't worn off. If anything, he has even been more difficult this past week."

The edge was gone from Sally's good feeling already. "Difficult?" She echoed that dread word that was always so vague and meaningless to her, but laden with such terrible possibilities.

"He keeps entirely to himself," Miss Smith explained. "Although he is well enough for it now, he refuses occupational therapy, and he refuses to take advantage of any of the recreational facilities offered the patients. His attitude has become unhealthy again. I don't wish you to become alarmed. I only tell you this because I think you should make a special effort to cheer him up today, if you can."

"Yes, I understand," Sally said. Her shoulders drooped a little as she trudged up the next flight of stairs, and she had to cling to the faith and confidence she had brought with her today.

The nurse noted the dulling of Sally's face, and she said kindly, "There, now, I have upset you, haven't I? But, honestly, I don't think there is any need for you to be upset. Your husband's case has shown a steady line of improvement ever since he has been here, with just a few setbacks at the very beginning. I wouldn't be surprised but what this bad weather we have been having hasn't depressed all of the patients, shut in as they are. If it stays warm and sunshiny for a few days so they can all get out for walks, I'll bet you'll find a big improvement in your husband the next time you come."

"I guess you're right, Miss Smith," Sally answered with a determined cheerfulness. "Gosh, that bad weather even got me to feeling blue sometimes." Sure it could be partly the weather, Sally argued with herself. Dull nasty weather day in and day out did sort of get you after awhile, and it must be twice as bad if you had nothing to do all day but just sit around and look out of a window. That was just the trouble, Roy had always been used to such an active life. His work, driving a truck, had kept him on the move all the time, rain or shine. No wonder he felt blue. Probably the fact that he was blue like this was a sign that he was really getting better, wanting to get out of this place and back to work again. There wasn't really anything wrong with a person feeling blue, everybody had blue spells once in a while, it didn't have to mean that Roy was sick again. It was up to her to be extra bright and cheerful and loving today, the only way that she could think of to help him.

Sally listened again to the sound of her feet. Hey, hey, now, she told herself sternly, this will never do, no feet dragging along today! Confidence and strength and faith, remember. Sally smiled and straightened her shoulders and made her steps quick and light.

The turn in the corridor was reached, and Sally caught the familiar glimpse of Roy's thin, stooped figure waiting for her in the doorway.

"Roy! Hi, darling!" Sally called.

He called "Hi" to her, but he didn't come to meet her.

Oh, he looked so old and tired, with his shoulders stooped like that, Sally mourned. His face was different too, sunken a little, and all the life gone out of it, somehow. Aw, never you mind, my darling, Sally said deep within herself. This is a terrible place for anybody to have to live, anybody would be changed if they had to stay here. But some of these days you will be leaving here and coming home again, don't forget that, darling!

"Gosh, it's good to see you! Seems like it's been so long! How are you, darling?"

Sally stood on tiptoe, but his kiss was brief and perfunctory.

"Doesn't she look pretty today, Mr. Otis?" Miss Smith said cheerfully as she ushered them ahead of her into the plain little room. "I told her on the way upstairs that she was just like a breath of spring weather around this place and that there was nothing that we all needed more."

Sally laughed a little as the nurse pulled the chairs around in front of the high-legged metal table. "Well, I wish I could bring about a week of spring weather along down here and we could use some to home, too." In the face of Roy's silence, Sally spoke a little awkwardly and self-consciously.

They sat down, and Sally put her magazines and candy on the corner of the table. The nurse adjusted the door wide open and then smiled at them over her shoulder. "Have a nice visit now!"

When she was gone the room was very still momentarily. Roy sat stiff and straight on his chair without speaking. He was looking at Sally, but his face was blank and expressionless, and he sat so still that he hardly seemed to breathe or wink an eyelid.

Sally fumbled for a package of cigarettes automatically. "Well, gosh, it's good to see you," she said again. "How have you been feeling, honey? Why in the world don't you write to me? What have you been doing this week?"

"Nothin'," he said. "Just settin' here."

Neither the words he spoke nor the tone of his voice gave Sally much to go on, but she spoke again with an effort of determined cheerfulness. "I know, Roy. There isn't much news with us, either. We're all well, and the kids are in school every day, and I keep workin' same as always, that's about all."

Roy's face was blank and set. He made her no answer; he showed no interest in what she was saying.

Aw, poor darling, Sally thought, with a little sob deep inside of her. You're so blue and so discouraged that it is all you can do to sit there without crying out loud. If I could only help you, if I could only think of the right things to do or say that would make you feel a little better.

"You want a cigarette, dear?" Sally said brightly, holding out the fresh package to him.

"No, I don't!" he said, and there was something cold and strange in his voice.

"My golly, don't tell me you're cuttin' down on your smoking, after all the talkin' I've done for all these years!" Sally's laughter sounded warm and natural to her ears. "Here you are cuttin' down, and here I am smokin' more than I used to. First thing you know, I'll be the one in this family that's smokin' a couple cartons a cigarettes a week!"

Roy broke in on her with laughter of his own, but unnatural laughter, with the strange cold quality about it. "Yeah," he said. "I guess you're doin' a lot of things now you never used to do when I was to home."

His words chilled and frightened Sally, so that for a moment she could scarcely breath. But I mustn't pay any attention to it, she told herself desperately. He didn't really mean that the way it sounded. It's because he's blue and unhappy that he says things like that. He doesn't really mean it. There could never really be words like that between Roy and me, never in the world. Out of the hurt inside of her, Sally said the words that Miss Smith and the doctors would never approve of her saying.

"Aw, Roy, honey, what's the matter? You don't feel good today, do you? You act so funny. You're just blue and discouraged, I know, but you mustn't be, darling. Everything is all right. You're gettin' better and you're gonna be comin' home pretty soon now. Darling, don't get blue and discouraged and act funny like this. Tell me what's the matter, can't you?"

"Nothin's the matter. I'm fine." He smiled a little, a secretive smile, as if he savored some joke that was unknown to her. That smile frightened Sally even more than anything he had said to her today. Because that smile was familiar to her, because it belonged to dark days long months ago when Roy was not himself at all, when he was a frightening tormenting stranger to her.

Sally lighted her own cigarette and dropped the matches back in her purse with fingers that trembled. Words came from her in a gay chattering unnaturalness. "Gee, isn't this a swell day out, though? It's so warm, with the sun shining like this. The snow and ice is meltin' fast. Gosh, I hope it stays like this a day or two, then you could be gettin' outdoors to take some walks. That would seem good for a change, wouldn't it? The weather has been so horrid lately, you're lucky you didn't have to get out in it. Everybody keeps gettin' colds all the time. We been awful lucky though, none of us has had a sign of a cold since Virginia had the flu that time. I guess I oughta knock on wood, though. Gosh, I guess this table isn't wood, though, is it? Oh, well, I'll knock on my head, that's as good a block a wood as you could find anywhere, isn't it, darling?"

Sally stopped for breath momentarily, and Roy kept smiling at her, that tormenting secretive smile that struck terror to her very heart.

Sally caught her breath and went on talking. "Roy Otis, you never said a word about my new hat! A fine thing! Here I get a new hat and I save it to wear down here to see you and then you never even notice it! A fine thing!"

"Oh, I noticed it all right," he said, with the odd smile at his lips.

"Do you like it?" Sally chattered on desperately. "And this is new too, and this, see?" She indicated her bag and scarf as she spoke. "Petey gave them to me. Wasn't that sweet of her? I've been saving them all week to wear down here to see you."

"So Petey gave 'em to you, huh!" Roy said with the sardonic, secretive amusement.

"Uh huh, it was awful nice of her, don't you think?" Sally was running out of things to talk about and she picked up the magazines desperately and held them out to him. "I brought you some candy and magazines. Honest, hon, I have the worst time pickin' out stuff for you to read. I wish you'd tell me once which magazines you like best, it's so hard for me to pick 'em out for you, I . . ."

With one abrupt motion he pushed the magazines out of her hand back onto the table, and he caught her wrist tight in his fingers, pulling her toward him. Out of balance as she was, Sally scrambled to her feet to keep from falling. But still the relentless pressure on her wrist, pulling her toward him.

"Roy, stop, you're hurting me, please!" Sally's breath came short and loud and uneven in the quiet little room. He stopped pulling on her wrist, but he held it tight with fingers like steel. He kept smiling up at her with the crafty secretive amusement.

"You don't even want me to touch you, do you?" he said softly. "You belong to him now, don't you?"

"Him?" Sally stammered over the word, her face pale and bewildered.

"Jesus Christ, you think you could fool me forever," he said in soft amusement. "I guess I'm smart enough to know you couldn't keep goin' on the money you claimed they paid you at that restaurant! I guess I know who's givin' you money and buyin' you hats and stuff, an' I know why he's doin' it too! You can't fool me! You thought you could, but you can't. I know all about it now. I got the proof!"

Sally was faint and sick with the words that he was saying to her, the fear and despair that she felt. Suddenly she remembered something that had happened a long time ago. She remembered Lee, the dark-haired girl at the restaurant weeks ago, before Christmas, and before Petey came to town, back in the days when Nicky Toresca had hung around and the girls there thought that she had been dating him. There was something Lee had said then, something nasty about suppose somebody wrote a letter to Roy and told him about it, something that had been said to Sally a long time ago and had frightened her then. She thought of it now, as Roy said these fantastic monstrous things to her, and, before she thought, the tell-tale words were out of her mouth.

"Roy, stop! You don't mean these things you're sayin'. Somebody wrote you a letter maybe, but you know . . ."

He was on his feet instantly, his face twisted into leering triumph. He shook Sally hard with both hands and then flung her away from him. "Oh, no," he said, "nobody wrote me no letter. Nobody had ta! But I know just the same. I knew just how the land lay when I found out how you fixed it so I couldn't come home for Christmas. I always knew what you was like; you're just like that sister a yours, you're a good pair, the both of you, go to bed with any guy that comes along that's got the dough to . . . I know why you're keepin' me locked up here!"

Sally crouched at the end of the table, clutching it tightly with both hands for support, her face turned toward him, white and flat, her eyes enormous and half-blind in her face.

"You bitch! You goddam bitch!" His voice rose and he lunged toward her. "Comin' down here, smilin' and showin' off in the hat he bought you with the money you earned in bed!" He grabbed at the hat with rough clumsy hands, tearing it from her head, and twisting it out of shape before he threw it to the floor.

Sally backed away from him on clumsy, numb feet, her hair hanging disheveled over her white face and down into her eyes.

"Bringin' me books and cigarettes and stuff with the money he give yuh!"

He scooped them up from the table and threw them directly at her. Sally ducked instinctively, and one of the magazines sailed out over her head through the open door.

"Christ, women like you ain't fit to live, to marry decent guys and be the mother a little innocent kids! You bitch, you dirty little bitch!"

He lunged toward her again, and Sally was too stupefied and paralyzed to elude him. He shook her roughly with one hand, and slapped her hard across the face, and then tore at the front of her dress with rough furious fingers.

At that moment the ward helpers came, and somehow, Sally would never know just how, she was loosened from his frenzied hands and hustled out of the room, away down the corridor, leaving a sound of shouts and struggle behind her. Roy fought them off desperately, crying in his rage, his thin body twisting and thrashing from their grasp, upsetting the chairs and table in the little room. A part of him that was quite removed from all this that had happened, that had sat back and watched and listened to it all and was quite powerless to stop any of it, was sobbing and sick with shame. Jesus, how could I say things like that to Sally, how could I use words like that, how could I hit her? How could I hurt her so, when I love her so, when she is the dearest and the best person in all this world? Jesus, no wonder they say I'm crazy, no wonder they keep me locked up in this place. They ought to keep me locked up here, they ought to never let me out. I'm crazy, that's it. Jesus, I must be crazy to act like this to Sally. I'm crazy! And I don't want to live, I want to die. I'm not fit to live. Jesus Christ almighty, I'm crazy, you hear me, and I want to die!

Quite awhile later that day, Sally sat beside the desk of the young doctor in his office off the corridor on the main floor. She sat very quietly, listening to the words he said to her. Her face was a little pale, her hat was set firmly on her head, bent slightly, but still becoming. Her face was quite steady as she listened, and so were her eyes, with no traces of weeping about them, because, as a matter of fact, Sally had not wept.

The young doctor stopped talking and leaned back in his chair, folding his hands together easily. The late afternoon sun from the window behind him turned him into a dark silhouette of a figure.

Sally slid forward on her chair a little. "I guess I'll have to go now," she said softly. "It's time for my bus to go. Was there anything else you . . ."

"No, I think that's about all," he said. He studied her white, drawn face, and his own face softened a little, except Sally could not see that, silhouetted against the window as he was.

"Mrs. Otis, may I say again how truly sorry I am that you had to be subjected to such an experience this afternoon," he said gently. "As I have told you, such an outbreak is beyond our powers of prediction or prevention."

"No, it's all right," Sally said in her clear voice as she stood up from her chair. "I don't blame any of you or anything. How could you tell or know? Besides, I don't care about myself. It's—it's him I'm thinking about."

"As I have said, you are not to take this outbreak too seriously," the doctor said. "It may not be in the nature of a serious setback, only time will tell. I can't deny that it is a setback in his case, but I can say that such a setback at this stage in the progress of his cure is not unknown, by any means, nor hopeless either. But for the time being I am suspending your visiting privilege entirely. I think you understand that that is for the best?"

"I understand, Doctor," Sally said.

The doctor rose from his chair unexpectedly and ushered Sally to the door himself. Just as she went out he dropped his hand on the shoulder of her old tweed coat, his fingers warm and reassuring. "You are a very brave and loyal woman, Mrs. Otis," he said abruptly. "I only wish that the relatives of more of my patients exhibited the intelligence and patience and understanding that you do. I will send you a report on your husband's condition within two or three weeks. Good-bye."

"Thank you, doctor. Good-bye," Sally said. She hurried off down the corridor toward the big glass door through which she saw the lumbering old car which was to take her to the main road and her bus.

All those words the doctor had used echoed in her ears, brave, loyal, intelligent, patient, understanding. Sally felt a little amusement that was sadder than tears as she tugged at the heavy door and stepped into the warm moist air. All of those fine words for her, because she clung to the only faith that she lived by, the faith that Roy would some day be cured and return home to her and that they might resume their life together where it had been broken off. All of those fine words because she had to believe that what had happened this afternoon between her and Roy was beyond Roy's control and part of his illness, because she had to believe that or die with her hurt and despair. You did and believed what you had to, and someone used fine words about it: bravery, loyalty, intelligence, patience, understanding!

# 27

A S SALLY CLIMBED THE STAIRS AT HOME THAT NIGHT, the door to the O'Connor apartment swung open and Johnny stuck his head out into the hallway.

"Well, if there isn't Sally Otis!" he said cheerfully.

"Hi, Johnny, how are you?"

"And if she hasn't got a brand-new hat on!" Johnny went on. "Sure, now, my girl, and ain't you a sight for these tired old eyes! You career women with your fancy clothes and fixin's! Would you have a minute to spare for a poor tired housewife and father like me?"

"Well, sure, I would, Johnny," Sally said.

He flung the door open for her with a flourish and, as she walked in, Sally said, "Well, gosh, this place looks swell, Johnny! Everything looks as clean as a whistle. I guess you're doin' fine as a housekeeper."

Johnny surveyed the unusual tidiness of the small room with pride. "Yes, sir," he said. "And, would you believe it now, the baby is fed and to sleep and I got my dinner dishes all done."

"Good for you! Where's Gloria tonight?" Sally sat down on the chair just inside the door with a little unconscious sigh of weariness.

"Oh, she's out gaddin' again," Johnny said cheerfully.

In the face of Sally's silence he added a little defensively, "She and her girl friend Marjorie had something on for tonight. You know how it is. Now she's got that job tying her down every day she kind of likes to get out with the girls of an evenin' once in awhile."

"Does she still like her job all right?" Sally asked.

"Yeah, she seems to be crazy about it." His face was suddenly sober. "She gets such a kick outa working I guess it's gonna seem pretty tame to her to stay home and do housework again after I get back on the job."

He got up and crossed the room with his package of cigarettes, and, as Sally took one, she said, "Look, Johnny, any time you wanta get out with Gloria in the evening, or go out yourself some night when she's out like tonight, I'll be glad to keep the baby. I mean, it must seem kinda funny to you being tied down to home every day like this."

"Thanks a lot," Johnny said as he struck the match. "Naw, hell, I'm gettin' used to staying home. I guess maybe I'm just a housewife at heart."

He wasn't smiling when he said it, and he changed the subject abruptly. "You went to the hospital today, huh?"

"Uh huh." Sally's face was very sober and still, and her eyes dropped to the burning tip of her cigarette as she turned it a little in her fingers.

"And what did Roy think a you all dolled up in a new hat like a picture in a magazine?"

For a moment there was a sort of flutter of the muscles around Sally's mouth, and then she said evenly, "Oh, I guess he liked it all right."

Johnny looked at her sharply. "Did you have a good visit today?"

"Uh huh."

"You wouldn't try to fool your Uncle Johnny, would you, honey?"

Sally smiled briefly and twisted around in her chair to the ash tray on the table behind her.

"He isn't comin' along so good, is he?" Johnny said to her gently. "The visit today was pretty tough."

"Yeah, that's right," Sally said, and suddenly her voice broke. "Oh, gosh, Johnny!"

"As bad as that?"

Sally nodded her head, blinking back the tears.

"Jesus, Sally," he said soberly. "It sounds so damn silly to say words like 'I'm sorry.' But keep the old chin up, honey. Maybe today was just kind of an off day for him. Why, probably the next time you go down next week . . ."

Sally got up from her chair suddenly, and her voice tightened. "That's just it, Johnny. I won't be going back next week. Maybe I won't be going again for months. The doctor suspended my visiting privilege today."

She turned around again to the ash tray, and Johnny was silent for quite awhile.

"Yeah, I guess I get how you feel," he said at last. "Jesus, if that was Glory off someplace and I couldn't . . . But Sally, if the doctor wants it like that, it's because it's the best thing for Roy, you gotta believe that."

"Yeah, I know." In a minute Sally turned around, and there was desperation on her face and in her voice. "But, Johnny, how can it be the best thing for Roy? It always seemed like me goin' down there and the letters I wrote to him was the only tie he had with his family and all the life he had before he went to that place. Now he's shut away from everything in the world, locked up in that place with those—those—crazy people! My God, Johnny, you don't know what it's like down there! You don't know how awful it is! Even the ones right there in that ward where Roy is. I've seen 'em! They creep on the floor and yell and sing and talk crazy and try to kill themselves! They got Roy locked up with 'em, day in, day out, and I can't get to him, nor nothin' nor nobody. Johnny, it's terrible, how can he ever get better, how can he keep from . . . ?"

Johnny was across the room and had tight hold of her shoulders. "Sally, stop, don't talk like that! Don't say no more. You can't talk things like that! You can't even think things like that!"

"But it's true," Sally said. "Everything I said was true. How can I help but think things like that?"

"I don't know," Johnny said. "All I know is you can't do it. You mustn't let yourself. You just gotta snap out of it somehow. Jesus, Sally, you're just flesh and blood and nerves like anybody else. If you let yourself keep thinking about that all the time, why, you can't stand it, you'll . . ."

"Yeah, I know," she said, with her voice little more than a weary whisper. "Or else I'll go crazy too!"

Johnny's face was tragic and baffled. "Sally, honey, I don't know what to say to you," he said finally. "I know how much you love that guy, so I know what you're goin' through. But he loves you too, and he couldn't stand havin' you hurt and goin' to pieces like this either. I don't know what to say to you, except that you've got to start thinking about yourself too. You got a life of your own now, you got three kids to home there that worship the ground you walk on. When you feel like this you've got to think of them, and of yourself that's got to go on from day to day providin' for 'em, and bringing them up. They're his kids too, and you and them are what he's gonna be comin' home to when he gets better."

Sally was silent a moment more and then she straightened her shoulders and raised her face to Johnny's. Her eyes were bright with tears, and, although her face was pale, some of the strain had gone out of it. "Aw, I know, Johnny," she said. "I'm sorry I went to pieces like this. I never done it before. I guess I just come home all nerved up and kind of lost hold of myself there for a minute. But I'm all right now, honest. You been swell, Johnny, I'm sorry I . . ."

"For Christ's sakes!" Johnny grinned as he fumbled for his cigarettes. "Look, Sally, how about us getting Virginia to keep an ear out for Bevvy and you and me'll step out someplace for dinner, for a change."

Sally shook her head as she started for the door. "No, thanks a lot, Johnny. If you wanta go out I'll be glad to watch the baby, but I think I'll feel better goin' home and gettin' supper for the kids, honest."

"Well, you know what you feel like doing," Johnny said, "but come in again, why don't you? Don't stay away so long."

"I'll come again," Sally said from the doorway. "And you come over, Johnny. And thanks a lot for everything."

Sally hurried down the hall and opened the door to her own apartment. Buddy and Marilyn swarmed across the living room to meet her, and Sally knelt, her arms outstretched to them. Between kisses Sally said, "Well, how you been? What you been doin' today? Gosh, I bet you thought I'd run off and left you. I bet you're starved to death, unless maybe you ate already. Where's everybody?"

"Virgie's in the bedroom and she won't come out," Buddy announced importantly, as Sally took off her coat and hung it in the closet.

"Well, what do you know about that!" Sally said, smiling a little as she watched their bright animated faces. But, as she turned away from the closet, she rapped on the bedroom door and called Virginia's name softly. The room was dark and Virginia did not answer.

"I guess Ginny's to sleep," she said. "Come on, let's us get out there in that kitchen and see about gettin' some supper around here. My gosh, about time we did it too, if poor Fred's gonna get anything to eat before he has to go to work."

Later that evening, as Sally and Fred Foster lingered over second cups of coffee, Mrs. Gideon called up the stairway. "My land, I thought you was all dead up there," she called good-naturedly when Sally opened the door. "Virginia's boy friend's on the telephone!"

"Thanks a lot," Sally said. "I'll call Virginia right away."

Sally opened the door to the bedroom and she saw Virginia lying across the bed, her face hidden in the pillow. Sally went to her and shook her shoulder gently. "Ginny, wake up, honey!"

Virginia rolled over instantly and sat up. "I'm not asleep."

"Gosh, I thought you was sleepin'," Sally said pleasantly. "You missed your supper, you know that? Your boy friend's on the telephone, honey."

"I don't want to talk to him," Virginia said, her voice flat and lifeless.

Sally was silent for a moment. "Aw, honey, I knew that you two had had a fight, the way you was actin'. Now, why don't you go on down there and talk to him and make it up with him?"

"We haven't had any fight. I just don't want to talk to him."

Sally dropped her arm around Virginia's shoulders. "Ginny, it'll only make you feel worse if you don't talk to him. Now he's willing to make up and he's called you, you go on down there and talk to him and make it up with him. There isn't any sense you kids making each other unhappy when . . ."

"He's not my boy friend! We haven't had any fight, and I don't want to talk to him," Virginia said again in the curiously flat voice.

"But he's waitin' on the telephone. What am I going to tell him?" Sally coaxed.

"I don't care what you tell him."

"Well, I'll tell him you've gone out for a minute and he better call back later. How'll that be?" Sally said, with a tinge of exasperation in her voice. "Now, you come on out and eat your supper, you're never gonna feel any better mopin' around in here alone in the dark. Come on now."

She pulled Virginia up from the bed and led her out into the living room. "You go on out in the kitchen, and I'll fix you up some supper when I come back."

Virginia stood still and listened to the patter of Sally's feet going down the stairs. Why can't she let me alone? Virginia thought without emotion. Why can't everybody let me alone? Why can't I just drop through the floor and disappear?

She didn't go out to the kitchen. She went into the bathroom instead, bolting both doors securely. Then she stood still again, in the middle of the bathroom floor. Jimmy Terwilliger on the telephone. Jimmy Terwilliger, somebody she had known several million years ago in a different life, in a different place, when she was a totally different person. How could she have talked to him? What could she possibly have to say to him, or he to her? Except that he didn't know yet, Virginia's mind patiently answered the last half of the question. Nobody knew yet, but they would all know pretty soon. When they found out about her having a baby she supposed everybody would blame Jimmy Terwilliger because she had been having dates with him and they thought he was her boy friend. How terribly unfair to Jimmy, Virginia thought dispassionately. The thought aroused no particular emotion in her. She was quite past that. It simply occurred to her as another facet to her horrible and inescapable predicament.

The stiffening went out of Virginia's knees suddenly, and she sat down on the edge of the bathtub and buried her face in her hands.

In a moment or two the doorknob to the bathroom door rattled and Sally's voice said, "Ginny, you come on out and eat now. It'll make you feel better, honey, honest."

"I'll be out in a minute," Virginia said automatically.

She stood up again and listened to the sound of Sally's feet going back to the kitchen. If they would only let her alone! If there was only some way that she could sneak out of the house without anyone seeing her or knowing that she was gone—except that there was no place for her to go to. If she could only drop through the floor and disappear before anybody knew about what had happened to her.

Virginia opened the door to the little medicine cabinet and, as she opened it, a tiny bottle fell from a crowded shelf. She caught it in her hands before it fell and broke in the washbowl.

Iodine, Virginia thought as she returned the phial to its precarious place. But there wasn't enough of it left in the bottle. There wasn't enough iodine left for what? Virginia's mind had no answer, and her hands were busy with the accumulation of bottles, boxes, tubes and jars that cluttered the cabinet. It needed cleaning out, Virginia thought objectively. Sally was always saying that she was going to do it, but she never seemed to find the time.

There was an old comb with most of the teeth missing lying on the top shelf. Virginia pulled at it and dislodged a cold-cream jar from a corner. She managed to catch that, but the tiny box which had been wedged in behind it fell into the washbowl. Virginia didn't notice it for a minute, and then she picked it up and turned it over curiously. Sedative, the writing said, prescribed for Roy Otis. The dosage was one, and if relief did not follow another one could be taken after two hours. But never more than two, the writing made that quite explicit. Virginia slid open the little box curiously and folded back the thin piece of cotton. Capsules, little blue capsules, and more than two of them left in the box, quite a lot more. A lot of fragile little blue capsules between the thin layers of cotton, maybe eight or nine of them, maybe more. Oh, yes, ten, eleven—a lot of them, enough, oh, yes, enough of them, without a doubt. Virginia did not hesitate a second. She filled the water glass under the faucet and dumped all the capsules out of the box into her hand. She dropped the little box into the washbowl and picked up the water glass in her free hand. She put a lot of the capsules into her mouth at once, they were so small.

Out in the kitchen Fred Foster was saying to Sally, "So I said to her, I said, 'Now look, dear, you may be a flower of the Old South, but now you-all is up North where we-all is havin' a hard winter. I take you out drinkin', that's fine. But that ain't no sign you can pick out the most expensive liquor they got in this joint and order drinks for all your goddam friends and expect me to pay the bill! Christ,' I says to her . . ."

"Wait just a minute, Fred," Sally said, getting up from the table. "I want to get Ginny out here and make her eat something. Gosh, she probably hasn't had a thing to eat all day, if she was moping around by herself like that."

Fred stretched luxuriously, reaching his hand out to the coffee pot on the corner of the stove. "Jesus, I forgot about Ginny! Where is she, she musta fell in or something. She's been in there in that bathroom a hell of a while."

"I know," Sally said from the doorway. "I was listening to you talk and I sort of forgot about her. She probably went back in the bedroom and crawled in bed with Marilyn. Now, when she comes out, don't kid her too much about having a fight with Jimmy. Let's see if we can't cheer her up."

"Sure, you betcha," Fred said, as he poured his coffee. "Regular little ray a sunshine, that's me. Christ, Virgie and her love-life!"

The bathroom door was still closed, the light shining out from under it. Sally took hold of the knob and rattled it in her hand. "Ginny, come on out now, honey. Ginny! Aw, Ginny!" Sally stood quite still, the fearful sound from the other side of the door loud in her ears. The sound of spasmodic vomiting, together with an agonized dull moaning. "Ginny, why didn't you tell me you was sick? Aw, Ginny, let me in! Aw, honey, you're terrible sick, let me in, let me help you! Ginny, can't you hear me? Honey, open the door, let me come in! Ginny, Ginny!" The fear clutched Sally suddenly, and she beat on the door with both fists. "Fred, Fred, come here quick!"

Fred came, the sound of his chair toppling behind him. "For Christ's sakes, what's . . . ?"

"It's Ginny," Sally said wildly. "She's in there and she's terrible sick. She's got the door locked! We gotta get in there!"

"Well, now, wait a minute, take it easy," Fred said. "Maybe she . . ." His voice thinned out as he came close to the door and heard the sound that came from the other side.

"Christ, I guess she is sick!" he said. "No wonder she didn't wanta eat nothin'! Virge! Hey, Virge! Come on now, open up that door!"

"It isn't any use yellin' to her, Fred," Sally said in a shaking voice. "Maybe she's too sick to open the door! Maybe she's too sick to even hear us. We gotta get that door open, we gotta get in there."

"Maybe the door on the other side . . ."

"Aw, no," Sally said. "She'd have both of 'em locked. Anybody that goes in and locks one door always locks the other. No use wasting time, we gotta get this door open."

"Hell, there ain't nothin' to that if you wanta break it open," Fred said. "Them bolts don't amount to nothin', and the wood's all soft and rotten. A couple a pushes and . . ."

"Well, go on and do it!" Sally said.

"Well, okay," Fred said, "if you wanta bust it . . ."

He slammed his heavy shoulder against the door two or three times, and the door gave perceptibly.

"Oh, Fred, hurry," Sally said. "It sounds like she's gettin' worse."

Fred was breathing heavily as he backed a couple of steps away from the door, and the perspiration shone on his face. "This time oughta do it!"

That time did do it. The door swung open, catapulting Fred into the bathroom, and Sally right behind him. Virginia was crumpled on her knees on the floor at the foot of the bathtub, her head and shoulders hanging over the edge of the tub. Sally bent over her, tugging at her shoulders.

"Aw, Fred, she's terrible sick, look at her! She's all stiff. It's like convulsions! I guess she's unconscious. We gotta get a doctor quick. Aw, Fred, what is it you do for convulsions?"

"Jesus, I dunno," Fred said. "She sure don't need nothin' to make her vomit. She's like to tearin' her insides out, vomiting, right now."

Sally was tugging Virginia into an upright position. "Oh, we'll have to have a doctor, but if I could just remember what it is you do for . . ."

"Christ, I guess she is sick, look at her face!" Fred said in an awed voice. "We better call a doctor quick!"

"Oh, gosh!" Sally hugged Virginia's twisted and ghastly face tight against her for a minute. "Here, Fred, you stay with her, keep her head up so she don't strangle. I'll call him right away."

But Fred was bent down, his big fingers clumsy with something on the floor. "Look! She musta felt this comin' on, she musta been tryin' to take some medicine . . ."

He straightened up and held his hand out to Sally, the tiny blue capsule rolling on his palm.

Sally stood transfixed, her eyes staring.

"Yeah, see, here's the box in the bowl."

"Let me see that box," Sally said, her voice a whisper. "No, the top of it."

They read the writing on the cover of the little box together.

"Jesus . . ." Fred said wonderingly.

"Oh, God," Sally said. "Roy never used more than one or two of 'em. The box musta been full."

They looked at each other then, and each of them read the confirmation of his own thought on the other's face.

"Aw, Ginny," Sally said with a little sob. "Stay with her, Fred!"

After her call to the doctor, Sally telephoned Toresca's on the chance that Petey had already arrived for work. Luck was with her. Petey walked in just in time to take the call. In response to Sally's frenzied voice, Petey promised to come immediately. She stopped long enough to leave a message with the bartender that she would be back to sing later, and then she caught a cab for Horton Street.

Just as she was climbing the porch steps, the front door opened and Fred Foster came out, his lunch sack in his hand.

"Hi," Petey said. "How's Ginny?"

"I dunno," Fred said gloomily. "The doctor come a few minutes ago. Christ, she sure is sick. I sure hope the doc can fix her up."

Petey made the last two porch steps in one bound. "See you later, Freddy!"

Inside the door she nearly tripped over Mrs. Gideon, prowling at the foot of the stairs.

"For goodness' sakes," Mrs. Gideon began, "Sally says that Virginia is just terrible sick. Why, I can't hardly believe it. I seen her just the other morning, and I said to Harry, Mr. Gideon, you know, I said, 'why, I never seen Virginia Braun lookin' any better in her life since she been here than she did this morning.' The doctor's here already . . ."

Petey had no chance to say a word to her, so she never even paused, and Mrs. Gideon called after her, "If there's anything in the world I can do to help Sally, you tell her I'd be glad to. I'm just awful sorry that . . ."

"Sure, I'll tell Sally. Thanks a lot, Mrs. Gideon."

Just at the door of Sally's apartment, Petey met Johnny O'Connor coming out, Buddy and Marilyn clinging to either hand, bundled in bathrobes and stumbling along beside him sleepily.

"Hi, here you are," Johnny said. "Sally's been worrying about why you didn't get here."

"How's Ginny?"

"I dunno," Johnny said. "The doctor just took her in the bedroom and Sally went in with 'em."

"What's the matter with her?" Petey said. "Is she really bad sick?"

"I don't know," Johnny said. "I guess she must have been pretty bad, the way the doctor flew into it when he got here. Sally seemed worried half sick herself."

"Poor Sally!" Petey said.

"Yeah! Her trouble always seems to come double double, don't it?"

Petey was silent a moment, pushing back her heavy hair on her shoulders. Her face looked a little pale above her dark fur. She was wearing huge earrings, great rough clusters of irregular-shaped aquamarine crystals that glittered in the dim light.

"I better go on in," Petey said.

"I'm gonna put the kids to bed over at my place," Johnny said. "If there is anything I can do, just holler."

"Thanks," Petey said automatically. She stepped into the living room and Johnny and the children went down the hall, the sound of his cheerful voice as he talked to them fading out with their footsteps. The living room was deserted, the bedroom door closed, and lights were blazing all over the tiny apartment.

There was a faint mumble of low-pitched voices from the bedroom. The living room was very warm and still and a faint antiseptic odor that Petey always associated with hospitals and doctors hung in the air.

Petey fidgeted and, just as she was fitting a second cigarette into her black holder, Sally slid out of the bedroom and closed the door softly behind her.

"Hi, I heard you come in," Sally said. Her face looked tired, her hair was disheveled and the sleeves of her old red jersey dress were rolled up from the wrists.

"Here, sit down here on the davenport," Petey said. Sally took a cigarette from Petey's package, and Petey struck the match for them both.

"Well, I guess she's goin' to be all right," Sally said, with a tremulous relief in her voice. She leaned her head back on the cushions momentarily and closed her eyes.

Petey looked at her affectionately. "Well, fine," she said. "What was the matter with her?"

Sally sat up straight on the davenport again, and her face looked even more tired. When she spoke, the words came slowly and unwillingly. "It was—it was some sleepin' pills the doctor gave Roy last year just before he went to the hospital. They was awful strong. Roy never used more'n one or two of 'em. There was a whole box full of 'em left there in the cabinet in the bathroom. I guess it's my fault for keepin' stuff like that around, specially when there's kids in the house, and everything."

Petey's face looked puzzled and alert. "You mean she . . ."

Sally nodded. "She took just about all of 'em."

Petey's face was suddenly incredulous. "Jesus God, Sally! You don't mean she . . ."

"Yes, I guess so," Sally said wearily. "It couldn't have been no mistake. It was written right out plain on the box so you couldn't miss it, what they was, and how you couldn't take more than two at one time. She took just about all there was of 'em in the box, it couldn't have been no mistake."

Petey loosened the hair at her neck with one slim glittering hand. "Aw, Christ!"

"Petey, what are we ever gonna do?" Sally said softly.

Petey's face was still incredulous, her eyes wide. "But why, Sally? What made her do it?"

"Well, I don't really know for sure," Sally said. "But she's been actin' terrible funny around here for a couple days now. I figured it out that she'd had a fight with that Terwilliger boy. Then tonight when he called up she wouldn't talk to him on the telephone, and it was right after that that she went in the bathroom and . . . So I figured . . ."

"Oh, hell, no," Petey said. "She hadn't had any fight with Jimmy Terwilliger. Jimmy was in at Toresca's this afternoon at rehearsals to see his father. I had a drink with him. They hadn't had any fight. They had a date all set for tomorrow night. Everything was fine with her and Jimmy!"

Now Sally's face was blank with puzzlement. "She hadn't been fightin' with him, you're sure? Then what in the world . . ."

"You said she was actin' funny. What do you mean 'funny'?" Petey said rapidly.

"Why, I don't know," Sally said. "She just kept all to herself. Most of the time she was in the bedroom there with the door shut, just laying on the bed. She wouldn't talk to nobody or come out where we was or eat or anything. I talked to her tonight. I was tryin' to get her to come out and eat some supper when she . . . She just acted funny when you talked to her. She didn't look you in the face, her voice sounded so funny. She was kind of—of—all froze up."

"How long has she been actin' like that?" Petey wanted to know abruptly.

"Why, I don't just know, two or three days, I guess."

"No, Sally, now think!" Petey said. "When was the first time you noticed her acting like that? Yesterday morning? Last night? The night before that? When?"

Sally tried to think, rubbing her forehead with her palm and pushing her hair back from her face. "Gosh, I'm so tired and all upset I can't remember nothing. Let's see—it was—no—it was . . . Oh, sure, now I know! It was last night! When I got home here, she wasn't here, and I kind of worried because she's never late like that. She never got home till quite late. We was eatin' supper when she come in. She was actin' funny the minute she come in the door. She wouldn't eat or nothing. She went right there in the bedroom and laid down on my bed."

"Last night!" Petey turned around suddenly and went to the window and closed it with a little bang. Then she just stood there for a moment with her back to Sally.

"I don't know where she coulda been yesterday afternoon so late," Sally said. "She claimed she met this Terwilliger fellow downtown, and she said she'd had something to eat, but of course you can't tell nothing from that. Had she been over to your place yesterday doing the cleaning?"

"Yeah, she was there," Petey said. Petey turned around again, picking her skirt out of the way impatiently.

"What in the world ever made her do it?" Sally said softly. "What are we ever gonna do with her?"

Petey squeezed Sally's shoulder tight in her fingers, but before she had time to answer, if she had an answer to give, the bedroom door opened once more and the plump, oldish doctor came out, leaving the door a little ajar behind him.

He went immediately to his bag on the chair and began to pack in the bottles, stethoscope and other paraphernalia he had brought with him from the bedroom.

"How is she, Doctor?" Petey asked.

He looked around over his shoulder in surprise, as if he hadn't noticed Petey's presence there and was startled by the husky deep voice behind him.

He looked at Petey for a moment before he answered, a flamboyant glittering figure there in that faded, dingy little room. His face looked faintly disapproving, and his voice was dry when he answered her. "She'll be all right now. She's not feeling very good, no better than you'd expect her to."

"But she's going to be all right?" Sally repeated with the warm relief in her voice.

The doctor looked at Sally sharply too. "Yes, she's going to be all right," he said, sighing a little as he snapped his bag shut.

There was an awkward silence in the room as he put his bag on the floor and reached for his overcoat flung over the chair. "I left a bottle of medicine in there on the bureau," he said. "The dosage is on the bottle. You can start giving it to her tomorrow when she wakes up. You're going to have a pretty tired, sick little girl on your hands for a few days."

"Doctor, is it all right if I go in and talk to my sister?" Petey said tersely.

The doctor folded his woolen muffler precisely across his neck.

"She needs to rest," he said. "I've got her all fixed in there to sleep. She can't be more than half-conscious right now. The best thing to do is leave her alone."

"I think under the circumstances it would be best if I talked to her tonight," Petey said levelly.

"Well, then, go ahead," he said. "You'll do it, anyway, the minute I'm out of the house. Why do you ask me?"

"Then I think I'll go in a minute right now," Petey said. "I haven't much time. Sally, my purse is right there by my coat. If you'll please pay the doctor before he leaves."

Petey walked across the floor slowly, a frown on her face, and just at the door she hesitated, looking quickly at the doctor once more. The doctor was struggling into his overcoat, holding his muffler in place with his chin clamped tight to his chest. "I know what's on your mind, young woman, so why don't you come out with it?" he mumbled querulously. "You want to know if I'm going to file a report of attempted suicide on this affair, only you're afraid to ask me, on the chance that I'm such a doddering old fool that I don't know what went on here tonight."

"That's exactly right," Petey said. "Well, are you?" Sally stared white-faced from one to the other of them.

The doctor did not answer Petey's question. His face suddenly looked old and tired. "Whether you know it or not," he said, "that little girl in there had a pretty close call tonight. You can always be thankful that she didn't know there is any such thing as taking an overdose and that that box was full of capsules. If there had been five less capsules left in that box, maybe even four less, there wouldn't have been anything that I or anybody else could have done for her."

The room was very still and the doctor turned his hat in his hands wearily. "About my report? Well, I don't know. I don't think she's going to try it again. She did some talking in there a few minutes ago when she wasn't fully conscious and didn't realize what she was saying. She wanted me to go away and let her die, she said, because she was going to have a baby."

He paused again, and there was the sharp sound of Sally's breath caught in her throat.

The doctor turned to her, then, smiling a little. "Well, that doesn't seem likely, does it, Mrs. Otis, according to what happened along with all the other excitement tonight? If that had happened just an hour or so sooner, I think her mind would have been at rest, and she wouldn't have been hanging around the medicine cabinet swallowing everything she could lay her hands on."

The doctor put his hat on and picked up his bag from the floor. "Notify the police? No. No, I don't think I'm going to. I don't see where the necessity is, do you?"

"Thank you, Doctor," Petey said. The muscles around her mouth were curiously set, and she turned away instantly, her hand on the door.

"I thought maybe after you heard that you wouldn't have to disturb her, trying to talk to her tonight," the doctor said mildly.

"I won't talk but a minute. I won't upset her," Petey said. She pushed the bedroom door open and went in.

Petey hesitated a moment at the foot of the bed. The little lamp on the bureau was turned on, the light dim through the thick shade. Virginia lay very still, her body unbelievably slight in the middle of the big bed, her face unbelievably white against her dark hair scattered on the pillow. Her eyes were half open, but she gave no sign of seeing Petey.

"Hello, Ginny," Petey said gently. "I thought maybe you were asleep. I just stopped in to say good night to you." Petey sat down on the edge of the bed beside her and took one of Virginia's limp cool hands in both of her two warm ones. "Darling, this is Petey, and I've come to say good night to you before you go to sleep."

"Petey," Virginia said, a tiny drowsy whisper through her lips.

"That's right," Petey said. She bent suddenly and kissed Virginia's still face. "Aw, honey, you scared us so. Don't ever do anything like this again. Sally and I are your family, don't you know that? And don't you know that there isn't anything, no matter how bad, that you couldn't tell us about, and we would help you?"

Petey's eyes were fixed anxiously on Virginia's still face, and she kept rubbing her hand gently. "But it's all over now and everything's all right. You know it's all right now, don't you, honey? The doctor told you. You're not going to have a baby. Everything's all right, isn't it?"

"It's all right," Virginia said in her drowsy whisper.

Petey was silent a moment, her eyes never leaving Virginia's face. And then she spoke again softly. "It was what happened yesterday in my apartment, wasn't it, darling? It didn't have anything to do with Jimmy, did it?"

Virginia's head moved a bit on the pillow and her voice was a shade stronger. "Not Jimmy! Him!"

"Yes, dear. I know, it's all right now."

"Him—up there to your . . ." Virginia's voice trailed out, but she tried again. "I didn't want to! He grabbed hold of me and . . ."

"Yes, darling, I know. Now don't talk any more. Everything's all right, and you've gotta go to sleep now. Tomorrow you'll feel better, and I'll come and see you again tomorrow. You go to sleep now. Good night, darling!"

Petey kissed her again and then sat still a moment on the bed beside her. Virginia's eyes were almost shut and her breathing was deep and regular. Petey got up from the bed suddenly and left the room.

Sally lifted her head as Petey closed the door softly. "Is she all right? Is she going to sleep?"

Petey nodded. "She's just about asleep now." Petey fumbled with her cigarette holder, the huge rings glittering on her hands.

"Gosh, isn't it funny?" Sally said. "I was just settin' out here thinking. These kids. They seem so awful young, running around the way they do. You never think they got anything more on their minds than their ball games and dancing and coke dates. But they have trouble too, and they take it so terrible serious."

"Yeah," Petey said.

"Wasn't Dr. Bates wonderful, though?" Sally said. "I thought he was just wonderful about it, the way he talked to us and everything. I never give it a thought about him being supposed to notify the police or nothing like that. I thought he was awful nice. He certainly is a wonderful man."

"Yeah," Petey said again. She picked up her coat suddenly. "Looky, I gotta scram," she said rapidly. "I'll call the agency tonight and have 'em send a nurse over here tomorrow to look after Ginny and give her her medicine and stuff. I'll come over to see her tomorrow afternoon after rehearsals."

"Aw, Petey, I hate to have you go to all that expense of a nurse. I could lay off my job, or else . . ."

"Naw, forget it," Petey said.

Sally stood up from the davenport. "Gosh, Petey, you've sure done an awful lot for Virginia."

"Yeah," Petey said, and she smiled briefly. "Now look, baby, you go to bed right now and get some sleep or you're gonna fall flat on your face over there to that restaurant tomorrow. I'll see you tomorrow, or else I'll call."

She kissed Sally lightly and was gone.

Petey got back to Toresca's in plenty of time to sing for the late crowd that was just coming in, and she stopped off at the bar for a drink. When her spot came on the program she sang the numbers she had rehearsed and the encores, but no more. She didn't think about much of anything, she didn't notice much of anything, except that Gloria O'Connor, with a great sprawling showy corsage pinned to one shoulder, was sitting at a front table with a prosperous-looking, rather handsome dark-haired man, who had a noticeable habit of not being able to keep his hands off Gloria, even in public. Jesus, there's a dumb sister, Petey thought objectively, but without much interest. She knows that I work here, and she knows that I know her husband at least well enough to tell him stories. Not even a quarter of a brain under that pretty blonde hair!

Once she was through singing, Petey didn't even wait for a drink. She walked out of Toresca's without a word to anybody and caught a cab.

When she walked into her apartment the living room was deserted, one soft light on in the corner. But from the bedroom, through the partially open door, came brighter light and the sound of music from the radio. Petey loosened her cape, so that it dangled from one shoulder, and went into the bedroom.

San was sprawled comfortably across her bed, pillows crammed behind his head, a magazine propped on his chest and cigarettes and tray within reach of his hand.

"Hello, darling."

He looked up, his face expressionless as usual, and stretched out his arm to her. Petey went to the bed and stooped down to kiss him. He held her tight in the circle of his arm for a long minute. "You're tired," he said, his mouth moving under hers.

Petey stood up, flinging her hair back on her shoulders. "Christ, yes!"

She moved away from him, tossed her bag and cigarette holder on the dressing table, and went to the closet to hang up her cape.

"You're not barrel house tonight," he said. "You're a blues song."

Petey laughed a little, the sound of it echoing in the tiny closet. "Yeah, that's right."

She came back from the closet and sat down on the bench in front of the dressing table. She looked at her reflection in the glass momentarily, and then she slowly began to remove the heavy crystalline jewelry from her hands and ears.

"Could you use a whisky sour?"

"Aw, couldn't I!" Petey said. She gestured toward the radio suddenly with her slim nervous hand. "Listen! Louie Armstrong!"

"Yeah. Recordings." San hoisted his big body up from the bed with a smooth easy motion. "Get in bed, I'll fix a drink."

As he passed behind her he touched her hair lightly with one of his big muscular hands.

When he came back with the drinks, Petey was still sitting on the bench in front of the dressing table. She had undressed and put on a white chiffon negligee over a heavy white satin nightgown, both trimmed with slashes of dark lace. She was brushing her hair, and it moved on her shoulders, crackling with electricity.

She put the brush down to take the glass he offered her. "Um, wonderful!" she said. "Thanks, darling."

"You wanta get in bed now?"

She shook her head. "Not yet."

He went back to the bed himself then, doubling the pillows behind his back this time. He set his drink down on the table in front of the radio to light a cigarette.

Petey sipped her drink and the room was very still, except for the music from the radio. After awhile Petey put her drink down and reached for her cigarettes. "Bet you that's Joe Sullivan on that piano."

"Could be Fats Waller," he said.

"Aw, no! Never in this world!"

She moved her cigarette holder nervously in her hands, and pushed at her heavy hair. Suddenly she snuffed out her cigarette and took a long drink out of her glass. She put it down and turned around a little on the bench. She picked up some of the clusters of the odd aquamarine crystals and turned them in her hands, watching the flat surfaces sending off myriad little flashes of light.

"San," she said suddenly.

"Yeah?"

She took a deep breath and spaced the words evenly in her deep husky voice. "San, my kid sister Virginia tried to kill herself tonight."

The room was still and Petey kept watching the crystal jewelry in her hands, flashing out the sparks of light. "She took a whole box of sleeping pills, but it was an overdose, so she's all right now. She thought she was going to have a baby."

Petey looked up suddenly into the mirror in front of her. She could see his reflection there plain, from the bed behind her. He was sitting quietly, with his own terrific stillness, no motion, no expression, no anything.

"That's a laugh, isn't it?" Petey said, with her voice breaking all at once. "The whole thing makes me laugh! That poor little dumb kid! And you! You, the big sex menace! Jumpin' on little kids and scarin' the life outa them! You, that ain't even a normal man, that ain't enough man ta . . ."

Then Petey stopped talking, and after that she just sat there, staring at him in the mirror in front of her. A couple of minutes went by like that, and then he moved. He got up from the bed all in one smooth easy motion as he always moved. He picked up his old coat, where it lay crumpled in a chair beside the bed, and flung it over his arm. He stood still a moment, his hand fumbling in his pocket. He brought out a key and dropped it on the table. It fell with a clattering sound, a small flat apartment key. He walked out of the bedroom without looking back and Petey heard the sound of the outside door when it closed behind him.

Petey took a drink out of the glass beside her. Then she sat still for quite awhile, and just kept looking in the mirror at the bed where he had been sitting, the pillows still wadded together from the weight of his body, his glass with a little ice and liquor in the bottom standing beside the radio, her key where he had dropped it, a fine wisp of smoke lingering over the ash tray.

That isn't Sullivan on that piano, Petey thought suddenly, it is Fats Waller.

The music kept playing, and Petey emptied her glass with one long drink.

Oh, yes, she thought, I had to come in here tonight and say those things to him, didn't I? I knew what would happen, but I had to say it. The meanest, nastiest thing I could ever say to him, the one thing that would hurt him the most, the one thing I always swore I'd never throw in his face, no matter what happened. But tonight because I'm hurt and jealous and upset, I have to do it! I have to throw that in his face, I have to do the cruelest, most unfair thing I coulda done to him, I have to hurt him like that! Aw, Christ!

Petey stopped looking at the empty bed reflected in the mirror. She picked up the clusters of crystalline jewelry once more, turning and twisting them in her hands, staring without winking at the sparks of light reflected from the numberless little hard polished surfaces.

# 28

THE NEXT AFTERNOON PETEY CANCELED A BEAUTY-shop appointment and took a cab out to Horton Street to pay a call on Virginia before rehearsal time. To her surprise, it was Sally who opened the door for her. Oh, Virginia was fine, Sally explained hurriedly. It was just that she got to thinking, and the more she thought about it, the worse it seemed to leave Virginia alone with a stranger to look after her. It wasn't that she didn't know the nurse would look after Virginia all right, take better care of her than Sally herself could, but Sally just felt that she would like to do it herself, that Virginia might feel better about it. So she had explained to Sam Toresca that her sister was sick and he had given Sally the afternoon off.

How was Virginia feeling, anyway? Petey wanted to know. Oh, pretty good, Sally said, she just seemed to be completely tired out and so weak she could hardly lift her hand.

That could be the shock from what had happened, Petey ventured.

Yes, Sally said, that was just what the doctor had said last night. As far as Virginia's state of mind was concerned, Sally thought that she was quite easy now, and perfectly relaxed about everything. She had slept most of the day.

In that case there was no point in disturbing her, Petey said. She couldn't stay long, anyway, and she could come out again any time.

Petey brought with her a stack of magazines and a large cone-shaped bundle loosely wrapped in florist's paper. Sally volunteered to look for a vase. She was afraid she didn't have one big enough, but they could always borrow from Mrs. Gideon.

Petey loosened the underwrapping of thin paper carefully, and Sally craned her neck for a first glimpse of the flowers. "Oh, pretty!" she said as she caught sight of them. "Gosh, those are swell, Petey. Ginny couldn't help but love 'em. And just smell 'em!"

"Say," Sally said hesitantly, as she watched Petey arrange the flowers in the vase, "that Terwilliger boy called up today. Seems he called last night and Mrs. Gideon told him Virginia was sick. He called up again this noon to see how she was."

Petey's eyes were on the flowers. "No, I know what you're thinkin', but you're wrong. Jimmy Terwilliger didn't have anything to do with what happened around here last night."

"But then who . . ." Sally began in soft incredulity.

Petey frowned a little over an iris that drooped in the wrong direction, no matter how many times she adjusted it.

"Virginia just had a little accident, I happen to know," Petey said tersely. "It wasn't even quite what she thought it was."

Sally's face was bewildered and troubled. "But, Petey, I don't get it. What happened? I mean—who . . . ?"

"It's nothin' that will ever make any more trouble for Virginia," Petey said. "She'll never run into him again, so let's skip it."

"But, Petey . . ." Sally said softly and questioningly.

Petey's face was suddenly strained and her fingers closed too tightly on the soft delicate green stems of the flowers. "Sally, honey, I'm sorry. It's—it's just something I don't want to talk about, see?"

Before Sally had a chance to speak again, Petey broke in. "Oh, while I think of it! Guess who was at Toresca's having herself a time last night? Little O'Connor, down the hall here."

"Gloria?" Sally said vaguely, obviously reluctant to leave the subject of Virginia. "Yeah, Johnny said she was out with her girl friend last night. He said she . . ."

"Girl friend, hell!" Petey said. "She was at Toresca's alone with a man. They had a table on the floor and they were smooching around like a couple of high-school kids."

"Aw, no!" Sally said in a horrified voice. "Oh, my gosh!"

"So I guess I was right about little Beautiful. How much did we bet on that, anyway?" Petey stepped back a little to survey her handiwork. "There, I guess that does it," she said, looking at the bouquet critically.

"Why, that's awful about Gloria O'Connor," Sally said in a hushed voice. "Poor Johnny. Why, if he knew he'd feel terrible. Why,

I don't know what he'd do. What in the world's happened to Gloria to make her start running around like this, and lying to Johnny and . . ."

"Like I always said," Petey said. "She just never got a good chance before."

"You know," Sally said with sudden energy, "I think you ought to tell Johnny about this. Gloria's an awful funny girl. In lots a ways she ain't got any more sense than some little kid. I bet you anything this is the very first time she ever stepped out on Johnny like this. If he knew about it and he sort of clamped down on her and give her a good talking to, why, it might be the best thing in the world for her, and she might never do nothin' like this again."

Petey balanced her slim cigarette holder easily in her fingers. "You could be right," she said. "So if you feel like that about it, why don't you beat it over there and tell him right now before you start thinkin' about it, and get to puttin' it off."

Sally thought that over a minute. "Honest, I don't dare," she said at last. "Johnny's gonna feel just terrible. I honest to goodness don't dare go over there and tell him that about Gloria!"

Petey's eyebrow doubled against her forehead in amusement.

Sally laughed ruefully herself. "Yeah, I guess I'm a good one, trying to get other people to do things I don't dare do myself. But look, Petey, you could do it so much easier than I could."

"Yeah, sure," Petey said. She stood with her back to Sally, looking out the window. The sun was already near setting, the sky bright and glowing in the West. There wasn't any snow on the ground, just the drab frozen dirt, as colorless and unyielding as the cement sidewalk. The trees stuck up against the pale sooty-looking sky, bare and motionless. Ugly frame houses stretched away down the street to a background of factory chimneys, begrimed with smoke. "Jesus, sunset over Horton Street!" Petey said softly.

She turned around quickly and picked up her coat.

"Gosh, you don't feel good today, do you?" Sally said anxiously.

"Don't mind me, honey. I got the leapin' shakes today," Petey said. "I gotta scram downtown. Give Ginny my love when she wakes up and tell her I'll come to see her again."

"Then you're not gonna stop to see Johnny?" Sally said timidly as she followed Petey to the door.

"Yeah, sure," Petey said. "I'll talk to Johnny. I got the time to spare, and they do say the devil finds work for idle hands."

"Aw, fine," Sally said. "Come out again real soon, won't you? Honest, Petey, I'm worried about you, the way you look today. I think you're workin' too hard!"

"Will you please sign a statement to that effect and send it to the Nicky?" Petey laughed, and for a second was her old self again.

When Johnny O'Connor opened the door to Petey's light knock he was carrying the baby's bottle full of milk in one hand. "Well, hello there, Petey Braun," he said cheerfully, "and the top a the mornin' to yuh! Come in!"

"Shure now, let me be thankin' yuh," Petey said, smiling. "An' the balance a the day to yourself!"

"Hey, hey!" he said. "Why didn't yuh ever be tellin' me that your mother come from Ireland? Jesus, I'm glad you stopped in! I'm just a lonesome housewife, and company is more welcome around here than sunshine. Sit down. If you'll excuse me, I'll go in and put the feed-bag on my offspring and I'll be right out."

"Mind if I tag along?" Petey said. "I never laid eyes on that young daughter of yours, you know."

"Sure, come on along." Johnny ushered her before him into the bedroom with a flourish. "This is it! Beverly Kathleen O'Connor! Beverly, meet Petey Glamiferous de Lovely Braun!"

The baby, after no more than one brief glance and her incredibly wise look, ignored both Petey and her father in favor of the bottle which Johnny propped up for her with a couple of wadded diapers.

"Hello, Beverly." Petey bent down over the bed and touched the baby's downy dark fuzz of hair with her fingers. "Well, Johnny, I'd never have to look twice to tell this was your daughter."

"Yup, that's right." Johnny watched the baby's face as it wrinkled and twisted enthusiastically as she sucked on the bottle. He shook his head dolefully. "Sometimes it makes me lay awake nights worrying over whether she's bright or not. With a chance to look like a mother like hers, she decided to take after a mug like mine!"

They left the bedroom together and back in the living room Johnny said, "Here, let me take your coat. No? You sure? Sit down. There's a couple other bottles around this house besides the milk bottles. Could I interest you in a drink?"

"Fine. I'm on my way to rehearsals," Petey said. "This is just the spot in the afternoon when I need a drink."

Johnny hurried out into the kitchen, and after an elaborate exchange of banter over the clatter of removing the ice-cube tray from the refrigerator he came back into the living room.

"Jesus, I'm glad you stopped in. I get so lonesome, I talk to myself!"

"I saw your wife last night," Petey said, moving her glass idly in her hand so that the ice clinked a little.

"Is that right?" Johnny said, smiling. "Yeah, she was out having herself a night on the town. She's got a girl friend that's secretary in an office downtown, name of Anderson. Glory likes to . . ."

Petey slid forward to the edge of her chair and broke in on what he was saying. "Look, Johnny, I'm no good at bluffing a story, nor I'm not really one of these well-meaning friends you hear about that come and tell a guy something he doesn't want to hear because they claim it's for his own good. So I'd rather put the cards on the table, see? I happened to mention something to Sally, and Sally thought you ought to know about it and she could be right, so I said I'd tell you about it because Sally didn't feel like doing the job."

Johnny took a slow, deliberate drink out of his glass, and his eyes were very bright. "So what is it that you're wantin' to tell me now?" he asked softly.

Petey looked at him hard for a moment before she spoke. "Just this, Johnny. Your wife was at Toresca's last night with a man—alone. By the looks of the way they acted together I'd say that they knew each other pretty well. The reason I think you ought to know about it right away is so that maybe you can do something about it. The guy she was with was a rat, if I ever saw one."

Johnny's face was perfectly blank and he sat very still in his chair. "Is that all that you wanted to say?" he asked with a kind of over-controlled politeness.

"Yes, I guess so," Petey said, smiling a little wryly.

"Then there's a couple things I'd like to say," Johnny replied in the same polite, soft, over-controlled voice. "First, I'd thank you not to go any further with a story like that about my wife. It's exactly the kind of story I'd expect a woman like you to tell after she saw two people just happening to have a drink together someplace. You'd have to make something wrong and dirty out of it, because that's the kind of a woman you are. You'd have to judge her by the kind of a woman that you are yourself, you couldn't help but do that. You wouldn't know anything about how a woman behaves when she's decent and . . ."

Petey stood up suddenly and put her drink down on the table. "Okay! So I knew when I came over here that I was leadin' with my chin for this! Jesus, men like you are funny! You're not thinking about her right now; all you're thinking about is your own goddam pride! You can't stand to think that any woman that had the chance to be married to you would even want to look at another man. It nearly kills you to think that anybody knows that your wife is steppin' out on you. Well, I didn't come over here and go into my little song and dance because I was thinking about you. I don't give a hoot in hell for you nor your pride, either. I come over here because I was thinkin' about her, just a dumb kid that's got herself mixed up with a slick rat that she hasn't got any business gettin' mixed up with . . ."

"I guess we've finished talking about my wife now," Johnny said with his deadly politeness.

Petey's eyebrow doubled against her forehead, giving her face the expression of devilish amusement. "Before you toss me outa here," she said pleasantly, "there's a couple more things I'll say. I get a kick out of hearing you keep calling her your wife. Hell, she's not your wife. You never gave her a chance to be your wife, even if she had it in her to be a wife to any guy. She's just a pretty little gal that you liked to pet and spoil and play with, and that you gotta kick out of walking down the street with because the other guys all whistled. So don't get all hot and bothered now all of a sudden and expect her to act like a wife should. It just might be that she's found another playmate that she likes to play with just as well as she does with you."

Johnny started to speak again, but Petey stopped him. "No, we better skip it, I'm leaving. Don't bother to get up, I'll find the door." Petey adjusted her tiny hat to the correct angle and tucked her big purse under her arm. "Well, so long, Johnny, and no hard feelings. You know, it just might be that down underneath all the rest of this stuff, you really love that kid. But I doubt it. I don't think you know what love is. Why don't you grow up, Johnny?"

Petey went out the door, a last swish of a short full black skirt and a slim silken leg. Johnny was up out of his chair as if tight coiled springs had suddenly released him. He went straight to the kitchen and mixed himself another drink. He came back to the living room, the glass in his hand. He didn't sit down again. He walked the floor restlessly, his face strained and tight. He switched on the radio, and then, after spinning the dial, turned it off again. He picked up magazines only to drop them. All the time he kept watching the clock, and time after time he stood still, his ear cocked toward the door, listening for the steps on the stairs. And once he wiped perspiration from his face with his handkerchief.

After awhile came the sound he was waiting for. The thudding shut of the front door downstairs, light steps on the stairs that were unmistakably Gloria's. Johnny stopped still in front of the radio, and turned around toward the door. There was an expression of something close to fear on his face as he kept looking at that plain wooden door. The footsteps came nearer, and Johnny began to light a cigarette hastily. Then the door opened suddenly, and Gloria came in. "Hi," she said, closing the door behind her. She slid her arms out of the short, black fur jacket. "I got hot comin' up them stairs," she said. "What you doin'?"

"Nothing," Johnny said.

Gloria smoothed her blue crepe dress over her hips and rattled the heavy gold necklace at her neck before she took off her hat. "You look funny just standin' there," she said. "I thought you was doin' something."

Johnny didn't say anything, and Gloria yawned with her mouth wide for a moment. "Gosh, I'm sleepy!" She stood on one foot, weaving a little on her high, run-over heels, and examined the hat in her hand. A blue felt hat with a big bow of ribbon and a lot of veil. Gloria tugged at the ribbon, spreading out the ends of it, and then she began to adjust the veil. She looked at Johnny suddenly and then back at the hat. "Gee, I had more fun last night," she said with something mechanical and dutiful in her voice. "Marjorie and I had dinner'n then we went to the movies, the last show, and then we went home to her house. We had somethin' to eat an' some folks come in and we talked. That's why I got home so late, and . . ."

"You don't have to tell me any more of that stuff, honey," Johnny said. He dropped his cigarette and walked across the room to her and there was no mistaking the fright on Gloria's face.

He took hold of her shoulders tightly, and there was a nervous tremor in his voice. "Glory, baby, there's something I'm gonna say to you and then we're never goin' to talk about it again, ever. Everybody makes mistakes, see, and this never happened before, so maybe you didn't understand how I felt about it. I don't want you to ever have a date with some other guy again. I don't even want you going out someplace to have a drink with another guy."

Gloria started to speak, and he laid his finger gently over her lips.

"No, we aren't gonna talk about it at all," he said. "The first time, why, maybe you didn't understand, but now you know how I feel about it. You aren't to do it again, ever."

Gloria looked at him, her eyes big and still in her face. Johnny took her in his arms and kissed her hard for a minute. When he released her he was smiling a little, and he brushed back the heavy hair from her forehead tenderly. "Well, what are we gonna have for supper?" he said. "You go set down and rest them tired little feet a yours and I'll get it. What do you feel like eatin' for supper, honey?"

Gloria stepped away from him and picked up her coat from the chair. "I don't feel like eatin' nothing," she said slowly. She walked across the floor into the bedroom and shut the door behind her, hard.

# 29

PETEY BECAME A WELL-KNOWN FIGURE IN THE LATE bars, the illegal side-street places that stayed open till the dawn. Several times she started to pack her suitcases, and then slowly unpacked them again. She lost four pounds in weight and realized that she was becoming a little haggard.

There was a night at Toresca's, maybe a week and a half later. Petey was finishing her first songs of the evening. She picked "I Don't Want to Cry Any More" for her last extra and sang it blue, with a sob in her voice, clipping off each line:

*"Each day long about sunset*
*I watch you passin' by my door.*
*It's all I can do*
*Not to run to you*
*But—I don't want to cry any more . . ."*

She finished it, took her bows and walked away from the microphone. She was all in white that night, with the bracelets glittering on her arms. She looked well, except that she looked tired. But when she walked her head was lifted, and she walked with her long strutting stride.

Nicky Toresca came over, smiling, and asked her to join him in a drink. He chose a table toward the back, which, Petey thought idly, meant that he wanted to talk rather than to dance. While they waited for their drinks, Petey glanced up to find him looking at her steadily. His dark face was carefully expressionless, but Petey could tell that for some reason he was feeling very good this night. When he met her eyes he said, "You look fine, Petey." And he straightened one of the bracelets on her arm with a proprietary gesture. Petey answered him with the mocking little half-bow as she lifted her cigarette.

"It's been a long time since I seen you, is that right?" He stuck his hands in his pockets and leaned back in his chair, still watching her. Petey waited, her eyes narrowed against the smoke. He kept looking at her, and the waiter set their drinks down. The orchestra was playing the "St. Louis Blues" and Petey sang a line of it softly . . .

*"Feelin' tomorrow lak ah feel today . . ."*

"Course, you been pretty busy lately," Nicky said. "Or at least you was, up to a few days ago."

Petey picked up her drink and her face was quite unperturbed. "Some day I have to teach that new bartender Joe how to mix a drink for me," she said idly. "He dumps in half the ice wagon."

Then Nicky went on talking easily. "You know, I been thinkin'," he said. "It's too bad we don't see more of each other lately, and there isn't no reason why we shouldn't; now, is that right? I been thinkin', too, maybe what we both need is a little vacation . . ."

"So?" Petey said casually.

"So I have to go to Chicago on some business," he said. "I thought maybe you'd like to come along. We could maybe combine business with pleasure, is that right?"

Petey laughed a little, softly. "That's right," she said. "My contract did run out last week, didn't it?"

He answered her in a hurt voice, with delight and mockery just behind it. "Petey, I'm surprised at you! Talk like that between old friends like we are!"

"So you think I need a vacation, huh?"

He leaned closer to her across the table. "That's right. I been worried about you, Petey."

"That's very nice of you, Mr. Toresca," Petey mocked. "You take such an interest in your employees. Is it my health you're worried about?"

"Well—yes," he said.

Petey's eyebrow bent up against her forehead.

"Yeah, Petey. I never did figure it was healthy to live like you do now. Everytime you get up there to sing I worry that maybe you'll bust out crying and start singin' the 'Empty Bed Blues.'"

Petey set her glass down on the table too hard, and she looked away from him to the dancers on the floor.

"So I can't sell you a trip to Chicago," the Nicky said sadly. "The Braun sisters are certainly hard to get. Well, too bad. Maybe some other time, is that right?"

Petey picked up her drink again without looking at him.

"You know," he said suddenly, "I really think you gotta yen for the big dummy. That's too bad, Petey."

For the second time, Petey put her glass down too hard, and she picked up her purse from the table and shoved her chair back. "It's been nice having a drink with you," she said. "I might see you around again sometime."

The Nicky caught hold of her wrist as she got up and pulled her down to her chair again. "Wait a minute, Petey," he said caressingly. "You don't wanta rush away like this. There was something I was gonna tell you that I bet you'd like to hear about."

"It don't seem likely, does it?" Petey said.

Nicky leaned back in his chair again, smiling. "Oh, you never can tell. I know a lot of interesting things."

Petey looked at him suddenly with speculative narrow eyes. "So?" she said softly, waiting again.

"Yes," the Nicky said musingly. "I know a lotta interesting things. It's funny the things you get to know about in a business like this. Seems like you get to know all there is about everybody all the time."

"Yeah," Petey said abruptly. "So why don't you get on with it? You didn't keep me here to tell me all this stuff. I ain't got all night."

"That's right, Petey," he said. "But I bet you would like to hear where your big dummy is right tonight!"

This time it was something Petey couldn't hide or control. She went stiff in her chair.

Just then the dance floor emptied. The orchestra leader looked out over his shoulder and gave the sign for the introductory cue to Petey's next group of songs.

"Go on and sing, Petey," Nicky said softly. "I'll wait right here for you."

Petey hesitated only a moment, and then she got up from her

chair and walked up to the front of the room. She got through her songs all right, but she didn't sing any extras. She left the microphone and walked back to the table, her vital flamboyant self.

The Nicky waited and the fresh drink was there on the table for her. He kicked back her chair with his foot, his slim body sprawled back in his chair, his hands deep and still in his pockets.

Petey sat down, her white dress shimmering in the dim light.

"You know, you sing nice, Petey," Nicky said. "I been thinkin' that . . ."

"Now, look," she said. "You had your fun. Either you know something or you don't, either you're gonna tell me or you ain't. Make up your mind!"

"Okay," he said readily. "You want to know something bad, so I'll tell you. Your big dummy is over at Kalamazoo Johnson's. He's been stayin' over there two weeks."

Petey's face was alert. "Kalamazoo Johnson's?"

"I guess you wouldn't know about Kalamazoo's," Nicky said. "You ain't been around town long enough. It's on Water Street."

Petey had been around town long enough to know what the Water Street section meant.

"As a matter of fact," Nicky said, "Kalamazoo's place is way out Water Street."

His voice was meaningful, but whatever significance he intended was beyond Petey's knowledge. She had taken a cab ride once through that section; she even remembered "way out Water Street" just at the city limits. She had seen a row of drab, tumble-down frame shacks fronting on the dirt road and the railroad tracks, and nothing more. She even remembered the curious deserted appearance out there by daylight, as bleak a landscape as she had ever seen. But the Nicky was driving at something, and what it was precisely Petey could not fathom.

Nicky was looking at her. He caught the puzzled look on her face and he went on talking. "Kalamazoo's quite a girl," he said. "Maybe I'd worry, if I was you. There's a lot a folks that might think Kalamazoo was a whole lot better-lookin' than you are."

The Nicky was smiling and down in the very depths of Petey's thinking something fell into place.

"A course, Kalamazoo's no fancy high-yellow gal, but . . ."

Even before he said it, Petey remembered "way out Water Street" as the most down-at-heel part of a down-at-heel Negro section.

"There ain't no explainin' some guys' tastes. Me, I can't understand that." Nicky closed his hand over Petey's. "Jesus, Petey, knowin' the way you feel about the dummy, I hated ta have to tell you this— and it ain't the first time he's hung around Kalamazoo's . . ."

Petey pulled her hand out from under his and turned her face toward him slowly. "Christ, you're a slimy little rat," she said, without animosity.

"Petey, you're all upset," he said solicitously. "I understand how you must feel. But if you think I'm lying about him being out at Kalamazoo's, why . . ."

"No, I know you're not lyin'," Petey said. "That wasn't what I meant."

She got up from her chair and walked away from the table before he had a chance to say another word. She went toward the powder room, moving leisurely, waving her hand in answer to greetings and invitations from various tables. She found the powder room crowded with chattering women and strong with the smell of perfume and cosmetics. She went out to the combination toilet and dressing room reserved for the employees. The room was bare and cold and empty, except for one of the bleached-blonde chorus girls. Petey searched her lipstick out of her bag and made up her lips in front of the big mirror. The air was cold against her bare shoulders and she shivered.

"Christ, you'd think they'd get some heat in here!"

"Yeah," the girl said. She was in costume for their next number and she stood shivering, her coat wrapped around her shoulders. She wore only the briefest blue satin shorts and a scant brassiere; her rather thick body and legs were mottled and purplish with cold.

She sniffled a little, and Petey turned to look at her curiously. The girl's face was miserable under the heavy make-up in startling contrast to the stiff light hair, and the mascara at her eyes was becoming a little blurred with tears, although she dabbed at them carefully with a piece of paper towel.

"What's the matter, kid?" Petey asked.

"Aw, I dunno," the girl said with a little gulp, her voice dull and spiritless.

"You're due on right now," Petey said gently. "You better get out there, honey. The other girls will be lookin' for you."

She shook her bright metallic head. "They're both in there," she gestured toward the row of cubicles. "They're sick," she added.

The sounds of their sickness were obvious enough through the little bare room.

"They both sick? What's the matter with 'em?" Petey asked.

The girl dabbed at her eyes again and threw the little mascara-blackened piece of paper towel away. "June's been drinkin' too much. I guess Doris just don't feel good."

There was a knock on the outside of the door just then and a voice called, "Hey, you girls, you're on!"

Petey's face was concerned. "Jesus, the orchestra's playin' your entrance!"

The girl dropped her coat on the top of the tall waste can and grabbed a couple of paper towels out of the metal container. She pounded with her fist on one of the cubicle doors, and her voice was shrill and desperate. "Come on! We gotta go on now!"

Both doors flew open at the same time to emit two more girls with bleached-blonde hair, coats pulled around their bare shoulders. One of them was sobbing out loud. The first girl dabbed frenziedly at the damaged make-up on their sticky faces with her towels, and Petey plucked the coats from around them and pushed the door open. They ran out into the entranceway, all three of them, and Petey watched from the open door. They fell into line just in front of the other door, heads up, the bright alluring smiles on their faces, their feet moving together in the concerted shuffle of their entrance step. They danced out through the door onto the dance floor.

Petey sat down at the mirror and picked up her lipstick. She added a touch more color to her full underlip, and suddenly the tears came up in her own dark eyes. Her shoulders slumped suddenly, and Petey pressed her forehead hard against her doubled fist. "Aw, Christ! Christ!" she whispered.

That night was a long one for Petey. At last she was through and she took a cab to a little beer place where she had gone once with San. It was at the other end of town among the factories, a maze of narrow, dark, unpaved streets. The cab stopped at last in front of the little building with one lighted plate-glass window fronting on the long brick side of a factory building across the street. The small room was all but deserted, the graveyard shift had gone on across the street long ago, and only a few stragglers from the second shift lingered over their drinks before they went home. A little bare room, a few booths, a couple of tables, a pinball machine, a juke-box, a little bar at the back with a scant row of bottles and a decoration of flashy metal beer signs around the speckled mirror.

Petey took the table against the window at the front and ordered a beer. This place seemed good to her. After no more than one curious glance at her long dress the men ignored her. The room was very warm; the corny juke-box music somehow soothed her. Across the street was the dark bulk of the factory building, strings of windows emitting their peculiar blue-green light, and the sound of machinery pounding at the ears, loud and continual. Across the windows at the far end, some huge machine threw a great leaping shadow, a fan maybe, or a big piston. Petey watched it for a long time, a gigantic twisting leaping shadow flung across the windows time after time.

A nasal hillbilly vocal came out of the juke-box:

*"If you wanta make me believe in you*
*You gotta quit cheatin' on me.*
*Now I come home at five o'clock*
*To greet my honey lamb,*
*I come in the front and hear the back door slam.*
*Oh, if you wanta make me believe in you*
*You gotta quit cheatin' on me . . ."*

Petey sat there for a long time and then she ordered a cab from the pay telephone on the wall. She went home then. She climbed the flights of stairs and opened her door to the quiet empty darkness. She turned lights on all over the apartment and found a recorded program of music on her little radio. She changed into a full-skirted satin housecoat and went to sit in the big chair in her living room in front of the window. She just sat there, lighting a cigarette from time to time. As daylight came she slept.

She awakened before noon, stiff and cramped in the chair. She was tired, weary to the bone, and her eyes were enormous with shadows. She got up and turned out lights, and shut off the droning of a soap-opera on the radio. She took a shower and dressed for the street, in the gay, full-skirted, red wool dress and the ridiculous hat that was nothing more than several big red felt flowers and a great deal of black fishnet veiling.

After she had eaten breakfast she walked slowly back toward her apartment again, stopping at the drug store on the corner to buy cigarettes and papers. She climbed the flights of stairs once more, and once more fumbled for her key. Inside, she lay down the papers, and wandered from room to room, without taking off her hat or furs. She came back to the living room and stood still in the middle of the floor, her face expressionless and marred by fatigue. She lighted a cigarette and put it out after the first drag on it, with a little wry face. She went into the bedroom then and came back with her black cigarette holder. She rammed several pipecleaners through it, fitted a cigarette in the end and struck the match. She stood still and lifted her heavy hair back on her shoulders. Suddenly with a great burst of vitality she scrabbled cigarettes, matches and door key into her big black bag and went out again, slamming the door behind her. She went down the stairs fast and out onto the street. She walked to the corner rapidly with her long stride, her skirt swinging, the long end of her veil billowing behind her. She waved down a cab just as she got to the corner. The driver pulled up to the curb and swung the door open for her. As Petey stooped to get in, she said, "Look, Joe, do yuh know where Kalamazoo Johnson's place is? It's somewhere way out Water Street."

"Yeah, I know where Kalamazoo's place is," he said with a faint surprise in his voice. "You wanta go out there, lady?"

"Yeah," Petey said as she slammed the door, "and step on it, will yuh?"

"Yes, ma'am," the driver said obediently, but with a trace of doubt in his voice.

The driver turned the cab off Main Street and, after fourteen or fifteen blocks on side streets, he turned into the labyrinth of unpaved streets hemmed in by squalid houses that made up the Water Street section, and was transected by Water Street itself. He had to slow down speed here, but before long he turned onto Water Street and headed out of town.

He cut speed still more, and Petey caught a glimpse of his puzzled, embarrassed face in the rear-vision mirror at the top of the windshield. He licked his lips and opened his mouth three or four times before he actually spoke to her. "Look, lady," he said with embarrassed hesitancy, "it ain't none a my business, but are you sure you ain't made a mistake? This Kalamazoo's place ain't no place for a lady like you to be goin'. Honest, lady—you sure you ain't . . . ?"

"Yeah, I'm sure," Petey said. "Take it easy, Joe."

With that reassurance his embarrassment vanished, leaving him merely puzzled. The road was narrow here, gullied out in little perpendicular ruts, washboard fashion, and it ran parallel with the railroad tracks on the right-hand side. The roadbed was built up here, high above the street level, and the steep embankment made a sort of wall. Some of the white crushed stone had washed out from the ends of the ties and lay scattered along the edge of the road itself. To the left the land was flat, and she saw a scattering of sagging, tumbledown houses, miserable places with little sign of life around them.

At last the driver slammed on his brakes, and Petey caught a glimpse of a big, sprawling frame house, paintless, sagging. There was no porch or entrance of any sort, merely a door set flush on a level with the soggy, soot-covered dirt that answered for a front yard. She only got a glimpse of the place, however, for at that moment a train thundered by on the tracks above them and the drift of white smoke scooped down the embankment, as if it were pressed down by the dull, overcast gray sky, and billowed thick around the cab.

The cab driver said something, but Petey couldn't hear it. She glanced at the meter and opened her purse while the white smoke swirled around the windows. It was gone in an instant, moving rapidly toward the left, traveling a few feet above the ground with an incredible speed and with a strange, silent appearance of purposeful being. When the train was gone the driver said, "There, that's Kalamazoo's joint," indicating with his hand just as the outline of the building emerged from the smoke.

There was no sign of any life about the house. The door and all the windows were closed and no glimpse of motion or of a living creature could be seen anywhere.

Petey pulled the handle of the taxi door and let it swing open. "Wait for me," she said tersely to the driver.

Petey got out of the cab. The driver shut off the motor, and there was no sound any place but the faint rumble of the train that had disappeared down the tracks. Skirting mud puddles, sinking into the soggy dirt with every step, she approached the place. A raw cold wind was blowing that made Petey duck her face down into her furs, and it caught at the yards of coarse veiling on her hat and lifted it behind her, a black web silhouetted against a gray sky.

At the door Petey didn't even hesitate. She took hold of the nicked, white crockery knob and turned it, half experimentally. It turned and she walked in. The room was dimly lighted, so she got the smell of it first—stale air, pungent with cooking smells, smoke, cheap cloying perfume and other things Petey couldn't identify. Soon she could make out the outlines of the large room. The floor was bare, the walls of scarred unpainted plaster were broken by big windows with tattered green shades pulled to the sills. To the right, there was a battered old piano with a stool in front of it and some other chairs around it. To the left was a big juke-box, silent and dark. Petey made out a lot of little tables and chairs at the far end, and an immense kitchen range cluttered with kettles, the rusty stovepipe rising above it length after length. On one side of the stove there were four or five shallow, sagging steps up to a door that stood half open. Right in front of Petey, in the middle of the bare floor, a slender Negro boy with a broom gaped at her, open-mouthed.

Petey shut the door behind her and advanced a couple of steps, slowly. "Hi," she said.

The boy didn't answer; he gripped the broom until his bony

knuckles stood out against the bright-yellow handle, and only his eyes moved, the whites of them flickering. There was not a sound in the room other than the roaring and crackling of the fire in the stove. Suddenly the boy broke and ran, his broom clattering as he dropped it, and then his old tennis shoes slapping against the floor. He made the short flight of steps at the far end of the room in two leaps and disappeared through the door.

Petey looked after him and then, in the silence that followed his departure, she walked farther into the room. A board squeaked under her foot and that sharp sound seemed fairly to echo through the house. Petey stopped still again. She fitted a cigarette into her holder, her hands a trifle clumsy in the long black gloves she wore, and then she lighted it.

"What you-all want around here?"

Petey jumped at the sound of the heavy hostile voice, and fanned her match out abruptly. A big Negro man stood in the doorway, so big he all but filled it. He wore a light-tan suit and tan shoes. His face under a brown felt hat was unfriendly. He didn't move down the steps.

"Hi," Petey said. "I . . ."

But she didn't get the chance to finish what she started to say. There was a sudden flurry of high heels behind the man, and he looked over his shoulder into the room behind him. "Look out the way, Jode!" a husky fluting woman's voice said impatiently. She was a tall woman. She elbowed past him, and came down the steps and across the room to Petey with a long quick stride. Maybe three feet away from Petey she stopped still abruptly, teetering on her heels, but perfectly graceful and balanced. She looked at Petey from head to foot, leisurely, intently and unashamedly.

And Petey looked back at her with an equal curiosity. She was fully as tall as Petey herself and only a shade heavier, her figure well-proportioned, long-legged and sinuous. Her blue-black hair was straightened into a shining sleek cap on her well-shaped head. Her skin was very black, her features strong and regular. She wore a short black crepe dress, with a deep insertion of black lace in the front with some silver metallic threads running through it. Her legs were bare, and she wore bright-red sandals trimmed in gold, with tall, gold-colored heels.

"I'm Kalamazoo Johnson," she said abruptly to Petey. "You got business?"

"My name is Petey Braun," Petey said. "I'm lookin' for a guy. I heard he was out here."

The room was very quiet then, except for the roaring and popping of the fire.

Kalamazoo spun on her heel suddenly. "You, Jode!" she snapped in her deep husky voice to the man in the doorway. "Get to hell outa here. Don't stand around gawpin'!"

The man grunted disapprovingly, but he moved back through the doorway ponderously and slammed the door hard behind him.

There was an alert wariness on Petey's face when Kalamazoo turned back to her.

"You're lookin' for San, ain't you?" Kalamazoo said gently. "You're his woman."

Petey took a quick deep breath. "Yeah," she said simply. "Is he here?"

Kalamazoo nodded and smiled, showing strong white teeth. "He's upstairs sleepin', dead to the world!"

They looked at each other for a long moment. It was Kalamazoo who broke it. With a little motion of her hand and a real friendliness in her voice she said, "Come set, huh?"

"Thanks," Petey said slowly.

Kalamazoo led the way to one of the tables close to the stove and she shoved out a chair for Petey, brushing the seat of it quickly with her hand.

Petey sat down, and Kalamazoo hesitated by the corner of the table. "Would you—I mean—maybe you'd just as soon—" Kalamazoo was stumbling over words in sudden self-consciousness. She stopped altogether and threw back her head and laughed, warm rich laughter there in the dim hot room. When she was done laughing, she said simply, "Would you like to have a drink?"

For the first time, Petey smiled. "I'd love to."

"I keep liquor out back. I'll fetch it." Kalamazoo went up the steps in her quick stride and flung the door open with a bang. In a minute she was back again with a little round tin tray with a bottle and glasses and a pitcher part full of water. She put the tray in the middle of the table and pulled the cork out of the whisky bottle.

"Help yourself," she said, as she pulled out the chair across the table and sat down.

"Thanks." Petey poured a little whisky in the bottom of one of the glasses and handed the bottle to Kalamazoo before she picked up the water pitcher.

Kalamazoo poured her drink. "That San!" she said. "He sure do like his liquor, don't he?"

Petey leaned back in her chair and loosened her furs a little in the heat from the stove. Some of the wariness crept back into her face again.

Kalamazoo glanced at her quickly and down to the glass in her own hands. "You come out here aimin' to fetch San?"

Petey was silent for a long moment and then she said honestly, "I don't know. I . . ."

There was a look of understanding on Kalamazoo's face. When she spoke again her voice was warm. "You suit yourself, you know best, but he ain't doin' no harm here." Kalamazoo hunted a package of cigarettes out of her pocket and Petey struck a match for her. She nodded her thanks. She took a deep drag on the cigarette and she looked at Petey levelly. "Sure funny about San comin' out here like he does. He jus' wanta set at a table and drink his liquor all by himself and listen to the music and watch the people like, kinda soakin' it all in like he do. When it's mornin' somebody help him up to bed. He never makes no trouble about it. Come night he do the same thing all over again. Maybe he stay three days like that, maybe a week, once he stayed three weeks. He don't make no trouble here. He jus' set down here and drink his liquor and then go upstairs to sleep there."

Petey took a long drink out of her glass and set it down on the table again.

Kalamazoo stole another quick look at Petey's face. "I been tellin' you all this," she said simply, "because I figure you think somethin' funny, San comin' here like he do."

Petey's face was expressionless as she lifted her cigarette holder to her lips, and then suddenly she smiled at Kalamazoo again. "It's all right," Petey said. "Maybe I did think something was funny. But I didn't know nothing about the place, I didn't know . . . But it's all right now."

Kalamazoo smiled too. "That's good," she said. "I jus' didn't want you to think nothin'." She shrugged her shoulders. "Why San come here? I dunno. I guess he jus' come down here when he get to feelin' bad a certain way."

Kalamazoo paused and pushed the bottle toward Petey.

"Course," she went on slowly, "it get pretty lively around here at night. A lotta music, a lotta dancin', a lotta drinkin', 'n lovin' an' fightin'—seem like he jus' like to be here soakin' it all in, times when he git to feelin' bad."

Petey nodded her head slowly. "Yeah. I think maybe you're right. I think maybe I'm beginnin' to get it a little. There's a lotta living goin' on here. It's somethin' he could feel'n . . ." Petey nodded her head again. "Yeah, it's beginnin' to make a little sense. You been nice about it."

Kalamazoo answered her with her ready smile. "That's good. I like San. He's a funny guy, but he don't make no trouble down here. An' now I seen you, I like you too, an' I don't want you thinkin' anything is like it ain't. I take you upstairs where he is, if you want."

She darted another of her swift glances at Petey, and poured herself another drink. "I tell you," she said delicately, "I dunno nothin' about it, whether you and him had trouble or what. Me, I don't tell you what to do or not. If I was you, I wouldn't try to fetch him. When he get done here, he leave again. I figure when he get done here he come right straight where you are. He couldn't help it."

"It's nice a you to say that," Petey said. "About today, I guess you're right, I shouldn't try to fetch him. I—well—I guess I just wanted to know if he was all right, and—and what he was doin', and if I couldn't talk to him and if I couldn't . . . But now I come down here, I feel different. He'll be all right here. And when he's ready to leave he'll leave. And when he does leave—well—then I hope you're right. I hope he comes home to me."

"He come all right!" Kalamazoo said with her wide smile. "He couldn't help but come. You wait'n see."

Petey emptied the last of her drink and pulled her furs closer around her shoulders. "Well, I gotta scram now," she said. "Thanks a lot. You been pretty swell about it."

Kalamazoo stood up too, with an easy sinuous motion.

"Aw, that's all right! Look, I take you upstairs an' see him if you want?"

Petey was silent a moment and her face looked a little pinched and tired suddenly, as she pulled on her long gloves. "No," she said at last. "Thanks a lot, but—but I guess I'd rather not."

The quick sympathy flickered over Kalamazoo's face again.

They walked slowly toward the door together. "He's a lucky guy," Kalamazoo said. "You're a swell woman. What you do? You in show business, maybe?"

"I sing," Petey said. "I got a job singin' in Toresca's place here in town."

"Good," Kalamazoo said. "I heard about that place. They say it's a swell place, all right. Look, how you gettin' back to town? You gotta cab waitin'? I gotta telephone, I could . . ."

"Naw, thanks," Petey said. "My cab's waitin' out here."

Kalamazoo pulled open the door for her, and Petey stepped over the threshold out into the raw cold air. She turned around then, and held out her hand to Kalamazoo silently. Kalamazoo took it and they shook hands, looking at each other, and the smiles on both their faces were curiously alike.

"I don't know about San," Petey said softly, "but that man Jode a yours is a pretty damn lucky guy."

Kalamazoo laughed her warm husky laughter.

"G'bye," she said. "An' don't you worry no more. No harm ain't comin' to your man here, an' he be comin' back to you right soon, you wait'n see!"

"Good-bye," Petey said. "And thanks for everything."

"Don't you worry no more!"

Kalamazoo stood quietly in the doorway as Petey picked her way back across the yard. Her waiting taxi driver dropped his newspaper to start the motor and wheeled the cab around in the road, heading it back toward town. He opened the door and Petey got in. As the cab pulled away, Petey looked back out of the window. Kalamazoo Johnson was still standing in the doorway. She smiled and waved her hand high above her head, and Petey waved back to her.

The look of curiosity on the taxi driver's face deepened. He stepped on the gas a little, the cab skidding along over the rutted road. He cleared his throat loudly. "Well, this war business sure looks bad, don't it?" he said. "I was just reading there today. Sure looks like this country is gonna be in the war by spring, all right."

# 30

SEVERAL DAYS AFTER HER CALL AT KALAMAZOO Johnson's, Petey telephoned Virginia that the doctor had requested that she come in for a physical examination, and that she had made the appointment for her early that afternoon. Virginia agreed somewhat unwillingly and promised to meet Petey for a cup of coffee when the examination was over. The checkup was entirely Petey's idea, though she had not thought it wise to tell Virginia so.

Late that afternoon, Virginia met Petey at a drug store. "Hi," Petey said cheerfully as Virginia slid into the booth across from her. "Now that wasn't so bad, was it? Aren't you glad it's all over now?"

"Yeah," Virginia said. She shivered, her hands deep in the pockets of her shabby tan coat.

"You better take that coat off, it's all wet," Petey said. "Your feet aren't wet, are they? We don't want you catching cold again. How about some hot coffee? They make good coffee around here."

"All right," Virginia said as she struggled out of her coat. Petey signaled the waitress.

"Well, what did the doctor say, honey? Is everything all right?" Virginia nodded. "Uh huh."

"Did he give you the works? I mean, internal examination and everything?"

Virginia nodded again. "I'd never had an examination like that. I guess that's why I was scared about going."

Petey took hold of her hand and squeezed it tight. "Sure you were scared! But aren't you glad it's over now? And don't it make you feel better to know that everything's all right?"

Virginia sighed a little. "Sure."

The waitress brought her coffee, and Petey watched her keenly as she bent her pale serious face over the cup.

"How's everything out on Horton Street?" Petey asked as she lighted a cigarette.

"Oh, fine," Virginia said.

After a thorough canvass of family matters Petey switched to a new topic.

"And how is old Giddy? Is she still playin' bingo as much as ever?"

Virginia smiled a little faintly, for the first time. "Yeah, I guess so. Right now she's all excited about a new fortune-teller she found that she thinks is really good. Some kind of a spiritualist minister, or something like that. She's real excited about her."

Petey laughed her soft husky laughter. "Jesus, everybody in this town seems like is chasing to some fortune-teller someplace. Does Sally ever go?"

Virginia nodded. "Sometimes. She's been talking to Mrs. Gideon about this spiritualist woman, and now she says she is going to save up her money and go to her the first chance she gets."

"Well, I'll be damned," Petey said in half-amused incredulity. "What's the name of this woman?"

"A Mrs. Thorpe on Bacon Street," Virginia said. "She gives her readings right in her own home, I guess. She's a licensed fortune-teller, and everything."

"Did you ever go and have a reading?"

Virginia shook her head.

"You're a skeptic like me, huh?"

"Oh, I don't know," Virginia said. "I don't know whether I

believe in that stuff or not. But I wouldn't care anything about going. I guess I wouldn't want to know about my future." She looked into her coffee cup, and her dark silky hair fell over her cheeks.

Petey looked at her, and her face was thoughtful as she took a drag from her cigarette.

"Things have been lookin' pretty tough to you for quite awhile now, haven't they, Ginny?"

Virginia shrugged her shoulders a little without looking up.

"You can't fool me, honey," Petey said gently. "I could come right back at you and say 'buck up, everybody's got trouble,' but it's more than that. It's just something that's sort a part a bein' young, honey. It's feelin' like you don't belong no place in the world, and all the years stretchin' out in front a you, and you keep wondering how you're gonna live 'em all, and what you're gonna be doin' to make a living for yourself, and what you're gonna be doin' to make a life for yourself. I know. It ain't any joke."

Virginia kept looking into her coffee cup. "No, it isn't any joke," she said softly, with a little tremble in her voice.

"And the funny part about it, it don't do a hell of a lot a good to worry," Petey said. "You just keep muddlin' along the best you can, and it kinda solves itself and the first thing you know years go by, and all of a sudden you kind of wake up and say to yourself, 'Jesus, this is it, this is what my life is, this is my place, this is how I make my living!'"

Virginia looked up at her suddenly, took a drink of her coffee and her eyes followed the cup down to the saucer again.

"Some a these days, when you're feelin' better, you'll get a break and get a job someplace, and that'll help a lot, you wait and see. And something else, honey. The way I say it, it won't make good sense maybe, but you just try it and see! Don't get all bottled up inside a you, honey. When you got trouble and you feel bad, come out where people are. They got trouble too, and, if you listen awhile, first thing you know you don't notice your own trouble so bad, you learn how to get along with it, or you learn how to solve it, maybe. It's only when you get all bottled up inside a yourself that things get so bad for you that you can't stand 'em any more."

Virginia was tracing little patterns on the table with her finger-nail. "I guess I know what you mean," she said softly. "You and Sally both been swell. You never said a word to me about—about—you know. I—I—know that was wrong now. I'd never do nothing like that again, no matter how bad it was. I—I wouldn't a wanted to have died."

Petey looked at her again keenly, and said cautiously, "Well, I wasn't talkin' about that in particular, honey, but I'm glad you told me that. I'm glad you feel that way about it."

Virginia went on talking with a little effort, but as if it was very good for her to talk. "It was awful silly for me to do something like that. Because, well, because what I thought, wasn't even going to happen. And I wouldn't have wanted to have died. I caused every-body a lot of expense and worry and everything. I—I was just so scared and I felt so awful about—about everything—and . . ."

"Aw, Ginny, of course you did," Petey said. "It was pretty tough going. I'm not gonna say, it's over, so forget about it. Because you can't forget about it, but don't think about it too much. Don't let it spoil things for you. There ain't any reason for you just setting around home and feeling bad about it now. When Jimmy calls you up, why don't you go ahead and have a date with him the way you used to, or when . . ."

"I know," Virginia said softly. "I suppose Jimmy and everybody thinks it's funny, the way I act. But it's just that—that—I don't feel the same any more. Things seem all different now, as if I've changed, as if . . ."

Petey lighted another cigarette and fanned the match out. "Sure, I know how you feel, Ginny. It's only natural for you to feel like you've changed. Well, you have, but, honey, things happen to us every day, all kinds a things, and we change and sometimes we know it and sometimes we don't. This ain't no different or any more important than any one of a couple a hundred other things that could have happened to you."

Virginia looked up at her again briefly, her eyes wide and ques-tioning. "No, I suppose it isn't. It's just that it made me feel so—so . . ."

"Aw, honey, I know! But you shouldn't feel that way. It ain't nothing for you ever to feel ashamed of, or anything like that. It was tough, sure, but so are a lot of things. It was just one of those things that happen sometimes.

"There's another thing, honey . . ." Petey took a deep, quick breath. "I don't know just how to say this to you, so that you'll understand. What happened there in my apartment that afternoon, well, it was awful for you. It wasn't—pleasant. But, darling, just try to remember that what happened then doesn't really have anything to do with the way it is when two people that love each other are together and it's right. What happened that afternoon—well . . ." Petey's face was tense and strained. "You won't understand what I say, but you gotta remember it. It wasn't the way it should have been, see? It wasn't really . . ."

Virginia was flushing all over her face and Petey was floundering for words. She took hold of Virginia's hand and held it tight. "I know. I'm doin' a lotta talking you don't understand. Just remember one thing. Some day you will meet someone you really love and—and things will be different. You mustn't be scared or dread it, and then you'll find out that it isn't anything like what happened that afternoon, honest."

Petey stopped talking then, and Virginia traced invisible patterns on the table that never seemed to end.

After quite awhile, Virginia said, "I wanted to tell you. I—I—wanted to come and clean your apartment again for you, but—I know it's silly—but it seemed like I never wanted to see that place again. I know that's silly, well, because I know that he'd never be there any more . . ."

Petey's face was completely expressionless. "I tell yuh, honey. Let's let that ride for a few weeks, huh? I don't want you workin' too hard till you feel real good again, and you got enough to do around Sally's. Let's let it wait a few weeks and then maybe you'll feel different about it, and we'll talk about it then. Is that all right?"

"Sure." There was a little smile across Virginia's sober face. "Gosh, I guess I better get home now. I sort of like to get things straightened up before Sally comes home."

Petey twisted around to see the clock. "Oh, Christ, yes, it's get-tin' late. Well, look, Ginny, I'll see you again. Don't work too hard, will you?"

They walked out to the street together. The rain was coming down hard, blanking out even the store fronts just across the street. "We better get a cab," Petey said. "You can drop me off and go on home."

Petey hailed a cruising taxi and, at her place, she paid the driver the fare out to Horton Street. The car went on then, splashing through the rain.

# 31

PETEY AWAKENED THE NEXT MORNING IN A VILE temper, which progressed with the day. She made a scene at rehearsal, which amused Nicky Toresca immensely. When rehearsals were over she refused his dinner invitation and strode off grimly to the telephone booth. She called the spiritualist fortune-teller whom Virginia had mentioned the day before, scowling ferociously into the telephone.

Did she want a reading with cards, tea leaves, handwriting or palm? Well, what the hell did she care, Petey said dangerously. Dust off the crystal ball for all she cared, she'd be there at seven o'clock.

She caught a cab in front of the restaurant. The address on Bacon Street was of great interest to her driver. He sure hauled a sight a people out there to Mrs. Thorpe's, he confided in Petey. Did she consult Mrs. Thorpe regularly?

Between her rage and her humiliation Petey answered him with a dangerous meekness, to the effect that this was her first visit to the Reverend Clara Thorpe.

Well, the reason he asked, he explained, a lotta people went to her every week. He hauled a couple old ladies from the other end of town out here Monday night every week as regular as clockwork.

Petey had a sudden vision of the Reverend Thorpe's clientele as consisting of vast numbers of doddering senile old women with quavering voices and high-topped shoes, and now herself among them. Was he one of Mrs. Thorpe's regular customers? Petey asked.

Nope, he answered her cheerfully, he himself went to a little guy name of Gus out on Morch Street that he figured was the best there was. His grandmother was a Gypsy and Gus was the seventh son of a seventh son. Gus didn't have a license to practice on account of he never got the money to go to that regular fortune-telling school in Detroit. Without a license he never dared charge more than a quarter or fifty cents for a reading. Gus sure was good, though. He combined your stars with palmistry, and he couldn't be beat. For a slight extra charge Gus also gave you advice on what numbers to play. He personally had never won following Gus's advice, but he knew a woman that had. If Petey would like to go out and see Gus for a reading sometime, he would be glad to fix it up for her, he volunteered. Gus, for his money, couldn't be beat.

No, thanks, Petey said. Her head was whirling. She felt as if she had suddenly acquired the knowledge that all the local citizenry that she had hitherto thought of as being relatively sane were actually stark, raving mad, and that her own sanity was toppling in a crazy world.

About Gus, her driver said cautiously, he hoped she would be careful about whom she talked to about Gus. Gus had a pretty tough time of it, practicing without a license the way he did. All the licensed fortune-tellers in town stuck tight together, a closed corporation, and they sure raised hell with anybody they found out was doin' readings without a license. Why, just the other day a woman was arrested for that. He sure hoped she'd be careful who she mentioned Gus to.

She sure would, Petey said.

Oh, he knew he could trust her, all right, her driver hastened to assure her, but he just thought he oughta tell her how it was. He sure would hate for Gus to get into any trouble on account a him.

Petey was seething. How the hell much farther to Bacon Street, she wanted to know.

Finally he stopped his cab before one of a row of neat, rambling frame houses along the sedate dark street. Petey glanced at it suspiciously as she paid off her driver. He wished her luck with her reading and drove off down the street.

Petey climbed the porch steps. There was a little name tag over the doorbell announcing the occupant's name and profession. This was the right place, all right. Petey rang the bell with a definite pressure of her gloved finger on the button. There was no response, and, after a moment, Petey rang the bell again. The door opened suddenly to reveal a mountainous fat woman in a neat print dress.

"Come in, please," she said in a pleasant, low-pitched voice.

Petey walked into the hallway without a word. The woman wiped her nose carefully on a piece of tissue and gestured toward a door on the right. "I'm just finishing a reading," she said. "If you'll wait in there."

Petey murmured something and opened the door indicated to her. She stepped into the room and closed the door again. A floor lamp gave a soft light in the room. There were several chairs and racks of magazines. Petey chose a huge, raspberry-colored, overstuffed chair under the floor lamp and gazed around the room in amazement. It was not a small room, and it was cluttered with a great amount of furniture and bric-a-brac of all kinds. Apparently fortune-telling was a lucrative profession. The rug on the floor was soft and thick, but the pattern unfortunately consisted of the largest and gaudiest flowers Petey had ever seen on a rug before. The tall windows were curtained in sheer lacy material and maroon brocaded satin drapes hung stiffly to the very floor. The furniture consisted of an overstuffed set in the raspberry-colored mohair, but such an overstuffed set as Petey had never dreamed of. Each piece was huge and distorted weirdly with ornate padding. In addition, the room contained full dining-room equipment, each piece carved and ornate, two colors of wood polished like glass. And the walls were solid with pictures, and over the top of everything were doilies, dishes, vases, lamps, figures, ash trays in wild profusion. And good things, too;

Petey's eyes lingered admiringly on a silver coffee service on top of a flat buffet, hemmed in by vases, candelabra, trays, bowls, lamps and an ornate samovar.

The room was warm and very still. There was not a sound from any place in the house. Petey got to her feet restlessly. The room was suffocating to her. She could look in no direction without seeing a piece of bric-a-brac that she had failed to notice before, and it gave her the odd sensation that more and more objects were filtering into the room even as she sat there, crowding in about her silently and imperceptibly.

Jesus, Petey thought with disgust, it's bad enough to lose my grip like this and come sneaking down here to have my fortune told like a regular loony without me going all to pieces and gettin' the shakes waiting around here.

She lighted a cigarette and walked about the room in such narrow space between articles of furniture as was afforded her. The stillness was uncanny, not even a noise of traffic from the street, and the warm, incredibly cluttered room, and the thick rug under her feet that absorbed the sound of her footsteps and felt altogether too soft and cushiony.

I'll give that dame five minutes, Petey thought grimly, and then I'm gettin' to hell outa here if she don't show up.

Just at the moment when Petey was trying to decide whether the Reverend Clara Thorpe had been kidnapped to another world by her own spirits, or murdered by a client whom she had been attempting to blackmail, the door behind her opened suddenly. Petey jumped perceptibly and turned around to face the huge woman in the print dress.

"You can come in now," she said in her low-pitched, placid voice.

Petey followed her out of the room and across the hall to a small room on the left. This room, in startling contrast to the other one, was small and almost empty. A silent radio sat on a small table in front of a window, the shade drawn to the sill. In the middle of the floor was a cheap card table and a floor lamp beside it. There was a sort of cupboard along one wall, and that was all.

"If you'll sit down, please," the woman said.

Petey pulled out the straight wooden chair in front of the card table and sat down. "Thanks," she said.

Mrs. Thorpe lowered her great bulk ponderously into the chair across the table. The table was bare, except for a box of pink Kleenex at her elbow. The Reverend Thorpe pulled another sheet of tissue from the box and held it to her nose. "I have a bad cold," she said. "I hope you'll forgive me."

"Oh, sure, that's all right," Petey said. She looked at the woman curiously as she bent to drop the wad of tissue in a little tin waste-basket beside her chair. Her size and her placidity were impressive. Her face was fat and smooth, her thin dark hair drawn straight back from her face and twisted into a little knot. She wore no make-up on her face; her skin glistened and her lips were straight and rather thin. If there was anything uncanny about her, it was her eyes. She had very large and very dark eyes, prominent in her face; and in direct contrast to the rest of her, her eyes were as sharp and alert and quick-moving as any eyes that Petey had ever seen. And there was something a little uncanny about her voice too, so low-pitched and controlled. Petey suspected that voice and mannerism of speaking as a professional acquirement.

Mrs. Thorpe sat up in her chair again and fixed her large eyes on Petey, missing no single detail of Petey's face or clothing. "You didn't specify what type of reading you wanted," she said with a faint accusation in her voice.

Petey forgot everything suddenly in an absorbing interest in this woman and the lucrative profession that she followed. "Well, whatcha got?" Petey said cheerfully.

Mrs. Thorpe answered her with dignity. "I am able to establish contact with my guide through a study of either cards, tea leaves, palms, handwriting or flowers."

"You better make mine cards," Petey said. She refrained from saying that her luck ran well with cards. She decided suddenly that Mrs. Thorpe was going to get no information from her to help her act along. You're on your own, old girl, Petey thought with grim glee.

Mrs. Thorpe pulled a pack of worn cards out of her pocket

silently. "Did you want the dollar reading, or the dollar and a half one?" she inquired delicately, snuffling a little.

"You can give me the works," Petey said, her eyes on the pack of cards. Mrs. Thorpe's hands were somewhat surprising too, long slender fingers tipped with broad, flat, colorless nails. Her hands matched her eyes, but nothing else about her; they were amazingly quick and dexterous.

Mrs. Thorpe hesitated, the pack of cards in her hands. "You'll have to put out that cigarette," she said with the faint accusation in her voice. "The spirits cannot come through smoke!"

"Oh, excuse me!" Petey said, smiling. While she stepped on the cigarette on the bare floor, Mrs. Thorpe wiped her nose on another piece of tissue.

Mrs. Thorpe frowned a little at a last wisp of smoke drifting over the table and shuffled the cards rapidly and expertly.

Hummm, Petey thought, watching her quick fingers with the cards. I bet you deal off the bottom too, sister!

Mrs. Thorpe put the cards down on the table in front of Petey with a little snap. "Cut the cards, please."

Petey cut them obediently.

"No, no," Mrs. Thorpe said tolerantly. "Have you luck to throw away, young woman? Next time cut them toward you, not away from you."

"My mistake again," Petey said with her cheerful smile.

There was no answering smile on Mrs. Thorpe's face. She shuffled the cards again thoroughly. "Now," she said.

Petey carefully cut the cards toward her on the table.

"You may turn up the one on top."

"Deuces wild?" Petey asked with interest.

Mrs. Thorpe's eyes were momentarily accusing. "You certainly are in a better humor now than when you came here," she said mildly, ignoring the question.

The question answered itself as Petey turned over the card. They were not playing cards at all, although they were the same size. The card was bent and slightly dirty and covered with a jumble of symbols that were unintelligible to Petey.

"These are fortune-telling cards, as you see," Mrs. Thorpe said to Petey. "You may keep that card you have turned up on the table in front of you. In that card lies the key!"

Petey put it down obediently and watched the woman with interest as she dealt out the strange cards face up in a great fan shape across the table.

With the cards dealt, there was a silence in the room. Mrs. Thorpe studied the position of the cards with concentration, sometimes shaking her head, sometimes pausing to wipe her nose on tissues from the box in front of her.

"First I must orient you a little, then we will talk of the future," Mrs. Thorpe said at last solemnly.

"Okay."

"You are a stranger in this town. You have not been here long, months, but not long. Just how long I cannot say, but less than a year, a great deal less. Before you came here you were—yes—I see it here—you were in the South."

Petey smiled at the card Mrs. Thorpe indicated with her finger suddenly. Uh huh, Petey thought, did you get that out of the card, old girl, or did you just make a note when you saw my sun tan when you was looking me over a minute ago?

"Before the South," Mrs. Thorpe went on, "you have been many places. I do not need to tell names to you. You know it well yourself, though you have been so many places you have forgotten some of them, maybe. For a long time, why, for all your life nearly, you have been moving, first one place, then another. You never stayed long any place, but then you had nothing to hold you in any one place, did you?"

Petey didn't answer her. Well, score one for a pair a good eyes and a lot of experience with people, she was thinking.

"Always on the move. But you liked it that way; you have had a good time. For some people it wouldn't do, always moving like that, but for you, you liked it that way. You like new places, and new faces. You like people. You make friends with people easily. Wherever you go you make new friends. Friends come to you quick and easy. But you are a good friend to have. You are loyal and you are generous. You keep friends, but they never tie you down."

Mrs. Thorpe stopped talking and wiped her nose and looked at the cards again. She indicated another card with her finger.

"Your work has kept you moving, too. You work with people because you like people; you like to be where they are. You are in show business—it isn't quite clear here—but you are in some sort of show business. An actress, maybe, but I don't think so. A dancer more likely, or a singer. Do you remember Carlo?"

"Carlo?" Petey echoed the name that was meaningless to her, and tried to think obediently. "Nope. If it's a place, I was never there. If it's a person's name, I never knew anybody by that name."

"Carlo means nothing to you!" Mrs. Thorpe said with a little smile. "My guide brought me the name just now. Well, you have forgotten. I don't suppose Stella means anything to you, either. No? No, it is as I said, so many places, so many people, you have forgotten."

You'd have a hell of a time proving that, sister, Petey was thinking.

"You are skeptical," Mrs. Thorpe said inexorably. "Well, I cannot help you. It isn't quite clear; there are disturbances. But remember the names, Carlo and Stella. Perhaps you will remember them later, if you think about it. You have simply forgotten them."

Mrs. Thorpe went back to a long silent study of the cards, and to her box of Kleenex tissue.

"I am trying to understand the forces that brought you to this town," she explained. "It is here in the cards. I see it, but not clearly. You are working here, yes, but that is not why you came here. I doubt that you ever expected to work here when you came. No, it was something else that brought you here. Old friends, no, closer than that. Relatives, I think. Somebody close to you. Not parents, but someone close. Perhaps a brother or a sister, relatives close to you who you had not seen for a long time. That is why you came here, but you have stayed on longer than you intended. You have even found work here, which you certainly never intended to do when you came. You found an unexpected reason for staying. It could be an illness in your family, yes, I think it is an illness."

Petey's face was alive with interest. Mrs. Thorpe stole a quick glance at her.

"The outcome of that illness I cannot say. But you will remain on in this town for a while longer, not much longer but for awhile, and then you will be on the move again."

Mrs. Thorpe changed the positions of some of the cards and studied them all again.

"You came to me tonight unexpectedly, too. You often do things like that, quick, without thinking much about it. Something has upset you. I see it here, something upset you very much. Something out of the ordinary that upset you and frightened you. Because you have never been to a reader before, you are a skeptic, you do not recognize powers such as I make use of. But something happened to you that frightened you and upset you and for the first time in your life you felt it necessary to seek aid outside yourself, even to seek aid and assurance from powers you have never believed in. It isn't any ordinary thing, like worry about your work, or worry about money, nothing like that. Your life has been full of ups and downs, this thing that has happened is something different.

"You have been to a party recently," Mrs. Thorpe said with an abrupt change of subject. "A big party. I see the candles burning on the table. A very big party. Is that right?"

"Nope, I'm afraid not," Petey said. "I guess the wires got crossed there for a minute."

"No? Well, it doesn't matter. You will go to such a party then within six weeks. There will be candles on the table—a big party you will remember that I told you. It is easy to make mistakes like that, there is such a thin line between what has just happened and what is soon to happen. It is a line that my Indian guides do not recognize at all, of course. You will go to a big party soon, and even sooner, even before the party, you are going to get a long-distance telephone call. You will be very surprised to hear from this person, an old friend, a very close friend, but someone you haven't seen or heard from in a long time. You will be surprised to hear from him, surprised that he knows where you are. You will talk together on the telephone, although there are a great many miles between you. It will be very pleasant for you, he will have pleasant things to tell you. I see another phone call too, but not a long-distance one, and this one is not pleasant, like the other one. This one will be bad news. It will mean that you have to take a trip, just a short trip, and you will come back here again. But it is very bad luck, it will be most unpleasant for you, and bad luck will come of it. You must be very careful, but even so, I don't think you can prevent the bad luck that will come from that trip. There is someone close to you that you trust, and you should not trust that person. If you will think very hard you will know whom I mean. Not that the person is bad, nothing like that. It is just that the person whom you trust will do something that will mean a great deal of bad luck and unhappiness for you. There are many people close to you that are bad, that you must be very careful of. But this bad luck ahead of you won't come from any of them. It will come from someone close to you that you trust, but who is not a bad person. Perhaps you want to know specific things. If you could ask me a few questions, if you could tell me what it is that you want to know about?"

"No, I'm afraid not," Petey said. "You go ahead, you're doing all right."

The faint accusation crept into Mrs. Thorpe's voice again. "You are determined not to trust me, aren't you?" she said, wiping her nose brusquely. "Well, without questions from you, I can tell you little more, and very few definite things. I see a great deal of trouble about you. All of your life there has been trouble around you, more trouble around you than actually in your life. Well, I see a great deal of trouble ahead, around you and in your own life, too. Yes, a great deal of trouble. Yes, death, even. Certainly death, it is unmistakable. Does the name Raymond mean anything to you? Raymond, or maybe it's Randolph or Rudolph, something like that? No? Well, he has not come into your life then, but he will very soon. He will be a person that you can trust, and there are not many in your life that you can trust. The advice he gives you will be good, you would be wise to listen to him. But you are not good at taking advice. You are too headstrong, too quick, too sure of yourself. That makes trouble for you; it will make even more trouble for you soon. Yes, a great deal of trouble ahead and unhappiness for you. You have not been happy lately, that is why you came to me. Well, there is more unhappiness to follow. I cannot see it clearly, but I know that it is there. There is a man, I think, whom you love very much. He brings you unhappiness; he will bring you more. You will not marry him. You would not be happy if you did. You have never been married; you would find little happiness in marriage. This man that you love can only bring you unhappiness, there is no use for you to go on hoping for any happiness from him. He cannot give it to you. I see him very plainly. A slender, dark-haired man, am I not right? He is very slender and dark, no taller than you are. I see you together. I see you dancing together. You dance very well together. I see you dancing, just you two alone on a shiny floor. You have a white dress on and flowers in your hair. You are smiling, but he is not smiling. He is angry, and, even though you are smiling, neither one of you is happy. I see the picture very plain, the two of you dancing across a small shiny floor. You have the long white dress on and bracelets shining, and white flowers in your hair. And his face is very angry. No, there is no happiness that this man can give you. You love him very much, perhaps more than you have ever loved before, but there is no happiness in it. There is trouble ahead and death. And then you will leave this town, and you will leave alone. No matter what you hope now, you will leave this town soon and alone."

"And then?" Petey said softly.

Mrs. Thorpe shrugged her shoulders. "Then? More of the same, the moving, here and there, and never long anywhere. Your work? It will go on. You are not ambitious for your work, and therefore you will have no great success with it. You will have more success even than you want, because you are not ambitious for success, and it can bring you no happiness."

"That's a gloomy picture," Petey said. "If you can't see anything good ahead I only ought to have to pay half price."

Mrs. Thorpe's voice was severe. "Well, can you see great happiness or great change ahead of you? No, of course you can't. If you could you wouldn't have come here. The picture looks gloomy to you? That is because you are hoping for something that cannot happen, you know it yourself. You love someone and you think your life will be changed because of it, or at least you hope so. That cannot happen. I have told you, that man has no happiness to give you. But the picture need not be gloomy. You are young and beautiful and healthy. Did I warn you about your ankle? You must be careful; soon you are going to have an accident and sprain your ankle, maybe even break it. You love life, you like people and excitement and clothes and music and gaiety. Well, it is there ahead of you. You can still enjoy it, unless you make yourself miserable over something that you can't have, something that would only bring you unhappiness if you had it. I don't say that you will find that life satisfactory to you, as you used to. You will be lonely, but then a number of us do not find our lives particularly satisfactory. Fears you have and uncertainties, and you will not lose them overnight, you will carry them with you when you leave here; you will carry them for a long time. I see . . ."

Petey struck a match abruptly and held it to a cigarette. "Never mind the spirits," she said. "I've had enough of them, anyway. Well, I asked for the works and I certainly got it. Loneliness, fear, uncertainty, trouble, death, unhappiness—all for a buck and a half. And here I thought you'd tell me about the nice trip I was gonna take on a boat, where I'd meet a pretty man and get married and have three kids." Petey put the dollar bill on the table, and a fifty-cent piece on top of it.

"I can only tell you what I see and what my guides help me to know," Mrs. Thorpe said with her closest approximation to good humor.

"Indians, huh?" Petey said with frank interest, as she fastened her furs at her throat.

Mrs. Thorpe hoisted her great bulk out of the chair. "You won't come again, so I will say good-bye and good luck to you," she said, holding out her hand. "I am glad you came. You are a very interesting person. You are a very unusual person, too. I saw many, many things in your life, past and present and future that I did not tell you. I shall think about them, and about you many times."

"Thanks," Petey said. "I had fun too. Except it was my funeral you was talking about."

"No, not your funeral," Mrs. Thorpe said seriously. "The death I saw was not your death."

"Well, that's one thing to look forward to then," Petey said wryly. "Thanks for the reading. Good luck to you. I'll send you a post card after I get married to the pretty guy I meet on the boat. I won't wait until I have the three kids."

The door closed behind her, and, as Petey went down the steps, she was thinking, Christ, it would be just my luck to pick up that dame's cold. I shoulda asked her how the spirits could get through all that Kleenex. There was a little grocery store less than three blocks away. Petey had made note of it on the way out here, and she headed for it now, to telephone for a cab back downtown.

Petey was in better spirits now. Thorpe is a funny old girl, she was thinking. I wonder where she got that dope on me dancing with the Nicky with a white dress on—and flowers. It must have been New Year's Eve. But I'll swear she wasn't at Toresca's kicking the gong around, and I don't think she knows me. I wonder where she finds out things like that. She's a smart old gal. She can read people like a book. But then, that's her business. I bet she knows a lot of things about a lot of people.

Petey felt pretty good as she hurried along the dark street. Her ill humor had vanished, and the gloomy future that the Reverend Clara Thorpe had foreseen for her did not trouble her at all.

# 32

PETEY FINISHED HER FIRST GROUP OF SONGS AT Toresca's that evening and made her leisurely way toward the bar, pausing to talk at several tables on the way. As she walked along the bar she saw Johnny O'Connor sitting there alone with a drink. "Hello, Petey," he said. "Would you do me the honor now a havin' a drink with me, maybe?"

"Hi, Johnny." Petey slid up on the stool beside him. "Go easy on the ice, Joe. How are the hands comin', Johnny?"

"Fine," Johnny said as he struck the match for her cigarette. "The doc says in a couple weeks they'll be as good as new."

"Jesus, no rest for the wicked!" Petey said cheerfully. "First thing you know, Johnny, you'll have to go back to work."

"Yeah, ain't it a shame!"

Johnny's face sobered suddenly and he looked down to the drink in front of him on the bar. "Petey, I got an apology to make to you," he said briefly. "Somebody oughta punched my head off for talking the way I did to you the other afternoon."

"Aw, skip it, Johnny," she said. "Remember what I said that day when I left--'no hard feelin's.' It's all right. I had it comin' for sticking my nose in where it was none a my business. I did quite a lotta talkin' that day myself."

"Yeah," he said with his quick grin. "And what you said to me was the truth. I even knew it then while you were saying it."

Petey laughed. "Hell, Johnny, since when has the truth been an excuse for shootin' your mouth off? Let's forget it, huh? What's news with you?"

"Oh, hell," Johnny said. "I'm the original stay-at-home, play-at-home boy! Tonight I got fed up. Glory was out gaddin' someplace so I got Ginny in to keep an eye on the baby and I come out for some air and a little night life."

Because she was looking in that direction Petey saw them when they first came in together—Gloria O'Connor with an orchid on her jacket and the man with the dark hair and the round, unpleasant face. Petey's fingers tightened around her glass. Gloria said something to him, and he laughed, and dropped his hand on the back of her head, pulling at her thick blonde hair playfully, an intimate and possessive gesture. His arm dropped to her waist as she turned around and they came up the ramp together.

Petey caught her breath silently and turned around to Johnny on the stool next to hers.

He had seen them, all right. His body was rigid on the stool, his face tense, his eyes very bright. Just as Gloria and the man with her passed a group at the end of the bar, Gloria saw Johnny too.

She stopped dead still and then stood there with her face suddenly pale and frightened. The man stopped too, a little behind her, so abruptly that he stumbled against her. He looked at her questioningly and he started to speak, but at the sight of her face his voice died out, and his eyes slid along the bar in the direction that she was looking. His eyes came to rest on Johnny and stopped. The laughter went out of his face and he withdrew his arm slowly from Gloria's waist.

Johnny O'Connor caught his breath audibly. He put his glass down and slid from his stool all in one motion. But Petey was quicker. She moved just as Johnny did. In two strides she was across the floor and her hand dropped lightly on Gloria's arm, in a natural and friendly gesture.

"Well, hi!" Petey said with a friendly warmth in her voice. "Where you been? Johnny and I been waiting and waiting. We thought you two got lost or something. Come on over and have a drink before you go!"

Gloria's face was blank and stupid, but Petey slipped her hand through her arm, and another through the arm of Gloria's escort and led them toward the bar.

As they approached Johnny, Petey said lightly, "Johnny, you and Gloria don't have to go home right this minute, do you? Gloria hasn't had a drink yet. You stay and have another drink while she has one, huh?"

Johnny's voice was controlled and toneless to match his face as he looked at Gloria. "You wanta drink, Gloria?"

Gloria had no voice to answer him, but Petey said genially, "Of course she wants a drink! Sure, and a fine question to be askin' a lady! Set 'em up all around, Joe, the drinks are on me."

Petey led them straight up to the bar. She landed Gloria on the stool beside Johnny's with a deft shove, she herself stood next, and Gloria's friend on the other side of her.

"Whatcha drinkin', honey?" Petey said to Gloria as the bartender waited.

Gloria was still speechless, and Johnny said, "She drinks Manhattans. Make mine the same."

Petey caught a nod from the man beside her. "Okay, Joe, four Manhattans, and make mine with rye, will yuh?"

Petey passed her cigarette package in both directions. "No takers, huh? Christ, this is a slow night in here tonight! Of course, it's early. Maybe it'll pick up later. Just look, about eight of us here at the bar, and maybe nine or ten down there at the tables. If the Nicky ever took a peek in here right now, he'd faint. You know the Nicky, don't you, Johnny?"

"I used to," Johnny said. "I haven't seen much of him lately."

"Too bad you missed the early show," Petey went on, including Gloria and the dark-haired man. "Tommy was in top form tonight. You was here when he played, weren't you, Johnny? He was doin' all right tonight, didn't you think?"

"Yeah."

"And when Tommy's in form, there ain't nothing around this town that can hold a candle to him!" Thus Petey kept the conversation alive. There was a little sound from Gloria, and Petey looked at her quickly. Gloria's face was puckered. She was trying very hard not to cry, but there were tears shining on her face.

Petey tasted her drink and cocked her ear at the orchestra. "Hey, that's all right!" she said. "There's a number I never do sit out unless I have to." She turned to the dark-haired man, meaningfully.

"You care to dance this one?" he mumbled.

"Uh huh." He followed her toward the stairs obediently. "Don't go away," she called back to Gloria and Johnny.

Gloria's friend proved to be a heavy and methodical dancer, and Petey thought the orchestra would prolong the number forever. From time to time she caught glimpses of the O'Connors sitting together in apparent silence.

When the number was over at last, Petey led the way back to the bar, the dark-haired man at her heels. Gloria was losing her fight against tears, and Johnny stood down from his stool as they approached.

"I guess we have to run along now," he said to Petey quietly, and he turned to help Gloria down from her stool.

"Aw, I'm sorry you gotta go," Petey said. "You come in again soon when you can make a night of it, huh? Good night, honey." She squeezed Gloria's arm tight in her fingers as she spoke.

"Good night, Petey," Johnny said, "and thanks—for everything."

Petey stopped him with a quick little gesture of her hand.

"So long. Take it easy, Johnny!"

Johnny and Gloria walked down the ramp together, and neither one of them even looked at the dark-haired man who stood back at the bar again, a little behind Petey. When she turned he was taking a great drink, emptying his glass, and there was a little perspiration shining over his heavy face.

Petey said impersonally, "See you around again. I have to see a couple guys." She swung around on her heel, the full silken skirt of her gay, flowered dress billowing.

There were no words spoken between Johnny and Gloria during the taxi ride out to Horton Street. Once Gloria was in the cab she began to cry, a soft miserable sniveling, and she kept it up all the way home. Johnny didn't speak to her or touch her. He didn't even look at her.

When they came into the apartment, Ginny was curled up on the end of the davenport, her head bent over a magazine. She looked up to them, her face a little surprised.

"Gosh, you scared me!" Virginia said. "I didn't think you'd be home this early. I couldn't imagine who was walking in here." She got up from the davenport slowly as she spoke.

"Glory isn't feeling good. We came home early," Johnny said briefly.

There was a little curiosity on Virginia's face in spite of herself, but she walked toward the door hurriedly. "Beverly's been fine. She never woke up once nor made a sound in there. I'm sorry you aren't feeling good, Gloria."

"Thanks a lot, Ginny," Johnny said. "I'll see you tomorrow."

"All right. Good night!" Virginia closed the door softly behind her.

After she was gone, Gloria began to cry again. She stood there just inside the door, one hand lifted to her face, her whole body shaking with sobs. Johnny took off his coat and hat mechanically and dropped them in a chair. He stood still, his back to Gloria, his hands thrust deep in his pockets, for several minutes.

He turned around at last and his face looked as if he, too, was trying very hard not to cry. "Glory," he said, with a little catch in his voice over her name. "Glory, I don't know what to say. I don't even know what to think. We talked about this. You knew how I felt about it, that I didn't want you running around with that guy. But you didn't pay any attention to me, did you? You kept right on going around with him, and you kept lyin' to me, didn't you?"

"Johnny! Aw, Johnny," Gloria sobbed out loud. Her voice was heavy and broken with her crying. She cried hard, just standing there inside the door, with one hand lifted to her face, and the other hand hanging limply at her side.

"Glory, I don't know what to do nor say nor nothin'," Johnny said miserably.

Gloria moved suddenly, she ran across the room and flung her arms around Johnny and clung to him tight, her face burrowed into his chest, her hat slipping back, so that her soft fragrant hair brushed against his chin. "Johnny, don't be mad! I'm sorry, Johnny. Aw, don't get mad!"

"Then why do you do this, Glory? Why do you go out with him? Is it just because you like to go out and have a good time? Can't you have a good time with me? Or do you like him? Or what is it?"

Gloria sagged under his hands. Her face was wet and flushed, and the orchid on her coat was crushed and torn. "Johnny, I didn't want to—honest, I didn't—want—to. Johnny—I love you so!"

She was crying too hard, and Johnny took her back in his arms again and held her tight. "Then why did you go with him? Why? What made you do it, Glory?"

Gloria was close to hysteria, her crying came harder and harder, and her voice was labored as she went on. "But—but when I'm with him—I love him too! Aw, Johnny! Johnny!"

Johnny stiffened, and then he struggled with her, trying to push her away from him. "Glory, stop cryin' like that! Stop it! You hear me! Don't hold your breath like that! Glory, honey, stop it now!"

He held her away from him. She caught her breath and held it, her mouth wide open, her face flushing red and her eyes wild and unseeing.

Johnny's face was grim as he loosened one of his hands from her grasp and slapped her hard across the side of her face.

She let her breath go, and her knees buckled under her. Johnny half carried her to the davenport, and when he set her down, she toppled over, her face buried in her arms. Her body was still shaking with sobs, but her crying was only a sort of whimpering now.

Johnny backed away from the davenport, rubbing his face a little with his hand. "Aw, Jesus, Glory!"

"Johnny!" She stretched out her hand for him, but when she didn't find him, she pulled herself upright slowly and raised her face to him. "It's all right, Johnny," she said softly, with a little sob like a hiccough. Her eyes were all but closed, the reddened lids twitching a little.

Johnny stood in front of her, his face bleak. "All right? How can it be all right?" he said. "What you just said to me, if that's true, why, how . . ."

"It's all right," Gloria said again brokenly. "I ain't never gonna see him no more, Johnny. He's a designer to the corset factory. He's got a new job in Chicago. They're gonna move down there next week, him an' his wife an' kids. I ain't never gonna see him no more. It's all right, Johnny."

"Yeah, sure!" Johnny backed up and sat down in a chair as if all the strength had left his legs suddenly. He dropped his head onto his hand, his fingers covering his eyes.

"Johnny, don't be mad! Please, Johnny!" Gloria knelt beside him. She pulled off her hat, breaking the little elastic band, and threw it over her shoulder. She burrowed her head along his knee under his arm to raise her lips to his.


Later on that night, Petey finished her work at Toresca's and took a cab for home. There was rain pattering down gently. Petey watched it through the cab window, soft rain falling slowly and easily in the darkness: It made her think of spring suddenly. Spring was something special and good to Petey. First warm weather and Easter, and the crinkling tissue in a brand-new hat box, a gay new hat with a knot of pastel veiling, and furs into storage and a trim-fitting suit instead. She wished spring would hurry up and come, Petey thought with a sudden longing, she'd had enough of winter.

And, in the meantime, Petey told herself practically, she was going home and soak for a long time in a warm bubble bath. Her body ached with fatigue, her make-up felt smudged and sticky on her face. She wished this really was a spring rain, warm, sweet-smelling, rather than the raw penetrating cold. Petey sighed a little and straightened out her legs wearily. Another night's work done, and here she was on her way home through dark empty streets with a cold rain drizzling down. She was tired, her throat was strained from singing, her mouth raw with the taste of too many cigarettes. It didn't seem to add up to much, did it?

The cab drew up to the curb in front of her apartment house, splashing water out of the gutter onto the sidewalk. Petey climbed out and dropped her cigarette to sizzle in the wet at her feet. She shivered a little as she fished the change out of her bag to pay her driver. The wet crept up through the thin soles of her pumps and her whole body was chilled in a minute.

"There you are, Joe," Petey said with a cheerfulness she didn't feel. She held her skirts up high. She felt the rain on her face and it caught and shone in her curly dark hair.

"Thank you," her driver said, and she stepped back quickly to avoid the water that the wheels churned up as he pulled away. Petey turned around and walked slowly toward the entrance.

And then she stopped dead still, the rain forgotten. Because San was standing there, close up against the wall of the building, to the right of the entranceway. He wore the familiar light gabardine rain-coat, and his head was bare. He stood with his broad shoulders flat against the brick wall, a cigarette burning in his fingers, his other hand deep in his pocket, and a little pool of water forming around the toes of his shoes.

Petey just stood still there in the rain and looked at him. He moved suddenly and came toward her. Petey took a step to meet him.

"San," she said, and her voice was shaking. He kept looking at her, and Petey lifted her hand and took hold of the sleeve of his coat uncertainly, the fabric of it wet and cold in her fingers. He steadied her, his hand on her side just below her armpit.

"Well, what are we standing out here for?" Petey said tremulously. "Jesus, you're soaked."

He followed her into the building without a word. He waited behind her in the dimly lighted hallway, while she unlocked her door, and they went in together. He slammed the door shut behind them, and Petey moved in the direction of the patch of dim light that was the window and turned on the floor lamp in front of it. The soft light flooded the apartment and Petey turned around to San, who stood just in front of the door. She dropped her hat in the chair and her purse and key and gloves with it.

Petey caught her breath a little and wiped tears off her cheeks unashamedly. She laughed, a soft shaky bit of laughter. "Christ, I'm a dope! Look at me, I'm cryin'!"

He was looking at her all right, his strange pale eyes on her face. His hair was slick to his head with water, and water shone on his pale eyebrows and glistened over the rough contours of his face. He was looking at her, and suddenly his lips moved a little, as if he had intended to speak to her but no voice had come.

"Aw, San! San!"

Petey was across the floor in two strides and in his arms, the whole long slimness of her body stretched up high and her arms tight around his neck.

# 33

EARLY MONDAY MORNING, JOHNNY O'CONNOR BROUGHT the baby and all of her feeding paraphernalia over to Sally's. By prearrangement, Virginia was to mind the baby for the day while Johnny started job-hunting. He was aware, before he started, that, due to the circumstances under which he lost his job, there weren't going to be many shops in town willing to hire him. He had a long, hard, fruitless day of it. It was eight o'clock before he trudged up the stairs on aching feet. The door to the apartment was locked, and, when he opened it, the room was dark and still and empty. Johnny was puzzled momentarily, and then he concluded that either Gloria was at Sally's or else she had made plans unexpectedly to remain downtown for the evening.

At Sally's he found the entire family eating supper in the kitchen. Why, no, Virginia said, she hadn't seen anything of Gloria all day. The baby had been just fine and not a bit of trouble. She had had her bottle and she was asleep. Johnny frowned a little. Had there been any telephone calls? It wasn't like Gloria to stay downtown without letting him know about it. Neither Virginia nor Sally had heard anything about any calls.

Oh, well, Johnny said, he'd go down and ask Mrs. Gideon in a minute. In the meantime he'd take his infant home and put her in her own bed.

"I always told you, Johnny," Fred Foster kidded him good-naturedly, "that you oughta keep that wife a yours under lock and key, or somebody would run off with her. But you wouldn't listen to me, and now it looks damned like that's what's happened."

Johnny laughed, but he made Fred no answer. Well, he'd take the half-pint and go on home now, he told Sally. He'd come over and get her feeding stuff later.

Johnny went into the dimly lighted bedroom and picked up the warm small bundle from the bed carefully. He never picked her up these days without the little shock at how she was growing, at the weight that she gained steadily from week to week. He could remember when she had been a scrap of nothing in his arms, mostly a bundle of blanket. But now she was getting some size to her. Babies didn't stay little for long. They grew up before you knew it, just like he'd always heard other parents say without thinking much about it. Johnny felt a lump of tenderness in his throat for this young daughter of his, who moved forward into childhood now almost with every hour, it seemed. She had been a very tiny baby, a miracle of tiny, perfectly formed hands and feet and arms and legs, but she wasn't going to be a baby much longer. The placid routine of eating and sleeping that made up her cradle days was all but over. Sometimes, when he caught that odd look of profound wisdom on her face, he thought that she knew all about what was happening to her. That she accepted these last days of her little babyhood with amused tolerance, while she gathered strength and knowledge against the day when speech and locomotion would be hers, and she would be a little girl instead of a baby. Johnny wondered if all babies were so darn mysterious.

"There you are, honey-baby," Johnny said softly, his hands gentle and clumsy with her blankets. She awakened a little, her face puckered and her lips sucked energetically on a bottle that was no longer there, but her eyelids never fluttered open. Johnny felt among the blankets expertly. No, her diapers were still dry. Just as he stood up and straightened the blankets over her again, something caught his eye that stopped him dead still. The light was shining in from the living room and, in that shaft of light dissected by the half-open door, his eye caught a bureau drawer pulled out so far that it was about to fall. The next drawer was partly open too, and the drawer below that.

Johnny dropped the blanket, pushed the button on the wall and flooded the bedroom with light. The drawers of the bureau were all pulled out, all right, and their contents spilling out of them. The bureau top was littered with clothes, and the bed was a welter of dresses and housecoats thrown every which way. The clothes-closet door stood wide open. There was a noticeable empty space in it now, and there were black wire hangers strewn over the entire bedroom floor.

Johnny stood still and looked around the bedroom. He never seemed to breathe, and it seemed to him that after that first quick flurry of beats his heart was still and waiting, too.

Next he saw the envelope propped up against the mirror on top of a Kleenex tissue box—a plain white envelope with his name written across the front of it—"Johnny"—in Gloria's rounded, childish script.

He walked across the floor and picked up the envelope. Suddenly his hands were shaking so that he tipped over the Kleenex box, and dislodged another box without a cover in which Gloria was wont to keep little sample boxes of face powder, rouge boxes, creams, lipsticks, eye-shadows and other cosmetics. Johnny caught at the box deftly, and only a few of the little tubes and jars fell out and rolled noisily at his feet.

He looked at the envelope and at Gloria's rounded, scrawling writing, the pencil lead smudged a little already. The envelope wasn't sealed. It wasn't very thick, no more than one sheet of paper inside. Johnny found a level, secure place on top of the bureau for the cosmetic box and pulled the paper out of the envelope. One full sheet covered with Gloria's childish pencil scrawl:

> *"Dear Johnny:*
>
> *I hope this don't make you feel too bad or awful sore at me. Alex and I are going to Chicago on the morning train today. Like Alex says we don't want to hurt other folks, but we gotta think of ourselves too, we got a right to be happy too. I hope this don't make you terrible mad, I want us to always feel like we're friends. I got to think about myself once in awhile. Alex thinks he can get it fixed for me to model in Chicago and get my picture in magazines, so I got to think of myself, and like he says, me and Alex got a right to be happy too. I hope you see how it is, why I'm leaving like this. Don't try to make me come back because I won't.*
>
> 

*With love*

*Gloria*

>
> *P.S. Kiss Bev goodby for me."*

Johnny read it over a couple of times until all the writing blurred and ran together in front of his eyes. The baby stirred in her bed suddenly, half crying softly in her sleep. Automatically Johnny bent over her, and then switched out the bright overhead lamp that poured glaring light down upon her. He stood beside her bed for a moment, the letter still in his hand, and then he walked out into the other room stiffly. He started to read the letter over again, but he stopped himself and threw it onto the top of the radio. Johnny looked about him suddenly as if the very silence there had startled him. He took a couple of steps across the floor uncertainly, but he stopped again, as if he couldn't remember where it was that he had started to go or what it was that he had intended to do. He lighted a cigarette then, and in a minute he went back to the radio and picked up Gloria's letter. He held it in his hand without reading any of it, and then he dropped it again. After that he sat down in his chair and dropped his head on his hand.

It was quite a few minutes later that the knock came on the door.

He said "Yes?" with a kind of wonderment and impatience in his voice.

It was Sally who opened the door and stuck her head in. "Hi," she said. "You mind if I come in a minute? We just got the dishes done, and I kinda wanted to talk to you about something. Gloria's out tonight, huh? You weren't plannin' on goin' out, were you? Because if you are, why, it's perfectly all right, and I could come in some other time."

"No, come in, sit down," Johnny said. His face gave Sally the odd sensation that he was not looking at her really, and that he was not somehow aware that he had even spoken to her. Sally looked at him curiously, and she said, "Johnny, what in the world's the matter with you? You aren't sick or nothin', are you?"

"It's all right," Johnny said. "Sit down, Sally."

Sally was not satisfied. She sat down on the very edge of a chair and she kept looking at Johnny. "Well, how did the job-huntin' come out today?" she asked him. "Did you have any luck?"

"No, no luck today," Johnny said in a strange voice.

Sally jumped up from her chair. "Johnny, something's wrong! I can tell the way you're actin'. What's the matter? Has something happened? What's the matter, Johnny?"

He looked at her then as if he were at that moment seeing her for the first time since she had entered the room. "The matter?" he said. "Why—why—" Johnny laughed suddenly and dropped his head back into his hands. "Go ahead and read it," he said, his voice muffled. "On the radio."

Sally opened her lips to speak again, but she went to the radio instead and lifted the sheet of white paper. It didn't take her long to read it, and her face turned horror-stricken.

"Aw, Johnny," she whispered. "An' that little baby in there in that bed! Why, Johnny . . ."

She stopped talking and turned to him. Johnny didn't look up at her, and her face was suddenly warm with sympathy, and quick tears came to her dark eyes as she looked at the miserable slump of his back.

Sally put the paper back on top of the radio silently. She stood still a moment longer and then she walked over to him and dropped her hand on his shoulder, and squeezed it tight.

"Johnny," Sally said quietly, "Johnny, if you should—should want to go out someplace a little later, why, I'd be glad to look after the baby. If you do decide to go out, why, you don't need to come in or ask or nothin'. You can just knock on my door and I'll know it's you and I'll come over here and wheel her little bed right over to my place and she can just as well stay over there all night. I got her feedin' stuff over there yet."

Johnny didn't answer. Sally waited a moment, gave his shoulder a last little squeeze and slipped out, closing the door softly behind her.

Quite awhile later, nearly two hours, Sally heard a quick, light knock at her door. When she opened it, there wasn't anybody there. She stood still, puzzled for a moment, and then she caught a glimpse of Johnny in his hat and overcoat going down the stairs.

# 34

JIMMY TERWILLIGER WAS NOT ELIMINATED IN THE first semi-final bouts of the Golden Gloves contest. No contender in his weight class managed to stay with him more than seven rounds, and he accumulated a clean record of kay-oh's and technical knockouts. The local daily newspaper was generous with publicity.

Jimmy was picked as the city's best bet in the state finals at Grand Rapids and a sure thing for the national finals in Chicago. Although Jimmy's father still disapproved, his pride and excitement got the better of him, and everytime Jimmy fought, his father was to be found in his corner. As the semi-final eliminations narrowed down, Jimmy too became excited, and his school work was all but forgotten.

Nicky Toresca had been generous in his support of Jimmy from the very beginning. Whatever monetary investment he had made in Jimmy's career brought him good returns, although the betting odds on Jimmy dwindled fast as his victories mounted. The Nicky was present at the ringside each time Jimmy fought, and the elegant blue satin robe that Jimmy wore into the ring bore Toresca's name across the back.

Petey, too, was one of Jimmy's most loyal supporters. Petey was a fight fan, anyway, and she came early and stayed late. She sat at the ringside and chewed her way through packages of chewing gum and gave vigorous and vociferous support to her favorites.

But Petey was not able to persuade Virginia to attend the bouts with her, even on those nights when Jimmy Terwilliger was fighting. Virginia saw Jimmy infrequently these days. She did not exactly approve of his fistic career, and she had no inclination to see him fight.

The night of the final eliminations came at last. This would see the selection of contenders for the state finals in Grand Rapids. It was a heavy card, and many contestants would be required to fight several times before the night was over. The bouts were to begin promptly at seven-thirty, and were going to last indefinitely. Ringside seats were sold out for days in advance, and the lucky possessors of such tickets were rumored to be making fabulous sums on surreptitious re-sales.

The day itself could hardly have been less auspicious. Several weeks of wet gray weather culminated in a thick fog that dropped over the city like a smoke screen early that afternoon. The local radio station begged fight fans to leave their automobiles at home. About five o'clock a light rain set in, but strangely enough, although the fog thinned a little, it did not lift.

Petey sprayed her throat with antiseptic every hour during the afternoon. She would be singing that night in a late show for an anticipated capacity crowd after the fights.

"Hi yuh, Joe," Petey greeted the bartender cheerfully as she strode up the ramp at Toresca's. "Christ, ain't this fog awful!"

"Hi, Miss Braun! Still soupy out, huh?"

"You better tell the boss to hang a couple lanterns out there on the door. If he don't, some of the best customers are liable to miss it, like I pretty near did and ram into the wall and knock their teeth out!"

The bartender laughed appreciatively, and Petey shook drops of water out of her furs in all directions. Tommy Terwilliger was sitting down at the far end of the bar with a glass of beer in front of him and Petey waved her hand at him.

"Hi yuh, Tommy! Well, tonight's the big night! You nervous?"

"Hello, there, Miss Petey." Tommy grinned across his battered features and looked at his glass self-consciously. "Naw, I feel fine. It'll be all right till I get over there tonight, and then I'll get the shakes right."

"Good for you," Petey said. "Look at me, I'm shakin' like a leaf! Jesus, I don't know what we're worrying about! The kid's got it on ice."

"Well, you never can tell," Tommy said. "A fight ain't never won till your man is down on ten or the decision's in, I told him."

"Well, I guess you got something there, all right." Petey flung her fur cape over a stool, and climbed up on the next one beside Tommy.

"Make mine a beer, Joe." Petey was all in black, with a dusky rainbow of sequins on the collar of her dress, on the pockets, and on the wide cuffs of the soft black gauntlet gloves that matched the dress material.

"I don't know just what time Jimmy's bout'll go on," Tommy said worriedly. "He probably gotta fight a couple times. He might go out first before nine o'clock even."

"Well, I'll be there, all right," Petey said cheerfully. "I'll be there at seven-thirty on the dot. I wanta see how that little Andrews kid makes out, you know, the little Negro kid in the bantams. He oughta go out one of the first bouts."

After rehearsals Petey had a drink with the Nicky and then went around the corner for a sandwich at a drug store. She killed time over coffee until it was time for her to go, and then walked the short distance through the wet foggy streets to the Elks' Temple Auditorium where the Gloves contest was held this year. The steps, the entranceway, and the corridor of the middle-sized building were jammed with people: those fans who were still in line and hopeful of general-admission tickets due to the bad weather, groups of overcoated men smoking their cigarettes as they went into the auditorium and discussing favorites and picking winners. Petey shoved her way through to the door and pulled out her white ringside ticket. They couldn't have picked a worse place for the contest, she thought, as she followed her usher down the central aisle between rows of folding chairs already filled with people.

It was just an ordinary auditorium, and the ring had been set up on the main floor, away from the stage at the far end of the room. A few chairs on the stage itself were reserved for timekeepers and judges, and such few newspaper reporters and photographers as were present. Ringside seats consisted of five rows of chairs set up on the three sides of the ring away from the stage.

The ring itself was empty, save for an official in white shirt and trousers, who was testing the floor and the ropes while he traded jokes with a few officials and newspaper men who were already in their chairs on the stage. The bright overhead lights had not been turned on yet.

Petey's ticket was for the second row ringside, just beyond a corner. Nicky Toresca held the tickets for that entire row of ringside seats. They were all empty now, except for Al Riley and another man whom Petey recognized as also being an employee of Nicky's.

"Hi yuh, boys," Petey said as she scrambled over their feet to her chair. "I like this seat, so why don't you move on down here and be sociable?"

They moved down beside her, and Petey draped her furs over the back of her chair and passed her package of chewing gum to them.

"Well, what's cookin' around here?" She wanted to know. "Who's winnin' what and why? Much money on Jimmy?"

"Aw, so so," Al Riley said, as he stripped the paper off a stick of gum. "Course, you can't get no odds on Jimmy no more. There ain't so much bettin' goin' on around here this year, nothin' like I've seen it some years."

"Looky," said Petey, "I gotta tip for you. Keep your eye on a little Negro kid named Andrews down among the panty-weights. He sure has got a cute left!"

More and more people were crowding into the auditorium. Ushers were kept on the run locating the chairs for those people who had reserved seats and came late. The glaring overhead lights above the ring were turned on suddenly, and the hum of voices in the huge room rose a couple of notches in excitement. Soft-drink and peanut salesmen were already doing a rush business as the temperature rose.

Al Riley yawned with his mouth wide open. "Hell, I don't care nothin' about seein' these kids bat around," he said disgustedly. "The boss was so damn scared he'd miss seein' the kids he sent us down here at seven o'clock, so he'd be sure we'd know what was going on an' telephone him so he could get down here in plenty a time for Jimmy. The way I figure, there ain't nothin' worth seein' till you get up into the middle-weights."

"Oh, I dunno," Petey said. "I get a kick outa the little kids. They put up a real scrap; they got their heart and soul in it. Maybe they ain't got much steam behind the gloves, but they sure put everything they've got behind it, every punch they throw. Some of these big CCC boys are gonna do the real fightin' around here tonight in the heavyweights. I wouldn't be surprised they turn up some real competition for Jimmy in his division."

"Here go the announcements," Al said in disgust as a gray-haired man with a sheaf of papers in his hand climbed in between the ropes. "Old drizzle-puss'll get up there and spout for a half hour yet."

The man in the ring droned through his announcements while the crowd moved restlessly. At last the announcements were over, including the announcement of the first bout, and the fighters were coming through the ropes. They were a couple of kids, maybe fifteen or sixteen, gangling, immature bodies in the scanty ring shorts, and the gloves looked ridiculously large dangling from the ends of their thin arms. One of them had a sweat-shirt draped around his scrawny, pinkish shoulders, the sleeves knotted loosely under his chin; the other had a faded blanket bathrobe wrapped about him awkwardly. Al Riley dropped back in his chair at the sight of them, and apparently fell asleep immediately. The referee, too, seemed profoundly bored as he read off their names to a faint scattering of applause. The boys took their corners awkwardly and leaned back against the ropes, uncertain what to do with either their feet or gloved hands. The seconds assigned to their corners took no interest in them.

The gong sounded and the referee moved easily on his feet, back from the center of the ring. Both boys hesitated for just a fraction of a second, long enough for a wave of laughter to start among the crowd. Then both of them bounded out of the corners at the same time, taut with nervousness, awkward in their footwork, feinting with the oversized gloves cautiously.

By the middle of the second round the crowd was noisy again, restless for action. Boos and catcalls, and instructions to do a little fighting were heard on every side. The boys' initial nervousness was wearing off now. One of them landed a lucky punch that pinkened the skin of his surprised opponent, and after that both of them swung wild rights and lefts in reckless abandon for the remainder of the bout. The judges made a decision, and the referee read off the winner's name from the center of the ring. There was a slight burst of applause in which Petey joined enthusiastically, and the boy grinned in embarrassment at the audience. His opponent was scrambling back into his bathrobe. He hesitated a little uncertainly, and then met the winner in the center of the ring and slapped him on the back with his gloved hand. That drew a greater wave of applause from the audience, and the two boys left the ring together.

A couple of similar bouts followed, and then a bout in a slightly heavier division was announced. Petey slid to the edge of her chair, and chewed her gum a trifle faster. Sure enough, the Negro boy named Andrews climbed through the ropes behind a white boy in an orange bathrobe.

The Andrews boy was short and well built. He was very black, his body glistening and smooth, his hair was very curly and he had a bright, infectious smile. He did some limbering exercises on the ropes briskly while his opponent was presented. When his own name was announced, he spun around, clutching his flimsy purple robe, and held one glove high above his head as he smiled broadly at the crowd.

Petey applauded vigorously. "Hi, Andy! Go get him, kid!" she yelled.

The white boy used a tooth guard. He mouthed it nervously after the whistle, as he crouched in his corner, his arms spread out wide, his eyes focused on his opponent.

At the gong, Andrews was out of his corner like a shot before his slower opponent hardly had time to move. Andrews came to meet him, still grinning. His foot work was rhythmic, he ducked and bobbed smoothly, feinting with his right expertly and carrying his left high and cocked.

His opponent made a more professional appearance in the ring as well. He was taller than Andrews and had the advantage of a longer reach. But he was much slower and he lacked the perfect, smooth co-ordination of the Negro.

Toward the end of the round he landed a right high on Andrews' face, and Andrews rode the punch back a step, still smiling.

"Never hit a Nigger in the haid!" a man roared behind Petey.

She turned around indignantly. "Why don't you button your lip, mister!" And the next second she was on the edge of her chair, yelling excitedly, "Atta boy, Andy! Let him have that left. Go get him, kid!"

In the fifth round, Andrews' left sent his opponent to his knees. Andrews backed away to the neutral corner briskly. The white boy was up at the count of seven and Andrews came after him with his brisk businesslike duck and weave, the left cocked and waiting. There was fight in his opponent yet. He landed a flurry of light blows to the body, and, as he forced Andrews into the crouch, he landed a heavy one on his face that hurt.

Andrews rode it all right, but it slowed him down momentarily. His gloves dropped and his opponent stepped in.

Petey shrieked like a banshee. "Get 'em up, Andy! Watch it! Get away from him! Get those gloves up, kid!"

Andrews got his gloves up, but he didn't back away nor did he take a clinch. He let his opponent keep on coming, a rain of blows to the head, the body and then the head again. He ducked and bobbed and waited. He got his chance. His opponent let go a long right that didn't quite connect. It was a hard blow; it glanced off his ear and kept right on traveling. Andrews suddenly puffed his cheeks out wide, and his left came up from the floor someplace like lightning. It landed neat and on the button with all the strength of his short compact body.

This time the count of ten found his opponent on hands and knees in the middle of the ring, shaking his head, half-stunned. Andrews waited in the corner, the wide grin on his face, and the referee lifted his glove. Petey bounced on her chair and howled her delight and approval.

"Didn't I tell you watch that kid?" she babbled to Al Riley delightedly. "Didn't I tell you watch that left? Jesus, he's gotta sweet left! He gets it up from the floor in nothin' flat, and once he lands it, oh, boy! Didn't I tell you watch that kid . . . ?"

"Yeah, sure," Al said without enthusiasm. He looked at Petey in wonderment and slight disgust.

# 35

JUST AT THAT MOMENT AN ANNOUNCER OVER THE local radio station gave the estimated attendance figures and the names of the winners of the first two bouts of the evening. Since they did not have the facilities for broadcasting from the ringside, they were forced to report the news as it was relayed from a telephone at the auditorium.

Nicky Toresca listened to the announcement over the portable radio that stood on the corner of his desk. He swore a little under his breath and turned the dial down as the program of recorded music resumed. "Christ, they just got the fights started over there!" he said disgustedly. "The kid won't be goin' out for a hell of a while!"

Joe Braun lounged in a chair in front of the desk, his overcoat on, his hat pushed to the back of his head. He was reading a newspaper by the soft light of the ornate standard lamp on the desk, and he grunted a little by way of answer, without looking up.

The Nicky, in immaculate shirt sleeves, twitched at the radio dials and then put out his cigarette in the heavy glass ash tray in front of him. He leaned far back in his chair then, doubling one knee against the edge of the desk top, and crossing his wrists behind his sleek dark head. The room was very still and warm and dimly lighted by the one desk light with a thick opaque shade. The Nicky yawned and the rain pattered suddenly on the glass of the window behind him.

"Joey," he said lazily, "I gotta job for you. You can handle it on accounta you're a bright boy, is that right?"

Joe stifled a half-yawn of his own, his eyes still on the newspaper. "Yeah? What's that?"

There was a shade of amusement over Nicky's smooth dark face. "It's a nice job, Joey, you'd be surprised. Maybe I wouldn't mind doin' this job myself. You know the little dame upstairs?"

Joe frowned over the newspaper. "What little dame upstairs? Oh, you mean the little blonde! She still here?"

Nicky jiggled his chair idly. "Yeah, she's still here. She acts like she's settled down here for life. Well, we gotta get her out a here."

Joe flapped over the sheets of the newspaper and started in on the comic page. "Oh, I dunno," he said. "She's kinda nice to have around. She might come in handy, you never can tell."

Nicky yawned again. "Oh, she's handy to have around, all right, but just the same we gotta get her outa here. Hell, she been here three or four days now, and that's even too long already. She's no floozy to begin with. She's just a dumb kid. She's just the kind that might turn into jailbait, Joey, you never can tell."

"Yeah," Joe said, "I see what you mean. Well, what am I supposed to do with her? Where does she live? What am I supposed to do, slug her over the head and drag her out a here and take her home to her mama?"

Nicky smiled. "Well, that's just the trouble, Joey. She claims she ain't got any place to go, that she don't live any place no more. She claims she's gonna stay here." Nicky laughed a little. "She says she's gonna stay here on account of she has so much fun here."

Joe laughed his dry, mirthless laughter. "Well, she sure's been havin' fun around here, all right!"

Nicky sat forward in his chair suddenly and picked up his cigarette package. "Just the same, we gotta get her out of here, is that right?"

"Well, hell!" Joe said plaintively, his eyes still on his newspaper. "What am I supposed to do, take her out and drown her?"

The little flare of light from the match revealed the faint, half-mocking amusement on Nicky Toresca's face. "Well, I wouldn't go so far as to say that. Just get her outa here."

Joe pondered over the last comic strip and then suddenly he tossed the paper away and groped for his own cigarettes.

"Right now, Joey," Nicky said, with the half-mocking patience in his voice. "You got time before we go down to the fights."

Joe's face was aggrieved. "Well, where she come from? Hell, she must live here in town someplace. How'd she get here in the first place?"

"She come in with a party, two, three nights ago," the Nicky said idly. "They hada lotta liquor up there and the little blonde passes out cold. So when the rest of 'em come to leave, they just left her here. I don't figure they know her, anyway, maybe. Maybe they just picked her up someplace. She been here ever since, and she's been having a hell of a time for herself. She ain't been sober since she been here, and every party comes in upstairs she plays with the boys free for nothing. She's good for business, but she's jailbait. Like I said, she ain't no floozy, she's some dumb kid. Those clothes she's wearin' cost money."

"She gotta purse with her?" Joe said. "Maybe there's some address in there."

The Nicky snapped the button on the radio again. "Naw, I

already looked," he said. "No address, no money, just powder and junk."

Joe stood up leisurely, and stretched his long arms before he pulled his hat down over his eyes. "What you want I should do, dump her off at some hotel?"

The Nicky leaned forward to read the numbers on the radio, and he turned around to look at Joe with a kind of mocking, patient tolerance. "For Christ's sakes, Joe! I said we wanta get rid of her like she never been here. Take my car, ride her around the block a few times and drop her off on a street corner. Then we never seen her before in our life, is that right?"

He turned back to the radio. "They oughta have some more returns from the fights pretty soon now. Maybe we can get a line on how soon the kid'll be goin' out, huh?"

Joe was frowning a little. "Jesus, this is a helluva night to drop nobody off on some street corner! She's higher than a kite, an' you claim she ain't got no money an' . . ."

Nicky didn't turn around from the radio. "Joey, I'm surprised at you! Regular little Boy Scout fella! Go ahead, get her outa here like I say. Maybe the fresh air will put some sense in her head, and she'll remember where she lives and go on home, like she oughta. Anyway, get her outa here like I tell you."

"Okay, you're the boss," Joe said with a sudden loss of interest.

Just as he went out he turned around with a grin on his face. "She's a nice little dish, too. Jesus, I could go for her myself. Maybe I'll drive outa town and park someplace before I dump her off, huh?" Joe laughed his dry laughter.

Nicky cocked his head at the radio. "So go ahead, what the hell," he said indifferently. "Everybody else around here been layin' her, so why not you? Just get her outa here, is that right?"

Joe climbed the stairway to the third floor, which was divided off in rooms for private parties. The corridor was dark on the third floor, and Joe hesitated momentarily. The door to the first room on the right was open, the light pouring out, and Joe stuck his head in. A table and chairs were pushed to one side of the wall, and a waiter was sweeping up the floor.

"Hi," Joe said. "The little blonde kid still around here?"

The waiter stopped and leaned on his broom handle. "She's still around, all right," he said, grinning. "She's down in that bedroom at that enda the hall. She's got the light on. What's the matter, Joe, you come up to have a piece?"

Joe grinned back at him. "Naw, the boss wants I should get her outa here."

The waiter started pushing the broom again, and Joe walked down the corridor until he saw the slit of light under a closed door.

Joe rapped lightly and then opened the door. It was just a little room, with a bed and a chair beside it, and a door to a toilet that opened off the bedroom. The little blonde girl was half-sitting, half-reclining on the bed, with the pillows doubled behind her back. There was a bottle of cheap whisky, about half full, together with cigarettes and an ash tray on the chair beside the bed, and she had a glass in her hand. She was a nice-looking kid, all right, Joe thought, and young. She couldn't be more than seventeen, maybe eighteen, and maybe a whole lot younger than that. She had on a slip, a low V at the neck between her full, round breasts, and one of her stockings was missing. Her hair was dark blonde, and it curled around her face. Her eyes were bright blue, and a little bleary, like the rest of her face. Her lipstick was very red, but it was on crooked. She smiled at Joe, a nice wide smile that revealed her even, white teeth.

"Hel-lo," she said, and she ended it with a little chirruping giggle. She put down her glass on the chair unsteadily and held out her arms to him. "What's your name? We gonna have a party now?"

Joe went over and put his arms around her and kissed her. She was a nice kid, all right, her flesh was firm and soft and warm under his fingers, and her hair was sweet-smelling. Not now, maybe later, Joe told himself. Right now he had to get her to hell out of this joint, or the boss would raise hell with him.

Joe loosened her arms and straightened up, still holding both her hands. "Look, baby, how about you comin' out for a little ride with me, huh?" Joe said easily.

She shook her head vigorously from side to side. The effort

apparently disturbed her narrow margin of equilibrium. She closed her eyes tight, screwing up her face into a gay little grimace. "Oh, my!" she said when she opened her eyes again. Then she giggled again, the funny little chirrup of laughter.

Joe tugged at her hands. "Come on, be a nice girl," he said patiently. "Don't you wanta go for a nice ride?"

She smiled again, her irresistibly gay and good-humored smile. "Nope," she said. "I don't wanta go any place. But you stay here and we'll have a party. Come on, you have a drink."

"Naw, come on now, we're gonna go for a ride," Joe said. "Where's your dress? Come on, you get up and put your dress on like a nice girl."

She jerked her hands away from him suddenly and doubled her arms behind her back. She stuck out her full lower lip in a pout, with laughter not far behind it. "No, I don't want to go for a ride. I'm gonna stay ri-ight here."

"Sure, you can stay here," Joe wheedled. "We'll just go out for a little ride, and then we'll come right back here and I'll have a drink with you and we'll have a party."

"We-el," she said, teasingly, but then her little giggle came suddenly in spite of her.

"That's a good girl," Joe said quickly. She stretched out her hands and he pulled her up onto her feet. When she stood up she rocked a little unsteadily and she took hold of Joe's arms for a second. "My goodness!" she said in her gay, clear, piping voice.

"Some fresh air gonna be good for you, honey," Joe said easily. "Now, where'd you put your dress? You gotta put your dress on!"

"I know where it is," she said. "I bet you can't find it. I know where it is, but I'm not gonna tell. I don't wanta put my dress on. I'll go for a ride all bare!"

She started to haul up her slip as she spoke, and Joe made a grab for her and pulled it down again. She struggled in his arms, giggling again, her contagious, little-girl laughter.

"Now, looky," Joe said. "You get that dress and put it on, or I'm gonna spank your behind for you, and I'm not just talking. Cut out the funny stuff now."

She stuck out her lower lip again, ducked her head and put her arms behind her back.

Joe looked around the room, but there wasn't a sign of any clothes, just a pair of navy-blue suede pumps with high heels that lay tipped over beside the bed. He had an inspiration and walked into the bathroom and switched on the light. Her blue leather purse was in there, with combs and cosmetics spilled over the washbowl, but that was all. There might be a hook on the inside of the door, though, Joe thought suddenly. He went in and closed the door a little and sure enough there was a dark-blue dress hanging over the hook, and a heavy brown fur coat over it. He took them down and carried them out into the bedroom.

The girl skipped around to the foot of the bed, hanging onto the footrail for support, to meet him. "Aw, you found them the first thing," she said gaily. "You're awful smart. It isn't fair."

Joe threw the coat on the bed and shook out the dress in his hands. "Yeah, I'm a pretty smart boy. Come on, let's put your dress on now."

"All right," she held up her arms obediently like a child. She hiccoughed all of a sudden. "Oh, my," she said, and she put her hand over her mouth.

"You gonna get sick?" Joe asked suspiciously. "If you gotta throw up, come on, let's go in the bathroom."

She thought it over a minute, her eyes shining with amusement over her hand. Then she took her hand away and held up her arms again. "Nope, I guess not," she said. "Come on, put my dress on, and we'll go for a ride and then we'll come back here and we'll have a drink and then we'll have a party, huh?"

"That's right," Joe said. He found the front of the dress and eased it down over her head and tugged it into place smoothly over her breasts. There was a zipper gaping open at the side of her dress, and Joe closed it and smoothed it down over her hips. She certainly had a nice figure, all right.

"Now we gotta put your shoes on," Joe said, picking them up from the floor.

She had her hand over her mouth again, and the amusement was gone from her face. "Oh, my," she mumbled. "I guess maybe I am gonna be sick."

"Here, you better come on in the bathroom," Joe said.

She pushed his arm away, and she walked unsteadily toward the door. "I can do it," she said.

She closed the door behind her. She must have got there just in time, Joe reflected. First there was the sound of water running, and after that the sound of her vomiting. Joe put her shoes back on the floor and sat down on the edge of the bed and lighted a cigarette while he waited for her.

After awhile it was all quiet in the bathroom, and in a minute Joe called to her. "Hey, how you comin' in there? Are you all right?"

For an answer he got a chirrup of a giggle, and he decided that that must mean she was all right. Anyway, she hadn't passed out, or anything like that.

A couple of minutes more and she opened the door. She had combed her hair, and put powder on her face, and fresh, bright lipstick.

"About time you was gettin' out here," Joe said, getting up from the bed. "Come on, put your shoes on."

"My goodness," she said. "Can't a girl have time to put on some lipstick?"

She took hold of his shoulders as he bent over and held out one foot obediently. He pulled the pump on. "Come on, other foot!"

She stuck her foot out, and then she went off into a whole series of giggles.

"What's the matter now?" Joe said. "Wrong foot?"

"Uh uh," she said. "Look!" She wriggled her bare toes. "No stocking on this foot."

Joe stood up and looked around the room again. "Yeah. What did you do with that other stocking?"

She thought it over, and she apparently found it very amusing. "I dunno. It musta got lost."

"Okay," Joe said, bending down again. "So we go with one stocking, what the hell."

"No, silly!" she piped in her clear, high voice. "And here I thought you were so smart." She let him put the shoe on and then she pushed him away and sat down on the edge of the bed. "See, this is what we'll do," she said. She pulled the other pump off and stripped the sheer stocking from her slender, well-formed leg and then put on the shoe again. "Not just one stocking," she said accusingly. "Two stockings, or no stockings, see?"

"Yeah, I see," Joe said. "Well, you can learn somep'n new every day, can't you? Come on, get your coat on. You didn't have a hat, huh?"

"No hat," she said gaily.

Joe helped her on with the coat. The Nicky was right about it, that coat cost a lot of money, he was thinking. He'd sure like to know where this kid came from. She was class, all right; it was easy to see that. A good thing the boss was getting her out of here, too. She could turn into jailbait as easy as dynamite.

"Hey, wait a minute," Joe said as they started for the door. He went back to the bathroom, scooped up all her stuff and put it into her purse and fastened it. "Here you are, you pretty near forgot your pocketbook," he said, offering it to her as they went out the door.

"Silly," she said again. "I don't want it. We're comin' right back here again."

"Oh, yeah, that's right," Joe said. "Oh, well, you better take it along, anyway. You might wanta powder your nose again, or something."

They started down the corridor. She wasn't any too steady on her feet yet, and Joe slipped his arm around her. "How you feel now?" he asked.

"Ah, I'm fi-ine," she said cheerfully. "My goodness, though, I certainly was sick there for a minute, wasn't I?"

"Yeah, you sure were. Here, we go down this way." He guided her down the stairs, but he had to half carry her.

"What's your name?" she asked him.

"Huh? Oh, just call me Joe," Joe said. He was thinking suddenly that he certainly hoped he got her out of here without running into the boss. It took such a long time to get her dressed that Nicky might think he layed her upstairs before he took her out, and that might make the boss sore on account of he'd told him to get her out of the joint right away.

But they got out of the building without running into the Nicky. Joe opened the little door into the alley, and shoved her ahead of him. The fog was drifting through the alley in streamers, and the rain was coming down steadily, gathering in pools between the uneven bricks of the pavement. It was hard walking on the bricks, so Joe kept his arm around the girl and hurried her along, half carrying her.

"My goodness, it's wet," she said accusingly. "This isn't any kind of a night to go for a ride. See, I told you. We should have stayed home and had a party."

"Where's home?" Joe asked automatically. He kept looking ahead of him up the alley, trying to see through the fog. He supposed the boss wouldn't care to have anybody see him taking the kid out of here, but the car was parked right there at the mouth of the alley, and with the fog like this, and the darkness, nobody was likely to see anything, anyway.

"Home?" she said, with her funny little giggle. "Oh, I haven't got a home any more. I meant back there. That's where I live now."

"Oh, I see," Joe said. "What's your name?"

He got the giggle first. "Just call me Marjorie!"

"Okay, Marjorie," he said. "Don't talk so loud, huh?" They were almost at the car now, and he didn't want to take any chances on anybody seeing them.

"Why not?" she said gaily. "Why can't I talk loud? Maybe I feel like making noise. Maybe I'll holler!"

Joe grabbed her tight and got his hand over her mouth before she really got started, and the sweat came out on his forehead. Jesus, this dame was crazy, he was thinking. Suppose she'd started hollering and raising a rumpus, anybody could a heard her, maybe a cop, maybe anybody, and the boss woulda had his skin on a board for it, as sure as all hell.

Joe shook her a little and his voice was harsh. "So you cut out the yellin' and the funny stuff, see?" he said.

He took his hand off her mouth cautiously and they started walking again. She didn't say a word. Joe figured maybe she was pulling that pouting act again, but it was too dark for him to see her face. She nearly fell just as they came out of the alley and he had to grab her in both arms.

"My goodness!" she said softly.

Joe shoved her onto the front seat of the car and slammed the door. He went around on the other side, got in and switched on the dashlights. Joe found the keys and switched on the ignition in a hurry. He gave it the gas away from the curb, so that the whole car jerked, but that was because he was nervous, and he wanted to get to hell away from here before that crazy little kid took it in her head to start yellin' or something.

Joe didn't draw an easy breath until they were a block away, and then he relaxed a little and turned on the radio. He wanted to get the reports from the fights, because he'd have to be back with the car in plenty of time for the boss to go down there to see the Terwilliger kid fight. But it was early yet, he had lots of time, Joe figured. He turned on the local station, but there wasn't anything but some music playing. He left it turned on there, anyway.

The little blonde girl beside him was just sitting there with her hands stuck in her pockets.

Joe looked at her sideways as he swung around a corner, feeling the easy power and motion of the big automobile. "How you feelin'?" he said. "What in hell's the matter with you? You ain't said nothin' for five whole minutes!"

The chirruping giggle came out of her coat collar. "I thought you were mad at me."

Joe leaned over and patted her on her knee. "Naw, hell, I ain't mad at you, baby," he said. Joe felt fine now they were in the car, and with every block he put between them and Toresca's he felt better.

"Ah, goody," she said. She slid over in the seat, pressing her body close against Joe. Joe put his arm around her so that her head and shoulders were on his chest, because he didn't want to take any chances driving the boss's car with one hand in this fog.

"Uuuuum!" she said, snuggling down against him.

Her body felt warm right through the heavy coat, and her soft, fragrant hair brushed his chin. Joe wanted her all of a sudden, and he wanted her badly. He stepped on the gas and he said, "Baby, let's you an' me have that party right away, huh?" He knew just the place, too, between a couple of vacant lots out by Water Street. It was a good place to park, no cops ever around there, not even any cars, and with this fog it would be a cinch.

Joe stepped on the gas and guided the big car through the traffic expertly. He swung off into the dark tortuous streets in the Water Street section, sending the car hurtling over the bumps into the fog. "It won't be long now, baby," Joe said, stumbling over the words. He dropped a kiss on the top of her head, and she twisted around and raised her face and kissed him two or three times, her face warm against his chin.

Jesus, it hadn't better be long, Joe was thinking, as she wriggled against him. This little babe was dynamite, for his money.

A few minutes later Joe stopped the car. It wasn't exactly the place he had had in mind to park, but it would do. It would have to, Joe thought exultantly. He switched off the lights, and the darkness and fog settled down. He put both arms around her tight and started kissing her. "Let's you and me get in the back seat, baby," he mumbled.

She giggled her funny little giggle as Joe pushed the door open.


A little while later, Joe helped her to the front seat again. He slid her in back of the wheel, and then he got in after her and slammed the door shut and started the motor. She leaned against him, one arm around his neck, the other hand on his knee. "You're nice," she said. "I like having you. What's your name? Joe? I like you, Joe. Let's go back there and have a drink, and then you stay with me, Joe, huh?"

"Sure, sure," Joe said. He had to turn the car around. He took it slow and easy because of the fog. The boss was pretty particular about this car. Once he got turned around and started up the narrow, unpaved street again, Joe turned the radio up louder. He better keep an ear out for announcements about the fights. The boss would certainly be burned up if he didn't have the car back there in plenty of time to go over to the Elks' to see the Terwilliger kid fight.

Marjorie's head bobbed against his shoulder. "My goodness, I'm getting sleepy," she said drowsily. "When we get back there I'm gonna go to sleep for awhile. You stay with me while I sleep, huh, Joe?"

"Sure, I will, honey. Don't you worry about nothin'," Joe said automatically. He wasn't in anywhere near the hurry that he had been when he came out here, and he found the dark narrow streets tricky in the fog.

All of a sudden she started giggling again. "My goodness," she said.

Joe eased around a sharp corner slowly, straining his eyes ahead of him into the mist and rain. "What's so funny now?" he asked her.

"Well, I just shut my eyes on account of I was sleepy. It isn't so good when I shut my eyes. Everything goes around and around and I see stars, and my tummy comes up. Ooooooh!"

"Then you better keep your eyes open," Joe said. "Here, I'll put the window down a little, maybe the fresh air will wake you up." He didn't want to take any chances on her going to sleep on him. He'd got to start thinking about getting her out of the car any minute now.

Marjorie had her chin on his shoulder and she moved forward a little, and kissed him lightly on the side of his face. "You're awful smart, Joe," she said in her clear, piping voice. "You're nice too. I like you. After this you're gonna stay with me all the time, aren't you, Joe?"

"Yeah, sure." They were coming back now into street lights and traffic. Joe still drove slowly. He'd have to dump the kid out along one of these street corners pretty soon.

Her chirrup of laughter was close to his ear. "F'rever an' ever an' ever! Amen!"

"Now look, kid," Joe said suddenly, his voice harsh over the splashing of the rain and the soft music of the radio. "I'm gonna talk a minute and you're gonna listen, see? Now cut out all the funny stuff an' pay attention. The party's all over an' I'm gonna take you home. You got folks and a home to go to around here someplace, and that's where you're goin'. You tell me where you live an' I'm takin' you back there right now, see? No more funny business."

"Nope!" Her voice was gay, but it was positive, too. "I haven't got a home. I used to have, but I haven't any more. They wouldn't want me now. They never liked me very much, anyway. Soooooo, we'll go back there where I was, that's where I live now. Unless you want me to go where you live, Joe. I'm gonna stay with you, Joe."

"Okay, have it your way," Joe said shortly, and he stepped on the gas a little. Christ, she was certainly one crazy little dame, Joe was thinking. So okay, it was her own funeral. He gave her a chance and she wouldn't take it, to hell with her. The boss was probably right about it. Let her run around the streets awhile in this rain and she'd get some sense in her head; then she'd beat it for home and damn glad to go back. But getting her out of the car was going to take a little doing. Let's see, he was pretty close to Main Street now. Well, he'd give her one break, he'd drop her off right in the downtown section, instead of leaving her way off out in the sticks someplace all by herself.

Marjorie nestled against him contentedly. "Oooh, look!" she said suddenly, pointing. "Funny lights!"

She meant the headlights of cars they met along the street. Those headlights even looked funny to Joe, too, the way they came out of the fog all of a sudden, two glaring yellow eyes, and then were gone again.

Marjorie started counting them. "One, two," she said, "well, buckle my shoe! Three, four, well, shut my mouth!" Then she started giggling.

Any place along here would do, Joe was thinking. One good thing about it, with the weather like it was the sidewalks were practically deserted, and as far as the traffic in the street went, nobody was going to see anything in this dark and mist, nor pay any attention if they did. At a busy intersection right in the downtown area, Joe slowed up and crossed Main Street cautiously. The fog made driving tricky and he didn't want to take any chances on maybe crumbling a fender for the boss.

Just across Main Street he saw a parking space along the curb. It was near a hydrant, but that was all right, too; this wasn't going to take him but a second. Joe slid up to the curb and stopped, but he left the motor running.

"Well, here we are," he said to Marjorie. He shoved her over on the seat a little and leaned in front of her to turn the door handle.

"Well, here we are," she mimicked him gaily. "It was a nice ride, but I like it better up there . . ."

"Come on, let go a me, now," Joe said impatiently. "We gotta get outa the car, come on."

He slid over on the seat, shoving her out ahead of him. It was a good thing he had hold of her, because she nearly fell when she stood up on the curb.

"My goodness," she said gaily, as Joe put one arm around her and hustled her along the sidewalk toward the corner. "My crazy old feet aren't good for much, are they? I guess I need a drink." She giggled her funny little chirrup of laughter. Just before they got up to the corner on Main Street, Joe stopped. As soon as he stopped she put both arms around his neck and leaned against him. "Nasty wet!" she said, cuddling her face away from the rain against his overcoat. Joe loosened her hands quickly and spun around and made off for the car, running easily and lightly, his feet spatting on the wet sidewalk.

"Joe!" Her voice behind him was a whimper with a lot of fear in it. "Don't leave me, Joe! I don't feel good! Joe, don't leave me all alone, Joe!"

Joe made the car in one bound, and slid over under the wheel, pulling the door shut after him with a slam. He was looking in the rear-vision mirror when he pulled away from the curb, and he looked a fraction of a minute longer after the car straightened out and he saw it all. Two glaring yellow eyes of headlights came out of the fog suddenly and for one second he saw her very plainly, silhouetted right in front of those lights, because she was in the street, running after his car, or trying to run, staggering, her arms outstretched. For just a second Joe saw her plainly silhouetted in front of those lights. Then, with a terrible suddenness, she just wasn't in front of the lights any more. Joe heard the thud; he heard the screaming shriek of brakes as the car behind him stopped. He heard voices. But that was all he heard. For just a moment he closed his eyes, but he opened them the next second and stepped on the gas hard, everything a jumble of fog and traffic and Neon signs and rain in front of him. Joe was cold all over and clammy with sweat. He could feel his legs shaking, too. His mouth was dry, but all the time he kept feeling as though he wanted to spit. "Aw, Christ, Christ," he said hoarsely. He said it out loud, because he heard his voice saying it. He kept driving fast through the fog and rain. He kept turning corners. He didn't know where he was, and he didn't care. He kept on driving like that for five or ten minutes. Then he had to stop at an intersection because a policeman was directing traffic there. All of a sudden the policeman lifted his arm, the wet black rubber of his slicker gleaming, and waved Joe ahead. The policeman was a big man. He had a cheerful, florid face, and he gave Joe a friendly smile as he gave him the signal to drive on. Right then something clicked for Joe, and he started thinking again. Well, what the hell was he driving around here for, what was he running from like this? The police weren't after him. Nobody was after him. Why should they be after him? He hadn't done anything. It wasn't him that run over the kid. Joe switched his thinking away from that quickly, because he saw again with terrible clarity the image of the little blonde girl with her arms outstretched, silhouetted in front of those headlights and then just disappearing with a terrible suddenness. It followed through, Joe heard that thud again, and the screaming brakes. It made him prickle all over and the cold sweat came out again.

He'd got to get hold of himself, Joe told himself wildly. He hadn't had anything to do with it. He'd done just like the boss told him; the boss had nothing to get sore about. It wasn't his fault if she got herself run over; it had nothing to do with him. It didn't make no difference to him, anyway. It didn't make any difference to the boss. Nobody had nothing on him; he hadn't done nothing. Besides, nobody knew nothing about it. That reassured Joe more than anything. The boss didn't know anything about it, nor he didn't have to know because there wasn't any way that he could find out about it. Joe took his first easy breath. He felt better; some of the terror was gone, but he was weak and trembling. He was beginning to feel sort of sick. He figured he better get this car off the streets before he cracked it up and really had something to worry about.

The radio was still playing softly, although that was the first time he had noticed it, and it wasn't music any more. It was a man's voice, and he was giving returns from the fights. That gave Joe a bad start too. He had forgotten all about the goddam fights. He'd got to get the car back to Toresca's quick. If the boss had got ready to go down to see the Terwilliger kid fight and then had to monkey around waiting for a cab, he was going to catch plenty of hell about this.

Joe turned a corner and headed for Toresca's. He was weak with relief when he switched off the ignition at the curb, but the silence after the motor stopped closed in on him. Jesus, that rain! Patter, patter, patter! Enough to drive a guy bats, Joe thought wildly. Now you better take it easy, he warned himself. You can't go to pieces.

When Joe got out of the car he discovered that the stiffening was gone from his knees, and he stumbled over the rough bricks going down the alley. "My goodness," he heard the clear, piping voice and then the funny little giggle. He heard it plain right there in the dark alley, where there wasn't anything except the rain and the fog and some ashcans. Joe discovered that his skin didn't fit his body, and it crawled along raw sensitive nerve ends. Christ, that rain, Joe was thinking, drive a guy nuts, patter, patter, patter . . .

He went in through the alley door and walked along the corridor to the Nicky's office. From out front, he could hear the muffled sound of the orchestra playing. He knocked on the office door and then opened it.

# 36

WHEN JOE ENTERED TORESCA'S OFFICE, THE NICKY was standing in front of the window, back of his desk. He had just put on his suit coat and was fussing with his shirt cuffs. The portable radio on the desk was playing some music, and the room was full of drifting spirals of cigarette smoke. There was an odor of perfume in the room, too, sharp through the smoke.

"You got here just right, Joe," Nicky said, smoothing his cuffs. "Al just called, the kid is goin' on in a few minutes. Christ, where you been, Joey? You and the blonde musta had quite a party, is that right?"

Joe didn't say anything. He was looking at the chair in front of the desk. Just four steps away, maybe five. Just five steps and then he could sit down, just five steps, if he could make his legs hold him up that long, and move with him.

"You got her outa here, didn't you?" Nicky said with a sudden faint suspicion in his voice.

Joe kept his eyes fixed on the chair, and he took a deep breath and decided to try it. He made it all right, too, except that the top of his head jarred so when he walked. Have to get rubber heels on my shoes, Joe thought idiotically. Joe sat down in the chair, and then his whole thin body seemed to fall to pieces. He raised one hand to his face, but when he got it there he didn't know what to do with it. So he doubled it into a fist against his mouth, and gently chewed at his knuckles.

The Nicky stopped still and looked at him. "Christ a'mighty, Joe, what's the matter with you?"

The sound of Nicky's voice pulled Joe out of it a little. "Nothin's the matter," he said through his dry lips. "I got her outa here all right."

Nicky wasn't satisfied. He was still looking at Joe curiously. "I believe that little blonde was too much for you, Joey," he said mockingly. "Maybe you can't take it any more the way you used to, is that right? Yeah, she was a nice little number, all right, that is, if you like 'em young and ripe. She make much trouble gettin' her out of here?"

Joe wished to hell that the Nicky would stop talking about the little blonde. Because if he didn't stop, Joe had the feeling that any minute now he was going to have one of those flashes, see her plain again in front of those yellow headlights, see her disappear with that ghastly suddenness, and hear again the sounds that came after that.

"What the hell, Joe," the Nicky said impatiently. "You're white as a sheet and your eyes are hanging out on your face. I think maybe you're allergic to blondes. I think maybe you better have a drink before you start screamin' and I have to call the wagon."

Nicky bent down and pulled out a desk drawer. He lifted out a bottle of whisky and poured out a shot for Joe and handed it to him across the desk. "Can you make your mouth, or shall I pour it down you?" he said mockingly.

Joe took the glass and swallowed the liquor gratefully.

The Nicky filled the little glass again. "Better make it two, it wasn't full."

Joe downed the second one and coughed a little. The liquor didn't feel warm in his stomach. It merely seemed as if all the rest of his body except his stomach was shivering with an unbearable damp cold.

Nicky returned the bottle to the drawer, pushing it shut with his knee. Joe wiped his mouth on the back of his hand, his eyes staring straight ahead of him. Nicky lighted a cigarette and left it in his mouth. He put his slender, well-manicured hands flat on the desk and leaned over between his arms toward Joe.

"Joe," he said softly.

He waited a minute and then he said, "Joe, when I talk to you, you look at me, is that right?"

Joe turned his head around, and it felt crazy, just turning his head like that, as if his neck were rubber and if he weren't careful his head would go right on the whole way around and then just keep on going around and around like that, like a slow top spinning. He stopped his head from turning all the way around by focusing his eyes on the Nicky. By some trick of the lamp, all the light was glaring on his immaculate soft white shirt and maroon necktie, and his face was completely in shadow. His face was lost in dark shadow, just the red end of his cigarette bobbing in front of his lips when he talked.

Nicky Toresca looked down into Joe's lifted white face, with the distended dark eyes, and he repeated his name again softly. "Joe, something has scared the hell out of you, is that right? Maybe you better tell me what it was. Maybe you got into some trouble. Maybe I better know all about it, just in case. You better start talkin', Joey."

Joe continued to stare in fascination at that shining white shirt front, and at the dark face lost in black shadow. He licked at his lips before he answered. "No trouble," he said thinly.

"Is that right?" the Nicky said gently. He waited just a moment and then he spoke abruptly, the words like whiplashes in Joe's face. "So maybe you accidentally dumped the little blonde in the river after all, Joe!"

Joe cowered away from him. Some of the fear came back to his face, and he stared at the Nicky in a kind of goggle-eyed incredulity.

Nicky moved around the corner of the desk closer to Joe all of a sudden. "Joe, what become of the little blonde, anyway?"

Joe moved his lips, but no sound came out of them. The Nicky waited, and, while he waited, he moved his right hand just a little, flexed the fingers, and the heavy cameo ring moved on one of them.

Joe started talking desperately. "How the hell I know what become of her? I got her outa here and I dumped her off on a street corner, like you told me. Then I got back in the car and drove off. How the hell I know what become of her?"

The Nicky thought it over a little, his face impassive. "So maybe that's all right then," he said at last. "So maybe it's something else."

"It ain't nothing else! It ain't nothing the matter," Joe said wildly. "I just got the jumps tonight, that's all. It's this—it's this goddam rain! Patter, patter! It's enough to drive a guy nuts. Rain, fog! Jesus!"

"It might be the rain, at that," Nicky said with sudden and unexpected amiability. "Christ, Joe, sometimes I think you are half nuts. With a guy like you, it wouldn't take nothin' much more'n the rain going patter, patter to send you off your nut, at that. The rain goin' patter, patter!" The Nicky laughed softly. "Christ, let's go on to the fights. We probably fooled around here till the kid's got his kay-oh and it's all over with. They're about due for some more announcements on this goddam radio! We might as well wait."

Nicky went over and turned up the radio a little. He laughed as he turned the dial. "The rain goin' patter, patter. Jesus, Joey, some a these days they're gonna lock you up in the loony bin!"

The music played on, and Joe straightened up in his chair a little. Some of the strain was gone from his face, but he still looked jittery, as if at any moment he would jump right out of his chair, or right over the desk, maybe, chair and all.

The Nicky waited, and in a minute the music faded out. The voice of the announcer cut in.

"Well, Ladies and Gentlemen, the big news right at present from the final eliminations in the Golden Gloves Contest that are going on right now in the Elks' Temple Auditorium is that Jimmy Terwilliger of this city just scored a knockout over his opponent, Jackie Warren of Collinsville, in the fourth round of an eight-round bout. Jimmy, as you probably know, fights in the middle-weight division, and his victory doesn't come as much of news to anybody. Only one other contestant now stands between Jimmy and that coveted trip to the state finals in Grand Rapids . . ."

"Aw, hell," the Nicky said disgustedly, as the announcer went on talking. "Christ, I knew we'd fool around here and miss the kid." He threw a cigarette into the ash tray with a sharp flick of his fingers. "Christ!"

The voice of the announcer cut in again.

"Bad weather conditions in this vicinity claimed a third traffic victim in this city a few minutes ago. Earlier this evening, a car driven by Andrew Wankers, 916 East Caspar Street, collided with the rear of a truck stalled at the edge of the pavement on Dennis Road, just north of the city limits. Both occupants of the automobile, Wankers and his wife, Genevieve, died before an ambulance could reach the scene of the accident. The third fatality occurred a few moments ago on Jones Street just north of Main when a young girl, who has not yet been identified, stepped directly in the path of an oncoming automobile and was instantly killed. No detailed description of the victim is available at the present, except the fact that she was young, blonde hair, and that she was wearing a dark-blue dress and a brown fur coat at the time the accident occurred. This station will co-operate with the police in an effort to identify her as soon as possible. A complete description will be broadcast as soon as it is available. The identity of the driver of the death car has not yet been ascertained. Eye-witnesses to the accident attribute the victim's failure to see the oncoming vehicle to the poor visibility due to the heavy fog that has blanketed this city since early this afternoon. For further details stay tuned to your home station that gives you the local news as it happens."

Joe Braun stiffened in his chair and he sucked in his breath audibly. Nicky softened the music following the announcement; and when he turned around, his face was taut and furious with anger.

"Joe, it couldn't be you accidentally ran over the little blonde, could it?"

"Aw, God, no," Joe said wildly. "I swear to God, I . . ."

"You talk, Joe, and you talk straight and fast," Nicky said.

Joe's face worked convulsively, and he grasped the arms of his chair tight with his hands as he started talking. "Jesus, I done just like you said. I drop her off there on the corner and then . . ."

"What corner?"

"Like the radio said, the corner a Jones and Main, on the north side, and then I . . ."

The Nicky was trembling with anger. "Christ, you pick the busiest corner in town, with about ten cops and a hundred people to see what you're doin'! Go on!"

"There wasn't nobody around, honest!" Joe said desperately. "Well, I dump her out like you say and then I beat it back to the car and drive away. I was looking in the mirror to see if it was all clear when I pulled out, and I—I—seen it happen."

"Seen what happen?"

Joe licked his lips and got his voice started again. "Well, you couldn't see nothin' on account a the fog, just like the guy said. All of a sudden I see these headlights come up out of the fog, and just when I see them, why, I see the kid. She was—well—I guess she was trying to run after your car . . . She was tryin' to run out in the street. These headlights come up fast, that's how I happen to see her at all and then—then—that was all."

"Did the car stop after it hit her?"

"Yeah, it stopped all right." It was all going on there inside of Joe's head again. He heard it all again, the thud of her body under that automobile, the screech of brakes as the car skidded to a stop on the wet pavement. Joe held onto the arms of his chair as tight as he could, and the sweat broke out on his forehead. More than anything in the world he wanted another shot of that whisky in the desk drawer.

Because of his anger, the Nicky's studied suavity was cracking.

His face was twitching with rage and he walked the floor in front of his desk.

"You're lyin', you bastard," he snarled at Joe. "The car didn't stop. You heard what the radio said. They didn't know who hit her. The car didn't stop. Maybe there never was another car. Maybe you're lyin', maybe you run over her with my automobile."

"No, honest, I swear to God. It's just like I said it was," Joe said. "I seen the car when it hit her. I heard the brakes when the car stopped. I seen it stop, I heard voices yellin' around and stuff after the car stopped."

Nicky stopped his floor pacing and turned a furious face toward Joe. "You heard voices! Jesus Christ, a minute ago you try to tell me there wasn't nobody around there seein' you dump her out of the car, now you tell about hearin' voices!"

"I did hear voices," Joe said, his voice quavering. "But, honest to God, there wasn't nobody around when I dumped her out. If there was, I couldn't see 'em in the goddam fog, and if I couldn't see them, Christ, how the hell could they see me? Nobody seen me!"

The Nicky paced the floor again, his hands deep in the pockets of his trousers. Joe sat there and licked his lips, watching Nicky's feet walking back and forth over the rug—small slim feet in expensive black shoes with pointed toes that gleamed in the light. Just watching Nicky's feet, Joe could tell that he was angry, more angry and upset than Joe had ever seen him. Joe was scared, and after awhile he spoke defensively, forcing a kind of bravado into his voice.

"Hell," he said, "I done just like you told me. You tell me to dump her off on a street corner, so I do, and nobody seen me do it. I didn't run the hell over her, so what we got to be worried about?"

Joe looked at the Nicky anxiously, but the Nicky didn't seem to be impressed with his logic.

Joe tried again, his voice unnecessarily loud and blustering with his nervousness. "Hell, you wanted to get rid of her, didn't you?" Joe made an attempt at laughter that was not a marked success. "Well, she sure is rid of now, all right!"

Nicky whirled on him in a fury. "Christ, you bungling, crazy, dummy bastard! So now you think we're rid of the little bitch, huh?

You ain't even got the brains to know what's gonna happen. Well, I can tell you what's gonna happen, all right. Somebody must have seen you dump her off down there, hell, right downtown on Main Street. Somebody seen you, and somebody spotted my automobile, as sure as hell. You think it's gonna be hard to spot that automobile of mine? Christ! There ain't another one like mine in the whole goddam town. And that's just the beginnin' of it. The next thing you know, somebody's gonna identify that kid. I told you, she wasn't no floozy, she was class; she's liable to turn out to be dynamite. She's gonna turn out to be somebody's dumb little kid that's been missin' from home three or four days. Christ, that's gonna be nice, ain't it? Then them smart doctors are gonna spill the news that she was soaked in liquor when she got killed and they're gonna spill some more things about her too, maybe. Then the whole goddam bunch a them are gonna come after me. Hell, there's a lotta folks in this town that don't like me; they been lookin' for a chance to run me to hell outa here for years. This is just what they're lookin' for, maybe. Jesus, you wouldn't think a nothin' like that, would you?"

Joe was completely silenced, his face apprehensive. The Nicky stood still a moment, and then, as if the full import of his own words had just come to him, his eyes widened in his face, and he smacked his fist hard into the palm of his hand. "Christ!" he said. He got around the corner of the desk in a couple of strides and yanked open the drawer. But this time he poured the liquor for himself. His hands were none too steady with the bottle.

He had a couple of shots of the liquor and it seemed to steady him. He sat down in the chair behind his desk. "We gotta think a something, is that right?" he said, more to the empty air than to Joe. "We gotta get an angle on this. We gotta think a something quick before the police and the WCTU an' the DAR an' the YWCA an' all them bastards come bearin' down here!"

While he waited for the Nicky to pull a solution out of the air, Joe unobtrusively slid the bottle toward him across the desk and poured himself a shot.

Just about then the announcer's voice came over the radio again, and Nicky nearly jumped out of his chair, turning up the volume dial. The announcer gave some more news from the fights, and Nicky waited impatiently, leaning forward in his chair, his fingers on the dial. The pleasant radio voice said:

"Police have made known further details concerning the death of an unidentified girl who was struck and killed by an automobile at the corner of Jones Street and Main, this evening. The car, owned by Theodore Vaspanski, East Adams Street, was being driven at the time of the accident by his nephew, Stanislaus Vaspanski of Dearborn, who was not carrying his driver's license at the time the accident occurred. Vaspanski will not be held, police said, on the evidence of several eye-witnesses to the accident who testified that the girl stepped directly in front of the oncoming vehicle. Effort is still in progress toward the identification of the victim. Police Sergeant Williams of the city police department has authorized the following description: Height, five foot four, weight, one hundred and twenty pounds, dark-blonde hair, blue eyes. She was wearing a dark-blue dress, a brown fur coat and blue shoes, and she was carrying a blue leather purse. Her age was estimated at sixteen. Any listener with information that might speed the progress of her identification is urged to contact either the police department or this station immediately. Witnesses recount that several minutes prior to the accident the victim was seen to alight from an automobile in the company of an unidentified man wearing a dark overcoat. Her escort left her on the corner and returned to his automobile and drove away. It is alleged that in her attempt to rejoin him, the young woman ran out into the street directly in the path of the Vaspanski vehicle. After preliminary examinations, it has been alleged that the victim was under the influence of alcohol when death occurred. For further details, keep tuned to your home station which . . ."

The Nicky turned the dial down, his face suddenly livid.

"Jesus, see what I told you!" he said to Joe, his voice high and out of control. "It's just like I told you it was gonna be. Hell, them bastard cops are gonna trace down my automobile in no time, and then they gonna come bustin' in over here. We gotta cook up something fast."

Nicky's forehead wrinkled and he fumbled for his cigarettes. Joe watched him apprehensively from his chair, his face frightened and miserable.

"We gonna say you picked her up in some bar, see?" Nicky said rapidly. "She was settin' there drinkin', see, so you buy her a couple drinks. You offer to take her home on accounta it's a bad night. But she don't wanta go home, she wants to keep drinking. So you let her off on the corner like she says, an' you drive off and that's all you know about it."

Joe crouched farther back in his chair. "You mean I gotta talk to the police? You mean I gotta . . . ?"

"You gonna do just like I tell you to," Nicky said, "is that right?" The Nicky thought it over some more, his hands fiddling his cigarette nervously. "Except we gotta have witnesses," he said. "Hell, I can get a dozen witnesses, except I gotta have a bartender from some bar someplace . . ."

Joe made an obvious effort to pull himself together and be helpful. "What'sa matter with the bartender out here? I could say I picked her up out here at this bar, couldn't I? Jesus, why can't you . . . ?"

Nicky gave him a look of furious contempt and loathing. "Christ, keep your mouth shut. Do I have to draw a map for you? The kid never set her foot in this joint, nobody around here ever saw her before in their life. How many times I have to keep telling you!"

"Naw!" Joe quavered. "Nobody around here ever seen her before in their life! Except me! Christ, I don't wanta get mixed up in nothin'! I ain't gonna . . ."

"You're gonna do like I tell you! Hell, what you got to be scared of? They can't get nothin' on you!"

Just at that moment the phone rang, and the Nicky jumped in his chair noticeably. He looked at it, and it rang again, and after that it kept ringing. Nicky took a deep breath, and his face all of a sudden was a shade paler. He stretched out his hand and picked up the phone cautiously. The ominous jangle of its ringing stopped. For just a moment the Nicky hesitated, then he lifted it and said, "Yeah?"

It was Petey's excited, exuberant voice that came bubbling out of the receiver into his ear.

"Christ, I thought you was dead!" she said cheerfully. "What's the matter you weren't over here to see the kid fight? Jesus, you oughta seen him, he never looked better. Four rounds it went! Aw, he's in swell shape! Looky, you better get over here. He might come out again anytime now. The heavies are out now, and it don't take 'em long. The kid might fight again anytime now. You better git on over here if you . . ."

A curious look of relief came over the Nicky's face as he listened to her voice.

He broke in on her sharply. "Look, cut out the yellin', will you? I want you to get outa there and catch a cab and get to hell over here just as quick as you can. You hear what I said?"

"Hey, what gives by you?" There was surprise in Petey's voice.

The Nicky never hesitated. "Joey's run into a mess a trouble. I want you over here right away!"

There was a moment of silence from the other end of the phone, and he said impatiently, "Quit wasting time, you hear what I said?"

"Okay," Petey said disgustedly. "Keep your shirt on, I'm comin'."

She slammed up the receiver, and Nicky put the phone back in the cradle.

"Hey! What you mean, I run into a mess a trouble?" Joe said with the nervous querulousness in his voice. "What you mean, sayin' I run into a mess a trouble? They can't get nothin' on me, you said so yourself. Hell, I ain't done nothing! What you mean, tellin' her?"

"You gonna shut up!" Nicky got up from his chair again, and walked the floor restlessly.

"Yeah," Joe muttered, his eyes on the shiny pointed toes of Nicky's shoes again. "But what you want her comin' over here for? What you wanta tell her . . . ?"

"I ask her to come over here because I want her here, and what's it to you, is that right? Now you keep your big flappy mouth shut and let me think!"

Nicky trod back and forth across the floor. Joe muttered something under his breath and kept staring at the bottle of expensive whisky on the desk. Out of the radio a girl's voice wailed about being nobody's baby. Cigarette smoke spun around the lampshade slowly in flat, two-dimensional arabesques. The rain was still pattering against the windows softly.

"What the hell's holdin' her up? She shoulda been here by now," Nicky said impatiently.

Joe didn't answer him. The rain blew softly against the windows and Joe shivered all over. His eyes looked queer and dull. It was one of the times when he saw it all over again, saw the headlights out of the fog, and the girl in front of them, disappearing with ghastly rapidity. But this time instead of a thud and screech of brakes, he heard a clear, piping voice saying, "My goodness!" then her gay, childish, little chirrup of a giggle.

After that Joe forgot his temerity about drinking the boss's good liquor, and poured himself another shot.


Petey paid off her taxi driver and walked across the sidewalk to the entrance. There was no sign of Nicky's doorman tonight, and she didn't blame the guy for taking the night off. The rain was still falling softly, and although the fog had begun to lift, it still drifted in eerie long streaks and streamers.

Petey strode up the ramp, shivering a little. The blonde hat-check girl was leaning forward on her shelf, her shoulders hunched disconsolately.

"Hi yuh, honey," Petey said cheerfully. "How's business?"

"What business!" the girl said disgustedly. "And I don't bet we have a late crowd either! How's the weather?"

"Still raining," Petey said, "but the damn fog is going. It's still plenty nasty out."

She walked across the dance floor to the little door on the right. She pushed it open and walked down the corridor. Even the click of her high heels sounded irritated. What all this amounted to was that she was going to miss Jimmy's last fight. Whatever was eating on the Nicky and Joe better be good or she would personally knock both their heads off.

She rapped on the door, a loud impatient tattoo, yanked the door open and went in, letting it slam behind her.

Nicky was walking the floor. He stopped and said nastily, "Where the hell you been? I told you to get over here, didn't I?"

It all looked a little peculiar to Petey. There was Joe, collapsed in a chair with his overcoat still on, and a look on his face as if he were a fish that had been out of water for quite awhile. There was the Nicky, walking the floor as if he couldn't sit still, and the smooth mask of his face split wide apart by something she recognized as fear. Besides that, the room was so warm and so full of cigarette smoke that the air was unbearable.

"Jesus, you could suffocate in here!" Petey said. She dropped her purse on the desk and opened the window a little, banging the Venetian blind.

"Okay," she said, as she turned around. "What's the idea? Come on, tell mama where it hurts!"

They told her, all right. That is, the Nicky did most of the talking. Ever so often Joe would break in and Nicky would tell him to shut his mouth. Between them Petey got a pretty straight account of what had happened and what was happening. While she listened, she sat on the edge of the desk and crossed her legs. Her face was scowling. She took her black cigarette holder out of her bag, cleaned it and fitted a cigarette into the end. She pulled off her hat, threw it on the desk, and shook out her long heavy hair impatiently.

Nicky stopped talking and Petey looked from him to Joe and back to Nicky again. "My God," she said contemptuously. "You're a nice pair a rats! Regular little Helping Hand Society! You sure handed that poor little kid a break!"

"This is no time to be funny, is that right?" Nicky said. "What you think I shoulda done with her, run an ad in the lost and found column?"

"Aw, skip it," Petey said. "I don't wanta hear you talk any more about her. It makes me sick. You always got enough floozies around here to keep this joint going. She was some poor little dumb kid, why couldn't you give her a break?"

The Nicky's face was livid. "I give up goin' to Sunday School years ago," he said, and, in his effort at control, he stumbled over words. "I don't want to start in again tonight, is that right? So maybe you don't think I'm in a spot! The law always played ball with me pretty around this town, but if they get in a spot now, they'll throw me to the wolves as sure as hell!"

Petey looked at him for a minute, and then she laughed quietly. Her voice, when she spoke, was just as quiet. "You know," she said, "if this whole thing didn't make me sick, I'd get a kick outa you right now. You've had a hell of a time for yourself around here, pretendin' you was a big shot! You've had a lotta fun crackin' the whip over a lotta dumb bunnies like Joe, and thinkin' what a big hard tough guy you was. But the first time some trouble comes along and it begins to look like maybe the heat might be on, what do you do? Why, you fly all to pieces and start shakin' and shiverin' like the little yellow rat you are!"

For a minute it looked as if the Nicky was going to hit her, but he didn't. "Okay," he said. "Go right ahead and shoot your mouth off. Go right ahead, laugh and have fun. You think I don't know what I'm talkin' about, maybe. Ever so often the law around this town has gotta have a big clean-up crusade to keep the people happy and keep their own goddam jobs. They're about due for another one. And I ain't gonna be it, is that right? Hell, they could ruin my business, they could run me outa this town. You better get this through your head, if they throw me to the wolves I ain't gonna go alone, is that right? Maybe you think I couldn't slap a kidnappin' charge on Joey, and some others that ain't even that nice! Maybe you don't think I couldn't send you right along with him as an accessory, if I wanted to! Don't get any wrong ideas about this, baby, if I wanta I can . . ."

Joe Braun was out of his chair suddenly, his eyes bulging out of his face. "Hey, what you mean slap a kidnappin' charge on me or something? Hell, I ain't done nothing. I never had nothin' to do with none a this! What you mean, sayin' you gonna . . ."

The Nicky whirled on him. "Joey, I'm gettin' goddam sick a you! You're nothin' but a crazy, dummy, bunglin' bastard. You got me into this mess, goddam yuh! So maybe you're gonna be the one to get me out! You keep your mouth shut an' . . ."

"I ain't a gonna do it," Joe shrieked. "Hell, I ain't done nothin'. You get in a jam, an' if you think I'm gonna set around and let you hang something on me, you're crazy! Hell, I ain't gonna . . ."

"Take your dirty hands off my coat, you bastard," Nicky said. "You're gonna keep your mouth shut and do like I tell you or I'll knock your . . ."

"You ain't gonna do nothin'! You ain't gonna hang nothin' on me! Why, you sonofabitch! You yella rat! You coward!"

Joe lunged forward, his arms flailing, knocking Nicky backward, off balance. Petey swung her legs around instantly, and came up on the floor the other side of the desk. Joe grabbed Nicky, half by the neck, half by his collar and shook him with all the strength he had, cursing between his whistling breaths. Toresca got his feet solid under him and ducked away out of Joe's hands. There was the loud sound of his shirt ripping away at the neck. He came up from a crouch like a rubber ball bouncing, and his doubled right fist caught Joe at the side of the chin. It was a hard punch, and it knocked Joe backward against the desk. The cameo ring ripped the skin away along the side of Joe's jaw. Joe clawed at the desk for support, but it moved away with the impact of his body and he fell to his knees. When the desk started moving, Petey moved too. Just at that very moment the music on the radio gave over to a newscast. Petey pulled the cord on the portable radio and grabbed it by the handle on the top. She scrambled over the fallen chair and around the corner of the desk toward the door. There she stopped, the radio in her arms, and threw the button that switched it over on batteries.

"You bastard!" the Nicky shrieked. His sleek hair was mussed, his shirt was torn down the front, his tie askew. His face wasn't a mask any more. It was alive and livid with hate and fear, fury and spite. Joe was trying to scramble to his feet, half dazed. The Nicky's breath came in sobs. He caught up the whisky bottle from the desk by its neck and balanced it in his hand for the swing. Joe saw him grab the bottle just before he straightened up, and he shot forward off his feet, the whole lean length of his body in a clean flying tackle. He caught Nicky just above the knees and they both went down onto the floor hard. The bottle shot out of Nicky's hand away from them and broke on the floor almost at Petey's feet. She wasn't paying much attention, though. She was holding the portable radio in her arm, her head bent with her ear against the speaker. Nicky and Joe rolled together on the floor. There was the sound of their loud, uneven breathing, their grunts and curses, the thump of bodies on the floor, the smack of a hard fist against flesh. The chair in front of the desk went over, crashing. The next moment the desk rocked on its legs, and the high standard lamp fell off the corner and the room was in darkness. Petey pushed the button beside the door automatically. The overhead lamp came on and poured light through the room again. Nicky was on the bottom, but he kicked Joe away from him, a well-placed hard kick with one of his neat slender pointed-toed shoes. Joe went over backward, grunting, and struck against the overturned wooden chair. As Nicky came for him again, Joe got hold of the chair clumsily by the legs, and swung it with all his strength directly at Nicky's head. His aim wasn't very good and Nicky ducked, the back of it just glancing off his head. He ducked away again and rolled over, agile as a monkey. His fingers closed over a jagged piece of the glass from the broken bottle at Petey's feet. He whirled around on Joe, the jagged glass ready in his hand.

"Hey!" Petey said. She kicked Nicky's hand hard with her black pump, so that the glass flew out of his fingers and away from him. She opened the door into the corridor then and called loudly, "Red! Gus! Somebody! Hey!"

By the time the red-headed fellow and another one got there on a run, there wasn't much happening. Petey stood in the doorway, the radio in her hand. The room was a shambles, and the Nicky was just scrambling to his feet. Joe was half crouched on the floor, his face and torn shirt and coat streaked with blood, and his mouth wide open for his hoarse uneven breathing.

"Holy Christ!" the guy named Red said, staring in from the doorway.

Petey's face was impassive. "Get Joe outa here," she said shortly. "Get him cleaned up. And take a look at his chin, he might have to have stitches."

The men hesitated just a moment. The Nicky got onto his feet and turned away, his back to them, his shoulders heaving with his breathing. Then they went into the room, kicking the wreckage of the chair out of the way. They helped Joe onto his feet; they led him out and he went with them without protest, half dazed, his legs tottering under him. When they were gone Petey slammed the door shut. The Nicky didn't turn around, nor did he say anything. Petey walked over to the desk and put the radio down on it. The rug was wrinkled up under the desk. She tugged at one end of it and kicked the other out straight. She looked around the room a little, scowling. She righted the chair behind the desk, which was unhurt, and she picked up the lamp. The shade was ripped and flattened, and so she set lamp and shade on the floor along the wall. The wastebasket had overturned and rolled under the desk. Petey picked that up too. There had been only a couple of wads of paper in it besides the emptyings from the ash tray. Petey picked up the paper and put it back in the basket.

Just then a knock came at the door. Petey waited a minute, looking at the Nicky, but he didn't turn around or pay any attention to it.

"Yeah?" she said.

One of the waiters opened the door cautiously. "You want I should clean this up a little?" he said, his voice and face both impersonal.

"You might pick up some of them hunks a glass in front of the door there, and get that chair outa here," Petey said. He went to work swiftly, with no more than one glance at the Nicky's back. Petey stepped out of the way, and fitted a cigarette into her holder silently. When the man was done, his dustpan full of glass and the wreckage of chair gathered up in his arms, she said tersely, "You better bring in another bottle, a pitcher a water and some ice, too, huh?"

"Right," he said.

She held the door open for him and he maneuvered his armload out. When he came back she took the tray and slammed the door shut with her foot. She hesitated a little and then she walked over to the Nicky. "Come on," she said with a sort of weary gentleness in her voice. "Come on, set down and have a drink."

He took a deep breath and held it for a minute, and then he walked over and sat down in the chair behind the desk. As he sat down he struggled his arms out of the wrinkled, ripped and blood-smeared coat, flinging it to the floor behind him. His shirt was torn and dirty, the tie hanging loosely on the front of it. His hair was tousled, his face was bruised, one eye was blackening, and there was a cut in his eyebrow over it. He didn't look at her, and he put his elbow on the desk and dropped his head onto his hand, his fingers over his eyes. His knuckles were scraped, and there was a cut around the big black cameo ring.

Petey mixed two drinks. When she was done she shoved the tray over and made herself comfortable on a corner of the desk.

"Here's your drink."

He made her no answer. He didn't even move.

Petey took hold of his wrist gently with her fingers. "Come on, here's your drink."

His hand dropped away from his eyes then and he straightened up a little in his chair. "Thanks," he said. He picked up the glass and took a drink, but he still didn't look at her.

Petey smoked silently for a couple of minutes, turning her own glass in her fingers. "Looky," she said at last. "I hate to bring the glad tidings like this, but you might want to know about it. They just give some more dope over the radio a minute ago. It seems there is some big shot around this town, name of Amhurst. Seems he owns a factory or something. Well, come to find out he's got a sixteen-year-old daughter named Marjorie that's been missing three or four days. Police said he had been informed and was gonna take a look at the kid. In the meantime the radio Joe said the police were busy tracing the car she got out of just before she was killed, and they expected to get a break on that angle any minute."

He didn't say anything. His eyes were staring straight ahead of him. He took another long drink out of his glass and groped in one pocket.

Petey lighted a cigarette for him out of her own package and handed it to him.

"If I was you," she said, "I'd just sit tight, see? I'd wait an' see what happens. Let 'em come over here. The best they can do is play a long shot on identifying your car. Maybe there were some witnesses, so what? It was a rainy, foggy, dark night, and nobody was going around writing down license numbers. All you gotta do is sit tight. Hand 'em a good strong alibi, if they come pokin' in over here. Tell 'em you and two or three of the boys were out a town with the car all evening. Jesus, you got connections out a town that will alibi you to hell and gone. And stick with it. Let 'em blow their heads off. They can't get anything on you. Besides that, I gotta feelin' you ain't gonna hear nothin' from 'em. It could be you're just borrowing a lotta grief for yourself. Sit tight and take it easy, and you ain't got anything to worry about. If you want an alibi you can get one. Hell, you don't even have to bother to give 'em an alibi. If this Amhurst guy identifies her and he's as big a shot as they claim he is, he isn't gonna be a damn bit crazier about gettin' any publicity on this than you are, you know. You might just as well relax. Unless I miss my guess, this thing is never gonna blow up at all."

He still didn't look at her; his eyes were dark and brooding.

After a little, Petey said, "Why don't you go get cleaned up and change, huh? I gotta change myself and do some singin' around here tonight."

"In a minute," he said, reaching for the bottle. "You stick around for awhile after the show, huh?"

"Okay," she said as she slid off the desk. "See you later."

# 37

ASSISTED BY THE ADORING COLORED MAID FROM THE powder room, Petey changed in the bare and bleak employees' dressing room. Her dress was made out of yards of soft gray chiffon, with slashes of dark gold in the same material, and a liberal sprinkling of dusty gold sequins. For all of the yards of material that went into it, when it was in place, the last cunningly concealed zipper closed, the soft material draped close to Petey's body in incredible slimness.

Sadie adjusted folds of material with trembling, reverent fingers. "My Gawd," she said softly. "Miss Petey, you sure look wonderful in this dress. I never seen nothin' like it before in my life. When you get this dress on, my Gawd, it's—it's—like little, old, wet chunks a wood a burnin' up, all smoke and a little bitty fire in it!"

Petey looked at Sadie's rapt face in the mirror, and she smiled a little. "Thanks, Sadie, that's an awful nice compliment." Petey felt in a queer mood of suspension. It seemed to her that already this night had lasted for several days, that somehow time had stopped, and as near as she could tell this night might go on for a long time more, too—days or weeks.

Sadie helped her with the jewelry that went with the dress, heavy wide wristlets on either forearm, made out of dull gold and set heavy with simulated moonstones; a huge, elaborate hair clip suspending a glittering spraywork of fine gold wire covered with myriad topaz-like stones and gold-colored paillette sequins, holding all her hair back in a heavy, tight, slim snood.

Petey stared at her reflection in the mirror. With her hair drawn up and back like that, her face looked slimmer, and a lot different, somehow, contours that were unfamiliar to her. She was beginning to feel a sense of unreality about this night, and this elaborate, exotic costume she was wearing seemed infinitely appropriate.

Petey went out to sing, and, as she adjusted the microphone, she reflected that the weather must be a helluva lot better, because there was a pretty good crowd in the place all of a sudden. She took the songs that she had rehearsed, and she got some good requests for encores, good old songs that she never could work enough times.

> "Nights are long since you went away.
> I think about you all through the day,
> My Buddy, My Buddy,
> Nobody quite so true . . ."

For a last encore she did "It Had to Be You," and by that time Petey was feeling fine about everything. It was a good number to sing. Petey liked to sing songs like that one. She took a second chorus over hot, and she swayed in front of the microphone, a kind of caricature of her own style of presentation, and did a few bumps for the boys.

When she was done she went up to the bar for a drink. She didn't see the Nicky around, and for two cents she thought she would walk out on him, what the hell. All this was his headache and none of hers. But then she thought better of it. She had promised him to stick around and she better do it, he was about fit to go off into the screaming shakes. If anything should happen around here, he would probably fly into a million pieces and he was as apt to get Joe into a jam as not. She caught a glimpse of the clock just then, and it gave her a shock. It was quite a bit later than she thought it was. Time still didn't make sense to her. She was surprised that it was so late, but, on the other hand, it seemed like about a week ago that she had been over there at the Auditorium watching the fights. She had a date to meet San and she was late for it already. Petey thought that over for a minute. She wanted to go, but, on the other hand, she'd told Nicky she would stick around. She got a couple of nickels change from the bartender and went over to the telephone booth. She looked up the café where San was waiting and dialed the number. She asked if San was there and the bartender said, yeah, just a minute. Soon she heard San's voice. "Yes?" he said.

Petey was scowling and she fumbled with the other nickel in her fingers. "Darling, I'm awful sorry. I hate to stand you up like this, but I can't make it for awhile. Something come up, see?"

"Aren't you done working?"

"Well, not exactly," Petey said. "Something's come up, and I gotta stick around here for awhile. The Nicky . . ."

"The Nicky," San's voice said in her ear. "Yeah, I understand that all right!" After that came the soft click as he hung up the receiver. He didn't slam it, he just hung it back on the hook with a soft little click in her ear. For a second Petey didn't get it. "San," she said, and she rattled the hook with her fingers. Then all of a sudden she knew that he had hung up on her. She waited a minute and then she dropped her other nickel in and started dialing the number again with hurried, fumbling fingers. In the middle of dialing her lips tightened and she slammed up her receiver and thumped the side of the telephone impatiently to get her nickel back. She pushed the door open and stepped out of the booth.

The Nicky was waiting for her at the bar. He had changed into immaculate evening clothes, and he looked like himself again, except that his face was bruised, and his eye discolored and swollen. Even though his face was a little battered, it was a smooth, controlled mask again, and he stood very stiff and straight in front of the bar. Well, she'd hand it to him for that much, Petey thought, as she walked over to him. She never thought he'd get up here in the bright lights looking like this. He had a little bit more guts than she thought he had, anyway.

He turned around to her as she came up beside him. "You want to finish your drink or shall we dance now?"

"Let's dance," she said. He followed her down the steps, his body stiff and upright. Petey marveled at him a little. He certainly had pulled together into a controlled and deadly sullenness. Nobody would dare to kid him about that black eye either, or even laugh at him behind his back.

Nicky was a smooth and expert dancer and it seemed to Petey that tonight he was much better than usual. Petey was aware that they attracted a great deal of attention without thinking much about it. She was used to people staring after her, and when she was with the Nicky they stared even more, and they talked too. Nicky guided her over to a spot on the floor that was empty.

"I heard something interesting on the radio," he said softly into her ear.

"So?"

"Yeah. It seems this guy Amhurst had a look at the kid, but he said she wasn't his daughter."

The next chance he got, the Nicky spoke again. "I figure if those big-mouthed bastard cops had had a lead on my car like they claimed, they'd a been over here before this. So it looks like I'm all out in the clear now, is that right?"

Petey's eyebrow bent up in her amusement. "I figured you heard something that made you feel a helluva lot better!"

That didn't seem to make him mad. He smiled his faint mocking smile at her. "So maybe I just sort of went to pieces there for a minute!" he said. "I was feeling kind of jumpy tonight, anyway. It must have been the rain goin' patter, patter." That seemed to amuse him inordinately. He laughed out loud.

Petey smiled. "Jesus, I getta kick outa you," she said to him. "You're like some kid playin' cops and robbers. Now the heat's off, you're a big-shot tough guy again, aren't you? It wouldn't make no difference to you that little kid got bumped off tonight."

"That's right," the Nicky said. "Why should it?"

Petey was still smiling, but her eyes were looking far away, some other place and some other time. "Yup, that's right," she said. "Why should it?"

The Nicky looked down at her for a moment and then he drew her close to him, his lips brushing her hair. "You look different tonight, Petey. You look even better, is that right?"

"You can skip the conversation," Petey said shortly. "Let's dance."

"All right, so we dance."

In a few minutes the floor thinned out a little, and Nicky gave a signal to the orchestra leader that meant he wanted a rumba. He spun Petey out the length of his arm, and her eyebrow bent at him mockingly as she caught the rhythm in the flat muscles of her body above the waist.

When they were tired they sat down at a table for a drink. Petey sang again after awhile, and just after that Jimmy Terwilliger came in with his father, and a celebration was in order.

Jimmy had won his last fight, and he had the trip to the finals sewed up. Tommy was bursting with pride and trying not to show it. Jimmy was elated and grinning, big and good-looking in his evening clothes, a piece of tape over one eye and another on his chin.

Tommy and Jimmy sat at the Nicky's table. There were free drinks coming and going in all directions. Jimmy was introduced to the crowd, and took his bows with a new professional ease, his hands clasped over his head. He looked fine in the spotlight, taking his bows like that, but Petey caught a look on his father's face that made her lean over in her chair and squeeze Tommy's hand hard. It could be, she realized suddenly, that Tommy was seeing this all over again, nights years and years ago when people had applauded him like this, a time when he had had some local fame in this same profession, a profession that left him an old man with a battered face marked with scar tissue, a couple of cauliflower ears and a pair of busted hands—and that was all. Petey danced with Jimmy a couple of times. When she came back to the table, she asked Tommy to play. She had a feeling that she was right about it, Jimmy was having the time of his life, but the celebration had gone sour for his father all of a sudden. Tommy agreed to play, and she knew that it was because he felt like playing, that he had a lot of things in his heart all of a sudden that he couldn't tell to anybody except a piano.

The waiters hauled the piano out, and the Nicky excused himself to make some phone calls. When Tommy got up from his chair, he caught Petey by the hand. He wanted her up there by the piano, he said. And Jimmy said, sure, go ahead, he could join another table with some friends of his.

So Tommy played, with Petey leaning over the corner of his low, upright piano. And his hands were very sure this night, and the music was right. It was so right that Petey wanted him to go on playing forever, the perfect rolling rhythm, power-house, so that the whole piano shook and vibrated under her arms. The right hand that did strange and wonderful things, cross rhythms, notes that were good, sometimes blue, sometimes hot and always incredibly right and alive.

Because the music was so right, Petey wasn't thinking about anything else. But she saw the man come in and she watched him quite awhile before she was aware that she was watching him. There was something odd about that man, because he came in and sat down at a table alone, and he still had on his overcoat. He ordered a drink, but he didn't touch it. He said something to the waiter, and the waiter went out back, but when he came back to the table he shook his head at the man. The man just sat there then, without touching his drink, his hat on the table in front of him, and his overcoat still on. He was middle-aged, short, but powerfully built. He had thinning gray hair and a clipped, smooth gray mustache. There was something queer about his taut drawn face, his staring eyes and his hands that kept fidgeting with his hat, a great diamond gleaming on one of the fingers.

Suddenly he got to his feet, stood a minute and looked around in all directions. He seemed to take a deep breath and his hands went deep into his overcoat pockets and he walked across the floor rapidly, skirting the edge of the tables. He went directly to the little door at the end of the orchestra stand, entered and closed it behind him.

Petey wasn't aware that she had been watching him, until he had left the room. She knew it then and stood up to look at his empty chair, as if to reassure herself that he had been there at all. He had been there, all right, because his drink was still sitting there on the table. Petey stood up straight at the end of the piano and looked around. The room was full of Tommy's power-house piano and nobody was paying any attention. The waiters were all clustered around the big table where Jimmy Terwilliger was, and where the voices were the noisiest. She never thought much about it, nor did she hesitate. She walked across the floor quickly, and out through the little door into the dark corridor. As she closed the door behind her she stood still a minute, shivering from the chill air on her bare shoulders. She could still hear Tommy playing, and the whole thing was part of the nightmare of this night. She couldn't tell what she was doing here, nor why she had come. She walked quietly along the corridor to the door of Nicky's office. The light was on there, for she could see a streak of it shining under the door. She came up close to the door and then she just stood there. Her breath was coming hard and short.

The man was in there, all right. She could hear his voice. She could tell it was his; it was the sort of voice that went with his appearance. He wasn't talking loudly, but he was talking clearly and distinctly, with terrific tension and control, so that she could understand every word he was saying right through the door.

" . . . and what do you suppose I thought about while I stood there looking down at her?" he was saying. "What do you suppose I thought about? She didn't die easy. An automobile can break and tear a little soft body. What do you suppose I thought about then? But how would you know that, a filthy little rat like you! You couldn't understand how I felt, but before I'm through with it, you're going to understand. I had to stand there and look down at her, and I had to shake my head and say no, no, that wasn't Marjorie, that wasn't my daughter. I had to stand there and just look at her a minute, and then turn away while they pulled the sheet up over her. Then I had to walk out of there and leave her alone. I don't know why I tell you this, because you couldn't understand. There's only one thing a scum like you can understand, and, by God, you're going to get it now.

"I don't know how you got her here. Oh, I've heard about this place of yours. It's notorious; I suppose you have your methods. You got hold of her someplace and kept her here as long as she was of use to you and your goddam business, and then you threw her out. It didn't matter to you, whether it was under an automobile's wheels or where it was, did it? Well, you've done that for the last time."

Petey opened the door, turned the knob carefully in her fingers, little by little, carefully so that it did not make a sound, and then she let it turn back just as carefully, leaving the door open a crack. She was very careful. The timing was just right. The knob turned back into place without a click and then she pushed the door open, little by little.

His back was to her, a broad, overcoated back, as he stood there facing the desk. The Nicky was crouched back in his chair behind the desk. He didn't see her, either. His face was a livid white, his mouth a little open. She could see sweat shining all over him, and his eyes were narrowed down to two pinpoints that were focused on something in front of him that Petey couldn't see—not the man's face but something that he held in his hand, perhaps. Petey slid past the door and moved up behind him, carefully, making not a sound on the soft rug. When she was right behind him, she said, "You better drop that gun, Mr. Amhurst!" in her cool husky voice.

She never had a chance to finish all the words. He whirled on his feet and, at the exact moment that he started moving, Petey shot forward, catching his right arm in both of hers, holding onto it with all the strength she had. He struggled and tried to shake her loose. Petey felt his clenched fingers and the cold steel of the butt end of the gun against her bare shoulder. She hung on with all her strength, her knees sagging, pulling his arm down. When the gun went off, the report was deafening in her ear. Jesus, go around carrying a goddam cannon, Petey thought crossly, probably singed all my goddam hair off!

The report was very loud in the small room and, as if it had stunned the man, his fingers loosened and he dropped the gun. It glanced off Petey's back and she felt the cold steel as it fell. Then, for the first time, she thought, hell, it was a good thing my head was down, coulda blowed my damn fool head off with that cannon!

She scrabbled the gun from the rug and gingerly balanced it in her hand as she stood up. She needn't have bothered. The man in the overcoat just stood there. His face looked as if he had been stunned— as if, Petey thought, the bullet had killed him maybe, except he was still standing there. But the bullet hadn't killed him; Petey didn't quite know where it was, except that it wasn't in her and it wasn't in him and it sure as hell wasn't in the Nicky. She figured maybe that grazed place in the plaster of the wall had something to do with where that bullet was.

Petey just stood there, too, and not one of the three of them moved. She looked down at the gun in her hand. It was heavy. She had been right about it; it was a cannon, all right. When this Amhurst Joe packed a gun he really wasn't fooling.

Then the door opened and a waiter stuck his head in, his face white and frightened.

"You can relax, Joe," Petey said. "We was shooting tin cans out in the alley." Then Petey laughed a little, shakily. "Here," she said, "take this thing out for me and get it cleaned, will you?"

The waiter's eyes darted around the room and he looked scared to death. She offered him the gun and he gingerly took it out of her fingers. Then he just stood there with it as if he were afraid that if he moved it would explode in his hand.

"Go on, get out!" Petey said sharply.

He went, and closed the door behind him. Petey moved then. She went over to the desk and poured herself a shot of whisky and took it neat. It didn't look to her as if either the Nicky or the man ever intended to move again. This whole night was a nightmare— that and a bad Hollywood motion picture, Petey was thinking; and she was getting sick of it.

"You better go home, Mr. Amhurst," she said wearily, listening to her own voice.

Still he didn't move, and Petey said, "Or maybe you better have a drink first."

She held it out to him, and he took it from her. "Thank you," he said.

He downed it and put the glass down on the desk like a sleepwalker. But he still didn't move.

Petey leaned both hands on the edge of the desk suddenly. "You better go home, Mr. Amhurst," she said again. She had a feeling that she was going to talk too much, but there wasn't a thing that she could do to stop herself. "I don't like you," she said. "You're a goddam fool runnin' around with your great big guns. Oh, don't git me wrong. I wouldn't a cared if you put a bullet through the Nicky here, maybe two or three of 'em. I wouldn't a cared. Hell, he's got it coming to him. He's got it coming for a lot of reasons. But you're a goddam fool goin' around shootin' off guns when it's too late to help anybody. You make a fine figure of a father standing there with a gun in your hand. You're too late for that, mister. The time you coulda made a fine figure of a father was years ago. I guess you ain't so much of a father, that a kid runs away from home in the first place, and then, when she gets in a jam, don't feel like she can go home and tell you about it. Besides, all I want to know about you is what you did tonight. You'd let 'em ship the kid off to the morgue, wouldn't you, before you'd let down your goddam pride and let 'em know that kid there was your daughter, no matter what she'd done or what had happened to her. I kept you out of a bad jam tonight, but it wasn't because I like you, nor it wasn't because I'd of cared if you'd pumped the Nicky's carcass fulla bullets, either. I done it on accounta Marjorie. That's funny, because, hell, I never set eyes on Marjorie in my life. All I know about Marjorie is, she sounds like a nice little kid who got a pretty bad break from you in the first place and from the Nicky here and some other people. Well, she's dead now, nobody can help that. But her picture and a lot of stuff about what happened to her isn't gonna be dragged through a lotta goddam newspapers when her father goes on trial for murder, see? Hell, that ain't much to do, it don't matter to her now. But it's just a little present from me to her, insteada sending flowers. Besides, who knows, maybe she'd still care what happened to you, though I don't see why the hell she should, do you? I don't like you, Mr. Amhurst. You go on, get out of here and go on home."

Petey stopped talking, and the funny thing about it was, he did go. He stood there just a minute more; he looked at her, he looked at the Nicky still crouched there in his chair, and then he looked back at Petey for a long minute. He turned around then and went out, slamming the door behind him.

Petey hung onto the edge of the desk with both hands. This night was a nightmare, and she was tired, terribly tired. Furthermore, she had just missed having her goddam head blown off. Her ear still ached from the report of the heavy caliber revolver and the smell of powder was still in her nostrils. Her knees felt loose, and she couldn't get enough air into her lungs. Petey made a deliberate effort and stood erect. Her dress was torn a little at the shoulder. With fingers that she kept deliberately slow and controlled she adjusted it so that the rip didn't show.

She looked at Nicky, and he wasn't a pretty sight to see. His face was still pasty and he was concentrating his every energy on pulling himself together. Every once in awhile his body would shake a little, convulsively, and he would stiffen out rigidly in his chair to stop it, his hands clenching and un-clenching over the chair arms.

Petey looked at him and she said patiently, "I don't like you, either. The next guy that comes bustin' in here tonight with a cannon can drill you for all I care, and the hell to him and the hell to you."

She walked out of the office then. She had lost all sense of reality and she wanted to be where San was. But when she thought of him something stirred within her. This night wasn't over yet; this night had to go on for a long, long time. Because there were still things that she had to do. Something had happened between her and San. She had got to find San and she'd got to find him quick.

There were still a few customers in Toresca's, though most of them were leaving. Petey went straight to the powder room where

Sadie drowsed on a chair, waiting for the last customer to leave so that she could tidy up the place and go home.

Petey listened to her strange voice speaking, "Sadie, would you get my coat, please?"

"Huh—oh, that you, Miss Petey? I get your coat, wait just a minute."

# 38

SADIE LEFT THE POWDER ROOM AND PETEY WALKED up to the mirror. She looked white, and her face looked funny and unfamiliar, slimmer, somehow, and strange. But that was because her hair was all gathered back like that, Petey told herself with an idiotic carefulness. She had left some cosmetics in one of the dressing-table drawers the last time she was in. She pulled the drawer open now and took out her lipstick. She went back to the mirror, took off the cap and screwed out the red crayon. But when she lifted her hand, she got things a little mixed up; she lifted the lipstick to the pale lips in the mirror in front of her. Petey stopped herself, just as the lipstick smeared the smooth glass in front of her. Petey laughed out loud. Christ Jesus, she thought mockingly, will you look at baby! She moved down a little, and this time she put the lipstick on her lips.

Sadie came back in a minute with Petey's fur cape and the yards of chiffon, which made the headgear that went with the dress. She put the furs over Petey's shoulders and she said, "How you work this other, Miss Petey?"

"Aw, to hell with it," Petey said.

"Aw, put it on, Miss Petey, please," Sadie said. "I sure would like to see how it looks. You sure would look fine with that on."

"Okay," Petey said wearily. Petey took it out of Sadie's hands and shook it out a little, frowning. It was probably the whackiest piece of headgear that a designer ever dreamed up out of a nightmare. So why not wear it, what the hell. She adjusted fold after fold of gray chiffon dotted with sequins far back on the head like a hooded cowl and then a streamer length of it across the lower part of her face, up to the eyes, loose, so that it could be pushed down below the chin or raised to cover the entire face like a veil. All the ends of it were caught together at the back, to be held with a little clip. Then yards of chiffon fell over the shoulder to the floor, like a half of a very full cape.

Sadie adjusted the falling folds of material with careful fingers. "My Gawd," she said reverently, "would you look at that!"

Petey waited while Sadie packed some articles from her purse into an evening bag, and then she tipped her and left the powder room.

The bartender was just cleaning up as she started out, and he called to her, "Hey, Miss Braun, wait a minute. The doorman ain't on. I'll get you a cab."

"Thanks a lot, Joe."

When he came in, he said, "It's rainin' hard out, Miss Braun. I sure woulda hated to see you get all them fancy clothes wet, walkin' around lookin' for a cab."

Petey hesitated in the door. It was raining hard, all right, drops coming down like millions of little silver lancets, gashing at the cement so that the gutters ran with water. The fog had hung on to the very last like a malignant presence in the city and eerie streamers of it still floated here and there. The cab waited at the curb, the door open, and Petey crossed the sidewalk and got in.

She gave the number of her apartment automatically, although even then she knew quite well what her ultimate destination was to be tonight. When the cab stopped in front she told her driver to wait. She climbed the stairs with the knowledge that she was merely wasting time. Sure enough, when she pushed open the door the apartment was dark and still and empty. She didn't go in. She just stood there on the threshold for a second, face to face with all that darkness and stillness. She closed the door quietly then, and went down the stairs to her cab.

"Kalamazoo Johnson's place," she told the driver. "You know where it is? It's way out Water Street."

"Yeah, I know," the driver said. He wheeled the cab around, directly into the hard plunging rain, and drove fast through the empty streets.

"And step on it, will yuh?" Petey said.

The rain was pouring down with a vicious abandon. Petey's clothing was damp, the soft material clung to her body, sticky, she thought, like cobwebs. The driver had the window on his side down a little from the top, and the cool air blew in against her face. It was good, except that nothing could take the feeling of fatigue out of her, the odd feeling of unreality, and the feeling that this was a nightmare which would go on forever, time in suspension.

Petey discovered then that her arms hurt under the wide tight metal wristlets. She supposed she had bruised the flesh underneath them. She chafed the skin around the edges with her fingers, but she was too tired to manipulate the intricacies of the fastenings to take them off.

It seemed as if she had been in the dark cab for a long time with the rain pounding down, when the driver turned off on Water Street. The cab bounced over the bumps, splashing water from the wheels. There was a freight train pulling in on the track above them, the wheels grinding along slowly and monotonously. However bad the weather had been in town, it appeared worse to Petey out here. The rain seemed to come down harder, the darkness a thick, tangible blackness, the rain lost in it. The fog had hung on here longer. She could see it in front of the car lights sometimes, long streamers of it hanging over the marshes along the road. The cab moved more slowly, the rain buffeting it, and the headlights seemed inadequate in the blackness that closed in around them. This was a bad night, Petey thought suddenly with a little shudder, it was an evil night. There was something bad in the way the rain lashed at the earth, there was something bad in the tangible blackness that followed after the cab like a great, soft-footed, clumsy beast. There was a badness in those tentacles of fog that still clung to the marshes as if they never would let go. This night could breed unheard-of evil and violence in people. Or was it the other way around, Petey wondered, was it the evil and violence that people did that crept out from them like a bad odor to tincture the very atmosphere sometimes? Anyway, it was a bad night. Petey knew it, and it wasn't over yet; there were hours to come before the dawn, that is, if the dawn ever came again.

The cab moved slower and slower. The driver leaned forward over the wheel, straining his eyes ahead into the blackness and the slashing rain. The freight train had gone on now, and there was just the sound of the rain, loud over the motor. Petey leaned forward on the seat, too, looking out toward the left, trying to see through the steam on the window and the wash of water on the other side and the blackness beyond that.

"Kalamazoo's is right along here someplace," the cabby explained. "It's kinda hard to find it at night like this."

Petey saw it first, just the familiar outline of the sagging frame building, stark in the wet and black.

"That's it," she said. "Stop right here, huh?"

"Right," he said, and he brought the cab to a halt, at the edge of the road.

He shut off the meter and Petey handed him a bill from her purse. "You wait," she said. "I may be in there quite awhile, but you wait right here."

"Okay." And then he said, "Jesus, you're gonna spoil your clothes gettin' over there. I'll leave the lights on, maybe that'll help a little."

Petey swung the door open, and then hesitated a moment, getting her direction, before she stepped out into the rain. The headlights weren't much good in the blackness, but they helped a little. The house was dark and deserted-looking, not a stir of life nor a sound around it, but the windows were gray, as if there were lights on behind the drawn shades, and Petey caught the smell of woodsmoke that must have come from the chimney. The yard was a sea of mud and water, rippled by the driving rain, and fog clutched at the corners of the house.

Petey gathered up her skirts and stepped from the running board. Her feet sank into the mud until she thought she would never find a solid footing, and she grabbed hold of the door to get her balance.

"Can you make it all right, lady?" the driver asked her anxiously, peering out of the window, his face a flat white blob on the other side of the glass.

"Yeah, sure," Petey said. She got her footing and slammed the door shut. The cold rain caught her before she took another step, and it felt as if buckets of ice-water had been poured over her. Petey struck out diagonally across the yard. It was slow going, her feet slid and caught in the mud, the water cold against her bare ankles and the rain beating so hard against her body that she had the odd sensation of swimming in dark cold water, against a current.

But she got to the door all right. She groped for the white crockery doorknob in the darkness and felt it at last, cold and clammy wet in her hand. She turned it as far as it would go and she pushed on the door, but it didn't open. For a moment she thought that it was locked, but it finally gave inward under her hands, and she realized then that the water had warped the wooden door. Petey held the knob in both hands, and flung her whole body against the door. It opened suddenly, and Petey was catapulted into the room, hanging tight to the doorknob to keep her footing. Petey's eyes were blind with water and sudden light after darkness, and, like the other time, it was the odor of the room that she caught first. Here was hot, stale air, full of cigarette smoke and liquor, the smell of sweating bodies, woodsmoke, and over everything the sharp sickening sweetness of cheap perfume.

Petey closed the door behind her and leaned against it. She wiped water out of her eyes, and peeled the wet chiffon down from her face impatiently.

The room was dimly lighted and very hot. The room was packed; all the tables were filled with drinkers, men in suits, men in shirt-sleeves, men in undershirts, and scattered among them were the girls, dancing with them, drinking with them, making love with them, light girls, dark girls, attractive girls and ugly ones; girls in short, flashy silk dresses, and bare legs and glittering fancy sandals.

The music started all of a sudden, a great loud burst of it. The piano was right in front of Petey as she stood by the door. In addition there was a guitar for rhythm and the raw burst of brass came from a fat man who leaned back in his chair against the wall, holding a battered trumpet to his lips lovingly. The music caught at Petey. The rhythm was right. Through all the smoke and the milling bodies in the dim light, she tried to catch a glimpse of San, but she couldn't see him any place. Nobody paid any attention to her. It was as if she were not here at all, as if she were a ghost and invisible to their eyes. The fatigue caught at Petey again so that her knees almost sagged. She felt the fatigue in terrible contrast to all the life and vitality in that room. A lump came up in her throat, pity for herself and an awful longing and wistfulness.

All of a sudden Kalamazoo herself was in front of Petey. She was dancing with a man, pressed so tight in his arms that when she stepped away from him it was as if one body had divided into two. She came to Petey with her long quick stride, her hand outstretched, a wide warm smile on her face. She wore the same black silk dress tight to her long, well-shaped body, and her sandals were silver colored.

She caught Petey's hand in both her warm ones for a greeting, and she raised her husky voice over the music. "You're soakin'! It's a bad night out, huh? Your man's right over here, lemme take you."

She kept hold of Petey's hand and she led her past the musicians, through the melee in the little space cleared for dancing and in among the crowded tables.

"Right there," she said pointing. San was there all right, his pale bleached hair gleaming in the dim light, his familiar gabardine raincoat stretched over his great shoulders. He was sitting alone at a table against the wall, hunched over his drink, his pale eyes staring straight ahead of him.

Kalamazoo squeezed Petey's hand tight. "There's a chair," she said. "Go set with him. He'll be glad."

"Thanks," Petey said. Kalamazoo nodded, her eyes warm with more than mere friendship; it was nearer kinship. Then she turned away to the man who had followed at her heels.

Petey pulled out the chair across the narrow table from San. There was just room for her to slide into it. When she sat down, San's eyes shifted ever so little toward her, but no sign of anything changed his face.

Petey felt as if she were suffocating, and she threw her furs over the back of her chair. The soft folds and draperies of her clothing stuck fast to her body in great wet patches.

She leaned across the table then, close to him. "Aw, San!" she said, her voice all but lost in the confusion of voices and the loud music.

"Why did you come?" he said in his flat voice, his lips hardly moving, without any motion in him anywhere.

There was such a great dumb aching misery in Petey that she couldn't answer him.

She just sat there, how long she didn't know, and then a waiter slid a tray down on the table in front of her. There was a bottle of cheap whisky on it, and a pitcher full of water, and a couple of glasses. Petey fumbled for her purse, but the waiter shook his head, grinning, his teeth white in his dark face. "Uh uh," he said. "Miss Kalamazoo, she say you drink what you want."

"Thanks a lot," Petey said. "Tell her thanks." She dropped a coin into his hand, and his grin widened. "Thank you," he said.

The music was right, but it was unbearably loud and the brass tore at Petey's nerves. Beside the heat and the crowd, there were strident voices and high laughter, chairs scraping on the floor and the slapping of dancing feet.

Petey mixed her drink suddenly with unsteady hands. "San, come home!" she said.

"Home!" He took the bottle out of her fingers and poured himself a stiff one and drank it neat.

"Aw, San, San," Petey said softly, her voice lost in the noise. "Aw, darling, what's the matter?"

"You know what's the matter. I suppose you want to hear me say it."

Petey was all but crying suddenly. "No! No, never, San. Never those words between us again. Not ever!"

"Why not?" His pale eyes were on her, and his voice was inexorable. "Why shouldn't we talk about it? You think we should go on pretending that there isn't anything wrong with me?"

"No," Petey whispered. "Don't, San, please!" She closed her

eyes, and her face was like a tragic mask with eyebrows and mouth etched into it.

"Tonight you were with Toresca," he said steadily and flatly. "Well, why shouldn't you be? You have to have a man sometimes. You're a normal woman with a fine, healthy body. You have to have a man sometimes."

"San, darling, don't!" Her voice was just the dry whisper, and she caught at his hand on the table with both of hers.

He jerked his hand away from her. "No, don't," he said. "There's been enough of that."

Petey fell back in her chair then. Her eyes were wide open now, and she stared straight over his shoulder and her hands were limp and crumpled on the table.

"You must have known we couldn't go on like this," he said patiently. "What can I give you? I'm not a man. I'm not anything. Have you ever been completely happy with me? No, you couldn't be. You must have known this couldn't go on. Think of me, too, along with everything else. Your pity didn't make it any easier for me."

Her hands moved a little then. "No, San!" she said. "Don't say that!"

"No, I don't blame you," he said. "I was a fool to have started this. But I wanted you. I still do, but we can't go on with it. There's more to it even than that one thing. I haven't anything else to give you either to make you happy. You ought to be happy, Petey. It's your turn. I can't give you anything now, believe me. My life all went to smash and ended years ago. I'm no more alive than that fog out there. Sometimes you can make me alive, but it wouldn't last. I'm not a good person any more when I am alive. I'd hurt you too much. It's no good." His voice was suddenly harsh. "You know all these things, why do you make me say them?"

Petey made an odd little sound almost like laughter. "No, you're right, San. It's no good. It's too late," she said. "It's too late for you to leave me. I won't forget about you. I won't get over this."

"You might," he said, "and, even if you don't, you'll be better off alone than you would be with me."

"San, don't you think I should be the one to decide that?"

For the first time something moved in his face, muscles tightening around his mouth. "No," he said, flatly. "I have to think of myself, too. You make me live again. I start to think about things and want things. I can't stand that. I'd rather be dead like I was when you first saw me."

Petey was sagging in the chair, but she pulled herself upright and reached out for her glass on the table and took a long drink. They didn't say anything more. Petey followed the confusion of people with her eyes, and the beat of the music inside of her. She saw Kalamazoo and the man sit down together at a table without really seeing them. They sat with their chairs pulled close together, their bodies leaned forward, their hands clinging. It wasn't the man Jode, it was another, a big, handsome man, younger, and very black. He wore a light polo shirt, knitted in bright stripes of color, the fabric pulled tight over his wide muscular shoulders. They kissed, their faces together for a long time.

Petey saw it, and a little spasm of motion went through her body. "San, what's to become of us?" she said.

He didn't seem to hear her. He poured another shot of liquor, and after a little he said, "I don't know. I don't know as it matters much. Me, I'm going to catch a freight train out of here tonight and I'm going a long way before I stop."

The rain lashed at the window over their heads, but the next minute the music started again and the brass came in hot on the beat and drowned out the rain.

After a while Petey had another drink, and she searched for cigarettes automatically. He watched her, and although a cigarette burned in his own fingers, he didn't offer her one, nor strike a match for her. His light eyes were still upon her and in a minute he said with a queer irrelevance, "I knew you a long time before I met you, and I'll be with you a good many times after I'm gone. All places like this are like you."

Petey's shoulders moved a little on the chair back.

"Tonight it isn't barrel house or boogie-woogie," he said. "It's the blues, isn't it?"

Petey watched the cigarette burn down in her fingers, her eyes narrowed against the smoke. She picked up the bottle to pour herself another drink.

When things started to happen they happened fast. There was a girl's high, thin scream over all the noise first of all, a scream that went on and on for a long time, and then just stopped without warning, and voices thinning out. Petey twisted around in her chair to see, the bottle still in her hand.

It was the man Jode, the same light suit and tan shoes but plastered with mud and water. He pushed his way down the room, and bodies melted away in front of him, and a table overturned. His face was twisted and ugly.

Petey saw all that in a flash, and then another table went crashing over in the sudden silence there in that room. That was the table where Kalamazoo and the man were sitting. It crashed over as the Negro jumped to his feet, his face terror-stricken, his eyes distended, wide whites around the pupils against his face. He might have started to run, but his feet got tangled in the table legs and he reached for the wall with flat palms to keep himself from falling. Then he just flattened out against the wall where he was, his great chest swelling in spasmodic breaths, his arms outstretched from his wide shoulders in the attitude of the crucifixion.

Kalamazoo was still in her chair, and Petey had one glimpse of her. There was no fear in Kalamazoo's face, just a great alertness. At that moment Kalamazoo was out of her chair in one lithe bound, the chair overturning behind her. Jode lunged for her, but she was away from him, running around in front of the stove, and up the short flight of steps at the back of the room. He was at her heels, and she whirled around suddenly right at the top of the steps, her face contemptuous. "You, Jode!" she said fiercely. "Be careful what you do here!"

He lunged up at her, Petey saw the shine of it in his hand, a knife maybe, or a long slim razor. He caught her throat first with it, a powerful slash of steel, and then across her face, again and again. The blood gushed out as she crumpled, splattering over him, as if her head were nearly severed from her body. She fell on the steps, and the room was full of the girls' thin screaming and hysterical crying and the hoarse shouts from men, all against a background of crashing furniture and crowding, shoving confusion for the door.

Petey couldn't take her eyes away from the stairway. Kalamazoo's crumpled body, and more blood than it seemed possible, and the man Jode spotted over with the crimson stream standing there over her, sobbing and cursing, kicking at her limp body time after time with short vicious kicks of his tan pointed-toed shoes.

San overturned the table between them and pulled her to her feet. Just as she got her hand on her furs the lights went out and the voices in the room rose in terror. After that it became stark horror, the dark hot room, furniture overturned, the pressing, trampling pack of bodies directed toward the door. The door was open and it showed a light patch in the darkness. San had his arm tight around Petey, and he dragged her after him, his huge shoulders bucking a slow path toward the door. Petey felt only a great sharpening of sensation. Bodies crowded against hers in the darkness, hands clutched at her and she felt the sharp pain when the leg of an overturned table scraped the skin off her shin. Always there was the screaming and shouting, and somewhere among them a voice yelling "Police, police!" over and over again, whether into a telephone or not Petey couldn't tell. But she had the fleeting thought that the police couldn't have arrived here already. She nearly fell once, and for a moment the fear of trampling feet in the darkness clutched at her, but San yanked her back onto her feet again, and pulled her along with him. After what seemed like a very long time they made the door and she felt the wash of cold rain over her, and the soft mud under her feet. She had a confused sight of people running in all directions, some of them falling in the slippery mud, in the darkness.

"You all right?" San said sharply. "You gotta cab? Is it those lights down there?"

She couldn't answer him. She clung to him, and he shook her hard by the shoulders.

"Is that your cab? We haven't got all night, the police will be here in a minute!"

"Yes, that's it," Petey said automatically in a dry voice.

"Can you run?"

"Sure, I can run."

They ran together toward the headlights, his arm still around her, their feet sliding in the mud and darkness, and the rain pouring down on them.

Almost at the headlights, San stopped, his arm still around her. "Is that you, cabby?"

"Yeah," the man's voice from the cab sounded frightened. "Is that you, lady? What the hell broke loose? Is . . . ?"

San grabbed the furs out of her hands and wrapped them around her shoulders. "Tell him to get out of this section as fast as he can. You don't wanta run into a police car!"

She knew somehow what was going to happen, and she clung to him with all her strength. "No, San," she whimpered. "Come with me, please. Don't go like this, please. Not like this, San."

"The best time," he said shortly. "There ain't all night, you know, the police'll be here."

He held her tight in his arms for a moment and kissed her short and hard, and then he let loose and was gone, sprinting away in the mud and water, and the rain and the blackness swallowed him up.

"San, no! San! Aw, San!" She tried to run after him, just a few steps, and she nearly fell in the mud and she stopped.

"Jesus, lady," her driver yelled. "Let's get to hell outa here if you're goin'. Looks like all hell busted loose around here!"

Petey stood still a minute in the rain and she knew she was crying. "Okay," she said.

She scrambled over to the cab. He had the door open and as soon as she was in he stepped on the gas.

"You better take the first side street no matter where," Petey said rapidly. "There'll be police cars headin' this way."

"Aw, Christ!" the driver said.

He sent the cab hurtling over the bumps into the darkness. "Christ, what happened in that joint?" he said. "Musta been a fight, huh? Maybe some fancy razor slashin', huh? Well, it wouldn't be the first time that happened out this way, nor in Kalamazoo's joint, either."

He took the first side street all right, and in a minute he said,

"Well, I guess we can relax now. We're in the clear with a lotta time to spare. I ain't even seen a sign of a police car yet."

He drove on fast in the rain, and after awhile he said with faint disgust in his voice, "Hell, lady, there ain't no sense you cryin' like that. Jesus, I always say, if you're gonna go around to joints like that, why, you gotta expect things like that to happen!"

# 39

PETEY GOT OUT OF BED IN MID-AFTERNOON. THE fatigue was still with her, as if her body had been pounded and bruised. She didn't stop for breakfast. She went about her packing with a relentless speed and efficiency, stripping the apartment of her belongings, and packing them away in a trunk and suitcases. Even after her trunk and bags were sent off to the station, there were things to be done. The rented radio returned to the shop, and last bills to be paid. Petey worked fast, her face white without make-up and great dark shadows ringing her eyes. There were no rehearsals today, and so she worked straight through until dinner time. By that time everything was done. The apartment, stripped of all her belongings, had a strange neat impersonality about it. For dinner she ate the last scraps of food left in the kitchen. After that she had a long warm bath and then she dressed for Toresca's, the slim green dinner dress which she had left outspread on the bed when she did her packing. One last job of packing after that, a complete change of street clothing packed away in an overnight case, and cosmetics gathered up into her big purse. Petey slipped her furs over her shoulders and carried the little suitcase and a hat out into the living room. She put them down on the end of the studio couch, and then she stood there a moment and put a cigarette into her holder. The rooms were very still, all the lights on, everything neat and in place, just any furnished apartment in any city. Petey made the last tour of the rooms, a last look in the clothes closet, a last glance at the empty shelves of the bathroom cabinet, pulled the empty, paper-lined drawers of the dressing table out for the last time, turning off lights behind her. The kitchen last, and she picked up the brown paper sack from the shelf, containing a couple of bottles, the end of her liquor supply. Then she turned out the light and went back into the living room, her heels clicking smartly. Not even a last look here. She picked up the suitcase and hat, pulled the chain on the floor lamp and went out and closed the door behind her. On her way out of the building she stopped at the janitor's room and turned in her key and made him a present of her sack of liquor. Then she caught a cab at the corner for Horton Street.

At Sally's she found the living room deserted, except for Virginia kneeling on the floor beside the davenport, holding a bottle of milk for young Beverly O'Connor.

"Hello," Virginia said without getting up. "How are you? We haven't seen anything of you in a long time. Sally was saying so just the other day."

"Hi," Petey said. "How are you? Where is everybody?"

"Well," Virginia answered her, smiling. "Let's see. The kids are eating out in the kitchen, and Fred's in bed, and Harold's out someplace and Sally's to the hospital and Johnny hasn't got home from work yet."

Petey smiled too as she dropped her furs over a chair. "Just one great big happy family, huh?"

"Yup." Virginia bent over the baby lovingly. "That's right, isn't it, Beverly?"

Petey looked at Virginia curiously as she lighted a cigarette. Virginia was wearing the soft pink sweater that made her look very slight and young, but her face and hands were extraordinarily gentle and tender over the baby.

Petey moved about the room restlessly. "So you're baby-tender now along with bein' chief cook and bottle washer around here?"

Virginia's eyes were on the baby's face. "Well, Johnny had to have somebody to take care of the baby, you know," she said. "He's got a job now. So he offered to pay me if I would do it. I didn't know much about babies, but he and Sally showed me a lot, and we get along fine now."

"Good." Petey plucked the curtain back from the window and stared out over the rooftops into the darkness. "Jimmy won both his fights last night, did you hear? He'll be goin' to the state finals now."

"I read it in the paper tonight," Virginia said with polite interest. "That's fine, isn't it? Look, have you eaten yet? Don't you want me to get you something? It wouldn't be any trouble, some coffee, anyway."

"Just a cup of coffee if you have it made."

Virginia propped up the bottle and rose to her feet lightly.

"Don't bother," Petey said. "I'll come out."

"No bother," Virginia called back over her shoulder. "I'll bring it in here."

While she was gone, the baby lost the bottle and she began to whine a little.

Virginia hurried in from the kitchen and handed the cup of coffee to Petey and flew back to the davenport.

"Aw, did the nasty old bottle get away? Well, there, here it is, right here!" Virginia tipped up the bottle and rested her chin on her hand, her eyes on the baby's face again. "I'm spoiling her," she said ruefully. "She always used to be so good about taking her bottle alone, but I love to give it to her, and now she's getting spoiled about it. Oh, I know I shouldn't, but . . . Of course I know she's really too little to miss her mother, but just the same . . . Babies are so terrible little and helpless and . . ."

"Yeah," Petey said. "I guess maybe they need love to grow on, all right." Even with her coffee Petey didn't sit down. She stood up straight and slim in the sleek green dress, her hair heavy and fluffy on her shoulders, and the long earrings glittering.

"It's kinda nasty out, isn't it?" Virginia said idly. "But nowhere near as bad as it was last night, though. Doesn't this damp nasty weather make you sick? Last night was terrible."

"Yeah."

After that the room was quiet, except for the noise the baby made sucking on the rubber nipple, and the chatter of the children's voices from the kitchen.

A minute or two later the door opened quietly and Johnny O'Connor stuck his head in. He looked toward the davenport first, and his eyes warmed as he looked at the baby with Virginia bent over her.

"Hi yuh, Johnny," Petey said. "I hear you're back in the harness again."

"Well, if it isn't Petey Braun! Oh, God, yes! I'm just a workin' man again. What's the news from the home front, Ginny?"

"Everything's under control," Virginia said happily.

He went over to stand beside her in front of the davenport. "Hello there, half-pint! Got a smile for the old man?"

"Pooh!" Virginia said. "You expect a girl to take time off from her supper just to smile at her father!"

He got a smile all right, but it was more Virginia's than it was his. "Will you look at that?" he mourned. "Look who's stealin' whose heart away from who!" He patted Virginia on the back affectionately as he said it. "Well, how's the hard cruel world treatin' you these days, Petey?"

"I'm not complainin'," she said briefly.

"Is that coffee I smell?" Johnny said with an exaggerated sniffing. "Ginny, could you spare another slug a java for a broken-down old bum like me?"

"I certainly could," she said. She propped up the bottle again and hurried out to the kitchen.

Johnny looked after her and he said to Petey in a soft voice, "Jesus, that kid's a wonder, isn't she? The way she took hold here with the baby! Why, now you'd think she'd been taking care a babies all her life."

"Ginny's a sweet kid," Petey said. "They don't come better."

"Well, it could run in the family," Johnny said. "You know the more I see a you Braun girls . . ."

Virginia came back with a cup in one hand and a sugar bowl in the other. "Here you are."

"Thank you," Johnny said as he took the cup and saucer. He

paused a moment, the grin across his face. "Well, shoot the sugar to me, kid!"

Virginia's face was glowing, and there was something a little special in her eyes and in her smile when she looked at him. "Sweet, white, or granulated?"

"I got some orders for you, Ginny," he said as he stirred his coffee. "I gotta pay check today, which means a pay check for you, and I think that calls for celebratin', you just ask Petey here. So the idea is this, you git your coat on and we're goin' stepping. We'll park the offspring with Sally, and we'll go out and eat in a classy restaurant, and then, by God, we'll go to the movin' pitchers, that's what we'll do."

"Aw, Johnny, I'd love to," she said as if she meant it. "But Sally's not here. She oughta be here any minute, she's late now—and . . ."

"Go ahead, Ginny," Petey said. "I'll be here till Sally comes, and I never got my diploma for baby-tender, but I guess we could make it."

"There, you see?" he said. "No excuses."

"Well," Virginia's eyes were shining, "I'd have to change my dress and . . ."

"Uh uh," Johnny said. "If you don't wear that pretty sweater I won't go. Go on and get your coat, I'm a hungry man."

"You're sure you don't mind, Petey?" Virginia asked. "I think it's awful to run off like this when you come and . . ."

"Naw, that's all right," Petey said. "Go on now, powder your nose and put your coat on. Don't keep a gentleman waitin'."

While Johnny drank his coffee Petey moved back to the window again, as if there was something in the landscape of rooftops and lighted windows that was special to look at. When she put a cigarette in her holder, Johnny set down his coffee cup and struck a match for her.

"Not so good, huh?" he said sympathetically. "Somebody must be trampin' over your grave tonight."

"Yeah, I got the shakes tonight!" Petey smiled suddenly as she inhaled the smoke. "Must be the weather's gettin' me—this rain goin' patter, patter!"

Virginia came back all in a rush, with her hat and coat on.

"About time," Johnny said. "Here we go!"

"I hate to run off like this, Petey," Virginia said penitently. She took a last look at the baby, dropped a kiss lightly on the top of her head. "She's pretty near asleep right now. I guess she'll be all right."

"Sure, she will," Petey said. "Run along and don't worry."

"Thanks, Petey," Johnny said as they went. "Let us know in time and we'll tend a baby for you sometime."

"Can I count on that?" Petey said, laughing. "So long, have fun!"

The door no more than closed than it opened again and Virginia stuck her head in. "Petey, will you tell Sally that Fred's in bed and she's supposed to call him in time for him to get to work? He was out with some girl drinking all afternoon, and he didn't want any supper. He went right to bed, and he'll never wake up unless somebody calls him."

"I'll tell her," Petey said. "Good night, honey. Have a good time."

"Thanks a lot. It's awfully nice of you to stay with the baby like this. I'll be seeing you. Good night."

The door closed again, and Petey listened to their footsteps down the hall. She moved about the room restlessly, and she walked over to the davenport once and looked down at the baby. Her eyes were nearly closed. Petey looked at her a minute, and then she bent down and touched her fuzzy head gently with her hand. The baby's eyes fluttered open and she looked at Petey momentarily. She smiled her odd, wise smile suddenly, La Gioconda in miniature, and closed her eyes again. Petey caught her breath a little and walked away, back to the window, her fingers nervous with another cigarette.

It was maybe five minutes after that that she heard Sally's quick light feet coming down the hall, and the door opened and there was Sally herself, in her old tweed coat.

"Well, hi!" Sally said with her wide warm smile. "Surprise! Where you been keepin' yourself? Gosh, it's good to see you, stranger! How are you? What you been doin' that kept you so busy you couldn't even telephone once in awhile?"

"Aw, I'm fine," Petey said. "How are you, honey? What's cookin' with you?"

Sally closed the door behind her and came into the room. "Look," she said, holding out the letter in her hand. Petey took it and glanced at it curiously, and then she nodded her head slowly and knowingly.

"It must have come today," Sally said. "It was on the table down there when I came in. Gosh, I don't even know where Joe is, but he ought to have this right away. I guess it's his questionnaire, all right."

"Yeah," Petey said. "It looks like the army can't get along without Joey any longer. You think he'll pass his physical all right?"

"Oh, sure," Sally said from the closet as she hung up her coat. "You know, I know Joe hates to go and all that, but just the same I'm glad about this, awful glad. I think it'll be the best thing in the world for Joe."

"Could be," Petey said briefly. She walked over to the table and put the envelope down. "If you call Toresca's tomorrow somebody could probably give you Joe's address. I'm not just sure that he's working for the Nicky any more, but somebody around there would know where he's livin' now."

Sally's face was surprised. "What do you mean maybe he's not working there any more? Did he have trouble over there or something? Why, gosh, I thought . . ."

"Looky, honey," Petey said. "I haven't got much time and I wanta talk a minute. While I think of it, Ginny said to tell you . . ."

Sally settled into a chair comfortably, brushing at her tousled little-girl hair. "Why, I was gonna ask you where Ginny was. Where is everybody, anyway? Are you baby-tender around here?"

"Ginny and Johnny went out to dinner and the movies to celebrate his pay check. The kids are still eating, I guess, and Ginny said to tell you that Fred was in bed and was supposed to be called in time to get to work."

"Petey, are you feelin' all right?" Sally said, looking at her anxiously. "Seems like you look a little peaked. You haven't got a cold, have you? This weather so awful and everything, why, it seems like . . ."

"Naw, I'm fine. Looky, honey . . ."

"I get to talk first," Sally said. "Remember how we used to always say that when we were kids? Well, anyway, I get to talk first because I've got news. I've got a new job!"

"Well, good! Tell me!"

"Well," Sally said, the grin way across her face, "it seems Mr. Toresca figured business is so good he needs a full-time cashier at the restaurant and I'm it! That means five more a week, and it's ever so much easier than hopping tables, on your feet all day long like that, and the hours aren't any longer. He told me today, and I was tickled to death, honest."

"Aw, swell, honey," Petey said. "I'm awfully glad."

"Yeah, it sure is gonna help a lot," Sally sighed a little.

Petey looked at her hard for a moment. "You was at the hospital today, huh? How's everything?"

Sally took a deep breath and lifted her chin. "Well, I didn't see Roy, of course, but I talked to the doctor. You know Roy had kind of a setback, but he's coming along. It's awful slow business. It's just gonna take a little longer than we planned but . . ."

"Sally, honey, why don't you snap out of it?"

Sally's face looked very serious suddenly. "Snap out of it?"

"Honey, you're young. You've got to think about yourself. You've got a life of your own to live and it isn't fair to you, going on like this. I don't think Roy's ever going to be any better. I don't think that you do either, way down underneath, do you?"

"Petey, don't say it, please," Sally said; her eyes were very wide, and her lips unsteady. "Of course I think he's gonna get better. I know he is. Why, if I didn't think that Roy was gonna get better and come home here and things be like they used to, why I—I just couldn't go on, that's all. I've got to think that or I couldn't stand it! It's—it's—what I live by!"

Petey smiled suddenly, and shook the hair back on her shoulders, her eyes affectionate on Sally's face. "Aw, I know, Sally. I shouldn't have said that, should I?"

"I better take a look out there in the kitchen and see what those kids a mine are up to," Sally said rapidly. "Just a minute, I'll be right back."

Petey saw the tears in her eyes as she left the room, and Petey smiled a little thoughtfully over her cigarette holder.

Sally was back in a minute, her own smiling, cheerful self again. "They're just eatin' their pudding like regular little lambs," she said.

"Petey, why don't you sit down? Though, honest, I don't see how you could in that dress, without splitting the sides of it."

"No, I can't, Sally. I've gotta go in just a second." Petey hesitated for just a little and then she said, "Looky, dear, I'm no damn good at saying good-bye. I hardly ever do it, but I couldn't leave without tellin' you . . ."

"Petey!" There was consternation on Sally's face. "Aw, Petey!"

Petey nodded. "Yeah. I'm all packed and everything. I'm gonna catch a train after the show tonight."

"Oh, gosh! But . . . Why, where you going?"

Petey smiled. "Well, I can't really say. I won't know till I come to buy the ticket. I gotta hunch, maybe Chicago. I haven't been in Chicago in a hell of a long time."

"Aw, Petey!"

"Yeah, I know," Petey said. "It's always like this when you try to say good-bye to somebody. That's why I never do. Somebody says they're leavin' and then everybody gets all tongue-tied, and nobody knows what to say or nothin'."

"But Petey, why?" There was real consternation in Sally's voice. "I thought maybe you'd sort a settle down here for awhile. You got a good job here and everything—why . . ."

Petey was smiling. "Yeah, I know. It must sound crazy to you."

"But to leave like this, without even knowing for sure where you're going, or whether you'll get a job or nothing!" Sally insisted. "You haven't got anything more to take you one place than another, and I sort of thought, well—I'm here—and Ginny and Joe now, and . . ."

"Yeah, I know," Petey said. "Honey, I just got train whistles in my ears, I guess."

"Well, I don't like it," Sally was close to tears. "Petey, what makes you! Always movin' like this! Why, it's—it's—no kind of a real life at all. Not for you, anyway."

"I'll write as soon as I get located," Petey said steadily. "Honey, I hate to bail out on you, honest I do. I know the spot you're in, and I want to help. As soon as I get a job or located someplace, why, I'll send you . . ."

"It isn't that," Sally said indignantly. "You've helped me a lot and it's terribly sweet of you, but it isn't—isn't—money—I'm thinking about. I'm thinking about you! Petey, don't go like this. It isn't right for you. Maybe it's a lot of fun now, but in a few years, what are you going to have? If you could only . . ."

Petey laughed her deep laughter. "I know, get married and settle down and have a family! Sally, honey, I love you!"

"No, now don't laugh at me!" Sally said. "But, really, Petey!"

Petey caught up her furs from the chair. "No more lectures," she said cheerfully. "And if we don't lecture we're gonna start snivelin', so I'm gonna run. I'm gonna be all right, don't worry about me. And you'll have a letter from me in just a few days. This time I won't stay away for so long, I promise, cross my heart. You take care of yourself, won't you? Don't work too hard, and write sometimes, and if you ever get in a spot, no matter what it is, you holler loud, won't you, and I'll be right here before you know it. No, don't get up— and say good-bye to everybody for me, huh?"

Petey stooped and kissed Sally and hugged her tight. "Be good, honey, and—and keep 'em flying, huh?"

The next moment she was gone, the door banging behind her.

She stopped off at a florist's on the way over to Toresca's and bought herself orchids. She sang her last show, and when it was over she picked up her last check and a substantial bonus from a quiet, sullen Nicky. The bonus was Petey's own idea, and he gave it to her without a word.

She made a quick change in the washroom, and Sadie tearfully packed her evening clothes in the overnight case. Then she caught a cab to the depot just in time to get her luggage aboard the midnight bound west for Chicago.

Everything quick with no time to spare. It was only after the train had pulled out and she sat there with a magazine in a quiet coach full of sleeping passengers, with nothing but darkness on the other side of the window and the endless clickety clack of the train wheels that she had time to think.

Petey took a deep breath, got to her feet and made her way through the endless narrow passageways of swaying Pullman cars, between the empty white tables of a darkened diner to the club car. It wasn't much of a club car, a moth-eaten rug and a few chairs and a radio, a card game in the corner, and a few men over drinks, and it was chilly cold.

Petey took a chair in a corner and ordered her drink from the waiter. While she waited, she slowly fitted a cigarette into her holder. Just darkness the other side of the windows, and the momentary pin-pricks of the lights of small towns. Always the clickety clack of the train wheels, the weaving small room that the club car was, a swing band on the radio, and the idle, soft-voiced conversation of the drinkers. Just any club car on any train bound for any place, an interval out of living when people are neither here nor there nor this thing nor the other.

The whistle wailed at a crossing, and the train pulled together for the leap and plunged across into the darkness.

# ABOUT THE AUTHOR

MARITTA WOLFF was born on December 25, 1918, in Grass Lake, Michigan, where she grew up on her grandparents' farm and attended a one-room country school. At the age of twenty-two, after graduating the University of Michigan as a Phi Beta Kappa with a bachelor's degree in English composition, her Hopwood Award–winning novel *Whistle Stop* was published by Random House in 1941, going through five printings and earning glowing reviews for her raw, vital characters. A special Armed Forces edition of *Whistle Stop* brought a flood of letters from servicemen and began her lifelong practice of writing to her fans.

Wolff moved to Los Angeles in the late 1940s. A year after her first husband, author Hubert Skidmore, died in a house fire, she married Leonard Stegman. They had one son, Hugh. Between 1941 and 1962 Wolff wrote and published five more novels. After a disagreement with her publisher, her seventh novel was not published and languished in a refrigerator until after her death on July 1, 2002.